THE VENGEANCE SERIES

BOOKS 1-4

M. SINCLAIR

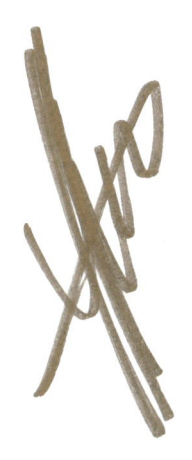

Copyright © 2020 M. Sinclair
Published by M. Sinclair
In the USA

All rights reserved.
All rights reserved. No part of this publication may be reproduced/transmitted/distributed in any form. No part of this publication shall be shared by any means including photocopying, recording, or any electronic/mechanical method, or the Internet, without the prior written consent of the author. Cases of brief quotations embodied in critical reviews and certain other non-commercial uses permitted by copyright law are the exception. The unauthorized reproduction/transmitting of this work is illegal. This book is a work of fiction and any resemblance to persons, living or dead, or places, events or locales is purely coincidental. The characters are products of the author's imagination and used fictitiously.

Edited By: Chantal Fleming
Formatted By: Kassie Morse

The Union of Love & Madness

CONTENTS

The Vengeance Series ix

SAVAGES

Prologue	3
1. Gray	5
2. Adyen	9
3. Gray	14
4. Athens	23
5. Gray	25
6. Rhodes	30
7. Gray	34
8. Adyen	40
9. Gray	43
10. Neo	50
11. Gray	53
12. Taylor	61
13. Gray	63
14. Gray	66
15. Gray	71
16. Gray	77
17. Adyen	86
18. Gray	89
19. Athens	93
20. Gray	100
21. Gray	104
22. Athens	107
23. Gray	111
24. Gray	114
25. Neo	120
26. Gray	124
27. Gray	130

28. Gray	140
29. Adyen	149
30. Gray	155
31. Rhodes	172
32. Gray	179
33. Taylor	187

LUNATICS

Blurb	193
Prologue	195
1. Gray	201
2. Taylor	210
3. Gray	213
4. Gray	227
5. Rhodes	233
6. Gray	237
7. Gray	242
8. Gray	251
9. Gray	273
10. Gray	287
11. Gray	301
12. Adyen	325
13. Gray	338
14. Athens	346

MONSTERS

Blurb	351
1. Gray	353
2. Taylor	368
3. Gray	375
4. Adyen	390
5. Gray	398
6. Gray	405
7. Gray	419
8. Neo	434

9. Gray	447
10. Gray	455
11. Gray	465
12. Rhodes	471
13. Gray	485
14. Neo	492
15. Gray	501
16. Gray	508
17. Gray	516
Epilogue	520
18. Bonus Scenes	523

PSYCHOS

Blurb	541
Prologue	543
1. Gray	547
2. Rhodes	560
3. Gray	570
4. Gray	589
5. Gray	601
6. Neo	614
7. Taylor	619
8. Gray	626
9. Gray	635
Epilogue I	643
Epilogue II	649
Ending Note to Readers	653
Sneak Peek	654
Exclusive Bonus Scene	661
M. Sinclair	669
Also by M. Sinclair	671
Stalk me... really, I'm into it	675

THE VENGEANCE SERIES

Join Gray and her guards on a journey filled with adventure, steam, and vengeance...

I have a secret. Okay, probably more than one. I live a delicate balance, living with the evil I know than the one I don't. I accepted that. Until they showed up. Until they brought my secret and past into the light. Until I had no choice but to accept my true fate. Sh*t. This is why you punch first and ask questions later.

Fantasy RH Our bad*ss heroine and guardians swear a lot. As well, please be advised that the book contains darker themes including assault, PTSD, and violence. Additionally, sexual themes are suitable for mature audiences +18.

This Completed Series Includes:
- Savages
- Lunatics
- Monsters
- Psychos
- Bonus Scene - *exclusive to this box set!*

SAVAGES

BLURB

I had been found feral, and despite their beautiful home... their beautiful facade - they were the same. Savages. Feral Savages. So I would treat them accordingly. I would live accordingly. I would kill accordingly.

I have a secret. Okay, probably more than one. I live a delicate balance, living with the evil I know than the one I don't. I accepted that. Until they showed up. Until they brought my secret and past into the light. Until I had no choice but to accept my true fate.

Sh*t. This is why you punch first and ask questions later.

PROLOGUE
GRAY

I touched the rim of my porcelain coffee mug to my lips as the taste of orange blossom tea exploded on my tongue. The morning traffic, heavy with small sedans, flew by the gates of our academy. What did the humans driving past our school think about when they looked upon the dark foreboding gates? Did they think it was odd that a tiny collegiate academy decided to pick a small suburb of Colorado for its location? I thought it was odd and I attended the damn place.

It didn't help that our walls were so heavy with secrets that they shook with tension. A safe haven. That was the meaning it held for so many of its students. Could it truly be a safe haven though? When the walls inside were so frail they would break upon impact? When everyone was so terrified to say anything. To admit to anything. So instead, silence rattled the walls in fear like a pair of knocking knees.

My manicured hand pressed against the thick glass of the dorm window as a pair of warm muscular arms wrapped around my waist comfortably. It was a friendly gesture that made me sigh in content. He rested his head on my shoulder and pressed a kiss to my clothing covered scars.

"So you're positive? Do we know their names? Or anything useful?" I asked with a raspy voice that spoke of my exhaustion.

"No, not really… but I am as positive as I can be," he mumbled and pressed his forehead to my shoulder. "It means your time here is shortening."

My hand reached up to rub his soft hair absently.

"We knew this would happen."

"I just thought we had more time," he grumbled while turning my shoulders gently so that I faced him. My back pressed into the cold glass behind me.

"We are going to be just fine," I reassured him with a tight smile.

His warm tanned hand cupped my jawline. "I know. I just can't imagine going a day without being us."

I grinned at that.

"*Us* isn't us though, You know how much I hate those assholes."

A low, comfortable chuckle filled the air as his lips pressed to my forehead. It was soft and warm, like melted chocolate. How could I not love him? He was the balm to my dark soul and the shelter within my storm. This connection had been predestined. It ensured that at least one person would love me without reserve.

"One day, Gray," he whispered before pulling me into a hug, "this will all be over. We just have to be strong."

"And until then?" I swallowed my mounting fear.

"Punch anyone who gives you a problem." He stated with a grin.

That I would.

1
GRAY

Monday was my favorite day. It was the day I looked forward to because of this moment. *This moment* being the ever consistent event that highlighted the lack of understanding between Bobby and I. He had his stupidly muscular arms crossed and his face twisted in a confused expression. My blank expression and sarcasm seemed to have stopped his onslaught of 'witty' remarks regarding my scars.

"What?" he asked with a tilt of his head, reminding me of a golden retriever.

"Bobby," I groaned as his friends snickered. "You asked me if I noticed what I had on my face. I responded with, '*What do you mean? What's on my face?*' It's pretty clear what I was asking."

His honey-brown eyes darkened, "How do you not know what's on your face?"

He seemed genuinely concerned that I didn't know about the scar that held the center spotlight on my cheek. I bit my lip as a genuine laugh almost escaped.

God damn it, Gray. Keep it together.

"Bobby, she's being sar--" His lanky, red-haired friend, Jason, finished in a mumble because of my narrowed eyes. This was my game with Bobby. He wasn't about to fucking ruin it.

Jason paled as he worried his lip ring. Good. Be nervous. I turned my eyes back to my large 'friend' and spoke quietly.

"Now, Bobby, please continue to explain what is on my face because I am clearly at a loss here."

I grinned and motioned to the other women around me, "I know I am not the only one who is curious, correct?"

A series of murmured agreements and laughs sounded. Esme laughed from behind me at our usual table. Her cigarette smoke clouded the area in a perfume of tobacco. The entire front lawn of the estate, from the dark gates to the main building, had been landscaped into a series of gardens. Our garden, with our specific table, was surrounded by terraces of black roses that formed a protective visual wall. The roses perfumed the air and made our lunchtime rather enjoyable and picturesque.

Bobby's eyes narrowed as the cogs turned in his brain. One of these days he would understand sarcasm. *One of these days*. I kept telling myself that.

"Your scar--"

There it was! I let my fist collide with his beautifully tanned face and felt something crunch. It was only a very small smidge of my physical power, but enough to make him grunt while holding his bleeding nose. I had to retain the small giggle of delight from my inner savage before turning on my black leather heels. Like every damn Monday, Jason led him toward the medical wing.

Routine. Every Monday.

Routine. Different dialogue.

Routine. Same fucking result.

"I think he likes you," Esme teased as she turned to face me.

We sat across from one another at our benched table. Her messy dark waves formed a halo around her smooth, mocha colored skin in the afternoon light. I felt a slight tug of jealousy, as always, at her clear complexion. Not one single scar.

"Probably," I offered while adjusting my cropped leather jacket. Lunchtime was the only time of the day that residents of the academy could actually relax. One hour out of 24. It seemed inhumane. Unless you were me, of course, and had more fucking time than you knew what to do with.

"Are we still on for tomorrow?" Esme asked with curiosity as she hit the ashes off of her cigarette. It was nearly out, which meant our lunchtime was almost to an end. I smiled as a brief moment of appreciation cycled through me at her fantastic memory. Of course, she would remember my birthday. She was fantastic at this friendship shit.

When I first arrived at the academy with a chip on my shoulder, Esme had looked me right in the eye and told me to 'calm my shit.' Something about her straight forward attitude and genuine interest in my well-being eventually broke through my little black heart. We had been best friends ever since. Her loyalty was something I never questioned. In fact, she was one of the only two individuals that I trusted with anything worth mentioning in my life.

"You only turn 21 once," I sighed.

She smiled, humor sparkling in her amber eyes.

"Well, twice, if you count your fake ID."

"As if I need it," I smiled in jest. My eyes caught movement near the gates. My heart jumped from my chest into my throat. At first, I thought it was *them*, but my contract hadn't mentioned them visiting today. When I didn't see a black SUV, I relaxed back into an indifferent posture. I continued to watch the guests as my lips curled into a small smirk.

"I hadn't heard we were receiving any new transfers." I mumbled quietly while looking at Esme. "Have you heard anything about this?"

Esme turned to peer past the usual group of women gathered in the surrounding gardens to see five large, suited men talking to security. They all ranged in height, but their massive builds and expensive clothing told me that they were definitely not human. Instinctively, every part of me was *very okay* with that. Self-preservation told me to go fucking hide because these weren't normal men by any standards.

"Should we say hi?" Her smile was dark and contagious. Esme was a lunatic like myself. Her scars were emotional, rather than physical though. The woman had survived 18 years in a religious cult while hiding that she was madly in love with the cult leader's daughter. In my opinion, she deserved more fun in her life. I had the power to provide that fun.

Unfortunately the fun would be for *us*, not the hot new guys. We had a reputation to maintain. They disrupted our carefully built hierarchy by showing up here. I had made a promise to myself, long ago, that I would always be the queen of my own damn castle. I would not be ruled over. I motioned to one of the girls around our table. Her blue eyes widened in surprise.

"Go invite them over here," I nodded to the gate. The girl nodded and adjusted her uniform as if she were on a mission for the gods themselves.

I nearly smiled at that.

If she only knew.

Esme lit another cigarette before grinning.

"Ready to have some fun?"

2

ADYEN

*H*oly motherfucking shit.

Now, I wasn't a shy guy. There wasn't a shy bone in my body. I was usually very secure in myself and my ability to talk to others. However, for the first time in my life, I was speechless. Every possible point of conversation in my mind was gone. All because of her.

In fact, the only sound I could possibly produce would be a growl. *If that.* My dragon was creating a rumble in my chest that I attempted to silence with a cough. It only brought her attention to me as we approached.

She couldn't have been more than 5'3, yet her entire body radiated a dangerous tension that I had only seen on a defensive cobra. I suppose it was pretty accurate since we had just watched her break the nose of some guy twice her size. As we followed the large eyed girl to the table where we had been '*summoned*,' I felt my eyes widen in realization. This was her.

Taylor, tell Rhodes. This is her.

Rhodes shot me a look and nodded in understanding. We had been sent here for her. I wasn't sure what I had been expecting, but it wasn't her. It wasn't this.

"Hello, boys." She purred in greeting and caused her friend, the only one sitting across from her, to smirk. I imagined this was similar to being summoned to a queen's throne, every surrounding face watched us narrowly with suspicion. It seemed they were very protective of her, which made me want to chuckle. She had created her own following, even on the Earth realm.

Rhodes stepped forward, his body tight with tension, but eyes curious.

"Nice to meet you, I'm Rhodes."

He offered her a hand and she simply grinned like it was fucking Christmas. It was a dangerous grin that spoke of a predatory nature.

She exuded anger, power, as well as sexuality. Her hair was so dark that it had hints of navy blue. It hung in a straight, silk veil down to her waist. While she was short, her entire body was perfectly curved and fit like she spent everyday running and working out. That same tight, curvy body was dressed in painted on jeans and a half top. I was not complaining about the lack of uniform. Yet, it seemed to only apply to her. It was when I met her gaze and saw the annoyance on it that I realized I had been caught staring.

"You done?" She asked through a tight jaw while standing up from the table.

I felt myself smirk at her frustration.

"Done with what?"

Why was I antagonizing her? It wasn't in my nature to do that. At my center, I was protective and reliable. Yet, somewhere in my fucked up brain, I wanted her to react. Instead of apologizing, I kept smiling.

I blamed my dragon, the fucker was an antagonistic and aggressive bastard.

As she stalked forward with precise movements, the scent of ashes and something uniquely *her* surrounded me. Those eyes fixated on me with frustration. I couldn't help but examine her unique coloring. Her eyes, a stunning rich indigo, had a silver edge that surrounded her pupils. They were framed by thick lashes that brushed her cheeks and brought my attention to her lips that, while plump and deep red, were pressed in a thin line. My god, she was beautiful - absolutely fucking beautiful. Annoyed at me, but nonetheless, beautiful. Possibly more beautiful because of her annoyance.

After all, it wasn't everyday that a woman scowled at me. Most wouldn't have risked it.

"Are you done examining me?" She growled, a cute sound, as she tilted her head up. My dragon answered her anger with a rumble that made her pupils dilate. I knew she very much understood that my dragon wasn't threatening her, but it seemed the other answer wasn't preferable to her. She ignored my obvious reaction and narrowed her eyes.

I was impressed by her, considering most people didn't stand toe-to-toe with me. I wouldn't lie. This woman was intimidating and I imagined that she faced the same problem. Instead of backing down, I continued to offer her a challenging gaze. Her confidence and poise only affirmed what I knew of her heritage.

"Maybe," I offered with a singular shoulder shrug. "Maybe not."

I thought I saw amusement flash through her eyes, before she offered an eye roll and moved to sit on the edge of the table. Her friend, currently smoking, rose a brow at all of us with an unimpressed gaze. Gray looked at her and then tucked her silky locks behind her right ear. It was then that I noticed her scar. I tried not to react, but her eyes were trained on us as a group. When I heard Neo make a pained sound, I sighed. Fucking idiot.

I understood it, though. My dragon wanted to know what had fucking caused that.

The scar was a silver color that trailed from her temple to

curve along her jawline. It reminded me of a crescent moon, adding to her beautiful, ivory skin. She narrowed her eyes at Neo and raised her long nails for inspection. The hand had scars on it, smaller round ones. I took in the contrast of her scars next to her set of diamond rings.

She was baiting us. She wanted us to react. To see the contrast.

She screamed wealth and power, yet those scars... *Where the hell did those come from?* Every protective instinct inside of me roared up. I swallowed hard and kept my eyes on her gaze instead of the scars. I knew she wasn't doing this for pity.

A smile crossed her lips.

"Let me make something very clear, boys. I don't really give a fuck about who you are or why you are starting the semester late. Just make sure to stay away from my people and we won't have a problem - got it?" Heads nodded around her.

Rhodes frowned as Taylor offered me a raised brow and an amused smirk. The fucking demon found everything funny. I noticed her entire group was made of women that were staring at her like she was some kind of deity. She probably was to them. Hell, she was like nothing I had ever seen. I wondered why she had placed such a purposeful distance between herself and the other men on campus? At least, I assumed that was the case. She had, essentially, a wall of women surrounding her. Shit, maybe I didn't want to know.

Fuck. No. Now I *had* to know.

"Shouldn't we know the name of *who* we are avoiding?" Athens asked with a coy smile.

He needed to watch himself. Both he and Neo were absolute idiots at times. It was stupid to rise to her challenge when she was this defensive.

This caused an authentic smile to flash onto her face. It was stunning and nearly caused me to lunge forward so I could see it better. It was in my nature to like shiny treasures, after all.

"Gray," she offered and locked eyes with me.

But we already knew that.

3
GRAY

"Who the hell are those guys?" Esme asked curiously while echoing my thoughts. "They seem way older than college kids."

"I would bet 24 or 25. That one asshole seemed younger though," I murmured.

They did seem older, stronger, and bigger… I let out an exhale. My anxiety felt like a constricting snake around my throat. I was terrible with change.

"Come on. Let's get to our classes." She offered with an understanding look of sympathy.

I didn't do well around men and sure as shit not men that big. It was why I offered protection to the women at this school from assholes like them. Even if they were who I suspected, men had fallen into predictable patterns my entire life. Men that big and dominant? They were absolutely nothing but fucking trouble.

"Gray!" A voice called out as we moved down the hall that parted for us.

"What's kickin' Mr. Jackson?" I asked our Dean of Students.

Other than the president, he was the only one I needed to worry about. I made him a deal last year he couldn't refuse.

Mr. Jackson, a young fae himself, was in love with Jason. I had caught the fae and the shifter in a fairly compromising position. That position was the basis for our deal. My deal. The deal stated that I could wear whatever I wanted in exchange for my silence. It was a very small price for their massive secret.

I was perfectly happy to let them live their lives. Plus, I hated the uniforms for the academy and much preferred to wear an outfit like I had on today. My leather heels were classic stilettos with red bottoms and paired with light wash retro Calvin Klein jeans. A white half top fit under my leather jacket. It was a solid outfit, like most of the clothing I wore. I had a thing for clothes. I found them therapeutic.

I'm sure there is an issue somewhere in that concept, but… oh well.

"Could you provide a tour to the new students this next period?" He pleaded.

His eyes were a bright green under those glasses. I nearly snickered at how young he looked. He was a hardass though. Esme had even put distance between us. She didn't want a lecture on how she had altered her uniform skirt.

I nodded once. "Sure, but will it get me out of Theoretical?"

He groaned softly, "You know you still need to be in attendance, even if you have an A."

I patted his shoulder, "Let me worry about that. Where are they now? At the office?"

He nodded and I waved goodbye to Esme. I followed Mr. Jackson to see our new students. Truth be told, spending the afternoon with the hot guys wasn't a problem. No, it was being completely alone with them that was the problem. I did my best to avoid that type of situation.

Mr. Jackson opened the office door and I was immediately met with five different gazes. I smirked and caught Mr. Jackson rolling his eyes. It seemed my amusement wasn't received well by at least half of the men present.

"Ms. Gray will be showing you around today." He explained, his voice sharp. "She is our top student here, so I would suggest showing her the respect she deserves."

Mr. In Charge, as I dubbed him, although his name was Rhodes, snapped his gaze up at me from where he sat. I saw a million questions in those pale green eyes that made my grin grow in size. I really was an asshole. I supposed my ego and cockiness had to make up for the obvious physical size difference between us.

It was very clear these men were warriors, which only cemented my belief that they were from the Fae lands. Humans just weren't built to contain that much power and grace.

"Let's go, boys," I motioned to the hallway with a wave of the hand, making them all walk past me.

Rhodes was first and I didn't hide my analysis of each of them. Why bother? *Big guy* over there had done the same.

Rhodes passed me, staring down at me with a peculiar, pensive look in those pale green eyes that reminded me of mint leaves. They were framed by the same golden lashes as his silky blonde hair. The blonde hair that was tied up in a man bun provided contrast to his dark blue suit, but matched his golden earring in his left ear. If he wasn't someone from school, I wouldn't have hesitated to take him home and climb up that impressive muscular body like a fucking monkey. The man was fucking gorgeous.

He offered a hand once again, "Rhodes."

I took his hand this time and instantly let go, without offering a greeting back. This made him smile. I should have punched him right then, just to reinforce my point. Although, to be fair, I really only did that to Bobby. It was a special relationship.

"Adyen," The next guy offered as I looked up at the man I had dubbed *big guy*. I know I am a literary genius. A nickname master. The CEO of nicknames. The point? I am fucking awesome.

At least, that was my humble opinion.

While Rhodes was lean and around 6'2, this man was massively muscular and nearly 6'7. It was why I had chosen to focus on him first in the gardens. He was the most physically intimidating and not just because of that look in his eyes. That look was dangerous. Actually, he was dangerous. As always, I liked to tackle the scariest threat or problem first.

I took his hand and met his honey colored gaze. He put pressure on our grip and a smile snuck onto those perfect lips. Yep, I needed to punch him. These men had way too much confidence.

"*You* can let go now," I commanded with a raised brow before forcing him to step away.

He offered me a perfect white smile and ran a hand through his short neat black hair.

I looked to the next person. Instantly, I felt my expression soften *which was stupid, of course*. Yet, I knew pain. This kid had a lot of it. He was the one that had grunted at my scar. Side note- who actually grunts? It's nearly as bad as growling. I had a feeling one or two of these men did that regularly, if my memory of shifters served correct.

Looking at him, I instantly thought of Esme. His skin tone was a deep mocha like hers but filled with chiseled hard lines. He didn't have the slightly older face of the first two. Rather, his sharp jawline seemed to be fixed in a perfect, angelic shape. Yet, I noticed a hardened pain that the first two men didn't have. I found myself fascinated by this man within the first few seconds of knowing him.

"Neo," he put out a large hand.

I noticed, examining him further, that his dark, impeccable face had an almost metallic undertone to it in the afternoon light.

He peered at me with large, dark eyes sparkling like onyx stones. I gave him an awkward smile and a handshake. This caused big guy Adyen to chuckle.

Yeah. I would punch him.

"My name is Athens," the next guy announced, pushing Neo out of the way.

I felt my eyes widen. This guy was much louder than Neo, but he was a near physical replica. He had been the one to ask for my name, even though I had been doing my best to intimidate them. Honestly, who the hell was I kidding? These men were huge. Oh fucking well. Fake it until you fucking make it.

"Hi," I nodded and shook his hand.

He grinned a brilliant smile and swung an arm around Neo easily. I looked up to the next guy.

Oh, wow. I couldn't tell if I hated him or loved him. Maybe... both?

"Taylor," he stated with amusement and darkness which lurked behind a pair of beautiful, emerald eyes.

I narrowed my eyes, not because he didn't offer me a hand, but because he seemed supremely confident. Those eyes. Lord, help me. Those eyes were lit with a fire that I loved and hated. He was sexy and that made me hate him. Honestly, it was probably why I hated all of them.

Wow. You know, even to me, that felt like a lot of hate.

"Isn't Taylor a girl's name?" I asked with amusement.

He narrowed his eyes. They cooled considerably which I considered a victory on its own. I ignored the laughs from the other four as we stared one another down.

"Isn't 'Gray' a color?" He shot back and made sure to emphasize my name.

I smirked. Okay, okay. Good response. I rolled my eyes before clapping enthusiastically.

"Come on, carrot top. Time to show you around."

Okay, so his hair was more of a crimson and he was probably the sexiest out of all of them but... like, whatever. Unlike Adyen and the twins who were bulky and nearly a full foot taller than me, he was lean like Rhodes. Both men still clocked in over six feet.

"Gray, you can bring them back here after the tour." Mr. Jackson said, looking at his watch.

I smirked with amusement, "...or I will let you know where the bodies are."

Mr. Jackson rolled his eyes, but Neo watched me with caution. I grinned stupidly.

"Alright, so welcome to Mera Academy named after said Mera Luna--" I motioned around the long hallway to a huge portrait. The woman was as boring as her name was interesting. It wasn't confirmed, but I was nearly positive that she had been a pixie. Or maybe a brownie? I just assumed because she was so damn tiny with frail white fair and massive white eyes.

Then again, no one ever confirmed 'what' they were here. Unless you knew someone well or caught them in the act, you just knew they were different. Hell. The only reason I knew Mr. Jackson was fae and Jason a shifter was because I had caught them in such an intimate moment.

"Why don't you wear a uniform?" Adyen gruffed out. I narrowed my eyes at the disruption. I had been giving them a very fascinating, interesting... yeah, the academy's history was fairly lackluster. I could feel them behind me, but Rhodes continued trying to walk next to me. Gods, I bet it bugged him to not be leading the group. I purposefully sped up. Shifters that had alpha tendencies were fun to fuck with, especially since I was a far more dangerous predator than them.

"As I was saying," I continued. "This is the academy and it consists of three buildings. The current building is called *Alpha* because of obvious reasons."

"What obvious reasons?" Rhodes asked.

"What was the first thing you saw when you arrived?" I sighed in resignation.

Athens's voice sounded like a smile, "You."

I gave him a deadpan look and began walking backward, "*Anyway,* this is Alpha, Beta is the dinning and rec area, and Gamma is the living space - unless you live off the estate grounds."

"We do, love," Rhodes offered calmly.

Yep, such a *Mr. In Charge*. Wait, hold up. Was that an accent? Oh, sweet baby Jesus, help me. I've always been a sucker for accents, especially since the Earth realm had so many interesting ones.

"First, not your 'love'. Second, good for you," I responded, trying to fight the urge to ask *where*.

"Moving on, the medical unit is to your left--"

"Gray," a voice called as my smirk returned.

Bobby walked down the hallway toward me. His shirt was bloodstained and his eyes were frustrated. Those large brown eyes were at odds with his hulking muscular form. I suppose a lot of people saw him as scary, but he *really* reminded me of a golden retriever. I just couldn't get that analogy out of my head.

Not that I had ever owned a dog. Or any pet. I didn't really do well with keeping things alive.

"Hey, Bobby," I spoke as he came to the head of our group.

His eyes immediately looked at the men behind me and his face changed from frustration to concern. Those eyes focused back on me with clarity.

"Who are they?"

I offered him a look, "New guys and I'm giving them a tour. Why? What's up?"

He looked behind me again with narrowed eyes, "Nothing, I just wanted to talk about--"

I placed a hand on his chest, "Your nose is barely healed. Let's not go there."

He chuckled while looking down at me, "Yeah, you're right. I wanted to apologize though. Dinner tonight?"

My eyebrow raised, "Bobby..."

Bobby placed a hand on my shoulder and I rolled them back to detach.

"Just think about it."

I barely heard him over the growl someone made behind me. Now, that was a beautiful sound. So unrestrained and primal.

"Go to class, Bobby," I stated simply.

His eyes narrowed behind me before he squeezed my shoulder again. I shook my head as he retreated. I tried not to think about his hand on my shoulder. I really didn't do well with touch.

"You are not going to dinner with him, are you?" Taylor, I think, asked as I turned around.

I raised my brows at the myriad of expressions. Neo and Athens were watching Bobby walk away. Taylor looked absolutely incensed. Rhodes's jaw was tight and had a hand on Adyen. I sighed before tucking my hands in my jeans and leaning back in my heels.

"*Who* I go to dinner with, Taylor," I responded quietly, looking at the retreating figure, "is none of your damn business. Is that understood?"

His eyes were on fire and his nostrils flared.

"But, come on. That guy--"

I put a manicured hand up, "Stop."

I continued in a calm tone, "I don't need this. I don't need you to worry, or even think about me, honestly. We don't know one another and I plan to keep it that way. Drop it now."

Rhodes went to open his mouth and I turned to cut him off with an indifferent tone, "I don't care what you are about to say. Understood? I don't give a fuck."

"Are you always such a bitch?"

I smirked at Taylor, "This is me on my good behavior, baby."

The tour is over. I turned on my heel and began to walk down the hallway. I ignored Athens's call to me. Instead, I went to get some fresh air. Who the hell did they think they were?

Unfortunately, I think I knew the answer to that question.

4
ATHENS

"I like her," I chimed in as the five of us walked around the campus mapping out our classes. Our pointless classes. Neo smiled while walking next to me, but I could tell my twin was nervous around her. In fairness, the woman was unpredictable. That was something Neo would find frustrating, no doubt.

My eyes tracked all of the tiny humans outside of the academy gates. Had humans always been this damn small? I laughed softly in amusement. They sure as shit built them larger in the Horde.

"Plus, she shut Rhodes up," Taylor snickered from nearby.

Rhodes let out a growl that sounded a lot like his animal and made me grin.

"She didn't *shut me up*," Rhodes offered as his English accent became more apparent with all of us being alone. "I just don't bother explaining myself to kittens."

I let out a loud laugh, "I get it because you're a bigger cat than a kitten? That was the joke right?" Everyone groaned as Neo rolled his eyes. Shifter jokes were the best, hands down.

"Do you think she will go to dinner with that Bobby?" Taylor asked as his eyes darkened.

"I don't know," Rhodes sighed. "Adyen nearly bit his head off, so knowing her... probably."

"Wasn't me," Adyen's eyes shone with mirth as his creature shone through.

Taylor shook his head, "That guy's head was all fucked up. I didn't like it."

Adyen growled in a low threatening tone, "How so?"

Taylor groaned, "Very twisted and dark like elaborate vines. Maybe too many hits to the head?"

I smiled with amusement, "From her possibly?"

"Hopefully," Taylor barked out a laugh.

"Neo, she seemed to like you," I encouraged nudging his shoulder. "You should go talk to her."

Neo made a sound in the back of his throat and shook his head, "Probably not a good idea."

"Why?"

He sighed, "Because she literally saw right through me. Like I was transparent. I fear going to talk to her would be a tad *intense*. Neither of us are ready for that."

I could feel my twin was hiding something. I hated that, but I understood how closed up he was. I knew he would tell me when he was ready.

"Plus, he would tell her everything," Rhodes offered knowingly.

I nodded my agreement. She would need to be told soon though. The woman was sharp and she would see through all of us with given time. I didn't mind that as much as I presumed.

5
GRAY

When I woke up in our dorm the next morning, I knew something was different. Esme was sitting in our kitchen with a big fucking grin. We had a beautiful two-bedroom, one bath suite with a window wall overlooking the estate. The fall sunlight shone through with hazy rays that were expected in the morning. I could smell coffee, which was always a good sign.

The entire room was a gunmetal grey and white, softened by large rugs and crystal lighting. I moved toward the kitchen table. I was dressed in a blue nightshirt and slippers. My eyes landing on the Starbucks coffee cup and a *fucking* bouquet of roses. What in the ever-loving Christ?!

"Who the fuck are these from?" I demanded while pointing to the offensive objects.

Esme burst out laughing, "*Not me,* unfortunately. Bobby dropped the coffee and roses off. Look at him being such a good boy."

"You're shitting me," I murmured and took a sip of the coffee. What was he thinking? Not to be difficult but this wasn't even how I took my coffee. So what was he up to? I examined the roses for hidden knives but found nothing. I suppose it was truly a nice gesture. One that I am positive he meant for anyone visiting my apartment to see.

"I think it's sweet! You punch him and he buys you flowers, especially for your birthday…" she cooed. "It's like some fucked up sitcom. *Join us this Sunday for the Bobby and Gray show*!"

I snarled and tossed a pillow at her mocking television host voice. I walked over to the fridge. I poured extra creamer in the coffee before even attempting to face the day. Esme was already dressed because despite both of our classes starting in the afternoon, she preferred to be productive each morning. I was a late sleeper. Sue me.

"I think he's an idiot." I finally growled. "Too many fucking punches to the head."

"Maybe he's into that?" She smiled coyly. "Maybe it's some weird kink."

I choked out a laugh, "No, that would be abuse." Before she could respond though, a knock sounded on the door and caused me to frown. Now, who in the hell would that be?

"That better be one of your girls," I stated evenly. I moved to the door and flung it open.

Taylor. Of course, it would be Taylor.

I was happy to say that he looked far more normal dressed in the standard uniform compared to the dark green suit that he wore yesterday. Still handsome though. Still completely sexy.

"What?" I snarled while taking another sip of my coffee.

Those emerald eyes sparkled taking in my outfit, or lack thereof, before he began speaking, "I wanted to walk you to class to apologize for yesterday."

"Apologize?" I rose a brow as Esme snuck up behind me.

"Well, hi there," Esme laughed, slightly nudging my shoulder. "Gray, I am gonna sneak past you to go grab breakfast. Be ready by seven tonight!"

I flipped her off as she slid her tall, slim form past me. I had always been jealous of her model-thin body. I looked at Taylor, expecting his eyes to be trained on her. I was secretly pleased to find them on me. I smirked.

"Like something you see?" I teased.

Taylor's eyes ignited and he stepped forward into my space. The scent of bonfire encapsulated all my thoughts. I didn't move and he took this as a sign to reach down, trailing a hand across my silk-covered hip. I tried not to flinch.

Now, a normal reaction would have been to lean into him. He was totally hot and did funny things to my body. Hot things. Instead, I took that hand and squeezed it hard enough that pain registered on his face. I placed it calmly back onto his chest.

"Do. Not. Touch. Me." I murmured, my eyes narrowed. A look crossed his face, fleeting but dark and concerned before he held up his hands in surrender.

"Sorry, Gray." He apologized sincerely. "For that and for yesterday."

Damn, I nearly felt bad at the sincerity in his voice. I couldn't get a fucking read on this guy. Half the time, I thought he was an ass. The other half, he seemed rather sweet. I noticed a small amount of reddish-brown stubble on his chin as he rubbed it in distraction. Shit, he was handsome. I pressed my lips together and tried to not jump into his arms.

Yes. I realize I just told him to not touch me.

Yes. I find him fuckable and want to climb him like a tree.

No. I never said I was consistent.

"You're welcome to come in, but I am not even close to ready to go," I stated softly. I didn't accept apologies, as a general rule, but he could make them all he wanted.

"I can just wait," he stated. His eyes took in the dorm. Did I really just let him in? Good idea, Gray. Absolutely brilliant. Yes, because no one has ever regretted letting a man they didn't know into their dorm.

"Alright. Just sit and stay or whatever," I growled defensively as his lips twerked.

"I'm not a dog." He answered while sitting down on the couch. His large arms went onto the back of the leather and I was distracted, momentarily by his muscles. He smiled brilliantly at my attention and it caused me to snap out of it. I rolled my eyes and muttered annoyances to myself as I slipped into my bedroom to get ready.

* * *

Nearly half an hour later, I was ready for class. My legs were showcased in a tight leather skirt and thigh-high flat black boots. I tucked in a silky plum top that had billowed sleeves and hung off the shoulders. Finally, I adjusted my leather necklace in place. The reflection in the mirror was smooth and beautiful, besides the scars that marked my shoulders and back. Small round ones and long gashes.

I had learned long ago not to hide them. It made people view them as a weakness they could exploit. Instead, I braided my silky hair into a waist-length style and wondered if this would remove the light in Taylor's eyes when he looked at me. Maybe it was more of a hope. I spritzed myself with perfume and left the sleek navy and silver bedroom I kept.

"Shit, Gray!" Taylor exclaimed with a dangerous smile flitting across his face. Not the reaction I wanted. I rolled my eyes at him and that, for whatever reason, caused him to chuckle.

"Why don't you have to wear a uniform?" He asked curiously as he followed me to the kitchen.

I shrugged my shoulder, "It's too much work to argue with me, so they don't."

Taylor smirked at that before his eyes snapped to the bouquet of roses on the counter. Forgotten along with my half-finished coffee cup.

"Secret admirer?" He asked with a dip of his brow that seemed almost contemplative.

I crossed my arms in a slightly defensive posture, "Not so secret. Bobby dropped them off."

"The pup from yesterday?" He asked as his jaw tensed.

Why was I explaining myself to him? More so, how did he figure Bobby a pup? Taylor couldn't have been much older than him.

"Nope," I wiggled my finger at him. "You have no right to get all 'caveman-ish' about him. I barely know you. If you get all weird, it will hurt any progress we've made."

His green eyes moved away from the flowers. He sighed, meeting my gaze, "Fine. Fine. Let's go before we are late for my *very important* first day of class."

"Bossy," I grinned at his sarcasm but appreciated the effort to move on. I knew it was difficult for men like him to not be bossy. We left the dorm, and for the first time since school began, I let a boy walk with me to class. I really should have just punched him instead.

6

RHODES

I had to grip the table as she walked into the computer lab. Her saunter causing the entire room to go quiet. She smirked as Taylor followed after her. He looked like a fucking puppy dog. His eyes showed amusement, but his body was tense. I noticed his eyes kept moving to her shoulders and then back to me. What was he trying to tell me? I didn't have time to listen to his mental nudges before Gray approached with her blue eyes trained on me with speculation.

"You're in *my* seat, Rhodes." She stated as the class watched in interest. Her skirt was skin tight. I could follow the long trail of her legs from the top of her boots to between her thighs with ease. Fuck. She was a hot little minx.

My jaguar made a purr in the back of my throat that I attempted to silence. Instead, I responded with normal confidence, "You strike me as adaptable, you'll be fine."

I had to stop my grin as her mouth popped open in surprise. Taylor wouldn't meet my eyes, but I could hear his laughter through our silent bond. I expected her to yell or get in my face. Instead, she lowered into the seat next to me, turning to face me completely. I watched her with interest.

A hand snaked out and grabbed my jaw gently with a fairly impressive strength that brought us face to face. I could feel the energy strumming off her in thick waves, and for just a moment, the room seemed to be bathed in silver. It was like the two of us were completely alone and it made it painfully clear just how much she was holding back.

She whispered quietly in my ear. Malice was radiating through her, "Let me make something very clear, Rhodes. I don't deal with bullshit from men like you. I don't let them, or you, push me around. I don't let anyone take what is mine. So I am going to kindly because you didn't know this, ask you to get the fuck out of my seat."

Our faces were so close to one another that all it would take to kiss her would be a slight surge forward. I could taste those soft lips and run my hands along her sleek, moonlit scar with ease. I also suspected I would get my nose broken in a second flat. That didn't bother me all that much, though. So what stopped me? The anger in her eyes, deep, ingrained, and ignitable. This was bigger than me. My jaguar paced recklessly through my mind. He wanted to retaliate against her dominance.

He wanted to pin her down and force her to tell us everything. He wanted her submission and for her to bare her neck to us. He wanted to understand her. Why did she not like being touched? Why did she flinch around men? Why did she have so many scars? Talking about scars, where the fuck did those scars on her shoulders and back come from?

"Do you understand me, Rhodes?" Her voice was lethal and dangerous.

"Tell me where the scars are from and I will move," I murmured. I was testing the waters and I think I knew it would backfire. I should have expected the hand that slipped around my throat as her nails pierced my skin with sudden violence. Still, I didn't move my gaze. She needed this control to feel better. If I easily removed her grip, it would only remove any chance of me finding out the answers I wanted. She would become defensive and back away.

"Do not ask me about my scars." She snarled quietly. "Ever."

I nodded and switched places with her easily. I rubbed my jaw to see if she had drawn blood. She had and a small part of my animal loved that she had marked us. Ah. Fuck. That was the last thing I needed right now. It was difficult as a shifter though. You were constantly fighting for dominance with those around you. When someone did best you, it was considered a good thing even though you didn't want it originally. A complicated dynamic.

As she passed me, her hair braid swung over her shoulder and my entire body began vibrating with anger. I felt my jaguar snarl at the extent of the horrible scarring on her shoulders and back. My eyes snapped to Taylor, who offered me a single head shake. When I first saw it, I assumed there had been only a few that covered her shoulder tops. Now. Well shit. Now I could see that they covered her entire bloody back.

As class started, my eyes continued to trail along the injured area. The scars were small and round on her shoulders. I knew those, I had two on my shoulder as well. Larger than cigarettes, but most definitely, cigar burns. The others though? They were raised like knife cuts and criss crossed over some thinner whip-like ones. What the fuck had happened to her? More importantly, who the fuck had hurt her like that?

The class continued to create more questions than answers. Why did every woman look at her with hopefulness? Why did every man stay away from her? Was she a protector? A bully? I couldn't get a read on the dynamic here. I mean, hell, why did the teachers speak of her with such reverence? Was she truly the best student here?

After nearly an hour, I turned to her. A strand of her dark silky hair escaped her braid. Before I realized what I had done, I tucked it away from her face. A look crossed her face as she flinched back and those eyes hardened into pure gemstones. Taylor made a worried sound in the back of his throat while pushing at my mental bond. I ignored him because I was very well aware of the mistake I had made.

"Rhodes, you *ever* touch me again and you will wish you hadn't." She growled, her eyes turning a deep, nearly midnight, color. I could feel the winds change outside, a thundercloud appearing and casting the sky in a deep rich grey color that made the room filled with shadows. I nodded as she stood up and walked away, her steps filled with tension. I looked to Taylor in confusion and he let out a deep exhale upon her exit.

"It seems our little kitten is going to be a tad more difficult to convince than we assumed," I responded to his concerned expression.

Taylor gave an amused, yet dry, chuckle as the thunder outside cracked through the empty classroom. Yes, I predicted that Gray was going to be something that we hadn't expected in the least.

7
GRAY

"Fucking stupid Rhodes," I growled as I sat outside. My fingers held a shading pencil as my eyes traced patterns in the leather-bound notebook. I was shaking from my interaction with him. I didn't even feel like drawing, but it calmed the vibrating energy that seemed to have grown more powerful under my skin.

Rhodes didn't scare me. I mean he was intimidating as hell, but it was the calculating gaze in his eyes that I didn't like. They scanned right through me. When I threatened him, he didn't blink from his dissection of my psyche. I felt as though he had not argued because he knew that I needed to be in control. I fucking hated that.

I hated that someone I barely knew had me pinned already.

I could feel the heat from his fingers when he had touched me. I could hear the interest in his slightly accented voice when he asked me about my damn scars. What I didn't see? Pity. Rather, there was interest and a controlled calm that reminded me of a therapist. I hated him more than Taylor right now. I should have marched my ass back inside to punch him. Instead, I thought about how good those warm hands felt on the part of me no one had ever touched with compassion.

"Gray," Bobby's voice sounded from the pavilion. I smirked as the big, puppy-eyed man came and sat across from me. His hair was wet from the sheets of rain coming down around the pavilion. Here, I felt centered. Why was he here though? He wasn't supposed to be here.

"Hey, Bobby." I answered quietly, my fingers closing the leather-bound journal.

"Happy birthday, beautiful. Did you get the flowers and coffee?" He asked curiously with a bright smile. There was humor in his eyes, making the normal brown turn into honey.

"I did." I answered quietly. "Why did you bring those over?"

He rose a brow with undisguised amusement, "Isn't it obvious? I *like* you, Gray."

I pursed my lips to not smile and looked at his puppy dog eyes. Why was that so cute? Why was everyone around me so damn handsome lately? Ugh. Bad thoughts, Gray. Bad thoughts.

"Well don't." I replied easily with indifference. "I will just end up punching you."

He grinned roguishly, "But that's *us*, Gray. I say something stupid and you punch me."

I rose a brow but was distracted by a large body moving through the rain with grace. Adyen appeared. He raised a brow at the two of us while shaking his hair like a wet dog. Why was everyone a fucking dog in my head? I had literally never had a dog. In fact, I figured myself much more of a cat person. He smiled at me, before shooting a look at Bobby.

"What do you need, Adyen?" I asked with interest while leaning my chin on my palm.

He smirked, "Came to see how my lil brawler is doing."

"Your brawler?" I asked with laughter bubbling up. *This guy...*

"Yeah, buddy. She hits me, not you." Bobby stated proudly. I lost it and began laughing. Was he jealous? Oh gods. What was even happening today? Maybe it was one of those odd human movies where everything gets fucked up on your birthday.

Both men looked at me. One looked at me with confusion, the other with contained amusement.

"Listen, Bobby," I said quietly with an undertone of warning. "I will think about dinner like you asked, but it seems that Adyen has something to talk to me about. I'll find you later, okay?"

Bobby frowned while standing up, "Fine. But remember, you don't get to take my place."

Adyen grinned a predatory smile that made me warm, "Don't worry. I would never dream of taking your place as her punching bag."

Bobby shook his head, spearing me with a glance that flashed with something dark, and jogged off into the rain. For a big guy, he moved quickly. Adyen sat across from me, effectively blocking my view, and fixed me with a penetrating look.

"What can I do for you?" I curiously asked, my eyes trailing along his handsome face. What can I do for you? Really, Gray? What am I? In an office? A secretary? Fuck. I needed to re-learn how to interact socially with the male species outside of punching them.

Wait. Why do I give a fuck?

He grinned as those amber eyes twinkled, "I really did come to see how you were doing."

"Is Rhodes being a gossip?" I mused with an eyebrow raise. I was glad my hair was down right now, covering my shoulders and keeping me somewhat warm. It wasn't that I wanted to hide them from Adyen, but he struck me as someone who would pitch a fit about the story behind them.

Adyen smiled, "Definitely. He is very interested in you."

I rolled my eyes, "Very cool story. I am *not* interested in him."

"What are you interested in?"

"Not making friends." I explained lightly which only served to make him smile.

"Crazy storm, right?" He changed topics like whiplash. My eyes examined the heavy rain and dark gray skies peeking out from around the pavilion.

"Seems about right," I stated dryly. "Matches my mood."

"Wet?" He asked coyly with a shocking, yet charming, smile.

I offered a frustrated smirk with an eye roll, "*Smooth*, but no."

As if directed, the weather let up and the skies lightened to a pale gray. I couldn't control the small smirk that appeared on my lips. Maybe the weather was a reflection of my mood? I bet I could make some hail come down if I was pissed. Oh! Better yet, lightning. Yes. That would be fucking awesome.

"Cool necklace," Adyen offered with a smile, changing the topic once again. I gave him one back because it was a cool necklace. Esme had given it to me. I tossed my hair back and slipped it off, so that I could show him the piece. However, as I went to pass it across the table, a deep growl took me off guard and forced me to stop. What had I said about growling again?

My eyes snapped up to see his eyes light with fire. Not in a metaphorical sense either. No, it was as if a roaring inferno had been shrunk down into his amber eyes. They were focused on my shoulders and it caused me to grimace with annoyance. I sighed while slipping the necklace back on. We were done here.

"Who did that to you?" He barely got out through a strangled voice, his entire body vibrated with a very animalistic energy.

I rolled my eyes, "How do you know it's a *who*?" I mean, I guess that was obvious but it could have been self-inflicted. Or maybe I had been in an accident? He had no idea.

"Gray, answer me." He demanded, with a dominance dripping from his tone that made me bristle.

"No." I snapped easily and moved from the table. Another, louder growl, sounded at the view of my back. Fuck my life. Mr.

Growly over here needed to get a grip before I hit him over the head.

"Gray... please?" He pleaded in a rough voice as my eyes tracked the pity growing in those angry eyes.

"Fuck you," I growled out. "Don't you dare feel pity for me."

I stalked past him with fury, embarrassment, and anger running through my veins. I hated that I was feeling the second. A searing hand snuck out to catch my wrist in a vice grip. It caused an automatic shiver of dread to crawl up my spine like a snake. My eyes snapped to his and his face completely changed from lost to something darker. We both stilled for a brief moment.

"I. Do. Not. Pity. You." He murmured standing up from the bench and moving closer to me. My throat closed up as he invaded my space with the scent of cinnamon and ash crowding my senses. I wanted to be scared, but something stopped me from truly fearing this giant. Instead, when my back hit the pavilion railing, a warmth exploded through me that caused my toes to tingle. *He couldn't hurt me.* No. That was stupid, he could most definitely hurt me, but he wouldn't.

"*Tell me* who did this to you." He whispered through a tight jaw. He used the hand not holding my wrist to brush against my hip softly. "Please."

Shit. Could he feel what his touch was doing to me? There was a deep-rooted connection inside of me, flaring to life in response to his animal. Unlike Rhodes and Taylor, I didn't bother telling him to not touch me. I wasn't sure why exactly, except that I knew I could trust him. He wouldn't hurt me. He also wouldn't ask to be in my space though, either. He just expected me to be okay with him being there. In my air. In my space. As if he fucking owned it. As if he had a right to it.

Maybe he did.

What the fuck was I saying? Had I lost my damn mind?

"It doesn't matter anymore." I responded breathlessly. I was shaking, just slightly, because his overwhelming presence was everything I should fear. Everything. Yet, I couldn't remove the desire building through my system and my power urging me to touch him. My fingers twitched to spread across that massive chest. I prayed I wouldn't have as strong of a reaction to the other boys in private, but knew that was probably a lost cause. The fact that I had even noticed them to begin with spelled trouble for me from the start.

"Fuck that!" He rasped out. "You flinch every single time someone touches you."

"Let it go." I stated evenly, my voice nearly catching.

"Only for today." he demanded softly. "You are going to tell me. Soon."

I let out a dark rumble, "You *do not* get to decide that, Adyen."

The searing hand dropped from my wrist and lifted my chin with a commanding force, "I am going to kill whoever did that to you. Understand?"

Oh man. Part of me totally wanted to punch him for speaking to me like that, but the other part of me was swooning. Who was this intense warrior man? Willing to avenge my honor and kill for me? ME?! I must have died. If he only knew what I was capable of.

Maybe I had died and gone to Gray's fantasy land? Yes, that made far more sense. I pressed my lips together with a dark smile.

"Can't kill the dead, Adyen."

His eyebrows shot up as I escaped his grasp with a quick turn. I gave him a light punch in the side for emphasis and escaped through the rain. It was only then that I realized I had forgotten my journal. Fucking shit. Today was not my day.

8
ADYEN

"Bloody hell." Rhodes murmured darkly. "You think she *killed* whoever did that?"

I shrugged, but watched her from across campus. I had her leather journal under my arm. I was waiting to see how long it would take her to come demand it from me. I wasn't hiding it at all and I knew she had seen it in my hand.

"Bastard seemed to deserve it, as far as I am concerned," Taylor grumbled.

My eyes focused on her. She was currently talking to a group of girls. One of them was in tears across the table from her. A soft look came over her face that I had yet to see anywhere else. It was odd seeing any softness cross that beautiful face.

"That is probably why she offers protection to all these girls," Rhodes mused while twirling his pen in a distracted fashion. Our spot across the courtyard allowed us direct access to see Gray in her garden of black roses. We probably looked like creeps. We had abandoned the pretense of homework long ago to watch her.

"From what?" I wondered out loud. "Bobby seems pretty harmless."

"I don't trust him." Taylor stated softly. "Kid's brain is all dark and messy."

"I still don't see him being a threat though." I explained with quiet certainty. I didn't get a good feeling from him either, but did he seem dangerous enough to threaten the population of women here? No. The threat was not him.

Neo walked over with Athens. They had finished a class early. Athens's eyes were bright as he announced some news.

"Rumor around campus is that Gray's birthday party is tonight."

"Fuck. Today's her birthday?"

Rhodes grimaced with a grunt, "We should have known that from the file."

"I bet you feel like a jerk, Rhodes," Taylor chided in amusement.

I found it amusing but also worrisome. I pushed her today as well. Now, I was holding her journal captive. Those eyes found mine from across the courtyard once more. I could feel that both Rhodes and I were becoming more restless as our animals began to show signs of acting out.

This behavior didn't bother me as much. I was very much used to acting on animalistic impulses. Dragons are taught to foster that. Shit, even members of Rhodes's community were taught to engage their animal and act on their will, occasionally. Unfortunately, our leader thrived on control and rarely listened to his jaguar.

I predicted it would cause some serious problems. I mean my dragon was telling me to throw Gray over our shoulder and take her to the Fae lands. Would I? Not yet. At some point though? Most likely. I had no patience.

"We should find out where it is going to be," Rhodes commented lightly.

Neo spoke up finally, "It's at a club in the downtown district."

Before I could say anything, the gates opened to the campus and sent a loud metallic sound over the grounds. Gray's eyes snapped up from the crying girl to the large dark SUV entering into the long driveway. Instantly, Gray dismissed everyone from the table including her friend Esme. They scattered. Quickly. Efficiently. Practiced.

My prediction was that *this* was the threat.

I was instantly up, as the doors of the large car opened. Bobby, a stupid smile on his face, got out and behind him were four other men whom I had never seen before. Rhodes put a hand on my arm as the car drove away and all five men approached her table. It was painfully obvious that the four of them, excluding Bobby, were fae.

"I don't like this." I growled out as one of the men sat next to her. He sat very close and caused her to flinch. Nope, I didn't like this at fucking all. The final straw though? One of the men, nearly my size, grabbed her neck in a commanding nature and forced her to look directly at him. All of that fight, that spark, in her eyes had disappeared.

Rhodes was across the grounds faster than I was.

9
GRAY

We lived in a complicated world. The academy wasn't well liked by many because we had a secret. Well, several secrets. All of them surrounded the 'gifts' that our students had. These talents, while not directly stated, made us different enough that human instinct told the rest of society that we didn't fit in. Mera Academy was for those of us with gifts and talents that wanted to be safe. For those of us that didn't want to be outcasts. We weren't here to develop our talents. We were here to go to college in a safe environment void of violence.

It wasn't like we had families to keep us safe.

We were a small group. Our female population was even smaller. It left us in a vulnerable position. Specifically, vulnerable to men who knew our secret, like the ones in front of me. Bobby, sitting on the far end, was essentially a punching bag to these four. Graduates and now huge donors for the academy, these four seemed to relish in using their status to harm others. I would tell them to fuck off, but I was afraid they would direct their attention elsewhere.

Instead, when they came onto campus for meetings, which

wasn't very often, they would bully me. It kept them away from the other girls. It made them feel like the strong tough guys *they thought* they were. The cost to me? Some measly PTSD from my years of extensive abuse. So yeah, I lied to Rhodes when I said no one bullied me anymore. These guys most definitely did. *I let them* because it saved other women here.

"Gray," Damon smiled as he pet my throat in a possessive grip. "I heard it's your birthday today. Is that true?"

In any other situation, I would have called Damon attractive. Actually, all four men were beautiful in the way fae tended to be. It was a raw, primal beauty that vibrated with dark power. Ivory skin, tall, lethal muscles, and dark hair with glittering eyes. It was the stuff books were written about, if you disregarded the evil sadistic flair. *You know,* the one where the guy gets off on hurting women? Yeah. The fucking one that has Damon's name branded all over it.

"Yep," I murmured as Bobby ignored all of us. His eyes on the brown table and his jaw clenched. Stupid. I knew he was the one who told them about my birthday.

"Want to celebrate?" Talon asked with a leering smile as his hair fell in dark waves around his face. Gods, no. *You creep.* The last thing I wanted was to celebrate with Talon.

"Not particularly," I responded simply.

Damon smirked his dark eyes sparkling with excitement.

"Ashford and Kennedy once shared a girl on her birthday. I am positive they would *love* to again."

I snarled as he tightened his grip. I tried to keep cool, but I was positive that he wasn't asking or gauging my interest. Kennedy chuckled, but Ashford looked over his shoulder at the sound of approaching footsteps. A dark smile appeared on his face.

"Are these your boyfriends?" Ashford asked as his eyes glinted maliciously behind his glasses.

"I don't have-" *Or shit maybe I did?*

Instantly, Ashford was caught up in a hold by Athens. The hold was practiced and showed the restraint of a trained professional. It looked as though he had done it a million times before. I had always thought of these brothers as huge, but in the twin's easy hold, I wasn't so sure. Athen's jaw was clenched tight. Neo had an impressive hold on Kennedy. Who knew the shy twin was capable of that? Scratch that. The more time I spent around Neo, the more I realized he was shielding what I assumed to be a larger reserve of power. How deep that power went? I had no idea.

I would have made a remark but both men were laser focused on Damon's hand. The hand that was more of a strangled grip on my throat now. Fantastic.

"What is this?" Damon asked with mirth.

I grimaced as I caught the gaze of Taylor. Oh, carrot top had a bit of a temper in an unsurprising turn of events. He rounded the table, flying over it with agility, and grabbed Talon by his neck. "You're going to want to get your hand off her now, understand?"

Talon snarled, but Taylor rolled his eyes and yanked him off the bench. I had nearly forgotten about his hold on me as well. It was terrifying that I had let Talon out of my watch for even a moment. The guy was creepy as fuck. My eyes went to Bobby who looked shocked. I tried to swallow, but Damon still had my throat.

"Touch me and I crush her throat," Damon offered with a devious glint. Of course, he was enjoying this. I looked up behind him to find Adyen. I had seen the man heated, but this was different. He was furious. His eyes burned into mine and I couldn't look away. Instead, I just made sure not to move. I really wasn't interested in bruises.

Rhodes stepped toward the table and I repressed a shiver. Clearly, I had underestimated these men. It was very obvious that Rhodes was a very powerful, lethal, and dominant predator in his human and shifter form. Like really, really deadly. He moved easily, like he was stalking his prey, and circled the table to stand behind me. I felt his hands on my shoulders, warm and comforting, as Damon looked up at him with humor.

I nearly flinched at his hands on my scars, but instead of rejecting the touch, I accepted it. I would take pity over my wind pipe being damaged right now. Plus, Rhodes's hands felt good on me. I would consider the implications of that later.

"Release her," He stated quietly. His voice was deceptively soft.

"Why?" Damon offered a dark laugh. "I have a deal with her. She's very much okay with this."

"I don't give a fuck what your deal is," Rhodes responded as if he was discussing local weather. "This is unacceptable."

"You're not SE, so calm your shit. She's my girl."

"Are you his girl?" Rhodes asked quietly as his hand smoothed over my skin. I tried to answer, but couldn't fully breathe. Instead, a pathetic wheezing of my breath came out. *Good job, Gray.* Adyen nearly lost his shit over that noise. I just knew he would be growling a lot when I met him.

"Well, Mr. Hollingworth, I am SE and this is my team," Rhodes stated taking out a badge with black raised edges and silver metal plating. *Oh fancy.* Those were totally only for Earth realm use only, no one in the fae realms would care about a stupid badge. "Unless you want to get the Horde leadership called, you will release her."

Fucking Supernatural Enforcement? The Horde? Yeah. That would be just my fucking luck. I always fucked myself over somehow. I nearly just let Damon choke me at that point. These guys were essentially the military of the Fae lands and it seemed they were specifically from the Horde.

Out of all three realms in the fae lands... the Horde lands was number two on which to avoid. Honestly, I hated all of them. But really? *SE from the Horde?* Let us give it up for irony.

Damon's hand released my throat as he let out an annoyed sound. Instantly, Adyen was on him, punching him directly in the stomach, and pulling him up by his hair. I appreciated it... but then, *I didn't*. I knew the consequences would be far worse if he got in serious trouble.

"Resisting arrest," Adyen murmured, hitting him again. As oxygen flooded through me, I began coughing a lot and I couldn't get out what I needed to say to him. I swallowed hard as Adyen pulled him up against his chest and locked his massive arm around Damon's neck.

"Hollingworth, we are contacting the Horde," Rhodes explained and took his hands off my shoulders. I suddenly felt cold without them.

Damon met my eyes and I felt fear push through me in a violent icy wave. *Nope.* That couldn't happen. If he went back to the Horde, then he would tell everyone where I was. He would be given back free rein after being released to the Dark Fae. I wouldn't be here to defend the women attending this school. In fact, Damon would probably bring along more individuals just like his brothers.

So, instead of letting Rhodes continue, I said something that made the boys furious.

"Let them go."

All at once, multiple voices started objecting. I just kept my eyes on Damon and repeated myself. Rhodes leaned over the table and forced me to look up at him with a long tan finger. I would have slapped it away, but we had bigger issues.

"This is SE business now," he explained. His voice was clinical and eyes blank.

Oh. SE business, you say? I wouldn't know anything about that. Fucking laughable.

"You report him and I will claim mate status with Damon. He will be essentially untouchable, unless you go back to the Horde for permission. By that point in time, both of us will be gone." I hissed.

I was making a massive assumption about their true reason for being here and betting that they didn't want to lose track of me. I also was taking a huge risk by admitting to them how much I knew about SE. I was essentially confirming what they probably assumed about me, them being from the Fae lands and all.

Rhodes snarled as his eyes flashed gold, "Why would you do that?"

Damon chuckled softly, "Maybe she likes it."

Adyen punched him in the side, causing him to groan as I snapped out, "Don't push your luck."

I kept my face perfectly blank, "Rhodes, release them now. You *do not* understand the situation."

Those pale green eyes scanned my expression as he let out a foreign harsh word.

"Let them go."

"The fuck?" Taylor sounded furious, but I kept my eyes on Rhodes. God, he smelled amazing. I tried to ignore the way his expensive cologne seemed to wrap around me in a blanket of safety. I swallowed and tried to ignore how much my throat hurt. It would heal in a day or so, even without using my powers.

"See you tonight," Talon stated with elation as the four of them were released. I could hear threats being made, but all of them scampered back into the estate like the little bitches they were. I noticed Bobby trailed after slowly. I finally lowered my eyes from a furious Rhodes and turned back into the table. An exhale pushed through my lips as I kept focused on the task at hand. I had to explain myself, but say as little as fucking possible and move on.

"*Do. Not.* Do that again. Ever." I started off looking at the five men around me. Rhodes stood over me, unlike everyone else sitting around me, and kept his gaze locked on mine with an indecipherable expression.

"Are you crazy?" Athens practically yelled. "He could have killed you!"

My eyes narrowed on his, but I didn't offer him a response. He knew damn well that Damon wouldn't have been able to kill me like that. I wasn't in the mood for fucking dramatics. Instead, I moved my hands from my throat causing a deep growl to come from Adyen. I reached into my pocket, pulling out my phone to check the camera. I had deep bruises lining my throat in the shape of Damon's hand.

Happy fucking birthday to me.

10
NEO

Gray sat at the table with her camera set up against her purse to apply makeup to her bruises. I was transfixed. Her eyes, usually fiery, were empty and cold. Absolutely empty. It was like a switch.

I knew Adyen saw it because he sat across from her with fury in every part of his body. I knew he could still hear the fae assholes scampering about campus. Hell, I could hear them and hearing wasn't even something I did all that well in comparison to him. Yet, none of us moved. None of us said anything.

Finally, she tossed her makeup in her purse and brushed out her dark hair. Athens was speechless as he watched her gather herself. I could tell he was outraged, but more surprised at her compartmentalization. Taylor was incensed, probably having read through their thoughts and intentions as well as hers. Rhodes? I could tell the man was barely hanging on. *That's* saying something because he was fairly known for his control. Although it seemed Gray had a very large impact on Rhodes's animal and continuously drew out reactions from him that no one else had ever managed. She probably didn't even realize the significance of how he interacted with her in comparison to anyone outside of our team.

"Gray," I whispered, calling her attention as those navy eyes snapped to me. "What was that? How often does that happen?"

I saw her eyes melt for just a moment, the blue softening, before a coldness took over again. She spoke quietly, "That was nothing you need to worry about."

"He left bruises," Adyen snapped out.

Her eyes slowly moved from me to him, "Better on me than other people."

"What the actual fuck?" Taylor let out, causing her to sigh in frustration.

She began to get up, but Rhodes took her hand, making her still as she looked up at him. I think I expected anger. Instead of snarling at him, she gave him a bone chilling look that made him let go almost immediately. Once she was up, those lips parted and what she said next had all of the horrible puzzle pieces fitting together like some disfigured jigsaw.

"I would let Damon choke me out every single day of the year if it meant he and his brothers left the other girls alone. *We* are the minority in our community here. I am not going to let them suffer for it. By arresting him, you would leave a power vacuum. I can't afford that. I can deal with the evil I know, so please, stay out of it before you permanently fuck something up. I am only asking this once."

"Gray," Athens began his eyes flashing silver momentarily.

She held up her hand in an elegant yet harsh movement, "No. You have no place in my life, nor do I value your opinion, any of you. I won't ask why SE team members are enrolled at school here, so leave me out of your drama. Stay out of it. Do we have an understanding?"

No one responded as Adyen stood up to offer a smooth leather journal. Those blank eyes suddenly filled with emotion that appeared like a damn tsunami. A heavy amount of pain mixed with several undetermined emotions flickering so fast they couldn't be categorized. I watched as she took the journal and snapped her expression to blank again. It was unsettling how easily she did it. Once the journal was tucked away, the air shifted and the tension broke.

"Anyway, if you live off campus, feel free to stop by the district," She smirked all the pain gone in her expression and replaced with an amused expression. "It is *my 21st,* after all."

She walked away then, leaving us all in absolute confusion.

11

GRAY

"Is it really sneaking out if Mr. Jackson knows?" Esme asked, laughing as we sat in the district bar. I sat in a high booth. My back was against the red velvet seat as I watched the room. My hair was piled on top of my head in a crown-like updo. I was the birthday queen, after all.

"Also, he's in attendance so that negates any ability for him to deny knowing," I snickered as the sea of bodies on the floor moved with pulsating energy. The music was deep and rolling with an energetic undertone. The entire club was lit up. The owner, Bruce Arnold, had come by twice to make sure my bottle service was up to par.

I only nodded in response. My trust fund had provided me the ability to buy ownership in the bar, but I never really brought it up to him. I didn't want the title of owner like he did. I just enjoyed the money it brought in and the influence within the community. However, it did mean my birthday had been publicized and the club had filled with academy members very early in the night. Specifically, the Hollingworth brothers, who sat across the room with predatory eyes on the crowd. I kept my alcohol to a minimum, so I could watch them carefully.

Our deal still stood. I kept their secret and they kept mine. Hopefully, Rhodes wouldn't ruin our simple balance. It was so much larger than protecting the girls here. Although, that was a large part of it. I nodded to Damon from across the room. A predatory smile slinked onto his face as he motioned to the open seating. I ignored it and him.

That was not part of the deal.

I crossed my legs and took a sip of my wine. My legs were bare and I was dressed in a simple silver cocktail dress. It was barely a dress, honestly. Especially with the stilettos I wore. I looked hot, though. I needed that with everything that had happened today.

"Think there is anyone here that would be up for a one nighter?" I pondered.

It couldn't be someone from school. Not only would that result in a clinger, but being involved with one of those men could hurt my ability to be unbiased when helping the other girls out.

Honestly, my job didn't require a lot in that aspect. Most of the men were easy going and I wasn't so rash as to assume every break-up was immediately the fault of the male. However, I had to intervene in a few instances when it came to some guy hitting around his girlfriend or calling her names. It was fairly easy to see abusive tendencies early on. Esme and I were easily able to catch on to it and usually stop it before anything terrible happened.

Esme leaned over and adjusted my chandelier earrings, "Probably. There are some older guys at the bar."

My eyes flit over to the bar, noting the lack of options. It wasn't that the population of our town was unattractive, but humans always posed a dilemma to me. Those not human even more so. Due to who I am, humans tended to become somewhat fixated after even an interaction with me, so that could result in something far more dangerous than a clingy one night stand. Not for me as much as those around me. I could just snap their neck, but that would attract unwanted attention. It was that need to stay under the radar that kept me distant from other supernatural creatures, except for Esme. It wasn't very hard to gauge my power level if you were around me consistently.

The minute they walked in my spine felt as though it was trickling with heat. Fuck, why had I invited them? I should have known they would show up. Yes, because, of course, in true Gray fashion, the only guys I am interested in fucking are quite literally the worst option for my plan to stay under the radar. Although, it was fairly unfortunate because I could very, very much assume what Rhodes would be like in bed. I have to say, I was a fan.

"Why not them?" Esme asked with amusement.

I chuckled softly, "Bad idea. Trust me."

It was a bad idea and those several bad ideas didn't seem to understand that. The five of them began to walk through the crowd, which moved seamlessly to accommodate them as my eyes narrowed on a smirking Rhodes. Honestly, though he had a right to smirk.

The shifter was wearing a pale gold shirt that was rolled at the elbows and showed off his extensive tattoos that also peeked out at the neck. It was a good look for him. He was followed by Adyen who looked on edge, but sexy, in his dark shirt and motorcycle boots.

Esme nudged my shoulder while smiling, "I know that look."

"Fuck you," I snarled as the twins came into view.

Fuck, they looked fucking fantastic in their light colored polos and dark jeans. Instantly, Athens smiled at me, causing my heart to warm just a little bit. Neo gave me a soft smile that seemed curious, yet reserved. I still felt on edge from earlier. I could tell that both of them knew it. Damn. Perceptive *and* hot.

Finally, Taylor came into view. I nearly crawled over the table to get to him. No question, the guy was hands down sex on a stick. Which was why I hated him, right? Which was why I had to practically pin myself to my seat to not move. He wore an open dark shirt. I could see an expansive tattoo on his chest that was a stark black. Those sparkling emerald eyes fixated on me in a way that made heat uncurl in my stomach as my toes curled in my heels slightly. Damn him.

"Hey, boys," Esme called out as the five of them walked up to our table. My 'friend', you know the best one? She winked at me and left me alone with the bastards.

I crossed my arms feeling annoyed. Sort of. Not really, though.

Rhodes slid into one side as Adyen followed onto the other. The rest followed. As they pressed me into the center of the red velvet booth, I rose a brow in question at their familiarity.

"What is this about?" I motioned to them in my space.

Adyen grinned a sharp smile, "Checking in on our lil brawler. We wanted to make sure your birthday party went smoothly."

I let out a short laugh as Athens smiled authentically.

"How's your birthday party going?"

I waved a hand toward the room which made Neo look over the crowd and ask, "All friends?"

Shrugging a single shoulder, "Sure." Not really though. I had two friends and neither of them were at this table currently.

"Why aren't you out there enjoying it?" Taylor frowned.

I leaned forward, "Celebrations aren't for the person they celebrate." *Especially me.*

Rhodes caught my attention as he leaned in my space, "Why is that?"

I took a sip of wine. It brushed over my palate, "Heavy is the responsibility of those in charge." My eyes caught Damon from across the room and the annoyance on his face. Fuckity fuck fuck.

"Hey," I started in a distracted tone, "you guys should go enjoy the party, though."

"We aren't moving because of him," Adyen responded with an even, yet rough, voice.

I narrowed my eyes on him, "You will have way more fun. Trust me."

"Why don't you go have fun?" Athen's wondered out loud.

I laughed out a sound that had a dark edge, my eye catching Neo's gaze before I could hide the slight pain from that question. His eyes were dark and glittering like onyx stones. He seemed to see completely through me. I had to avoid him from now on. He saw way too much. I had a lot to hide.

"I am a fairly neutral force here at the academy," I murmured in response "Please don't hang around me. I really don't need any more problems than I already have."

"You're stuck with us," Adyen offered calmly without any room for argument. "You don't have to tell us what is going on, but we are staying. So essentially, you need to deal with it."

I tried to not let those words warm me. In fact, I almost forced them to leave, but then the Hollingworth brother's left. *Well, shit.* That's a first. I watched them walk out as I signaled to Bruce. The man walked over quickly. His murky grey eyes avoided the men around me.

"Tell me if those four return, okay?" I asked him with serious dark eyes on the retreating figures. He nodded, shocked I spoke to him, and left again with the top of his bald head glinting off the lights. Like I said, he knew about my financial involvement in the club, but we rarely actually worked together. Despite that, he was reliable when I needed him.

"Who was that?" Athens asked with interest. Gods. He had a lot of questions, didn't he? Somehow, it managed to not annoy me completely. It was probably because he was so damn cute. I could see that the women here tonight noticed him. I wasn't sure how that made me feel and that conflict annoyed me more than this question ever could.

"Co-owner of the bar," I murmured as my eyes scanned the crowd. I was positive it looked like I was watching the crowd. Instead, I was focused on those looking at us. Their reactions were interesting. Lust. Anger. Confusion. Join the club. That's called my daily life, ladies and gents. Well, the first had been a recent addition at the appearance of the five men around me.

"Friend?" Taylor mused drawing me from my thoughts.

I chuckled at the bad boy, "Sure."

Neo spoke quietly, "Who is the other owner?"

My eyes narrowed on him as that deep gaze turned to intrigue. I leaned forward hoping to make him nervous, "I think you know the answer to that."

"Shit, seriously?" Neo asked, surprised.

Should I be offended by that? In fairness, the club was pretty popular in the district. A club in the metropolitan area of Denver? Yes, it cost money. It went by the official name of *Peak Top,* but I had always hated that name. I could probably have changed it, but I was really only interested in the income it brought and the influence within the community. I was also a chairman for several influential organizations throughout the city, so that I always knew what the humans were going to do before they did it.

"Wait. What?" Athens asked.

My eyes found Taylor, and then Rhodes. Were they silently communicating? It seemed like Athens was clued in as shock registered. I wondered briefly what abilities the twins and Taylor had. It was fairly easy to spot a shifter, but the other three were masking their powers enough that I couldn't determine. I also didn't want to make an assumption and be wrong.

So why didn't I ask? Because I didn't care. That's my story and I was sticking to it.

"You are a co-owner?" Athens asked with a hefty amount of surprise.

Yeah, I'm offended. I simply smiled and took a sip of my

wine. Adyen chuckled next to me, as I finally felt myself relaxing just a little bit. I didn't like that.

Around them, complete strangers mind you, a sense of calm overtook me. That wouldn't do at all. I watched Athens make stupid jokes to Neo. Taylor offered an eye roll at their antics. I could feel Adyen looking down at me with interest as both he and Rhodes attempted to not touch me, while maintaining a closeness. Rhodes was staring out into the wave of people like myself.

I wasn't sure how long I had been relaxing before Esme twirled my way. My beautiful, gold dressed friend signaled for me and I nodded.

"Alright boys, time for me to go to the floor," I sighed, finishing my wine in one drink.

"Why now?" Rhodes asked. Always curious, that one. Not as bad as Athens though.

I offered a full smile, meeting his pale gaze, "Ballroom dancing, *obviously*."

With that, the boys let me out of the booth. My smile was confident and the crowd parted with ease. The music decreased slightly as the MC stepped to the mic. I held myself back from looking at the men behind me. I bet they thought me odd. It wasn't often that I cared for others opinions, but I did find myself wanting to know what they thought.

"How are we doing tonight, Peak Top?!" Claudia asked into the mic and was met by screams and hollers. I loved Claudia's rich and deep voice. That was about all I appreciated about her, though. Usually, her personality left something to be desired, unless she was on stage.

"Tonight is not only Solar's preview performance, but our favorite girl's birthday! Happy birthday, Gray!" Also met by cheers. I found Esme on the dance floor, along with our two dance partners. My eyes locked with Alex as a smile stole over my face. I had met Alex last year when Esme and I had gone to a party off campus. Neither of our dance partners were from the academy. That was perfectly fine with me. It kept my worlds apart and very simple.

"Are you ready?" I asked moving into position.

"Absolutely," he smiled casually. "Are you going to introduce me to those babes after?"

I shrugged as he pulled me closer. *Would I introduce him?* I may mess with the boys a little, after all Alex was super handsome. Not into me or anything else with a vagina, but super handsome. Tall, dark, and with stunning eyes. So yeah, I would be making introductions just to see their reactions.

Damn, twenty-one felt good. I felt an authentic smile grace my face which should have been my first clue that something was fucked up.

12
TAYLOR

I couldn't believe what I was seeing. I swore the woman was the most fascinating and odd person I had ever met. So unique. So painfully different and extreme in every way. She was a predator and everyone around her was at her whim. Yet, she didn't abuse it. The opposite actually.

Yet, watching her dance, there was an odd sense of calm that fell over the crowd. She was like a siren. The entire room went still as a salsa beat came over the speaker system. That tiny silver dress began sparkling under the lights as her body pressed against her dance partner. Something about him being so close made me uncomfortable. Actually, not something. Fucking everything. I pressed into his mind and then felt a calm, reassurance soothe over me.

He's gay. Calm down, Adyen.

Athens jaw was slack, surprised by her movement. I managed to whip out a mental chuckle. Adyen relaxed, but his eyes were solely focused on her spinning body as the dance moves flirted on the edge of sexy and dirty. The dress never showed anything, but fuck, it was one breeze away from falling off. I felt a pang of desire course through me as I squeezed my fists, trying to keep cool and relaxed.

I don't think any of us expected this. Least of all Rhodes or Adyen. We had a job and if our assumption was correct about our client, it was bad. Worse than her finding out that we weren't just simple SE members. I pushed that thought from my head. It seemed that she barely had any knowledge of her heritage.

Nightmares more likely, if the stories were to be believed. The lights shone off her scars and a burning sense of pride pushed through me. *You go, baby girl.* I was proud that she didn't hide. She was clearly not a victim, but viewed herself as a survivor.

"Shit," Neo whispered as the song came to an end and her hair swung out like a black tornado. It was absolutely stunning. I felt mesmerized. So, of course, I didn't hear or react to the gunshot.

"Gray," Rhodes growled out, as the crowd broke out into panic. My eyes flew to her stomach, where a deep red was spreading. *What the fuck?*

A deep roar echoed through the bar as I felt Adyen shift next to me. Nothing like a dragon in a bar to ruin the vibe, right? He moved swiftly to block the door as I felt a red haze come over my eyes. I felt the darkness surrounding me as I slipped my knives from my wrist compartments.

Now, who the fuck was going to die tonight?

13
GRAY

"Kitten, you stay with me." Rhodes ground out. His eye lit with a deep pulsing gold. I had never been this close to him and I found myself shell shocked. How was he this beautiful?

I also felt annoyed. Where else was I going to go, Rhodes? I couldn't exactly move or use my powers. Or do anything fucking useful, without exposing myself.

"I am not a fucking kitten," I snarled.

"You can be whatever you want, just keep your eyes on me," He murmured quietly. It was an intense thing, eye contact while in pain. I could hear Esme and some other noises that made no sense. My eyes trailed away, for just a moment.

Holy shit, is that a dragon? It was beautiful, huge, and *totally causing damage to my club.* It was a deep gold color and was guarding the door with a deep growl and narrowed eyes.

Wow, now that's what I call a show with dinner!

"Gray," Rhodes murmured, but I was watching the fascinating show in front of me.

Ashford Hollingworth was on his knees in front of a shadow. The shadow was a deep pulsating red and was holding his neck in a deep bone crunching grip. The room seemed to flare with its power. It was forcing everyone around it to their knees. It was a heated show, like flames licking at my very being and I could feel the darkness whispering against my skin.

"Baby, this is going to hurt," Athens said as his face suddenly filled my vision.

"Shit, your eyes," I murmured as he offered an impish grin and put those silver eyes on my stomach. He took scissors and cut my dress in the center, peeling away the bloody fabric. No, it's cool, Athens. I didn't love that dress or anything. Thank the gods I wore a cute lace thong, though. I mean it wasn't that I cared what they thought, but come on, no matter who it is, everyone liked to look good naked!

"Gray," Neo drew my attention as he held my other hand. I stared up into his eyes that seemed to grow even darker, swirling with a power that felt like ice against my skin. He seemed to be shimmering like a wave of dark water. I squeezed his hand in comfort.

Look at me, comforting others with a bullet lodged in my stomach. Friend of the fucking year right here! Once again, not that they were my friends but it's the principle.

A scream tore from my throat as Athens placed a large hand on my stomach. A searing sharp pain began to delve through my abdomen. Oh shit, it did hurt! I also took the time to marvel that his hand literally almost covered my small waist. Guess who's workout plan is showing progress? Mine bitches.

"Dude, Athens," I growled after minutes of agony. "Hurry the fuck up."

Rhodes laughed in a strained voice, "Shit. You're tough."

I could feel Athens's silver strands moving through my stomach and surrounding the iron bullet. I groaned as he pulled it up through the muscle. I almost puked, but instead kept it together. Okay, so I may have let tears fall down my face in thin ugly streaks. My makeup was probably ruined, which was a damn shame because I looked fantastic before this.

On a completely unrelated topic, it seems that Athens is a metal mage. At least, I couldn't remember any other magic users that could control metal with this amount of ease. I was pretty impressed and would have said so, if I wasn't in pain.

"You owe me a fucking drink for not screaming like a bitch," I attempted humor. Rhodes just kept watching my face with an indecipherable look.

"You did scream--"

"Shut it," Neo growled at Athens.

I felt myself smiling. A deep cry came from Ashford and my eyes found the red shadow releasing his body, it went limp. I could tell he was still alive, but past that the room began to go blurry.

"Rhodes, heal her," Neo murmured.

I was suddenly in his arms as Rhodes left with me. My eyes flickered shut as a snarl echoed through the room minutes later. Now, that didn't sound like a dragon to me. Weren't they supposed to *roar* or something? Crap. What sound did dragons make exactly?

Before I could open my eyes, I felt a warm tongue, like an animal, touch my stomach. What in the ever-loving christ... nope too late. The darkness didn't care about my shock. My eyes fell shut.

14
GRAY

When I woke up, my body instantly began bitching. I let out a groan as I flung myself up, flipping open one eye and coming face to face with Adyen. His dark hair was freshly washed with some water droplets still present, but his face was smooth and shaven. It made those amber eyes brighter and more dangerous looking. I could even smell the cinnamon drifting off him in warming waves.

"Wow," I stated lightly as if it wasn't weird to wake up to him. "Hell of a way to wake up."

The big guy broke into a smile, "Seems like your sense of humor was saved, lil brawler."

He handed me coffee and I nearly kissed him. Instead, I took it and offered him a shy smile.

"You're my favorite now. Thank you for the coffee."

"I literally pulled a bullet out of you, baby!" Athens exclaimed from the door with unmasked shock. Both men were dressed in sweats and freshly showered, but still looked sleepy and cute. I liked them like that.

God damn them. No, I didn't. I didn't like them at all.

I rose a brow and ignored my inner conflict, "Is that *coffee*,

Athens? No. It was you saving my life and very much *not* as good as coffee."

He groaned and walked back into the other room. I stole a look at Adyen. His eyebrows were drawn, but his gold eyes sparkled. It reminded me of something.

"Oh, holy shit. You're a dragon, aren't you?" It dawned on me as I lightly punched his shoulder. That earned me a brilliant smile that I found myself enjoying.

"Yep," He sighed while reaching up slowly to tuck a strand of hair behind my ear. I could feel that it had curled just slightly in my sleep.

"That's really cool actually." I chirped. "So, you guys are sorta badass, right? I mean if you're part of SE and from the Horde? You have to be, right?" As if I didn't know how fucking badass they had to be…

Rhodes came to the door and paused my thoughts. Was the man ever *not* hot? He looked comfy and sleepy. Oh my gods, did they sleep here? I sorta loved that. It was like my own harem.

Taylor barked out a laugh from the other room.

"That was a loud thought, baby girl."

I blushed for once as my ears heated, "You didn't think it would be good to tell me that you read fucking minds, Taylor?!"

The man in question moved to the door, "I can't usually read yours, but you broadcasted that particular thought loud and clear."

I narrowed my eyes and scowled, "You keep that to yourself."

"Wait, but you were looking at me," Rhodes concluded with curiosity. "Why don't I get to know?"

I grinned and looked back at him, evil glinting in my eyes, as I pounced.

"Yes, I was looking at you," I stated coyly, "...and you don't get to know, just like how you didn't tell me that you were a jaguar."

I chuckled as his eyes widened and I nearly broke at his

expression. Did he seriously think I didn't put that together? I mean, true, he seemed more reserved and pulled back from his animal nature. But, that would mean I had an extensive 'dream' of a massive cat sealing my injury shut with its tongue and I knew it hadn't been a dream. I would have broken into giggles if it wasn't for the fact that it was really sweet. Not that I would admit that. Also, ew, I didn't giggle. Ever.

Rhodes narrowed his eyes and sauntered forward, all that deadly predator hotness moving toward me. I tilted my head up, curious to what he would say, or maybe do? A girl can dream. I almost hit myself on the head at that thought. When he crouched down to be even with me, there was a glint to his expression that made me smile with excitement.

"Did you like what you saw, kitten?"

I offered a coy smile, "If you keep calling me that, you will never find out."

He laughed as Neo walked in with a calm expression, but eyes darker than usual. I offered him a smile. He simply crawled onto the bed as Athens joined us as well. I felt Neo move closer, but he didn't touch me. I appreciated that he understood the unspoken boundaries.

"What happened to Ashford?" I asked suddenly. My eyes went wide as they stuck on Taylor. The man's emerald gaze was caught on mine. A dangerous smile formed on his lips.

"He's not dead." He assured me quietly. "But he will be out of your way for some time."

I swallowed hard as thoughts of retaliation from Damon filling my mind. Fuck. Why had they wanted to kill me? That wasn't part of our deal. It also frustrated me to no end.

"You need to report them." Rhodes started. My temper flared up quickly because of how concerned I was about our very delicate balance.

"I don't *need* to do anything." I began simply, my emotions emptying. "I will talk to them."

"You're not going near them." Adyen growled out softly.

I ignored how his eyes flashed gold and spoke evenly, "That isn't your decision."

Neo's hand grasped mine and I moved my gaze in his direction. He met me with an even, but knowing gaze. I worried my lip and pulled my hand away. It was hard to be around Neo. It was far too intense for just waking up and not having finished my first cup of coffee.

"I need to mull this over." I explained quietly. "Thanks for healing me and spending the night, but I need some time to think."

I really was thankful, it would have been a pain in the ass to pull out the bullet myself.

"Gray," Adyen began his voice rough. I knew what was coming and I really did understand. They were probably worried because they thought I nearly died. I suppose I would be worried also. I was more worried about why they were trying to kill me. Ashford knew very well what that iron bullet would have done if I were a weak fae, which he assumed me to be.

Rhodes let out a noise in his throat but spoke, "We will leave for now, but at least have dinner with us later to talk about what your options are?"

"Maybe."

He sighed, but stood up to walk toward the door. Taylor offered me a frustrated look as Neo squeezed my arm gently before leaving. Athens didn't look too worried, but pressed a kiss to my forehead that caught me off guard. Adyen didn't leave at first.

"What?"

Adyen spoke quietly, "I am not letting this go, Gray. I don't care if I have to lock you up to keep you safe. He shot you with a fucking iron bullet. You should be almost dead right now." I felt my face pale because he was edging very close to the truth.

I let out a quiet snarl, "Do *not* pull that dragon bullshit on me, Adyen. I don't need you to be protective over me. I've been just fucking fine on my own."

He spoke with narrowed gold eyes that began swirling with black on the edges, "Like I said, this is not over. Get some rest, but don't think that just because I leave this room, I am not protecting you." The infuriating, stupid dragon left then.

What the fuck did that mean? Why did I like it? That is the better question. I groaned. Fuck these guys. I needed a good glass of wine and a girl's night.

Esme peeked in once the door closed, "Holy shit, dude." She had obviously overheard.

I smiled and drank my coffee as she joined me on the bed. I loved coffee. I also loved Esme. She snuggled next to me as silence fell over the suite. We were both dressed comfortably and she flipped on my television to watch some Earth realm cartoons.

"Bomb ass party though," she offered with a grin before the opening tune to Spongebob started.

I grinned in agreement. Yeah. We were lunatics, alright. One question plagued me though. How were people not freaking out about the dragon in my club?

15

GRAY

The shooting was all over the academy as I walked towards class. There was no mention of dragons, red shadows, or jaguars though. Odd? Yes, I thought so as well.

However, I did notice people talking about me being shot. My stomach had a new pink scar that my body was turning a shiny silver as we spoke. It was one positive about my injuries, I suppose. This morning, I had decided to wear an oversized, deep blue sweater and leggings. It was casual, but I did get shot the night before so I figured people would understand. I even wore sneakers and oversized sunglasses. It was perfect for the type of overcast day it was.

"Gray," Bobby called out as I passed. I pulled off my glasses and faced him.

He saw the anger there and rose his hands, "I had no idea--"

It wasn't a Monday but I punched him in the side anyway, making him grunt. Usually, I would have stopped for more conversation, but I was angry. So, I turned and left. Oh, didn't know? Right, Bobby. You had only arrived with them and had been talking to Ashford all night. A small sense of inappropriate betrayal filled me.

He called out to me, but I ignored him. I made it to theories and became instantly aware that Taylor sat with Adyen in the back of the classroom. Yes, all I needed was another class with them, right? Actually, I was almost positive that I could hear the twins entering behind me. Fan-fucking-tastic.

"How are we doing, Miss Gray?" Barney asked from the front desk. I smiled and walked up while pulling open my bag. I knew I hadn't been to class, except once, but he wouldn't stay mad for long. Particle Physics was my shit.

"I have finished all written assignments," I handed him those, a large stack of data filled white sheets. Then, I pulled out my computer. "I will still take the exams, but I have developed that simulator we talked about over the summer to replace the several, smaller projects on the syllabus."

Barney rose his bushy gray brows in interest.

"The student classroom simulator?"

I offered him an authentic smile, "The very same one. Look at this."

The bell had rung, but our focus was on the laptop. I wasn't naive about the leniency I was granted here. However, it came at the expectation of finishing stellar work. He was smiling by the end of the program and his deep blue eyes gazed up at me proudly.

"Do you care if I show it to the class?"

I nodded my consent and went to plug it in as the class opened up their work. I didn't look at the boys because I was happy just being me for a few moments. The Gray who didn't get shot, but instead was fantastic at school and beat up Bobby because he was a snarky bastard. I took a sip of my travel mug as the scent of jasmine tea drifted through me.

"Good morning," Barney clapped with enthusiasm. "Please, pass forward your assignments. While I take attendance, Miss

Gray is going to showcase a developed simulator she created for students in the classroom."

I covered my face as a yawn broke and the class seemed amused by this. I supposed it did look odd that rumors of me being shot had been flying around, yet I was in class presenting new work. Mind you, it was a project that Barney had been working on originally. It went without saying that I could have graduated with a degree within a year flat, but had decided to stay for the safety of the school.

I started it up and gave my body a stretch. *Shit!* My injury still hurts. I winced, but kept my eyes on the laptop, ignoring the growl from Adyen that echoed in the back. The simulator took a few minutes and an enthusiastic clap followed that made me smile. I still didn't look at the boys because I didn't really want to see their reactions. I was exhausted and, for once, feeling fairly non-confrontational. I know, crazy shit, right?

That was the problem with friends though. The more people who cared about you meant the more people worrying about you. Talking to you. Asking you questions. Exhausting.

"You can sit down now, Miss Gray. Good work." Barney said with a smile. I was happy that it wouldn't be necessary for me to frequent this class very often. All five sexy SE Horde warriors in one class? No, thank you, I wouldn't be able to focus with one or two, let alone all five.

I gathered my bag and traversed to the back of the classroom. Finally, I looked up. Yeah, I nearly choked on my tea. It was priceless. Why had I avoided this? This was like some personal entertainment.

Neo and Athens were both looking at me with raised eyebrows. Only after a moment did Athens offer me a sly grin and wink. Adyen gave me a head nod as Taylor whispered '*Good job, baby girl*' which earned him a scowl. The best though? Rhodes.

Those pale green eyes were lit up with questions. Hungry curiosity. Didn't curiosity kill the cat?

"How did you--"

I turned and patted his hand, "Don't worry, Rhodes. I'll show you sometime."

Athens chuckled at my patronizing tone that made Rhodes shake his head. Honestly, it felt good. See? I wasn't just the girl who beat people up and wore nice clothes. I was smart as shit. Thank you very much. I supposed it helped that I wasn't human and restricted to the way they thought about the world.

It was around an hour later when I realized class was over. I looked up from the game of hangman I had been playing with Athens, to see someone standing in front of me. My head snapped up to catch a gaze I was unfamiliar with.

"Hi, Gray," The young man offered with a soft smile that made his brown eyes warm. "I just want to say I was really impressed with the simulator today."

I sat back and smiled, looking at the way his uniform fit his muscular lean body. He was cute in that boy next door way with his wavy blonde hair and tan skin. I knew he had more to say, but I went along with it. I could tell he was an earnest guy. It didn't surprise me because I could tell he was some type of shifter. Probably canine, but I had been wrong before.

"Thanks," I offered sweetly. "What's your name?"

I heard something behind me, but the man just answered, "Jordan Web."

"Well, Jordan, it's great to meet you."

He blushed, but offered a bigger smile, "Yeah, for sure--"

I could see it on the tip of his tongue, but then I felt a pair of hands on my shoulders. I nearly chuckled. God damn possessive bastard.

Taylor spoke, "Ready to go, *baby girl*?"

Jordan raised his brows at the hands on my shoulders, "Oh, I didn't realize..."

With a sigh, I shook the hands on my shoulders off to stand up. I realized Jordan's height towered over mine as I placed a hand on his shoulder. I tried to hold in my grin as someone with a growling problem practically jumped over the row in agitation. I smiled, "Let's talk later, cool?"

Jordan nodded and left quickly as my eyes sought out the men behind me. Neo and Athens hadn't done anything, each sitting on one side of me with amused, but innocent expressions. The other three? Yeah. They were being a fucking issue.

"What was that?" I asked with a raised brow. Taylor looked pleased, Adyen's eyes were on Jordan, and Rhodes was once again the winner of best reactions because he looked jealous. Gods, why were emotional displays on him so enjoyable? Probably because he was always striving for control.

"What did I do?" Taylor asked with feigned innocence that didn't match the glint in his eyes. His red hair was messy today in that way only men could perfect.

"You know he was working up the nerve to ask me out," I reasoned, crossing my arms. All of their attention went to my chest as I nearly snickered. Score: Gray 1, Boys 0.

Rhodes's expression morphed into humor, "You shouldn't be with a guy who has to 'work himself up' to anything regarding you, kitten."

I practically growled at that response, but instead, I looked at Adyen, "All three of you are on my shit list. Oh yes you, Adyen, I know the look you were giving him. I said no dragon bullshit. Now, we can try to be friends, but if you pull that bullshit again..."

Athens whined with big eyes, "But Gray, you're *our* girl. Don't go out with him. He was boring and doesn't deserve your attention."

That got a smile out of me because it was such a fucking ridiculous comment. I tapped his nose, "No, Athens. I am no one's girl." Athens didn't respond, but distracted me by nipping at my finger.

Rhodes simply chuckled while leaning back, "That sounds like a challenge, love."

I rolled my eyes at him, "Whatever floats your boat. I am heading to lunch. I will see you later."

As I left the room, I had the distinct impression that they believed it was a challenge now. I wasn't sure how I felt about that.

16

GRAY

It was late in the evening and I found myself examining a classic works coffee table book. I had purchased it nearly a year ago, but tonight, with the window open and a calm cool breeze in our dorm, it seemed like a good night to explore it. Until a knock sounded on my door.

It was a Wednesday, who the hell was at my door? Esme was on a date and wouldn't be home until the morning. I opened the door and frowned.

"Damon," I growled out quietly. Wonderful. This is just what I needed.

He was alone, but stepped into the space. The man instantly had me backing up as he closed the door. I swallowed hard. I honestly wished it was anyone but him. Especially alone. I didn't want to use my power in self-defense, but if it came down to it, my self-preservation would win out.

"Tell me what your demon did to my brother?"

Say what? Taylor was a demon? That made sense actually.

"The brother who shot me?" I frowned in distraction.

Damon caged me into the counter and pinned me with a glittering, dark gaze. I should have been scared, but instead felt a deep energy boiling through me. I waited for his response.

"It was a warning shot," he said with a shake of his head. It caused that ebony hair to go flying around his face, softening the effect of his anger. Over time, I had noticed small differences between the brothers. Damon was the oldest and had a polished, hardened appearance. Those eyes often reminded me of obsidian. At times, I thought I saw a sparkle of silver. It reminded me of sparks on a train track. Tonight, he was dressed in a loose shirt and jeans that seemed wrinkled and messy for someone like him. I could feel the tension rolling through him. Something was clearly wrong.

I tilted my head and narrowed my eyes, "To my *stomach,* Damon, Ashford fired an iron bullet into my fucking stomach."

It *sooo* wasn't the time to mention that it wouldn't have killed me.

He looked at me sharply and I saw his jaw was clenched tight, vibrating with energy. There was a paleness to his skin and circles under his eyes. It was unusual to see him this pale. He had a glow to him normally, unlike Talon. He was the second oldest and had the fairest skin out of all of them, paired with messy dark hair and a leering smile. Talon made me upset nearly all of the time because rationalizing with him was like talking to a child. A creepy fucking child.

"He didn't tell you he was going to? Is that the problem?" I asked.

Well, if that was the case, I supposed I would need to apologize to Bobby. *Or not.*

Damon lifted a hand to my stomach and gently pulled up my sweater. I was fascinated with what was happening, so I let him. His hand was ice cold and caused a shiver to rack through me as pain lanced his face. He let out a low growl before stepping away from me.

It was surprising because in all this time, he had never touched me like that. Ever.

Ashford, with his dark glasses and scruff, had come close to kissing me once, but it had been antagonistic. Out of all the brothers, I trusted him the least and it wasn't because he shot me. There was something unhinged about him that was completely unpredictable.

"What's going on, Damon?"

"He wasn't aiming for you," He murmured quietly. "At least, that's what I assume."

"What?" I felt dumb or really clueless at least.

His gaze pinned me again, "Ashford wouldn't have wanted to hurt you. Kennedy said he was jealous, but he wouldn't have tried to harm you. Ever."

"Jealous?" I raised a brow. The fuck was going on here?

I didn't trust Kennedy either, but it wasn't due to his calculating nature. No, the over muscular, youngest sibling was just dumb. He made up shit a lot. I didn't care for his opinion. Once again, except for Damon, they all seemed like overgrown children.

"We would never try to kill you," Damon growled out to himself.

Was this guy crazy?

"You almost crushed my throat dude," I stated quietly with a sigh.

He looked at me again. His eyes trailing along my throat bruises that were essentially gone with the level of heat.

"I like seeing you at my mercy, but I didn't mean to leave bruises."

Okay. Yeah. That's all kinds of fucked up, but I'm going to put that to the side for now. I mean with the right person that attitude could be hot. But with Damon? He was way more likely to kill me than to fuck me. At least, I hoped that was the case. The guy was not someone I wanted to wake up next to. A shiver rolled through me at the thought of that.

"What do you mean about your brother? What's wrong with him?" *Besides the normal.*

"He is all fucked up in the head, Gray. What did the demon do?" *He's always been fucked up.*

"Demon?" *I just needed clarification here.*

"Yes, the red haired one."

"That's what he is?" I asked with an amused expression.

So, we have a dragon, demon, jaguar, and then the twins. I knew that Athens was a metal mage, but I couldn't determine what type of mage Neo was.

Damon groaned at my lack of attention, "Listen, Gray, I am going to go, but stay away from those fuckers. Please."

"Uh--"

Damon pressed a kiss to my forehead and was gone then. What the actual fuck? My head spun with the weirdness of what happened. I mean, don't get me wrong. I hated the guy, but I understood what he got out of all this, keeping his secrets and feeling like the big man on campus.

It made me wonder why he wanted me to stay away from the other guys. I hadn't really questioned them on why they were here because I assumed I knew the answer. Yet, SE normally stayed away from this part of the country. The fact that they showed up at the academy was odd. I should have at least questioned them even for appearances. With that thought, I decided that tonight would be a good time for a glass of wine. Or a bottle.

My gaze drifted back to the classics book as I took a glass of cabernet to the couch. I had sat down and pulled a blanket over me when the door sounded again. Damn it.

"I swear to gods if this is you, Damon," I flung the door open to find an unamused Rhodes. I crossed my arms over my soft silk tank, "What's up, dude?" *Dude? Really Gray?*

Rhodes tilted his head. A strand of golden hair fell out of the knot at the back of his head, "Dude? Really?" *Yeah. Wasn't positive what I was thinking.*

I shrugged, holding back a smirk, "Don't take it personally."

He frowned, "Why did you think it was Damon?"

"He was just here..."

"The hell?" Adyen asked catching up to Rhodes. I always forgot how large Adyen was until he moved fast and into your space with very non-human-ish movements.

"No big deal. He left after a quick chat," I summarized easily. At least I thought I had.

Except Adyen didn't take that well and he walked forward, forcing me back, as Rhodes watched with interest. Cool, dude. I let out a pathetic squeak as Adyen caged me against the same counter as Damon. It felt way different though. I wasn't worried or afraid of Adyen, just overwhelmed by him. His size. His intensity. They were a lot to deal with. I mean, you try holding a conversation with someone nearly 15 inches taller than you.

My entire body was shivering as heat brushed over me. His head dipped and he began sniffing around my neck, face, and ending on my forehead. Oh wow. This was why I didn't usually hang out with a lot of predatory shifters.

"Did he kiss you?" Adyen asked with a deep growl vibrating through his chest.

"Just my forehead, big guy," I murmured, setting a hand on his rumbling chest. A dark part of me liked his reaction and the other part of me was very confused at its intensity.

Rhodes let out a low sound of his own, but covered it up with a cough before speaking.

"Adyen, calm down mate."

Except Adyen didn't calm down. Nope. He picked me up, one hand around my damn waist and the other under my butt, to hold me close while rubbing his nose on my neck. Instinctively, I locked my legs around his massive waist and clung to him like a fucking monkey. I found Rhodes's curious gaze and I just tried to stay still. Rhodes approached silently.

"Adyen--"

Adyen let out a threatening deep growl, very different than the one towards me, that brought unfiltered surprise to Rhodes's face. I was trying to catch his gaze, but the man kept nuzzling my neck and hair. Holy shit, was he scenting me? Uh-uh. Nope. This was not happening.

"Adyen," I gripped his chin making him look at me. "Are you fucking scenting me?"

Rhodes chuckled which made Adyen let out another deep growl. I just wrapped my arms around his neck because what the fuck else was I supposed to do? He pulled me closer and I could feel his hardness press into me. Holy shit, he was huge. I tried to contain my small squeak which only encouraged him to press a kiss to my neck as a deep rumble echoed in his chest.

"Are you purring?" I wondered out loud as Rhodes took a sip of *my* wine.

He looked so amused that I found myself wanting to punch him. Also, who the fuck drinks someone's wine without asking? That is like friendship rule number one.

"Baby!" Athens called sauntering in before raising his brows. Adyen let out a snarl as Athens rounded to view the dragon with wide eyes. I did take a moment to appreciate how cute he looked in a matching set of Nike white joggers and an oversized hoodie.

"Um, Adyen, be careful with our girl there," He mumbled out, but Adyen just leveled him with a very narrowed gaze over his shoulder.

It was sorta fucking funny, but now was not the time to laugh. I couldn't help my reaction though, primal displays of emotions had always been more natural to me than Earth realm expectations. I smoothed his hair, hoping to console him which made the purring start again. I saw Athens start to chuckle, but Neo showed up before he could make a noise. It was probably for the best. We wouldn't want Adyen getting jealous that someone was laughing in my direction or anything.

Neo narrowed his eyes at Adyen before looking at Rhodes, "What exactly happened to make him act like this?"

He was always straight to the point, I appreciated that from him. Everything that came out of his stupidly perfect mouth seemed important enough that I found myself listening.

"Damon showed up earlier, which let me tell you was a weird conversation in its own regard, but Adyen could smell that he kissed my forehead and freaked." I explained casually.

Rhodes let out a deep snarl before snapping his face back to neutral. How did he do that? I nearly snickered, but Neo's reaction shocked me the most. He went still as ice as those dark eyes began to glitter.

"He kissed you?" He murmured his eyes glinting with a similar darkness as Damon's eyes.

I didn't find myself threatened by it but rather intrigued. Yeah. I had always been a sucker for dangerous shit.

"Woah," Taylor strolled in with a smirk. "This is interesting."

"Tell me about it," I murmured.

Adyen picked me up from the counter and moved me away from everyone else. Literally putting distance between us and them. I was then placed in his lap, facing forward as strong, locked arms circled around me like pythons. I let out another surprised sound as all four other men looked on. I wondered briefly if this had ever happened before. I didn't think it had and the idea of another woman this close to him made me annoyed.

Ah. Shit. I was in no place to get possessive over Adyen.

"Adyen, you're going to have to let her go," Taylor explained reasonably.

"Mine," Adyen snarled, causing my head to snap back to look

at him. *Excuse me?*

Athens lost it and started laughing as Rhodes raised an elegant eyebrow. Neo looked lost, his body still frozen from the news Damon had kissed me. I wondered where his mind was. Taylor looked annoyed, but also amused.

"Okay, big guy. Listen, I am totally fine, but--" *How do I explain that I am so not his?*

"He touched you." He snarled and tucked my head under his chin. Well, shit.

Rhodes sighed and pulled up a chair, keeping distance as everyone else settled. Taylor leaned against the door, his eyes narrowed at Adyen with interest and... something else. I had a feeling being able to hear a person's thoughts made his life difficult. I wondered if it influenced his emotions?

"What exactly did Damon say to you?" Rhodes asked quietly.

I twisted my lips, "It's more what he didn't say. I wish you could see it--"

Taylor surged forward, ignoring Adyen as he came to kneel in front of us. He looked up at Adyen, "I am just going to grab the memory from her so we can see what this guy said to her. Is that cool?"

Adyen made a threatening sound, but kissed my neck gently before placing his head against my shoulder. I tried to ignore him as Taylor spoke to me.

"Run me through the scene mentally. I will pick it up if you direct it toward me and then I can broadcast it to them."

I sighed. This was going to be bad. So, I let him see. I knew that he was broadcasting it by the way his heated magic flew through the air. I knew they could see it because noises of annoyance came from his language about them and absolute tense silence came from the kiss. So, it seemed that not only Adyen was bothered by that. Taylor laughed at that thought and pulled away from our connection.

However, it seemed that Adyen had calmed down slightly, now that he had seen what had occurred. His grip was still ironclad, but when I looked up into his handsome face, he offered me a small, almost shy, smile. Well, shit. That's sorta cute.

"Out of my brain, Taylor!" I called out as he snorted at my thoughts.

"So, big guy," I murmured turning into him. "What was all *this* about?"

I could hear the other men talking briefly about the brothers behind us and probably giving us space. Instead of answering, he just put his head in my neck, nibbling the skin and murmuring 'mine.' It wasn't aggressive this time. He seemed to be explaining what had happened through that singular word.

I normally hated when people touched me, but this I could deal with. My body relaxed into him as Rhodes's gaze caught my eye. It was an interesting, odd look that crossed between confusion and curiosity. I felt a little of both as well.

"Gray," Athens whined out of the blue. "Can we sleep over and get pizza?"

I rose a brow, "Dude, it's only 10. You can easily get home."

Once again, I briefly wondered where they were staying off campus.

Neo sighed running a hand through his hair as he finally relaxed, "It's his way of saying he's worried about leaving you alone."

I wondered how often he had to translate for his twin.

Athens flashed me a smile and went to the area where I kept pizza menus. How did he know where that was? Taylor helped him sort through them for a few minutes as I finally gave in.

"Fine, whatever. I need more wine though."

Rhodes sent me a guilty smile as he put down my wine glass. Fucking wine thief.

17

ADYEN

I could feel Rhodes's concern from across the room, but I didn't care. I couldn't care. I was focused on her instead. A small smile played on her lips as she caught me staring at her. I tried to chastise my dragon, but he was thrilled she had all but accepted his play of dominance.

She isn't ours buddy, not really. I was smart enough to know you couldn't fucking own a woman like Gray. If anything, she owned you.

But she is, he responded flippantly.

Nope.

We already made our decision. She knows it. Just accept it.

Gray was talking to Athens with animation. Oddly, my dragon didn't react. He had viewed them as a threat initially, but now he didn't. After scenting another male on her skin, especially an unknown one, he would have reacted poorly to anyone. I didn't for a minute believe my lack of reaction was because they didn't like her. Hell, I knew Rhodes better than he knew himself. The man was obsessed with her like one of his complex puzzles.

I was furious Damon had been here and my dragon had reacted on pure instinct. It didn't need to be said that my dragon had claimed her as his mate. I had a feeling she didn't understand that. It was okay for now. Eventually, she would get it. I would need to control my reactions until then.

Rhodes finally gave up glaring my way and opened a new bottle of wine to fill their glasses. She offered us beer and an assortment of other snacks as we waited for pizza. It was entertaining to see her flit around the suite in a pair of deep blue sleep shorts and a tank. My eyes were trained to the way her hips curved and how the lights bounced off that dark hair. She was perfect. Simply perfect. It was also fucking hilarious to see the group of us sitting around a college dorm like we weren't a military unit on an essential mission for the Horde's future.

Athens was quick to turn on a late night comedy show once the pizza arrived. The entire group spread out as I pulled her onto the couch between Rhodes and me. She seemed to accept my touch with hesitancy, but I made sure to keep my hands off her shoulders and neck. The only person who had touched her there had been Rhodes. He didn't dare to touch her now. Instead, Athens put a blanket over her and sat on the plush rug next to Neo in front of her. Taylor had a beer slung between his fingers and had his chair angled to see the door. I could tell the Damon incident bothered him a lot, but he wasn't good at expressing himself in situations like that.

The night was relaxing. It was unusual for us, but I could tell she felt conflicted on the comfort level. I felt the urge to make her understand *why* we were there and to explain why she was comfortable around us. I didn't want her to worry or think something was amiss. Rhodes assured me that with time, it would be possible to tell her. I wasn't sure though... How could we serve our temporary duty if our primary duty clearly hated the temporary? My brain spun as I considered our many options. Except, I knew I would choose Gray over any mission assigned to us.

My body stilled as she let out a small content sigh and let her hand brush against mine gently. I peeked at her to find that her body had relaxed back into the couch and into Rhodes's side. Her silky black hair covered her closed eyes while her breathing evened out. She was sleeping and the best part was that it was on Rhodes.

Taylor, ask Rhodes if we should move her.

I met my friend's pale green gaze and he attempted to offer me a blank look, but I didn't buy it. Taylor didn't comment as he was used to passing along messages.

Maybe in a bit.

I took a sip of my beer as Rhodes shifted her slightly. She looked more comfortable now. He couldn't hide the slight upturn of his lips and it made me happy to see him smiling. Under our current assignment, he took most of the responsibility. It was good to see him feeling more comfortable around her. The two of them were combative, but she had a softer side that was begging to be explored. I hoped she would help him and help us, like we would help her.

After all, she had to trust us to some extent to fall asleep with us here, right?

18
GRAY

I didn't live in the past. I wasn't a victim.

I had my scars and I dealt with the anxiety that leeched onto me. I knew my place. I knew my purpose. I had control of it. My life. My fate. The terrified little girl had long been buried. I had buried her after running. After every beating. After every predatory glance. After every sickening touch. No. She was buried. The fear was buried.

However, like my scars, the nightmares and anxiety still thrived with the sickening energy that pain often had. I took it day by day and kept myself controlled enough to know when I wasn't okay. When I wasn't okay, when I wasn't strong enough... I stayed home. It happened every once in a while, when the numbness wouldn't come to hide the pain. On those days, I didn't leave my bedroom.

As I woke up in the early dawn, I knew without a doubt that it was one of those days. The beautiful silver and blue room felt bleak and my body was chilled like ice. I was wrapped in blankets and the soft sound of snores filled the room as my eyes tracked the five bodies spread throughout the room.

Rhodes was in the arm chair, a hand over his face. Adyen was on the floor near the bed. The twins were closer to the closet and Taylor was by the door. It was sweet and protective so, of course, I felt choked by panic. Absolute sheer panic and fear. My body turned cold with chills and I found myself scrambling out of bed. I felt bile rising in my throat.

I moved over the bodies with lethal grace and found myself in Esme's bathroom. The pink tile seemed to make me only more sick as I dry heaved over the toilet. I had turned the sink on, but my entire body was wracked with tremors. Fuck, I needed my medicine. The Earth realm beta blocker would help calm the physical symptoms for an hour or so.

The door opened behind me and a hot hand wrapped around my waist gently. A sob broke in my throat. Without tears, of course. I couldn't remember what it felt like to cry. Taylor turned me to him. Those dark green eyes were lit up with knowledge as I attempted to slam my walls back into place. It was too late though. Today was a bad day. A weak day. A day that was filled with darkness. Damn it. I should be stronger. I should face the day head on. I couldn't though. Today was a black day.

I didn't know how long we sat on the bathroom floor. I felt the tremors take over as he sat across from me and pressed his forehead into mine. He didn't say anything and I didn't contribute. What would I say? What could explain this, besides the obvious? I was broken. Thank gods I hadn't cried in years. Even now, they didn't come.

Eventually, he produced a bottle of medicine. It was very clear he had awoken to my thoughts. I took one pill and used a paper cup from the sink. It went down easily as I leaned over the sink. Behind me, Taylor's entire body seemed to move in a shimmered red haze. Those eyes bore into mine as I found myself looking at my own reflection.

Fuck. My eyes were filled with so much. I knew I couldn't face anyone else today. *I need everyone gone now.* Taylor's lips turned into a slight frown. He didn't break the silence. Instead, he wrapped his arms around my waist and pressed a kiss to my cheek. He was gone then and left me to my nightmare. I let out a deep breath and began to build up some defenses. Any defenses, really. Even one brick in the wall would help.

* * *

I took a shower in Esme's room. I pulled on a pair of sweats and a borrowed hoodie. She wouldn't mind, especially today. I wasn't positive, but I had a feeling it had been about an hour. I hoped they were gone, yet the feeling also made me sad. I left her room and went to my bedroom. *Shit.* Not gone at all.

Five pairs of eyes found mine with varying levels of emotion. All of them ranged from confused to concern. All of them made me uncomfortable. I wasn't positive, but it should have been obvious how close to the edge I was. My walls were barely up and I could feel Taylor attempting to push into them. I let out a pained sound and met his gaze as he immediately pulled back.

"Could you both," Motioning to Rhodes and Taylor with a rough voice that broke the tension, "tell our Physics teacher that I will be absent but to look for an email?"

Rhodes stepped forward, but I shook my head motioning to the door. I could see the pain in his gaze, but no one said anything. I forced myself to look at all five of them as they left, knowing it would be the last time they were in this intimate of a setting with me. It was far too overwhelming. Too many people to worry about, to disappoint, to lose...

I wasn't positive if Taylor could hear my thoughts, but I saw deep regret in his eyes. As Taylor passed me, he lifted a hand to my jaw and pressed a kiss to my forehead. I didn't respond, but let out a shaky exhale that made his eyes darken in pain. I closed my eyes until he moved through the door. I found Athens in front of me when I opened my eyes again.

His goofy, light hearted personality seemed heavy as those eyes churned with silver. He whispered, "Get some rest, baby." and squeezed my hand gently. I felt a searing pain of affection rip through me. Someone like him shouldn't be friends with someone like me.

Neo's gaze upset me the most. His eyes were glittering and his body moved with stealth that seemed unnatural. His shyness was gone. Instead, he tugged me into an embrace by my hips as I held back a sob. This wasn't like me. This was the Gray that couldn't keep her shit together.

This felt different than kicking them out of my room the other morning. Was this a goodbye? Of course, it was. I couldn't be friends with them. I was damaged and broken goods. Not friend material. I had a small amount of deja-vu remembering how they had walked past me through the dean's door when we first met.

Adyen's honey gaze was filled with flames as he pressed a kiss to the top of my head, once again overwhelming me with his presence. He murmured something in a language I recognized, but I held back my reaction. I turned to look away from his intensity and found a pair of green eyes that seemed more gold this morning.

Rhodes didn't hold back and instead invaded my space. Similar to the other day, his long fingers smoothed over my neck and shoulders. He was unapologetic and held me in a gaze that pinned my very soul to the wall. I could feel the walls wobbling as he whispered in my ear.

"There is nowhere dark enough that we wouldn't follow, Gray."

How very wrong he was.

19
ATHENS

Later that day...

I knocked on the door as I shifted the weight of my package to the other hand. I really wanted to stay and comfort Gray, especially after this morning. If she didn't want that, a care package was the next best option. My mom had always made them for my neighborhood friends before the guard. I suppose I picked the habit up from her.

I knew the homemade soup and fuzzy blanket I bought wouldn't do much to help the actual issue. I had seen how scared she had been this morning and how exhausted she looked. Taylor had explained he had woken to her pain and found her dry heaving over her roommate's toilet. My heart hurt at the idea of Gray suffering any more than she already had in this life.

I knocked again.

"Hold on," A voice sounded as the door opened. It wasn't Gray though. It was her roommate.

"What's up?" She asked politely. There was something off about her tone, though. It was a forced calm and her left hand was twitching just slightly.

"Is Gray home? I have something for her," I began slowly my

suspicion rising as she paled.

Esme licked her lips and crossed her arms, "No. Gray is not here."

"Where is she?" I asked quietly, my voice edging in annoyance. I tried to be an upbeat and happy guy, but at the center of my nature, I was very much a predator like the rest of my team. When Esme avoided my question, I grew angry.

Her roommate frowned, "None of your business. If she had wanted you to know, she would have told you."

"Did she leave?" I snapped out.

Esme's eyes went wide as she refused to answer. Instead, she slammed the door in my face. Shit. That wasn't good at all. I turned on my heel to find Rhodes.

Rhodes

"What did Esme say exactly?" I snarled out as I followed Athens and Neo back to her dorm. Athens had found me sitting outside at her pavilion and immediately blurted out his suspicions. I could feel my heart rapidly beating in my chest. This morning, Gray hadn't been in any condition to leave bed, let alone leave campus.

"She said *'if she had wanted you to know, she would have told you,'*" He muttered quietly. I could feel the tension and hurt rolling off of Athens. He may not admit to it being so, but I knew that if Gray left, he would take it personally.

Once we were at the dorm door, I banged loud enough that the sound echoed around us. It immediately flung open to reveal Esme and none other than Bobby.

"Where the fuck is she?" I demanded stepping into the room and focusing my glare on both of them. Esme looked pale and distressed. Bobby seemed to be more tense than usual. His eyes burned with more intelligence than I had given him credit for.

"I already told your friend," she motioned to Athens. "She

left. She didn't want you to know if she didn't tell you."

"Location. Now." I demanded sharply as Neo stepped toward Bobby. I could feel his power leaking out in icy tendrils and every shy bone in his body was quickly disappearing.

"No. I can't do that, even if I wanted to," she stated quietly. "She didn't give us any specifics."

Us? Why the hell was Bobby even part of this discussion?

"She was shot less than two fucking days ago," I growled out barely restraining myself. "And you let her just leave?"

Bobby shook his head, but kept an eye on Neo with trained caution as he spoke.

"If Gray wants to do something, she does it."

Who the bloody hell was this guy?

"This is ridiculous," Athens muttered.

I agreed. We weren't going to get anything from them. I looked at Neo to gauge his willingness to use his powers on the two of them. He met my eyes and offered me a small shake of the head. I turned on my heel and the two of them followed me out. This was some bullshit.

"Their minds were blocked. I couldn't influence them at all." Neo murmured, with a small hint of pride. I rose a brow as Athens shook his head in disbelief. Neo being blocked from influence was unheard of.

"Kitten is more powerful than we thought." I muttered quietly.

"She also inspires an impressive amount of loyalty." Neo added.

It was true. With the amount of power circulating through that dorm, a weaker loyalty would have broken. Easily.

"What do we do?" Athens asked quietly, his hands strumming a nervous pattern against his leg.

"Send Adyen and Taylor to corner Bobby and try again later today, Athens, go see if the administration has been contacted," I listed quietly. "Neo, you and I are going to go back to the house and see if any travel records match up."

We needed to find our girl.

Rhodes

Two Weeks Later...

"Gray is back," Adyen snapped out. It made a few people walking by jump.

At first, his words didn't make much sense to me. Mostly because... all I had been hoping for were *those* words for two weeks now. So... why now? Why would she back now? We had chosen to not leave our temporary rental, because we figured she would return here eventually. My eyes snapped up to the figure crossing the grounds, dressed in all black and walking next to Bobby.

"Where has she been?" I demanded. I didn't bother to hide my inner turmoil.

The morning at her dorm had been the last time anyone had seen her. Esme had still refused to provide me with any more details other than what we had gathered that first afternoon. The Dean had told Athens that she had taken a leave of absence. Neo had been able to track her movements to the airport, but after that she had disappeared. Her paperwork and files hadn't matched anything in our database. For two fucking weeks, she had been gone. Absolute radio silence. That was pretty fucking impressive, considering our tracking abilities.

I felt a deep anxiety fill my chest at the thought of her alone, unprotected. I had seen how the blackness had consumed her. Those blue eyes had darkened to black and stood out against her ivory skin. I hadn't wanted to leave her that morning, but pushing her would have been equally harmful. I wanted to demand answers, all of them, and have her bare her very soul to me. I needed it. I needed to understand her, but I knew it would have pushed her further away.

"I don't know," Adyen rumbled as his eyes filled with pain. I knew his dragon had tried several times to track her, but when Gray didn't want to be found, she wouldn't.

I had enough of this bullshit. I looked at Adyen and he nodded in understanding. It was time she and I had a talk. I wasn't going to deal with her distance and lack of answers anymore. I would demand answers. Demand her trust. Sounds easy, right?

"Morning," Bobby greeted me as I approached their table. Gray stiffened as her deep gaze found mine. I tried not to let concern flash across my face because I knew it wouldn't help. I wasn't sure where she had been the past two weeks, but she was thinner. Her eyes seemed far too large and her lips were pale. There was a haunted pain in her face that was barely covered by her smirk. A smirk that was unlike her coy sexy one. No, this was dark and forced, almost cruel.

She was drowning. There was no blank look, no emptiness. Her eyes seemed black and glittering with unspoken emotion. I wondered if Bobby could see it. Judging from his stupid grin, probably not. I needed her alone.

"Bobby, leave us," I murmured in a voice I rarely used, infused with a calm alpha power. She didn't stop me from dismissing Bobby as her eyes flashed with resignation. I didn't like that at all. A Gray without fight and power wasn't Gray.

"See you later, Gray," Bobby grinned and kissed her cheek. She didn't react, but she didn't push him away either. Her eyes were trained on my expression. I found my seat across from her.

"Gray--" I began keeping my voice even.

She cut me off with a sharp tone, "What do you want, Rhodes?"

"What do I want?" I leveled with a low rumble. "You *disappeared* for two fucking weeks."

"I didn't disappear," she explained nonchalantly. "The people who mattered knew where I was."

Somewhere in my chest that stung. I wasn't stupid, though. I had seen the peace we had given her in the few days she had known us. She was lying through her teeth if she was trying to convince me that she didn't care about us. I wasn't going to let her get away with it.

"Stop the bullshit," I growled out. "You ran away."

"From what? *Who* am I running from?" She snarled under her breath, those eyes swirling with pain. The woman was stupidly stubborn. At least she was reacting to this though.

"From us," I leveled honestly. "You ran away from whatever was going on."

A dark look broke onto her face, "*Yes,* because the three days I spent with you changed me, right? Made me feel things that I had never before. Is that what you wanted to hear?"

Her sarcasm spoke truth and she knew that. A dark look came over her face and she took a shuddering tiny breath without looking at me.

"Where were you?" I demanded.

"Why are you here?" She switched topics without an answer. "Why the academy? Why is SE operating outside of the Fae lands?"

I swallowed hard, but didn't respond. A glimmer of anger flashed through those eyes as if I had confirmed something officially. I wondered if we had been outed. I didn't think Bobby or Damon had recognized us, but I supposed it was possible.

"Was it them? Were you with them?" I growled out sharply, my hand catching hers in a demanding fashion. Those dark eyes flashed to my hand, but she didn't pull away.

"I was somewhere I could be left alone," she whispered softly, her voice portraying her exhaustion. "Do they strike you as the type to leave me alone?"

Relief poured through me at her statement. The Hollingworth brothers were dangerous and she knew that. My thumb smoothed over her scarred skin and she began to tremble just slightly. An idea came to fruition before I could think twice.

"Rhodes," she let out a small sexy sound as I unbuttoned my shirt, letting go of her hand. "I am not opposed to seeing you shirtless but..."

I chuckled darkly at her admission as a blush filled her cheeks. Shit, that was cute. I could imagine other places a flush like that would look good. Honestly, I was mostly glad to see some color back on her face. I pulled down the shoulder of my shirt and grasped her other hand.

"What are you--"

Her words stopped as I brought her soft fingers to trace the large cigar burns that mocked me in the mirror each morning. The expression on her face was enough to let her explore a little. The softness in her eyes filled with a deep blue as tears spilled down her angled cheekbones. I think she knew very well what it would take for that scarring to be permanent.

I grasped her long delicate hands and brought her knuckles to my lips gently, "*You* are not the only one running from things, Gray."

A flush of knowledge came to her cheeks as she let out a soft, shaky sound. Those beautiful eyes closed as she barely nodded. My thumbs smoothed over her scars again and again. While hesitant, she let me touch her scars. Maybe, she had always known subconsciously that our suffering was similar. Maybe, that was why she was comfortable with my daring touch.

"Are you done with classes today?" I asked softly as those eyes met mine again, filling with the lightning indigo and silver.

She nodded, wiping those silvery tears and then drying her hands. Those tears seemed to amaze her. A roll of thunder boomed through the entire space.

20

GRAY

I prayed to the divine goddess that they weren't what Damon had eluded to. Yet, his easy avoidance of my words left me feeling concerned. If they were, could I even push them away? Why wouldn't they have told me? Or was I just avoiding the truth? Damn it. I knew exactly who they were and they knew who I was.

We were just playing a fucking game now.

As Rhodes led me across the estate to Adyen, fear trickled through me. Rhodes had brought me to tears and opened my soul for his appraisal. I felt weakened and clingy, as if they could provide me with the joy and calm I sought. I had escaped to the East Coast for two weeks, to clear my head and bring forward the numbness.

Instead, I was left missing *them*.

Adyen's arms instantly wrapped around me without warning and I found myself curling into his broad chest. I let my arms wrap around his neck as the searing warmth of his body melted into mine. He didn't say anything and simply pressed his face into my neck and hair gently. I could tell he was scenting me. Fuck it.

I didn't even mind. I felt my soul warming up from the inside out. Adyen did that to me.

"Please don't ever do that again." He murmured in a rough voice against my ear.

It was the type of voice that sounded more animal than not and made me shiver. I pressed into him further by tightening my arms.

I heard his voice before I saw him.

Athens spoke loudly, "Rhodes, what's this all--"

"Fuck," Neo swore softly.

Neo never swore. Unlike Rhodes and I. Now that was a man who cursed a lot. Adyen placed me down gently as I turned nervously to face the twins. Something had shifted while I was gone and I found myself less concerned about why I cared about their opinion.

"Well, shit. I want a hug, baby," Athens recovered his heart breaking expression first.

He brought me into a tight hug and kissed my cheek. It lacked his usual enthusiasm but held a lot of heat. I should have considered how much this would have hurt him. Athens was an open book with his emotions. By leaving, I had stomped right on that damn book. I was a selfish bitch.

I felt like I was losing my fucking mind. When had I started caring so much?

Neo approached next and tugged me into another encompassing hug. I exhaled with relief when surrounded by the two of them. A part of my heart clicked into place and it made me consider Damon's warning that Bobby had passed along. I heard a click of a lighter and my eyes snapped to Taylor over Neo's shoulder.

I almost flinched back from the demon. His face was blazing and filled with an array of emotions that I didn't understand. *Except* the pain. I knew that one well. I saw it in the mirror every single day. He stalked forward and the twins left me practically trembling in my heels. Fucking traitors. I kept my face blank, at least I hoped it was, and crossed my arms.

Except as he got closer, I found myself taking a few steps back because of the intensity in that green gaze. Those eyes reminded me of emeralds on a daily basis, but today they seemed to be on fire. Taylor was pissed at me. Furious. Adyen went to move in front of me, but Rhodes stopped him. I felt my back hit the school wall as Taylor caged me tightly against the wall.

It wasn't the time *or* place to notice how hard his body was against my soft curves. I could feel every muscle and sharp edge radiating power and heat into my skin. It wasn't the comforting warmth that Adyen provided, but it still made my toes curl. It made a trickle of heat and excitement go down my spine in anticipation. I wanted to see how close the two of us could fit together.

I was so fucked.

His voice was smoky with anger, "Can you even comprehend what the past two weeks were like, Gray?"

I let out a pained sound in the back of my throat as he growled against my temple, "I. Felt. Everything. Everything, Gray." I loved his soft lips against my temple and the way they curved onto my skin.

"What?" I forced out in a strangled gasp as I processed his words.

He placed a hand on my chin, tilting me up so we were a breath away, "Everything, baby girl. Every thought. Every emotion. Yet, no way to find you." I felt tears well up in my eyes... again. Fucking fantastic.

"That isn't possible," I barely got out as my cheeks grew wet with tears.

The tears that Taylor rubbed gently into my skin with his thumb as he continued to hold my jaw. I felt nearly hypnotized by his closeness. There was no anger there anymore. His face was soft, yet filled with our shared pain.

"Sure it is," he murmured gently.

I knew it was possible, of course, but then, Damon would have been right and that would mean… Ah. Fuck. I hoped that the loyalty they had to me would outweigh the loyalty to their command. That's not asking a lot of the men I had just ditched for two weeks, right?

He pressed a soft kiss to my forehead and spoke quietly, "Don't overthink it, baby girl. Not yet."

Overhead the sky turned a dark gray as a droplet of water landed between us.

One droplet that was like a tear. I wish it would have ended there, but as I looked at the four other men around us, something snapped into place. Something clicked that fundamentally tied me to these men. I was positive that they felt it. I couldn't ask though. I wouldn't ask yet.

The sky opened up as thunder echoed around us, soaking the six of us in nature's tears.

21
GRAY

"Baby! Wake up!" Athens called while throwing open my bedroom door.

I let out a muffled groan as I curled further into my silk sheets. I had slept amazing the night before. It had been better than the previous two weeks by far.

"What do you want, demon?" I growled darkly. My stomach rolled with hunger. It was a positive sign that I was feeling better.

"That's Taylor, not me," he sang happily and rolled onto my bed which caused me to jump up. My eyes locked with his as he offered me a stunning grin. The warm honey scent of his natural cologne came at me in a large comfortable hug which he echoed.

"We are going out today. Get your cute ass ready." He declared happily. I noticed he wore jeans and a tight green sweater today. Be still my heart and ovaries.

I snarked with a smile, "You think I have a cute ass?"

Athens, my light hearted friend, went serious immediately as heat flashed through his eyes. I was still wrapped in a hug and rose a brow at the change. He offered me a sexy smile that had no amusement and all heat. It brought on a shiver that rattled my bones.

"Well, if you turn around, baby, I can evaluate my prior statement," He growled lightly as his hand grew tighter on my waist.

I blushed. Fucking blushed. I just hadn't expected it. Hadn't expected that from him.

He grinned with humor and light filled his eyes, "Now, go get ready. We are going out."

Athens was gone then, leaving me completely speechless. I felt like I was missing something about both of the twins. Something deeper than their light hearted antics and shy smiles. I tilted my head and finally gave up. I needed a shower. A shower and some coffee.

As jets of water pulsed against my body and steam filled my senses, I found myself thinking about the day before. Esme had been giving me a comfortable distance, but she had known where on the east coast I had been. She hadn't had enough information to give me away, but with some effort and well placed documents, I had no doubt she could have figured it out. While we never talked about our abilities, I knew hers had to do with tracking. I imagined she was some type of shifter. Unfortunately, at the academy, no one talked about what made them unique. It was far too dangerous to admit you were different and face possible rejection.

I promised myself to have a girls night out soon. Maybe after Solar's first show? Honestly, after two weeks of being alone, interaction of any kind seemed like a gift. It was one of the reasons that Athens's proposition seemed so tempting, even before having coffee.

"You almost ready, baby?" Athens drawled happily as I walked out of the bathroom.

I had brought my dark hair into a sleek ponytail and painted my lips a deep rose color. I had even put in my piercings so that they adorned one ear with a series of small silver rings.

"Nearly," I responded as he raised a brow at my navy silk robe.

"You should wear that out," He commented lightly as a glint entered his gaze.

"Oh yeah?" I chuckled. "All we would need is a big gust of wind and the police would arrest me for public nudity."

"I wouldn't let you get arrested alone." He wiggled his eyebrows playfully which caused me to laugh. I shooed him from my room and went to my closet.

In my self-prescribed exile, I had lost weight. I hoped this weekend to consume enough wine, cheese, and pasta to fix that. As I pulled on a pair of vintage high-waisted jeans and a black lace bra, I checked the weather. For September in Denver, it wasn't very cold. In fact, I was able to get away with a vintage half-top jacket and sneakers. After a quick look in the mirror, I left the bedroom feeling satisfied.

"Where are we going?" I asked Athens curiously as he handed me a coffee.

Bless his soul. I noticed the other men, who had slept over on my floor, had already left. I missed them already. I scowled at the thought while drinking my coffee. Of course, he made my coffee perfect. Typical. Isn't there some rule? If you're a hotter-than-sin man, you make awful coffee? I am positive that exists.

"We are going to the movies." Athens grinned a boyish smile and offered me his hand.

I locked up the dorm as he slung an arm over my shoulders.

"What movie?" I mused out loud.

"The date always picks," He stated with a playful wink.

Okay, I blushed. "Is this a date?"

Athens tilted his head at me, eyes roaming over my blush, and just answered with a *yes.*

Okay. I was going on a date with Athens.

Holy crap.

I didn't do dates. Ever.

22

ATHENS

"Baby, just pick a type of candy," I growled against her ear as she examined all the options.

She looked too thin after two heart breaking weeks of being away. There was more light to her eyes after yesterday and I had been assigned via Rhodes to 'keep a fucking smile on kitten's face all day.'

I, being the gentleman I am, accepted that challenge without a second thought. I loved nothing more than to spend time with her. While demon boy and Rhodes were brooding, Adyen was frustrated, and Neo was… well being Neo-ish, I had no issue showing her exactly how much I liked her. I didn't try to hide how much it had hurt when she left, but I also didn't want to waste my time with her being upset.

Life was short. I wanted to experience it. Live it. Especially with Gray next to me.

She was a dynamite. A survivor. She pushed through the hard shit and kept going. Even now, her tight curvy body bounced with energy and her smile at me seemed to knock down some of my own defenses. I could feel eyes on us and it made me proud. I knew I couldn't keep her to myself, but today, I was her date.

"M&Ms or Snickers?" She asked sincerely. Her eyes swirled with lightning.

"Both," I stated to the cashier as Gray made a humming sound of approval.

I felt my entire body tense and my cock jerk. Did she even realize how hot she was? From her husky voice to sassy scowl.

I was happily surprised when she pulled my arm more comfortably over her shoulder. I knew that the clothing made her scars feel more hidden, but it felt something akin to trust. We made our way to the line for the new movie that had just come out. The crowd was filled with people of assorted ages. We rested our backs against the wall comfortably.

It was about thirty minutes later that my back tingled with warning. My eyes found Gray's happy smile as an older woman came down the line, a deep scowl on her face and she was specifically set on our intertwined hands. I grimaced because *I knew* what this was about. I had seen this woman before when I was out with Neo.

Once the woman was in front of us and coughing to get our attention, Gray slid her eyes to the problem at hand. Her smile fell and her eyes went a deep blue, nearly black. Maybe she could feel the tension as well? Man, she was sorta scary. I loved that.

"Do you need something?" Gray mused out loud her voice icy. When not directed toward myself, the voice had a hypnotic quality to it. The scowling woman had pamphlets in her hand and shoved one toward Gray. I reached out to take it and the woman instantly drew back. Gray raised a single eyebrow.

"Our church is not open to your kind," She stated in a raspy smoker's voice as Gray's entire body tensed. That almost earned a chuckle because this was Denver and she 100% did not know what my kind was.

"Please," Gray seethed through her teeth with a predatory shift of her body. "Tell me. What is *his* kind?"

The woman's face softened in panic and looked to Gray.

"It's not too late to be saved dear, especially for a nice white-_"

"Fuck no," Gray commanded loudly. "Get the fuck out of my face. Now."

I felt pride surge through me, but I still brought a comforting arm around Gray.

"It's okay, baby. She's going to be who she is."

Gray turned her stormy eyes on me, "It's not fucking okay. You're fucking awesome and she's a piece of shit."

The woman gasped and Gray tossed up a finger at her without looking.

"Get your fucking pamphlets out of my face and take your racist bullshit away from me."

Everyone in line made sounds of agreements and I even heard a few claps. As the line moved forward, I pulled Gray to my chest and tried to not let the rumble of approval break through. I could feel it building in me. She was so strong and those harsh words coming out of her perfect mouth only turned me on more. Once we were inside, I pulled her to the back of the theatre. I needed to be alone with her.

"I can't believe her--"

Gray was trembling with anger, but I cut off her rant, determined to not ruin our date. I pulled her down into the seat while simultaneously raising the armrest between our seats. She let out a squeak as I pressed my lips to her gently in a chaste kiss of thanks.

"Thanks for sticking up for me, baby," I murmured, pulling away from her intense gaze.

She nodded and pressed her forehead against mine. I breathed in her rose scented perfume and twirled a single strand of silky hair from her ponytail.

"Now. Let's watch this movie, have a nice date, and ignore that bitch."

She laughed at that. Her laugh was beautiful. Yeah. No doubt about it. I liked Gray.

23

GRAY

"She was a total badass," Athens declared over dinner with Neo later that day. I flushed because Athens made me feel as strong as I tried to portray. At the same time, the man totally made me melt. The kiss he had pressed to my lips had been sweet and chaste.

Had he meant it as a thank you? Was it more than that? I currently sat between both twins at a pizza parlor and had no idea what to make of the situation. I didn't date. Ever. Now, I sorta felt like I was on a double date. Athens had his arm swung around the back of the booth and Neo was turned facing me attentively.

"I bet she was," Neo offered his eyes sparkling that midnight black blue.

I shrugged and smiled as the waitress put our large pizza down. I took a sip of my beer while filling my plate with pizza.

"How are you feeling today?" Neo asked curiously. "I am glad you're eating more."

I nodded happily, "Well, I lost like 10 lbs so my goal is to gain it back."

Athens chuckled lightly, "*Said no woman ever*. Glad to hear it though."

"You know, my body is something I have forced myself to appreciate," I explained comfortably. "Only thing you can really control is you."

Athens whined, "Why are you so smart?"

Neo sighed, "Or it's just shocking to you because you're so dumb."

I laughed at that. In fact, around them I seemed to laugh a lot. They weren't as intense as Taylor, as consuming as Adyen, or as confusing as Rhodes. They were just them. Goofy, and a little shy, but more complex than they let on. As we sat enjoying our pizza, I could feel eyes on us. Specifically our waitress, but I didn't pay attention to her expression. Instead, I let a calm come over me in waves. I needed this peace.

"How did you get all those piercings?" She asked at her next stop. "Sorry, I know that's super random. You just have so many of them and I have to imagine that hurt like hell."

I smiled, but met her blushing face. Was I making her nervous? Shit, I was bad at this.

"I actually got them all at once while in Amsterdam," I explained briefly.

"Did it hurt? It must have," she conceded. Well, considering I had to use a special metal…

I nodded, "Yeah, it hurt." See, I could be polite! Look at my manners!

Once she left, Neo leveled me with a knowing grin as I groaned. Pizza would save me. Pizza was always a safe bet to distract me from awkward social situations, sexy smiles, and hot twins.

"When did you go to Amsterdam?" Neo asked curiously, his eyes sparkling.

"Two years ago," I explained softly. "After freshman year."

"Any reason in particular?"

Athens snorted, "The Earth realm marijuana. Obviously Neo."

I rolled my eyes as he slid out of the bench to go use the washroom. Neo looked at me patiently, wanting the answer still. I grinned and took a deep breath.

"I went for drawing actually," I explained at my food. "I traveled through most of northern Europe, not just there."

Neo whistled, "You must have had a good job."

I brought my eyes up to him while attempting not to wince, "Actually, I have a trust fund."

He chuckled softly, "Now, that is interesting. What is the story there?"

There was a part of me that wondered how much of my history he knew. Neo would never assume anything though, even if he had knowledge on it. He would ask first. I met his eyes again, but narrowed mine just slightly as Damon's warning flashed through me. Neo kept his eyes blank, except for curiosity.

"I was adopted around six," I started at a lazy pace. "I was brought from Moscow and grew up in Los Angeles until my guardians died, I filed for emancipation and moved here."

Neo's lips twisted into a frown, "Shit. Gray, I'm sorry for bringing that up."

I shrugged as he asked the question I hated.

"Your parents. How did they die?"

A cruel, sad smile broke onto my lips as I kept my eyes on him.

"They were killed."

Athens arrived back at the table then. Neo didn't bring it up, but I was pretty sure he had a good idea of who had killed those abusive motherfuckers. I never felt guilty about using their life insurance or trust fund for personal gain. They took something away from me and left their marks, so I took something away from them and stole their life.

The only good thing they ever did?

They kept me hidden from the true evil searching me out.

24
GRAY

I woke up on Saturday with my bedroom and dorm empty. Esme had texted me about going out the night before and the twins had left near midnight. I had no plans and felt an anxious burn in my chest begin to creep up on me. Before I could let it bubble up, I sent out a text.

Me: Want to come by for breakfast?

Athens: Isn't breakfast usually for the morning after?

I snorted at that because I could imagine his flirty smile.

Me: *insert eye roll* I will make chocolate chip pancakes.

Taylor: Be there yesterday.

Adyen: Marry me?

Ah. It seemed food was the way to our dragon's heart.

Rhodes: Officially the worst proposal ever, mate.

Neo: Be over in about an hour, Gray :)

Me: Why can't you all be nice like Neo?

Athens: LOL she just called you nice. I'm fucking losing it over here.

I placed my phone down and brushed my teeth quickly. My hair was straight from yesterday and I shrugged on a pair of loose silky shorts and an oversized shirt. If they wanted to be my friends, or whatever the hell we were, then they would have to get used to seeing the real me.

As I began to take out the pancake mix, a knock sounded on the door. I chuckled, one hour my ass. With a quick skip, I swung the door open.

I let out a pained sound as something solid hit me in the face. *Shit.*

I guess I did have plans this morning.

Taylor

"Baby girl?"

I could feel bile thicken in my throat as I took in the unhinged door of her dorm. The hallway was silent and the pancake mix sat on the counter, viewable from the hallway. The guys were coming up behind me, but I didn't move. I was trying to smell her scent. My nose found the pool of blood on the floor that had soaked into the dark wood.

A deep growl came from Adyen as he took in the scene. I felt my breathing hitch as Rhodes's chest rumbled in anger. He jumped over the pool of blood easily and began to search the apartment. Silence echoed between the five of us. We waited for him to say something.

"Adyen can you get a tracking read on her?" Rhodes demanded his eyes pools of gold.

Adyen, his body tense and rigid, knelt down and sniffed the blood. I couldn't see his eyes, but from previous experience, I knew they had most likely turned black. He let out a low growl.

"I can't fully because we haven't mated," he sounded out with an unsatisfied voice. Shit.

I felt her regain consciousness as our connection lit up like an electrical board. My entire body became racked with pain and my knees gave out on me as I collapsed to the floor.

"Taylor?" Athens asked with concern, his hands grabbing my shoulders. My eyes glazed over as I felt her walls give way and pain invaded my body like a hot searing burn.

Baby girl? Gray? Where are you?

I was met with silence, so I pushed the connection further. I could almost smell her scent and the blood that was falling down her neck and face. Head injury, for sure.

Taylor? Shit. Her voice was so soft and raspy as pain made her entire demeanor change.

Let me in, baby girl. Let me see where you are--

I had thought her walls were down before, *but then...* She ripped them away without thought. Demolished them until she laid bare in front of me. I felt her momentary panic, pain, and self-hatred filter through me. I felt my sanity waver as I let out a cough of black tar onto the floor. The amount of pain held back by those walls, the fortress that was her, was undeniably impossible to describe. It humbled and terrified me.

Gray, we're coming for you.

She didn't respond and I felt her throw back up her walls.

Gray

I hoped that Taylor would allow me to explain everything he had experienced before allowing the other men to pour over my pain like a heartbreaking novel. If he had already shared it with them?

Fuck.

Hopefully, they will let me explain.

There was pain radiating through my entire body currently. The connection between Taylor and I was silent like the dark cold room I was currently in. My blood was trickling down my face and I could feel burns from the iron shackles that tied me to the stupid plastic chair I sat in. I knew my captors would be in soon now that I was awake. I wanted this over with. I needed to get out of here before I did something unforgivable.

"Damon!" I growled out my voice harsh. "Get your ass in here."

A deep chuckle radiated from the shadows as the dark fae guardian stepped out. Damn him, he looked completely unaffected as if his insane brother kidnapping me was nothing at all.

"What the fuck is going on?" I demanded, my entire body shaking with anger.

I was still dressed in an oversized shirt and comfortable shorts. I had been cozy in my suite, now I was fucking freezing. I hated being cold. Plus, this honestly wasn't the outfit to kick ass in.

I let out a deep growl, bared teeth and all, as the door opened and the other three brothers waltzed in. I kept my eyes on Ashford. You know, the one who shot me? Yeah. Fuck him. He kept his eyes on me with an intensity that made me feel sick to my stomach. Creepy motherfucker.

"You were supposed to stay away from them," Talon murmured.

His normal cocky smile was gone and he looked exhausted. Actually, looking around the room, I noticed a fatigue that surrounded their auras.

They had warned me to stay away from them. They warned me that they were guardians, like themselves. Only difference is... I knew exactly whose team these guardians were on.

If they knew who I was... Well, I would be dead before dawn.

"So your solution is to hurt me?" I raised a brow.

I had a feeling it wasn't that simple and cursed myself for opening my walls to the team. They would have figured it out eventually. Ashford hadn't been discreet, but it could have bought me time to escape. Instead, they would arrive here as the brothers wanted, I presumed.

"No, we want to get rid of those pesky guardians," Damon mused as Kennedy made a low unsatisfied growl in his throat.

Ashford just kept watching me like the creep he was.

"How do you even know they are the guardians?" I murmured.

I hoped they were wrong because that absolute confirmation was probably the most heartbreaking news I could receive.

He had hinted at it. So had they. Yet, I had ignored it. Why? Why keep away that connection? It was safer for everyone involved and admitting to it would mean returning to that world. It would mean returning to my family and my fiancé. It would mean returning to something I had been smart enough to flee as a child. I am smarter now. I had no fucking intention of returning.

Before now, Damon hadn't warned me specifically of them, but of any guardian outside of the four of them. Possessive bastards. It was going to kill them when they realized the truth. I would find it fucking hilarious though.

Upstairs, I could hear the front door break open and I made a worried sound in my throat. I didn't want them down here. I wanted them back at the academy. I had zero concern about my safety in this situation, I knew I could escape. I wasn't sure how they would fair.

"Ah! They *do* care," Damon snorted as my eyes fell on the door. It was thrown open as red mist swarmed the entire room. Honestly, if it wasn't for the pain I knew they were going to be subjected to, I would have admired their raw power.

I would never deny that my SE boys weren't dangerous. They were well-trained and lethal, more so than they even displayed. Their power radiated through the room like the predators that they were. None of us were human. No, we were far higher on the food chain so why try to pretend to be anything but the savages we were. Unfortunately, they had let their emotions get ahead of them and walked straight into this fucking trap.

"Damon, you're going to regret this," I murmured as Talon did the expected.

The men were brought to their knees as iron holds infiltrated the air. Unlike them, it only caused me mild irritation. I took stock of the men in front of me as concern pushed through my chest uncomfortably.

Rhodes looked furious and slightly unhinged. Frankly, it was a good look, more so than his usual calm. Adyen was already mid shift as his body shimmered in gold scales and his muscles swelled even bigger. Taylor was red from his eyes to the power surrounding him. It was frozen in a cloud like mist. The twins were both hyper-focused on my wrists and the damage I had incurred. I wondered if they noticed the minimal extent of it.

Ashford stepped forward his eyes on me, glinting through his glasses. I knew I didn't have time and there would be no long drawn out speech. Instead, he simply held up his gun with iron bullets and placed it next to Neo's temple. My eyes met the midnight gaze and the resignation I saw there made me furious. He knew I could stop this and he didn't expect me to. I spoke.

"Ashford, drop the gun or you die."

My inner power snarled at the concept that Ashford would even dare to threaten one of mine. Fuck, when had they become mine?

His voice was rough and raw, "As long as you're safe."

He pushed the safety down right as I snapped his neck.

25

NEO

I had expected to die.

My eyes had met hers knowingly. It was my job to sacrifice myself for her safety. By saving us, it would alert what she feared. I wasn't positive about what she feared, but I knew it had to be terrifying for her to be scared. So, I would die willingly. As the safety clicked, the very familiar snap of bones sounded throughout the cold room. *Shit.*

Gray was no longer tied down and instead stood next to me as Ashford's body slumped to the ground. I looked up at her to meet those beautiful dark eyes in surprise. It was the only physical change about her, yet the entire room was suffocating in a thick wave of power.

I had assumed she would be powerful, but I had no data to back up the extent of that power. No one knew what type of power she possessed. Even now, I could feel her power radiating like a heavy, mysterious presence in the room. It felt different than the five of us. It was as lethal and dangerous, but somehow more savage.

That was a good word. *Savage*. Wild. Untamable. Primal. Her magic was uncontrollable, even by her. It had its own mind.

"What the fuck?" Kennedy voiced as he urged the door open. My eyes tracked Gray as she lifted a hand and halted his progression. It was simply a flick of her wrist. That flick of the wrist brought the room to an icy still. It was a feeling I knew well. I wondered to what extent she could hold the room captive.

"You're fae. How did you--" Damon's voice was thick with fear and confusion.

"You should have done your homework better, Damon," She cooed moving to Talon.

He grit his teeth and tried to move against his icy restraints. The power she held was barely being utilized. I found myself almost hypnotized by the quality of it.

"Tell me, Damon," She murmured, her voice becoming layered in texture. "Did you plan on killing all of them?"

Anyone outside of this room would have lied. However, as he fell on his knees, it was clear his mind couldn't formulate a way around the truth. He was from the Dark Fae kingdom, and like the light, he was beholden to the truth. The man was frozen and pale. His fear brought me an absurd amount of happiness. Then again, was it absurd? He tried to hurt Gray. That was simply unacceptable.

"Yes," he breathed out as his body trembled.

Gray made an amused sound and closed a hand around Talon's throat. I let out a sound of surprise as he disintegrated. His body had turned to ash with a simple touch of her hand. It had been nothing to her.

"And then?"

"We would have kept you safe from any Horde members," He whispered with a pained voice.

It was clear that he was pleading for her to understand his motivations on some level. Kennedy was next as the sound of his body hitting the door echoed with the snap of his neck. It was a clean and practiced move. She let out a growl of annoyance and stepped around us to face Damon on his knees.

Her voice swam through the air in layers, "*Stupid, stupid Damon,*" she cooed softly and placed a hand under his chin from his position kneeling. "I wasn't running from the Horde. I was running from *your* sadistic fucking king."

Damon's eyes widened and he began to mumble out words quickly, "But you're a Horde creature. You told us to keep you safe from fae. You were running from their guard."

"I was running from a guard unit. *Instead,* your guard unit offered me protection while I existed right under your fucking nose."

Damon's skin turned even paler, "You can't be her. The heir was--"

I watched as his body burned to ash. I wondered briefly the difference between methods but didn't ask as her power receded back. All of us let out a sigh of relief and slumped forward slightly. The scent of ash permeated the air.

"We need to leave now," she stated quietly, her eyes flashing silver across the four bodies. "Tell me you have a car outside."

Rhodes recovered first in a calm voice, "Absolutely."

We moved past the bodies and up the stairs as my eyes fixed on her slim figure in front of me. I could feel her power being pulled in as if a vortex was consuming it and devouring it whole. I looked up as her steps faltered. It was a small misstep, but it showcased her exhaustion. Suddenly, her entire body fell back into my chest. Just like it had appeared, her immense power was gone and her snarky little smirk appeared. It was dimmed slightly by her half-lidded eyes.

"*See,* Neo," She smiled sleepily, her eyes turning back to a deep indigo, "I scratch your back and you scratch mine."

I snorted and lifted her into my arms. Her soft hair cascaded against my shoulders as her scent overwhelmed me with how delicate and soft it was. Fuck. How was this the same person? My eyes examined her critically and noted nothing but exhaustion on her face.

"That is not how that works, Gray," I smiled down at her and those thick lashes fluttered shut.

If we hadn't been sure before, we knew now. She was the one we had been built for. She was the one we had been brought together for. Gray was *ours*.

26

GRAY

My eyes fluttered open to meet a pair of beautiful honey colored eyes. They were surrounded by thick, dark lashes that were nearly feminine and darkened with various emotions. I could have described to you in a million ways how beautiful those eyes were. Not just because of the light yellow to rich amber fade within his pupil. Not just because of the shiny dark lashes that seemed to enhance his masculine face. No. They were beautiful because looking at them meant the boys were safe. We had gotten back to my suite alive. Well, at least for right now.

I felt a stupid smile break onto my face. God. My brain was being so mushy right now. Then my hearing returned.

Esme panicked, "Trust me, Rhodes. You have to get her out of here."

"We aren't running."

A pained sound came from my throat as Rhodes moved into my line of sight, "She's right. The academy is going to be swamped with activity by the Dark Fae in the morning. We have to get out of here."

Had he always looked so angelic? It was that damn golden

hair. Like a halo or some shit. I really was terrible with romantic literary shit. It was why I could never be a writer.

Rhodes met my confused gaze as panic filled me. My panic must have worried him. Instantly, his face became calm and unreadable. That was good. That was who I needed right now. I groaned and sat up as Adyen held me close by wrapping an arm around my waist. I motioned for Esme to come to me as her eyes widened with panic and skin grew nearly green. I had never confided in her completely. I wouldn't now, *but* she was in possession of some important information.

"I won't risk your safety by explaining everything," I whispered, clasping her soft hands to mine. "Please go grab the file I need. It is in the cabinet built under the head of your bed and should be a silver color. Leave the others. Give the silver one to Rhodes. It explains nearly everything. Please. Then, go get Bobby and his friend, Jason."

"Bobby?" Taylor asked in his gruff voice.

I was temporarily distracted by the handsome demon. He was shirtless. Could you blame me? His fair skin was shredded with lean muscle and freckles were scattered across the top of his shoulders. Damn, his tattoo was so much larger than I realized.

My eyes snapped to his emerald gaze, "Trust me, Taylor."

Esme was already coming back into the room and she handed the sleek silver file to Rhodes. I met his pale, green gaze and spoke quietly, "Esme, please go get both of them."

She did, leaving with urgency as I continued my directions.

"Inside that folder is the coordinates to several safe houses I keep. Pick one at random from the options on page four. I do not want to know where we are going until we are out of the area because if I am caught, I don't want them to know where you are headed."

I struggled to get up and ignored their protests, squeezing Adyen's shoulder.

"Esme and Bobby have been aware of my situation for some time now. He was keeping tabs on the Hollingworth brothers for years. They probably only kept him around because he let them treat him like shit."

Taylor moved in front of me with a distraught look, "The darkness in his head?"

"Mine," I admitted darkly. "To keep the brothers out of his head."

There was silence as Rhodes opened up the file and met my eyes again. I was exhausted and found myself leaning back into Adyen. The room seemed to swarm with lights.

"Baby?" Athens asked quietly, kneeling in front of me. I kept my eyes on Rhodes.

"I need this done correctly. Please, Rhodes. I'm trusting you."

The beautiful man kept his pale gaze on me and with a sharp nod, began directing the men throughout the room. Luckily, Adyen's warm body stayed tucked under mine as the room burst into action. I felt proud that I had been right to pick Rhodes. He was smart, capable, and understood that the time for questions would be later.

I had no doubt though.

There would be many fucking questions.

As I struggled to keep my eyes open, I heard Athens packing in my room. I had to assume he assigned Neo to manipulate the academy's database. Jason would explain what happened to the Dean, another reason I was glad to have helped their budding relationship. Taylor was on the phone quietly across the room. He was most likely demanding the private jet. Rhodes was on the phone as well, but his eyes were trained on my file. I wondered idly where he would pick to go.

"Gray?" A concerned voice said from the door.

I brought my eyes to a very concerned Esme, Jason, and Bobby. I pushed myself forward and motioned them toward me. I was wedged between Adyen's legs as his hand smoothed over my spine in a comforting motion.

Esme, large eyed and completely serious, brought me into a lung squeezing, tight hug. I spoke quietly to her.

"I need you to make sure the students here are safe. I need to erase your memory of me in order to do that. Do you understand?"

I pulled back and found her warm gaze thick with tears. I pressed my forehead to hers and spoke with confidence.

"I will have you remember when it's safe. This is not the end of our friendship. I promise you, Esme."

"Gray," she whispered with thick tears. "Do you promise?"

"I promise to always keep you safe."

"Do it," she swallowed with a nod. Her curls bounced. I pressed my forehead to hers and raised my hands to her temples. It was a light touch, barely there. I let a small smidge of my power out, enough to make Adyen grunt in closeness, and moved through her mind like a weaver. My string was a metallic silver that I twisted around my finger delicately, before pulling it from her consciousness. As I pulled away, I whispered for her to go to sleep. Without a second of confusion, Esme stood up and walked toward her bedroom. If the plans were followed precisely, she would have a new roommate by morning and my presence would be removed from campus.

"Jason," I whispered. "Come here."

The lanky redhead was far less emotional of an experience. In fact, his mind was so easy to mold that within seconds he was off to Mr. Jackson with a story in mind.

I hated this next part. I hated now he knelt in front of me with an expression of concern.

Concern that was for me, not himself. His large muscular shoulders were fitted in a beautiful, blue shirt I had bought him at Christmas. I had always loved that color against his tanned skin and light silky hair. My hand fluttered to his jaw as those brown eyes bore into me. The fake Bobby was gone and replaced with the serious loyal man I knew well.

"Bobby," I whispered quietly, bringing both hands to cup his face. His skin was warm.

His brow furrowed as his warm brown eyes clouded with emotion.

"Gray, don't make me forget you. Not like them. I can deal with you leaving, but not that."

I had never hated Bobby. *Sure*, I punched him because he was an asshole. He was only doing his job for the Hollingworth brothers. They wouldn't have taken it kindly if their punching bag was friends with me. Damn it. I hated this.

Bobby hadn't given it a second thought when I had enlisted him to aid me. The dog shifter was loyal and kind. He was also the only man in my life who I felt completely comfortable with.

"Bobby," I whispered, pressing my forehead to his. "It's for your safety, as well as theirs."

His face, normally open, became distorted with frustration, "Bring me with you, Gray. I can't lose you. Please."

I felt tears well up in my eyes as I brought him into a hug and Adyen released me into his arms. I let his warmth seep through me as the scent of my familiar surrounded me. I pulled back and pressed my hands to his temples. Gods. I wanted to be selfish. So selfish.

"I'll be back Bobby. Thank you for everything" I whispered quietly. "Please, keep them safe."

I pressed a chaste kiss to his lips softly and then to each of the tears coming down his tanned skin. He nodded sharply at the order and I delved into his mind easily to remove thoughts of me. A strangled sound came from his throat as his body slumped toward me in regret. I let out a whimper as I gathered him in my arms, officially completing the task at hand. I couldn't remove our connection because it was pre-fated. His memories of me were removable, though.

My eyes went from his soft messy hair to Rhodes. The man was staring at me with an indecipherable expression that bore into my very being. I couldn't look away from him. I couldn't escape the questions in his eyes. The best I could do was avoid for a small bit of time.

27

GRAY

"Mmm, good choice, Rhodes," I murmured from my spot next to him on the jet.

Now that we were in the air, I could see our destination and route.

"You had many interesting options," He stated quietly.

"All of which we will make use of until we can sort this situation out."

The large man next to me nodded and put his body at an angle to look at me. I faced him and took stock of his neatly pressed suit and messy shoulder length hair. Those beautiful pale green eyes were filled with questions, but he had dark circles under his eyes. Had he not been sleeping well? I reached out and squeezed his hand.

"You will explain."

"I will," I mumbled quietly in response to his command. "Once we are alone, Rhodes. All of us need to talk."

This seemed to satisfy our leader as he nodded sharply and squeezed my hand firmly. I let out a shaky exhale as my thoughts went to Esme and Bobby. I hadn't imagined my goodbye with

Bobby would have been so painful. Yet, I found myself missing him more than I expected.

"Do you love him?" Rhodes asked quietly. Could he read my mind?

"I love him, but I am not *in love* with him," I explained softly. "He is one of my closest friends outside of Esme. A confident and loyal friend. But no, Rhodes, I don't love him any more than in a family way."

"He feels differently."

"He feels nothing now, he doesn't remember me." *Keep it together, Gray.*

"One day, he will remember."

"So he will," I caught my strangled tears. Rhodes swiped a tear from my cheek as I crossed my arms. "He's my familiar, Rhodes."

Silence.

"And you refused him his memories of you?" He asked with wide darkening eyes. I understood why he was reacting like that. Familiars were very rare and normally not even given to fae. They were supposed to aid in focusing your power and serve as a support system. So Yeah. I had essentially told someone whose job it is to support me... to forget about me.

I nodded sharply, "Trust me. He's safer now."

Rhodes let out a deep growl, "Trust is earned, Gray. You have told us nothing."

I met his gaze with a narrowed look, "You are asking me to confirm your assumed knowledge, not tell you anything new."

Rhodes paled just slightly, "You know then?"

I grasped his face between my palms and met his eyes with a straight forward gaze.

"I had my assumptions. However, my mental connection with Taylor only solidified it."

"And the Dark Fae king? He is the one chasing after you?"

My skin broke out in tingles.

"Later, please." It was a pleading whisper.

"What do you need from me?"

I smiled sadly, "You are the head of my guard, Rhodes. I need you to be strong when I can not. I need you to advise me. I need you, when we are away from all this, to promise your life to mine. To give yourself to a cause, to a person, selflessly."

I hated this. I hated asking anyone for anything. I hoped he would say no. Except that thought left a massive hole in my chest of pulsating pain.

Instead, he leaned forward pressing a kiss to my forehead softly, "I told you, Gray. There is no darkness, no depth that you could go, that we wouldn't follow. I promised my life to you when we were young. It is no different now."

He meant it. I didn't move from his grasp as he pulled me onto his lap. I let my eyes closed as the exhaustion hit me like a freight train. The last thing I heard was his murmured words of allegiance in my ear.

Rhodes

"Rhodes, what's the plan once we arrive?" Adyen asked, his body tense and brow furrowed.

He was concerned about Gray and I didn't blame him. The woman terrified me as much as she concerned me. Her beautiful face was pale and breathing shallow as she slept on my lap. I bet she would make that cute, angry expression if she knew how kitten-like she looked curled up against me.

I had always heard rumors that she would be powerful. I had always known she would be strong and capable. Yet, Gray was all of that and so much more. Her power in the Hollingworth's basement was minuscule compared to her capability. Her wit and emotional strength were steely. If the scars on her back showed anything than that strength had been essential to her survival.

I wasn't sure how she had escaped the Horde. I had no knowledge of where exactly she had been since her sixth birthday and parent's death. I didn't know why she was running from the Dark Fae. All we knew was that her fiancé was requiring her presence, the Dark Fae were apparently after her, and the Horde needed her. Yet, none of that mattered because we were running. Her safety was the most important, most essential element. Her safety was the only thing that mattered anymore.

Our job was her. Keeping her safe. While I didn't very much understand it, I knew if she said to run then we would run. Still I, *we*, were owed an explanation. Yet, for the life of me, I couldn't bring myself to wake her up. She needed sleep.

If I was being selfish, there was a part of me perfectly okay with running because I didn't want to return her to the Horde for marriage. I was struggling enough with the information about her relationship with Bobby. He was an annoyance yet now I find out he's a fundamental piece to her. A familiar. A piece to the puzzle that was Gray.

"When we arrive in Estonia, I need the place secured. I don't know how long she will want to stay," I stated quietly.

"We are running from the Dark King then?" Adyen asked quietly his eyes sparkling with anger.

"Yes."

"Is he the one who--"

"No," I whispered, shaking my head. "Something happened between now and when she ran from the Horde. Something that left her with scars."

Taylor let out a deep sound from the row behind us.

"I want answers, Rhodes."

"Patience, Taylor." I snapped with annoyance.

I looked down as Gray turned into my chest and her hair fell from that jagged scar that ran temple to jaw. My fingers stretched out to touch her scar. The smooth moonlight texture made my healing powers spark dangerously.

I wondered briefly why she let me touch her scars, but didn't allow anyone else. It made me feel warm inside, like she was kindling a fire in my very being. A flame to my silent soul. I closed my eyes, ignoring my men, as my fingers stroked over her smooth scar gently. My powers seeped into her as sleep took over.

A whimper struck out against the silence of the room. My eyes snapping to a small, thin girl pressed against the living room wall. I felt bile rise in my throat. The little girl had black long hair and she was being held to a pale green wall by a monster. Her hand was wrapped around Gray's throat as tears tore down her young face in jagged patterns.

"Do you love him?!" The woman screamed in her face. I brought myself to stand next to the woman whose eyes were red with exhaustion and arms littered with needle marks. It stood in contrast to the beautiful home.

"No," Gray rasped out, "I don't want--"

A sharp slap hit Gray's face as another whimper came from her throat. I couldn't do anything but witness the horror that was occurring. The woman brought her hand forward and held it against Gray's temple. I felt nausea shudder through me at the sight of the kitchen knife.

"He won't want you after this," The woman whispered as her eyes darkened and her expression turned manic. I wanted to stop this. I knew what would happen. I knew what I was witnessing.

"I don't want him," Gray begged softly. "Please... Nia."

"I have to," she growled sharply and brought the knife down. "I have to take off this damn face. This cursed face."

I let out a roar lunging forward as the knife cut down her face. As I reached to grasp her, it disappeared and Gray's large eyes met mine. A look of horror flashing across her expression.

Everything went black.

Gray

"Shit," I flung up from my nightmare and slammed my head into his. He had been in my dream. I had felt him there. A flicker of rage grew in me.

I should have felt violated. I should have felt uncomfortable. Instead, I felt embarrassed and angry. I was angry that he had a front seat to the show that was my horrendous childhood. I felt embarrassed because Rhodes was strong and calm. *He was everything I couldn't be.* Why was it that after all these years, *he* had to be the one to delve into those memories? I could have dealt with Esme's pity or avoided Bobby's questions. I didn't know how to explain myself to Rhodes.

Except when I went to yell at him, I stopped dead in my tracks and let out a pained sound. His eyes were filled with furious liquid gold and those strong arms were locked around me like a vice hold. Inches separated those knowing eyes from my own. My position was not one that allowed for an easy escape.

"Don't," I growled out softly in warning.

I could deal with a lot. Not pity though. I couldn't deal with that. From Rhodes, our strong leader, it would feel even worse. There was a lethal, demanding power to Rhodes. He didn't just ask for answers, he demanded them. He saw through me like a clear glass pane. His entire demeanor demanded that you let him see exactly as much as he wanted, when he wanted. I felt hypnotized. I was thankful for the lack of pity I saw in his eyes.

"Is she dead, kitten?" He murmured, bringing his lips toward my ear so that it was in a whisper. His voice was thick and husky with his accent.

I nodded and pressed my forehead to his. It was dark in the cabin and the shades were pulled down. I hadn't even had time to appreciate the jet. I was positive it was beautiful. Instead, my attention was captured by the warm arms wrapped around me, keeping me locked against him.

"Yes," I mumbled softly as I moved even closer to him and to his soft sculpted lips.

At least I assumed they were soft. They looked soft. I wanted to see if they were.

Good Job, Gray. NOW is the time you want to kiss the handsome alpha shifter? Right after he saw your traumatic childhood? You fucking lunatic. Idiot.

"Good," He snarled softly. "If not, I would kill her myself."

The fierceness in his voice wasn't something I heard often, yet I couldn't help but appreciate it. It felt authentic and more than that, I believed he would follow that pledge. There was something very noble about Rhodes. He had a loyalty and meaning behind his words that you didn't see often.

"You would, wouldn't you?" I whispered through a thick voice.

"Anything for you," Rhodes vowed quietly. "But in return, I expect certain things, Gray."

"Like?" I could feel my nerves light on fire. I was terrified he would ask something of me that I couldn't give.

"Truth, transparency, loyalty," he murmured. "I need you to be open with me."

"I'm not good at that," I whispered as my face flushed.

What was it about these men making me all hot and bothered? This situation was extremely serious. And yet, I could feel every inch between us. The commanding tone coming from his tanned lips only made me more turned on. Shit. I really was screwed.

"I know, kitten," he purred and ran a hand through my silky hair. "And I'll be patient, but I need to know every part of you. Every little detail, every thought that crosses your beautiful mind. I need it like a fix. I want to protect you, to keep you and my brothers safe. In order to do that, I need to know every part of you. I need to know the puzzle that is you, Gray."

I think my brain sputtered and crashed. For such a calm and controlled man, his words were direct and intense. I tried not to mull over the beautiful comment and allusion to me being a drug to him. Did he also mention protecting me? Oh man. Be still my little, primal heart. The savage side of me was cheering at his archaic declaration.

"I can try," I murmured.

I should have argued with him about the kitten nickname or, you know, *punched him in the face*. Instead, my heart was beating at an uneven tempo.

"That's all I can ask, beautiful." He whispered.

He leaned closer while gently running a rough finger against my bottom lip. My breath caught as I met his eyes as they cooled to a beautiful, soft green. I wanted him to press those soft lips to mine and for him to surround me with his warmth. Rhodes was demanding, but he was a leader. Even if I didn't know him well, I knew he was trustworthy. I knew I could lean on him.

I leaned forward and closed the distance between us.

Soft. Damn, they were soft and sculpted… and he tasted amazing, like exotic spices and warm sugar. I let out a breathy moan as he pressed himself in between my legs so that I was straddling him. When he slipped his tongue into my mouth and deepened the kiss, my inner vixen did a little happy jig.

I let him control the kiss, his nature demanding and controlling as he kept a hand on my jaw and one on the back of my neck. I could feel him rumble softly at how I turned and offered my neck to him. It hadn't even been a show of submission, but I could feel how much he liked that concept. Fuck, why did that turn me on? I had never been one for controlling men. Or even sex for that matter... my childhood was thick with trauma. Yet like my scars, I felt emboldened to embrace this burning sexual desire that now coursed through my veins. I wanted to take control of myself and my sexuality. If that meant letting Rhodes take the lead, so be it.

I trusted him. I knew he would never hurt me and something about his nature made me think that he needed control as much as I needed to let mine go. I tugged on his lip experimentally and caused him to let out a deep, vibrating growl. The savage inside of me perked up happily.

My hands trailed over his neat suit and into his thick hair, the heat between my thighs pooling. I wanted to rub against him until I found release. I wanted to lick every inch of his golden skin. If not out of desire, then of gratitude. He handled everything with ease. He made me feel protected. Loved. I absorbed the groan he let out as it vibrated against my lips.

"Move your hair, kitten," He demanded quietly his eyes pulsating with power as we rested forehead to forehead. I bit my lip and lifted my locks into a tight messy bun on top of my head. I was wearing a tank top, so this move exposed my shoulders and therefore, my scars. I felt a nervous shiver wreck through me as he looked down at me. Even straddling his lap, he was so much larger than me.

"May I?" He whispered his voice tingling my ear gently.

I only offered a sharp nod. I felt my entire body tense as those soft lips began at the start of my long, jagged scar. The one where she had tried to peel off my *damn cursed face*. A pained sound came from my throat as he offered careful appreciative words and kissed along the scar.

"Rhodes," I murmured softly.

"Trust me," He demanded kissing my lips again and bringing a breathy moan out of my throat.

Those teeth began to nip at my neck, sharp little shocks, that he then smoothed over with his tongue. His hot, smooth, sexy tongue... Fuck. I rolled my hips without thinking it through. His hand snaked down to my hip, holding it in a possessive, unyielding hold. He held me like he couldn't bear to let me go, to let me move away from him.

"Gray," He ground out as his hardness pressed into my legging covered center.

He began to trail kisses down my shoulder which caused a moan to come from my lips. Fuck, he was the only one to touch me like that. He touched the scars with his lips in a worshiping way. I let out a sound that was pained and pleasured at the same time. I had never been shown affection in those areas of my body, only pain.

"So beautiful," He whispered quietly. "Every single one, kitten. Every single one."

Despite the desire coursing through me, tears welled up in my eyes and brought my lips crashing into his. It was in that dangerous way where teeth clashed and tears soaked my face. I was surprised no one woke in the cabin. Yet, I was grateful for this moment. I was grateful for him.

Shit. I should have punched him when I had the chance.

28

GRAY

"This is your place?" Athens asked with a low whistle. I grinned, feeling a surge of pride, as my eyes trailed over the beautiful stone estate. It was on a neat piece of well-maintained land that was edged with a large stone wall and a sprawling driveway. The driveway we were currently driving up led to a beautiful fountain and pair of deep onyx colored doors.

Despite the wealth I had, the pride I had in certain assets never seemed to fade. I didn't purchase pieces of property, art, or anything else unless it meant something to me.

"I bought the place right after my emancipation," I murmured simply.

Athens was behind me, his head placed on the top of the seat. Neo was next to him with a laptop open and his midnight eyes trained on the bright blue light. I could see the exhaustion on his face and wondered how much sleep he had gotten in the past day.

"How old were you?" Taylor grunted sitting next to me.

His legs were spread out and despite his gruff nature, his warm hand was gripping my thigh firmly.

"Old enough, but not legally an adult on the Earth realm."

There was silence in the car. I knew they had questions and, shit, I had some as well. For now though, I would keep it simple. I could hear their thoughts though, wondering *why* someone would need to be emancipated.

Adyen let out a sound and turned around from where he sat in the front with Rhodes, our designated driver, "I am going to do a security check. Do you have staff members?"

I nodded, "Yes. Only about five. Their names should be listed in the file."

As we pulled up to the estate an older woman, Tulsa, was waiting with a serious scowl. I chuckled because I knew without a doubt that it wasn't directed toward me. *No, no*, this was all about the men with me. I grinned at her and hugged her tightly. Despite her stuffy scowl, she hugged me close as the scent of expensive perfume came off her beautiful navy suit.

"These men," I gave her a coy smile, "are my guard."

Those steely gray eyes brightened and with a whisper, she responded, "Guard? Sounds like a special word for a harem, Miss Gray."

I chuckled at that and wiggled my eyebrows, "We will be staying here for about a week. This is Rhodes. He will be in charge of *stuff and things.*"

She smiled at that, "*Stuff and things,* you say?"

"Nice to meet you," Rhodes offered a hand as she nodded with a curious gaze on my smile.

Rhodes's lips twitched just slightly at my attempt to downplay his massive role as the leader of my guard. Had to keep his ego in check, right?

"This is Adyen." Rhodes explained while I was looking at the big, handsome man, his hands gripping my waist. "He is in charge of our security."

I leaned back into Adyen as his scent surrounded me. I wasn't completely used to the level of physical intimacy that these men showed me, but it was getting far better. I was getting far better at not shying away from them. Only them though. Everyone else can fuck off.

Rhodes continued, "Neo is in charge of our IT systems."

I nearly made a nerd joke, and would have, but *damn,* this was Neo we were talking about and he was so damn sweet. I could see some lingering pain in his eyes and hoped that one day he would trust me with it. *One day?* Damn it, Gray. Since when did we decide we were keeping them? Except I knew that my magic was possessive and it didn't surprise me in the least.

Athens grinned interrupting, "I'm Athens, the better looking twin and communication expert with SE."

I snorted as his interruption, but Rhodes didn't correct him. Tulsa offered him a smile while meeting his hand. I shook my head with amusement and looked at Taylor.

"Taylor," Rhodes explained, "is our weapons expert and sniper."

Taylor offered me a dangerously vicious smile and squeezed my arm in passing as he greeted Tulsa. Somehow, that position fits him perfectly. I wondered where my carrot top cutie gained his extensive knowledge of weapons.

I let her lead them through the large foyer as Athens locked his hand in mine. We trailed at the back of the group as she showcased the rooms off the foyer. The massive kitchen was well stocked and open at any time. The dining room could fit nearly thirty. The ballroom nearly 300. All of it was unnecessary. Yet I loved it. I loved it because of some repressed childhood subconscious need to live like a storybook princess. Happily Ever After and all that shit.

"Baby, this place looks like a fucking castle," Athens whispered in reverence.

I had a feeling the twins did not come from money. Not like the others at least.

"It reminded me of a story book castle when I bought it," I whispered quietly to him. "It was the first place I truly felt safe."

Athens smiled softly, "Baby, I will always keep you safe."

"I know," I mumbled while blushing.

"Is that a blush?" He chuckled, hitting my shoulder with his.

I bit my lip in a distracted fashion, "You're making me all blushy, Athens. Cut it the fuck out."

"Blushy?" He grinned, "You're cute as shit, Gray. Did you know that?"

"Cute isn't a term used to describe me normally," I mumbled again as we entered into a large hallway outside of the library. "Keep it up and I'll punch you."

Athens let out a deep throaty laugh that turned heads, "Threatening me, baby?"

I narrowed my eyes with a grin, "Maybe."

A dangerous look came into Athens's dark eyes as he smiled brilliantly, "Well, that deserves a punishment, don't you think? You can't go around threatening your friends."

I raised a brow and opened my mouth, only to let out a gasp. Athens had me over his shoulder easily and strode from the group toward somewhere in the house. I tried to wiggle to escape, but instead, he just let out his deep charming laugh. Damn him.

"Athens!" I yelped. "What the hell are you doing?"

He laughed again smoothing a hand over the back of my thighs, before playfully smacking my butt.

"Punishment time, Gray! You threatened your best friend. It's completely unacceptable."

"Oh, *you're* my best friend now?!" I exclaimed as he swung open my office door.

I didn't have time to look over the beautiful red oak wood and navy wall coloring. Instead, I found myself caged against the large doors by a massive and playfully vicious Athens.

"Are we not?" He asked, offended, his nose pressed close to

mine. I felt my breathing quicken at the turn of events. It was always like this with Athens, a hurricane of emotion and laughter.

"Are you friend zoning me?" I smirked playfully as a heat licked to life in those dark eyes, turning them a deep silver.

"Oh, is that what you're worried about, baby?" He cooed. "We can be best friends and I'll still kiss you."

Oh, be still my black heart.

I licked my lips and raised a hand to his chest.

"You haven't kissed me yet, so I'm not sure I believe your ability to multitask."

Who the hell had possessed my body? When had I learned to flirt?

"Let's correct that," He growled, leaning forward and taking my lips without a second thought.

My core melted. This playful handsome man was melting me. I let out a moan as his persuasive lips took mine easily, as if they were his to take. It wasn't controlled like Rhodes. Instead, this licked like flames at my soul. It fed and nourished me by fulfilling me with affection. I sunk my hands into his thick, curly fade, tugging his head closer to mine with a little extra strength.

"Athens," Rhodes growled lightly from outside of the door. "Now is not the time for this."

I pulled back and flushed. Fuck. Had I just kissed him? Did Rhodes know? What the hell do I tell Rhodes? I wasn't deluded enough to think we were together but still…

Athens chuckled, never looking away from my eyes before blasting my internal fears to the god damn house, "This is your fault, Rhodes. We all heard the delicious sounds she was making on the jet so I needed to taste her for myself."

Rhodes let out a laugh at that. A motherfucking laugh. It broke my embarrassment as I swung open the other side of the door, my eyes wide in confusion. I didn't ask Athens to move and he didn't attempt to, his hands slipping to my waist to pin me to the door. Rhodes stepped in and offered me a roguish smile. Oh man. I liked that smile.

"What's going on?" I asked, more confused than ever. I tried to ignore Athens as his lips trailed along my neck gently. I almost let out the breathy moan that caught in my throat. Rhodes leaned against the door to essentially finish boxing me in between the wall, door, and a very large, seductive Athens. Well shit. I suppose life could be worse.

"Well, kitten," he purred dangerously. "It seems I am not the only one on the team who finds you irresistible."

I swallowed, "Irresistible?"

Athens murmured his agreement as he trailed kisses against my collarbone, bringing me to squirm against him as my nipples hardened against his large chest. Rhodes stepped closer and tilted my head up with a finger under my chin.

"How do you feel about that, baby?" Athens wondered out loud.

"Feel about what?" I asked in avoidance. My face was flushed.

"Feel about *us* finding your irresistible." Rhodes clarified.

"You two?" I mumbled.

Rhodes grinned, "Now, I don't think Adyen, Taylor, or Neo will want to be left out of this."

"How would that even work?" I groaned as Rhodes nipped my bottom lip gently and Athens pressed his hands to my hip bones tightly. I could feel his hardness resting against my stomach and urging me to press forward. It wasn't unheard of to have multiple partners in the Horde.

Athens met my eyes, his gaze pure silver, "We'll figure it out, baby. We just need to know if you would consider something like that."

I licked my bottom lip as Rhodes tracked the movement, "Yes?"

"Not sure enough for my liking," Rhodes explained, his grin growing.

"There are five of you and one of me," I mumbled. "I suck at opening up and I am just becoming comfortable with the idea of being touched--" I moaned softly as Athens tugged at my bottom lip in a needy fashion.

"Why would you want me? I am complicated and messy."

I didn't want to down talk myself, but it was a valid concern. Not to mention my marriage contract... you know, the one that I won't be honoring? Not the point, but I briefly wondered if they remembered that small unimportant, stupid detail.

Rhodes smiled, "Trust me, kitten. You're perfect for us." He turned serious then. "I just needed to know you would be okay with this, before we go any further."

"So, there was no punishment?" I growled lightly at a snickering Athens.

A sound came from Rhodes's throat, "You sound disappointed."

I rose a brow, feeling bolder because of the idea the five of them liking me. "Maybe I am."

Athens grinned against my neck, "Be careful with Rhodes when talking about punishments. He's not as carefree as me."

I looked up at Rhodes, but swallowed hard, finding him a mere inch from my face and looking down at me in a consuming way. It was hungry and hot. I felt myself melt into both of them just a tad more. My face was flaming with heat as lust pooled in between my thighs.

"Do you like giving out punishments, Rhodes?" I murmured as his eye pooled liquid gold.

"Only if they are warranted," He growled against my lips. "Do you deserve a punishment?"

"Maybe," I whispered shakily.

"But do you need it?" He grounded out as his hands slipped into my hair dangerously tight.

"What?" I gasped as Athens pulled back from my neck to look into my face. Those perfect lips curled into a permanent smile.

"Do you need to be punished? Do you crave it?" Rhodes asked, pulling back my attention.

I was about to say *yes.* Damn it. I wanted to know what this punishment meant between the two of them. I was pent up from the amount of sexual tension in this small corner of the room.

"You never answered about *us.* Do you want *us,* Gray?" Athens reminded me.

"Yes." I murmured. I didn't know if it was to both or just one question. I knew I wanted them.

At that exact moment, the sirens went off. Specifically, the ward bells.

My body stilled as I ducked under both men and sprinted out of the room toward the foyer. I was fast, but I could hear Athens's curse at how I seemed to disappear. I didn't have time to enjoy that because if something made it past my wards, it was dangerous. I didn't like dangerous at all. Adyen was there already, his eyes a deep nearly black and his form surrounded by gold power.

"What the hell is going on?" I shouted over the warning bells from the wards. My dragon simply shook his head with a look of frustration as he placed me behind him with a sweep of his arm. The front doors flew open with a sweep of power. I let out a groan as I snapped to shut off the wards. Adyen wasn't attacking and I knew why. I knew that power and annoyance pulsed through me. Not fear. No, this was pure annoyance.

"Silas," I growled stepping around Adyen. "What the fuck are you doing here?"

The onyx doors were thrown open and the dusk lighting from outside highlighted the extensive guard units waiting outside. My eyes, though, were on Silas. He was standing in the door, looking every bit of the Horde King.

"Sister," Silas grinned viciously, his robes swirling around his feet in a deep silver and purple. "It is nice to see that you have *finally* made an appearance on everyone's fucking radar."

I heard Adyen growl, but I kept my gaze on his, "How did you find me, Silas? You shouldn't be here. You should have stopped looking."

This got a reaction out of the silver eyed man, "Stop looking for my sister? My only living relative? The woman who is supposed to be wearing this damn crown?"

He was angry, furious even, as he pointed to the onyx colored six-point crown on top of his head. I had heard that Silas was not fit to rule, but it seemed as though he truly had no intention of ruling. I didn't either, though. Well, that was a lie. It wasn't that I didn't want to rule. I just couldn't.

"Damn it!" I snarled. "Come inside, you fool."

The doors snapped as I commanded him to the library. Adyen stood looking at me with wide eyes as my petulant brother went to sit on the large deep blue sofas.

"Gather everyone, please," I murmured. "It's fucking story time."

Adyen rose a brow, "Alright, lil brawler, but you and I are having a talk later with just the team."

Fuck my life.

29

ADYEN

There was nothing I respected more in someone than a spine of steel. Gray had a spine of steel and a perfected scowl to accompany it. She stood at the front of the sitting room wearing that damn silk dress, as light as a tissue, while she narrowed her gaze on the Horde King. Her brother. Her twin. A terrifying man to most.

Yet, around her, he became a petulant child. He sat with his arms crossed and crown slanted as Rhodes watched him carefully. The two siblings were having some silent communicative battle as the rest of us lounged around waiting for story time. I tried to not let my mind go where it usually did when I was in her presence. I had to close my eyes so that I didn't focus on how her dress clung to her form.

"You understand why I am hiding, right Silas?" She demanded, turning as her hair floated around her like a waist length veil. Those eyes were sparkling with annoyance and her body coiled in anger.

"Because you don't want to rule." He grumbled.

"You are a fool." She growled out with narrowed eyes. "I can not go back. I *can not* rule without bringing massive war to the three kingdoms."

Silas frowned, "What the fuck are you talking about, Gray? We have no current wars."

Gray took a deep breath and looked up to the ceiling as if seeking divine inspiration. Hell, even in anger, she looked hot. Maybe, even more so. Her reactions were so raw and real.

"Because I am not there." She explained softly. "If I go back, the Dark kingdom and the Horde will go to war… the Light kingdom will aid us because of my..." she paused and clenched her jaw, "marriage contract."

I nearly snickered at that, but then again I also almost went to kill her fiancé. Either one would have worked... or both. Probably both.

"Why would we go to war with them?"

She sighed, her body slumping. "Because, Silas, the Dark King was the one who killed Mom and Dad. If I go back, my knowledge would have to be announced. We would have to go to war in order to show strength, or else, they will view us as weak because Mario knows that I am aware of his crime."

Silas let out a snarl leaning forward, "What? What do you mean he killed Mom and Dad? How would he know that we know?"

Gray licked her lips and tightened her hands, "*Because* he knows that I saw him! If I go back, he will know that I know and if I *don't* retaliate, we will look weak!"

Shit. The room went silent as I considered what she was saying. Silas let his fist smash onto the table. "Is that why you fucking ran? Instead of telling someone?"

"Who would I have told?" She mused angrily.

"Anyone! Me?" He growled as his power lashed out. "Instead, you left me in ignorance."

"I left you in safety!" She snapped with a snarl. "I didn't want him to subject you to what he subjected them to, just because of *my* knowledge. You were six! Instead, I left and brought the chase outside of the Horde lands."

My heart squeezed at the idea of her running. Alone. My dragon didn't like that at all, a small vibrating growl moved from my chest. I looked down at the ground to avoid Rhodes's sharp gaze in my direction. *As* if *he* was immune to his protective instincts, such bullshit.

"That's stupid, Gray." Silas muttered. "You are the rightful heir and are needed in the Horde, even if we do have to avenge Mom and Dad."

"It *wasn't* stupid." She retorted with a cold look. "He's a sadistic fuck."

"So, what? You got to live a fucking life of leisure after leaving me to rule?"

I nearly swore as Gray let out a deep animalistic, vibrating growl, "Oh yes, Silas. That's what it was for me. A vacation. You fucking fool!"

Silas must have realized something was wrong because he stood.

"I will give you two days to respond before I take all of my guard and leave."

Gray laughed sharply, "Go now. Please, fucking leave."

Silas grinned viciously, "No, no sister. *All* of my guard."

Her eyes sparkled with malice as she realized the implication. I met her gaze as she just let out an exhausted sigh and pointed for him to leave. All six of us watched as he left, her body slumped against the fireplace in relief as he disappeared.

"We won't leave you," Rhodes stated.

She shook her head, "It's in his rights."

Neo spoke quietly, "Actually, it's not. No offense to Silas, but he doesn't understand how guard units assigned to True Heirs work. We can't leave you, unless you order it."

She nibbled her lip, "So, you're stuck with me?"

Taylor growled, "Stop whatever you're thinking right now. We are here with you because we want you, baby girl. So cut it out."

A small grin came onto her lips as she shook her head, "Is the kingdom in that bad of shape in his hands?"

Athens spoke quietly, "It's pretty bad, baby."

Gray bit her lip, shaking her head with indecision. "Well, I will have to give it some thought."

The room was basked in silence before her face broke into a smile. It was a coy smile that spoke the amusement dancing in her eyes.

"What?" I asked quietly.

"Cat's out of the bag," She murmured. "No hiding that I am the Horde's True Heir now."

Rhodes chuckled, "Kitten, we sorta knew who you were. It's why we sought you out. We have been together for years, waiting to be assigned to find you as your guard."

Gray nodded, "I figured as much."

I spoke quietly, "We still need to talk about *what* that means, where you have been, hell, Gray! How you even managed to control your power up until now..."

She frowned and held up a hand in confusion, "Wait, you've been placed together for years?"

I looked to Rhodes who nodded, "Yeah, Gray. From before you even left."

Her eyes were stormy with thought and she let out a defeated sigh, "Shit. I have so much to tell all of you. So many years to explain."

Rhodes stopped her, "If you're not ready..."

She shook her head, "It's not that. Let's go eat dinner first. I won't feel like eating once I start."

This worried me, she didn't eat enough as it was.

Athens spoke then making me smile, "Pizza?"

Gray smiled, "We can't do delivery, but Tulsa should have the stuff to make pizza."

Everyone began to exit the room as I caught my lil brawler's hand, pulling her down onto my lap. She let out an amused sound, but wrapped her long arms around my neck comfortably, as if she had done it for years. I think it surprised her, but I didn't let her overthink it before I leaned forward capturing her lips. Her soft warm scent immediately tickled my senses as her velvet lips absorbed my growl. She tasted so perfect. Her skin was so soft against my hands as my dragon let out a deep, rumbling sound of recognition. Our mate. Our beautiful, fierce, little mate. My hands held her hips and moved her close enough to be pressed against one another completely.

"Adyen," She whispered pushing her long elegant fingers into my hair as my tongue moved into her cool mouth. I could feel the tension and power vibrating under her skin as a moan slipped from between her lips.

"Gray," I whispered, kissing down her sharp jaw to her neck. Her skin was smooth and cool to the touch. It reminded me of a precious stone. It had an intoxicating perfumed scent that made me want to run my tongue along each curve. Along all of her.

"Do you--" Neo's voice cut off as Gray leaned back with a small whimper at her self-inflicted separation. I didn't look away as her eyes met Neo's gaze. A pink flush filled her face.

It was always that way with Neo. He made her softer and it was unusual to see that dreamy, whimsical look on her face. I nearly felt jealousy at that notion, wishing I could make her feel that way. What did I offer Gray?

Gray smiled back down at me, "So, was that the talk we needed to have?"

I let out a low rumble and pressed a kiss to her lips, "No. I still need to spank you for stepping into the line of possible fire earlier."

The beautiful woman in the front of the room let out a sparkling laugh that made the room dizzy with power. I felt my heart warm at the sound and Neo shot me a look of understanding.

30
GRAY

My bedroom was silver and navy, a familiar pattern of brocade that I fitted to all my suites across the world. It made me feel at home, no matter how many different beds I slept in. Thoughts of bed… well, it brought my mind to who I would love to share my bed with. Rhodes totally had a kinky, controlling side to him. Athens was even more playful when teasing me. Adyen? Everything about him was possessive and full of depth. There was something he was telling me in those kisses that I didn't understand. They felt deeper and more serious than his words explained. I wondered what it would be like to kiss Neo and Taylor as well. I blushed at that and let out a small mutter of curses, feeling as though life was just getting more complicated.

The pizzas were downstairs cooking and I had come upstairs to compose myself under the guise of changing. I wasn't positive I was ready for their questions. It was a complicated story to explain to them. Yet, I owed them that. Their lives were contracted to mine and I wasn't about to back down. I never backed down and I wouldn't change that now.

"Baby girl?" A voice sounded from the door and my eyes fell on Taylor. He stood in a pair of low slung, dark jeans and a loose white shirt. Damn him for being so hot.

"Hey," I composed myself. "Sorry, I got distracted. I will be downstairs soon."

Taylor frowned as he closed the door, "I can feel your nerves from downstairs."

I groaned, "Does it surprise you? That I am nervous?"

He followed me to the closet as I yanked out a pair of spandex shorts and a half top.

"You don't have to explain yourself to us."

A harsh chuckle slipped from my lips as I moved past him, "Yes. Yes. I do."

Taylor growled, slipping a hand around my waist to tug me against him. He pressed a firm pair of lips to behind my ear, "We won't force you to."

My body turned in his arms as I slipped a hand to his cheek, "I know, Taylor. It doesn't change the fact that I need to tell you everything. You have given your life to protect mine and you deserve the truth."

"I would give you my life, even if it wasn't as part of the guard," He explained softly his words very quiet. "I would actually prefer that."

"You don't like the guard?" I asked looking up at him.

Taylor's eyes flashed defensively, "Something like that."

I wanted to know more, but the anger seemed to boil under his skin with each passing moment. Instead, I stepped further into his space and wrapped my arms around his waist. Taylor was quieter than the other guys and impossibly gruff and intense. Also sexy. I sighed breathing in his scent.

"Come on, baby girl," he commanded softly. "Let's go relieve Rhodes of his rampant curiosity before he dies of an aneurysm."

I snorted and moved to the bathroom to change quickly. I slipped into the new outfit and embraced the feel of the tight clothes against my skin. It made me feel sexy and empowered, something that hadn't been available to me for most of my teenage years.

"Shit," Taylor swore as I walked out. His comfortable stance against the wall faltered. I grinned before taking his hand to tug him downstairs.

I prided myself on facing my fears. I showed my scars and embraced the things that tore at my nerves. My sexuality had always been something I had needed to cover. My body something I hid. That was before I ended the abuse.

Now though? With those fuckers buried 6 feet under? I dressed in what I wanted, when I wanted. No question or second thoughts about it. I owed myself that. I owed my younger self to feel beautiful and wanted in a normal, healthy way.

Yet, despite this courage... I was scared. I was terrified to let them hear about my life.

The pizza was spread out on the kitchen counter and my hand was filled suddenly with a deep glass of red wine. Neo smiled and my face flushed at his kindness. Also, who is going to not smile at a man that handsome, handing her a glass of wine? He is a literal dream.

Athens was sitting on my side as casual talk overtook the group. I think all of us were doing our best to ignore the past few days. From my kidnapping, up to reuniting with my brother, I needed some damn sleep. Also, wine. A lot of wine.

Rhodes was quiet, but kept his eyes on Adyen and Taylor as they discussed Estonia. I keyed in as they talked about the local area and what is offered. They seemed to have a large scope of knowledge within the area.

"How do you know so much about the area?" I asked curiously, finishing a slice of pizza. The minute it was gone, Adyen replaced it without asking.

"Eat more." He demanded before softening. "Taylor and I are pretty familiar with the downtown area."

"Why is that? Do you own properties?" I wondered as all of them began to look at Rhodes.

Rhodes cleared his throat. "Yes. We own properties, everywhere you do."

I paled slightly, "I see. I have had those records buried, so that shouldn't be possible."

Neo spoke then, his face flashing with a darker wisdom. "And it isn't possible. For most people, at least. You have done a fantastic job of covering your tracks."

I frowned, "So, you knew where all my safe houses were?"

Rhodes nodded, "We have had eyes on you for a bit now, Gray. Although, determining where exactly you were took some time."

"What do you mean it isn't possible for *most* people?"

"As I mentioned," Rhodes explained, "we were put together for the purpose of guarding you and keeping you safe. It wasn't an accident that the five of us were put together. We have known from the time we were very young what our purpose would be."

"That is the most *detailed, vague* answer I have ever fucking heard." I muttered as he smirked.

"Let's move to the sitting room." Rhodes offered softly.

I let it slide and grabbed the bottle of wine as I walked to the sitting room. With an easy tug, I moved an armchair to the center, facing the couches as I dropped a fur blanket over me. No point in being uncomfortable while laying out my most painful memories.

"You look like a queen," Athens smiled playfully as he brought blankets down to sit against the coffee table facing me. I narrowed my eyes playfully.

"Yeah, Athens?" I bit my lip playfully. "Are you going to bow down?"

That heat returned as he cocked his head to the side, "Do you want me to, Gray?"

Did I want him to? I could get behind the image of Athens kneeling in front of me, as his hands trailed along my hips and thighs. Shit.

Adyen rose a brow walking in with a beer as he snagged the spot on the love seat on my left, taking up the entire deep velvet colored seat. I watched as his arms tucked behind his head and exposed those damn perfect abs. I saw those amber eyes spark with amusement. It reminded me of our kiss earlier. An uneasy feeling settled in me because I had left things unresolved and unanswered after talking to Rhodes. He wanted to know if I was okay with them... all of them.

As if summoning him, Rhodes stepped into the room and sat in a chair across from me. The king to my queen. I nearly snorted as he lounged back easily, a glass of dark, burning liquid in his hand. I noticed that his thick golden hair was loose around his shoulders as his pale green eyes reflected the burning light behind me. My thoughts went a little blank as he rolled his button down to expose dark, stark tattoos.

Finally, Taylor and Neo came into the room and the sitting room became warmer. The sun had set and the room felt intimate. Yet, I felt as though I was at a standoff with my past. While Neo sat down opposite Adyen, Taylor stood pacing along the back of the couches. I let my eyes trail from Neo's piercing gaze to Taylor's tense expression. God, he was a brooding bastard sometimes. I felt a smile slip onto my lips as I sipped on wine.

"Alright, bossman." I said softly. "Hit me with the questions."

"Why don't you start from where you left off with Silas?"

My neck rolled back as I sunk lower into the chair, letting out a sigh. I placed my metaphorical balls on the table and sat up after a moment. I nearly laughed at that thought because ovaries were way stronger than a metaphorical ball sack, but whatever. *Semantics.*

"The night of my sixth birthday party was a cause for celebration apparently, it was a huge event in the Horde lands and drew the attention of the Dark and Light kingdom. It was also the night my marriage…" I grimaced, "contract was signed with the Light kingdom. Apparently, since I had ovaries, my future had to be contracted out."

Taylor snorted at that.

"Anyway," I sighed, "something happened at the party that sorta put me on edge, or I assume it did, because I went searching for something. I wasn't sure what, I'm still not sure. I suppose it doesn't matter." My brain was telling me it was important, yet I continued. "I wandered through the castle and found myself at my father's office doors. Obviously, being who I am," I grinned, "I snuck through the hallway connecting from the library to listen and found them talking about my marriage contract with the Dark kingdom."

Memories broke through my consciousness as a sick shiver trickled over my spine. I spoke quieter, yet matter of fact, "Mario was furious that I hadn't been promised to one of *his* sons, so he killed my father, raped my mother, and then killed her as well."

Silence broke over the entire room as the memory of blood and limbs hitting the floor washed over me. I could feel every part of my stomach squeeze uncomfortably at the sound of her abuse. My stomach rolled as I knotted my fingers together to calm myself.

"Fuck," Taylor muttered. I snapped my head up and threw up my walls.

"Don't put them up," Rhodes growled out gently.

"I won't subject Taylor to that," I murmured quietly. "You

don't want them down. This - what I just told you - is absolutely nothing compared to what is to come."

Taylor spoke gruffly, grabbing the back of Neo's loveseat, "Put the fucking walls down. I can handle it. They need to understand how bad it was."

I shook my head in frustration, "That's called being a masochist."

After a second, I listened to him though and let my walls down, allowing memories of that moment to flood my system. My face was impassive as my body rolled with pain. I heard a number of pained sounds in the room, but ignored them completely and took another sip of wine.

"Tell me to throw them up if it becomes too much," I murmured embarrassed. "Anyway. I couldn't handle hearing my mom's screaming and attempted to run, but Mario heard me. He tried to chase after me, but someone had snagged me into a dark hallway. It kept me safe, nearly invisible, until he passed. I don't remember who it was that helped me. I think they were around my age, but it didn't really matter at that time. I just needed to get away from Mario."

The room went quiet and I found myself looking up. Except none of them were looking at me, instead their gaze was on Neo as Taylor frowned with interest. I noticed that Neo's skin was a tone darker, as if he was blushing.

"Am I missing something?" I murmured curiously. I was thrilled at the distraction.

Neo groaned quietly and sat down his beer. He spoke quietly, "We were there the night of your birthday. It was when we were placed as your official guard. We had our placement before training would even start."

"You were there?" I asked as my heart beat quickly.

Taylor spoke gruffly, "You probably don't remember when they branded us like fucking cattle then, either."

Rhodes snapped, "Taylor shut it."

Taylor pouted. He crossed his arms and looked at me with a sad, sorta lost expression. He didn't blame me, but he seemed annoyed. What had he said about branding?

"What brand?" I asked curiously.

"Later, baby girl," he murmured with a tired sigh.

I ran a hand through my hair, "Fine. So you were there, what does that have to do with what I was saying about my escape?"

Once again, all eyes fell on Neo. He spoke quietly, his eyes lighting up in the navy that seemed to always decorate my estate.

"Well. My powers range from mental manipulation to shadow manipulation because I'm an alchemy mage."

I tilted my head, "Shadow manipulation?"

Neo licked his lips in hesitation, "Yeah. The ability to hide in the shadows by making yourself essentially invisible."

"You?" I felt like my breathing halted.

He nodded, "I was the one who hid you from Mario and helped you escape."

Neo

"No shit," She stated with an amazed expression reflected in those silky, navy blue eyes. They were transfixed on me and it had me frozen to the spot.

"We had already made the initial bond, which is how we could find you. I sensed your panic and caught you just in time. I had enough judgment at my age to know something was wrong, so I helped you escape by pushing you rather forcefully into the Earth realm."

"Did you all know?" She asked quietly, knowing they were equally as shocked.

"I'm sorry, Gray," I whispered quietly with guilt, "I thought I was saving you."

Silence descended and I couldn't look away from her as she moved closer. I was trying not to focus on the way her hips swayed as she fell into the seat next to me. Her cool soft hands closed on mine as she spoke.

"You *did* save me, Neo."

I shook my head and her eyes sparkled faintly. "I know you didn't have it easy here."

She smiled then, shyly, "Better to suffer alive, than to be peacefully dead. I would always rather survive and move on."

My strength solidified as I boldly kissed her palm. My body reacted to the small breathy surprised sound that came from her. I nearly grinned, but instead allowed her to gently tug her hand away before moving back to the chair. No one said anything. Rhodes would later, no doubt.

I had always felt a huge amount of guilt over the situation. When I first saw her, at the celebration, my little heart had nearly collapsed at how beautiful she was. All of us had been enamored and hadn't questioned the process of receiving our blood ink tattoo and True Heir Guard branding so young. When I had felt her panic, my body had sprung into action and while I regret pushing her into the unknown... She was alive. Alive was good.

Rhodes spoke then, "What happened once you were in the human realm?"

Gray's face flashed white as Taylor let loose the pain flashing through her. I felt every protective instinct within me rise painfully sharp at just the thought of her pain. Our connection was growing in strength every moment we were together.

She licked her lips and looked at me dead in the eye, "Remember what I said, Neo. No matter what comes out of my mouth or what you feel. I would always rather be alive and trust me... if Mario had found me. I would have been dead."

I nod, not knowing how bad this is going to be. When she opened her mouth and the emotions began to stream out, I felt every part of my heart break for the beautiful woman in front of me.

Gray

"I lived in a forest somewhere in Russia for a month before being found. I was essentially feral, but luckily, the person who found me was from a wolf shifter pack and she brought me to a special orphanage. It was catered to children with supernatural abilities. I didn't show any of them my specific powers, but it was pretty obvious by how I looked that I wasn't human."

"How you look?" Adyen mused. I understood his confusion.

"I have a glamour on," I whispered quietly. All of them looked shocked. I wanted to delay what was next so I offered a small grin. "Want to see it off?"

Rhodes nodded so I placed my wine glass down and stood up. My eyes closed as I rolled back my shoulders and released the glamour. A glass dropped somewhere as I snickered in amusement.

Athens jumped up, "Holy shit, Gray! You're glowing! Not to take away from your beauty before, you're always beautiful, baby...but you're literally glowing!"

I nodded and examined my form. My skin was a shimmery pearl shade that seemed to make my body appear longer and leaner. My normal manicure had shifted to make it so my nails were long and a deep onyx black that matched my dark hand tattoos. I looked up to find all of them watching me.

"I like the silver in your hair," Taylor confirmed. I smiled at that because I did as well. It was in thick highlights throughout my deep, midnight colored hair.

"And your eyes are like three different colors." Neo whispered peering at the tri-color iris that went from silver, to navy, and ending with an almost midnight blue.

I ran a hand along my scars. They didn't ever go away. No matter the long, angular nature of my features or improved beauty, the scars were permanent.

"I would suspect that if we return to Horde lands, it would be harder to keep my glamour," I murmured.

With that thought, I snapped my glamour back in place. I saw a few of them sag in relief. I knew it was a lot to handle, the brilliance of my form. I snickered at that because it sounded conceited, but it was true. I wasn't human. I was a savage predator, even if I was a beautiful one.

"Anyway," I continued, "I was very quickly adopted. Most likely because of how unique I looked at first."

Memories flooded me as a painful sound echoed from Taylor. I closed my eyes.

"I learned very quickly to glamour myself after that. The couple who adopted me, Nia and Malvin, were Elven in heritage. They lived in a massive estate outside of LA. I didn't talk for the first year of living with them, scared to say anything. I did learn to glamour myself, though. Nia got jealous of the attention." I tried to keep my emotions numb. If I was numb, the memories hurt less.

"What made you finally talk?"

I didn't know *who* asked it, but I tried to breathe through the memory that assaulted me. I kept my eyes closed as I responded, "My first word in a year wasn't a word, it was a scream."

"I was screaming because Nia hit me over the head with a pan, fresh off the stove top. She was annoyed that I wouldn't respond to what she was saying. I think she had been on some rant about her and Malvin needing a new dealer. They were both into some heavy shit."

Adyen let out a deep vibrating growl, but I continued. I had to ignore their reactions. I went into my safe space. If I read into their reactions too much, I might consider what it meant for them to care about me on that level. I wasn't ready to handle the complexity of that.

"My first word was a scream at seven. I had learned English, even though it wasn't natural to me, because our language was far more familiar. Letting that language go was a regret I have still to this day. I didn't want to give myself away though. When I started speaking, I blamed the accent from being left in the Russian wilderness. They didn't really care enough to ask further questions. The only reason they had adopted me was because of the appeal I held, like a sparkly new toy.

"I started school that year and it kept me out of the house most days. Unfortunately, when I was home, it was hell. Nia was an angry bitch who liked to hit me when she was mad at Malvin. He was gone most of the time, thankfully, because when he was around...

Yep. Safe space, Gray. Eyes closed. You're alone.

"...When he was around, it was way worse. The bruising Nia caused was awful, but Malvin was the scars. He would have associates over and force me to sit on his lap, humiliating me, and burning his cigars into my shoulders and hands, time after time. When I complained, he would hit me with this stupidly small, wispy iron instrument that made all his friends fucking laugh. It went on like that for years, until I was nearly 12. By then scars littered my body."

I swallowed tightly, "Once I hit puberty, things got so much worse. I already had tried to have Nia get a lock on my door, but she said I was an attention whore if I was noticing any of the looks Malvin's friends gave me."

I ignored the snarl from Rhodes and opened up the gates.

"So yeah, not unimaginable what happened next." I growled softly, my eyes still closed, "Malvin's friends began forcing me to sit on their laps and when I didn't, it meant more marks on my body. When I tried to fight back once, Malvin beat me until I passed out in front of them. The next night, he started coming into my bedroom."

A repulsive shudder ran through me as I mentally chastised myself for letting him still have that power over me. I wasn't that girl anymore. *I wasn't a victim.*

"Nia, usually high and content with beating me, took notice. She became furious that her 'attention whore, adopted daughter' was stealing her husband's attention. So, when I came home from school one day..." I paused to swallow a pained whimper, "She tried to cut off my face and peel back the skin to my '*damn cursed face.*'" My words came out in a sneer.

For just a moment, I was suspended in the memory. The pain below me like a swirling massive black hole and my corporeal body floating painless amongst the stars. Numb and nonexistent. I forced myself back to earth.

"I was able to escape. I knocked her across the sitting room. With how fucking high she was, it should have never happened. I got my ass in her stupidly obnoxious car and drove myself to the hospital. I refused to tell them what had happened, mostly because I knew it wouldn't help anything..." Then, my lips curled. "Plus, then it would ruin my plans."

"Plan?" Neo said in a strangled voice. It didn't surprise me that he hadn't been able to hold back. I was actually surprised he and Rhodes had contained their questions so far.

"You have to understand. Nia and Malvin taught me that, despite the guise, they - and I - weren't human," I chuckled softly. "No, we were and are savages. So, I planned on acting like one from that point forward. I had been found feral, animalistic, and, despite their beautiful home, they were the same. Savages. So, I would treat them accordingly. I would live accordingly. I would kill accordingly."

"I left the hospital and went straight home. I walked straight into the estate and approached Nia from behind," I murmured with a sick thrill. "That was when I snapped a neck for the first time."

I let the thrill of pleasure pulse through me. My dragon's darkening eyes caught mine. I didn't feel bad. I knew it was sick and wrong. I knew that it should have made me *less* to enjoy what I did, but it didn't. I sighed and took a sip of wine. Neo looked at the glass with a pensive expression.

"It was easy enough to kill Malvin," I explained softly. "He came home shortly after and I used my power to threaten him. He signed over all his assets to me before I burnt him to ashes. Then, I burnt Nia's body and washed them down the drain." Finally, I let out a deep sigh. It was over. The worst was over. Neo murmured something about 'snapping necks and ashes'.

"I lived alone for three years before announcing their disappearance," I explained quietly. "I simply glamoured animals to appear as them when needed. Once announced, I applied for emancipation and was given the assets assigned to me. It was the same year that I began to purchase these estates."

I sighed, closing my walls up, brick by brick, "So yeah, I have been on the run ever since."

The room was silent as my eyes trailed over each of them. Taylor was pale and his hands were twitching with energy. Neo seemed transfixed and pensive. Athens had brought his head to my knee while my eyes had been closed. Adyen was furious. His eyes were a black storm. Rhodes, the master of reactions, was in complete control of his expression. Unreadable and terrifying.

"Sorry if that was a lot," I murmured, quietly stroking Athens's hair. "I know that the emotion I carry with it can be overwhelming." Wow. Was Athens's hair always this soft and springy? I loved this.

"Do. Not. Apologize." Rhodes forced out in a strangled voice from across the room.

The seriousness of his voice made me look up and I was glad

my walls were in place. All of them seemed to look frustrated at the small smile that came onto my lips.

"It happened a long time ago. I don't want you to be angry for me. It's sweet, but I am not a victim. I won't act like one. Ever."

Everyone seemed to collect themselves with small nods and muttered curses. I smiled happily and rolled my neck. There was still a tightness to the room. Oddly though, I felt relieved. I felt as though I could handle Silas and my future because my heavy past was in the open. No longer a secret.

"So, how did you find Bobby?"

I snickered softly, "I arrived at the academy and he immediately found me. He made some fucking comment about my scar, so I punched him."

"You do that a lot," Rhodes continued.

I smiled, "I didn't know he was my familiar at the time."

"What?!" Athens exclaimed looking up. The entire room stilled as I smiled. Rhodes flushed at the knowledge he hadn't shared.

"He's a dog shifter," I murmured. "He's my familiar."

"You hated each other!" Athens commented in complete surprise.

I shrugged, "Sorta. He was super loyal though. It's complicated."

I missed Bobby. More than I cared to admit, so I kept a pleased smile on my lips. I brought my hair over my shoulder and ran my hands through it.

"I think you just like punching people," Taylor offered, smirking dangerously. His eyes were still darkened with something that almost seemed like anger.

"Want to find out how much I like it?" I offered dangerously with a grin.

Taylor's eyes sparkled, "No, but Adyen would."

Rhodes cleared his throat, "Actually, that's not a bad idea. Training with us, that is."

I raised a brow at Adyen, "Yeah, big guy? Wanna fight?"

He grinned as his eyes grew warm, "Getting all sweaty with you? Absolutely."

The tension disappeared more as chuckles followed, but I looked to Rhodes, "Any other questions, bossman?"

His pale green eyes were pensive.

"No. Not tonight, kitten. Thank you for sharing all of that with us. I know it couldn't have been easy."

"It wasn't," I murmured softly. "But thank you for listening. I hope it fills in any gaps. It was the least I could do, since you are stuck with me, essentially forever."

"Or till we die."

My lips pursed at Rhodes, "Well, actually, that can't happen."

"Huh?" Athens asked quietly.

I grinned, "Please tell me I am not the first one to tell you that you're essentially immortal?"

There was that silence again. I stretched it out and let out a pleased sound.

"Immortality is only given to the True Heir and their guards, so welcome to the club. Now, we can still die technically, but it will not be due to old age. It's sorta complicated, but similar to how full blooded Light or Dark Fae have immortality, the six of us have been blessed with the same."

"Holy shit," Taylor offered gruffly.

I grinned standing up, "Well, boys. I think that is enough revelations for tonight. Yeah?"

Rhodes nodded, "I agree. We should go to sleep. Tomorrow, we have a lot more to talk--"

"Or we could drink," I interrupted with a grin. "Like go out."

"You want to go out?" Taylor asked with excitement in his eyes that was mirrored by Athens.

"I think we could use some relaxation," I explained softly. "What do you think, bossman?"

Rhodes sighed and ran a hand over his face, "I don't think--"

"Come on, bossman," Athens smiled brilliantly using my nickname. "We need this."

Finally, Rhodes groaned but nodded. The look Athens gave me and then Taylor spelled trouble.

31

RHODES

"This was a terrible idea." Adyen growled out as we watched her from across the pub. Despite Taylor and Athens being snug against her, the other men at the bar couldn't seem to stop staring. I didn't blame them, but damn if it didn't bother every possessive, animalistic bone in my body.

It didn't help that she had pulled on a pair of painted on jeans and a short, barely there t-shirt. It hung off her shoulder and exposed her slim fit stomach. Fuck. She was just perfect. So fucking perfect it hurt. Physically hurt. As in my cock was so hard it hurt.

"How was I supposed to say no, after *that?*"

Neo nodded, "I agree, Adyen. She may have been able to snap out of it easily, but that pain is still raw. I can't understand how she functions on a daily basis with that inside of her. I mean. Shit, I thought I had it bad."

Adyen rumbled, "She's a fucking survivor, that's how. But that's not the problem I'm referring to, the problem is that every motherfucker in this bar is staring at our girl."

I smirked at that as Neo spoke, "We need to talk to her about how we feel as a group."

"She knows," I explained quietly, "we talked briefly."

"When? You didn't say anything." Neo asked quietly.

I shook my head, "Happened today. *You* can't talk about keeping secrets. We will be having a talk about what you said earlier."

I felt bad about snapping at him but secrecy wasn't okay on our team. Neo rose his beer in understanding before looking at Adyen.

Adyen spoke, "What did she say?"

"She didn't get a chance to answer because of Silas, but she seemed interested."

I hoped that was the case. I also hoped that she was content with ignoring her marriage contract.

Neo groaned, "Good, because I'm done holding back."

Adyen chuckled, "Yeah. She may be a little shocked by your interests, buddy."

The fucker just smirked. His eyes moved to the beautiful girl at the bar. Our beautiful girl. I had been serious about punishing Gray, but my true interest laid in control. I wanted her subject to my ability to make her feel things and experience things she would never try herself.

Neo though? He loved punishment. He loved taking people to the edge of danger and holding them above it, I'd thought that was why he was so picky about anyone he showed interest in. I had another idea, knowing their history now, that he was picky because of her. At some point in time, all of us had dated other people, but Neo had only seen women exclusively for the purpose of sex. I think his only real emotional attachment was his brother and now us.

I watched as Gray carried two drinks, followed by Athens and Taylor. I saw Taylor offer one guy a look so dark that I felt his power levels rise just enough to have Gray raising a brow. Luckily, Athens diverted her attention by asking her a question. Thank fuck. I didn't need her catching on to how possessive we were of her yet. Something told me that, after tonight, she would take it as an offense to her strength. It wasn't that at all, but I could see how she would view it as so.

Unfortunately, tonight had made all of us more protective than we care to admit. I could read the group dynamic well. The pain that Gray has been through has united us. United us with Gray, for Gray. It became more than an assignment tonight.

I have always considered myself an honest person when it came to self-reflection. Not as honest as Adyen, who relied more on his baser instincts because of his dragon, but still honest. It was difficult to not be honest when there was a jaguar growling in my ear about his feelings towards our raven haired girl. The other men were less direct about their commitment levels to Gray, but I could tell that Neo and Athens were enamored with her. Taylor was far more difficult to understand. It probably had to do with his past. No matter though. She wasn't fully ready, most likely, for our emotions towards her. It was far too soon and too intense. She had larger issues to deal with, specifically from Silas and the Horde kingdom.

"Here we go!" Gray exclaimed her eyes sparkling as she slid the drinks across the table.

"You say you haven't been back here since seventeen?" Taylor asks gruffly. Adyen chuckled.

"Yeah, why?" she grinned sitting next to me. Athens joined her on the other side, facing the other three.

Adyen let out a low growl and mutter that had her biting down on her lower lip to stop a smile. I smoothed my thumb over her thigh as she turned her attention to Athens. He seemed like the only one who could successfully keep up a conversation without showing how on edge he was. Hell, even Neo seemed tense as his entire body went rigid and still.

My eyes followed his.

"Shit," I muttered. I was instantly annoyed as I saw the back of two familiar figures at the bar.

The five of us were a fairly insulated group because we had always known our purpose, even if we didn't join the academy for guard training until thirteen. As a result, the guard units with Silas yesterday were fairly familiar faces, including the two assholes sitting at the bar that we *just* happen to be at tonight. I could only think of one reason why they would be here and she was sitting next to me, laughing brightly and drawing attention from every corner of the damn room.

"Athens and I are going to dance!" She exclaimed.

I wasn't positive if she did it on purpose, but her eyes looked to me for approval which I granted with a nod. How the fuck was I going to say no to those eyes? The two of them moved out of the booth as I growled at a man walking by. His eyes snapped up from her ass to my expression as he fell in a pool of his own beer.

Gray shot me an amused look from over her shoulder. Damn little minx. "Adyen," I murmured as they walked away, "Go see what the two of them want. Bring Taylor. Neo, go join them in a bit. Try to keep her from noticing anything is wrong, I don't want to ruin her night."

My eyes trailed across Hathor and Jonathan to seek out any possible weapons. Not that they would need them technically, but my senses told me that most people in this room weren't aware of the supernatural. If they wanted to cause problems, they would most likely do it traditionally.

Gray had a natural grace as she moved with Athens on the dance floor. Her hair floated around her like a veil. Unlike with anyone else, her seductive twirl of hips against Athens didn't bother me. No, I knew myself well enough to understand that she needed all of us. The six of us were complete together. I just needed her to realize that.

"Rhodes," Hathor let out a deep growl as Taylor led him to

the table, along with Adyen and Jonathan. They did it in a manner that didn't seem forced, but I could see the tension in both of their forms. I nearly smiled at how uncomfortable they looked.

"What are you doing here?" I asked point blank as Taylor and Adyen blocked the exit to the booth.

"Watching Silas's sister," Hathor offered. His eyes were darker than his personality.

"Not needed."

"We don't follow orders from you," Jonathan said quietly, his eyes sharp and angry.

"Actually, you do," I state easily taking a drink of my beer. "Unless you have been promoted to Silas's personal heir guard, you do report to me. So, when I tell you something is not needed, you should listen and follow orders without question."

Hathor grunted, but Jonathan went silent.

"Now," I said, sounding bored to myself, "Please, leave. Gray came out tonight to enjoy herself and we don't need you ruining it."

Jonathan grinned a dark smile, "Are you afraid Gray will realize there are more guard options out there?"

I never claimed I had a good temperament.

My hand shot out as I closed it around his thick neck, causing an unflattering sound to escape his mouth. Hathor paled.

"Do. Not. Ever. Speak her name again. Understand?"

Adyen made a noise as my hand slipped off the man's throat. Gray, at that exact moment, returned to the table with unmasked amusement in her eyes. I didn't think she had seen my violent gesture, but I was curious about how she would react. The woman had easily killed four Dark Fae without a trace of concern. Yet, I knew a softer side of Gray existed. I was seeing it more often in the past few days.

"What are you doing over here?" She asked darkly toward

Hathor and Jonathan, "Did Silas instruct you to sit at our table and watch me? Or are you just being creepy?"

Okay, I nearly laughed at that.

"You knew?" Hathor asked quietly.

"Knew?" Gray asked her eyes sparkling silver. "I am the True Heir of the Horde. Do you think it would escape my notice when you walked in the door?"

"Silas--"

"Jonathan," She growled out a sexy sound. "I suggest you don't talk. Tell my brother that he better be prepared to give me the full three days he agreed to or I will punish him personally."

I felt my cock harden at her authoritative tone. Neo's eyes began to shine from behind her. See? The fucker got off on punishment. It wasn't even just sexual. He was just a vengeful motherfucker.

"Now," She growled pointing toward the door.

I did let out a chuckle at how fast they moved. She seemed to relax slightly as I tugged her waist toward me. I felt more comfortable once she was on my lap. Sometimes, when I held her she was like a kitten, right now though? She sat like a queen.

I gave Neo a nod before turning my attention to her soft red lips, "Kitten. That was sexy."

"What was sexy?" She asked quietly leaning into me as my hands clasped her hips tightly.

"You being all authoritative," I noted as Neo followed them out.

"Am I not usually?" She smiled. "I think I am usually great at being in control of situations."

"Sounds like a lot of responsibility. Wouldn't it be nice to not be in control for a bit?" I offered as her pupils dilated. I had originally meant this as a distraction, but my body didn't quite agree. I found my grip tightening as I hardened underneath her. I didn't miss how Adyen's eyes tracked the arch of her back and ass as he nudged Taylor to follow Neo. I brought my lips to hover above Gray's red lips.

"By the way, good sexy distraction, bossman," She smiled coyly as I snapped my eyes from her lips.

"You don't miss a thing." I murmured in appreciation. "Do you want to know where they are going? I didn't want to ruin your night."

"Not if I don't need to know," She stated quietly with a soft almost shy smile. "I trust you."

Well. Fuck. If that wasn't the most beautiful thing that had ever come from her lips, I'm not sure what was.

32
GRAY

I needed to get out of bed. Damn it. I knew I did.
Yet, getting up today would mean facing everything that came to light yesterday from my brother, to my guard, and my past. It was one day closer to making my decision about the Horde and more importantly, about my place as the True Heir.

Ah. Gods. See? A.P.F. should apply here... *always punch first.* Funny, right?

"Morning, Gray," The low smooth voice had me smiling. I looked up to see Neo holding a cup of coffee in a beautiful teal mug.

"Oh gods, I love you," I said motioning for the coffee as I rolled over. My hair was in a messy bun and I wore a super large shirt. I had fallen asleep right after scrubbing off my makeup and I was, in short, a mess. Not a hot one, either.

Neo chuckled softly, "For coffee?"

I snickered as he handed me the coffee, "No. I love the coffee, Neo. Gods, what an ego."

That earned me a beautiful grin as his dark eyes flashed with amusement. I took his hand in mine as I sipped my coffee. I let out a moan as my eyes closed. It was followed by a sound of pain as my hand scraped over a fresh wound on Neo's knuckle.

"What is this?" I asked, quietly turning his palm over. I knew exactly where it was from.

Neo didn't answer though. Instead, he got a darker look in his eyes as my fingers trailed over the cut. It was thin and, if I had to guess, was small in comparison to where it came from. I brought it to my lips gently as Neo's throat rumbled with a deep sound. I put down my coffee mug so my other hand could examine his palm as well.

"Did you and Taylor dole out some punishment yesterday?" I asked curiously.

I remembered exactly how Neo had sat up straighter at the prospect of pain. Who would have thought? I could have expected Taylor, but Neo? That had been a surprise.

"Yes," Neo murmured as I pressed my thumb into the cut just enough. I had meant it as a test. Curiosity kills the cat though, right?

"Fuck," I whispered breathlessly as my chest pressed against a very demanding Neo. My body was pinned against the sheets. I was beneath a completely different man than the Neo I had gotten used to. The softer, quieter, almost somber Neo was like a cozy fireplace. This new one? Shards of frozen glass piercing your skin.

Everything from his clenched jaw to his glittering eyes was hard. My wrists were pinned above me and being squeezed hard enough to draw a breathy sigh from my throat as he pressed himself against me. I was caught between the bed and him -- trapped, frozen in place. It was then I realized what a natural predator Neo was and how dangerous it was to be at the center of his attention.

"Dangerous game you're playing, Gray," He murmured, placing a soft kiss against my jaw and voicing my thoughts. My nipples began to harden against his chest as he further parted my thighs where I desperately wanted friction with his knee.

"I like dangerous things," I admitted, fascinated with this man.

"You want dangerous?" He asked quietly, switching my wrists to one hand as the other came to my throat in a gentle hold. "Make sure you're positive about that, because I can give you soft and sweet Gray, but I can't give you both."

"I want dangerous." *Jesus, don't sound too eager or anything, Gray.*

He smoothed over my throat gently and pressed another kiss to my nose, "You want to stand on the edge of pleasure and pain, my love? To be punished until you're red on the ass and dripping wet? You want to completely submit to however I want to use your body, even if it seems dangerous? *Especially* if it seems dangerous? Do you know what level of trust in me that would require of you?"

I was practically panting at his words as his hand closed on my throat. I found myself arching into it as he looked down at my lips that I had just licked. I wanted his lips on me. I want his body on me. Fuck. His words were like some magic I had never experienced before. Why did I like this? Why did I find it so exciting? I shouldn't, given my previous experience. Yet with Neo, it was different. It was like conquering my fears. Exhilarating and scary. An adrenaline rush.

"I do trust you, Neo," I whispered quietly as his lips claimed mine gently at first.

I did trust Neo. I was starting to trust all of them. How could I not? They had given and pledged their lives to a woman they didn't know.

It started off as the kiss I assumed would have come from Neo. Sweet, soft, and creating butterflies in my stomach, but only to be replaced and deepened. It became aggressive as he claimed my mouth and caused my entire body to whirl. Both. A taste of both. I loved both, but damn the second made me drenched with wet heat. I felt as though a serious case of Dr. Jekyll and Mr. Hyde was occurring. Damn, if that didn't just turn me on more.

"Maybe I can do both," he murmured to himself as his sparkling eyes traced over my face with thought. "I would do anything for you, Gray. You know that, right?"

I swallowed hard at his blazing intensity, placing my hands on his cut jaw, "I just need you, Neo. However, you want to give it to me."

Neo nuzzled my neck gently, "What you're agreeing to, Gray, is not just me. It's us. The six of us being together. Are you okay with that?"

Was I okay with it? If the five of them wanted me, wanted us, would I be okay with that type of relationship? I mean physically, can I get a 'fuck yes'? It was overwhelming, but it turned me on. We would need to go slow, though. In all aspects: physically, mentally, and emotionally. I was new to this.

"Before I say yes..." I whispered quietly as his eyes sparkled. "And for the record, if everyone wants this, not just to be with me but to be an *us*, it is a yes. I need everyone to understand that I have to take things slow, since my last few attempts at intimacy didn't end well."

Neo's face sharpened, "Of course, Gray. None of us would ever pressure you. You are the appeal here. We want you, however, and whenever you want us."

I bit my lip gently, "Even if you are assigned to me? I don't want to be a job and I mean, does everyone feel this way? What about Taylor? I don't think he likes the guard..."

"I don't, baby girl," His voice sounded from the end of the bed. Neo smiled, turning softer in the face as he rolled over on his side. I met Taylor's bright emerald gaze as he crawled forward onto the bed to hold himself above me on all fours.

"So, you don't want this?" I asked meekly.

He grinned, "No, I want you. I want what they are proposing, but I was answering the question about the guard. I hate the guard, always have, always will. I won't lie that when we got assigned as your guard unit I was pissed--"

"Taylor," Neo growled in warning. Taylor rolled his eyes.

"But, baby girl," he murmured gently. "It is for that reason, I would never be with you because it was part of the 'job' as you stated. I want to be with you because, for the first time in my life, everything isn't just violence and pain. That beauty and softness are because of you."

Damn it. Gruff Taylor being all romantic had tears coming to my eyes. My heart hurt though because behind his gruff beautiful words I could feel pain. Different than the somberness that Neo carried, but still laced with pain.

"I killed four men the other day," I murmured with a pained laugh trying to remind him that I was anything but soft. He flashed me a vicious smile as he leaned forward to kiss me gently.

"Abso-fucking-lutely," he murmured, "I would expect nothing else."

I felt a surge of happiness well inside me as I yanked on his shirt to connect our lips. I suppose I was testing the theory of us as a group, knowing Neo was there. As Taylor's lips connected with mine, Neo let out a rumble that vibrated to my soul. I moaned into my kiss with Taylor as his tongue demanded entrance into my mouth. A dark, passionate fire began to burn between us that willed me to run my hands through his thick, brightly colored hair.

"Well, this *is* a beautiful sight!" Athens's voice echoed as Taylor let out an annoyed grunt. Neo let out a sigh that encouraged Athens to laugh even more. I sat up as all three men moved to give me a bit of space which brought a soft smile to my face.

"When you said bring her coffee…" Athens chided.

I flushed as he pressed a kiss to the top of my head and offered me a hand to stand up. I did and stretched my legs out enjoying the groan Neo made at my lace boy shorts. Taylor just gruffly excused himself, muttering curses.

"You look delicious, baby," Athens purred. "But Silas is downstairs, so you may want to get your cute ass into some jeans."

The groan that slipped from my lips made both boys chuckle. It felt mundane, not wanting to meet with my brother. I decided, at that moment, to make him worry a little, I turned my grin to both twins.

"I am going to go shower and take some time getting ready. Let's have him stew for a bit, shall we?"

Neo chuckled softly as Athens nodded with excitement. I moved to the bathroom and left my twins with a dangerous wink. I blamed them for my playful mood. It was, after all, Neo's fault because of how he woke me up.

* * *

Neo

I usually hated Mondays. I was more of a Tuesday man myself, but this morning had been an unexpected delight. I had relayed what had happened to Athens and was now the cause of the shit eating grin on his face.

"Who knew our girl had a kinky side?" He mused happily, "I love how brave she is."

I rose a brow, "Love?"

Athens grinned, "Whatever, *love, like, appreciate*."

I sighed. Those were very different things. I was not surprised he chose the first. Athens hadn't been through the same torments as I had in our childhood. He had been sent to live with my mom, while I had been sent to live with my father. Our lives were very different until the age of thirteen and even now, his compassionate upbringing showed.

"Where is she?" Silas demanded. His silver eyes sparkled in annoyance. Rhodes, the bastard, sat across from him in the luxurious sitting room reading the fucking paper. Adyen stood by the windows watching the guard as Taylor ate some of the morning treats laid out by Tulsa. All of us knew Gray was purposefully making him wait.

"Calm yourself," Her voice sounded from the top of the stairs, causing my lips to quirk into a smile. I turned to watch her trail down the stairs, wanting to give her an Oscar for her performance. Silas looked like he wanted to disappear.

Gray was dressed in a silver gown that was cut into a deep V on the front and had a high back that created an elegant collar. Around her slim waist was a deep, black chained belt that hung in contrast to the soft material that formed her figure. She looked absolutely stunning and completely intimidating. Those eyes trained on her brother as she walked across the foyer towards the sitting room.

Adyen's eyes darkened on her outfit as he battled between his possessive tendencies and appreciation for how beautiful she was. Adyen dealt with the pressure. We could tell it was difficult for him to control his inner animal. I nearly felt bad for him, but then again, he's not the only one who has to fight his natural tendencies. Gods know, I was naturally a violent motherfucker.

"Thank the gods, you take forever--"

The explosion that echoed through the house had me flashing through the air in shadow form to Gray. My mind caught up to my body as I pulled her snug against me and the stairwell wall. My ears were ringing with the sound of the chaos raining down on us. I felt a sting of heat against the back of my neck and the breathy gasp coming from the woman pinned against me.

"Holy fuck," She murmured her darkening eyes meeting mine. I could tell the explosion had shocked her, which alone scared the shit out of me.

"I got you, Gray," I whispered, turning my eyes to the massive hole that was blown into the front of her estate. She had saved my life. My life, that I would have willingly given for her.

Now, it was my job to do the same.

33

TAYLOR

I knew, rationally, that I wasn't dying. I even knew that the amount of pain I was in could have been way worse. Yet, with a large shard of glass spearing my stomach and burns marring my face... My rationalization of this pain was fairly inaccurate. In fact, the pain was the only thing I was feeling as the world came to a spacey halt.

The front of the sitting room was blown open, exposing the massive estate lands. Chaos ensued. The jagged ends of the glass framed windows and exposed brick looked like angry teeth seared in black flames. Black flames? That didn't seem right.

I couldn't hear anything, but around me, the room seemed to jump into action. My eyes were trained on the sleek black and green figures that were battling Silas's men. It was a wave of chaos and blood that seemed to kill the bright, afternoon sky.

How was that possible? How was it sunny out? It shouldn't be sunny.

Rhodes was in front of me, yelling something, as his eyes flashed with anger. At me? No. That didn't seem right. I watched as he took hold of the massive glass piece wedged into my stomach. Then the fucker pulled it out, along with a scream of pain.

A flash of gold outside drew my attention as Adyen shifted. Black flames erupted from him, shadowing over the black and green sea. Fuck. Some of those were Silas's men… He would be pissed. Where was Silas, anyway?

My eyes tracked the room, past Athens, to a body slumped against the fireplace. He was knocked out cold. I looked back at Athens, hands extended up, as a spectacle of silver mercury laced up his arms to the ceiling. It looked like they were reinforcing the building.

"Shit," I murmured as the room began to flood with the dark and green men that were fleeing Adyen. Silas' men were trying to hold their own, *I think*. But there were too many of them. They would demolish us within seconds.

Someone was grunting in pain. My eyes shot down to Rhodes's hands, working magic on my injury. I realized with a start that I was making those noises. That was when my hearing came back to me.

"Stop."

The word was brilliant, loud and demanding. It was spoken from the lips of an avenging angel. My eyes found Gray and Neo. Holy shit. I had known Neo was powerful. We all had. But, until this moment, I had never realized the extent. I found myself frozen to the spot as the entire army of dark and green, along with Silas's men, froze. Absolutely frozen, mid motion. It would have been comical, if it wasn't for the pain I was in right now. Shit. That must have punctured something.

"Neo is holding all of them," Rhodes whispered his eyes wide. I saw blood covering him and briefly wondered if that blood was mine or his.

"Gray," Neo spoke calmly and drew my attention to the woman in question. She was completely unharmed as she stepped up next to him. Both of them had changed so drastically that it was hard to consider them the same.

It was like looking at the moon against a dark, endless sky. She was illuminated and her eyes were burning with a fury that I had never seen. I could feel her vibrating from here as Neo easily froze those under his judgment. He was glinting in a black onyx pattern that rippled across his skin like a dark wave. I could feel his icy calm from here. It was without a doubt terrifying. Both of them were terrifying.

Gray stepped forward and her hand rose with a beckoning motion. Instantly, the men in green and black rose to come to kneel at her feet. I briefly noticed Adyen was watching in dragon form for new arrivals, while Athens continued to reinforce the structure.

"Who?" She asked quietly. Her voice echoed around the room. Neo flicked one of his hands as Silas's men slumped to the ground, as if asleep.

"The Dark King," All of the men answered at once. Their faces were slack.

"Why?"

"The True Heir," All of them answered again.

Gray examined the large group of assassins. She carefully stepped to the back of the group. She grabbed the collar of his green armor and dragged him up to her face. Her voice came out cold and dark.

"You will go back to him. He will kill you. Not before you tell him that I expect to see him in my court immediately upon my coronation."

Gray tossed the man to the floor as he scrambled to flee quickly. His eyes met mine, but they were empty and void of any thought, except his purpose and direction. I watched as he left through the fucking front door.

"Gray," Neo stated once again as she looked back at him. At her careful nod, he lifted a hand easily and brought the men to stand.

"Gray?" Rhodes asked finally. She looked over. Rage filled her eyes at the sight of our injuries. I had never seen such a look of absolute fury. This is coming from a fucking demon, mind you.

"Now." She ordered.

A look of malice overtook Neo's face as he dropped his hand. Every single green and black uniform dropped dead. There was a heavy line of black bleeding from their nose and eyes.

He had liquified their fucking brains.

LUNATICS

BLURB

Mario has left me with no choice. He threatened my guard and my brother. My need to enact revenge for the brutal massacre of my parents is all-encompassing. If he wants war, a war he will receive.

The first order of business? Returning to a kingdom and home that I haven't seen in years. Will everything have changed? Will the politics of court allow for my shift in policy? Should I enact the Always Punch First rule? Why the hell are there still carriages here?

Will I even make it the coronation? Or will our merry band of lunatics break before I can even touch the throne?

The only question I don't have? How I will kill the dark fae king.

PROLOGUE

GRAY

I had always wanted to be taller.

Not stronger… because I was strong. I was also fast. But taller. Yes, give me an inch or two at least. *Please.* I scowled up at the man who brought these thoughts to the forefront of my mind.

Taylor.

"Weapons training is essential, Gray," The gruff bastard insisted. I was barely 5'3, without heels, and Taylor was a full foot taller than me. So how does one scowl correctly from a foot below? The answer: *with a lot of effort.*

We walked next to one another while pulling the heavily wrapped object across my Estonian estate grounds. I was confident that either one of us could have handled the task, but instead, we completed it together. The twilight sky, painted in hues of lavender and indigo, set a romantic scene that was perfect for dragging bodies. *See? This is the stupid shit love makes you do, kids.*

No. Not love.

Noppppppppppe. Ignore this crazy bitch.

"You don't need weapons when you are one," I responded with snark.

Taylor graced me with a booming chuckle that caused most of Silas's men to jump and shift uncomfortably. I scoffed silently. These were soldiers, right? Or was Taylor just scary and I didn't see it? No. My carrot top was a cutie.

I took a moment to appreciate his thick, red hair that lay in lazy waves on top of his angular face. It was the only thing about Taylor that was lazy. On a bad day, he had a sharp tongue and was amazingly quick-witted. His entire demonic aura was saturated with danger and seduction. Even the way he smirked, just a small millimeter smile, was enough to send my hormones into flight.

Those emerald eyes lit with amusement, "You are absolutely infuriating today."

I knew he meant that. The two of us hit heads on the best of days. We rarely agreed, but I respected him for his conviction regarding his opinions.

Even when it came to the useless act of weapons training.

"Today?" I scoffed with a grin. "Go to hell, Taylor. I'm infuriating every day."

Taylor bit his soft, pink lip before smiling, "Unfortunately, I went to hell and the devil sent me back to the Horde."

I only half heard his response because I loved seeing Taylor smile. It turned his devilishly handsome features to a brilliant masterpiece of crimson and emerald. Looking at him was an intense, albeit sexy, experience.

I chuckled at that. He always had some type of response. I envied him. Rhodes caught my eye and nodded to hurry. Now that we had arrived, the party could start. It was a fantastic night for burning the bodies of my enemy.

The closer I grew to Rhodes, the more magnetic his presence became. Those intuitive pale green eyes examined every part of my expression before instructing us. "Throw the last one on there."

Taylor and I both grinned at his masked impatience. Rhodes could be extremely intense when determined. After the events that had taken place today, he wanted this day to be over... preferably now. His masterful patience had reached an end. With one quick movement, we tossed the corpse on top of the sizeable mountain of dark metal and green leather.

Upon examining the many bodies, a deep rage surfaced underneath my calm facade. It felt like a tea kettle that was close to boiling. I appraised the clearing around us and leaned back into my heels. They sunk into the grass a solid inch, making me regret having worn them in the first place. Note to self: *Heels are not appropriate for body burnings*.

Rhodes offered me a small nod of appreciation before running a hand across his trimmed beard that surrounded his masculine sculpted lips. Those tiny, golden hairs sparkled under the setting sun and cast a gleaming halo around his silky waves. The man could easily be in a shampoo commercial. I envied his hand as it pushed through the thick strands like melted butter. I wanted *my* hands to do that.

Placing those thoughts to the side, I located the twins. Neo, broad-shouldered and bulky, stood in front of Silas's men. His expression was blank and even. One would never guess that he and I were responsible for these bodies. His short hair, like his twin, was worn in a fade that showcased their angelic, yet masculine faces. His dark obsidian eyes met mine for a second before a flash of white teeth graced my vision. Damn. He was just way too handsome. It was a good thing I had two of them.

Athens stood against the treeline with a cocky smile and bright silver eyes. It had been a change that had occurred after his extreme power usage earlier. I didn't mind the lack of glamour. I think it only added to his playful personality. Now, his eyes really did sparkle in amusement.

"Adyen?" I called out as a massive gold dragon shifted behind me. It cast a shadow that seemed to eclipse any of the beautiful evening light left. All of Silas's men began to shift uncomfortably once again, which caused a slow smile to graze my lips in a predatory fashion.

A golden tail, wrapped in metallic scales, secured my waist comfortably. I placed my hand along the smooth, warm texture of his tail as he shifted my position. Once I was set a few feet back from the body, *soon to be campfire,* pile he nudged my form gently with his massive snout. A sweet gesture from a gigantic dragon. He brought his chin to lay flat on the ground before releasing soft, swirling smoke from his dry, warm nose. The smoke smelled of cinnamon and ash. I pet his snout gently as those glittering black eyes watched me with interest.

I had never been this close to a dragon.

It seemed like things were going well thus far.

Despite their combined physical nature, I knew the two of them had very different personalities and thoughts. I suppose I had been a tad worried his dragon wouldn't like me.

"Alright," I sighed with dryness. "Let's do this shit."

The dragon fucking snorted at me. Was he laughing? The bastard was laughing. I let out a savage growl which caused Athens to grin from across the pile of bodies. I shook my head and turned my attention to Adyen's massive form. He towered over the clearing with vibrating primal energy that would make a weaker fae faint. *Literally,* one of the soldiers had just fainted. Fantastic. Cream of the crop over there.

As Adyen released a roar that shook the estate grounds, my eyes trailed to the treeline. Out here, I could almost forget what had happened. I could almost forget that these fuckers had tried to hurt my guard, my brother, and my favorite house.

How the mighty have fallen.

Assholes.

Adyen released an explosive stream of searing black flames that forced most of the group to back up. I didn't move from my position, although I did place a hand across my eyes so that my pretty long lashes weren't seared off. Rhodes advanced to stand by my side.

"That is a disgusting smell," He noted with a slight accent to his smooth words. I wondered briefly how he had developed a British accent, but figured there would be time for questions like that later. I searched the sparkle in his light eyes... *That liar*. He was enjoying this display as much as I.

"Now, don't go pretending you aren't a monster like the rest of us." I teased.

Rhodes sighed with a shrug, "Sometimes, the world needs monsters."

I laughed at his avoidance. The other soldiers shifted nervously at my laughter. I supposed it looked like I was smiling about the burning bodies. Eh. Not that far from the truth, to be honest.

"Now to anyone else, that might sound a little psychotic, Rhodes," I grinned like an idiot. Rhodes wrapped an arm around my shoulder gently and pressed a kiss to my temple. This time, I didn't flinch as I had in the past. He had scars like me. Pain like me.

Rhodes leaned into me, "I prefer inventive or creative, kitten."

The sound of his slight accent in my ear made my skin break out into small shivers. In what other ways could he be creative? My body clenched with pleasure as I attempted to focus on the bonfire in front of us.

Yes. You heard that right. I was getting all hot and bothered by Rhodes's voice while the distinct smell of my enemies burning flesh permeated the air. I wish I could tell you that I was sorry about that.

"I prefer 'psychopath'," I turned into his muscled arms. Those warm, golden arms tightened around me in security. While everyone else was still bloody and disgusting, Rhodes had changed into a fresh suit. Asshole.

"I'll be a psycho for you, Gray." He murmured, kissing the top of my head.

1
GRAY

"I'll order the repairs as discussed," Tulsa agreed from across the kitchen island.

Her hair was brushed back in a smooth, sleek ponytail, and those shrewd eyes seemed to be working overtime. I praised the fates that she had been gone during this morning's attack. Not only had I grown to care about the woman, but I also needed someone familiar with my situation to maintain the estate during my absence.

It was evening and, similar to Rhodes, she was impeccably dressed and already prepared to tackle the project at hand. She hadn't even asked about the many soldiers nor the smell of fae flesh burning. It was hard to find good help like her nowadays. The black leather binder in her hands would assist in the restoration of my property.

"Thank you, Tulsa." I nodded. "We will be leaving in the morning most likely."

"Baby!" Athens called out from the foyer. His ve¹ curled around my ears and caressed my entire ᴴ up. Tulsa rolled her eyes and turned to exit the that was my kitchen. Despite her attitude, I knew Tulsa didn't mind my men.

Hm. *My* men. When had that happened?

"In here," I called out while taking a sip of my tea.

It was a quiet response, but I had no doubt he would hear it. Sometimes I tested their abilities. I was sorta an asshole. I just didn't like to ruin the fun of figuring out what the twins were. I mean, I knew they were mages, but what type of mages? There were many options if I correctly recalled.

A pair of deeply colored arms captured my waist as I let out a small gasp laugh. The feel of his large hands against my waist caused me to wiggle against him. I placed my tea down as Athens moved me from my chair to the kitchen island. The movement elicited a laugh before I looked down at my playful guard from my new elevated position. *Hm, like the Queen I was soon to be…*

"You stole my seat," I offered a faux pout.

Athens immediately smiled, but grabbed my face, forcing it into a fishy face, "Oh, no. Fuck no. You do not get to pout. Ever."

I felt a laugh building in my chest.

"Why not?" Cue increase of fishy face pout.

"You're already a beautiful fucking warrior queen if we add 'cute' into your arsenal… Hell, Gray, I don't think I can handle that."

His face looked pain-stricken and it caused me to laugh even harder than before. I wiggled my face from his grasp and bit my lip to stop the laugh that bubbled up.

"I will try my damn hardest, Athens," I snickered while running my fingers through his thick dark fade, "to not be cute."

Athens sighed despondently, "No, it's too late. I've seen the pout. I'm ruined."

"My dearest apologies," I cooed. His eyes glinted with that r energy.

"I will forgive you, if… you make it up to me," He sighed dramatically while resting his hands on my bare legs.

I was dressed comfortably in a pair of shorts and an oversized sweater. Not my best look, but, oh well. It was worth it to feel his warm hands on my skin again. I knew he was hesitant to touch me, but I loved his touch… as long as it wasn't on my shoulders. I was getting better. Only with my guard, though. Screw anyone else.

"Oh?" I raised an eyebrow. "How so?"

"You can tell me how you're doing after today," He responded immediately.

I could tell the question made him nervous by how quickly he blurted it out. I wasn't the best at opening up and he knew it. My heart warmed at his concern. Out of everything he could have asked or said, he wanted to know how I felt after the attack today. I couldn't help the small smile that slipped onto my face.

Athens was playful in nature and usually optimistic. He tried to see the best in situations, nearly to a fault. I loved that about him. I envied that ability. I knew it took a lot for him to ask about such a serious and heavy topic.

My rage at our situation rippled through me like an angry wave. I inhaled a deep breath before responding, "Angry. Really fucking angry at Mario."

Mario. The King of the Dark Fae. The one who had killed my parents after committing acts of brutality so demented that I felt sick even thinking about it. Now that he had found me, I was forced to return to my position as the True Heir of the Horde.

I couldn't let him get away with what he had done.

Even if it meant war.

Especially if it meant war.

Silas didn't know what to do when it came to war.

"What about Neo? How do you think he's doing?" I asked quietly.

His eyes darkened in concern for his twin. "Neo won't talk about it, even if I asked," He muttered. "I don't think he's upset. I know I wouldn't be if it meant saving my brothers or you."

I liked that he thought of the other men as brothers. His comments were a sobering thought. I leaned my forehead down to meet his. The warmth that his body radiated was damn near supernatural.

"It'll be okay, Athens," I mumbled quietly.

It was odd to be in the position to comfort someone else, but I could tell he was worried. This was a side of Athens I had yet to see. It made me appreciate his optimism even more.

"If you don't want it to be okay," He whispered quietly. "I'm always here for you, Gray."

I could feel the heat between the two of us. Our lips were inches apart. Between them were phrases of comfort and security. I leaned forward to press a kiss to his warm lips. We had only kissed once and it had been playful and fun. This kiss though, which he deepened, was... something else. It was damn near therapeutic.

My arms wrapped around his warm neck as those large hands moved to hold my hips. His thumbs traced patterns on the skin above my shorts that caused my breathing to hitch. Slow and soothing patterns that were reflected in the movement of our kisses. I pressed deeper and let my tongue meet his in a tight embrace. The smell of coconut and something uniquely magical surrounded me in a soft caress.

"Shit, sorry," Neo mumbled from the doorway. I pulled away as Athens's mouth turned up in a playful smirk. I looked at his twin and felt myself sober slightly. Those dark, sad eyes held a glittering heat to them that caused me to go still. Neo often made me feel off-kilter with just a look. I supposed it was because I knew what those eyes looked like empty. Ruthless. I appreciated that about him. Usually, being a monster was a very lonely affair.

No more though. I had five of my very own monsters now.

"Nothing to be sorry about," Athens winked as Neo moved toward the counter.

He positioned himself behind me so that I was sandwiched between the two of them. I could smell his soft mint scent and the heat radiating from his bare forearms. They leaned close enough to touch and I was very tempted to do just that. To touch.

"Already packed and ready to go?" I asked him curiously.

I finally gave in and grabbed his wrist lightly. I just needed to touch him somehow. It had been an odd day for both of us, but I knew Neo wasn't used to touch like Athens. Neo's eyes glittered and shot to our combined touch.

He smiled slightly, "Never unpacked."

I shook my head, "I can't believe we are going to the Horde lands tomorrow... That is going to be--"

"Odd," Neo supplied.

His expression was replaced by a look of darkness that I didn't like. Athens's face didn't match his. He didn't seem affected by the prospect of going back home. Home? It didn't seem like my home.

"Hey," Athens drawled. "We can see mom. She would love to meet you, Gray."

I chuckled, "Want me to meet the parents already?"

Neo mumbled, "At least one of them."

One of them? Did their parents not live together?

"What about your father?" I asked because *screw me and my lack of filter.*

Athens stilled the pattern on my hip while Neo let out a low, pained sound. His eyes trailed from our joined touch, past my shoulder, and to my lips. Finally, he met my eyes with a look of deep sadness and fresh pain. I nearly gasped at the expression.

Neo's lip lifted in a snarl, "You will also meet our father, unfortunately. He is the lead representative for the mages."

I nodded. A million questions filtered through my brain, but I was nervous to ask. This was what happened when you started caring though. You thought of others and how your unfiltered questions would affect them. Hurt them, even.

"Yes. We did grow up separate," Athens answered my unspoken question.

I frowned as Neo's eyes grew haunted, "It was decided that I would grow up at our father's place and Athens would stay in town with mom."

"We still saw one another, because we didn't live that far apart," Athens mumbled before pressing his chin into my outstretched leg. Those hands wrapped around my waist as he held me securely.

I saw Neo frown. No, they may not have lived that far apart, but it had made a difference. I saw that now. I could only assume that Neo's dark, sad eyes derived from his experience growing up under his father's care.

"Why?"

My question wasn't merely directed toward their separation of residence. Who the fuck separated twins anyway? Was this why they were so different? Why did Neo's eyes look so haunted? What had happened? I wanted to know. I needed to know more.

I didn't get a response though. Instead, a very cut and shirtless Taylor strolled into the kitchen. He wore a pair of flannel bottoms that showed off his cut hips and dark tattoos. The tattoos covered every inch of his chest in a language I was familiar with but didn't speak. It didn't stop my eyes from seeking out every line and detail.

Okay. It was an excuse to check him out. Guilty as charged.

Those emerald eyes sparkled as the realization of our presence crossed his awareness. It was clear he hadn't expected us.

"Baby girl. Boys." He greeted, in a rough sleepy voice. "Am I missing out on some late night fun?" Those perfect lips tilted into a devious smile.

"Well, when you make it sound so dirty," I purred.

I heard Athens chuckle as Neo relaxed under the break of tension. Taylor's eyes tracked his relaxed posture and I realized he had done it on purpose. Sneaky, helpful demon.

"Is it dirty?" He asked suggestively while filling his water from the fridge.

Damn. He was a different type of muscular than the twins, not as bulky, but equally as hot.

"Not yet," I winked while slipping off the counter.

Athens let out a tired groan as Neo stretched his arms toward the ceiling. Both looked exhausted. Had it only been this morning that I had woken to Neo's intense kiss?

After a quick goodnight, I jogged up the large foyer stairs toward my room. My feet were bare on the smooth flooring as I met two familiar shapes lounging near my door.

"If it isn't my two favorite shifters," I mumbled sleepily.

Rhodes grinned, his eyes crinkling, as he stretched his shoulders in a sleepy motion. His hair was messy and mused as those green eyes traveled across my body in greeting. Adyen pressed a kiss to my head and slipped his hands into the large, comfortable hoodie he wore. It was clear the shift had taken a lot out of him today because his honey amber eyes were hooded as he ran a hand through his short, dark hair.

"Ready for bed?" Adyen mused.

"Sure am." I sighed. "Are you both ready to head home tomorrow?"

Rhodes wrapped an arm around my waist and kissed my nose. "Somewhat. Are you?"

I grumbled, "Yes. No. Maybe."

"Don't worry, Gray. We've got this." Rhodes assured. "Now, get some damn sleep."

Adyen and I watched him leave as he sauntered, like the predator he was, towards his room. He was lethal and sleek, similar to his jaguar form. A true feline.

"Come on, lil brawler." Adyen encouraged.

"Sleeping with me?" I asked. I was joking. Sorta. No. Okay. I was hoping. Honestly.

"Yes actually." He explained.

His massive arms wrapped around my center as we walked toward the bed. My chest was pressed against his and my feet hung off the ground. I didn't argue. Instead, I let my lips press into the warm skin of his neck in a gentle kiss.

"Thank you for today," I murmured quietly. My large navy brocade comforter was pulled back as he easily navigated the two of us under the warm covers.

I had only kissed him yesterday... Somehow, though, our physicality felt more comfortable than that. It was natural. His hands wrapped around my waist and my head tucked under his chin in a perfect fit. He was careful to not touch my shoulders. It was something I appreciated very much.

"Are you okay with me sleeping in here?" He asked in a quiet hum. His voice was a low rumble in my space that seemed to warm me from head to toe.

"Yes," I responded with sincerity. It made me nervous to have someone in my bed. How could it not? I was shit when it came to intimacy. "Are you okay with sleeping in here?"

Adyen was charming and protective, but he didn't often express how he felt about situations. I made a promise to ask his opinion on situations more often.

He chuckled in a deep husky tone, "Gray, I would prefer this arrangement every night if it were left up to me."

A shiver ran up my spine, across my shoulders, and brought a flush to my face. I could feel a vibrating force working itself out of his chest. Something about his reaction was primal, so it was unsurprising that I found it attractive. I felt reassured that my attraction to him was mutual. How would I know, you ask? The hard and unsurprisingly large element of Adyen's desire was pressing against my ass. I tried to not wiggle and clamped down on my subtle excitement. It was powerful to know I affected him that much. I must have been failing in the non-wiggling part though.

"Lil brawler," Adyen warned in a deep octave. "get some damn sleep."

"I'm not the only one excited," I grumbled. It earned me a chuckle.

I had no idea how I fell asleep. I had been trying not to wiggle and attempting to not work myself up over something that I wasn't sure I was even ready for. Did he even want that? I mean, hell, what would that mean for us? For the group?

Rhodes had encouraged a group relationship. It wasn't uncommon within the Fae realm. He had asked my opinion on it. Yet, that conversation seemed eons away. I tried to not let vulnerabilities and worries surface from my subconscious. After today, after our mass murder, did they want that anymore? Or had they seen the monster I was?

Those thoughts brought out some severe anxiety about not being wanted. Instead of letting it fester and grow in the darkness of my bedroom, I closed my eyes. I soaked in the intimacy of Adyen's large body against mine. It numbed the panic. It dulled the insecurities that I hid by day. It offered peace. Eventually, I fell asleep.

2

TAYLOR

The morning light peaked across the thickly forested skyline in a fiery, blood-red. It was my favorite color. The color of heat. The glow of fire. Gray would look fantastic in that color. Then again, she was the type of woman who looked good in anything.

"Smoking again, mate?" Rhodes asked. He had always been a morning person, like me. We were both dressed for the day in guard gear. It was standard black leather that would fit under armor, if necessary. The only thing that would set us apart from Silas's men were the custom deep navy and silver cloaks that Horde heir guards wore. Even Silas's men hadn't worn them.

"You know it doesn't affect me." I offered gruffly.

Rhodes sighed, sitting next to me, "I know, but it also means you're anxious."

We sat in silence for some time as I ignored his comment. Rhodes had brought out two cups of coffee and eventually, after two cigarettes, I drank mine. I would need caffeine to get through today. We were going back to the Horde, and I would have to resume my mild acceptance of the guard. It was bullshit. Hell, if it weren't for Gray and the close brotherhood I'd formed, I would be gone.

"Are you ready for today?" Rhodes asked.

The man had an uncanny sense of near mind reading. At one time, the ability had made me nervous, vulnerable. Now? I didn't mind so much. I trusted him.

"No," I groaned, stretching my arms above my head. "I hate the Horde lands and working with SE."

Instead of offering reassurance, Rhodes nodded, "Lots of political bullshit to deal with, but we'll be okay. We just need to get her on that throne."

I chuckled at that, "I don't see that being a problem. Gray is on a fucking warpath. She will walk right in and sit her hot little ass on that damn seat whether anyone wants her to or not."

Rhodes smiled, "Yes, I expect she will."

I frowned then, "This marriage contract, fiancé, whatever… what's the news on that?"

A shadow crossed over Rhodes's face with a sigh, "I have no idea about her thoughts regarding the subject. Since our conversation, she hasn't really decided on anything regarding us… and we can't really step between her and the responsibility to her kingdom."

I scowled, "How the hell did a marriage contract with the Light Fae come into existence?" The Horde tended to avoid the other two kingdoms.

Rhodes leaned back onto the stairs, "Her parents drafted it during the start of their rule before Gray was even born. It was supposed to foster the relationship between the Light Fae and the Horde. It was between the two future True Heirs of each kingdom, no names. I heard a rumor that her mother regretted it the minute Gray was born."

I nodded, "Can she get out of it?"

"Of course. She just has to deal with losing the potential Light Fae alliance."

"I hope we are ready for this, Rhodes," I sighed darkly.

"We don't have a choice. The only choice is Gray."

I had never heard more accurate words.

"Morning," A smooth sexy voice said from the doors behind us.

Gray was awake.

Today, we would leave for the Horde.

3
GRAY

"Tulsa," I hugged the impeccable woman, "if you need to contact me, use the numbers left inside the folder. I will get the message."

"I know," she assured. "Now, you be careful and don't let those boys boss you around."

Tulsa hadn't ever been told the extent of my past. When a 16-year-old hires you to run a multi-million dollar estate, you don't ask questions.

After a night of peaceful, dreamless sleep, I had awoken to my possessive dragon wrapped so tightly around me that I questioned whether he was a dragon or a python. It had taken twenty minutes to convince him to wake up. Even then, he had kept me in bed for another half hour. I hadn't minded one damn bit.

I was ready to face this predictably long day. I had even worn my favorite pair of heeled, leather boots. I knew, realistically, that my fashion options would change drastically once in the Horde. Today, I attempted a happy medium.

My small, slim form was fitted into a pair of kick-ass black lace-up pants that highlighted my boots. While the boots hit mid-thigh, you could see a sliver of skin through the laces of my pants that went up either thigh to mid-waist. My arms and chest were covered in a corset and matching jacket. It was black and lined in silver. I was feeling exceptionally badass.

Athens tugged on my dark, sleek ponytail and smiled at Tulsa. "Gray is the bossy one, Tulsa, not us."

Tulsa offered him a dry look and retreated back into the estate. My eyes trailed over the gathering in front of me. My guard stood outfitted in black leather on the stairs, while Silas stood with his, soon to be mine, army down below. I narrowed my eyes at my brother in annoyance. He was practically giddy at the events taking place. Asshole.

"Sister," Silas called out while stepping onto the stairs. "Are you ready to assume your rightful place?" He had hair that was so dark, it was nearly black, and large silver eyes. My eyes were often indigo, but they could darken in anger and lighten to silver in a moment of extreme power.

Before I could answer, Rhodes, stepped forward and offered me a silver cloak. I noticed, with deep satisfaction, that my guard wore a thick navy cloak lined in silver. They were masculine. Their cloaks marked them as the extraordinary men they were. That was the truth of it. They were exceptional. I couldn't even offer a sarcastic mental remark to that thought.

Damn them. Damn me. They were growing on me like mold. *Sigh.* I might keep them. They were mine, after all. My guard. See? I'm possessive already. This wouldn't end well.

My cloak was a deep silver that seemed to darken from top to bottom. It was without a hood but had black armored feathers that stretched from the collar to my shoulder blades. As Rhodes slipped it over my shoulders, he pressed a secretive kiss to the back of my neck that only my other men would see. It was reassuring.

"Silas," I called him forth.

"Yes, Your Majesty?" He grinned, with exceptional mirth.

He really got off on the idea of being lazy, didn't he? I looked to see if any of his soldiers could sense his underlying joy. Instead, I was met with stern trained expressions that were awaiting orders. I knew now that it was my orders they awaited.

"You will open the portal," I demanded simply. If he wasn't going to rule anymore, he would have to make himself useful somehow.

Silas hadn't understood at first why I had left the Horde lands. For a time, he assumed I was missing, or even possibly dead. Once I had explained my rather delicate position, the one where I had witnessed the Dark Fae King murdering our parents, he seemed to still not understand why I had left. The reasoning, that my presence would have brought war upon Horde lands, didn't seem to fit his plans of laziness. I had, initially, been given three days to decide my plans, but then the Dark Fae King's men had attacked. Now, it didn't matter if I stayed away or not, he knew that I knew.

"Of course," he grinned.

His angular face turned serious as he faced an open space to my left. His long dark hair began to breeze over his dark purple robes. It started out gentle but then turned ferocious in nature. I tried to not sway at the shocking amount of power my brother put forth.

I mean, I had more, but... Damn.

"You've got this, kitten," Rhodes whispered softly.

The strength he gave me was absolutely what I needed. The portal began to form as a small black crystal floated from my brother's outstretched hand. I knew it would harness his natural power. It floated gently off his palm and grew in size. It had been some time since I had seen my brother's magic. I was impressed by the level of skill he maintained. At least he worked at something. I'm sure he used it to get laid.

I stepped forward as the portal expanded into a long thin oval that shimmered in a cosmic pattern. I would be the first through the portal. I could already feel the exceptional power radiating from the Horde lands. It called to me.

This was the moment. The moment where everything would change.

"Shall we?" Rhodes offered. He and Adyen lined up directly behind me. I could tell they would have both felt more comfortable leading through. I also knew that it would show a weakness that I couldn't afford. It didn't stop Adyen's hand from twitching on my back as a low rumble echoed around us.

I didn't answer. Instead, I stepped into the smooth black surface and surrendered myself to universe travel. All at once, the world went dark.

Silence was not the enemy. No, I was familiar with silence.

The dark didn't scare me. I loved the darkness.

I worried briefly for the others traveling behind me, but I knew they were safe.

A natural wash of emotions crowded my senses. I could feel my glamour slipping off me like a silk scarf as my true form lengthened my limbs and turned my skin an iridescent silver. I was glowing brilliantly against the dark abyss. I knew I was moving, but I felt suspended in space, in time even.

My spine rippled in anticipation. We were drawing near.

The savage beast inside of me, the one that demanded blood from the Dark King, reared its head and smiled. It was a terrifyingly dark smile. She was back. The savage. I could feel her. She was everywhere. Inside of my head, in my skin, and watching through my eyes. A true predator.

Gods help them when she found her prey.

The first part of my consciousness that emerged from the dark void was my sight. As I pushed through the cosmic portal exit, my eyes were flooded with bright sunlight. It didn't affect my eyes though. I could still absorb the scene breaking out in front of me. And it was. It was a motherfucking ridiculous scene.

"Seems Silas sent out a motherfucking invitation to everyone," I murmured, stepping onto the soft ground. My heels didn't sink into this ground. It was made of tougher material than earth. Literally and figuratively. I wasn't about to complain.

Before I could speak, a gasp echoed throughout the entire clearing. It was filled. I could sense demons, shifters, and mages alike. All of them had been awaiting the portal and were now gathered behind their representative's families. Everyone seemed frozen.

"Kneel to your Queen!" A voice boomed from the shifter representatives. They were the first to kneel, followed by the demons, and lastly the mages. It didn't surprise me that the mages were the most stubborn.

I looked upon the booming voice and recognized a familiar pair of honey-colored eyes. Both Adyen and Rhodes's fathers both stood as representatives for the shifter population. It was unsurprising that they were still ruled by men. Where was the progress? Damn it.

Unfortunately, due to the creation of the Horde, we maintained similar ideals as humans. Before the time of the Horde, there had been only the Dark and Light Fae. Any creature not from a pure marriage had been considered a second class citizen. This included any offspring from the union of fae and demon, shifter, or human. It had been my ancestors, long dead now, that had broken away from that archaic notion. The Horde had been established as a sanctuary and kingdom for any half fae that was rejected in other established communities.

It was rare to find any communities that would accept someone who wasn't pure-blooded. As a result, the Horde kingdom grew to an impressive size. My bloodline hadn't been pure fae in some time, but every once in a few centuries, a True Heir was born. One that had pure fae magic. In this case, *me*. So what was the pure magic of fae? Some intense shit. That's what. It was a more normal occurrence within the other realms, but more unique within the Horde.

Essentially, I came from a long line of badass rebels. I would have been part of that history to a further extent if it hadn't been for that bastard, Mario.

Now I had a second chance.

I wouldn't run this time.

"Stand," I commanded softly.

Behind me, the portal let out another two shadows that I knew to be Rhodes and Adyen. Instantly, I felt at peace.

Without much prologue, I stepped forward with determination. The three sectors opened down the middle as figures began emerging behind us. An entire army would pass through this way, and I had no intention of spending another minute in this damn clearing. While the group seemed curious, there were too many eyes on me. Curiosity and an array of other emotions suffocated me.

I also knew that my scar, which shone from my temple to my jaw, was on full display. It was unsurprising, of course. It was a wicked scar. I kept my eyes ahead and walked boldly to the extensive line of travel carriages. Seriously? They were still using carriages. Okay. This needed to change.

"Taylor." Rhodes demanded loudly. "Travel with our Majesty."

I nearly let out a small laugh at that damn title. What, no kitten? I think I preferred that damn nickname right now.

I was terrible with change and this was a significant change. I could feel my inner bitch making an appearance. I kept my lips sealed and let Taylor take my hand to aid me into the carriage. It was a sleek, black carriage that shone in the brilliant sunlight. The outside lands of the Horde kingdom were filled with mountains and caves that provided defensive structures and room to expand. It was not unlike Estonia in temperament and beauty. Maybe that was why I had loved Estonia so much.

"You've got this, lil brawler." Adyen whispered. I knew the four of them would be close outside of our carriage. With a deep breath, I slid into the comfortably shaded space and let out a very unqueenly groan.

Taylor let out a gruff sound and offered me an exhausted look. Yep, there was my introverted, gruff, brooding, anti-social guard. While those descriptions sounded negative, I truly appreciated his nature.

"How do you think that went?" I asked quietly.

He was slipping off his coat and ran a hand through his thick dark red hair. My eyes spotted some adorable freckles along the bridge of his nose. Well, that is distracting and unfair. It also was a contrast to his badass persona, so I loved it naturally.

"I think," He mumbled running a hand through his hair again, "that it went exactly as we expected."

Instead of responding, I leaned back into the seat as Taylor squeezed my knee softly. I could assume our ride would take about half a day. It wasn't a terrible distance but would have been a hell of a lot faster through a portal. Why had we not transported into the castle, you ask? Because. Silas apparently wanted to make a scene. I should have expected that shit.

The Horde lands were beautiful. It wasn't nearly as terrifying as many assumed. In fact, the Dark Fae lands were hideously bare compared to the forested beauty around us. It was only rivaled by the Light Fae lands which existed on a large island that floated above a body of exceptionally clear water. I always considered that far more of a vacation place. Who could live on a beach year round?

However, no matter where you were in the Fae lands, it was beautiful. I had heard a rumor that the Elven lands were as stunning, but I had never visited. I wasn't exactly a huge fan of elves. My abusive caretakers had been Elven in heritage, so their species was sorta ruined for me. I know I'm a biased bitch, but I had no other experience to draw from yet.

I promised myself I would invite representatives from the Elven kingdom to my crowning... Maybe.

"How are you feeling about returning to your official guard proximity?" I asked Taylor. I knew he hated his place in the guard, as he pointed out often. It honestly made me trust his opinion more. He wasn't doing this for duty. He was in it for me. For us.

"Thrilled," he drawled sarcastically with that asshole smile.

It was the same one that he had used on me the day I first met him. I couldn't rationalize how it had been less than a month since that time. So I wouldn't. I would ignore it. Ignore the fast-paced nature of this friendship... relationship? Six-some?

Oh, that sounded dirty.

"So, how does that work with being Heir guards?" I didn't have exceptional knowledge of the SE Guard units. I didn't like to lack knowledge in any field.

"Supernatural Enforcement is no longer in charge of us," Taylor explained. "While the Horde guard is a sector of SE, the Heir guard is specifically 'contracted' out to royalty. However, the position is permanent and only for True Heirs. Silas's guard will stay with him but are replaceable to some level. Our unit was formed from a very early age and trained in a skill set compatible for the Heir."

Oh, a particular skill set for an heir? I bet you have a skill set for me.

"That is by far the most you have said at one time." I cackled.

Taylor glowered, but then grinned, "If you like my voice, baby girl, all you have to do is ask. I can whisper all types of things to you."

I made an appreciative humming noise and smirked. "I just bet you could."

A powerful fist on the door made both of us smile. Damn shifter hearing. I knew that was either Rhodes or Adyen.

"Freaking cockblocks," I growled. It earned me a chuckle from outside.

Taylor gave me a millimeter smile, "By the way, I like your glamour removed."

Instantly, I felt more self-conscious, but I continued, "Why haven't you let your glamour fall?"

"Demonic creatures have a full separate form, similar to shifters, so unlike royalty, they don't need glamour." His statement made me want to see Neo and Athens. Did mages have glamour? I had assumed they did, but now, I didn't know.

I loved that the Horde was different than that of the Dark and Light kingdoms. It had more diversity. More excitement. In the human realm, shifters existed due to the various strands of bite viruses that caused the infected to shift into an assortment of natural creatures. There were predators, such as wolves, and prey, such as deer. However, they had all been born human and made from humans. In the Horde, our shifters had all mated with pure blood fae at some point within their line. They had magic within their very souls. Due to the shifting ability of some fae in the Dark and Light kingdoms, the mythical shifters had been born. Dragons. Phoenix. An assortment of beautiful shifters that lived harmoniously next to naturalistic shifters. All of them were half fae and half shifter. All of them were welcome here.

Along the same notion demons, *the old world term of darkness seemed cheesy and overused*, were welcomed here as well.

Pure-blooded demons resided in a realm that humans often thought of as hell. They were oddly picky about who was let in. As a result, our population of half-demons had grown exceptionally fast. It didn't help that pureblood demons often vacationed to the Fae lands. Those lusty fools produced a lot of kids. I blushed at all of the devious and sexy things I had heard about demons in bed.

Taylor rose a red brow, "Are you blushing?"

"Fuck you," I snarled and looked outside.

He chuckled and continued his light ministrations on my knee.

The third group within the Horde were the mages. By far, the most difficult. They were the offsprings of human and fae, born with *magic sight*. What did that mean? They had an essential understanding of magic and could see it occurring despite glamour. However, unless they received a blood ink tattoo from an ink mage within the community, they wouldn't be able to practice magic. I had heard a rumor that human children born without sight could gain it. However, the mages in the Horde talked poorly about them, as if they weren't as good as them. Even though they would have to get the same damn tattoo as them.

I growled under my breath, "Taylor, can I run some details past you. I don't think much has changed since I left, but..."

"Of course, Gray," he nodded in understanding.

I explained everything I could remember but excluded the sexy demon part. No need to boost his ego.

"You've got it right," Taylor nodded. "My brother has been studying the mages' ability to impart their gift on humans. He's been obsessed with it for some time."

"I wonder why," I mused. "Oh, by the way, I saw your father."

He snorted, "Unfortunately, as did I."

My guard had been chosen at a young age from a selection of young men within each of the kingdoms three groups. I had to assume that their fathers, all representatives as I had been informed by the twins, had aided in that placement. It was considered an honor putting up with my difficult ass. I realized with a frown that I wasn't entirely familiar with how leadership was selected within each group. It was something that I lacked knowledge of.

"How are the leaders of each group chosen?" I voiced.

"The groups are essentially self-governed, but they look to Horde royalty for guidance in large scale country political and military matters," Taylor continued. "With Silas in charge, a lot of that had fallen on the representatives."

I leveled him with a distressed expression, "Be honest. How bad has it been?"

Taylor shrugged, which told me enough. Damn the guilt I felt for leaving the Horde lands when I had. Then again, I had not known what a shitty leader Silas would be. It wasn't like my 'human' life had gone exceptionally peachy.

I wasn't positive how long we sat in relative silence. It was comfortable and his presence was very reassuring. My hands, at some point, involuntarily snuck out from my control and claimed his. Taylor didn't waste time to move over to my side of the carriage. He must have been waiting for me to openly touch him.

My head fell back into his shoulder as those long fingers strummed a pattern on my waist gently. He was fantastic at not touching my shoulders. I wasn't sure if it would make me uncomfortable. I trusted him impeccably, but I didn't want to risk a panic attack before such a significant moment. We would be arriving at the kingdom soon.

The scenery grew more saturated in color, darker tones turned to jewel tones and lights turned into pastels. I found my focus on the massive castle that rested against a range of imposing mountains. It was exactly as I remembered it. I swallowed down the onslaught of painful memories.

I wouldn't think about my parents. I wouldn't think about the last time I had been here. The time I had escaped. Thanks to Neo mind you.

"Taylor trade with Neo," Rhodes commanded. Taylor sighed, pressed a kiss to my ear, and slid out of my space. I didn't have to wait long before Neo replaced him.

"Oh, wow," I sighed appreciatively like a fucking teenage girl.

His glamour was gone. Neo was stunning in his true form. The mocha color of his skin had turned into a brilliant onyx color that looked like stone. Those eyes softened in meeting mine but remained dangerously sharp and lethal overall. I noticed something unusual as he moved closer.

"You have a piercing?!" I asked in genuine shock. I found myself leaning forward to see the small piercing that glinted in his eyebrow like a black diamond.

Neo hummed and grasped my face gently before pulling me onto his lap. It was so unlike him that I began to worry. I could feel how tense and serious he was. I had to assume that this was due to his father. There was no other reason for him to demand such physical contact. Not that I minded. I pressed my thumb to his piercing and he let out a strangled sigh before responding.

"When a child is born, half fae and half human, no matter how long ago the union was in their family… they have the sight. To harness that sight, you need a blood ink tattoo that allows your body to harness the type of magic you are most inclined to use. The tattoo," He pulled down his collar and presented me a dark tattoo that looked like a circle within a triangle, "expands with your power. In the case of Athens and I, it expanded to the point that it resulted in a tattooed form. Something that was essentially unheard of at such a young age. They believe it is due to our branding as a True Heir guard member."

"How do you know which type of magic you're inclined to use?"

Neo smiled, "Ink mages are much better at that than me.

However, it didn't surprise anyone I was an alchemy mage. My ability came easily after my tattoo was placed on my skin. They usually wait until puberty, but for Athens and me, they did it before our ceremony initiation to become your guard."

"So, what's an alchemy mage?" I wondered. It was humbling to realize how little I knew about the members of my kingdom.

"Well, it's one of the most diverse abilities actually. We can perform everything from shadow manipulation to mental manipulation. One of Taylor's cousins, Edwin I believe, is fantastic at it. I worked with him once during a SE training activity."

"Does he have a tattooed form like you?" I continued.

Neo shook his head, "I don't believe so. It's interesting because, with most mages, the blood ink influences their body as an added benefit, like a mask... For Athens and I, it's almost like this is more of our natural skin than the other."

"So, it's not really a glamour then?" I motioned to his form. "Both forms are real, especially the other."

He nodded and looked back out the carriage window with a tense expression.

I realized then that Rhodes had switched out Neo for a reason. He was impossibly tense. I curled into his lap further and stilled when his chin landed on my shoulder. Neo instantly stopped his action to await my reaction. I knew he would back up in an instant if needed. It was an odd feeling. It was different than with Rhodes. My body was tense, but I forced it to relax. This was Neo. I trusted Neo.

"It's okay," I whispered. "I trust you."

Neo's arms wrapped further around my waist, and his chin tilted only slightly on my shoulder. I melted into his chest and my fears softened until they evaporated. Neo was complex and haunted. He felt so intense and so deep. He could be soft and sweet. Yet, hidden beneath all of that was darkness, there was a cold black shadowy void that I recognized. It was such an intense contrast.

He would never judge me. He would never count the lives that I had taken. There was an equality of power within our relationship that came from our primal beings.

When I gazed into Neo's eyes, I saw his monster looking back at mine.

4
GRAY

"Baby," Athens murmured quietly, "this place is crazy."

I grinned a small smile at his flashy tattooed form. Neo hadn't mentioned his brother's abilities, but I was nearly positive Athens was a metal mage. It helped that his entire form seemed to shimmer like cold steel. His eyes were like melted silver and his hair shone with icy, almost white, highlights. Even his dark skin was contrasted with silver metallic streaks that highlighted his muscular neck and big hands.

This reminded me of a conversation that had only happened two days ago. Somehow, it was exceptionally different. Now, Athens strode next to me and walked parallel to Neo. I could feel Adyen at my back with Taylor while I watched Rhodes off to my slight right. If we had been walking anywhere else, he would have most likely moved protectively in front of me. I could see his animal peeking out by the way his gold eyes tracked every movement that occurred in front of us.

Our carriages had stopped directly in front of the palace steps. I had heard greetings and the start of celebrations outside. It was somewhat more friendly than the reception from leadership before. It was probably because they hadn't seen my scars yet. Well, hadn't at the time, they would now.

The carriage was shaded, so I hadn't had the opportunity to see more than a glimpse of the dark stone castle we were approaching. I would want to explore later tonight. Maybe Adyen would fly out over the landscape? I bet I could hitch a ride. I would just have to ask him if I could ride him… *ha ha*! That would be interesting.

We approached the dark steps of the castle as the crowd behind us cheered in encouragement. Silas followed directly behind us with our guard. I knew today wasn't the day for celebration. I had yet to be officially crowned. An array of frustrating political bullshit awaited me from the representatives.

"Rhodes," I murmured, gaining his attention but not drawing the attention of the staff that lined the halls.

"I will tell leadership to wait in the throne room if you need a moment?" he offered, as a quiet suggestion.

Did I need a moment? No. I needed to get through the day without softening for even a moment. If I weakened, I would fall asleep on my fucking feet.

"No," I growled softly. "Let's get this done."

The hallway we traveled through led to a pair of navy doors that were opened by guardsmen. They bent their heads respectfully. My eyes instantly zeroed in on the occupants within the throne room. It was already filling with a considerable amount of leadership. Now, why did I feel like this was more of a crowd than usual?

The room was shaped like a giant white stone hexagon that had marble floors and massive windows. The throne, sitting at the tip of the hexagon, was a deep rich black that was accented by silver cushions. Outside of it were two smaller seats that were positioned lower. The room was empty of furniture outside of that.

My shoes sounded against the floor as I strode up to the impressive focal point. I could already assume there would be adverse reactions to my next move. Unfortunately, for them, I didn't really care.

No. If I was back, I would be handling this the way I saw fit.

I knew the moment everyone realized my plans because the room stilled. I felt my guardsmen expand out in a protective barrier along the upper step of the throne. Only Rhodes moved to stand near my seat. I offered him a short nod before sitting myself down. I tried to not smile at the sight greeting me.

The room was silent. I didn't cross my legs or arms but sat with rapt focus on the crowd. I could feel hundreds of eyes on me. I could feel the tension in the room as Silas approached the throne and happily took the secondary lower seat. It elicited a reaction of surprise from the crowd of onlookers. Okay, now my inner bitch really did want to grin. What had they expected? For him to fight for the seat?

I didn't rush to say anything to the growing crowd. Instead, I waited until the heavy dark doors were closed before I spoke. My eyes trailed along each group with interest.

The shifters were well represented and stood center to the throne. The mythical and naturalistic elements were evenly split down the middle. They wore thick, dark blue garments, similar to those around them, but were accented by the gold lining of their cloaks. Their two representative leaders stood with eyes focused intently on the throne.

Adyen's father, whose name I didn't know, stood larger than Rhodes's father. Both of them looked similar to their sons, except for a few distinct differences. Rhodes spoke quietly in my ear, acting as the support and knowledge I lacked.

"That is Raphael, Mythical Shifter Representative, and Adyen's father. I will introduce you to his family later." He whispered quietly. I could see the similarities shared with Adyen.

However, Raphael had a far more tanned face that seemed wrinkled with age and eyes that were darker than his sons.

"That is Alexander, Naturalistic Shifter Representative, and my..." he sighed, "father."

I could feel the tension radiating from him and could only assume that his feelings toward his father were lukewarm at best.

"Over to your left…"

My eyes barely moved to the large crowd of navy robes that were lined in crimson. They were led by two individuals at the front of the group. Men, of course, because apparently, equality had yet to reach this damn archaic kingdom. Shit was about to change. You knew you were in a dangerous place when humans did equality better than you.

"... that is Henry, Demonic Representative, and his son Palo," Rhodes explained softly. "Taylor's father and brother."

I could see the family resemblance, but it was far less than the shifters. Henry seemed like a barrel-chested version of Taylor with dark auburn hair and black eyes. Palo, on the other hand, had Taylor's trademark red hair with his father's black eyes. I wondered briefly if Taylor's mother had green eyes. I couldn't afford to search the crowd, but my instinct told me she would be looking back at me. I wondered briefly if she was half demon as well or a fae that left the Dark or Light kingdom. Lineage in the Horde wasn't well recorded for obvious reasons.

As the Dark King once said to my parents, "Fae don't like to be reminded of their transgressions." Apparently, that was what my kingdom was. A bunch of bastard children Mario didn't want to be reminded of.

Fuck him. I could feel my rage bubbling forth like an angry tsunami. I would show him. I stilled my body and realized how frightfully possessive I had become of this kingdom and its people already.

"Finally, all the way to your right," he sighed. "We have the mages."

"Neo and Athens's father," I murmured.

He nodded as my eyes focused on a man who already made me unnaturally angry. Well, that's not true. I was always fucking angry. However, this guy served as the cherry on top for the disaster sundae that the past 48 hours had been.

He looked similar to both of my twins but had a harsh sneer to his face that made him seem more shallow and dark. His eyes were narrowed on his sons and a cruel smirk was on his lips. It was clear he had a fucking problem. My problem right now was how he was looking at my two extremely tense guards. *My* guards.

"His name is Colliard," Rhodes explained softly. "Mage Representative."

I placed a hand gently on his and stood. My cloak fell around me and Silas offered me a subtle nod. I hoped he would understand what I said next. It was clear he hadn't wanted to rule and had let some dark tension form. The leadership of this kingdom seemed uneasy and uncomfortable here. I would bet the change that was occurring made them even more uncomfortable. Maybe even scared, at least for the few of them that had been benefitting from the chaos.

"For those who don't know me," I spoke clear and sharp. "My name is Gray. True Heir of the Horde and daughter to the late rulers of this land."

Silence followed.

"Why have you decided to come back now?" Colliard's voice rang out eventually. His eyes moved toward Silas. "We were perfectly fine without you."

I chuckled at that, causing many to flinch. Clearly, my laugh had sounded harsh and maybe slightly scary. Good to know.

"If I have not informed you of my purpose in returning now, rather than before, Colliard... there is a reason."

Colliard flinched at that. His attention was now on the marble floor instead of Silas or my twins. Good. I promised the Gods that if I found out, at any point, that he had used my brother... there would be no mercy. I would even ask Neo if he wanted the pleasure of killing him. After all, it was clear the man had caused him pain.

"Excuse him, Your Majesty." A smoky voice echoed from the demonic representatives. Palo stepped forward, "We welcome you back. Not all of our kingdom's members are skilled in normal interaction."

A chuckle sounded throughout the demonic gathering. I offered a slight nod to Palo. I tried to not let my amusement show through at his obvious jab. I could tell the man was attempting to be charming but I had a feeling it wasn't natural to him. Not that he was trying to deceive me, but maybe trying to impress me slightly. I really didn't need that.

"If we can aid your transition in any way, please let us know," Alexander offered. His hair was short and trim, unlike Rhodes. Those gold eyes were very familiar though. They reminded me of the way Rhodes's eyes often shifted.

"You can aid me in one way," I spoke softly, but with directness.

"Of course," he bowed.

With a small smile, I spoke. My words were sharp and delivered with a cruel note.

"You can start by explaining what the hell has happened to this kingdom?"

5

RHODES

My lips twitched at her direct and sharp question. It suffocated the room with unease and made my father shrink. I enjoyed that far more than I should have. His eyes kept finding mine. I offered him the blankest look I could manage. Bastard didn't deserve my politeness.

"Your Majesty?" Raphael asked in concern.

Gray's hair swung against her back in a dark, thick wave that sparkled with silver. She stood tall and confident. Her confidence had my cock hardening against my leather pants. It was common in shifter communities to have women serve as alphas. In fact, the only reason my father and Adyen's father were leaders had to do with the archaic atmosphere within the social circle of royalty, not our pack. Within our groups, most of the shifter groups were led by women. Her ability to command this room was doing very little to curb my desire for Gray. I tried to ignore the consideration that there were probably other shifter males who felt similar right now.

"I would like for someone to explain to me how within less than two decades, our kingdom has socially and culturally fallen behind. Despite my brother's self-proclaimed dislike of ruling and my ability to place blame on him, I know for a fact that it is not completely his fault."

The room fell silent as she continued.

"Two decades and positive growth within the economy should have led to growth within social and cultural fields, as well as technology. Instead, I have seen medieval carriages and archaic social expectations."

I was happily surprised by her extensive knowledge of the state of affairs. While she had not been present within the kingdom, it was clear she had been paying attention to an extent.

She turned and continued, "I wish I could say it had been put toward the military, which could be easily adjusted for, but I don't think that has been the case either. That leads me to wonder, who our economic growth has been benefiting."

Silas spoke then, "Economic responsibilities are mainly handled by the four representatives."

I wanted to hate Silas. He had thrown her into this mess and took absolutely zero responsibility for this kingdom. He didn't even have pride enough to argue for his reputation. Instead, he would just let her fix his mess. At least he was informative. There was no ill will or insult on his end. He just wanted the burden gone.

Gray's eyes narrowed on the representatives. I found myself moving toward her quickly. With a soft whisper, I spoke against her ear, "I would suggest instigating an investigation on the specifics of budgetary activities, instead of calling anyone out right now. They may run."

Her eyes flashed silver, but she offered a nod. She spoke then, "I will leave you with this thought, I plan on fully investigating this problem and correcting any… errors, whether it be on activity or character."

I could tell Gray was making sharp eye contact with every

representative. It must have been relatively intimidating because Colliard made an uncomfortable noise.

I spoke then, my voice commanding and loud, "Your Majesty will meet with the representatives for dinner tonight. Look to them for any specific changes."

With that, Adyen commanded the separation of the crowd. His voice was sharp and within the native tongue. Luckily, it was a language only used for military reference and positioning nowadays. There had been far too many crossover elements with the Earth realm and ours to not adapt to English. I figured Gray was far more comfortable in English as well.

I could hear whispers and words of concern as my hand pressed onto Gray's leather covered back. She offered me a softer look that couldn't be seen by the crowd. I shielded her quickly as we stepped through the separated shifters and were followed out by the rest of our guard. I could tell she was tired. Her body was less tense than before though.

"How are you, kitten?" I murmured against her ear.

The hallway was filled with servants and soldiers. They kept their eyes either ahead or to the ground. Good. I looked down at Gray and had a moment of actual concern.

I often forgot how small she was. A lot of it was due to her personality, her confidence, and cockiness, but also because of her pure fae magic. The woman was deadly. At this moment though, with the softness of her body against mine, I remembered. How small she was. How young she was. How much responsibility she had on those tiny shoulders. I wanted to wrap myself around her in bed and force her to relax. To take the day off. To forget about her problems. To protect her. It was easy to protect her when she was wrapped up in my arms.

Gray's soft lips tilted down just a millimeter, "Exhausted."

Despite her not feeling well, I appreciated how frank and honest she had become with us.

"Today will be the most difficult," I murmured while guiding her up a set of large stairs. "Just make it through today. I promise it will get better."

A coy smile appeared on her lips, removing the heavyweight over our conversation.

"Are you offering me a happy ending, Rhodes?"

Despite my attempt to keep professional in sight of everyone, I laughed. She had taken me off guard and I didn't feel bad in the least. Gray's returning smile was absolutely stunning. I saw a few of the building guards take note of it.

"You can't do that in public." Adyen grumbled.

His eyes were narrowed on the set of men I had specifically noticed. At the massive guard's appearance though, they averted their eyes.

"Make Rhodes laugh?" She grinned again while looking between the two of us.

Somehow the problem of other men seemed not as worrisome with her stuck between the two of us. I could hear the other three keeping pace behind us in a protective formation.

"Something like that," He grumbled again.

I shot him a smile that only increased his scowl. We were past the group of guardsmen though so he seemed to relax.

Suddenly, Gray was striding down the hall toward a very familiar pair of pale green eyes and long blonde hair. The two women met in an instant clash of hugs and greetings that caused most of the servants to gasp in surprise. I shook my head realizing who exactly had been feeding Gray information all these years. Typical.

I pulled up next to Gray as those eyes turned onto me.

"Rhodes!" She exclaimed and pulled me into a tight hug.

"Mom," I greeted softly.

6

GRAY

"Now, that is unexpected," I mumbled while looking at Clara and then back at Rhodes.

Both of them were offering me the same damn amused smile. How the hell had I not seen this before? Of course, maybe that was why I had been so comfortable around him. I had been working with his mother since my emancipation.

Initially, I had no contact with the Horde lands. Then around my 17th birthday, Clara had sought me out and explained she would provide me with updates in case I ever wished to return. I denied my identity to her for nearly two years, assuming she would give up or believe she was wrong. Instead, she continued to feed me details about the state of the Horde lands. However, she had never mentioned how truly medieval they were. Nor that her son was one of my guardsmen.

"Mom." Rhodes chided. "We should move to her quarters. There are a lot of people out here."

Clara looked at me with a silly smile, "I will see *you* later, Your Majesty."

She was gone then. Rhodes led me toward a massive set of

silver doors before I could even catch my breath. A whirlwind of emotions rushed through me.

Exhaustion from this day. Relief the hardest part was over. The excitement from seeing Clara. Disappointment for not noticing the familial connection. I was usually very observant. The feelings were overwhelming and exhausting.

Before I had a chance to explore my new luxurious room, the doors closed on all five of my guardsmen and I. Silence and relief flashed across each of their faces. Alone. The six of us were finally alone again.

"I vote to be anti-social after today," Athens started with a small grin.

Neo grinned, yet his body was still tense, "Yeah, that was a lot of people. Way more than the amount that usually shows up for Silas."

I let out a tired groan and stalked over to the bed, which caused all the men to chuckle. Adyen sunk down next to me on the edge of the soft material before throwing his arm around my shoulder casually. I didn't flinch.

"Don't worry, Gray. It really will get better." Adyen assured with a charming smile. "If not, I can always just shift and burn away your problems."

I smiled at him while leaning into his shoulder, "Yeah? Would you burn down this entire kingdom for me?"

"Absolutely." He admitted softly, lifting a finger to raise my chin. "Anything for you, lil brawler."

"Reminds me," I sighed dramatically, "I haven't punched anyone in a while."

"She's looking for volunteers," Neo explained from the massive living room arrangement to my left. The man was a Gray translator in training.

"You wanna fight, baby girl?" Taylor whispered from behind

my right shoulder. Surprised and having been focused on Neo, I let out an exceptionally girly scream.

Silence followed.

Then, all of those assholes broke into deep, loud laughter. Bastards.

I turned swiftly into Taylor and tackled him full force, catching him off guard and stopping his laughter. Rhodes shook his head in passing as he moved toward Neo.

"Come on, baby. You've got him!" Athens exclaimed from the foot of my bed.

I didn't have him.

I currently had his one arm. I was pulling on it in a desperate attempt to roll us, while he laughed and held himself over me. Without powers, our physical size made a huge difference.

"Taylor," I growled. "Let me up."

He grinned as those emerald eyes sparkled with fire, "Work for your freedom, Gray."

I briefly consider wiggling my way out of this or using my decent, *read: average*, seduction skills to distract him. Then I stopped struggling because I thought of something *so* much better.

"Adyen! Help!" I exclaimed with amusement.

"Ohhhh," Athens chuckled, laughing so hard that he had tears streaming from his eyes.

I even heard Neo laughing with Rhodes.

"Gray," Taylor growled, bringing his lips close to mine.

"Should have let me up," I chided with a giggle as my protective dragon appeared behind Taylor. In one swift movement, the lethal demon was extracted from my body and tossed to the ground.

I grinned, taking aim and landing a soft punch to his side. You know, as a reminder of what a badass I am. His eyes lit up with flames of vengeance and retribution.

"Lil brawler," Adyen warned at my cheap shot.

I barked out a laugh before jumping into Adyen's arms and away from a very aggressive Taylor. My hands clasped over his shoulders as I dangled like a monkey off his massive build.

"Hand her over," Taylor demanded. I could see amusement dancing on his lips, but it wasn't enough to trust. I scrambled to Adyen's back to further avoid the demon.

"Keep me safe from the demon," I cooed softly, causing Adyen to chuckle.

"Don't use that voice, Gray. It's not fair to either party, or us observers," Rhodes called out over the paper he had picked up. I blushed, caught in my distraction attempt.

"Make me," I teased, without looking back at him. I did hear Athens's snicker, following his retreat towards the living room area.

My eyes were still on Taylor and my body molded to Adyen, who took a firm step back to distance us. Both of them had distractingly handsome smirks on their face. I realized this had little to do with me and was now a competition between them. Males. Freaking males. Why does everything turn competitive?

"I will," A soft British accent whispered behind me.

A gasp tumbled from my mouth before strong, tanned arms wrenched me from Adyen. I cried out in defeat as Rhodes let out a deep husky laugh. He had me. Damn it. I had taken my eyes off all potential enemies. He walked smoothly towards the bed and deposited me firmly in the soft texture.

"What am I doing in bed?" I asked curiously, trying to not let particularly dirty thoughts cloud my mind.

Rhodes unhooked my cloak and then untied my shoes with an ease and speed that impressed me.

"Nope," He chided tapping my lip with his thumb. "You need to rest before tonight."

"What about all of you?" I asked curiously with a slow

eyelash bat. I knew my attempt at flirting was weak at best. Remember, I know my strengths… a badass warrior? Check. Good at flirting? *Nope.*

"We will take turns sleeping," He explained with an unimpressed expression. "Now get some sleep."

"Yes, sir." I mock saluted.

Rhodes let out a deep rumble and pressed a kiss to my forehead. He leaned down into my ear and spoke so softly that I doubted Adyen could hear.

"Be good, Gray, or else I will have to tie you down until you sleep."

"Ooh." I cooed, actually blushing. "Well, don't tempt me with a good time."

He shook his head and departed, replaced by Athens's sparkling eyes and a broad smile. The muscular man climbed into bed and plopped down into the pillows dramatically. I let out a groan and stretched my limbs under the silky silver sheets, promising myself that a small eye rest wouldn't really be napping.

"Get some rest, baby." Athens whispered against my ear. I felt the bed tilt as Neo climbed into the other side. He offered me a soft smile and kiss to my forehead. Despite such a large bed, I felt entirely sandwiched between the two of them.

If it hadn't been for my exhaustion, early dawn wake up time, and universe travel into a non-earth kingdom from that day… I would have made extensive twin sandwich jokes. Instead, I found my eyes closing like heavy doors and my body pressing into the bed with relief. The last thing that played through my head was the sound of both men breathing calmly and deeply.

Peace surrounded me.

7
GRAY

*E*ventually, a soft voice woke me from my slumber. I instantly recognized it as Rhodes and Adyen's voices. Clearly, the *turn-taking* on naps had been a bunch of bullshit. I would scold them later. I knew the older guys were making sure that the twins and I got the rest we needed. How dare they try to take care of us...

I didn't move to get up just yet. My first reason was due to curiosity. I had always wondered what they talked about when I was not around. While it seemed like these men were an intricate, important part of my life... I couldn't forget they were, in fact, a group of individuals I had known less than a month. Sue me for being curious.

The second reason was due to my placement within the aforementioned twin sandwich. It had gone from a neatly made turkey sandwich on fresh bread to a squished PBJ. I was suffocating in warmth and affection. Even in their sleep, the twins were aware enough to not touch my shoulders and extensive scarring from my childhood abuse. Instead, Athens's chest was plastered against my back with his legs intertwined in mine. Neo had both arms wrapped around my hips right below Athens grip on my waist. My face was buried in Neo's chest. His breathing had become a lullaby of its own. I was surrounded by the scent of coconut and mint.

"Tonight, at the dinner, Gray will need to make the leadership aware of her plans moving forward with Mario." Rhodes stated quietly.

"What is the best way to go about this?" Taylor questioned.

Adyen hadn't said anything, but I had heard his rumbling voice only minutes ago.

"She will have her official coronation in a few days. I think it would be a good time to test her allies and enemies."

"Test?" Adyen questioned.

"Mario is well aware of her knowledge. He knows that she will announce his traitorous actions the moment she sees him." Rhodes explained. "He will either show up and kneel before her with apologies or--"

"Or he won't show up and it means war." I called from bed causing both twins to grumble their annoyance at my loud voice. So dramatic.

"Exactly," Rhodes stated loudly. I loved that he was unsurprised by my eavesdropping. In fact, it seemed he had expected it. That was the odd contrast of Rhodes though, transparent in all things... except for himself.

Before I knew it, my three other men were standing over the bed. Taylor looked tired and leaned into the edge of the bed. Adyen rose his brow in surprise. Rhodes just seemed amused. I realize at that moment I probably looked pretty funny stuck between the twins.

"What time is it?" I asked quietly to not wake them.

"Nearly four, you still have time before dinner," He stated as Adyen offered me a hand.

I grasped it firmly and found myself being lifted gently from the masculine twin sandwich and into his scent of ash. I chuckled as Athens rolled into Neo's space. Taylor looked longingly at the vacated area of the bed.

Like the mind reader he was, Rhodes directed him, "Get some sleep, Taylor. Tonight is going to be long and I need you focused."

The demon didn't argue but crawled into the pile of puppies. I snickered as Adyen carried me over to the living room section. I took the time to look around my massive room in appreciation. Someone apparently knew my taste well. I was betting Clara had some heavy influence on the choices made for my room.

The room was an open layout that spread from the heavy doors to a semi-circle of windows that spanned the back wall of the room. The view, while darkening at dusk, was forested and lush with color. My white, sizeable, wooden bed sat to the right of the room. With a low base and lush carpets strewn across the marble floors nearby, it looked far more like a throne than a bed. The sheets were a beautiful silver paired with a navy comforter and accents. Currently though, the three accents I liked the most were Athens, Taylor, and Neo. Can I just crawl into bed now? Why was I eager to leave again?

Over to the left was a living space that was currently occupied by the three of us and an assortment of large dark velvet couches. I examined the massive, *like enough room for me to stand inside,* fireplace and matching bookshelves. Each bookshelf seemed filled and organized with an array of exciting choices. It took away any possibility of the room being sterile or cold.

Finally, the last element I noticed was a set of two large white doors positioned off to the side. If I had to guess, they consisted of a bathroom and closet. I would be checking those out soon, especially since clothes were involved. I really wanted to get out of this leather.

Exhaustion was one of the worst feelings in the world. I felt it less than a human would, but there was no escaping the raw numbness that spread through my body. My head hurt and my body felt tense. My clothes felt itchy and tight. A migraine was building in the center of my brow. I knew that I needed sleep, real sleep.

"It's impersonal, but I think you can add some elements to it." Rhodes offered softly about the room.

Adyen's arms tightened around my waist gently to remind me of his presence. I agreed with him that I could add some more personal elements to my space.

"Where will the five of you stay?"

Please say here. Please. Please.

Ah. Shit. Why did I care where they stayed?

Because you *likkkkeeeee* them.

"The doors, outside in the hall, are ours." he explained softly with a knowing grin. I couldn't help the small, barely noticeable pout, that formed onto my lips.

"Nope!" Athens called from the bed as he rolled off.

Instantly, he was stalking over with a grace I forget he possessed. I felt Adyen stiffen at his predatory movements, but I pat his hand. My playful guardsmen made my protective dragon nervous.

Males, am I right?

"What?" Rhodes wondered out loud.

Athens stalked up to me and pinched my cheeks together to create a fishy face. His eyes flashed a melted silver with humor.

"What did I say about being cute? Pouting is not allowed. I can't handle it. You need your guards sane and your pouting is going to make that impossible."

I couldn't help the laugh that popped out of me. It was echoed by Adyen's chuckle behind me while Rhodes shook his head. Athens, with narrowed eyes, let go of my chin and fell down into the couch. His eyes were heavy with sleep and those perfect lips were pressed together.

"I *was* going to say," Rhodes stated in that deep formal voice I loved, "that some of our living quarters, specifically mine and Adyen's, connect to your closet in case of an emergency or attack."

I knew I was in trouble the minute I broke into a smile. While Rhodes meant it to be a safety brief, my mind was only thinking of one reason for that door to open at night. Or any time of day. Adyen chuckled softly against my neck which sent a shiver up through my spine.

Athens tsked Rhodes, "See your giving baby ideas."

Rhodes frowned with a raised brow, "I am absolutely not. Those ideas already existed."

"Fuck yeah, they did." I whispered softly against Adyen's chest.

My eyes were half closed with exhaustion still. While the other two men didn't hear it, they heard the bark of laughter that reigned down from Adyen. I smiled in pride. I caused that damn laugh. All me.

My laugh. Adyen's laugh was mine. I claimed it.

"Kitten, anything you want to sh--"

Rhodes was interrupted by a loud knock at the door. I groaned before rolling off of Adyen and stalked toward the door. My overprotective dragon was hot on my tail and caught the door handle before I could. He offered me a narrowed look before stepping in front of me.

"What?" He asked. His charming, yet quiet, voice was replaced with enough gruffness to rival Taylor. I heard a soft squeak from the hallway.

"Adyen," I whispered softly. His shoulders relaxed. He stepped aside to reveal someone who could only be described as adorable.

"Your Majesty," The young female started clearly with only a slight tremble, "I was assigned to your quarters to help you get ready for dinner."

I couldn't place an exact age on the shifter standing before me. She was built like a bird, with a small stature and skinny frame, but her hair was thick and crimped. The shiny ash blonde color was as fair as her skin and complimented her wide dark eyes. Those massive thickly framed eyes were the key to my unanswered question.

"You're an owl shifter?" I asked curiously.

The girl beamed and offered a curtsey.

"Yes, Your Majesty."

"Come in," I offered.

Adyen grumbled which forced the girl to pale. I shot him a look that only made him huff in disagreement more. I grasped the girl's arm lightly and pulled her into the room.

"What is your name?" I asked curiously.

The girl's eyes fluttered around the room. I saw her take in a relaxed Rhodes and grinning Athens. As she avoided looking at Adyen, I saw her eyes land on the two forms within my bed. It caused her cheeks to flame a bright red.

Oh yeah. That probably looked unusual, didn't it?

"Marabella." She stated with more confidence.

Her eyes found mine, and she nodded as if she had come to a decision. With a fluid motion, she stalked toward my closet. I supposed this meant she was staying?

I followed her happily to my closet, glad to be distracted from a possible upcoming war and all that fun stuff. I stopped at the door as Adyen bumped into my back before grasping my waist.

"Alright, handsome. Please stop hovering." I turned to face him.

I could hear Marabella moving about the closet and examining the extensive wardrobe I had yet to see. Adyen's honey eyes glowed, but his lips slipped into a slight pout. I grinned at his reaction and leaned up to kiss him softly. Then I pushed him back with enough force to make him growl. The sound wasn't menacing at all, but it elicited shivers up my spine in a way that made me wiggle on the spot. Marabella swore behind me and dropped something. Apparently, she found it scarier.

Without any more conversation, I turned on my heel and addressed the wardrobe.

"Oh, thank the stars!" I exclaimed.

Marabella laughed as I took in the entire room. The room was impressive, even by my standards. My eyes trailed along the crown molding to the chandelier lighting that briefly flashed as a fire hazard in my mind. All of my garments were hung based on color and material from wall to wall. The only wall not filled with clothing showcased my shoes and extensive jewelry collection. Overall, I was far more impressed than I had expected to be. Someone had done their research and shopping. I could also see a tall door in the far corner… my door to Rhodes's room, possibly?

"Everything to your liking?" She asked happily and drawing me from my musings.

"Absolutely." I stated sincerely. "Now, what should I wear tonight?"

Neo

It had been two hours of watching Gray get ready. I could honestly state I had never been more fascinated by something so simple. The act of watching Gray interact with her lady in waiting was odd within itself, but to see Gray give over control was even more startling. Usually, Gray was rigid about completing tasks on her own. It didn't seem to apply to the process of getting ready.

Her eyes were closed as the woman, Marabella, smiled affectionately at her. She had already gone through the process of washing her hair and was now intricately weaving the dark locks into a damn floral arrangement. It was odd to watch. It made Gray more real. Sometimes it was hard to remember that, with how confident and self-assured she was.

My brother and I had let our tattooed forms slink beneath the surface once again, Gray though hadn't glamoured herself since arriving. I could tell she had grown more comfortable with her true self after only a few hours. Athens was sitting next to me and watching the display with a rapt focus in his eyes.

"No!" Athens whined. "Don't put makeup on her. The lipstick tastes funny."

Marabella's eyes went wide and Gray let out a laugh from across the room. I tried to hold in my laughter but failed when Rhodes gave us a reprimanding head shake.

"Pay them no mind, Marabella. You do whatever you think looks best." Gray stated peacefully. "Athens is just a big baby."

I snickered at my twin's mock flabbergasted expression.

"Baby, you wound me. I am not a baby. I am a man."

Adyen lost it right before Taylor did. Both of them laughing caused Rhodes to give in. Even Marabella laughed, which left my brother to feign dramatic hurt. Gray squinted open a single beautiful eye and let out a light giggle that seemed to infuse the room with lightness. Everyone seemed to listen appreciatively to the tinkled sound, something that Gray missed and Marabella definitely did not. She was observant and seemed admirably loyal to Gray already.

Gray did that though. She inspired loyalty. She knew when to be unbearably cold and when to sit back to let some young woman do her hair. It was a trait that many rulers didn't possess.

"Alright!" Marabella exclaimed softly. "Time to get dressed."

Rhodes locked eyes with all of us, "Let's go freshen up for dinner, shall we?"

It wasn't a question. It was an order. I saw the grumble on

Adyen's tongue, but I just shook my head in a small motion. The five of us walked toward the door and I found myself sneaking a last glance at Gray. Her peaceful expression was one I envied. I hoped I could keep it on her face for the duration of this evening.

Something told me, that wouldn't happen.

8
GRAY

"Fantastic choice," I praised Marabella. Her large owl eyes sparkled with unfiltered pride at my words.

It was a fantastic choice, though. I hadn't been lying. The dinner tonight was essential and she seemed to highlight that with a conservative yet beautiful dress. It was made of a thick dark gray material that was black and accented with a small silver brocade pattern. The form was fitted in my chest, waist, and arms, but flowed into an A-line gown that swept the marble floors. While it was still autumn, she had accented the waist with a black leather belt that was edged in fur. It brought the piece together in a very *Henry the 8th Hunter Chic* type of way.

Yes. That is a style. I promise you. It is. Yes, I may have also just created it.

"Let me find a necklace," she insisted.

The dress had a wide neck that rounded the tops of my shoulder but showcased my cleavage as well as my scars. Marabella had yet to bring them up. When she did, I would answer her questions. Until then, I merely confirmed that I was okay with an off the shoulder dress and my hair lifted off my back. She seemed to catch on quickly and jumped into the task efficiently.

"This should be perfect!" she exclaimed, while slipping a multi-stringed diamond choker around my neck.

It was a beautiful piece and delicate enough that it didn't take away from my dress. A knock sounded on the door, I spoke while offering a grin.

"That would be the impatient ones."

Marabella smiled with a slight head shake before exiting the closet. I stepped out to greet them and was instantly scooped up into a hug.

"I missed you so much, baby!" Athens exclaimed earnestly.

I let out an honest to gods giggle as he swung me around.

"Athens!" Adyen growled before detaching me. "You'll be with her all night. Don't break her."

I scowled at him, "As if I am that breakable!"

Rhodes smiled, "Kitten, put away your claws. No one is saying you're breakable."

"You do look beautiful, though." Neo offered with a smug smile.

"Be still my heart," I winked at him while bringing a hand up to my forehead dramatically.

Taylor pulled me away from Adyen gently while stalking toward the door. I grinned up at him.

"Hungry or something? What's the rush?"

His sparkling eyes narrowed on my face, "Hungry *for* something."

I bit my lip before I could stop it, "So, not dinner?"

"I'm sure it would taste fantastic." He rumbled appreciatively while looking over my body. I found my toes curling at the imagery he was painting.

"Alright, you two. Break it up," Adyen commanded with hidden amusement.

"Marabella," I turned around at the overwhelmed shifter.

"Yes, Your Majesty?"

"Will you be here tomorrow?" I asked.

"If you wish." She offered softly.

"See you then. I want you officially assigned to my quarters." I informed her.

I tossed her a grin before stalking through the main door. I was instantly assaulted by the many different sights and smells of the castle.

The hallway itself was relatively calm but lined with guards in anticipation of my travel throughout the castle. I didn't focus on the faces of those guards and instead made my way past them while feeling reassured by Adyen and Rhodes directly behind me. I could hear music coming from somewhere within the castle walls and the scent of food drifted ever so lightly to the upper floors.

"Sounds like a celebration," I murmured quietly.

"Leadership is still here from earlier. They are being entertained by Silas. However, the representatives await your call for dinner." Rhodes explained quietly.

"We will be taking the side entrance into the dining hall to avoid the crowds." Adyen spoke softly. I loved that he had thought of that because I wasn't in the mindset to be on parade like earlier.

"Alright. Let's get this over with."

Gray

Somehow this was precisely how I imagined this dinner going. Awkward. Terribly awkward and uncomfortable. There was absolutely no way it could have gone differently. Mostly because of Colliard. He was a problem.

The small dining room was lavish and lit with expensive

candles that accented the warmth of the fireplace. Everything was shaped by dark wood. My plush sapphire-colored seat was extremely comfortable. It was literally the only item or person that was comfortable in this room.

We were currently drinking wine and sitting around the sizeable furnished table that was set for dinner. I sat at the head of the table while Silas sat on the other end. He had a smile on his face that bore no resemblance to the panicked man I saw at my estate. Clearly, he was relieved of his panic and burden. Handing off an entire kingdom can do that. Asshole. I reminded myself to ask him later how he had found me. Right now, I wished he hadn't.

"Your Majesty," Colliard began again. "I do not understand the importance of evaluating the current positions within the kingdom's political sect. For the past twenty years, we have been perfectly fine."

I knew that his words were supposed to be an insult. I took a long sip of my merlot before sighing.

"Colliard. That is the exact problem. You may have been fine, but the kingdom has not been fine. About your previous question-- No, I do not trust the advisement of anyone currently at this table. I have no reason to trust anyone who has not earned my trust. Do you think that is an unfair statement? Do *you* trust the word of individuals you barely know often?"

"No," he muttered.

His jaw clenched and his eyes kept traveling to the perimeter of the room where my guardsmen stood. I had hoped he would be too distracted by the music and food to seek out his sons.

"Well then, we shouldn't have a problem." I commanded.

"If I may say, Your Majesty..." Alexander interrupted from the right opposite of Colliard. He seemed thoroughly annoyed with Colliard, similar to the expressions on Henry and Raphael's faces.

"You may."

"We have been made aware of the delicate issue regarding the Dark Fae King, Mario. Is it true that you bore witness to his massacre of your parents?"

"Absolutely." I confirmed.

"So, how do we plan on addressing this issue?" Raphael asked his voice low and deep. He reminded me so much of Adyen in his mannerisms.

"It's been twenty years, surely you are not..."

"Colliard!" I sharply demanded. "Do not tell me what I am planning *to* or *not* do."

"I think some form of action must be taken." Henry offered his voice smoky like both of his sons.

"I agree," I stated easily. "I think the upcoming coronation would be a perfect opportunity to analyze our true allies and enemies." *Not just the dynamics outside of our walls either.*

"How do you propose we do that?" Colliard asked. Good man. Way to join the party train. I could feel my blood boiling at the idea of Mario within my vicinity.

"It's simple. If Mario shows up, I call for his public acknowledgment of such a deed and his execution. One monarch's death for the murder of two monarchs is reasonable. If he doesn't show up or acknowledge his deed, it's war." The room was silent at my declaration. I hoped they understood how black and white this situation was to me.

"You believe we can win a war against the Dark Fae?" Henry asked carefully.

"Yes, I believe I can win a war against Mario." I stated quietly. "If it makes you feel comforted, we have the Light Fae kingdom as allies."

"The marriage contract!" Alexander exclaimed in remembrance. "You plan on honoring that?"

Oh. What a question, Alexander. I could feel every masculine ear in the room listening to my answer. Hopefully, they would enjoy it.

"No. I do not. However, I don't think that the Light kingdom needs to be made aware of that yet. The concept of an alliance proves more useful in the early stages of the plan than an actual marriage alliance. Besides, if we go to war, they will join sides with us whether there is a wedding or not."

"How can you be so sure? The game of war is not one you are familiar with." Colliard snapped.

Bad move Colli. I was done with this conversation and had permanently lost my appetite. I stood, causing the others to rise, as I made my way around the table.

"This was a courtesy to the four of you." I snarled quietly. "I was not asking your opinion or requesting input. This is how we will be handling this situation, so be prepared, come the coronation, to handle the outcome either way."

A series of nods and murmurs sounded as I placed a hand on Colliard's cloak-covered shoulder. I moved close to him and let out a menacing growl in response to his bullshit games. It wasn't polite, but it was effective.

"Do not play games with me, Colliard. Do not ever think you're even capable of playing on my level." I whispered, loud enough for everyone to hear. "The kingdom is changing whether you like it or not, so be prepared."

Without dinner in my stomach and a subtle migraine growing again, I made my way to the doors where my guard now stood.

"Enjoy your dinner, representatives. Silas, I will speak to you later." I called from over my shoulder. The sound of the door slamming shut filled me with relief. My entire posture dropped once surrounded by my guardsmen.

"You did fantastic, baby girl!" Taylor whispered softly. "Fuck them."

He slipped an arm around my waist gently as Neo brushed my cheek with long, warm fingers. Rhodes and Adyen began leading our way down into the hallway toward the music. Athens began to hum a soft song in response from behind our group.

"I *am* starving right now," I admitted quietly.

Adyen let out a quiet rumble, "How do you feel about a private balcony overlooking Silas's party?"

"The party he isn't at?" I chuckled. "Sure, why not."

As we turned the corner, a familiar face spotted us and made Taylor grow tense. I sighed as Palo drew near and stopped talking to one of the guardsmen nearby. It was clear these were the doors leading to the private balconies, so what was he doing here?

"Your Majesty!" Palo exclaimed, "I was hoping for a word."

"Speak," I directed in a near grumble.

Palo's eyes found Adyen and Rhodes before flashing me a smile.

"Alone?"

"Absolutely not," Neo spoke before Adyen did.

With a direct look to Adyen and then to Taylor, I nodded my head to the side. I stepped outside of the guard structure and walked with Palo maybe five feet. It was enough that when Palo smiled at me, Adyen let out a low rumbled growl. Protective bastard. I felt myself smiling almost.

"This better be worth my time," I stated.

Mostly, because I could be eating. Honestly, if I had to pick between Palo and food, food wins every time. You just don't interrupt a woman on the warpath for food.

"I know I am not a representative yet, Your Majesty," he stated confidently. "I hope to be in the future and am honored that there is even a chance to work closely with you. I can already tell that you are as smart as you are beautiful."

Teacher's pet. Teacher's pet. Suck up. Why don't you blow

some more smoke up my ass? Does this work on inflated egos usually?

My expression must have said it all because Taylor chuckled. I tried to be an adult and keep my face even, but something about Palo made me tense. His eyes were filled with wisdom and a secretive nature that seemed unnatural. Everything about him felt scripted and forced. I would much rather he be an asshole if that was his nature.

"If you become a representative, Palo," I spoke directly. "I would expect you to tell me your real thoughts. Not what you think I want to hear. More so, I hope that your goals would be aligned toward a better future for this kingdom and not an archaic past. It is a time for bold decisions, not the status quo. We are having that very issue with our current representatives. I hope to not repeat it. Do we understand one another?"

Palo's eyes sparkled with surprise and then something else. His face morphed from the forced mask into an authentic look filled with a serious nature. It was a far better look. He nodded in confirmation and I was glad he was so damn adaptable. I suddenly felt as though I had handed him the world on a silver platter. The unease in my stomach released though. Maybe he would put the mask away.

"Your Majesty," He stated softly. "My Queen. Thank you for your time."

I was about to respond. I was about to step away from him. Almost as if a premonition hit me, my nerves and anxiety sparked. It filled me with unease and caused a rapid release of memories. Of Damon. Of my adopted parents. Of those men. I was about to run from it all. Distance myself safely.

Then he did it.

In retrospect, I blamed myself for wearing an open neck and shoulder dress. I was asking for accidental touches, right? It wasn't unusual for someone to pat your shoulder or squeeze it in passing.

Except it was unusual for me.

It was my worst fucking nightmare.

My trigger.

I thought I was brave for wearing these dresses and felt as though I had improved so much. Except, Palo showed me how terribly wrong I was. How circumstantial my healing had been.

His hand slipped up to touch my bare shoulder softly before passing to leave. I didn't even have time to flinch before his skin was removed from mine. A shiver of panic pulsed through me. I distinctly heard a sharp snarl and growl, followed by Taylor's voice commanding him to leave. I must have looked amiss for him to stop his departure.

A chill wormed its way out of my gut and into my ribcage. I could feel myself shaking as my eyes fluttered shut. The memories of other hands began to crawl their way from my subconscious.

They unburied themselves like the living dead and let out roars of victory.

They craved a win.

They desired my demise.

This was what I had expected when Rhodes had touched me. Now, he touched my shoulders with such familiarity that I knew nothing else. I thought he had been erasing the harm done to me. No. He, *they* were the exception. An inaccurate test of my wellbeing.

"Gray?" Neo's asked softly, wrapping his arms around my waist gently.

I could barely keep my eyes open but forced my attention on him.

"He triggered her," Adyen snarled.

"What is going on?" Palo asked quietly.

I could hear the confusion in his voice. The question was followed by a loud growl and curse. I could almost feel the room shake with power.

I met Neo's eyes, but couldn't speak. I could still feel the distinct grasp of Palo's palm on my skin and it made my insides curl uncomfortably. I wanted to shave off that skin. I wanted to bleach myself and burn off any contact with him. I had forgotten how awful it was when others touched me. I had gotten used to my men, my guard.

"Let's get her upstairs," Rhodes demanded sharply.

I felt Neo lift me into his arms as my head fell to his chest comfortably. My panic was moderately better as his warmth seeped into where Palo had touched my skin.

"It's going to be okay, baby girl." Taylor stated gruffly.

We were moving, and my eyes were shutting. I couldn't feel Adyen or Athens around me. I had a feeling they were with Palo. A groan rumbled from my lips at the thought of him. His hands had been so cold. It had been awful.

"Is she okay?" A familiar voice asked. Clara.

"Mom," Rhodes began quietly. "Will you start a bath for her?"

"Of course." She whispered as I felt the world drop.

I was actually being lowered to the couch on Neo's lap, but my sense of everything was off. I could feel my heart beating fast and my head spinning. I needed the feel of him off me. I needed Palo off me.

"I will take her in there," Rhodes said softly.

"Adyen will freak," Taylor groaned.

"I will have my mom grab her a slip and I'll stay clothed."

I could hear the water running and my body began to tremble with shivers. I felt like a failure. What was wrong with me? Why didn't I have the capability of brushing off his touch, instead of acting like a freak? Tears began to well in my eyes. We were moving again.

"Test the water," Clara commanded softly. I was set down in a vanity seat as Clara began to help me out of my heavy dress. I couldn't see myself through the tears.

My skin was so cold. I could feel ice and darkness leaking from my inner sanctums to infect the surrounding area like a virus. My eyes fluttered and rolled back as I sagged in the vanity chair, my lace slip doing little to keep me warm.

"Mom, can you prepare some tea or get Marabella?" Rhodes asked quietly, his voice soft and soothing from behind me.

"Rhodes," I mumbled as my body was lowered into a pit of searing water.

"Don't worry, kitten," He soothed while stepping into the tub with me.

I briefly realized how funny he looked fully dressed in a loose top and leather pants. He pulled me into his chest as both our bodies became submerged in the bubbly lava pit. Why was he wearing clothes?

"Why do you have an accent?" I mumbled quietly instead.

It was a question that had been boggling my mind for some time. His mother, nor father, had an accent. Well, they did, but the Horde's accent sounded faintly eastern European, not British.

Due to the cross over between the Earth realm and Fae land, most of the Horde's inhabitants had adapted to English rather than the native language our lands were established in. The accent had derived from the area that the first human interactions had come from. Most individuals could barely notice the difference.

I was distracting myself and I knew it. Anything to keep the ice away.

Rhodes hummed while musing my hair gently, "SE starts training at thirteen, so Adyen and I started three years before the twins and two before Taylor. Unlike most units, we were separated often to ensure that we were prepared to protect the True Heir, no matter what. Around seventeen, I was sent to an Earth realm military base in England for three years and picked up somewhat of an accent."

I had to keep him talking. My pulse was slowing and body warming.

"Why thirteen?" I wondered and looked up at him. "Also, how old are you?"

Rhodes chuckled while kissing my temple gently. "Thirteen, because it allows most of our training to be finished by the time physical maturity has been met. As for my age, Adyen and I are both in our 25th year."

I hummed, "I'm 21, but I figure after some time we will stop counting with immortality and all."

He smiled, "Most shifters live an extended period, but we were never told the Heir guards were given immortality."

"It's a secret." I curled further into him. "I'm not sure how it is imparted, but I know that during your swearing-in, immortality is given to you. I believe it is similar to fae immortality. Once your body and mind reach maturity, you stop aging. It ensures that I will always have guards, prepared and youthful, to watch out for me. My mom told me that. At least, I think it was her. I can't remember if my father was part of the conversation."

"It may be part of our brand," Rhodes rationalized before pulling up his right sleeve.

My eyes trailed greedily along his dark tattoos to find a navy colored one amongst the black. It was a crown that wrapped around his forearm in carefully placed detail, I found my hand trailing along the pattern with absolute fascination.

My magic sparked in recognition as a soft purr came from Rhodes's throat. The sound sent shivers through my chest and heat between my legs. I looked up to find a pair of deep, gold eyes watching me with a hooded heat. I could feel warmth flooding my body as the promise of his hands on me became a reality.

"Kiss me," I demanded softly in a throaty voice. I crawled further between his legs as my knees parted to sit on top of his lap. Those golden hands curled against my hips in a bruising hold that made my throat go dry and mouth water.

"Kitten," He groaned softly as my nails dragged through his thick light hair. "You just had a panic--"

I silenced him before his words could be finished. I could smell his expensive scent that trickled through my nose and encouraged me to deepen my kiss. It took all of a second for Rhodes to take over. My control freak. Those hands pressed me into him as his tongue demanded my cooperation. I moaned as I felt him hardening underneath me. I moved against him, encouraging friction.

"Please," I mumbled against his jaw as I kissed toward my goal. I pulled lightly on his golden hoop earring with my teeth as a heated hiss came from his soft lips.

"Tell me what you need." He groaned while grinding against me with controlled movements.

I whimpered at the feel of his hardness pressing into my almost bare heat. I had no bra and no panties on, just a slim, silky slip.

"You," I gasped as his thumbs traced the underneath of my breasts and moved to tease my hard nipples. I arched back further into him as those perfect lips took control of my pleasure.

I moaned at the sharp feel of his teeth on my breast as he toyed with my nipple in a teasing and intoxicating manner. I could feel my icy power seducing his jaguar out to play. A low growl echoed against my chest and encouraged me to rub up against him. It was when I heard a rip that I realized Rhodes had shredded my slip down the middle, leaving me completely bear to him.

"Rhodes," I mumbled with my eyes closed in pleasure. "I want to feel you."

"I know, kitten," He whispered against my bare breast as a hand slipped between us. "I'm trying to keep some level of control for tonight, but I'll give you what you need."

I was about to ask, but then his tanned finger slipped into my wet heat. I cried out in pleasure as a growl echoed against my mouth. Rhodes held my body in complete control as he captivated my mind with soft heated words. Those fingers were practiced as they moved and easily pulled forward the climax he was looking for. I could feel it gathering power as my entire body rushed with our combined energy. His jaguar swam through the iciness that was my soul. He added heat to me that I didn't know was possible.

"That's right," He purred against my lips as his thumb drew wetness to my clit. "Come for me, kitten. I want to see you explode on my fingers."

His words brought forward an icy explosion, a rumble sounded through Rhodes'ss chest as I cried out his name. I could feel the lethal power of his jaguar roar in my head as his dominance filled my senses. For the first time in my life, I gave my power over to someone else. Someone I trusted.

My hand gripped his forearm as a trembling shiver of heat flooded me and sealed me into a hazy heated state. I swayed on his lap as Rhodes pulled me forward into his rumbling chest with affection soft words. *Damn it*. I was totally acting like a kitten right now. He was right. Of course, he was right. I was his goddamn kitten.

I wish I could have been more upset.

"Gray," he mumbled softly. "You are so perfect."

I nuzzled into his chest, "Thank you, Rhodes."

He grinned and tipped my chin up, "Who knew an orgasm would make you so agreeable, so sweet... like a cute, little kitten."

"Bastard," I yawned against him. His hands trailed my scarred shoulders and I didn't even have the energy to flinch. My body was filled with heat and happiness.

We sat like that for some time, both of us bathing in the tubs continual flow of hot water. I could feel my skin burning, but damn, I didn't even care. How could I? I felt so loved and comforted. For the first time in my life, I felt no need to rush. I appreciated that he wasn't pushing for anything else.

Due to the previous sexual abuse, I had endured, my confidence in my sexuality was a fragile thing. I knew that. Being around these men made me feel free of those demons. Liberated, even. I had been with a few people since my emancipation, but this was different. This felt loving and real.

"So if we are immortal," Rhodes started as he smoothed my hair, "what does that mean for our ability to die?"

So damn pragmatic, always thinking. I looked up and smiled softly.

"Ah," He grinned. "Now that is a smile I love."

I smiled more, "I smile a lot, you ass."

"Not like that," He murmured softly. "But the immortality thing--"

"Immortality doesn't mean invincible." I explained. "We can still die. It's hard because we are super powerful and all that shit… but we can still die like normal. *It just won't be by age*. Usually, we get killed by enemies… like my parents. "

"I'm sorry, kitten," he soothed. "I didn't mean to bring up bad memories."

I shrugged, but curled further into him.

"Most days it doesn't hurt."

There was a quiet knock on the door. Both of us looked up and Rhodes smiled.

"Adyen."

"Come in," I called out softly.

A massive dragon, in man form, filled the door. I instantly offered a small hand as he moved forward and sat on the steps leading up toward the tub. The entire space was a marble white with massive open windows that let in a breeze that fluttered the light sheer curtains. Adyen's dark hair and honey eyes seemed to contrast the whole room. My hands curled around his as Rhodes continued to smooth my hair.

"How are you?" He whispered quietly. I could see his body's tension and knew that it was taking a lot out of him to not haul my ass out of the tub.

I sighed, "Better. I need to talk to Palo, though. I don't want him to think this is about him."

"He's been dealt with," Adyen growled softly.

I rose a brow, "Adyen, if he's dead, I'm going to be pissed. It won't help my attempt to unite this kingdom."

Rhodes chuckled, "He's not dead, just a little bruised."

"He didn't do anything wrong technically." I pointed out but shivered.

Adyen snarled, "I would have kicked his ass for touching you anyway."

I grinned, "So possessive." My finger tapped his nose.

"No shit," He drawled with a smile, "I'm a fucking dragon, Gray. Hoard and all."

"Oh!" I sat up. "What do you collect?"

Rhodes chuckled as a blush stained Adyen's cheekbones.

"Um, it changed recently."

"What did it used to be?" I tilted my head.

"Precious stones," He explained softly.

"And now?" I rose a brow. Rhodes let out a louder laugh and tilted his head back.

Adyen twisted his lips, "Okay, so sometimes you leave stuff around... and it may have found its way into my possession."

"You're collecting my shit?" I grinned.

He groaned and flushed further.

"I like seeing your stuff all over my room."

I squeezed his hand, "Well damn Adyen. That's sorta sweet."

Rhodes chuckled more, "See mate? She didn't freak."

"Why would I freak?"

Adyen sighed, "I mean in the Earth realm, collecting a girl's shit is like… weird."

I laughed at that, husky and loud, "You are a dragon, Adyen. Rules are different."

"So damn perfect," Adyen muttered.

"I'll even add something to it for your birthday." I cooed and leaned forward to kiss his cheek, "When is it?"

"My birthday?" He asked confused. "Um... It's April 23rd, but we don't usually celebrate."

"Why not?" I frowned and looked to Rhodes, "What about you?"

Rhodes blushed this time, "Umm. November 12th and our birthdays have really never been a big deal."

If my birthday had been September 15… I looked up and scowled, "What is the date, Rhodes?"

Adyen laughed, "The 13th."

"What the heck?!" I exclaimed. "We should have done something to celebrate."

Rhodes shrugged and pulled me close, "This was enough for me, spending time just the two of us. Plus, I got to see my mom."

I frowned, "Fine, are you sure though? We could hold something."

Rhodes shook his head while placing it on top of mine, "I'm just happy you are safe and inside the Horde."

I sighed and looked to Adyen, "Fine, but I need to know everyone else's."

"Ours is December 6th!" Athens called from the bedroom. I

chuckled as the door opened and both sauntered in with relaxed smiles. I knew they were doing their best to keep me in a relaxed mood.

It was an odd feeling, being comfortable around a group of men. If you had asked me a month ago... this situation would have made me panic more than Palo's touch. Tonight? It felt perfect. Like they were the balm to my pain.

"Taylor?"

"He's with Palo," Neo explained. "But his is March 25th."

I nodded, "Well then, that's settled. Now, you can't escape a birthday celebration... Rhodes." I ended with narrowed eyes on the relaxed jaguar. He opened one eye and offered me a lazy cat smile.

"As much as I love this bathroom party," Adyen grumbled, "Can we move somewhere more comfortable?"

I nodded, knowing his big frame was uncomfortable on those tiny bath stairs. I motioned for a towel. Athens handed me one as I stood up. Adyen let out a low growl as Athens let out a small strangled whimper from his throat. I frowned and looked at Rhodes, his eyes on my shredded wet slip that was very see-through. I flushed as both men scattered, leaving Neo to help me down the slippery steps. Those black eyes sparkled with mirth and heat.

"I love that blush," He growled softly. The noise was unexpected from him as he left me to wrap myself in a towel. I rose my brows at Rhodes. He shrugged his shoulders in light humor.

After Rhodes left, I spent my time brushing and prepping my hair for the twisted braids Marabella would most likely do tomorrow. I wrapped myself in a soft cotton towel and applied rose water to the underneath of my hairline while brushing my teeth. I was hungry, but overall, I felt much better.

"Food," I groaned as I moved toward the living room. Everyone but Taylor was spread out and eating from the huge antipasto plate that had been delivered. I instantly spread brie cheese and jam over some fresh bread before stuffing it in my mouth. I sighed in relief.

"Baby," Athens brought my attention to him.

He stretched out and placed his head in my lap as Neo gently brushed through my wet hair. The two of them kept me warm like bookends. I could hear Adyen and Rhodes talking briefly, but nothing of vital importance.

"Yes?" I mumbled while stuffing another bite in my mouth.

"Come meet our mom tomorrow?" He requested with a slight plea. I smiled.

"Sure," I nodded. "Neo, will you be coming?"

Neo paled slightly, "No. I have to see my father, unfortunately."

"Do you want me to make a *Queenly decree* for you push it off?" I offered with a wink, trying to keep it light. He laughed but shook his head.

"No," he sighed. "I need to see the bastard, but give Mom a hug for me."

I nodded, "Will do."

The natural breeze that moved through the room smelled of flowers and moss. I could see the stars twinkling down upon the warmly lit villages that surrounded my castle. I was excited to see the Horde's citizens, to learn the problems plaguing this kingdom. I was already so possessive over this place and my people. I knew this was why I had avoided my position in part. It came far too naturally.

At some point, my head slumped into Neo's lap, and the warmth from Athens's body expanded to my waist as he wrapped his arms around me. I fell asleep quickly with the sound of Rhodes's soft words to Adyen about my coronation's security.

If immortality included this type of peace and security, maybe it wouldn't be terrible. Perhaps it would be filled with light and warmth, instead of my icy darkness.

Gray

"You little bitch. You horrible, horrible little bitch."

"Just stay quiet. Your daddy said I could hurt you as he does."

"We got this bitch from foster care, like a little puppy she followed us home. Now, she's ours."

"Baby girl," Taylor whispered while shaking me. I gasped as my back arched and eyes opened to a pair of concerned emerald eyes.

"Fuck," I whispered. "Sorry, what's going on?"

"You were whimpering," Taylor mumbled while pulling me from between the twins. Apparently, Adyen and Rhodes had retreated toward their room. I tried to ignore the loss I felt at that. My legs wrapped around Taylor as he walked toward the living room, pulling me down onto the couch.

"You heard that from your bedroom?" I smiled. "I think that's called screaming."

He chuckled, "I slept on your couch after leaving my brother."

I swallowed, "I didn't mean to react like that--"

"Hey," He whispered with an intense gaze. "Palo shouldn't have touched his Queen like that anyway. It was inappropriate. Expect an apology from him."

I pressed my head into his shoulder as he gently kissed my neck. He stilled at the assumed closeness to my scars. I pulled back and smiled gently, "It's okay."

Taylor looked exhausted, but he nodded before pulling a blanket around us. I curled into his chest. My head rested on his bare skin that showed through his opened shirt. I could see the crown tattoo that filled the center of his chest. It was surrounded, almost hidden by the other tattoos.

I pressed a finger to the artwork as his leather scent and power, a smoky haze of raw strength, jumped across my skin like a smooth wave of water. I drank it in and nuzzled his pale skin which was warm to the touch.

"How are you after tonight?" He asked gruffly. "Last time something happened, you left us."

The blunt gruffiness of Taylor was usually appreciated. Today, I nearly groaned because... Fuck, I hadn't even had a cup of coffee. The sun was still hiding. I looked up at his expectant gaze.

"I won't leave," I mumbled. "It's different this time. Everything is different."

He hummed his agreement, "You promise to tell me if you ever want to run? I can't deal with that shit, Gray. It scared the shit out of me."

He was pushing me. He always did. I sighed, "I promise, as long as you promise to be honest about how you're feeling."

"I'm fucking pissed at Palo and annoyed to be back here," he answered simply. "But I'm happy to have you in my arms."

I looked up at him, "You make it seem so easy, Taylor."

He flashed me a sexy grin and moved forward to nibble my lip gently.

"Baby girl, it is simple. I hate the guard, but it led me to you. You're my entire world now, so if it means putting up with the guard... so be it."

I blushed, "Your entire world, huh?"

He grinned and rolled his eyes, "Is that all it takes to make you blush?"

I scowled, "I am not blushing."

His chest rumbled, "Goodnight, baby girl. Remember your promise."

"Remember yours," I grinned before closing my eyes.

For the first time in years, I didn't worry about waking up to an anxiety attack. I had made a promise and I couldn't run away from it. I couldn't run away from them or the kingdom. I was in it for the long haul now.

I would be strong for this kingdom. For my people. For Clara and Marabella. For my men. For my brother. I would be the strength this kingdom needed.

9
GRAY

"Come on, baby!"

Athens pulled my hand as we walked through the front gates of my large castle. I smiled at his excitement and quickly caught up, my dress light and airy underneath my silver cloak. My men had decided it would be easier for me to observe the kingdom if no one knew who I was. I think they also thought it would be good for me to spend some time with Athens. I noticed he had been agitated since seeing his father.

It was early morning. The small road that led to the village center was bustling with foot traffic toward the castle. I noticed servants making their way with natural smiles and laughter radiating through the road. It seemed everyone was happy so far, except for the apparent lack of forward movement in technology and culture.

Seriously. This shit was medieval.

Athens began explaining, "The four main villages, each led by their representative, surround the castle and work together in almost everything. The representatives themselves have houses that rest along the castle's border wall. My father lives in a massive house there, and the hope is that they would be able to warn the castle of any offensive attacks."

"And your mom?" I asked curiously. My booted feet peeked out from under my silver cloak as we walked quickly along the sunkissed mud road. Athens was dressed more casual today, as well. He had a short sleeve white shirt and black leather pants. I nearly drooled at the way his biceps and chest muscles flexed under the cotton material. I could see a dark tattoo on his shoulder that peaked from under his cuff. I assumed it was a crown, but didn't stop to ask. I also wanted to know where his mage tattoo was… I would bet it was silver.

"Mom raised me in a small house." he grinned. "But she likes it that way. She is the best ink mage around. It's a shame that neither of us gained that ability."

"I still don't get it. How do you find out what type of mage you are?" I asked curiously.

"The gods choose," He grinned. "Apparently, something about me screams metal."

THAT IS SO NOT AN ANSWER DAMN IT.

I chuckled with masked frustration, "What does that even me? Can you control metal? Like, all metal?"

He nodded and smiled at my curiosity, "I will show off later. I don't want my tattoo form taking over in public. Then everyone will know who I am and who you are."

I sighed, "True."

After walking for a mere fifteen minutes, we came to a broad main street. It was paved with brick and shaded by massive trees that grew along the road. Every shop along the way opened to the bustling activity awaiting outside. It seemed the morning was a very popular time within the kingdom. We continued to walk down the main road toward a smaller, more residential section.

Then a soft meow had me turning on my heel.

I shot forward to save a small white fuzzball that was in

harm's way. I cursed as a carriage tumbled past in the exact spot the cat had been. A woman on board apologized, but I was captivated by the little fuzzball in my hand. Holy crap. A kitten. Well, that was ironic.

"Rhodes is going to get a kick out of this," Athens snickered.

I watched as the small little face tilted up to meow again. A pair of bright golden eyes sparkled at me underneath heavy soft fur. My magic sparked and I tilted my head getting a weird vibe from the little creature. I was distracted by its cuteness though.

"Hey, you," I cooed as Athens laughed again. "Aren't you a pretty..." I held up the cat and stared at its private parts, "Girl. You are such a pretty girl."

Athens slipped a hand around my waist, "A pretty kitten for a pretty girl."

I smiled authentically because I could. I was undercover, no one was watching, and for once, I felt as everyone else did. I was merely a woman going to meet her man's mother… With a kitten. Look at me being normal! Once again, showcasing my extensive range of talents regarding normality.

"We have to keep her," Athens declared quietly.

"Do you want to be kept?" I asked the little fuzzball. Its gold eyes sparkled as it clawed itself up my sleeve and atop my cloak covered shoulder. I grinned at Athens as he shook his head and pat the fluff ball.

"What should we name her?" Athens mused as he pulled my hand toward the residential area.

"We should have Rhodes name her," I responded happily. "Make him feel like the responsible cat parent he will have to be."

Athens chuckled, "I think out of everyone, Rhodes would be the most responsible parent, except for maybe you."

"I would be a terrible parent," I grinned.

Athens cooed, "I could imagine it now, 'Mom, little Suzy pushed me on the playground.' 'Well why didn't you punch her?'"

My head snapped back as I laughed loudly, "Very accurate."

It made my stomach clench in a nervous, yet exciting way, to think of a future with Athens and my men. I had never actually considered children. I had always just figured it would never be part of my life. Despite my shortcomings, I knew the five men in my life would be absolutely wonderful fathers, even my crazy demon.

I punched Athens in the side lightly as he led me toward a little house. It was made of sleek dark wood and had a beautiful garden that seemed to be continuously blooming. A smooth red sign sat in the garden that merely read, Ink Blood Tattoos. The scent of lilies and grass surrounded the entire building.

"Mom!" Athens called out as we approached the building with ease.

My little white kitten curled onto my shoulder, stretching against my neck, and began purring. It didn't bother me that the cat was touching my shoulders, oddly enough. The vibrations from her purring were relaxing.

The door opened as a short woman, maybe five feet in total stepped out. Her hair was a thick dark mass of curl, piled and held up with flowers. She offered a bright smile to both of us. Her face was so similar to her sons that I wondered what characteristics they had gained from Colliard.

"Mom," Athens pulled her into a tight hug with enthusiasm. "This is Gray. Gray, this is Laurena, my mom."

"Wonderful to meet you, Your Majesty," she bowed politely. "I hope my son has been the sweetheart I raised him to be."

Her voice was musical, and there was a youthful vibe that sparkled in her dark eyes. I could see laugh lines that encouraged me to assume she was the reason Athens was so playful.

"Call me Gray," I encouraged. "Thank you for having me over. As for Athens..."

Athens snickered as I rolled my eyes. His mom smiled and opened her door to welcome us. I was overwhelmed by the coziness of the small residence as I stepped past her. The wooden walls were covered in herbs and bookshelves that smelt of parchment. A compact kitchen and table sat near a comfortable sofa set that looked well-loved. I instantly set my eyes upon a set of doors that I assumed led to the bedrooms and bathroom. Other than that, an extensive collection of windows sat on the back of the house and overlooked a beautiful garden. This woman obviously gardened.

"Your garden is beautiful," I mumbled sweetly.

Laurena flushed, "Thank you, Your Majesty."

"Mom, do you have any of those cookies?" Athens wondered while spreading out in a chair. I sat down and watched his mom move toward the kitchen.

She chuckled, "You've been gone a month, Athens. It's not like a lot has changed."

"I didn't know," Athens shrugged. "Neo mentioned things would change when we left."

"How is your brother?" She asked quietly.

The plate she set on the table had small little cookies and an assortment of other fresh pastries. I didn't hesitate to take a small orange cookie that was shaped like a flower. It melted in my mouth as I moaned with pleasure. Laurena smiled and Athens winked.

"Good," Athens nodded. "Actually, way better since meeting Gray."

"Huh?" I asked confused.

"He's talking and stuff now," Athens grinned smoothly. "Like a real boy."

Laurena hit Athens's arm, "Stop it."

"Yeah, Athens," I teased. "Neo is just not as loud as you."

Laurena hooted, "Gray's got your number, Athens."

Athens rolled his eyes, "She's got everyone's number mom. She's a big bully."

I gasped and punched his shoulder as my kitten moved slightly, peeking out from my shoulder. "I am not."

"Don't worry about him." Laurena rolled her eyes. "He needs a good hit to the head."

I chuckled, "Well if your mom said so." I gently bopped Athen's head as he chuckled, loud and deep. The laugh caused my kitten to jump down onto the well-loved wood table and lazily stretch its legs.

"And who is this angel?" Laurena asked with a soft coo.

"First grandkid, congrats," Athens snickered.

I rolled my eyes as Laurena gasped, "Don't tease an old woman like that."

"You are not old." I smiled softly as Athens ruffled the kitten's fur.

"No, don't worry, Mom," he continued. "When we have kids, it will be all over the kingdom."

Laurena's eyes went wide, "Wait are you two--"

"Dating?" He grinned. "Madly in love? Something like that."

I shook my head and nudged his shoulder, "Stop it. But yes Laurena, we are dating, and I'm also dating--"

"Your favorite son," Athens whined dramatically. "All four of them actually. They are always stealing her attention from me."

"Oh, wonderful!" Laurena smiled with big eyes. "Your guard is made up of the finest men this kingdom has raised. Those boys have brought so much light to my life. I was thrilled when Neo and Athens got placed with them."

"Yeah," I smiled. "They are pretty fantastic."

A buzzer went off as Laurena stood, "Just a moment, I've been preparing a large batch of ink for a blood mage."

"How's business been?" Athens wondered.

I was still smiling from her easy acceptance of my relationship. Unlike the Earth realm, having a multi-partner relationship didn't seem odd to her. That acceptance was something I hoped would be universal. It wasn't like we could keep our relationship secret for long.

"Wonderful." She frowned though. "We actually have a large batch of new mages coming to get tattoos today."

"Why does that upset you?" I asked with no filter.

She sighed, "Well, they are humans who have the sight. I just am hoping to not attract attention from a certain nosy demon."

"Palo," Athens explained. "He's obsessed with the ability for humans to become mages. He's gone to the Earth realm several times in pursuit of understanding it better."

I nodded, "So these individuals are from the Earth realm?"

Laurena nodded, "I don't have a terrible amount of information, but that is what I presume."

As the morning progressed, pastries were finished, and tea made. I could feel the autumn weather rushing over the garden and filling the house with an overwhelming sense of rightness. I leaned into Athens as he softly played with my hair and talked to his mom. Laurena had an easy way about her that made you feel comfortable. She was relaxed, yet friendly. She was filled with stories and jokes, about Athens mostly. Her stories about Neo were from the past few years. I gathered he had started to visit around his mid-teens.

Once lunch came around, a knock sounded on the door. It caused Athens to grin as he stood up and Laurena began clearing the table. I aided her, despite the numerous times she told me not to. Queen or not, I wouldn't leave a dirty table.

Laurena turned toward me and took my hand softly, Athens could be heard at the door unlocking it.

"Thank you, Gray." She whispered. "I have never seen Athens this content. I can only imagine how you are affecting those other boys."

I blushed, "Honestly, Laurena, I rely on them a lot. Probably more than they do on me."

Laurena smiled and gently hugged me, barely touching, before a quiet meow sounded. I turned toward the table as we watched my small kitten jump into an empty coffee cup. I shook my head and picked up the small fuzz ball.

"Baby!" Athens's voice sounded. "The humans are out here!"

I jumped at his enthusiasm and moved toward the door, squeezing past Athens's massive form. I immediately swayed in surprise, my hood falling back down as the small cat on my shoulder curled underneath the falling material. I blinked while categorizing the woman in front of me.

Human? No, Athens had that wrong. I looked up at him and frowned before examining the power level of her group. Eight humans. Two mages. And I wasn't sure what the woman was.

We were the same height, exactly, and both squished forward so that we were nearly nose to nose. It was an odd feeling looking into someone's face at the exact same height. A pair of dark lashes fluttered in surprise as I took in her entire feminine demeanor that screamed delicate.

I felt a surge of protectiveness, similar to how I felt in meeting Marabella. She had no muscle, no fighting power physically. Yet she didn't seem weak. That wasn't unusual for me, really, but something about this woman screamed that she was a tiny flame in danger of being blown out. It didn't escape my notice that she was surrounded by eleven large males on all sides. I kept my internal snarling to a minimum and assumed that she wanted them there.

Her face was extremely angular, heart-shaped in nature, but was accented by a pair of dark raised brows. I could see her taking stock of me as I did the same. It was clear that both of us were keenly observant. I ran my gaze over her silver-white hair and almost frowned at the questions that formed in my head. Was that natural? It had to be because our hair was nearly the same length and you couldn't keep dyed hair healthy at waist length usually. Her violet eyes traced my scar without an ounce of pity. Instead, wonderment and blunt curiosity filled her face.

In some ways, the two of us were very similar... in others, completely different. The outfit she wore was casual by Earth realm standards. Then again, all of them were dressed more casually than Athens and I. I envied her comfortable jeans.

"Wow," Athens hummed with a laugh. "Do you have a long lost sister that we didn't know about, baby?"

I smiled at his words because, despite our hair color, we did look very similar. I briefly wondered if the possibility existed, I stuck my hand out to be polite.

"Gray," I offered while smiling. I didn't know this woman, but her power interested me. I couldn't tell what it was. That alone was a feat. Athens kept his chuckling low and deep.

"Vegas," She smiled with a bright flash of teeth. I heard the distant and muttered calls of my title and bows from her men.

"Your Majesty," A clear voice said that was echoed by another.

"Oh, Vegas," I purred with a smile. "I like you. Isn't it awful? And the carr-"

"Carriages?" She winced. "I know I was very confused by that."

I smiled broadly, "How long are you in town?"

Vegas looked up to pumpkin eyes, his smile familiar and his voice reminded me of Taylor's tone, "Your Majesty, we are only here for today. The sight holders are receiving their blood ink tattoos."

I frowned and looked up to Athens, not because of what he said, but his familiar voice. Athens smiled instantly.

"Edwin and Byron are cousins to Taylor."

My eyes went wide as I rose my brows. Was this why Palo

was obsessed with the human-made mage? I needed to figure this out. I looked back at Vegas.

"Stay an extra day? We can place you in the castle after you've been inked up. The coronation is tomorrow, and I would love for our newest mages to be there."

Vegas smiled, "I like 'inked up' way more than 'blood ink tattoo.'"

Her eyes went to the two mages that seemed in charge, but I noticed a tall redhead moving closer. She had a redhead too! We had a harem club in the making.

See? I could totally do friendship.

The blonde mage with soft brown eyes spoke. "We would be honored, Your Majesty."

I narrowed my eyes at him and wished that Vegas had delivered the news. I wasn't a fan of men answering for their women, but I also didn't know the situation well enough. Vegas smiled at me knowingly, so I decided to hug her.

"Fantastic," I grinned and pulled her close.

Once again our height made the hug odd, but I also noticed something else. The power that resonated within her chest seemed to burn against my ice like a beacon in the dark. I felt an odd, warm affection spread through the two of us that was familiar. I really would have to look into this possible relation thing. This connection wasn't normal. I wasn't confident how I would feel about either of my parents cheating on the other.. or maybe they hadn't? Perhaps she was a distant cousin? If cousins looked creepily similar... Hell, I didn't know shit about genetics, unless it was related to humans.

No. This was *other*. I felt as though I had been around her my entire life, more than Esme even. I didn't even know this woman's last name. Not that I had one either. I mean, I had a title… but still.

Athens chuckled, "Vegas, count yourself lucky. This one doesn't do affection."

I growled and hit his abs.

Vegas smiled, "I'm a hugger."

I shook my head, "You, Vegas, are fascinating, would you care to have dinner tonight? You can meet my men and it looks like yours wouldn't mind a meal."

She nodded, "Absolutely, my boys would love that."

A flush attacked her cheeks as a small chuckle echoed around her. Was it unusual for her to refer to them as a group?

With a nod, the three of us, Athens, my kitten, and myself, strode away from the group. I briefly heard Laurena greet them, but was far too enamored with my evening plans to listen. Athens kissed my cheek gently.

"Back to the castle?" I asked curiously.

Athens shook his head, "Not yet. I want to show you something."

Neo

As I approached the home I hadn't returned to in years, my entire body tensed as my power begged me to let loose. It felt my defensive attitude and tension. It wanted to defend me. If I had been this powerful those many years ago, Colliard wouldn't have had the opportunity to hurt me.

I could have missed the meeting today and joined Gray and Athens at my mom's house. I wasn't positive I could handle my mom's somber looks and Gray discovering the drastic contrast between the two of us though.

The truth was, I was ashamed. I was embarrassed because, many years ago, I hadn't stood up to my father. I had been powerful enough, yet every beating had left me feeling powerless. Every time he hit me, I remembered that if it wasn't for him, I wouldn't have even been alive. He told me it was a parent's right to treat their kid how they saw fit. Why did he see beating me as a solution? I hadn't been a bad kid. My disappointments ranged from an occasionally failed test to not attending a meeting my father wanted me to. Normal kid shit. Apparently not though.

Touch was hard for me. I understood Gray's aversion to it. I trusted her and my twin though. When they touched me, it didn't make me uncomfortable. I hoped that I could help Gray heal enough that she felt similar. Although, despite my heartache and abuse, I knew she had survived worse.

It wasn't that I discounted my pain, but rather, that I knew I could be strong like her. I sighed and approached the massive marble stairs that seemed to mock me. I had a feeling of how my father had grown to have such a luxurious house, but I wasn't going to like it. Fury at the possibility of him committing anything that could hurt our kingdom, *Gray's* kingdom, would push me to an edge I wasn't ready to jump off of. I was always there though. I was always on the edge of jumping.

No servants greeted me at the door. It didn't surprise me in the least that my father wouldn't have prepared for our meeting. I strolled through the ostentatious halls toward his office. I knew security would have warned him of my arrival. I rose a hand to knock on the familiar red oak doors.

"Come in!" A deep voice demanded, making me flinch. I cursed myself internally. I was much larger than my father now. I was also more powerful. This shouldn't be a fucking issue.

"Father," I kept my face blank as I strolled in, and stopped behind the chairs that faced his office. It was a small office and he liked it that way. He thought it made him seem larger. I wasn't sure it was effective.

My father smirked and looked up at me from his paperwork, "Ah, I see you actually listened to one of my requests."

I rose a brow, "You asked to see me and I had an opening.

What do you need?"

Colliard frowned, "I wanted your opinion actually."

So he wanted intel.

I sat down and leaned back, "Regarding?"

"Our future Queen." He muttered before flipping a page over. "She mentioned this possible war. How serious is she about that proposition?"

So fucking serious it would make your head spin.

"I don't need to rephrase Gray's opinions. She explained exactly how she felt about it to you," I was quickly growing tired of this.

My father smiled, "So familiar." He tsked, "Has my son taken a liking to our Queen?"

I groaned because *this* had been what he wanted to know. It was also a talking point I had very little guidance on. I didn't want to assume anything, but at the same time, I didn't want to discount our familiarity.

"Of course, Gray means a lot to me," I stated quietly. "I literally guard her with my life."

My father grunted and flipped through another page, "How is the finance investigation going?"

I rose a hand, "Stop. I am not here to give you intel. If this was all this was about, then I'm leaving."

My father's eyes widened, "I just wanted to see you and get your opinion on what was going on."

I rolled my eyes and stood, "If you have questions ask *Gray*. My loyalty is with her, not you."

I saw his jaw tick and temper jump, "Boy, your loyalty is *always* with your family."

My head was shaking before I knew it.

"My family is not you. Not anymore."

I left and tried to ignore the pen I felt hit my back. It was petty and ignorant. The minute I left the office I felt slightly disappointed in myself that I hadn't gotten more information, but... I just hated the man. I couldn't be around him. As I walked down the stairs I heard him start to yell in his office.

The old man had quickly become unhinged.

I checked the clock and headed down the massive marble staircase. For once, I didn't look back at my previous family home and looked forward to the enormous castle. My home was there.

For so long, I hadn't belonged. I hadn't had a home with my mother, nor my father. *Now* my brother and I had a home with our Gray.

10

GRAY

"Wow, Athens. This is beautiful," I whispered softly.

"Yes, you are," Athens teased with a playful tug on my hair. He stood next to me as we leaned over the railing attached to the massive metal deck that overlooked the kingdom. My kitten slept on Athens's coat, discarded a few feet away from us. Surrounding us was thick, lush greenery that surrounded and matched the Horde. The deck had been built into the vast mountainside that surrounded the land and looked down upon its lively vigor.

"Smooth talker," I mumbled softly.

"Not really," He smiled and pressed a kiss to my temple. "It really is beautiful, though. I used to come and meet Neo here before we joined SE."

"Why did you grow up separate?" I whispered, I regretted it as soon as Athens's face fell.

"When dad grew tired of mom, they separated us. It was around the same time as Silas took over. He assumed Neo would grow up to be more powerful because he showcased alchemy powers." He spoke in a low tone, "So, he left me with mom."

"Your mom would have probably loved to have both of you at home," I mumbled.

He nodded solemnly, "Yes. I assume she would have, but it ended up that I got the better end of the deal in some ways. My father has a bit of a temper issue. Neo has always blamed himself for *'leaving me behind'* but if anything, I feel bad that I didn't save him from our father. I know he hurt him."

I wanted to ask. I wanted to ask so badly and then kill Colliard. I also knew that was Neo's story to tell and I wanted him to tell me when he trusted me.

I soothed his shirt sleeve, "Well, now you can both be together. No more separation, I promise."

Athens flashed me his trademark smile, "I know, baby. You have no idea how much it means that we can finally be together as a family."

"Did you ever imagine you would be with the same woman as Neo?" I asked quietly.

His mom's easy acceptance made me wonder what his expectations had been about his future relationships.

"Baby," he purred nipping my ear and causing me to jump, "when we became heir guards, we sorta knew that if you wanted us, we would be yours."

I rose a brow, "But you didn't know me."

He wiggled his eyebrow, "Remember, we were all slightly older than you at your birthday celebration. When we got sworn in and found out we would be protecting such an angel, I couldn't believe my luck."

I scoffed at these words. *Angel?* I think not.

"Then I learned she punched people and was a badass warrior Queen, so I fell a little more." He whispered softly and pressed a kiss to my nose. "You are so much more than any of us expected, so to answer your question, I think I always expected to share you. I just didn't know about the unknown factor."

"What unknown factor?"

"*You*, baby," he mumbled. "We had no idea if you wanted us."

I leaned forward blushing, "I don't think this situation has a return receipt anyway." I felt like a teenage girl fawning over my first boyfriend.

Athen's chest rumbled as he nipped my lip gently, "No, we were part of a one time only sale."

I laughed, "Pretty high quality for a sale."

"Aww!" He cooed, "Thanks, beautiful."

I rolled my eyes and went to turn. Except Athens didn't let me, his hand slipping to my hip as he pressed me against his tall, hard, body. I let my head fall back as I looked up into his beautiful eyes that sparkled with silver.

"Do you trust me?" He whispered in a thick husky voice.

"Yes," I answered softly.

"Can I touch your back?" He asked with a soft kiss to my jaw. I nodded.

"What are you doing?" I whispered as he turned me in his arms.

I could feel his length against my back as his massive hands gripped my waist gently. My tongue moisturized my lips as he watched the action with heavy eyes.

"Showing off, remember?" He mumbled with a husky deep octave.

"What?" I frowned, but he nodded toward the front of us. I felt my mouth drop.

The railing from our metal deck had been deconstructed and laid flat in a delicate pattern. It spread out in a grating material that expanded out over the drop of the mountain. The only thing that would hold up an observer was that thin metal extension. Athens smiled and took a step forward, the material holding our weight perfectly.

"I've got you," he whispered and kissed my ear.

I could feel the wind licking any bare skin and moving my hair in a gentle pattern. I swallowed as we stood at the edge of his extension and looked out upon the afternoon landscape of my kingdom.

Mine. The primal savage inside of me rejoiced at my claiming of our land.

"This is all yours." Athens voiced, in a serious deep voice that was unusual for him. "Every person relies on you to be their strength and protection. You don't even notice the weight of that responsibility though because it comes so naturally to you. Baby, I have never seen someone so suited toward leadership. You are the True Heir, Gray."

I flushed and preened at his praise, "Thank you, Athens."

We stood there for nearly an hour, his hands smoothing along my waist and lips trailing against my neck in a gentle playful pattern. Despite the view, I grew distracted by his lips and turned to feel them pressed against mine. He groaned as our lips met in a playful match that had me pressing into his broad chest.

"Taking us to stable ground," Athens chuckled as we walked back toward the deck. I could feel his magic surrounded us and reforming the metal railing with ease. I doubt the move would make him break a sweat even.

As we met the metal desk, Athens gripped my thighs and brought them to wrap around his waist. He sat down and he kept us locked in the intimate and loving position. My hands spread across his massive shoulders as he trailed kisses along my face and neck. I could feel our bodies molding together with heated energy.

"I'm suddenly regretting taking you to a metal overlook and not somewhere softer." He teased before leaning me back onto my cloak. I stretched underneath him as Athens's lips trailed along my neck and chest. He unhooked the cloak and kissed me once again, a playful nip.

"Why is that?" I mused, feeling completely comfortable with him.

"Baby," He whispered above my softly parted mouth. "I need to taste you. You smell so damn good and your skin is so soft."

I felt a whimper escape at the thought of his lips and tongue on my skin. I nodded yes and ran my hands through his soft fade. Athens kissed along the neckline of my sheer dress as he nipped gently at my skin. I squirmed at the feel of his big body caging mine and his teeth against my flesh.

"You are so soft." He mumbled, while his hands trailed along my thighs and up to the hem of my dress.

I moaned softly as he pushed up my dress and licked down my stomach in a heated pattern. I could feel heated desire flood my center at the feel of his hard muscles under my hands.

The taste of Athen's power was metallic and seemed to vibrate the air itself with energy. I could feel his lips trail the heated skin that laid near my black lace thong. I thanked the gods I had put on cute panties today. I may have to live in a medieval town, but my undergarments had a standard.

"Athens!" I whimpered with heat. "Please."

"My Queen," He purred gently against the lace material at my center.

I could feel how soaked I was and moved against his lips to encourage friction.

"Tell me, what do you want me to do, Gray?" He whispered quietly.

I leaned onto my forearms and looked at Athens between my legs. I squirmed at the view but licked my lips in contemplation. With Rhodes, it had been different. Rhodes had wanted control. Athens was a different game. He was playful and I knew me telling him what I wanted was part of that game.

"Taste me, Athens." I purred gently. "Taste all of me."

He groaned and pulled the wet material from my body with

enough force that it ripped. My back arched in pleasure as his tongue met my damp heat. I let out a cry. His tongue's movement had my core tightening.

"Fuck!" I whispered as his thumb gently strummed my clit like a damn instrument.

I could feel my body tightening in arousal, from my nipples to my shaking legs. The heat from his body was overwhelming and melted my natural inhibitions.

"You taste like fucking sugar." He moaned in a low throaty sound that vibrated my skin. "Does that feel good, baby? Do you like it when I taste this pretty pussy?"

"Yes," I whimpered and clasped his head to my center.

I could feel my body jumping toward a release as he continued to playfully lick and nibble my center in a mindless pattern. Every time my body tightened for release, he removed his thumb and tongue. He would work me back up again and occasionally slip in a finger for my body to tighten around. I couldn't stop moaning and his name easily echoed off the forested area around us. I was positive a mental break was in my future if he didn't let me come.

"That's it, baby," He purred, "cum for me. Scream my name and cum for me, I love hearing those damn noises, Gray."

I gave in to the pleasure and let out a scream. My body flooded with heat and the taste of metallic filled my mouth. I had bitten my lip so hard it bled. I could feel the metal biting into me through my cloak and it brought a deep trembling shiver to my skin. The climax tore through me like a freight train and had my back rising off of the ground in ecstasy. Fuck.

"Oh, wow, Gray. You are so fucking perfect." Athens cooed softly and continued to lick me gently. I whimpered at the pressure as my body began trembling in post-orgasmic exhaustion.

"Damn!" I muttered. "That was something else, Athens."

He grinned, "I should be thanking you. You taste so amazing, baby."

I found my arms wrapping around his neck as he rolled us. His soft affirming words made me feel damn near angelic in his arms.

Athens smiled up at me as a soft 'meow' cried out. Both of our eyes opened in shock as we looked to our left. Our kitten temporarily named Fluff, jumped down from a thick forested bush where she had clearly been exploring. Which was good because I had totally forgotten about her. I shouldn't feel weird about getting all sexy with Athens in front of our little kitten… but still. I let out a small laugh at the thought as Athen's chest rumbled undermine.

"I can't wait to have Rhodes name her," I commented with a soft smile.

"After our little dinner? It's like a double date. I'm excited," Athens commented.

I laughed, "Except I have 5 boyfriends… and she has?"

"Eight, plus the two mages." He mumbled softly. "I don't know their relationship with her."

"What was she?" I mused out loud while resting my head on his chest.

"Isn't that a good question." Athens chuckled. "Maybe we can ask tonight."

"I don't want to move right now," I mumbled against his chest. He laughed and smoothed my hair.

"Baby, we can stay here all night if you want."

I felt my heart glow at his words. It was a soft feeling invading my heart, a dangerous feeling. A very dangerous feeling indeed.

Rhodes

I leaned back into my velvet chair and watched Gray dance with her new friend, Vegas. The two of them really did look related. I agreed with Gray. It would have to be something we looked into. Although family lineage was hard to track in the Horde and if Gray had escaped to the human realm… I supposed this woman could have as well. I turned away from Gray.

Lately, I nearly groaned at the thought of her. Since touching her yesterday, I couldn't stop thinking about her soft skin and persuasive lips.

"You're Rhodes, correct?" A voice sounded from nearby. I knew it was none of my guard units, so I plastered a welcoming smile on my face. A muscular man grabbed the chair next to me and sat down with a blank expression.

"I am, and you are?" I asked quietly, taking a sip of my ale.

"Grover," He answered with a friendly grin.

I nodded, and we sat there quietly as the music absorbed our thoughts. I was confident that he wanted to ask me something, but I wasn't sure what. I noticed that all eight of the previous humans, as Gray informed me, had fresh blood ink tattoos. Neo and Athens were talking with a few of them, specifically a tall blonde kid and a redhead. I thought their names were Rocket and Blue, but Athens was far better with names.

"Do you know anything about being a mage?" He finally asked quietly.

I rose a brow, "No, I'm a jaguar. However, we have two very capable mages here. If you want, I can introduce you."

He sighed, "I don't know, man. It's just a lot. I was human only hours ago."

"Sorta," I conceded. "But if you had the sight since you were young, you were always *other*."

"That's true." He nodded as my eyes fell upon Gray's bright

smile and smooth movements. She had even pulled Marabella into the mix. The small woman looked very overwhelmed, but happy.

"What type of mage are you?"

"Metal." He groaned. "I don't know what that means or how it was chosen. It seemed random to me."

"Athens," I called out. The man in question grinned and jogged across the small entertainment room. The entire room was filled with only essential help and a lot of food and ale. Music played softly from the stage and Gray's laughter filtered through every moment of quiet. I liked this. It was peaceful.

"This is Grover," I explained. "He's a metal mage and has no idea what to expect."

Grover grunted as Athens nodded, "Have you tested out any cool shit yet?"

"Like what?" The man seemed more intrigued.

Athens snickered, "Like this." I sighed as he flicked a hand out and Adyen's metal cup flipped onto his shirt. Grover let out a chuckle as the dragon's eyes narrowed on Athens with pure annoyance.

"Come on." Athens encouraged, "Let me show you a few other things while I avoid the pissed off dragon."

"He's a dragon?" Grover's eyes widened.

"Yep." He waved him toward the stage. "Come on."

Adyen scowled as they left and my chuckle filled the space around me. Neo, finally tired of being away from Gray, moved toward the dance floor and stole her. Vegas and Marabella laughed as they strode off. Well, Vegas strode toward me and sat down a few seats away. I noticed her adjusting one of her heels. I also took notice of the ten pairs of eyes that tracked her movements.

I smirked, understanding the feeling well.

"You can take them off," I offered. "Gray already has."

Vegas snorted in humor, "Dude, she's the Queen. It's sooo different."

I smiled, "I see why she wants to be friends with you."

"It's because I'm funny, right?" She wondered out loud.

"It's because your normal. Gray is being tossed into a very non-normal world," I sighed, "but you know what that is all about, don't you?"

Vegas nodded, "Yes, very much so. It's overwhelming. You all put off a lot of power, especially that guy up there."

"Neo," I explained easily, "is one of our most lethal team members."

I could see the confusion on her face as she observed the softness in his eyes and hold on Gray's body. The affection he held for her was written like a map across his skin.

"They are both predators. All of us are, Vegas," I warned quietly. "You and your men are as well now."

Vegas nodded with understanding, "It's hard to see that, though. When I look at them... the two of them seem to just melt together perfectly."

"She does that to all of us," I responded.

Vegas smiled nervously, "So this type of relationship isn't unusual here?"

I grinned softly, "The only aspect that is unusual is that we are her guard, not future kings. However, having multiple partners, husbands, or wives… that is not unusual. At least not in the Horde. It is completely dependant on the persons involved. If you have enough love in your heart to share it with multiple people, why limit it?"

Vegas's eyes went wide, "Yes, that makes perfect sense--"

"Princess," A dark-haired man called. *Decimus I believe?* "Come dance with me."

Vegas lit up, "Nice talking to you, Rhodes."

I nodded as she skipped off and left me to my curious

thoughts. In the time that I sat with her, it was impossible to determine what she was. I could smell magic on her, but it was undefinable as if it was everything and nothing. I couldn't tell if the magic came from her or if it came from somewhere else. I did notice that she didn't bare a new tattoo unless it was somewhat hidden.

I looked at Taylor and found him talking with his two cousins. Both of them looked defensive and quiet. I could see Taylor's temper leaking out.

"Taylor!" I called out. "Come have a drink, mate."

The demon grunted and came over. He spread out in a chair near mine and shook his head with disgust, "I fucking knew they, along with Palo, were doing something odd in the Earth realm."

"Odd as in a threat? Or just annoyed?" I asked feeling alert.

"Not a threat to Gray," he responded. "I don't question their loyalty, but I do question Palo's curiosity. Of course, due to their power levels, I can't read shit unless they project."

"Let's do our best to figure it out," I managed quietly. "From what I gathered from this group, they are fairly normal or were normal, at least. Not including your cousins. They were all foster kids placed within the same home after being found to have the sight. I don't see anything particularly odd going on yet, but we should continue to monitor the interest the mages and your cousins place on them."

I knew it wasn't of immediate importance, but I could tell Gray had taken a liking to Vegas. I needed to know if any safety concerns existed. Her safety and protection were immensely important to me. I felt a pull at my heart, knowing this peace and lighthearted fun weren't destined to last.

I promised myself that once this war was over, I would take steps to ensure the smile that graced her face would always be there.

Gray

This had been the perfect night. Now, I stood side by side with Athens, devious grins on our faces. Rhodes and Adyen were spread out on the couch facing us as Neo stood by the window, a small smile on his lips. I tried to ignore the tingle in my body from our dance earlier. Taylor's soft mumbled tones could be heard from the door, instructing Marabella on the times for tomorrow's coronation.

"We need to talk before tomorrow," Rhodes announced.

I rose my brows and became distracted from the situation at hand.

"About?" I mused.

Rhodes frowned, "You mentioned that you don't plan to honor your marriage contract--"

I smiled, "Of course not. I'm dating you five. How in the heck would a marriage to some random dude work?"

All four of them including Adyen rose their brows.

I frowned, "Are we not dating? I mean, unless something changed since the attack, I thought--"

"No!" Adyen practically yelled. "We are dating, for sure."

Rhodes nodded with bright gold eyes, "Just wanted to make sure you wanted that, kitten."

I smiled at Neo and Athens before looking back at them, "Yeah, I mean, I sorta like you guys."

Everyone laughed and my face flushed thinking about my time with Rhodes and Athens. Then, a small *meow* sounded, causing me and Athens to still.

"Why do you both look like you've done something terrible?" Rhodes mumbled quietly.

The kitten began to move in my hand and crawled up my back in a feat that would impress most mountain climbers. I tried to keep a straight face as a small white fluff ball tumbled onto my shoulder.

I wish I could have captured the expression on each face. Neo had already figured it out, sneaky bastard. He now sat with an amused smirk aimed at our shifters. Adyen let out a strangled cough of surprise as Rhodes's light green eyes expanded into large circles.

"What is that?" Adyen chuckled with a loud boom of laughter.

I looked right at Rhodes, "It's a kitten I found."

Rhodes's eyes lit up with humor as he sat back on the couch, "We are about to enter into a war with the Dark Fae... And you want to adopt a kitten? Or I should say, you *have* adopted a kitten?"

"I saved her!" I exclaimed and pulled her to my chest. "There isn't a right or perfect time for a kitten, Rhodes."

Athens grinned, "Yeah, can't control nature *Rhodes*. The kitten just happened."

Neo smiled, "Rhodes, you should have been more careful if you didn't want a kitten."

Adyen was laughing so hard that tears filled his eyes. Rhodes just looked utterly shocked. I smiled a winning grin.

"I got her for you, babe! I want you to name her."

"Fuck," Adyen coughed and laughed so loud he had to get up to leave.

I brought her toward Rhodes as the lethal man extended his hands with a narrowed gaze on her.

"I have no idea what to name her," Rhodes admitted and narrowed his eyes up at me. "You sure you want this, kitten?"

I kissed his cheek before placing the kitten in his hands.

"Of course, Rhodes. I always wanted a little kitten in my family."

He scoffed, "This is payback for the nickname."

"Yep," I cooed while petting her.

"Hey there," I cooed as she opened her eyes.

She looked around sleepily and took in her surroundings. Specifically, the one where she was in Rhodes's hands.

"Shit!" Rhodes exclaimed as the cat caught sight of him.

She hissed and flew out of his hands with her fur standing straight up. I grunted as her claw made contact with my nose. Oh good. That's what I needed. Another scar.

Athens chuckled, howling with laughter, and pulled the cat into his arms with a soothing motion. Everyone else was laughing as Rhodes and I shared a grumpy look. Taylor had graced us with a beautiful smile from across the room as he finished talking to Marabella.

"Fine. We will keep the little lunatic." Rhodes growled. "But you're changing the litter, Athens." I winked at Athens who looked bemused with mock horror.

"Lunatic!" Adyen said with a deep laugh. "That's her name."

Rhodes sighed taking a big stretch, "It fits."

Taylor grinned, "Plus, she's a little like Gray and Gray is a lunatic."

I narrowed my eyes at him and smirked, "If I'm a lunatic, I don't know what the heck you are, dude."

Taylor swiped my nose to reveal blood from my cut. He pressed a kiss to it. I tried to not blush, but he was stupidly sweet. Athens grinned and continued to make stupid cute faces at the cat. He looked insane. Crazy. An absolutely adorable lunatic.

11
GRAY

I woke to fur above my head and three muscular bodies in my bed. Wasn't this every woman's dream? I could feel Athens's arm wrapped around my center and Neo's chest to one side. Taylor starfished next to me as he mumbled some unfamiliar words and rolled over. Lunatic purred softly and clawed my hair.

It had been surprisingly easy to get someone to bring a modernized litter box and pet care supplies to the Horde. Until then, we were making do. I had also ordered a black studded collar for when she got larger. As of right now, she wore a black bow that said sassy badass. I may have been projecting with this cat.

I knew it was early, the dawn crisping over in a cool breeze that could be felt through my one open window. I had the coronation today and felt a level of tension expanding throughout my chest in a nervous wave.

Would I be a good ruler? I hoped to be. Would Mario show up? If he didn't, when would I make the announcement of war? I was nervous about what that would mean. I had only been here days. My investigation into the kingdom's finances hadn't revealed much yet. I just knew that there was something odd going on here and I was determined to figure it out.

"Your majesty?" A soft voice echoed through the room.

I squinted an eye open at Marabella. She wore a deep blue gown today with a little white hat. The girl was adorable.

"Yes?" I mumbled.

"I have started a bath so that we can begin the process of you getting ready. The coronation will be at 11 today."

"At night?" I asked hopefully.

She smiled sweetly, "Unfortunately not. Shall I have breakfast brought up?"

I nodded, "Yes, please."

"Alright, boys," I groaned once she left. "Gotta get up."

They all exchanged mumbled responses as I crawled out of bed and walked toward my luxurious bathroom. I closed the door and slipped off my sleeping shirt. The bathtub was filled with fresh flowers and essential oils that enticed me. I moved across the cold tile and slid into the heated water. Fuck. I needed that.

"Breakfast?" Marabella offered, as she slipped a tray onto a small table near the tub. I could smell fresh pastries, meat, cheese... and coffee. Thank gods. The first order of business, getting a motherfucking Starbucks here.

"Oh, Marabella!" I remembered. "Vegas and her men are attending the coronation. Will you make sure someone attends to them? I invited them last minute. You can even put her in one of my dresses."

Marabella smiled, "Any color? I am putting you in crystal and black."

I grinned, "Oh, just put her in a lighter color then. You know if you want, you can borrow a dress as well."

Marabella blushed, "I don't know. I'll be so busy during the ceremony."

"Do it anyway," I encouraged with a smile. "Do you have

anyone you want to look special for? Not that it has to be for someone other than yourself."

This was good. It was distracting me. I would have to be a badass bitch soon enough. Right now, I was 21 and talking to Marabella about boys.

Marabella blushed.

"Tell me!" I exclaimed while eating some fruit. Mmm... Strawberries.

"Okay," she smiled. "It can never happen, though."

"Forbidden love?!" I practically inhaled my fruit.

"Or he doesn't notice me." she sighed. "His name is Palo..."

"Shut the front door!" I breathed and smiled. "That is so cute."

I had my reservations about Palo, but he didn't strike me as dangerous. Moreso just sort of a politician type. Then again, once I asked him to not feed me bullshit, he seemed more authentic. I wondered what their history was.

"He's super charming in public." She sighed. "Total representative material. But, one day, I was working in the library and I came across his office. The demon is super smart. He has every text available and has a ton of earth realm contacts." I was now glad he had been assigned to the finance investigation. Apparently, he was a smart dude.

"Well, have you ever talked to him?" I asked quietly.

"Of course," She mumbled, "We have a bit of a difficult past, haven't always gotten along... plus I can't think straight around him."

I pursed my lips, "This is what we are going to do then, you are going to borrow a dress of mine and during the coronation procession, I am placing you two next to one another. Deal?"

Marabella bounced on her toes, "Okay, deal. Thank you, Your Majesty."

"No problem. And hey, in private, call me Gray."

Marabella nodded and skipped through the bathroom doors. I inhaled my food and coffee at a rate that was probably unladylike. Did I care? *Nopppppe.* Fuck that.

My bath left my skin feeling soft. Through the open doors, I could hear an abundance of activity and noise. I let my calm last another minute before I rose and walked toward my mirror. Marabella would be handling my hair and makeup, but I efficiently prepped my skin and brushed out my hair to condition it.

"Are we ready?" Marabella asked as I wrapped my body in a comfortable robe.

I nodded as she began her work. I closed my eyes for the majority of my prep and listened to the soft noises of my men eventually waking. They grumbled about getting ready but left through the closet door towards their quarters. I knew they did it to keep appearances up, but I honestly didn't care anymore. It was my kingdom and the men I lov… liked should be able to express that. I decided I would dance with each of them tonight, come hell or high water.

"Perfect!" Marabella sang happily.

I opened my eyes to find my hair pulled back in a graceful waterfall that showcased my thick silver highlights and black hair. My brows were shaded in slightly to showcase the diamond eyeshadow that surrounded my tri-layered blue eyes. I allowed her to apply a delicate, deep red lipstick on my lips before offering her an authentic smile. Looking good was always the positive side of an event.

I noticed that while Marabella hadn't changed yet, she had fixed her hair to showcase it's natural pale blonde, crimped texture. It reminded me of the waves you had after braiding your hair and brushing it out the next day. She had weaved in a soft ivory ribbon that pulled back some of the front strands and showcased her massive dark eyes. The styling made her seem older, especially with the light purple lipstick she wore. She could be described as almost ethereal.

"You look great," I commented authentically. She flushed and led me toward my closet. I gasped in excitement as soon as I saw my dress.

"Let's get you into it for the full effect!" She commented.

It fit like it was made for me. Probably had been. The body had a v-neck with small straps that were barely noticeable. Honestly, it looked like my skin faded into the same obsidian color as my nails at my neck and trailed down my entire body. The mesh straps made it appear that the gown was being held up seamlessly and the whole body of black silk sparkled with dark crystals. There was no hiding any of the curves or lines of my body within this dress. My dark heels only heightened that awareness. I loved the dress. Absolutely loved it. I took pride in my body, even though I had once wanted to hide it.

"The crown will complement these," Marabella explained while placing an assortment of rings upon my fingers and a pair of dark earrings. I dripped in shiny things and by gods, did I love it. I really sounded like a dragon.

"How's our girl doing?" Taylor called out from the door.

"Come in!" I smiled.

Taylor blew me away. I was confident that all my men were dressed similarly, but seeing him in the dark onyx armor that was a trademark to the Horde was satisfying. It was medieval, but beautiful. He had also placed his cloak on to accent the outfit.

"Baby girl!" He groaned and rose his brows. "You look--"

"Like she needs a cloak," Adyen grumbled in passing before squeezing my waist.

I chuckled at the two forms, him and Rhodes, moving through my closet. Marabella smiled and walked back into my bedroom.

"Do I look like a Queen?" I spun on my toes as my dress spread out around me.

"Kitten, you look stunning," Rhodes murmured and pressed a kiss to my temple.

Adyen nodded but narrowed his eyes at my dress as if it was evil. I snickered as Taylor moved out of the door. My footsteps took me toward my bed. Both twins were lounging in their outfits with Lunatic playing across their armor.

"She's so cute," Athens cooed, "even Neo loves her."

Neo flashed a smile, "It's true. She's perfect."

Rhodes scoffed, "This is ridiculous. My guard unit has been turned into--"

"Pussy cats?" Athens snickered. "Get it? Because you're a cat?"

I rolled my eyes as a knock sounded on the door, Adyen opened it and nodded toward someone outside. He closed the door, as Marabella slipped in, and offered me a smile. She had changed her dress.

"Holy crap!" I nearly shouted. "You look great!"

She did. Her slim body now showed off light curves in a bright pink dress that had cap sleeves and a long skirt. It was tight at the waist and showcased a bodice that had white lace appliques and small daisies that trailed down the skirt. It looked fantastic on her.

Marabella did a small sweet twirl, "Thank you so much, Gray. Really."

I grinned, "Just remember your mission tonight." She blushed as I winked at her.

A knock sounded, and her eyes went wide, Adyen went to the door. He growled lightly but opened the door as Palo strolled in with all the confidence he probably had. That was until he saw Marabella.

"Your Majesty..." He bowed, but stopped midway as his eyebrows shot up, "Marabella?"

I nearly jumped onto my toes as I watched the scene in front of me unfold. Palo's face went from charming to intense, those eyes raking over her small form as he reached out to her.

"What are you doing?" He asked in a strangled voice. I felt Athens laughing silently as Adyen grunted in understanding. I could read this situation from afar. Marabella couldn't though.

"What do you mean?" She asked quietly, with authentic confusion.

There was a light pink blush that seemed to fill her entire face as he pulled her close.

"I mean, you look stunning." He swallowed hard, "You always do… but let's get you a cloak or something."

Her lip trembled as she frowned, "Do you not like the dress?"

"No, I do," He rumbled instantly. "I just don't want anyone else…"

Marabella crossed her arms with a spark flaring in her eyes, "Well, why not?"

Rhodes shook his head as Palo frowned, "Nevermind."

"Fine, then." Marabella turned toward me. "Your Majesty, I will be waiting in line for your departure."

I watched as she strode from the room with more confidence than I expected from her. I was proud and knew she was on the track toward progress.

"Shit," Palo groaned. "Your Majesty, I was coming to say sorry and wish you luck, but if you don't mind…"

"Go," I pointed with an understanding smile.

"Yeah," Taylor teased. "Especially with all those guardsmen out there."

Palo snarled as he stalked out of the room with determination. I waited till the door shut before letting out a laugh and causing the others to smile.

"My job is done." I nodded in confidence. "Now, who is ready to get my crown?"

Gray

I had never been to a coronation. Apparently, it was a huge deal. As in the entire kingdom, and then some more showed up. I knew the Light Fae royalty had made an appearance, their quarters made ready the night before. I hadn't heard the Dark Fae were here yet, but I was giving them until tonight. Every member of the surrounding villages was in attendance and would be celebrating in local venues during the kingdom's feast tonight. I could feel the power coursing through me from the compounded amount of energy that could be found in the room up ahead.

The main hall was filled and I stood on the second level of the staircase, my guard surrounding me. Before us was a very graceful Marabella and frustrated Palo. I was proud of her for showing her backbone. If he wasn't going to admit his apparent feelings then screw him. Not literally though. Ahead of us was the main castle guard and I hoped to see, once we turned the corner, my new friend Vegas. The night before had taught me that I was capable of having friends.

Yeah! Go, Gray! See, I could be semi-normal. Actually, I was starting to think being normal had been boring compared to this. Plus, I get to wear fancy dresses here. Can we say the same about Denver? No.

Once the music began, I felt the entire crowd shift as our party started moving around the corner and into the long hall that would lead to the throne. I took reassurance from Taylor's hand on my lower back. It would stay until it couldn't anymore. I took a deep calming breath and strode forward.

The energy of the room was vibrant and each window along the long hallway vibrated with music and sunlight. Honestly, it was a goddamn beautiful day. But wasn't it good luck when it rained? Oh no. That was for weddings, nevermind.

My cloak, a sleek silver that floated around me, kept my body warm, but still showed off my black crystal display. I tried to tell myself that this was like prom. I hadn't gone to that, but it was similar right? Big dresses? Dancing? Celebration stuff? Okay. It was nothing like a prom.

Unless I was Prom Queen. Okay, I liked this idea.

My entire body stilled as I noticed the overwhelming amount of emotion displayed on the faces around me. The hallways were filled with mostly villagers, of all of whom had expressions that were filled with hope and pure excitement. Tears filled the eyes of many adults. Smiles crossed the faces of excited children. Why were they reacting like this? They had no idea who I was.

"You represent change and hope." Rhodes explained quietly. "It's exciting and overwhelming."

I nodded briefly as the music continued and the crowd changed from ordinary folk to the representatives and their clans folk. I noticed the material of dresses became more expensive as facial expressions grew more cautious. I found Vegas standing near the front left side in a large, light-colored tulle gown that made her appear to be floating. I wanted to thank Marabella's brilliant eye for fashion. It was always a good thing for friendship when you made your friends look good.

I was surrounded by friends, family, and allies. My curiosity laid in the non-friendly faces, a devious smile slipped onto my lips. Where, oh where, were my enemies?

At the top of the steps, stood Silas with a substantial lazy smile on his lips. I knew he had planned to serve as the coronation's administer and I had been happy to have him as part of it. I wanted our people to see us united. The music paused as I reached the top of the steps and my guard moved to spread across the top step.

"Citizens of the Horde!" Silas called out, in a voice that was smooth and happy, I turned to face the crowd as he stepped forward to a small table that the crown sat on. It was a beautiful crown, made of black onyx, with deadly savage points to it. It could be used as a weapon on its own.

"I have the absolute pleasure of introducing to everyone here our great land's True Heir. In her previous absence, I was honored to lead our country further. However, I think we can all agree that this is what a true Queen looks like. Gray is one of the most brilliant and fierce leaders I know. It is for this reason that I will be crowning her as monarch of our lands. Gray, if you will?"

His words, while charming and confident, hit home. I knew he meant them. The lazy son of a bitch was warming my heart just a little bit.

I approached him as he rose a hand to hold mine. I held it in unity as he spoke in a loud, brilliant tone, "True Heir, will you solemnly vow to lead the creatures of the Horde, and the lands thereto belonging, according to our law and statues?"

"I solemnly promise to do so." The words came out stronger than I thought.

"Will you, to the best of your ability and within the law, execute justice and mercy in all your judgments?"

"I will." I would. I could do that.

"Will you honor and maintain the desires of the natural gods that blessed this realm we now inhabit?"

"All this, I promise to do so."

Silas smiled, his dark eyes twinkling, as he lifted the crown upon my head. My eyes fluttered as words tumbled forth in a natural instinctual way, "These things I have promised, I will perform and keep: so help me, Gods."

As the obsidian material hit my head, a spark of power shot through me like a lightning bolt. My darkness shot out in relief as it filled every limb and nerve of my body. The room exploded in applause as stars danced behind my eyelids. Contentment filled me as my power collided with five branded souls.

My men. My guard. Their brands reacted and swelled with

relief. Metallic vibrations. A liquid drop of lethal, gold power. An icy blanket. A roar of black flames. A thick red smoke. All of it was mine and I, in turn, belonged to them.

I could barely hear the crowds exclamations because I was so in tune to the five men near me. My eyes opened as I faced my people. My kingdom. My responsibility.

Silas was smiling as he offered me a hand and led me down the steps. There was no sound, only a hazy warped sense of reality that had me watching every face I passed.

Marabella's wide, dark, eyes caught mine as a small frown dipped her brow. I assured her with a nod and tried to do the same with my men. Something had changed though, I could feel it. My eyes landed on my new friend and sound returned in full force. I noticed her panicked expression as she tried to hide near her men.

Something was going on.

Something had happened when my power had exploded.

Her power crackled through the room like a low ember and I wasn't the only one noticing. The bottom of her dress had been burnt, seared, and Edwin looked panicked. At least, I thought that was pumpkin eyes name. I nudged my head to point toward the door. She nodded in relief and rushed to escape, her entire dress producing tendrils of heat. I looked around and saw that only Palo and Marabella seemed to have noticed. However, her panic wasn't my first pressing concern. I was glad she had been able to escape though. I would have to ask her later what had happened.

"Tell Marabella to go find Vegas," I whispered to Rhodes in passing.

I felt odd, absolutely odd. A curious feeling invaded my chest. It was like my power had been extended and filled to a new level.

My jaguar nodded and moved his golden eyes to the couple. I continued my descent as Silas performed social graces. I needed to get somewhere private. The sound from the room was overwhelming and the scent of everyone's excitement was making my head hurt. Understatement for my migraine, but it worked.

"Silas," I mumbled. "I need to sit down."

He smiled through clenched teeth, "We have a private suite to overlook the celebrations."

Instead of traveling down the massive hallway, Silas turned the corner before the massive dark doors and led me toward a far more narrow entrance. I could feel my men behind me. Once encased in a dark, cold hallway, I stumbled and leaned into the stone wall. Instantly Adyen had me in his arms and was carrying me forward, toward another narrow set of stairs.

"Silas," Taylor snarled. "What the hell was that power surge?"

"No fucking clue," He mumbled. "Maybe a True Heir thing? Mine was nothing like that."

"The crowd got worked up into a frenzy because of her power," Athens muttered.

"I need to sit," I mumbled feeling dizzy.

I could feel the five of them under my skin like a snake that was wiggling against my very bone structure. I let out a series of curses that would make a sailor blush. My entire back began to burn.

"Fuck," I gritted out and pressed a hand to it.

"Nope!" Neo said and stopped my hand from touching my shoulder. "Sit down."

I frowned as he began to shimmy off my straps, I sat in a comfortable chair that overlooked the room that would soon hold the feast. It was an open-air balcony that showcased multiple couches and seating options. It was a place made for relaxing.

"Well, that is fascinating," Neo mumbled. "It seems that you are getting some new ink, Gray."

"What?" I frowned.

"That is sick," Athens chuckled. "You have one for each of us."

"Athens, I'm going to punch you. This hurts like a bitch," I complained.

Silas sighed, "This is 100% because you are the True Heir. I didn't get any unique markings."

"Now everyone knows she's connected to us," Adyen smiled as he pulled up a chair to face me. "How are you feeling, lil brawler?"

I ignored his possessive comment, "Depends what my back looks like."

"It looks like five small tattoos that span shoulder to shoulder," Rhodes explained calmly. "I don't recognize the symbolic language they are written in. It's most likely fae."

Silas nodded, "I would have to confirm, but I believe they are the traditional runes for the types of mages both twins are, as well as the shifter and demon clans."

I put my head down on Adyen's shoulder as he rumbled quietly. His vibrations made my body warm comfortably. I could feel the same type of connection that Rhodes's jaguar seemed to form with me. It brought a sense of peace forward within my heart and head. I knew I was safe with Adyen.

"How long until the feast?" Rhodes asked quietly.

"Less than an hour," Athens commented quietly. "The Dark Fae have yet to arrive, but the Light Fae are here, and Gray's fiancé--"

"Ew, please stop." I muttered as Adyen let out a growl. I would have snickered if it wasn't an accurate title currently.

"So what's our plan for him?" Rhodes asked quietly. I could feel his tension.

"Pretend there is a possibility and when war breaks out, which it will, I have an excuse to put it off. Then, I'll break it off eventually," I explained quietly. "Until then, we just need to avoid him understanding the scope of our relationship."

"He's going to want to spend time with you..." Athens complained quietly.

"I could just kill him and solve the problem," Neo muttered, which made me snort.

I looked up and he offered me a quiet shrug before looking over toward the balcony. Motherfucker was serious.

"Adyen," I narrowed my eyes at the dragon in front of me. "I'm going to have to dance with him, I need you..."

A low growl echoed through Adyen's massive body, his eyes bleeding to black, "No."

I frowned, "Adyen..."

Rhodes frowned and sat down near me, "I actually agree."

"Both of you are thinking irrationally. Ignore your animals for just a moment," I reasoned.

Adyen snarled, "My fucking mate isn't going to be dancing with some half-brained prince..."

"Mate?" I asked, my mouth opening in surprise.

What the heck?

Gray

Adyen flushed as Rhodes shook his head, "For shifters--"

A knock sounded on the door of the suite as Taylor, showcasing a bemused expression, went to open the door. I immediately stood as Marabella walked in with graceful strides. I wasn't confident what had changed about my lady in waiting, but something had. Her eyes were dark and concerned though.

I mentally placed our current conversation for later, piercing Adyen with a gaze that promised questions. I needed to know what a mate was precisely. It sounded very serious to me.

"How is Vegas?" I asked with rapt attention.

Marabella frowned, "She's fine. No one in her group will talk about what occurred at the ceremony, Palo is staying nearby to gather information."

I nodded, "I trust her to tell me if something is truly wrong."

Marabella nodded, "As do I. Now," she looked around, "we need to get you downstairs… The Light Heir Prince…"

Adyen snarled as she jumped slightly. I shot him a narrowed look. I stood up and adjusted my dress, leaving the cloak, "I'm ready."

"Here," Taylor offered me a dark glass that I shot back. The alcohol burned on my tongue as I straightened my shoulders.

We entered the same way we left, the entire room filled with staff and long tables. The guests hadn't been allowed in yet, but I strode toward the throne and made a slight adjustment to my crown. It felt permanently attached to my head even though I was positive that it could be taken off. Shit, I hoped it could be. I didn't want to sleep with this shit on. It was heavy.

My guard spread out along the top stair as Marabella moved to work behind me at a table that served my food and drink. Silas sat at the small throne and smiled broadly as the music began. The doors opened and a stream of people started to enter. Rhodes guided the representatives who wanted to meet me into a line. It was like a goddamn wedding reception.

Despite the overload of power and energy streaming through me, I felt exhausted. I felt like I was on display. I hated it. I wanted to get to the part where I cut off Mario's head.

I did have to admire the particular fashion that was being worn. Everything seemed to be in deep jewel tones and burnt reds. I had to assume it was paying homage to the season, but I wasn't sure. All I knew was that the colors were beautiful.

Adyen announced each person as Rhodes guided them toward me. At first, I was entertained by the apparent political masks being worn. I didn't mind talking to the representatives of my country, but after a few families, it grew tiresome. The shifter community seemed extremely receptive to my place on the throne to the point that both of my guard's fathers offered a place in their family homes whenever I traveled to the outside borders of our country. The demonic community seemed friendly as well. Although Taylor had explained that their hierarchy was based heavily in power, rather than birthright. I must have passed both tests in some way. When the mages approached, I could feel my entire body tense at Colliard.

"Your Majesty," He bowed with a tightness to his eyes. "Your coronation was wonderful, as much so as our new monarch."

I smiled with as much effort as I could muster, "Thank you, representative."

"I hope to be of help in all future endeavors regarding movements involving the Dark Fae," I examined his words and found them to be a playful lie. It wasn't a pure lie, but he was only promising to be helpful in the situation with the Dark Fae. He did not mention which side he would be helpful. Fae were taught tricks like that, but half fae folk weren't exactly held to the same rule biologically. Although it tended to be harder for them to lie well, they seemed to talk in beautiful circles.

I nodded as he continued on. I groaned internally at the approach of the Light Fae heir and company. Taylor tried to keep a straight face at my obvious internal commentary. I let a small smirk fall onto my lips. Apparently, I was projecting.

"Heir to the Light Fae Kingdom, Rainer, Your Majesty." Rhodes announced in a gruff voice that sounded like a growl. I wanted to eye his jaguar with humor. Rhodes always had the funniest reactions.

My eyes and mind categorized every feature of this supposed fiancé of mine. I was pleased for three reasons. It had nothing to do with his looks either. He was very handsome though. His skin, like most Light Fae, was a deep rich color that seemed almost burgundy in the right light. He had a face that was structured and showcased a beautiful set of hazel eyes. The dark braids that adorned his head were left to hang down to his waist with accents of gold spread throughout. Yes, he was beautiful. However, my reasoning for being pleased was more complicated.

First, he was very powerful. I could feel his pure fae magic radiating throughout the room. Only to be matched by his father, the King, who stood in line behind his son with a satisfied smile. I would have to get a read on him later as well. There was no doubt though that my supposed fiancé was very powerful.

Secondly, I was pleased because it was apparent that he was as uncomfortable with this situation like me. I appreciated the fresh wave of honesty that radiated from him. It was clear that those hazel eyes would express every feeling or thought. He was predictable.

Finally, I was pleased because his eyes continued to flash toward Silas. I smiled authentically because I was very aware of the fact that my dashing fiancé was more interested in my brother than he was me. This caused my defenses to lower because I knew that the two of us could figure out a way to make this work, even before speaking a word to him. This marriage contract wouldn't be necessary.

"A pleasure to meet you," I smiled to accept his bow.

"The pleasure is mine," He laughed as Silas approached. "I only recently learned of your return, until then I had only been in contact with his previous majesty, Silas, through letters."

I nearly snickered at the lack of technology.

"Well, I do trust Silas with most of our communication with other realms."

Silas offered me a lazy smile but preened at the compliment.

"We have been truly blessed that Gray has returned."

Rainer smiled at him, both of their faces changing, just slightly.

"Well, if you would like, Your Majesty, I would love to

request a dance from you later." Interesting. I looked at my brother. Had he ever dated anyone? I knew so little about my own family.

"Of course," I nodded with amusement. I could see Adyen frowning and it was clear that Taylor was unable to get a read from him.

Taylor, tell Adyen that Rainer is more into Silas than me or else he is going to shift… and then call him a possessive bastard. Wait. Don't, my teasing might not come across well via mind speak.

Adyen grinned as Taylor rose a brow. Apparently, my entire message had been broadcasted. Good. Everyone seemed less tense now.

The procession of greeting continued until I found myself in my throne once again. My mind stuttered as I took in the scene around me with amazement.

Somehow I had always known I would end up here. On this throne and protecting these people. The savage predator that lived inside of me was protective, possessive, and obsessive with the people it considered ours. Most monsters were like that. Every smile and happy peel of content laughter that echoed through the chamber reinforced that. I wanted to protect these people. No other fae, whether it be Mario or another threat, would hurt them. I was obsessive about keeping them safe and possessive over my people. I felt as though I was moving through thick honey as I looked around with emotion building in my chest. The change in power made everything more brilliant and intense. I could feel the energy of my people and their current contentment. I knew a change was needed, but whatever had changed during coronation had brought me into a perceived sense of understanding. I was the representative of my people. They needed me.

I knew, as of now, who my enemy was. King Mario wasn't here and that didn't surprise me. I would make the declaration of war tomorrow. Marabella offered me a glass of wine before her eyes returned toward Palo. He was sitting near his father with a distraught look on his face, focused on her.

"How are things going?" I asked quietly. She smiled a secret grin.

"Well," She sighed. "It's more obvious to me that he feels something... I just don't know what's holding him back. It's not like our social rank is very far apart."

I frowned, "I hope it has nothing to do with that. I would skin him alive if that was the case."

My lady in waiting paled as I offered her a small smile.

"Oh!" She said in a quiet whisper. "Vegas wanted to apologize for earlier and tell you that she wished to have a conversation with you later, if possible."

I found my new friend in question and beckoned her over. She smiled and gracefully made her way across the marble floors toward me, now dressed in a pale crystal dress that fit her form. I felt a small surge of pride that my friends and I looked so fantastic.

Yes. I realized I was retreating to fashion in order to cope. It's just what I do.

"How are you?" I asked quietly. Her large violet eyes widened as she smiled.

"Better now. I'm not sure exactly what happened." She whispered with confusion. "Edwin told me he would explain better later."

I nodded, "I trust you to tell me if it's anything serious."

Plus, it wasn't like I had a lot of time to overthink her situation when mine was so... war-ish. You know?

"Absolutely," she stated before her eyes flicked up to the window behind me.

They grew impossibly wide as she reached forward to pull me

from the throne. It was an abrupt movement, but my eyes turned to track her viewpoint.

"How many dragons do you have?" She asked in a rushed manner.

"What? One--"

Fuck a duck. I yanked Marabella and her behind me as the main window, behind my throne, crashed inward to reveal a massive black dragon. I swore as the entire room broke out in chaos, the windows shattering inward to reveal units of black metal and green leather. Glass and heat echoed through the small room as the beast sent black fire toward the ceiling to sear the room with ash.

"Mario," I hissed.

He was a bastard like that. I assumed he wasn't even present. I shouted to my men. I felt a ripple of power leak through the room as Adyen shifted to attack the dragon behind him. The primal power that left his form during a change was enough to make me grit my teeth.

"Hide," I snarled at the girls as I strode forward, trusting Adyen to handle the dragon behind us. Its tail was damaging my goddamn room.

I could see the Dark Fae fighting with magic and physicality as my temperament flew out the window. I didn't think we would lose since we were aided by the Light Fae forces, but I felt a surge of protectiveness stream through me. The primal instinct, which protected me, rose forth as a cruel smiled pulled on my lips.

"Now, boys!" I felt my power ripple outward in a dark wave that seemed to freeze the room momentarily. "That is not how you attack a damn kingdom. This is how you do it."

As if reading my mind, my guard tackled the room in an easily calculated methodology. Neo's skin rippled with black as he instantly liquified the brains of half the forces nearby. He let out a cold smile as our people backed up to the wall. Good for them, giving Neo space to work.

Taylor sliced through the forces in front of him, thick in numbers, but with a graceful elegance that made it seem like melted butter. His fair skin grew spattered with blood as he let out a laugh that had the Light Fae pausing their defensive attacks.

Rhodes's roar of contentment echoed through the room as he ripped the head off of a soldier near Edwin and Byron. Both mages seemed stuck in shock at the power display occurring.

Athens smiled, "Now, come on. Why are we still using metal swords and armor? How antiquated."

I watched as the metal on their skin melted into the soldiers' forms and burned them until death. The swords they had, twisted to press into the center point between their eyes. Still more soldiers flooded in and Athens refocused their weapons to do a dance of assault.

I closed my eyes as I released a burst of raw fae power that was targeted at the stream of people entering into my throne room. I couldn't snap their necks all at once, but ashes would do nicely. I heard Vegas curse as the entire force before us turned to ash. The savage inside of me pulled forward in a fashion that was so powerful it blew out candles throughout the room.

I felt everything inside of me shift as the predatory side of my senses grew more prominent. I knew without a doubt that if I so wished, I could devour the room whole in a natural powerplay. My teeth felt far sharper and more deadly in my mouth as my nails extended out. I stepped forward and took care of a few nearby soldiers.

Snap.

I made sure to toss the body away from me, ignoring the screams.

Snap.

I added to the pile of bodies that Rhodes was creating.

Snap. Snap. Snap.

"Oh no, no," I chuckled at a man trying to run. "I didn't give you permission to live, silly Fae."

Snap.

It wasn't enough, though. I was livid. I pushed my hand through his chest cavity and tossed his heart back toward the throne. I prayed to the gods my friends would duck or something. I didn't want to ruin their outfits.

Snap.

Snap.

"Tell Mario!" I hissed at a group of soldiers. "The next time he sees me, he will know true darkness. I will swallow him whole and burn down his entire kingdom with a fucking smile on my face."

They wouldn't have a chance to tell him. I turned them to ash as I snapped the front man's neck for fun. I snarled at the continued onslaught of soldiers.

"Gray!" A voice shouted as heat licked the back of my arms… but was deflected. I turned to see Marabella curled upon herself as Vegas stood defensively behind me with hands filled with black dragon fire, like a mirror bent backward. Adyen let out a roar as he snapped the neck of Mario's dragon. I wasn't confident if he was a shifter or not. I didn't give a fuck.

"Vegas?" I asked in curiosity as her hands absorbed the fire and a look of pure relief filtered through her expression. "I totally told you to hide."

"Yeah, not positive what that shit was. I need to talk to Edwin," She frowned and looked up at me with a slightly unhinged smile. "But, hey! I just saved you. Look at me being a badass. You must be rubbing off on me."

Marabella shook her head with a small laugh. I grinned, "You're sorta crazy, aren't you?"

She nodded with knowledge, "Oh for sure, I blame my boys."

I had met some of her boys during our dinner the other night. My opinion of them had changed. It was hard to keep track of them all. I honestly wasn't positive how or if she did deal with it… but they adored her. I was still hoping we could bond over our harems together.

"Don't worry. That's not a bad thing," I pointed out as I turned back to fight once more. Except there was nothing to fight… we had demolished the forces easily.

"Well, shit," Palo muttered approaching the throne. Silas stood up from his place behind the throne and looked around with a smile.

"See, Gray, you are total Queen material," He smiled. I snickered.

Maybe this would put the leadership's minds at ease about wartime?

Rhodes approached me in lethal form. His gold and brown pattern made those melted gold eyes stand out. I heard Marabella swear as I petted the underneath of his chin and knelt down so that he could lick my chin, avoiding his large bloody fangs. Oh, non-shifted Rhodes would be having none of that. He rolled his eyes and I once again questioned if he was a mind reader.

Adyen rumbled behind me as his tail pressed my back in a smoothing motion. Taylor's dark grin made me smile as he slipped his knives into his wrist compartment. Both twins approached and casually took a seat on the throne steps. I was confident we looked like lunatics smiling like this. In fact, if the expression of my people and the Light Fae told me anything, that was precisely what we looked like. The only people not looking at us oddly were Vegas and her boys. Then again, I had gotten an odd vibe from them as well. Maybe not a primal power, but just a little unhinged. A little crazy.

I looked around at the frightened, yet determined faces around me and opened my mouth to begin.

"I need to know how they got past our defenses," I called out calmly. "We obviously have a traitor in our midst and that will not, I repeat, will *not*, be tolerated, so that is our immediate focus--"

"Colliard," A voice stated quietly. It was Palo, "I couldn't stop him at the moment, but right before the attack he left."

"Fuck," Neo swore louder than normal.

"We will discuss this in private. Thank you, Palo," I stated. "As for the rest of everyone here, I would encourage you to go home. For the safety of your families, prepare for war. I will absolutely not tolerate this type of treatment of our kingdom. King Mario may want to assume we are weak or can be bullied… but we can not. The truth is, today was about giving him a chance. He killed the late King and Queen on my sixth birthday. I gave him the opportunity to turn himself in, without war, and the chance to save his people. He chose war. So we will give him a war!"

I bellowed the last part, and it was met with determined nods and booming cheers. Apparently, I had won them over to the war concept.

Good. I need to remove some heads.

I felt my body tense as the exhaustion worked its way through me, I knew I was going to crash soon. Silas took over, "If you would please exit the chamber so it can be restored, news will be brought via--" I was really starting to like my brother. He seemed like a perceptive ass. Also, how was this the second room I had destroyed this week?

I blanked out after that as I turned toward my throne. I could feel my body shaking as I sat down in my throne, a leg stretched out as I looked over the broken throne room. Well, better now than later to change the decor.

12
ADYEN

I was furious. Despite having shifted back to human form, my primal instincts were screaming at me to find King Mario myself. My mate sat sprawled in her throne in a brutal expanse of chaos.

Her hair was covered in ash and dress splattered in blood. Those dark nails and eyes watched the clean up process of the throne room as her lady in waiting attempted to offer her water and food. I noticed her teeth shrink back down from slightly pointed to normal as her eyes grew blue once again. I could feel the tension from the other guard as the five of us awaited news about Colliard.

If he had indeed left, if he had truly been behind this… It would hurt Neo and Athens. They hated their father, but being the child of a traitor was never easy. I could already see the hate burning in both their eyes at the mere possibility of his crime. I walked toward Gray, over several dead bodies and ash. This was becoming a habit, the bodies and ash, wasn't it?

I knelt down in front of her as those altered eyes found my gaze.

"Lil brawler, you don't need to stay and watch this."

Gray leaned forward and pressed her head to mine in a gesture that made my dragon relax.

"Yes, I do. Their attack may have not been successful… but it could have been. The rage, Adyen, it's building. I want-- No, I need to kill this bastard. He already took away my parents. I will be damned if he takes my kingdom."

"None of us will let that happen." I spoke softly. "Although I have to warn you, the men he has been sending are his lowest guard. His least powerful men-"

"Sacrifices and bait," She muttered with realization.

"He wanted a reaction from you, wanted you to call a war," I explained softly.

"He will get a fucking war, Adyen. I'm tired of his foolish games."

I nodded, "Just say the word and we will do what needs to be done."

The doors opened behind us as Palo walked in, followed by Silas. Both of them looked at the twins with guilt, before a set of guard units followed in afterward. I watched with caution as they approached us. I would be lying, though, if I said I wasn't turned on by how close Gray was to me.

Despite the blood and ash… or maybe, in part, due to it, Gray always turned me on. Her confidence and 'no shit' attitude was refreshing. On the same level, like the first day I met her, that tight little body tempted me and enthralled me. I watched her more than she probably realized and bathed in the scent that was uniquely her. Despite the perfume she occasionally wore, she smelt of ash and magic. It was a smell that I had never scented before and allowed me to find her anywhere. I wish I could have described what magic smelt like, but it was impossible. There was a small part of me that was happy I had slipped about her being my mate... I wanted to be able to explain to her what that meant. I wondered why Rhodes hadn't. I knew his jaguar had decided the same.

"Have you found him?" Gray asked almost hopeful.

I knew she didn't want the twins to suffer. I wasn't positive when we had earned her trust and loyalty, but it was an honor. I noticed that she no longer shied away from our touches and, despite her natural discomfort, didn't get upset at the occasional touch that occurred on her shoulders. It was why Palo's accidental movement, leading to her panic attack, had made me so furious.

I didn't want anything to hurt Gray. Ever.

Silas frowned, "No."

Palo spoke, "I have news that I believe is about this, directly and indirectly."

"Speak."

"Colliard has been found, according to the financial reports I was asked to review, to have been siphoning funds," He drawled. "I had gone back to my office and found last night that I had missed something... I planned on keeping an eye on him this morning, Your Majesty, and to tell you, but then--" I saw him look up at Marabella, "Anyway, it is my fault."

Gray sighed and nodded, "Thank you for being honest, Palo. He is gone then?"

"Fled before the attack," one the guards spoke. "He mentioned going home to retrieve a gift for you and, since he is a representative, we thought nothing of it."

Neo spoke with obvious tension radiating through him, "It explains why my father was so guarded during our meeting. He attempted to ask some questions about you, but other than that didn't offer much."

Gray offered him a look of understanding, "So, we can assume then that he has been working for Mario and siphoning funds."

Silas knelt down, "I am truly sorry that I didn't see this."

Gray placed a hand on my shoulder to stand and kiss her brother's head, "It's okay. As you said, I should have been here."

I didn't like her taking the blame, but it showed her natural ease of taking responsibility and ability to lead. I could see respect, and unfortunately, lust radiating through the guard's eyes at their Queen. If they didn't seem so useful, I would have burnt them to a crisp.

Gray seemed to collect herself then.

"Place out an official declaration of war. Inform the Light Fae. Let the guard units know to be prepared. I want a strategy meeting first thing this morning. Additionally, let any border guards know that if they see Colliard--"

"To fucking kill him," Neo snarled before walking away with a shimmer effect of power. Athens looked on at his brother with a deep understanding. Gray swayed toward him and looked at her guards.

"I want him brought back to be tortured," She snarled feeding off Neo's anger. "We should have the pleasure of hurting that bastard." The guards flinched.

Athens spoke, "I will start vetting for a proper representative replacement and let you know the possibilities."

Gray narrowed her eyes in thought and nodded, "Talk to your mother about the position, possibly."

Athens grinned and I took the cue to lead Gray toward the exit of the room. I looked down at her hardened face as she met my eyes.

"I need to find Neo." She whispered quietly.

"Check the training center," I answered knowledgeably.

Gray stopped, once we turned the corner, and pulled me down, "Thank you for killing that bastard."

She pressed her lips to me in a soft kiss after I admitted, "I wish I had done it sooner. You almost got hurt."

I growled at the scent of her desire and she offered me a small smile.

"No, I didn't. Plus, Vegas helped somehow… Anyway, I will have to thank you better later."

"Don't tease me, lil brawler," I growled as she walked away, sauntering with blood and ash marring her skin. Or maybe accenting it? Damn, she drove me crazy. It was probably because we were all a little crazy.

Gray

I moved toward the training center. The brisk autumn wind whipped over my skin as I rushed toward Neo's energy. I could feel his anger and frustration. Our connection was tight and tense. I hated that. I hated that he hurt. I paused only to toss off my shoes and ran barefoot across the thick, green grass.

The training center, used to keep our guard in shape, was a dark stone building that had two massive doors sitting near the center of the front. No trees or flowers were surrounding the building and it was void of windows. I used my energy to throw open the door and stormed in. My eyes locking onto Neo's furious form.

I wish I could tell you I knew how to handle this. I could feel his cold fury circulating through the room as he demolished a defensive structure that was used for practice. His entire body moved like obsidian liquid and those muscles seemed to radiate a primal intensity that should have scared me. Instead, I was turned on… because that's me.

I had a feeling that this was the place Neo went when he could no longer be silent.

"Neo," I growled, storming toward him with predatory steps. I placed my crown, which popped off my head like a suction cup, onto a shelf. I knew I would never forget it here. As it was, my natural instinct was to be close to it.

"Gray," He snarled in a tone that was so unlike Neo. Although, right now, I would take fury over silence or his blank lethal power.

"You need to calm down," I whispered and stood my ground against the assault of his icy power. It hit me like a dangerous weapon. I grit my teeth and found my hand holding me against the wall behind me, trying not to fall over. I could feel the predator inside of me attempting to lash out and fight. She knew we were more dominant and powerful. She wanted to make Neo submit, especially because of his impressive strength. I forced her down and faced him without power. I was just Gray right now.

"Calm down?" Neo whispered with darkness that seemed to focus entirely and intensely on me.

Yeah, being at the center of his attention was intimidating... at least right now.

"Yes," I demanded through a hiss, "We need to talk about Colliard--"

"I will not talk about that man!" He roared and demolished a fighting dummy in front of him before stalking forward. "He is a traitor, Gray. And I should have expected it."

My eyes were still trained on the dummy that he had just exploded, literally into pieces. Holy shit. I snapped to attention.

I growled softly as he cornered me into the wall and pricked my skin with icy power, "Neo."

"No," he mumbled and brought a hand to my throat. "I can't. I should have known, Gray. He has always been an abusive bastard, but this? This is different... You could have gotten hurt, I should have tried harder to get more information at his office--"

"No!" I snarled. "I am fine. He is the only one who won't be fine, Neo. I ordered them to bring him back. If you want revenge against him, then save your anger for that. Beat him as he beat you."

Neo's eyes flashed with a primal danger, "I will kill him, Gray. I will kill my own father. I want to reach into his chest and pull out his spine. I want to drag his corpse through the kingdom's grounds because that is the respect he deserves."

I placed my two hands on his angular jaw, "He will get what he deserves. We will get vengeance against those that have hurt us." We would, the two of us.

Neo's nostrils flared as he swallowed hard before looking down at my lips. I realized that our position was very intimate. I could feel how sweaty and massive his body was. My nipples hardened against his chest in a natural response.

"Neo," I mumbled quietly.

His lips covered mine as the scent of mint and sweat invaded my senses. I whimpered as he bit down on my mouth and used his fingers to peel my dress down the center. My clothes were always being ruined around these men. I groaned at the feel of his thigh between my leg, the friction causing me to pant and shiver.

"I need you." He muttered against my skin. "Please?"

I moaned into his lips again and pressed my tongue against his teeth as he opened his mouth. My primal instinct purred happily at his possession as I lifted my legs to wrap them around his thick waist. The dress I wore fell off as he groaned at the heat of my center pressed against his leather pants. I urged him closer by tightening my legs. A primal sound escaped his chest as he pushed me between the wall and himself.

"I should take my time with you," He muttered in contrast to his massive hands holding my smaller waist.

"No," I groaned as my connection with him snapped tighter. "I need you, Neo."

"The things I want to do to you, Gray," He whispered against the hollow of my neck as my pulse beat rapidly, "are twisted."

"As long as I get you, I don't care," I admitted softly.

It was true, between the pounding in my ears and trembling heated skin. I really didn't care. I needed him. I trusted him. He would never hurt me.

I felt liberated and freed by this thought.

I felt loved.

Neo groaned before turning me into the wall, my toes pressing into the matt of the gym. I hissed at the raw power that circled around me. Phantom hands pulled my arms up as Neo's hands pulled against my thong and ripped it off. I gasped at the ruin of my undergarments but was distracted by another set of phantom hands moving toward my breasts.

"What is this?" I mumbled in a moan.

A pair of invisible shackles held my hands above me in a hold as another pair smoothed and tugged at my nipples. I could feel wetness coating my thighs as I trembled.

"Magic," Neo mumbled against my skin as he bit into my ass.

I gasped at the feel of his teeth on my skin and his warm hands moved from my ankles to the heat between my thighs.

"Oh fuck, you are so wet," He nuzzled the in-between of my thighs as I sighed in relief. The ache that had started to form had become unbearable. Our magic tasted like darkness and ice shards. It was painful and assaulted my body like punishment. Sweet, amazing punishment.

"Do you like these hands on you?" He whispered in a husky throat sound. "Someone to hold you down while playing with those beautiful breasts."

Yes. Yes, I fucking did.

I moaned at his words as the phantom hands teased my nipples into diamonds points that had me panting. A sharp slap hit my ass as Neo groaned and licked a long line of my exposed heat while his thumb toyed with my clit. His tongue was oddly cold against my heat and it caused my eyes to roll into the back of my head.

"I want this ass nice and pink." He murmured softly. "Gods, you have a great ass, Gray."

I hummed as another set of hands pulled gently back on my hair, exposing my neck. I could feel Neo rising behind me and stepping against me in a predatory move.

"But playtime will have to wait for later, beautiful," He murmured against my neck.

Gone was the sweet, quiet Neo. This version was his dual and primal nature. I surrendered to his icy will.

He continued, "I need you, Gray. Do you need me?"

"Yes," I panted as those phantom hands were replaced by his.

I felt my core tighten as his large length slid between my thighs. I groaned at the friction against my wetness.

"I don't have any protection on me." He murmured in a raspy voice against my ear. "What do you want to do, beautiful? I would love to take you bare, feel every inch of you. I haven't been with anyone for some time."

I barely gasped out, "I'm on birth control."

I was thanking the gods for that damn birth control spell I had gotten years ago. It lasted until you decided to have it removed. Nifty magic seemed to have a lot of uses….

"Please, fill me up," I begged as his teasing continued.

"You don't ever have to beg, Gray." He soothed and in one swift movement, thrust into me. My head fell back to his shoulder as a cry of his name echoed throughout the gym.

Fuck. He was huge.

"So good, Gray. So fucking good," Neo groaned.

His length was massive and I hadn't had sex in so long… fuck. It was amazing. There was something so primal about being entirely filled by a predator that was dangerous and lethal. Something hazardous about being cared about by a deadly creature.

Neo gripped my hips in a bruising grasp, "Oh shit, Gray, you are so tight. Fuck, I love being inside of you."

I couldn't control my moans as he began to slide his rock hard length in and out of me with a furious and punishing pace. I closed my eyes and allowed his heated kisses to overwhelm my senses. I wasn't delicate normally, but fuck, I felt delicate in his arms. I whimpered as his rumbles grew louder.

"Faster," I encouraged as he bit down on my ear.

I screamed as his bite flared up my power and caused a mark on my back to heat up to a burnt sizzle. It felt so good, so damn good. I let Neo continue to pound my body into a deep, liquified state as I shivered in anticipation of my climax. I could feel him using my body as I used his. His fury and frustration encouraged me to lean back into him as I cried out his name through the moan. Throughout all of it, I felt a delicate thread of affection that surrounded me through the fury.

It was what made this even better. I could tell how much Neo cared.

He was punishing my body and punishing himself, but he would never hurt me. He would kill anyone who ever touched me. I knew that. It made my body tremble at the protectiveness that came out in the low growl that slipped through his teeth.

I had never known sex could be like this. I had never known I could be liberated and freed from my demons. At least for a time.

"Neo!" I cried out as my back arched at the sensation of my climax approaching. My toes curled as he let out a deep growl that had my body pushing forward.

"Come with me," I begged. "I want to feel you fill me up."

"Your wish is my fucking command," He snarled and quickened his fast pace.

He was drilling me to the wall. I felt my center explode as a raw cry came out of my chest and Neo let out a loud, primal yell. The brick in front of us crumbled slightly from his fist pounding against it. Dust fell on both of us as his hardness tightened and exploded within me, in an intense and primal marking.

Both of us were breathing so hard that my limbs seemed to rattle against his. Silence echoed through the room as our hearts beat nearly out of our chest. Neo lifted from my back and turned me, a gentleness in his eyes that surprised me. I offered him a soft, lazy smile.

Damn. Sex was fantastic. Brilliant. A wonderful, wonderful thing.

"Gray," He mumbled quietly and drew me to the floor. Our bodies pressed together in a sitting position.

"Neo," I kissed his jaw gently. I could see my quiet, intense guard make a return as I kept my face gentle.

"I'm sorry," He muttered. "I didn't mean to be so rough. I just was so angry and then knowing you knew about his abuse--"

"I didn't know exactly, but I know what abuse looks like," I whispered gently. "And hey, I liked it, a lot… Neo, that was mind-blowing."

He offered me a brilliant smile, "Yeah?"

"I mean we could do a repeat--"

He chuckled kissed me and then his face tightened, "When my father separated Athens and me…"

I opened my mouth to stop him, but he placed a gentle finger against my lip.

"I was heartbroken. He had been my best friend, my only real friend, considering our father's position. It didn't help that the other heir guards had been older than us. I didn't visit him or my mom until I was in my late teens."

"Why?" I whispered. It was then that I had noticed his tattooed form had faded into his warm dark skin and dark shiny eyes. I missed the absence of his piercing a little.

"I was ashamed. I knew Athens and mom would see right through me. They would have seen the pain. It wouldn't surprise my mom though. I assumed for years that he beat her as he beat me. When I finally asked her about it, she told me that he had tried once and their divorce was put into motion the next day… She felt immense guilt because she hadn't known how bad his temper had become."

"He used servants for a time. Eventually, it turned to me. I remember every beating, every time I disappointed him or didn't achieve something within the guard… a beating was sure to follow. My punishments weren't nearly as cruel as the servants he bought, but it was as if he was trying to release something inside of me. He didn't realize, though, that thing inside of me always existed. I was just too weak to use it on my father. I didn't want to put that weakness on my brother and mom, so I stayed distant."

Note to self - remove the ability for anyone to 'buy' servants. What the hell?

"Have you ever told them that?"

Athens voice sounded soft as he strolled into the gym, "No, baby, he hasn't."

Neo tensed, but took the robes that Athens offered us with a small smile. We both stood and wrapped it around ourselves as Athens approached Neo.

"I would absolutely never be ashamed of you. He was our fucking father, Neo. I would have never risen a hand to him unless my life was at stake. Even then, I might not have. We worshipped him before you left. You can't put this on yourself, just like how I can't continue to think that I was never 'good' enough for him. He's a rotten bastard."

Neo nodded, "I know…"

Athens pulled him into a hug as Neo blinked his eyes rapidly as if he was blinking back tears. I stood there with a soft smile as Athens pulled back and pushed his forehead to his brothers.

"Now, no more of this bullshit. When we find that abusive motherfucker, one of us is going to kill him--"

"Or I will," I voiced with a soft lilt.

Both twins looked at me with expressive and beautiful eyes. I stepped forward cautiously as Athens squeezed me into a bear hug. I laughed as Neo smoothed my hair gently.

For just a moment, the three of us relaxed in the peaceful love and affection that strummed between us. Athens finally got that sinister grin on his face as I looked at Neo's amused face.

"So, baby... now that you've had my twin, you sorta know what you've been blessed with, huh?" He winked with a coy smile. I rolled my eyes and punched him in his impressively hard abs.

Neo lifted me onto his shoulder and I stuck out my tongue, "Now you get no love."

Athens held his heart, "Baby, you can't deprive a man, I know what you taste like."

Neo perked up and looked at him, "Doesn't she taste good?"

"So good," Athens moaned. I flushed and wiggled down from the two of them with narrowed eyes.

"I'm supposed to be preparing for a strategy meeting tomorrow. Stop distracting my sexed up brain." I made sure to grab my crown. I must have been a vision in just a robe, messed up lipstick, and sex hair. I slipped my crown on and raised my chin.

"I'll sex up your brain further," Athens laughed. "I sorta like you post-orgasm. You're all cuddly and sweet."

I rose a middle finger as I reached the door.

Neo smiled in a predatory way, "Maybe she needs two of us to make it permanent, like a double dose?"

Athens threw his head back at my shocked expression, "What do you say, baby? Want the two of us at once?"

I squeaked while blushing and jumped through the door. I ignored the cold blast of air and laughter that followed me. I was so not ready for that... yet.

13

GRAY

"Taylor," I grunted, "just tell me what changed?"

Taylor bit his delicious lip and raised a dark red brow, "One of your tattoos is colored in. It seems as though something made it change…"

I blushed, "Which one?"

He snickered, "Well, baby girl, it looks like it's Neo's tattoo. Any reason for that?"

"Nope," I smiled with a coy glare.

"So, no reason Adyen tried lecturing Neo like an upset parent?"

I cackled, "How did that go?"

Adyen growled from the doorway, "Not well. It wasn't even about the sex. I just wanted to make sure he understood the importance--"

"Hey, big guy," I stammered through a blush. "It's really okay. I think he knows."

Adyen grumbled and returned back into the bedroom, Lunatic trailed after him with wide eyes. She had taken a liking to my dragon.

Taylor snickered, "Now that is great. I love that."

I rolled my eyes, "I need to get ready for this meeting. Out you go, trouble."

"I do not start trouble, I take advantage of it," He growled with a nip of my lip before leaving.

I sighed and watched him walk away, my legs shaking with the reminder of yesterday's fun. I shimmied on the loose dress I planned on wearing today. Last night, everyone had stayed in my room and I hoped that the trend would continue.

After the twins and I had returned yesterday, I wasn't confident what to expect. I knew that the dynamic of our relationship was changing, but I wasn't sure how others would react. Surprisingly, there hadn't been a grand reaction. Everything had been so crazy that I hadn't realized the lack of reaction in response to my intimacy with Rhodes in the tub either. They didn't know about Athens and I, but I assumed it wouldn't have caused a reaction. It made me realize that these men really meant what they said. They wanted this relationship. They wanted whatever I wanted. They wanted to make sure I was happy and to protect me.

Considering my previous experience, the feeling was odd. I still had no idea what to expect in this type of relationship, but I knew my closeness with each person would develop differently. I didn't feel guilty that I felt closer to Athens and Neo right now. I knew things would develop how they were supposed to with my men.

My men.

I had claimed them mentally, like my throne, crown, and kingdom... Once I settled the Light Heir marriage contract problem, it would allow me to move forward with telling everyone how vital my guard was to me. I didn't want to hide how happy they made me.

Marabella was sleeping in, I hoped near Palo. I snickered but adjusted the loose grey dress that fell off my shoulders and fitted my waist. I placed a small strand of diamonds around my neck and let my hair hang loose in a silky wave. Today, I needed to be comfortable and focused.

"Are you ready?" Athens asked with a lazy smile from the door. I nodded at his sleepy eyes and took the soft, dark shawl he offered.

"Why do you look so happy?" I asked quietly.

He grinned, "I have a bit of a surprise for you."

It was a surprise, a pleasant one, to find his mother at my strategy meeting awaiting my arrival. I offered her a brilliant grin before we sat at the long dark table. Morning pastries were spread around the massive map of the fae lands on the table.

After last night's events, our guests had made a quick retreat. Unfortunately, this had included the Light Fae. They had been made aware of our declaration of war sent to the Dark Fae. Their messengers delivered their news of alliance. The village outside the open windows of our meeting room was quiet as the early morning sun began to heat the cold stone flooring. I hadn't had a chance to ask or see Marabella, but I had the suspicion that Vegas and her boys had left.

I had really begun seeing both her and Marabella as sisters. I wondered if they felt that closeness to me. Maybe it was just my naturally protective instincts that had me looking after them. Then again, I was terrible at friendship. My only two friends had essentially forgotten I had existed. I hoped to be able to continue to see these two. I would have to make plans for Taylor to contact his cousin to arrange a more extended visit. Hopefully, this war wouldn't take a tremendous amount of time.

Strategy meetings were an exercise of listening. In some ways, Colliard had been correct, that bastard. I didn't have extensive knowledge about the formal works of the military, but that was why I had my guard and specialty teams. Athens had mentioned briefly that Edwin was part of a specialty team that included Vegas, so I held my tongue. I didn't want to encourage the concept that my new friends be put in danger. It was fascinating to take everyone's opinions into account, and it made me realize that despite my natural stubbornness, I had adapted slightly.

There was a vulnerability in caring about people, more than just protecting them. I could no longer deny how I felt about my men. I wasn't confident how love felt, but the warm wave of affection that expended in my chest made me think that I may just love them a little. My eyes fell on a pair of glittering black eyes that held familiarity and made my body squirm.

Neo had opened up to me. It seemed to lift the somber sadness that clouded his quiet and natural intensity. It was like a cloud had moved from his starlit eyes to reveal the fathomless primal nature of his personality. It was chaotic and beautiful, like a galaxy or an unexplored cosmos. The night sky was intimidating and so expansive, like his eyes. I knew that if I weren't careful, I would fall. He could devour me, swallow me whole.

Athens flashed me a smile as his playful optimism rose out to voice his strategic opinion. Despite his playful smile, I knew he had a depth to his genius and it didn't surprise me that he led most of our communicative efforts. He was fantastic with people and seemed to know exactly what to say to ease their minds. He was indeed the sunshine that appeared to shed some of the darkness on my broken, dark soul. Even Bobby, my familiar, hadn't been this much of a balm to my soul.

If Athens was my sunshine, Neo was the endless cosmos surrounding our eclipse... we were together. One unit. One family. Safe.

Rhodes made sure of that. I watched the dignified man stroke his scruff with frustration as his eyes scanned the map in front of us. In some ways, Rhodes was an open book that encouraged my trust. He answered every question and every concern. Yet, I felt like I knew so little about the lethal predator. I wanted to break that control. At the same time, I craved it. I liked his ability to draw a reaction from me and that I had enough trust in him to allow him to dominate me.

Instead of punching him and all that shit. I almost patted myself on the back for my mature thoughts.

Adyen watched from the window with a dark look in his honey colored eyes. Out of everyone on the team, I knew he warred the most with this. He didn't want to put any of us in danger but knew it was necessary to face Mario. I could see his dragon pacing furiously as those eyes sifted from amber to black. Again and again. Despite his natural possessiveness, or maybe because of it, Adyen was reliable and secure. I knew exactly where I stood with him and his dragon. Their loyalty was without question. It was something that I wouldn't ever take for granted.

I needed to talk to him about this mate thing though. I didn't know a lot about mates. It seemed very permanent. Was I ready for that? I mean, hell, I sorta already had five live-in boyfriends, so I guess we would see where that went. Very confusing. Then again, so was my life.

A pair of hands brushed onto my arms gently as I looked up at Taylor. He placed a glass of tea down. Despite the loss of his hands, I could still feel his delicious heat. I watched him saunter towards the windows like Adyen. I knew our weapons expert would hold more importance in the war conversation later. I watched the curl of his lip as he laughed at something with Adyen. The bastard always pushed me on things, but it made me respect him. Plus, when we did get into arguments, they always were fascinating and witty. If only we could get that temper in check... I smiled. Maybe not.

I looked at my men. Adyen, my protector. Rhodes, my fearless leader. Neo, my night sky. Athens, my sunshine. Taylor, my passionate flame.

Ah shit. See, they got in my head? I'm starting to really like them and shit.

"We need more allies," I concluded softly. "Maybe we should draw from outside the fae. Consider the elves possible." Kill me. I would do it for my kingdom though.

Athens grinned, "Actually, I may have something for you in the other room that would help that issue."

I rose a brow and stood to follow him. Laurena walked next to me and offered me a soft smile.

"He brought this idea to me last night. I thought it would be a wonderful plan. It would make you happy and keep them safe. Athens mentioned that they weren't able to fully express themselves before. Well here, they can find sanctuary and aid our cause, if they want of course."

My mouth popped open as I walked into the throne room and was assaulted by around one hundred of familiar faces. I stepped in front as the room stilled.

"Gray?" A familiar voice chuckled. Esme stood before me looking every part the supernatural that I hadn't realized she truly was.

I looked at Athens, "How?"

"I may have had my mom make something to remove the hold you had on them," He blushed. "I just knew they wouldn't be safe once war broke out and you cared so--"

I cut him off with a hug that had the royalty behind me gasping and Athens chuckling. I pulled back with tears in my eyes.

"Genius. You are a genius."

Something very real passed between the two of us that had my heart beating faster. I couldn't say the words I felt, but I think he knew.

My eyes then took in Esme. Her willowy frame was dressed in a silk tan dress and those amber eyes were more cat-like than ever before. I noticed her hair had been interwoven with gold strands.

"You're a shifter?" I asked curiously.

She grinned, "Lion."

I put my arms out and was met with a hug, "Holy shit, it's so good to see you."

She pulled back with a twinkle in her eyes, "Don't do that mind shit again. I had a terrible headache."

I threw my head back and laughed as the crowd began to get worked up with chatter. These were the women and academy students I had loved and protected for so long. Looking down at them, I realized I must have been practicing to be Queen.

"Gray," A deep masculine voice that filled me with warmth called. Esme parted as Bobby, my golden retriever familiar, approached with easy steps. He offered me a cheesy grin that had his tan face wrinkling in happiness and those warm brown eyes softening.

"Hey, you," I grinned and lightly punched his side before he pulled me into a hug.

"Well, this is sorta cool," He said bluntly. "You're like, a *Queen*. I'm a familiar to a Queen, Gray."

I nodded with a smile, "I'm so glad you are here. Both of you, really."

"Told you I would figure it out," He flashed a smile. "Did you follow orders on what to do until then?"

Esme rolled her eyes, "Let me guess you told her to Always Punch First?"

I chuckled as Bobby nodded, "Damn right, I did."

The familial acceptance of these two made my heart fill with joy. How could I not love them? They were two parts of my soul that had healed. My fun-loving, best friend and my loyal familiar. Bobby's eyes took in the hall as Esme began to chat with excitement.

I looked around the hall and was filled with hope. I could do this. I could really do this. Especially with my guard and my friends by my side. I had no doubt that King Mario would be a difficult enemy to defeat, but a woman on a mission was a dangerous one. I smiled as the music began playing.

I knew my time to celebrate was nearly at an end, but tonight, I would enjoy our minor victory.

14
ATHENS

"That girl loves you," My mom stated quietly.

"Mom," I muttered. "She doesn't love me. She's not stupid."

My mom hit me upside the head as I chuckled. She spoke. "Don't speak like that about yourself, Athens."

I shrugged, "I'm just honest. Gray is perfect, I don't doubt that she cares about me, but she cares about everyone. I'm just lucky to spend time with her. Really."

My mom shook her head, "You are loved, Athens, by many people… including her, trust me."

Gray talked with interest and vigor to both Bobby and Esme. I was thrilled to see an authentic smile on her face. I hadn't believed it when she had all but jumped into my arms in front of everyone. Her scent was intoxicating and I found myself even more attracted to her after this hell of a week.

I knew my brother felt similar. His eyes were on our girl. She was happy, which made everyone else happy. I knew this war would take away some of her calm, but I had no doubt we would be able to get through it.

My mom was right about one thing, I did trust her. If she was sensing love, it was from me though. I knew I loved hard and intensely. I wasn't one to question my feelings. Within the past month, I had fallen entirely for Gray. I loved her intensity. I loved her rare smiles. I loved her attitude. I loved her compassion. I loved her loyalty. Fuck. I just loved her.

I was in love with Gray.

I wanted to tell her. I wanted to swing her around and plant a kiss on those red lips in front of everyone. She looked like every storybook princess with an attitude that would scare most warriors. Our girl tasted like blood, ashes, and battle… but she loved like pure sweetness.

When I had found her with Neo, I couldn't help the warmth that spread through me because of her peaceful and open expression. The demons and darkness had been put away and what was left was *just* as perfect. There was nothing about Gray that I didn't love. Even her flaws were perfect, a primary and fundamental staple of how strong of a person she was.

She conquered everything. She took every fear and set it on fire until it listened to her. I found her to be someone I admired, respected and loved.

Wow. I really did love her.

This was putting aside the fact that I found her body tempting and mindblowing, to say the least. I just wanted to take her by that tiny waist and sling her over my shoulder. The woman made me feel like an absolute caveman. I looked to Adyen's rapt focus on her and snickered. *Okay, maybe not a complete caveman.*

I knew that the upcoming months would be hard, but I had no doubt that Gray would be able to lead us. Maybe then, I would also get a chance to express to her how much, *how deeply,* I loved her.

"Athens," She called out with a beautiful smile, "come over here."

I couldn't refuse the call of my Queen.

MONSTERS

BLURB

If King Mario wanted a war, he would get one. It has been one week since I promised war against the Dark Fae. One week of planning and aligning all the pieces on my board to assure victory. Then he did something unexpected. Now, I have no idea which way to move. Offense? Defense? Offense? Defense? Good news? I've got some quality drama to keep me entertained. From the Marabella and Palo show to Bobby and Esme's return, my days have been filled. What about time with my boys though? No worries! Even in war, we have time for romance. *Right?*

At least I have my cat Lunatic. Though, I have to admit she sometimes seems more human than cat. Is there something I'm not seeing? Hopefully, we will figure it out because if not… well, I would rather not consider that! Stay positive… right? I have only one rule and I plan to follow it. Always punch first.

A note to readers of both the Red Masques & Vengeance: There will be spoilers!!! The plotlines intertwine so I am releasing both books at the same time. Feel free to pick either release but I just wanted to give you a heads up! Enjoy!

1
GRAY

He was here.

I could feel him stalking me through the forest, my footsteps silent and eyes watchful. His energy felt lethal even from afar and I felt a smile tilt my lips in excitement. It was rare that someone could actually hunt me successfully. Honestly, the picture would be complete if we could get that National Geographic voice-over actor to narrate this. My magic pushed against me in protest but I kept it reined in.

It wasn't time yet.

With an easy movement, I grasped one of the many massive trees that inhabited the forests in the Horde. I loved how the tree changed at my touch and tipped just enough that I could scale it and sit comfortably on one of the branches. Despite being the end of November, the Horde was painted in stunning fall colors and the pines a thick healthy green. The land had begun to flourish and I didn't want to toot my own horn or anything, but it was totally because the True Heir, me, had taken the throne.

Palo had explained that my ascension to the throne did something to the magic in the land and after about one moment of soaking in the ego-boosting, I zoned out. I didn't feel terrible, however, because Taylor had as well and Palo was his own brother. Plus, if I ever needed anything repeated I could just ask Marabella. The woman was sharp as a tack with an amazing memory, which could have its drawbacks.

As in, sometimes she would remind me of something I'd said despite me wanting to change my opinion.

"Gray," she chided. "Hadn't you just said you were going to give your brother a chance to prove himself?"

"I said that after a glass of wine and a family dinner!" I exclaimed. *"I was just feeling sentimental. The guy sucks."*

Shit like that.

Silas wasn't a bad guy but he was just a lazy piece of shit. Still, I had found a job for him and, oddly enough, it was coordinating large events. The man had a knack for party planning. It was also why I'd been kicked out of my own damn castle today.

My own castle!

Despite being the *only* one from the Earth realm and it being Thanksgiving, Silas didn't want me to help plan the festival. It was bullshit. Although I had felt pretty proud of myself for bringing such a fun holiday to the Horde. Now if we could only get some cars and equal rights here.

I was still surprised I was even allowed to be Queen with the sexist undertone of this place.

Yet, there had been no riots thus far, so I had to be doing something right. Or, and this was likely the better guess, the inhabitants were scared shitless and didn't want to risk getting their asses handed to them.

You know, because I'm a total badass.

My head whipped to the side as a small noise down below caught my attention. I knew he was close but for the life of me, I couldn't find him. If I expanded my power, I might be able to…

"Fuck!" I squeaked, at the same time that a pair of strong arms snapped around me.

I'd been caught.

"Got you," the deep and rumbling voice whispered against my ear.

I turned to look up at Adyen with a scowl. How the hell did someone fifteen inches taller than my five-foot-two-inch-self move so quietly? The dragon offered me a dangerous smile as he leaned closer his nose trailing my cheekbone.

"How did you do that?" I demanded, feeling rather inadequate in my hide-and-seek skills.

Adyen's honey-colored gaze looked over my face affectionately as his slow, blinding smile grew and made his beautiful, golden, face light up. God-damn handsome bastard. Honestly, I wondered why there wasn't a rule regulating how attractive someone could be. I mean it just made sense. What if he caused an accident? It was inconsiderate if you really think about it.

"You're actually upset I snuck up on you?" He chuckled while lifting me so I was resting more securely on the branch. I ignored how the tree shifted so there were more branches to cradle us whilst thirty feet in the air. Gods. Good thing I like heights, huh?

"No," I denied, but put my chin up anyway. "I just want to know. For tactical purposes."

A cool breeze blew over both of us, that shifted his short, dark hair as the scent of ashes and cinnamon wrapped around me in a comforting blanket. Despite wearing only a pair of leather hunting pants and a light sweater, I wasn't cold. Although I totally moved closer, as if I was.

"Right," he offered me a patronizing look before those eyes smoldered. I stilled as he lifted a thumb to my lips and smirked. Lately, I felt as though I was going crazy and had no release from it. Every single touch or smile from the boys made me feel like a teenager with a stupid crush. I blamed my total lack of sexual attraction to anyone before meeting them.

Now they had all of my attention and the bastards knew it.

"So, what do I get for winning?" He goaded in amusement. I couldn't help but get distracted by how massive his hands were on my waist. Their mere touch made me want to squirm. Who knew my type was massive warrior men with rough hands and perfect smiles?

Said no one, ever.

"The feeling of accomplishing such a daring task." I winked.

A low rumble sounded in his chest and as he lifted me easily I straddled his large form. I shivered as my hands steadied on his shoulders.

"I don't think that was what we agreed on, lil brawler." He responded, in a deeper, more serious tone.

"We didn't agree on anything," I accused with wide eyes.

"No." He shook his head. "I think we did. Now, hand it over."

What was he talking… oh no.

I felt my eyes widen as I tried to escape. "No, Adyen."

His booming laugh scared some birds as he kept me trapped with a knowing gaze. "Come on, Gray. You have to play fair."

"This is the fifth one this week. They don't even sell them in the Horde," I complained in a soft whine.

Instead of responding he just fixed me with a look. I reached behind me with a grumble and pulled out the elastic band that held back my veil of dark hair. Until recently, the dragon possessed a treasure hoard that used to be made of precious stones. Now, however, it was all my fucking shit.

It was totally cute until he started taking all my hairbands.

"Fine," I growled.

His eyes flashed black as his dragon took it before drawing me closer so that my pelvis pressed against his own. I let out a small sound as he began tracing my collar bone with his nose. I didn't bother pulling away knowing his dragon was more in control than he was.

It was a dangerous game to play with shifters because, while fun, if they were antagonized enough, they got a bit crazy. Adyen was a perfect example. The man was loving, reliable, and persistent in his affection with me. He didn't always say how he felt but I could feel it in the way he acted and looked at me. I could also feel other things that made me want to just spend all day up here. Preferably naked.

Anyway. The point is that he is all of those things and so much more. His dragon, though? That motherfucker is one possessive bastard. I mean truly. Even now, I could hear a low rumble trying to escape his throat and Adyen really wasn't fighting it all that much. I swear if I let him, his dragon would add me to his hoard of things.

"Mate." He nipped at my neck as my core melted and I felt the rate of my breathing increase.

"Adyen," I cooed, while I gently leaned forward to kiss his nose. I had figured out that trying to break away from his hold was a futile effort, and I really had no reason to. There was nothing but food and celebration on my schedule so his dragon could love on me all he wanted.

In fact, I preferred that.

It had been a long fucking week since the last coronation. I mean truly. I was thrilled to have the academy members here, mostly Esme and Bobby, but it was a massive job to get everyone situated. That was in addition to the numerous logistical meetings I had held to plan for the pressure I intended to put on Mario's army. We needed to act soon before we had to play defense at our borders.

Every night, I tended to just collapse in bed with exhaustion. So, yeah. Time with my men? It had been nonexistent. It was odd because I lived so long without any affection. Now that they'd been in my life all of a month or two, I was attached. It didn't bother me so much as surprise me. The sneaky bastards had just slipped through the cracks in my defenses.

Sneaky, sexy bastards.

"Kitten," A voice prompted both of us to look down as my smile grew. I placed my head on Adyen's chest and he fingered my hair with massaging patterns.

"Yes, Rhodes?" I asked curiously, with a small smile. I knew exactly what I had done.

"Any chance you want to explain why I was tied to my bed this morning? Lunatic sat on my chest staring at me like she was plotting my demise."

Lunatic was our adorable kitten.

"Maybe she didn't want you to leave," I noted with amusement.

"I am finding it hard to believe she was the one who tied my wrists to the headboard." He growled softly, I felt my excitement jump at that. I. Wanted. His. Control. Gone.

Mission in motion.

"You're always teasing about tying me up." I drawled as I stood. Adyen followed, holding me protectively. "Maybe, I just wanted to see what the big fuss was about."

The tree shifted, the branches creaked to form makeshift steps that allowed us to descend the thirty feet and I came face to face with our lean and lethal leader. I loved the heat in his eyes.

"Adyen took my hair tie," I complained, as my dragon's eyes reverted back to honey. He winked as they did.

"Wasn't me." He shrugged and began trailing towards the castle with a proud smirk. I turned to look back at Rhodes. My heart jumped as my spine hit the tree and he loomed over me.

"If you wanted to know what the fuss was about," he purred gently, "I could have just shown you."

I bet you could have.

My pulse jumped as he easily stretched my gathered wrists above me. A tremble worked through my system. I let out an eager gasp as his lips found my neck and he trailed soft kisses along my carotid. His knee separated my legs. I absolutely loved being pinned like this. By Rhodes specifically.

"Rhodes." I made a soft noise. "Stop teasing me."

He chuckled against my skin as goosebumps broke across my entire body. The man with pale green eyes pulled back and I saw his jaguar break through, just a bit, as gold grew more apparent.

"I'm not teasing," he grinned. "I would gladly tie you up, kitten. You just aren't ready for what that would mean between us."

"You don't know that," I muttered, as a strand of golden hair fell from his sexy man bun. Words I thought I'd never say, I might add. His golden, shadowed beard and strong jaw looked especially hot this close up. It really didn't help that the man had a crisp English accent.

"I do." He grinned. "Because when *not* if, I claim you as my mate, it's forever. I'm going to bury myself deep inside your tight body and mark you, head-to-toe, with bites."

My breathing ceased as I struggled to hold in a moan. His primal declaration had me squirming and feeling flushed.

His lip twitched. "Just say the word, though, and I'll trust you're ready."

"Bastard," I muttered. He was right. I saw them in my future, all five of them, and it wasn't going to change. I wasn't naïve, though. I knew that we were still working through things not only from my past but theirs as well. It didn't stop me from falling in love.

Ignore that.

Love? After all, what's love? I don't love anyone.

Lie.

I totally do. I was completely and hopelessly falling in love with them. Every last one of them.

Gross.

A small meow had me chuckling as Rhodes sighed, hiding his

amusement, as a fluffy white fuzzball trotted out across the forest floor. She was so sassy. Lunatic's golden eyes narrowed at Rhodes as he scoffed. He shook his head. Despite acting like she hated Rhodes, she followed him around nearly as much as Adyen. I leaned down to pick her up. She curled around me and fixed him with a glowering stare.

"She thinks you're her mom." He rationalized humor in his tone.

"How do you know that?" I kissed her head as she purred in this small humming noise.

He chuckled. "I'm a feline shifter, kitten. Of course I can tell what our kitten is thinking."

Got him.

"*Our* kitten, you say?" I grinned. He grunted at my catch. "I had no idea you thought of her as ours. I like that, Rhodes. Although, you should have asked me to marry you or something to make it official. Make an honest woman of me and all."

He put his head skyward as if the Maker would help.

"Meow," Lunatic stated emphatically as I tried to not bust out laughing.

"I know!" He snarled quietly at the small cat.

"What did she say?" I tilted my head.

The man's ears turned pink. He shook his head. "Not important. Come on let's go back."

I gasped as I trailed after him. "Rhodes! You can't do that. I need to know. This is every cat owners' dream! I have to know what she is thinking at all times. Is there a way for me to talk to her? Please, Rhodes! Tell me!"

"Sorry, love," He grinned, firmly aware he had regained some degree of control. "Can't do that."

Lunatic huffed and stretched across my shoulders as I pet her. My plan was to annoy him more but as we reached the clearing behind my private quarters, I was distracted.

What in the ever living hell?

"Bobby?" I tilted my head as he met my gaze. Marabella stood between him and Palo as the two men exchanged low, harsh words. I'd never seen my lady-in-waiting and friend look so frustrated.

"Will you both stop!" She yelled, her dark eyes flashing as that crimpy, wheat hair blew out of its up-do. It was sort of glorious. The shy woman was slowly becoming a total badass and it looked awesome on her. Just today she'd finally, after much convincing, tried on a pair of leather riding pants. Bitch looked fabulous.

"What is going on?" I frowned as Lunatic sighed. Yes, sighed.

True cat, or opinionated small person in a feline body? The jury was still out.

"What's going on is that he's being purposefully obtuse!" Bobby exclaimed, motioning to Palo.

Maker. Some heavy vocabulary for this early in the morning.

"Explain." I looked at my friend.

"Palo," Marabella drawled, staring accusingly at Taylor's brother. The demon was nearly ethereal looking - lean muscular body, crimson hair, and black eyes. Eyes that were possessively trained on the woman he'd crushed on for years, but regrettably had done little about it. Also regrettably, he wouldn't let her move onto anyone else either.

"Is refusing to hear Robert out." Marabella continued. She referred to my familiar who held her arm gently as if she was a precious treasure. I considered the role my familiar played in my life. Honestly, he was one of my best friends. I suppose it is different for everyone. Some fall in love while others train together. Robert and I were good friends. If he liked Marabella, I was supportive of it.

Wait. Robert?

Ewwwwwwwww.

No. His name is Bobby, I refuse to adapt. Hell, I'm the Queen. I can make that a thing.

"About?" I forced the issue.

"She's my mate." Bobby stated, his brown eyes and warm complexion filled with more emotion than I'd ever seen from him.

Oh, shit.

"I don't give a fuck!" Palo swore and my eyes rounded. Well, that is a first.

"I do!" Marabella shot back with a scowl. "Stop acting like children. If you want to talk this out, I will be in the gardens. And don't kill one another. I won't clean it up!"

I watched her stalk away and without a word both men followed after.

"Well..." Taylor offered a cheeky grin. "That was more entertainment than I expected for this morning.

"When did *that* happen?" I frowned curiously, as Rhodes began to absently pet the cat on my shoulder. She purred loudly. I nearly rolled my eyes. Told you they liked one another. Adyen was stretched out on the grass, his eyes closed.

Taylor stretched his arms above his head, flashing me his lean abs and marble-like skin, before winking at where my attention went. I wasn't even embarrassed because my demon was just sexy. There was no way around it. His emerald eyes, dancing with hellfire, lit up as he drew closer. A small playful smile tugged on his lips. Over a foot taller than me, I could barely see the crimson texture of his messy hair which was a damn shame because I loved his hair. In fact, I could do a lot of things involving holding his hair…

Focus, Gray.

"Baby girl," he chuckled in a rough voice, "keep thinking like that and I won't be responsible for my actions."

I hummed innocently as if I didn't know what he was talking

about. He sauntered across the clearing and I tried to ignore the curl of desire that was exploding from my center. Today he wore a tight, fitted tank top that showed off his extensive tattoos and a pair of dark pants. Personally, I found it to be far too many clothes.

"What's she thinking about?" Rhodes questioned his lips on my ear. I felt my body light up as I leaned against the jaguar shifter's chest. Lunatic trotted off towards Adyen leaving me.

Tiny little traitor.

Taylor moved closer. His smile grew bigger as a flush took over my cheeks.

"No you don't." I wiggled my finger away from him. His dangerous allure, a soft haze of raw power and red smoke, wrapped around me gently.

"Don't do what?" he teased. "Rhodes, am I doing anything?"

Rhodes nipped my ear and I jumped. He groaned. I couldn't help the small whimper that escaped as he grew hard against my ass. Taylor totally heard it.

"You look flustered Gray." The demon whispered, lifting my chin up, "What's wrong baby girl?"

Absolutely nothing with you this close.

The fucker let out a bark of laughter. Mind reading happened to be his specialty. Fuck my life.

"What's so funny?" Athens chirped as he walked through the stone archway from the castle with a massive handsome smile on his face.

"You," I quipped back. A dangerous light entered those metallic silver eyes. He didn't even bother to glamour his tattooed form anymore. The form was an expression of his full power and it made it so that his dark fade was now tinted with metallic highlights and his dark rich skin was patterned with silver runes. It was beautiful. A stunning masterpiece.

"Oh, yeah?" One eyebrow arched high as he strode closer. "I can show you funny, Gray."

Taylor laughed. He shook his head and gave a mocking chide. "Gray is just all sass today."

Rhodes distracted me with his light touches and kisses. Normally, the man was so serious and stoic. Except where I was concerned. I think it was partially his animal because lately he'd been extra physical. I was completely into it.

"Sassy? Am not!" I put up a hand to my chest dramatically.

"Somehow, I find that hard to believe." Athens's coconut scent, the smell of summer, effectively pushed out Rhodes's expensive cologne and the subtle hint of leather from Taylor. I breathed it in as he challenged me with a gaze.

"I'm an angel." I stated, with wide eyes. "Why would I ever act sassy?"

Athens moved to respond but I was gone in an instant. Neo, his brother, had managed to steal me from both men. He had me enveloped in his cool icy shadows and mint scent nearly twenty feet away. His chest rumbled with contained laughter as he nuzzled my neck.

"Well, good morning to you too," I smiled affectionately.

"I am being selfish right now, I know." He began to run his thumbs over my cheekbones, meeting my eyes with a glittering onyx gaze. "I wish I cared more."

"You should, you bastard," Athens murmured, but all of them stayed where they were.

Neo and I had a special relationship. It possessed a more serious tone and not because we'd slept together. His shadows caressed me gently, reminding me of that small detail. My skin shivered with pleasure.

No. We shared a non-physical connection. Neo understood pain, one I was intimately familiar with. Despite Colliard's betrayal, I was glad the bastard was gone. I didn't want Neo to have to see his abuser every single fucking day. I would go crazy if I ever had to see... *them*. My adopted elven parents had abused me for the majority of my childhood until I killed them.

I know. Peachy, right?

I shook my head and as if he knew, Neo gently lifted a hand. After my nod began, he gently ran his fingers across my upper back where scars marred it. The boys tried to be careful around my shoulders and back but I was becoming far more comfortable with it. I wanted to trust them with my physicality and its flaws. Neo had shown me that nothing bad would happen if I did.

When his lips trailed my crescent-shaped scar that marred my cheekbone, I tilted my head to the side. A low growl caught in his throat because I was all but exposing my throat to him. Despite not being a shifter, Neo had a raw power that sometimes felt very animalistic. I liked it. A lot.

Neo, much like his twin brother, was a bulk of muscles at 6'4". His voice gave it a nice contrast with its smooth, gentle cadence. He had a quiet disposition that I'd foolishly mistaken for shy and a penchant for doling out punishments, mostly to me.

I really should do more bad shit.

His eyebrow piercing glinted like the rest of his obsidian skin and if I didn't know him so well I'd say his tattoo form was a bit scary. It was, but in a good way, you know? In a 'I want to be all over that sexy monster' kind of way.

What? You don't have those thoughts? Right. Okay.

"Hey, Gray?" Neo spoke softly while a thoughtful look passed over his face.

"Yeah?" I snuggled closer.

"I know Thanksgiving was just going to be our small group but would you mind if I invited my mother?" His words were hushed as my heart squeezed. I knew how big of a deal it was that he wanted his mom at our celebration. While a kingdom-wide festival would occur, we were also holding a private dinner with just our little family.

"Absolutely," I nodded. "You should invite her."

His lips quirked up as a flash of perfect white teeth nearly blinded me. The alchemy mage kissed my forehead and departed, striding across the lawn towards the castle.

"Where is he going?" Athens called out.

"He's inviting your mom to our dinner," I chirped with a big smile.

The angels began to sing as Athens graced the world with one of the most charming and beautiful smiles I'd ever seen. I wanted to pepper him with kisses. Truly.

I also wanted to fuck him. Two drastically different vibes.

"Gray?" Athens whisked me up so that I was eye level with him. "Thank you."

I tilted my head. "For what?"

"For mending my family," he whispered softly.

Oh, shit. Fucker was going to make me all emotional.

"Athens," I whispered. "You know how much I care about you, right? Both you and your brother mean so much to me. I will always do anything I can to show that."

His eyes rounded as the silver melted into something more possessive. The metal mage pressed me against one of the closest trees in a second flat to afford us some privacy. Oddly I wasn't nervous about my words despite how lighthearted I usually kept things. I had only known him for two months but I knew in my heart that I loved Athens. I also loved Neo. I just didn't think they were ready to hear that yet and didn't want to rush things.

I know I sound probably crazy but what can I say? I'm a tough cookie to break but then every crumb is yours.

I knew that in some ways Athens required more words than his brother. Neo's pain lay in his father's abuse and I could understand that. I could help him heal as I healed. Athens had a different kind of pain. When his father had chosen to abuse his brother over him, despite the pain Neo faced Athens felt as though he wasn't good enough for his attention. It's messed up. Despite knowing it wasn't true, I could still feel the pain lurking right under the surface.

His eyes trailed over my face as if searching for any lies. Any hesitancy. There was nothing to see but affection. It was so easy to care about Athens. He was playful and optimistic. I felt lucky to have someone like him in my life.

"Gray," he swallowed. Words seemed right on the tip of his tongue but then my eyes closed as our lips melded together. The metallic ringing of his power wrapped around me. His kiss was playful and teasing, but there was a depth to it. An emotion fueling his lighthearted attitude.

Love.

It was love making us so happy.

Now, how in the heck did I tell him that?

2
TAYLOR

"So I don't mean to break up the very apt rendition of Sleeping Beauty's love scene in the forest," I drawled in amusement as Athens flashed me a smile. I offered him one back because I was genuinely happy he was receiving the love he deserved. Both the twins were.

Gray flashed those stunning tri-colored eyes at me. "I am not Sleeping Beauty and besides, the bitch pricks her finger on a needle and falls into a magical coma. How weak is that shit? And on top of that, in the real story the prince gets her pregnant *while* she's passed out! I mean there are just so many issues…"

In a flash, I sealed my lips over hers as she leaned back into Athens. Her babble of words stopped and when I pulled back from her soft warm scent, she narrowed her eyes.

"That," she pointed at my chest, "was sneaky."

Before I could respond, the three of us heard Rhodes calling us back. Athens squeezed her hand before walking ahead towards Neo. The two men shared a look that I had to assume related to either their mother, Gray, or both. I slipped an arm around my baby girl and tugged lightly on one of her midnight blue strands of hair.

"Are you excited about Thanksgiving?" She asked enthusiastically.

How could I deny her anything? How could I ever look into that stunning face and tell her no? The woman was like a whirlwind when excited. For the millionth time in my life, I sent out a thanks to the Maker that I'd been chosen to be part of the True Heir Guard. I mean, sure I hated it at the time, but this right here? It made it worth it.

"I could go for some food," I responded with a smirk. "Although, I'm not sure how I feel about this pumpkin pie you want. It sounds sort of gross."

It didn't. I just wanted to see her get worked up.

"Taylor!" She exclaimed in horror. "What you just said could be considered treason. That is the best type of pie in the world you are talking about."

I offered her a disbelieving look as she huffed.

"Just try it okay?"

"I guess," I murmured in an unenthusiastic drawl. "But I should get something in return for my adventurous spirit."

She snorted with a suspicious look. "What do you want?"

"A date," I responded quickly.

Her eyes warmed as she tried to hide a smile. "Where would we go?"

"It would be a surprise."

She nibbled her lip as if she was undecided but then flashed me a wide smile. "Fine. I agree."

I loved pumpkin pie so this wasn't an issue.

I was about to tease her more when something chilled the air. It was an actual sensation that crawled against my skin as the predator within me sharpened its gaze. Gray's eyes darkened and it felt like time slowed. In a movement so sharp I couldn't believe I'd done it, my body rolled hers to the ground as a low thud hit the tree behind us.

Fuck. I looked up to see a crossbow bolt sunken into the tree. *Holy shit. A crossbow?! Really!*

Luckily, Adyen had been waiting for us and he began barking orders. A call went out around the castle. I just kept Gray under me as her breathing attempted to slow. I wish I could tell you I wasn't squishing her but I wanted every single part of her body covered. I didn't want any chance of anyone being able to hurt her, even if it was irrational to think my body alone would stop them.

"Who the fuck was that!?" She snarled, struggling under my weight. I pulled away, smoothing out her hair. My eyes ran over her beautiful face and fierce expression. I didn't see any sign of injury. Fury rolled through me. Gray had been so stressed lately and the one day she has time to relax, someone attempts to fucking kill her.

"Let's get inside now," I gritted through tight teeth. Hellfire jumped through my skin as my demonic nature let out a snarl. Her magic, like ash on my tongue, struggled against me as I picked her up but I didn't pay her any mind. I knew she hated being picked up, but I hated the concept of her dying. I win. I know she said we were immortal, but I'd rather not risk it. My baby girl could act as tough or weak as she wanted. My position didn't change. I'd protect her until my dying breath and if we're immortal, she better get used to it.

"Taylor," she snarled as guardsmen ran past us. "Put me the fuck down."

Instead of responding I crossed into the stone archway and breathed a little easier except for the boiling rage under my skin. Someone had just tried to kill her. I clutched her tighter as she struggled against me. Before her magic could react, I wrapped my red smoke around her like a cocooning prison. She'd have to hurt me to get out and I was hoping she'd realize I was just doing my job.

"We're inside now," she pointed out in command. I ignored it, my ears trained on the outside. They had yet to find anything. How had someone gotten across our borders so easily? Unless it was someone from within the kingdom, a possibility I'd hate to consider.

"Let me do my job, baby girl," I commented lightly, despite my boiling temper.

Her eyes scoped out my face and she must have seen something there because she didn't say anything. I carried her through the halls and up towards her quarters. We had been near her private suite anyway. This simply made it easier. The stairs were numerous but it felt like nothing compared to the feeling crawling under my skin. I needed to calm down.

This was why I didn't let myself get upset about things. When I did it was explosive.

"Taylor," she spoke my name softly. Almost cautiously.

Once inside her room, I sat her down on the velvet couch and distanced myself. My feet took me towards the windows as I looked down at the clearing nearly seven stories down. Soldiers scouted the woods. I could see Rhodes and Adyen talking to some of the Red Masques that had been working on the border. It was odd because the border that backed up to the castle was a mountain range that didn't even access the Dark Fae lands. Any attacker would have had to go far out of their way, and besides, how had they known she'd be outside today? Maybe it had been pure chance?

"Taylor," a soft voice whispered, I shook my head and looked down at our small queen. Her silky hair was loose and free but her red lips were pressed together in concern. I tried to ignore my body's natural response to how those leather pants fit her hips. I would love to peel those off her…

"Taylor," she demanded my gaze as I tried to restrain a growl. I wasn't very often controlled by more basic nature. That was a good thing because demons could be far worse than shifters. Shifters at least respected dominance, no matter the gender, of their mates.

Demons didn't.

Demons didn't give a fuck. I tried to breathe through the urge to lock her in this room until every threat was taken care of. It wasn't that my demon nature didn't respect her authority. It just considered it his right to protect her. However necessary. A tad possessive? Yeah. You could say that.

Okay. It may have even been past possessive.

"I'm going back out there." She stated as she turned. In a blink, I had her pinned to the bed as a low sound came from my throat.

See what I mean?

"Dude!" Gray pushed my shoulder as I held myself over her and tried to keep calm.

My voice was rough as I spoke, "Baby girl, I'm going to need you to stop struggling. I'm trying really hard to not lose my shit and go all Neanderthal, but my powers are very worked up right now."

"Oh." She whispered, and instantly stopped struggling.

My forehead pressed against hers as her scent washed over me, creating an entirely new hunger that was probably far safer. She released a small sound at the change in my body language as I kept my eyes closed, trying to resist the urge to flip her on her stomach and slam into her.

"Taylor?" she whispered softly.

Her voice calling my name made me groan as I began to trail kisses and nibbles across her jawline. I could feel a shiver break across her skin as my demon gladly traded this for violence. Either way she was protected. Except from us of course. No one would keep her from us.

Yeah, that was probably as fucked up as it sounded. I never claimed that side of me was rational.

My movements were slow but I locked onto her gaze as I knelt between her spread legs and slid the material of her sweater from her waist across her ribs and over her head. I couldn't contain the pained sound that came out of me at the sight of her tiny waist and breasts covered in black lace.

This woman's curves were going to kill me. Honestly, I could spend years kissing and tasting every part of her skin and it wouldn't be enough. I never knew where I wanted to look or touch and it really was unfair to make me pick. The woman was a masterpiece. I kissed her softly on the lips, tugging and torturing the velvety skin, before moving to her neck. I grasped the back of her head and sucked, feeling the pulse of the blood just below the surface.

"Taylor!" She exclaimed, I kissed the hickey gently.

I was already feeling far better.

"Baby girl." My voice came out like gravel. "I want to see you."

Something dark slid behind her eyes and she smirked just slightly. "Well, what are you waiting for?"

Hadn't I said I wanted to peel the leather off? Her whimper at my heated hands on her cool skin had me moaning. I almost lost it when I saw that she had a matching pair of panties. The waistband that rested against her porcelain colored hip bones. Her leather pants dropped to the floor as I peeled off my own shirt, needing to feel her skin against my own.

Downstairs I could hear the chaos. I knew they would be back up here soon.

I tugged off my own pants, leaving only my boxers, as I completely confused her by tucking us both under the blanket. She started to speak and I simply pulled her against me so her head was buried in my chest. My thumb stroked over her hickey.

It wasn't that I didn't want to drill her into the bed. I just wanted more time and I knew we would be interrupted soon. Plus, nothing compared to the feel of her against me like this.

Well, besides being inside of her I assumed.

"I'm confused." She stated breathlessly.

"We don't have much time alone." My voice was hoarse as I grabbed a handful of her perky ass. "And I needed to feel you, skin on skin, to know you're alright." My magic hummed in contentment as her mouth popped open and a blush filled her face.

"Oh!" She whispered, then looked back up at me with a coy smile. "But later?"

I kissed her hickey to avoid chuckling. "Later, baby girl, you're all mine."

I just hoped later was soon. If not it meant we had far larger issues.

3
GRAY

"I *reallllyy* don't want to wear this," Marabella blushed, "I look stupid."

"Wrong!" Esme stated as she looked over my friend. "You look awesome and those boys are going to wish they hadn't been such dumbasses earlier."

Her dark eyes took on a frustrated glint as my slender friend looked over her modern clothing. I figured we had to set the trend somewhere and this festival seemed like the right place to start. That was *if* my men let me go to the festival. Not that they could actually stop me, but I suppose if their fears were valid, I might *consider* listening to them. Besides, the city was essentially on lockdown but I was assured the celebration would still occur followed by a massive meal, all organized by my brother.

I closed my eyes and tried to keep my mind "free of distractions" as Esme put it. Except getting ready for a party was the last thing on my mind right now. As I mentioned before, my coronation had made me realize how possessive and protective I felt over the kingdom. While I knew today had been an attack specifically on me, I was far more concerned about the kingdom as a whole. It felt like there was something brewing and despite being assured that Mario had yet to leave his kingdom, I felt off.

Maybe Esme was right and I needed to just take today in stride. These problems would be there in the morning as she had stated several times. Honestly, I hadn't realized just how much I'd missed my stunning friend. I loved Marabella and the boys but no one called me out on my shit like Esme.

"I like it." I stated while looking over her outfit. Marabella was wearing a pair of leather jeans and an oversized, off-the-shoulder green sweater. I'd compromised allowing her wearing black sneakers but only because they were velvet. She looked beautiful and I could tell she needed it with how everything had gone down between her and Bobby. The confusion was etched into her face.

Esme had been a far better friend to her today than I had, so I wanted to assure her of something even if I couldn't seem to give advice to save my life. My sarcastic friend sat on the edge of the tub as she re-painted her nails a different shade of gold for the hundredth time this week. She repeated her mantra of "I'm over this color" and the process of completely re-doing them. Honestly, it was sort of funny. The dress she wore was tight and warm looking, a cream-colored sweater material, and it highlighted the chandeliers of gold earrings and curly ringlets of dark hair.

At least I wouldn't be the only one with a good sense of style now. I mean I loved the concept of being a leather-wearing badass but that shit *did* get uncomfortable.

"I just don't get it," Marabella frowned, her eyes filled with trepidation. "I have been crazy about Palo for over two years now, but he's done everything from absolutely nothing too confusing me about his thoughts about us. Then I find Robert, and actually connect with him. Plus, Robert really likes me and isn't afraid to admit to it! It is so flippin' refreshing."

"And you're his mate," Esme offered a satisfied grin at her

friend's potential happiness. I felt the same. I was honestly thrilled the two of them had hit it off so well and I think it was partly because they were both shifters.

"But now," Marabella rolled her eyes, "Palo is acting like I belong to him. Well, he had his shot. I just feel like this sudden push is for the wrong reasons."

"He's being possessive," I commented.

"I would totally be okay with being with both of them, obviously." She turned pink but was on a roll. "But I don't want to be with Palo if he only likes me because someone is stealing his metaphorical toy. I never thought that was the case but in the entire time I've known him, he has never acted like such a jerk."

I nodded as I stood up on my heeled boots as I crossed the room. My jeans were a dark almost midnight color and I wore a vintage corset with it so that my waist was highlighted. Honestly, it was super badass. I even liked how the blouse underneath hung off my shoulders with loose sleeves. It was sort of pirate-like but in a Versace meets *Pirates of the Caribbean* way.

"You need to tell him that," I stated, softly. I had never gotten the full story regarding the two of them. My understanding was that they had met by accident two years ago and created a bit of a messy history. Everything from not talking at all because he hurt her feelings to just trying to be "friends." Honestly, I'm terrible with emotions so I have no fucking idea how she does it. Everything is very black and white for me, no shades of grey… we all see the humor in that, yes?

She shook her head. "No. Then he's just going to tell me what I want to hear. Smooth-talking bastard."

I let out a bark of laughter at her mild curse word. A knock on the door from the main suite made us freeze. Esme moved ahead as we followed. When the door opened my smile was nearly unstoppable.

Speak of the devil and a demon may appear.

I realize that is not the saying but, I'm the Queen. Sue me.

"Palo," Marabella's face was blank but her large dark owl eyes held hurt.

Palo's obsidian gaze flashed over her outfit as he swallowed and his fists clenched. "Can I talk to you?"

I thought she'd go. She was always so focused on making others happy that I figured she would let him say his piece. Then the bitch went and surprised me.

Her back straightened as she crossed her arms. "No."

Actual surprise filtered across his face as Esme and I backed up towards the couches but stayed within hearing distance. This was some quality shit right here.

Like you wouldn't eavesdrop? Liar.

"What do you mean, 'no?'" The demon growled as his power filtered over the two of them. Marabella was an owl shifter and while not extremely powerful, dusted the energy away and leveled a glowering stare right back at him.

Bad bitch in the making right there!

"I mean no." She stated, with a low sound. "We've been through this. You don't get to act differently now that someone else likes me. I said we could be friends and then you wanted to make it something more, only to hurt me again. So, I'm not going to sit around and wait for you to 'decide' you are ready for a relationship. I like Robert and if he is sincere about me being his mate I want to see where that goes. Owl's don't work like that as you know but I could feel a connection even if it was small."

Oh, Palo did not like that.

"Maker," he growled and cursed under his breath. Then he fucked himself over.

"What are you wearing?" He demanded.

Oh, the fool.

You see, I did feel bad for him because Palo was very clearly obsessed with Marabella. He was also an intense, blunt asshole. The two didn't mix well.

"Clothes," she quipped.

Hm. Someone's attitude has been rubbing off on her.

"No." He stepped closer as I watched from the corner of my eye. "You are not going out like that. I won't let you."

I think she had finally realized that this had nothing to do with him thinking she looked bad like last time. She sighed and shook her head. "You don't get to make that decision."

"I swear to all that is holy, little lamb. If you walk out the door wearing that tonight, I will lock your ass in my room for the night."

Well, now I saw the family relation between Taylor and him.

"Your threats don't bother me." She stated softly. Anger filled her voice. "You know, you really suck, Palo. You know how much I've liked you and after the second time of screwing me over, you have no right to dictate anything anymore. I'm sorry if you had the impression that I was a given or that I'd always be around. I'm not your property and I won't be ordered around like I am. You chose Trinity over me. You chose work over me. In fact, you seem to always pick something over me! One date, Palo. You asked for one date and you didn't even have the courtesy to let me know you wouldn't show up? You know how long I sat at that stupid pub? Two hours. Two fucking hours."

I had no idea what was going on but I'd never seen her this upset. All I could gather thus far was that there was a bitch named Trinity and that Palo had failed to make Marabella a priority? And the asshole stood her up on a date. Who fucking does that?

"Lamb…"

"I am *not* your lamb!" She snapped as the door slammed shut.
Damn.

Esme began a slow clap as Marabella stalked over to the

couch and huffed. Her eyes were excited and heated but she seemed sad. I slung an arm around her and gave her a nudge.

"Cheer up, hun. I'm sure it won't be that bad. He is all bark and no bite. Besides you stood your ground. If he didn't understand what you were saying, the man is obtuse."

It was that bad, for the record.

Around four that afternoon the three of us had been escorted downstairs by Adyen. My poor dragon had a mask of tension and concern that I wanted to kiss away. I'd squeezed his hand and offered him an understanding look. Those eyes turned nearly black and I knew his dragon was fighting for control.

I had been impressed that my brother, the lazy piece of shit who now smiled proudly, pulled off such a fantastic fall festival. It helped that it was actually the harvest in the Horde so the area surrounding the castle was filled with food stands and many other purchasable options. A metal mage, based on a picture I'd found, had crafted a Ferris wheel that looked far safer than the earth realm ones. Soft music played, competing with boisterous bagpipes. Overall audience laughter from some local comedy shows rang true.

It was fantastic.

Honestly, it was difficult for me to enjoy it though. Not only were my thoughts on the safety of my kingdom but it felt wrong to be relaxing when Mario was probably planning my demise. Not to mention, it was difficult to do or say anything remotely normal because everyone and their fifth cousin wanted to talk to me. Or stare at me. Like creepy staring. I felt bad for thinking that but come on, I love my kingdom but shit, please stop staring at me. That alone rankled my mood. Then add on the tension radiating through my boys. It was just a disaster waiting to happen.

Taylor seemed the most tightly wound. He continued to randomly touch the mark on my neck in an affectionate brush. I really didn't get it but neither of the shifters thought it was odd. Adyen's eyes were more black than honey-colored, meaning he not only felt defensive but that his dragon was calling most of the shots. Then Rhodes, bless his soul, kept trying to keep our little family upbeat but no one was really making it easy on him. Quite the opposite. Athens was uncharacteristically quiet and Neo had an arm wrapped possessively around my waist. He kept a wary eye on everyone we passed. I surmised we would be leaving the festival within the first two hours.

Turned out we only lasted an hour. Stupid assassin messing up my festival vibes. I think all of us lost interest when we got hungry. Then the Marabella situation exploded into a technicolor mess of drama. I wasn't one for eating popcorn while drama occurred but with the wars and vengeance plans, a girl's gotta do something to keep relaxed. So, when Palo stalked toward Marabella and Bobby, my eyes grew wide with interest.

"Shit," I murmured as Rhodes followed my gaze.

"Marabella," Palo growled softly but with our enhanced hearing we could totally hear. "What did I say would happen? Go change."

"Hey!" Bobby snapped. "She looks great. Leave her alone."

I'd never seen him actually pissed off. Sort of scary.

"Leave her alone?" Palo stepped nose to nose with Bobby as Marabella shook her head, annoyed.

Palo continued. "You know absolutely nothing about her, Robert. I bet you couldn't even tell me her favorite fucking color. You've been around all of two minutes so don't fucking tell me to leave her alone. If you had half a brain you'd see all of the men looking at her and agree with me instead of being a fucking problem."

Robert let out a low sound as I watched Palo nearly unravel. I was expecting a fight.

Of course, unfortunately for my entertainment, Bobby had to be rational. His eyes met mine as he rolled them to the heavens. He stared at Palo and pulled Marabella closer. Not away from Palo, as one might have expected but, rather, more securely between the two of them. Palo frowned. I'm sure my familiar was confusing the shit out of him.

The truth? Bobby was one of the most calm, light-hearted, and good people I'd ever had the pleasure of calling my friend. I love Esme but Bobby has her beat in being nice to others. He hated tension and arguing so I'm sure he wanted this resolved.

"Happy?" Bobby queried. "Now no one can look at her. You're right. I don't know her like you do. I never claimed that was the case. Hell, you can even ask her. Today I told her that she should spend some time with you, didn't I, birdie?"

Marabella flushed but nodded.

"I am not trying to take your place but I care about her also." He finished with a sigh.

Fuck! This was so not the drama I wanted.

Jersey Shore! Jersey Shore! Not some sappy, romantic soap opera. As a friend I was happy for them. As a salacious voyeur? I was disappointed.

"Can we," Marabella spoke quietly before clearing her throat to start over, "can we talk alone boys? I don't think everyone needs to hear this."

Palo held Bobby's stare, communicating something or another. Then the demon sighed looking away just after smoothing a thumb over Marabella's lip. She was bright pink. Fucking adorable.

"We can go to my office." Palo grunted as he led the two of them towards the castle.

Esme tossed out a "Go Team Marabella!" I dissolved into laughter. I could tell the boys were amused and Taylor was practically in tears.

He chuckled while burying his nose in my hair. "Fuck. I don't think I've ever seen my brother so worked up. Cold bastard. Maker, but that was amazing."

I was just happy to see the tension had disappeared from his body and expression.

All of us nodded our consent and began trailing back to the castle, officially done with the festival but glad to see the Horde citizens enjoying it. My hand slipped into Rhodes's as he tossed me a smile. It was my favorite smile because it was authentic and made him look even younger than he was. Sometimes the man looked exhausted and I wished that I could take that from him, even if I was tired myself.

"I smell food," I bounced on my toes as we made our way towards the private dining room. Had it only been a week ago that Vegas and I had dinner there? Crazy. I missed her which was saying something because I didn't make friends easily. My magic encouraged it though and I had grasped there was something not being said yet between us, something unknown.

I was cool with waiting. I had a lot of shit going on.

Silas, my brother, stood waiting for us with a big grin. I loved my brother but he annoyed me. Today? He did the opposite of annoying me. I nearly jumped at him when I walked into the room, my mouth popping open.

"You like it?" He preened, smoothing a hand over his dark nearly purple hair as it glinted in the candlelight of the small luxurious room. From the ceiling to floor it had to be a twenty-foot drop. Each arch of the gothic room was covered with festive fall garland that matched the fiery color of the two roaring fireplaces on either end. The massive table sat squarely in the center with a setting that could rival most Pinterest boards. Gold. Orange. Red. All of them mixed with silk napkins and porcelain plates. Wine and appetizers were already being served, all topped off by the autumn sunset that peeked through the windows, setting the room ablaze in a fiery hue.

I loved Thanksgiving. Usually, it was just Esme, Bobby, and I celebrating, so I was totally being an over-emotional little bitch right now. I turned towards my brother.

"This is amazing, Silas, thank you." I gave him a hug that left him speechless before turning back around. I walked towards the head of the table between Rhodes and the place reserved for my brother. A content smile took over my face. Music played in the distance. The sounds of the festival echoed from below.

As food, elaborately done and well-made, was served I let my eyes trail over everyone. From my men to Esme and Laurena. The evening was packed full with laughter and lighthearted conversation. Even the arrival of the three who'd been arguing wasn't a big deal. It was clear from the pleased smile on Bobby's face that something had been worked out and based on Marabella's pink cheeks, it must have been good. Palo looked far calmer with his arm wrapped around her chair while Bobby kissed her hand gently as they laughed about something. My heart squeezed affectionately.

"Hey." Esme narrowed her eyes at me. "Are you getting emotional? Because you know what happens when you cry. I cry. And I'm an uglier crier."

"Isn't everyone?" Rhodes stated, amused.

Esme shook her head. "No! Not to be weird, but Gray even looks like a fucking supermodel crying. I think it is the only thing I truly hate about her."

I snorted and flipped her off. She was right though, I needed to focus on food.

In the time I'd been in the Horde, I hadn't maintained my weight. That concerned me because that meant losing muscle, which I needed. I was small enough. I started to cut into the food and found myself in a very special heaven when they served pumpkin pie early. I began eating it and narrowed my eyes at Taylor who had easily eaten his within a minute.

"Tricky bastard," I muttered, not minding because now we would have a date night.

It was such a peaceful evening that I began forgetting about nearly being shot earlier. I temporarily forgot about our war. I started to rest easy. So, of course, that *would* be when trouble happened. God forbid I have a peaceful thanksgiving.

Honestly, it was times like this that I wish I had a normal life. Like Vegas! She was probably relaxing at home enjoying her Thanksgiving. Then again, she didn't have an entire kingdom to worry about so I suppose our priorities were a tad different.

Around midnight, a comfortable easy pace had everyone tipsy and well-fed. I was now curled up on Adyen's lap as the twins sat with their mom sharing childhood stories. It sounded like, and not to judge, they were annoying little shits. I'd never say that to their faces though. Or maybe I would, but not with their amazing mother around.

Taylor chuckled at my thought, but continued to sip on his ale. Rhodes had a distant look on his face as if he was trying to figure something out. Overall, though they seemed much more relaxed.

It was just past midnight when the boom of an explosion rocked the Horde.

"What the hell was that?" I snapped as the eruption burned fire along our northern border. It was a violent shade of black and red. Dangerous and set to harm as much as possible.

Rhodes instantly barked orders as I moved closer to the window, my brow furrowing as I tried to grasp what was occurring. It was clear no large army stood on my land, so who the hell did this? It wasn't King Mario's style to send out single units to pick away at my border. He was more of a "big show" type of guy. An over-compensator if you ask yours truly.

"I want to go with you," I commented to Adyen as he tossed

on his jacket. Had I ever mentioned how handsome he was? How handsome all my boys were? Even after a night of celebrating, Adyen had only a slight scruff to show for it.

Damn him.

"Baby," he tilted my chin gently. "I would really rather you stay here, but I won't stop you."

My lips quirked up in an appreciative smile as I walked towards the door. Smart man. I tossed my heels to the side and sprinted, ridiculously fast, towards the riding stables. I didn't run very often because, frankly, it seemed a bit childish to sprint down my castles hall without shoes, but if there was ever a time it would be this. It felt exhilarating in a way.

The corridors of stone were dark and I found myself sprinting through the shadows that the oil lights didn't reach. Damn we needed more electricity around here. I had long given up on my hair and the normal silky texture was wavy and dancing with my movement. If I didn't take a moment like this to appreciate my agility and abilities, I'd never do it.

I entered the stables and slid to a stop in front of the correct stall, my boys following behind. My boots were already there and I slipped them on as I swung myself up onto my midnight colored horse. Her name was Midnight. As I've said I am very creative with names. It should be my second job.

"You should stay here," Taylor muttered. I smiled. I had never thought of the demon having a protective side because in normal life he is the adventurous one. Right now though? I could see the authentic concern all over his face. It was quite sweet really.

"It's going to be fine," I promised before offering him a confident look.

Rhodes shifted with a loud echoing roar into something far more vicious than a normal jaguar. His massive long teeth were deadly as daggers but when he nudged my leg I didn't flinch. The twins were already on their way out there with the guard. The four of us left to catch up to them. I grasped the reins on Midnight and with a gentle movement against her side, the bitch took off like a bat out of hell.

I lied. This was better than running.

Despite the circumstances, a smile crawled onto my face. I could have traveled by foot but I'd always enjoyed riding and the muscles that worked felt good. A howl echoed through the forest that had the savage in me wanting to hunt. I knew our guards who could shift had to track scents. The explosion cast a massive red light with the fire that hit our border. I didn't hold out hope they would actually find anything useful. No doubt most of it had been burned up by now. I jumped off Midnight right as I reached ten yards out. Rhodes had kept pace with me the entire time. He had worn one of those special uniforms that stayed on despite shifting.

It was a shame because I would much rather he shift back naked but I suppose this wasn't the time.

"What the hell happened?" I demanded from Neo.

His glittering eyes met mine as the soldiers around him scattered. Athens watched for the soldiers crossing the border just in case more laid in wait. It was odd seeing such a serious look on his face. I felt compelled to remove the tension from their lives. Unfortunately, we all knew damn well that would never happen.

"Bomber," Neo stated, his voice rough. "Probably a suicide bomber, but we won't know for sure."

"What?" I demanded. "Do we know if it was one of Mario's men?"

My alchemy mage shook his head. "It was dragon fire so there was nothing left of him or her. I fear that this had nothing to do actually causing harm. He didn't even cross the wards on our borders. He just blew himself up to make a fucking point."

The wards on our border were strong but if someone was

determined enough they could fight through the pain. Especially if they were skilled. It made me cautious that Mario's wards were so weak of late. The fucker probably wanted us to leave our land so that he was in a landscape he understood better.

I could feel the magic inside of me growing furious as a snarl nearly broke from my throat. "Any update on what the scouts have said?"

Athens spoke as he walked forward. "They've been prepping but no movement yet."

Well, that would take them a bit. Hopefully. Unless they portaled but, shit! An entire army? That would take time as well. My heart started to beat more rapidly as I shook my head. I really hadn't wanted to go on defense but it seemed that if we didn't make a move soon, we would be forced to. My biggest problem? I didn't want to leave our land because it left it weak and undefended. Yet, staying here exposed the entire kingdom to war. My hair whipped across my face as the cold wind howled with anger. The fire died down along with my spirit.

I needed sleep. I needed to think this over.

"Rhodes," I said softly. The man appeared at my side, his eyes darkened as if he knew what was going on in my head. "Call a meeting with the commanders of SE and the Red Masques tomorrow. I need to change our strategy."

He didn't ask questions that might change my mind and I was thankful because I had no idea what he would change it to. Without another word, I made it back to my horse and swung myself up. I began to ride back home. The only comfort I felt was the sound of Adyen above me in the skies, his heavy wing span looking black instead of gold. The longer I rode the more livid I became. I hated Mario. Gods, I hated him so much. I would kill that fucker for what he'd done to my mother and how he'd murdered my father in cold blood.

No matter how long this took, I vowed to see his heart ripped out from his body.

Savage, you say?

He had no idea what was coming for him.

4
ADYEN

I landed and shifted back but Gray was already inside. She had been for a time and while I'd wanted to follow, my dragon had been far too worked up. I sighed, feeling her indecision and frustration through our bond. It made me furious. Furious that she had been saddled with all of this on top of becoming queen.

My dragon let out a deep growl and I tried to calm down before I ventured inside. In and out. Slow breaths. I breathed until my dragon felt more rational. Without another thought, I went to Gray's chambers. I didn't bother knocking before letting myself in. What I saw there hurt my heart.

Gray, our fierce little queen, was curled up on the bed sleeping. It was clear she'd been crying. A single track of smeared mascara was on her cheek.

My lil brawler.

I pulled off my uniform before tossing on a pair of shorts. I kept extra clothes everywhere. Right now, I was thankful for it.

I knew the other men wouldn't be back for a bit and that when they were she would want to handle the plan moving forward. Her breathing was deep so I didn't fear waking her as I slid off her boots and peeled down her ridiculously tight pants. I should have felt bad about that, but for me, there was nothing wrong with making my mate more comfortable. She could punch me later if she wanted.

I sort of hoped she did because then I could pin her down. I shook my head at my own thoughts.

A soft sigh came from her lips as I tugged my massive shirt over her and reached along her spine to undo the crazy corset she wore. I relaxed once it slipped off and I made sure the large shirt was comfortably around her. My entire body was fucking hard and my dragon was grumbling about claiming our mate but even he understood right now was not the time.

My yawn was genuine as I crawled into bed with her. She rolled so that her body was intertwined with mine. Our mating bond hummed and I breathed in her scent before letting my fingers trace her waist over the shirt I positively hated right now. I wanted her skin against mine.

Eventually, I was comfortable but I still couldn't sleep. Gray seemed tense even in sleep and it made me overprotective. Like, really, really overprotective.

Probably unhealthily so, honestly.

"No," she whimpered against me. I cursed knowing that she'd been having nightmares every night this week. It had been getting better but her long term abuse had left a scar on her subconscious that would never go away. All we could hope to do was surround her with enough love and safety so she could heal. I wanted to replace all those damn nightmares with so many good memories she couldn't remember the bad.

I tugged her closer and pressed a soft kiss to the back of her neck where her scars began. She whimpered in her sleep and as much as I wanted to shake her awake, the last time we'd done that it had made it worse. She also had punched me right in the jaw. It fucking hurt.

It also turned me on which is an entirely different issue. My dragon purred contentedly at the idea of how strong our mate was. One day, she would be an amazing mother.

That thought alone had me cursing. I mean we already had Lunatic... So was it that farfetched to consider?

When all of this was over we would have to talk about what this was. I mean the Horde hadn't had a True Heir in such a long time. Would the kingdom accept us being with their Queen? Did it matter to Gray what they thought? I grunted and squeezed her closer. Hopefully we'd figure it out, because the one thing I did know? I couldn't see myself with anyone but her.

A soft whimper broke from her throat as she began to shake in earnest. I felt my chest tighten as I smoothed back her hair that grew damp with the sweat breaking out over her entire body. I knew she'd only gotten about an hour of sleep before I had come in. I wanted her to sleep but if she was this worked up, was her body even resting?

Before I could decide whether to wake her up, she let out a sharp cry and shot up in bed, panting. Her body shook. Her hand reached to touch her scar. I swallowed knowing she was thinking of the woman who'd cut her face like that. The woman that, if still alive, would have a short time left before I snuffed the life out of her myself.

"Li'l brawler," I whispered gently. Her head snapped towards me. Her eyes were a true, deep sapphire blue filled with distress and unshed tears. Like the tough woman she was, Gray blinked back the tears. I didn't push. I knew she needed to move past the dream. Move past the nightmarish things that tainted her memories of childhood.

"Adyen," she sighed. She crawled forward and laid directly on top of me so I could keep my arms wrapped around her. Her chin tilted up so that I could look into her beautiful face. A face that slowly reverted back to her normal calm. One day, when we weren't in a war, I wanted her to feel comfortable crying openly. Not just from nightmares. I wanted her to feel comfortable enough to share that side of herself, even if it was painful. Until then, I would be here for her as much as possible but I wouldn't push it. I wanted *her* to make the decision to open up to us.

"It's okay," I kissed the top of her hair.

"I don't know what to do," she spoke, her voice pained with indecision.

"Yes, you do," I confirmed without a doubt.

Her lips thinned as she shook her head. "I don't though, Adyen. If we go on the offensive and attack we risk going into their territory and leaving ours open. If we go on the defensive we can fortify everything here but it puts everyone at risk when the battle comes to us."

I had an answer but she needed to process this herself. I added something helpful though. "There are lands to the north. Not in the forest area but further east, that has an open field. It is far enough from the kingdom that most people don't even know it is there unless they've done patrol for SE."

"What if they don't go there though?" She whispered as her brain began moving a mile a minute.

"Force them to." I stated.

"Lower the wards in just that area?" She murmured thoughtfully.

"I think that is a great idea." I admitted. I was glad she'd come to the conclusion herself. It was hard to remember that despite her fierceness the woman had only been a queen for a short amount of time. She had no formal tactical training. Her power was raw and unformed. My dragon practically preened at the thought that we aided her. It only made sense. What else are the True Heir Guard for, if not this?

My chest hurt a bit at that. Proud as I was, I needed this to be more. She was my mate. I wasn't positive she knew the affection, love, and devotion that came with that. It was hard waiting for her to process through all of our connections but I was determined to take it slow, knowing it would be worth the wait. I had already seen my brothers heal so much because of the love she offered.

We need affection and love too...

I rolled my eyes internally at my fucking dragon's whine of self-pity. What was his actual issue?

You sound like a bitch.

He snorted.

What would that make you then?

"Adyen?" Gray prompted frowning.

I grunted with a sigh. "Sorry, my dragon is being a bitch."

She snorted. "So what does that make you?"

I barked out a laugh because of the similarity in conversations. It only reinforced how fated our bond was. My hands wrapped around her waist as I sat her on top of me. Despite how small she was, straddling me like this, I never felt she was weak. There was an energy and confidence to Gray that made her fill the space. Her size was no matter because her energy made her ten times taller than me.

She put her elbows on my chest. "I need to plan for this meeting."

"You need sleep," I retorted.

"By the way..." she suddenly frowned, looking down at my shirt on her form. "Who changed my clothes?"

My lips curled up into a smile. "I did."

Gray's cheeks filled with color as she tried to act mad but couldn't help smiling. "Oh? Did you like what you saw? Pervert."

I'd show her how perverted my thoughts were anytime.

A low sound broke from my chest. "Now that is a ridiculous question, I fucking loved what I saw. You're fucking stunning."

A dangerous glint entered her eyes as she moved her hips so that she wiggled against my hardening cock. I didn't even try to stop the pained sound that came from my throat as she trailed a nail up my chest and broke my skin, causing shivers to travel up my spine. Fuck, this woman was something else!

I also could not keep up with her emotional range. I loved it though. Always kept things interesting.

"Well," she purred, "maybe I should show you more."

I had her flipped on her back with myself over her in a quick movement, my mouth molding to hers. Her taste was sweet on my lips as her nails bit into my neck and her legs wrapped around my waist. I'd been around for a while now and there had never been a woman I'd met that had invoked the reaction in me that Gray did. She was like an addiction. You just kept wanting more and more of her until you realized she was your entire life.

I didn't mind one bit.

A soft sound from her throat caused me to pull back from her lips and watch her soft, relaxed expression. I liked her like this. I liked that it seemed I could distract her from everything.

"What do you need, lil brawler?" I whispered softly in a heated tone.

She shivered and shifted so that we were locked even tighter together. I could see a slight vulnerability in her eyes. I knew damn well that she didn't have a lot of experience with a healthy sexual relationship. It made her nervous but she was so brave and tried to move past it. Still, I wanted to tread lightly and only do what she wanted or needed.

Her lips moved to open but nothing came out. My nose nuzzled against hers as my hand skimmed down her thigh and her breath hitched.

"Gray," I murmured against her neck, "you need to tell me what you need."

Her eyes darkened as she breathlessly responded. "I don't know, I feel different. I think it's your dragon."

Ah! Yes. The mate bond that was driving me fucking crazy. I wondered if it would affect her.

"What does it feel like?" I began to nibble along her neck as my tongue brushed over the skin in a healing way. She let out a small moan of desire as she tilted her head to the side baring her neck to me. She was going to kill me.

If I died with my head buried against the soft skin of her neck I would be a happy fucking shifter.

"Like I want you to bite me," she whispered shyly.

My entire body froze. My smile grew because dragons didn't need to rush things to claim their mates. If she wanted a mating mark then I would damn well give her one.

"I'll give you what you want sweetheart," I murmured, "but you know what that will mean, right?"

Her brow furrowed. It was clear she didn't completely understand how all of this worked. I couldn't blame her. Despite knowing the basics of the Horde and Fae lands, there were still things she wasn't well versed in. It wasn't the type of knowledge that existed in books. I suppose that was just one more reason she needed us.

Yes. I was grasping at reasoning for her needing us in her life. It was hard because the woman was just so damn capable.

"If I bite you Gray that means I'm claiming you as my mate. Is that what you want?"

Her breathing hitched. I continued. "We don't have to go any further now but once we start the mating process, the two of us will be bonded no matter what happens in the future. I need you to be damn sure about this. Shifters only place a mating bond once in their life, so I don't want either of us to take this lightly."

Please be sure about it.

Also, I didn't think it was necessary to state that I was essentially proposing to her. That is what this would be. A lifelong commitment.

A soft look filled her eyes and a heart clenching sensation moved through me. My entire life I had been wanted by my family because of the place I held in society. I am sure they loved me but after all I was a True Heir Guard and a dragon. That was a lot of fucking power and influence, so I was important to them.

When Gray looked at me like she was right now, it made me feel like she would care about me whether I was who I was, or just a normal shifter.

"I'm positive, Adyen."

Thank the gods.

I wasn't about to ask twice.

5
GRAY

"Adyen!" I let out a small cry right as his teeth clamped down on the space between my neck and shoulder. An electric shock filled my entire system and my eyes fluttered shut. His scent of ash and cinnamon had me falling into an almost sleepy state. I felt all the energy and need for dominance flush out of me momentarily as a ridiculous amount of peace and contentment filled me. Adyen's soft lips pressed against the mating mark and my eyes opened.

Woah. Holy shit.

His eyes were black with power and his primal energy wrapped around the two of us as he placed a gentle kiss on my lips. I wanted to deepen it but he just kissed my face in small light affectionate brushes. I couldn't speak and for once nothing concerned me. I couldn't worry because my mate would take care of it.

Mate? This was some trippy shit.

"Gray," he murmured gently. "Open your eyes, sweetheart."

My eyes fluttered open as I looked at the handsome bastard. A grin spread onto my face as one of his eyebrows shot up. I just feel so cozy and hazy, how could I not smile at him? My body was safe and warm, trapped under him. This homey, almost languid feeling worked its way through my bones.

"You're so handsome," I placed a finger on his nose and poked gently.

His dangerous white teeth flashed as his body rumbled with laughter. I frowned. "Why are you laughing at me, big guy?"

"Because you're fucking adorable." He watched me with a soft look. "And I'm not laughing at you, lil brawler. I just had no idea how the mating bond would affect you."

I hummed as his energy coursed through me. I spoke, resting a hand in the center of my chest. "I can feel you inside of me."

That sounded way dirtier than I'd meant it. Oh, well.

He smirked. "Oh? What does it feel like?"

Instead of playing into his devious glint, I kissed his nose. "Like magic and love. Like us."

Adyen stilled but I was already falling asleep. I felt him wrap himself around me as he rested his lips against the bite. It sparked under his touch. He murmured a series of soft words that made my heart soar but knew I'd forget in the morning.

The one feeling that was undeniable? The one I wouldn't forget? Adyen was mine.

My dragon. Forever.

I figured I would only sleep for an hour or so.

I woke up to the sound of voices, humored but hushed. Rhodes's accent was nearby as he presumably spoke to the man wrapped around me. "You put the mating bite on her?"

"Of course I fucking did, I wasn't about to ask twice."

My jaguar chuckled. "You know how difficult it's going to be until you complete the bond right?"

He buried his nose in my hair. "I know."

Rhodes was silent for a minute and then he spoke quietly. "I wish it worked like that for naturalistic shifters."

"Have you ever heard of any cases where the mating wasn't paired with sex?"

"Not that I've heard of and I don't want her to ever feel rushed." He murmured in a rough voice.

I felt pain surge through my heart at his sad tone and before I could stop myself, I squirmed against Adyen and caught him off guard. In my sleepy state I thought it was a good idea to crawl into Rhodes's lap and curl my head in his neck to show my affection. After a frozen moment, Adyen chuckled quietly and Rhodes wrapped his muscular arms around me.

"Good morning, kitten." He whispered softly.

I purred with pleasure at the sound of his voice and it was echoed by a small meow. I would have laughed but my body was too relaxed. Lunatic crawled into my lap and it made a cute little tower of cuddling. Rhodes, Lunatic, and me.

Adyen continued to laugh. "Oh god, I need a fucking camera."

"I got you," Taylor said with a rolling chuckle. "Now, that is what I call a Christmas card quality photo."

"Let me see," Rhodes said his voice amused but filled with something else. Something more emotional. I could briefly see the twins relaxing near the living room area but I was to sleepy to say anything.

My eyes opened as I peeked through my hair to see a photo on Taylor's Earth realm phone. In the photo, Adyen sat laid out on the bed with his arms behind his head laughing. Rhodes looked down at me affectionately where I was curled into a small ball in a massive shirt. Lunatic, the sassy bitch, had her eyes on Rhodes while sitting on my lap as if daring him to say something.

I fucking loved it.

"Print out a copy of that." I whispered and Rhodes squeezed me affectionately.

"So, I love this," Athens chirped, "but baby, it is almost nine in the morning."

Oh, crap.

I jumped up. Rhodes grunted. I immediately looked at Neo who watched me with an intense yet affectionate look from the end of the bed near where Taylor sat. Athens stood and offered me a cheeky smile.

"I missed the meeting," I frowned and looked at Adyen. The cocky bastard smiled. *"You* did this!"

He chuckled. "I don't feel guilty. You look well rested for the first time in weeks."

"We took care of the meeting, baby," Athens added.

I started to be sassy. Instead, I yawned and brushed the bite mark by accident. The unintentional brush caused Adyen to let out a low rumble. Rhodes grinned. My lips curled at the edges. I winked at Adyen before my eyes trailed to the window where the sun brightened the fall day.

"What did they find?" I asked quietly.

"Nothing." Taylor sighed, his voice gruff. "Absolutely fucking nothing."

So the fire had either been set from afar and exploded or the person responsible had been incinerated right there on the spot. Either scenario was awful.

I felt like I was missing something. I felt Mario was going to do something besides attacking directly. An assassination attempt and a bomber were not quickly made decisions. It was in these moments that I was glad my good friends were either here in the castle or on Earth realm. I didn't want Vegas being caught in any more of this after the coronation. I wouldn't forgive myself if her or her boys were hurt. My protective side had already claimed them.

Wait.

Oh, shit.

"Colliard," I hissed as Neo grunted. Neo and Athens's traitor father had escaped but not after seeing who I was close with at the coronation. Who I cared about.

Nevermind. The Earth realm wasn't sounding safe enough.

"We need to get Vegas and her men here," I stated my frown growing, "I don't trust Mario to not go after them."

"We would have to portal into the Earth realm," Taylor stated in a serious tone, "and then portal again all the way to…where the fuck do they live?"

Everyone paused as we realized we had no fucking idea.

"Get your brother," I encouraged. Taylor disappeared in a cloud of red smoke and we waited in a comfortable silence for less than a minute.

"Maker!" Palo hissed. I snorted because the demon looked like he had just woken up, his shirt unbuttoned with…lipstick on it? My lips parted.

"So..." Taylor had the biggest fucking grin. "You will never guess who the fuck I just found in this man's bed. In all fairness, I have to give you more than one guess, because it wasn't just one person."

"Bobby?!" I exclaimed. Good for them!

I was jealous. Marabella was getting more action than me.

Palo offered his brother a dark look. "What do you need, brother? And, yes, Your Majesty, it seems that the three of us have worked out our differences."

So formal.

Then Athens lost it to laughter. "Yeah, I'll bet you fucking have! Tell me was that before or after the two of you..."

I punched his shoulder to stop him from uttering the dirty words he was about to spew out. The mage fell to the floor in dramatic, mock pain. I focused on Palo. "We want Vegas and her men here for safety reasons, we are going to portal but we need to know where in the heck they live."

Palo's eyes lit with humor. "Boston."

"Oh!" I nodded. "That's a groovy place to live."

"Who the bloody hell says 'groovy,' Gray?" Rhodes questioned.

"Shut it, kitten man," I nodded towards the kitten boa wrapped around his neck. He narrowed his eyes and my mouth twitched in a teasing smile. I totally wanted to see what he would do.

"Should I let them know you are coming?" Palo asked.

My lips peeled back. "No, I think it will be way funnier to surprise them. Best case they are just lounging around. Worst case, we interrupt an eleven-person orgy. Who knows! Either way, it should be a blast."

"They are an interesting group," Neo added with a thoughtful expression.

"You mean fucking crazy!" Palo growled. "Those ten mad men, specifically and including my cousins, are actually insane. Like on Tamara and her men's level. I know they seemed nice here but let me just tell you the things I've been told and seen."

Taylor snorted. "Why does this surprise you, Palo? Have you met Edwin? Or, better yet, Byron? Our cousins are the very definition of unstable. Fun, though. Really fucking fun to hang out with."

"Wait. Who is Tamara?" I asked Adyen because he was the only one looking at me.

Everyone got suddenly quiet at that question.

"I really don't know how to explain that mess," Palo frowned.

"I've got this," Athens smiled and looked at me. "Tamara and, far more specifically, her demonic husbands are nightmares. I mean they are very literally the inspiration for the seven deadly sins."

"They also act like children," Neo drawled. Mirth danced in his eyes.

If Neo thought they were funny that was probably bad. He isn't amused easily and when he is? Well, it probably isn't a good thing. He flashed me a smile as if he knew my thoughts.

"Essentially," Rhodes sighed, "they are extremely powerful and don't give a bloody hell what happens to anyone else. For example, Tamara has made it so that Cain is not allowed to kill anyone, which is difficult considering his wrath, unless she places them on a list."

"Why?" I raised a curious brow. I already loved this girl.

"The story goes, now mind you they've been around 200 something years, that she flirted with a couple of shifters and he slaughtered all of them."

"Because?" Adyen asked clearly not having heard this story.

"He was jealous that they were talking." Palo finished the example.

Well, shit.

"Yeah, I'm going to need to meet her," I offered a devious grin.

All my men narrowed their eyes at Palo who put his hands up. "That was supposed to scare her off, not make her want to be Facebook friends with them!"

I stood up and offered a morning stretch.

"Come on, boys! Let's go bother Vegas!"

I was totally using this as a mini-vacation.

6

GRAY

*P*ortal travel, without a doubt, always left me feeling odd. Especially considering the short turn-around time from leaving the Horde to landing in Boston. I probably could have figured out a way to jump realms but that shit sounded dangerous. So, instead, we landed our asses in the snow of Estonia and, after a momentary reprieve, we portaled again to Boston.

Originally, I had wanted all the boys to come with me but by the time Friday evening rolled around and we prepared to leave, there had been another border attack on the other side of the lines. It was smaller and, once again, didn't cause any major damage. I almost felt as though they were trying to gain our attention. As if we hadn't assumed they were coming already. Either Mario was beyond dense or he was attempting a distraction technique. It worried me to leave but the boys assured it would be fine. Adyen and Taylor were with me and, while the portalling was exhausting, I was happy they were in tow.

At this point in time, I would take any alone time I could have with any of them.

Focusing on the location Palo had provided was easy enough,

but the energy to actually portal took a lot out of me so it took much longer than normal. Along with the difference in time zones, it felt as though we'd had a million lay-overs in bad airports and had been traveling for hours on end. When the Earth realm air hit my nostrils, I smiled and sucked it in greedily noticing how different it was from the Horde. Also not nearly as clean, but I didn't have the time to reflect on the substantial pollution issues plaguing Earth this morning. I was *sans* coffee and feeling it.

Both boys grunted to a halt behind me. We were greeted to a pretty fucking funny if not downright ridiculous sight. Palo might have been right. These fuckers were insane.

First, I would like to note that the gothic monstrosity Vegas and her boys lived in looked like something out of a horror movie. Eerily beautiful, but totally creepy. And that's coming from a woman living in a massive castle without modern luxuries. The entire garden around us was dying under the chilly Boston sky. The air seemed thick with the smell of ash. My eyes trailed to a large tree bursting with red and orange flames. They didn't seem like normal flames. Once again I felt as though my friend was hiding how talented she was. The woman just smelled like fire and magic. Or maybe I still didn't know enough about the people I was supposed to be leading.

Second, several men, Vegas's men, lounged on the stone patio pavilion watching the scene unfold before me with keen interest. The long-haired blonde man laughed at something being said as the elemental mage held Vegas on the ground with grass cuffs.

Grass cuffs? Kinky.

She laughed about something but then looked super emotional the next second. Edwin, the commander of the Red Masques, crouched down beside her with an expression so focused it bordered between obsessive and sweet. Fucking weird shit.

"Fuck," the elemental mage released her and yelled at Edwin.

"Edwin, dude, don't make her sentimental. You just said she's emotional! Now you are making her cry and shit. Bandit may actually kill you. He hates Vegas crying more than anything."

Was Bandit the scary one? I tried to remember. Blonde hair and green eyes? Made you feel like you were staring into a massive void. He was possibly the only person I'd ever met in my entire life that scared me. Mind you, it wasn't much but still. What did it matter, really? All of them were a bit intense. Yeah, I know. *Takes one to know one.* I was well aware that I was more powerful than them but, fuck, if they ever got strong enough, I'm not sure the Fae world would survive their particular brand of crazy. My flavor was fairly strategic but just happened to include a growing bloodlust and an interest in all things violent. It was a primal energy. This? This was just some odd fucking shit.

I wondered briefly if we had landed on the wrong realm. This shit was Wonderland worthy.

Edwin winced and paled. "Sorry, *dolcezza*."

"Oh, great!" Adyen grunted in a dismal whisper. "Our special forces commander is using pet names. Fantastic."

I looked at him with an ironic brow raised. "What do you call lil brawler?'"

My dragon's eyes flashed darkly to my bite mark causing Taylor to laugh quietly. We continued to watch the scene as some of the men noticed our presence.

"No!" Vegas exclaimed while chuckling tears dripped down my cheeks. "This is fucking ridiculous, I need to get this shit under control."

Was she laughing?

God I picked the weirdest friends.

"What's ridiculous?" My voice boomed as their heads whipped towards us.

"Gray?" Vegas echoed.

I smiled and stepped forward as she jumped up, eyes filled

with emotions and body with intense power levels. My magic sought out hers. While I encouraged it to figure out what the hell she was, my magic just gave hers a high five and started shooting the breeze like old friends.

Good. So helpful.

"Hey," I pulled her into a hug. She squeezed back, bouncing on her toes with excitement.

"What are you doing here?" She asked excitedly as her other men walked over.

"We need to talk," I spoke, feeling oddly hyped up instead of tired. It was her fault. She was jumping around like a bunny.

"Sorry." Edwin grunted while trying to hold her in place. "Her magic seems to make her a bit more reactive to emotions."

One of the boys snorted and I narrowed my eyes, their eyes snapping away immediately. Good. Only *I* was allowed to poke fun at my friends.

"Let's go inside," Vegas tugged on my hand and I followed. I noticed that she was dressed in workout gear and felt a small tug of pride knowing she'd been training. I wanted to think it was because of the problems in the Horde but maybe she was just enjoying a casual workout.

"Nice place," I commented as she led me down a hall.

"Right?" she chirped. Her hair whipped around in a ponytail. Must be nice to be able to keep one of those in. I tossed an accusing look toward Adyen.

I meant what I said about the gothic mansion. It seemed lived in and despite being a tad shadowy and dark, there was a warmth to it. It's totally possible that it wasn't imagined. The warmth could be coming from my friend. Either I was really fucking cold or she was searing.

"So, what's going on?" She sat down on the couch and I moved to the seat across from her. I started feeling badly, considering taking them away from here, now that I'd seen them in their everyday life. Her boys filed in. I felt Adyen sit next to me, he wrapped an arm around me possessively. I knew he understood, as well as I did, that none of those boys were a threat but it didn't stop his dragon.

Taylor sat on my other side and wrapped a hand around my leg. He stroked it gently with his thumb. I leaned forward slightly, speaking to Vegas. "I hate to do this, especially after seeing all of you so happy here, but we need you to come to the Horde. There have been more attacks from the Dark Fae and since you were seen with me last…"

Vegas's eyes flashed a deep purple, nearly amethyst, with understanding and something else I didn't understand. She offered me a look that seemed far too knowing. Finally, she spoke.

"We actually had decided to leave for the Horde within the next day as it was."

Oh.

Taylor groaned dramatically. "Gray, we just wasted so much time."

And energy. So many hours and energy. That bastard Palo had been right. We should have called ahead.

I scowled at Taylor's smirk regarding my thoughts. "Taylor, this was not a wasted trip! We had a mini vacation and now we are perfectly refreshed to kill Mario. Plus, how would we have known they were planning on returning anyway?"

All right. Most of the relaxing part wasn't true, but I didn't want them to feel bad about it. Taylor offered me a raised brow. He started to say something but Commander Edwin spoke. I focused back on the group. Within a minute I'd sized them up and found myself surprised by their dynamic as always.

I loved…really *liked* my boys. A lot. I considered us to have a healthy love, er, liking relationship. We all respected one another and I felt safe around them. We were normal. As normal as Fae can be. Admittedly slightly scary and violent. But, trust me when

I say that their group was centered around Vegas, I don't mean how the boys are my guard and I'm their Queen. No, I mean they are *literally* centered around her. Like she is their universal focal point and the only thing that has existed. Ever.

Even food. She existed more than food. That is fucking terrifying. How the hell does an individual become more important than food?

I tried not to let my analysis show as I categorized each of them and tried to understand their dynamic because it had to be something other than boys like girl. Commander Edwin, his eyes not on Vegas but the three of us, had his hand wrapped around her thigh possessively. Not very different from his cousin, my demon Taylor. The alchemy mage, according to Neo, was one of the strongest in the Horde yet he used pet names? All right. That was sort of cute.

Then you had his brother, Byron the blood mage, who had a vicious reputation. The Horde equivalent to Vlad the Impaler. Even my boys tried to steer clear of him. Not because they couldn't overpower him, but because they said it would be a "messy affair."

Next, there was the man sitting on the other side of her who didn't move his eyes away from her face. Oh! That was the scary one! His intensity was some shit, man. I frowned momentarily because his magic felt almost too intense for a human turned mage. Hell, maybe too intense for even a natural born mage. Fascinating.

Then there was the red-headed blood mage who looked far too happy for this conversation. I think he might have been broken. Maybe just a bit? Behind the couch was a man nearly as large as Adyen. I could fucking feel his animal roaming around under his skin. I was worried he might randomly shift. He kept staring at Vegas's necklace every few minutes.

Weird.

A man with long dark choppy hair sat on the floor by Vegas's feet and would randomly roll the back of his head against her leg as she ran her nails through it like she would a cat. The long, blonde-haired mage stood off to the side watching the action as if he wanted her to do the same thing to him.

Finally, you had the three near the door. One was the elemental guy who'd yelled at Edwin and another was a man whose power reminded me of Athens. Finally, there was Rocket. I *did* know this guy's name because he was a necromancer. That was a dangerous power and, while I trusted Vegas, I didn't trust her men completely.

I tried to focus back on the conversation.

Commander Edwin was speaking. "Your Majesty, we do actually have some news that we've been meaning to tell you." I kept my eyes on Edwin but noticed Vegas tensed just a bit.

She definitely had something going on.

"Vegas's stalker," he continued as instant anger for my friends boiled through me, "has been using a human at the local campus as a puppet to get past any magical barriers we've constructed for safety."

Motherfucker.

I felt my magic rise up under my skin. "How do you know that?"

Vegas spoke. Her words were tired. "On Thursday we were at a party and the man, who we assumed to be a local drug dealer, confronted me. I am not entirely positive how I could tell but it became obvious to me that Gabriel, the human physically in front of me, wasn't my actual stalker. There was no way that type of power was consistently contained within his body on a daily basis."

Before I could respond, Taylor did. "You could tell that without any interaction?"

My lips pressed together as I thought through the bigger

picture of what she was saying. I didn't discount the importance of Taylor's words but the fact that some mage, with the ability to possess a human vessel, was targeting her concerned me. Greatly.

"Yes. Only since I received my tattoo," Vegas explained. "That night, Gabriel spoke to us and announced his true identity and how he had come to find me."

True identity?

I knew this was going to be bad.

"Who is he?" I let a small growl slip out.

"Victor. Mario's son. The Heir of the Dark Fae," Byron spoke, his voice rough.

My anger and fury at Mario freaked out the Earth realm weather. A massive clap of thunder sounded as rain poured onto the house in sheets. I tried to take soothing breaths. My fury wouldn't solve anything at this moment. My hands found my dark outfit and I adjusted slightly before looking back up.

"You are leaving tomorrow," I demanded softly. "I am so sorry for bringing this burden on you, Vegas."

Vegas immediately shook her head. "I think he was watching me long before we met."

That didn't change anything really.

Adyen kissed my shoulder directly on our mating bite in order to center me. I breathed in and nodded as our odd connection flared to life.

"Come see me when you arrive," I commanded.

I pulled Vegas into a hug, hoping that they would make it safely to the Horde. If not, Mario and his fucking son would have hell to pay. Maker. I am so overprotective lately. Could you imagine if I was a mom? I would be a monster.

"Baby girl?" Taylor tried to distract me and it was sweet. "Can we stop in New York and see one of the shows where the humans sing and dance like little puppets?"

I found it hard to believe the bastard didn't know what a musical was called.

Adyen shook his head in amusement. "It was good to see all of you."

I summoned my magic and the three of us were swept up into a portal that would take us to Estonia and then back home. I wish I hadn't been lying about taking a vacation. The six of us and Lunatic needed one desperately.

Yes. I did include my cat.

* * *

It was late when we got back. I slipped into the large tiled bathroom before any of the boys could stop me or wake up. I felt tired and shaky. Portaling was exhausting and right now, all I wanted was to stretch out near my boys.

My skin felt gritty. I slowly began to take off my earrings and other jewelry. My makeup was essentially gone as it was, so I simply washed my face and brushed my teeth. I smirked as I took a hidden hair tie from the vanity and pulled my long hair above my head into a ponytail. I braced my hands on the counter and took a deep breath.

We were going to be fine.

Sure, this was stressful but I'd known what I was asking for when I declared war on Mario. I just needed to be a big girl about this and continue to channel my inner badass bitch.

"Baby?" Athens stepped into the bathroom and offered a soft smile.

Athens.

"Hey," I offered a sleepy grin as he walked over and tucked a piece of stray hair behind my ear. I didn't hesitate to bury myself in his chest and let out a sigh. His arms felt so right around me and I let out a deep breath I'd been holding.

"Come on." He motioned to the tub. I hadn't even realized that it was filled with warm, steaming water and a lavender, milky mixture that kept the small flowers floating on top looking picture perfect. I smiled at Athens as the bastard's eyes sparkled.

The man didn't do well with negative emotions. When he was worried about me, he tried to do sweet things like ordering pizza. Or drawing me a bath. More importantly, ordering me pizza. The man knew his way to my heart.

Without even a moment of shyness, I let Athens begin undressing me. A soft look of affection and unabashed heat smoldered in his eyes. I shivered as his massive hands skimmed across my skin and left me standing in just a lace bra and underwear. It felt so fucking good to be out of those clothes.

He paused and looked up at me with a head tilt, asking permission.

I nodded. He offered me one of his beautiful smiles as he stepped forward and took my lips. I breathed in his coconut scent as he unclipped my bra and let it fall to the floor before sliding the rest of my undergarments off. I shivered but the sexy bastard pulled back and yanked off his own shirt, one-handed, before tugging me against him.

I never felt shy around Athens. I wasn't positive why exactly. It was just who he was.

A string of hot desire uncurled within me. I began shaking just slightly. The metal mage lifted me and placed me in the water. I watched as he maintained eye contact and slowly unzipped and kicked off his dark pants. Oh, Maker! I don't think I'd ever get over how sexy he and Neo were naked. Ever.

"Don't look at me like that, baby." He let out a small growl as he stepped into the massive tub. Instantly, he pulled me on top of him so I was eclipsed by his arms and surrounded by warm water. I could feel how hard he was beneath me and despite my wiggling, Athens seemed perfectly content with how close we were.

I had to admit I understood the contentment. It felt intimate to be like this in the late hours of the night with the hot water against our skin and the open windows allowing a cool breeze to shift the white curtains. Even the lights were lower than normal. I had the distinct impression that Athens was trying to make me as relaxed as possible.

So fucking perfect.

"Stop wiggling," he chuckled softly. "I'm trying to behave."

"I don't want you to behave," I complained as his hands began skimming my body in a gentle, shiver-inducing pattern. I rubbed myself along his length slowly. He let out a guttural groan. His hand grasped my ass in a firm grip. I no longer felt tired.

I was wide a-fucking-wake.

"What do you want, baby?" He asked, tilting my chin as he gazed at me with bedroom eyes.

What did I need? I needed him. I was tired and stressed. I wanted his love to heal me and to take this day away. To take everything away since the explosion on the night of Thanksgiving. I mean, shit! It was already early into Sunday and I felt as though only a single, chaotic second had passed. I hadn't had any time to enjoy the people around me and I was over it.

Before anything though, I needed to tell Athens how I felt. It was a leap but… fuck it.

"I need you," I answered shly. "I need the man I love."

His eyes flashed a shiny metallic silver as he processed my words. A steamy look flashed over his face. With no words, Athens grasped my face and ran a thumb along my lip gently.

"Repeat that, Gray." His voice was raspy and his eyes tumbled with so many different emotions.

Here we go.

"I love you, Athens."

I think I broke him.

His lips met mine, hot and molten, and for once our kiss was not playful. It was deep and fulfilling. I felt my heart flutter as he pulled back and I wondered if I'd said the words too soon.

"Gray." He pressed his forehead against mine as he intertwined our hands gently. "I love you so much, baby. So much more than I could ever express properly."

Fucker was going to make me cry.

"Really?" I whispered as he nuzzled my nose gently and pulled me closer.

"Yes." He murmured against my lips. "How could I not? You are the strongest and most unique woman I've ever had the pleasure of having in my life."

All right. Screw self-control.

I couldn't stop anymore. I yanked him tight against me. His moan against my mouth fueled my inner fire. Excited and passionate lust ignited both of us as my legs pressed together. My hips ground against him as a hot curse fell from his mouth.

"I need you," I whispered in a soft, imploring voice.

"Are you sure, Gray?" he asked seriously. I nodded fast enough to get whiplash.

Without another word, Athens lifted me. I shivered from the cool air against my heated flesh. I let out a small whine of need as his massive length began to slide into me. My body shook as he let out a low, dark sound. My head fell back as my hair cascaded down my spine into our hot bath. I gasped at his large length as he seated himself fully inside of me.

For just a moment, everything froze in a pleasure-filled, euphoric silence.

"Fucking shit!" He murmured finally with an exhale. "Baby, you are so tight, it's almost painful."

I nodded with a whimper as he began to move, lifting me easily and bringing me back down on his cock with easy slow movements. The pace was deep and rhythmic causing everything in my body to tense with pleasure at each thrust, again and again. Each time got deeper and harder until I felt like he was trying to bury himself within my very fucking soul.

Joke's on him. He was already there.

"Faster," I begged. His eyes flashed white hot. He tugged me closer by the back of my neck. I tightened my legs around him. The next thing I felt was the cold tile as he laid me out on the edge of the tub. His length pulled out of me and I let out a cry.

"Patience," he teased, but I could see how hard he was holding back.

When his large hands gripped my thighs and spread them apart, I shivered again. When he pressed back into me, I felt as though I was going home. I cried out his name as his movements became a smooth pattern distracting me from his teeth on my breasts. My legs trembled, but he just kept going. As his speed increased, so did his name on my lips.

"Athens!" I cried out as he began to slam into me in earnest. My back arched as I gripped the tile edge behind me. His teeth bit down on my flesh.

"Fuck, baby." He growled. "You feel so fucking good, Gray. I should just stay in you for fucking ever. Would you like that? If I just kept myself buried inside of your tight pussy?"

Oh, sweet gods.

I could barely keep my eyes open as I shouted out an unintelligible "Yes!" Back and forth, back and forth. I cried out loudly as he slammed into me so hard I climaxed on the spot.

Fuck.

Somehow, romantic and slow had turned into hard, deep fucking. I loved it. Everything in me released as he continued to fill me like he had been made to.

"Baby." His mouth pulled away from my abused nipple. "You are so fucking beautiful. I love you."

"I love you," I barely managed to gasp as his thumb pressed against my clit. My scream was so loud, I was sure my other men had woken up. A burst of pleasure soared through me as I climaxed around him, wanting him to sink further into me. I could feel Athens's release as he cursed and roared out my name in the crook of my neck. My breathing was rough as I melted into the ground.

Shit.

"I love you," he murmured against my skin. Again and again, praising my flushed skin with kisses and soft words.

"I love you too," I whispered as he offered me a blinding smile. He moved both of us back into the tub as I clung to his form, my eyes closed. He began humming softly. I couldn't help but think how amazing this man was.

A burn on my back had me knowing that another of my marks had filled in. His warm finger began to trace it and I had a feeling that he knew it had changed. I curled myself against his body and the two of us soaked in the sweet smelling hot water.

I have no idea when the metal mage dried me off but before I knew it I was curled between him and Neo. I could feel the other boys nearby, particularly Adyen, who was stretched out across the end of the bed, his breathing deepended. One thought permeated my mind after this long fucking day.

I needed a bigger bed.

7
GRAY

"**F**ucking shit, you've lost it, woman. You're insane!"

I grinned as my sword hit Taylor's with an ease that made it seem I'd been practicing for years. I turned on the ball of my foot and my metal clanged against his in the early sunrise. This was what the demon deserved. If he wanted to wake me up at dawn on a fucking Sunday, then I would kick his ass.

It was really fun actually.

"You can admit defeat at any time, honey." I tossed a careless smile and didn't allow myself to get distracted by how stunning the man looked outside in this blood red light. He moved with lethal energy that forced me to focus. Yet, I was still winning.

"You aren't even following rules of combat," he chuckled as his eyes lit up with fire, "plus, I've accomplished my goal."

"What was your goal?" I frowned as we clashed together again, my eyes drawing to his body. His loose shirt was unbuttoned and showed off his dark tattoos and muscles. Not the time to be distracted, dammit.

"Weapons training. I told you it was important."

That bastard! I had promised myself I would never do it, simply on principle.

I gasped in indignation and he had me. His arm slipped around me and my sword was knocked nearly ten feet away. His own blade pressed against the length of my back like a metal spine. The cool metal felt good through my loose white tunic and pants.

You couldn't blame me for the foible. You could blame the fact that I hadn't had coffee yet. My sword wielding abilities are only so good without the nectar of the gods.

"Tell me this isn't fun," he offered a cocky smile as he let my hand rest on his impressive pectorals. There was a dark shadow that made me wonder exactly what was on his skin. I frowned as I peeled back his shirt and found his tattoo. The tattoo that branded him as an Heir Guard. I frowned knowing that he had never wanted this.

"Hey," his voice was like a soothing melody, "don't give me that face, baby girl. Just because I didn't like the circumstances doesn't mean I'm not happy I'm here."

I nodded and sighed. "None of you had a choice, though. I feel like that is unfair. I mean, this is the rest of your lives, not just some regular 9-5."

He grunted. "Did you have a choice to be a True Heir? No. Some things aren't a choice. It is just what we are meant to do in this life."

He was right.

My lips twisted in a wry smile. "You're sounding awfully wise for someone who hasn't had coffee yet, Taylor."

The demon winked and pulled away. "Who says I haven't?"

"You did not! Tell me that you did not have coffee without me!" I begged as he grabbed my sword and nodded towards the castle. We'd walked a bit far out, so we took out time walking back, enjoying how the land seemed to respond to my every step. It was peaceful.

The morning was bright but it was clear since it had rained

last night. A slight, damp mist covered the ground. As we trailed through the higher grasses towards the forested exit, I let my hands trail across it.

"When my father first told me about joining the True Heir Guard," Taylor began, breaking the silence, "I had been thrilled. Really. I was obsessed with SE as it was and then to also be chosen? To be a protector for the True Heir of the entire kingdom? I was in heaven. Then, when we arrived at the coronation ceremony I couldn't believe that you were the little thing we were protecting. It was clear why there were five of us."

"I was not that little!" I punched his shoulder lightly.

His forehead crinkled in amusement but he moved on. "The branding of the tattoo was difficult but it was amazing to have the ability to practice the full extent of my powers so early on."

"So, when did you stop liking it?"

"For the longest time, I felt as though we were somewhat pointless honestly. We were too special to interact with the normal SE population but we had no official job besides attempting to find you. We didn't know if that would ever happen."

"I'm sorry." I squeezed his hand after a moment. He shook his head and smiled.

"I just got fed up with it. I was young and stupid, but I'm glad that I made the effort to maintain my status as your guard. I can't imagine life without you, baby girl."

"You're making me blush and shit," I muttered playfully. He chuckled and pulled me close, his lips pressing to my temple in a warm, affectionate gesture.

After a few moments of walking, he asked a question. "Do you remember meeting us that night?"

I tilted my head meeting his eyes. "What?"

He nodded. "Yep. All of us. I remember it really fucking vividly."

"Show me!" I stopped him from walking forth. I would take any happy memories from that night to replace the horrible one.

Taylor paused. "You know, I think I may have something better than just showing you. How do you feel about retrieving your memory through our bond?"

"Will I be able to stop *it?*"

I didn't want to get to the fucking awful part with King Mario.

After a moment of thought, he swept me up and sat us at the base of a massive tree. The autumn winds brushed past us and as the sun kissed my skin. I closed my eyes as he spoke. "I will watch along with you. Just try to think back to that day."

Honestly, I wasn't positive it would work but as I felt his magic wrap around me, I took a deep breath. I could smell and taste the air of the castle before I let the vision in front of me grow to life.

"Your Majesty," an older voice spoke as I looked away from Mommy and Daddy. *"Would the True Heir like to meet her guard?"*

"Gray?" My father asked, his eyes sparkling despite his grumpy expression. I offered him a serious look, like the one mommy gave him when making an important decision. I nodded and he signaled towards the children in front of me.

"Hello," I said softly while looking them over. They were big. Way bigger than me.

"I'm Rhodes," a boy with blonde hair offered. I could hear Mommy and Daddy talking to someone over our heads, so I stepped closer. His eyes widened as I rose up on my tip toes and frowned.

"What are you doing?" Another boy, taller and with gold eyes, asked bluntly.

"Don't be rude." A third, smaller boy with warm brown eyes corrected. Next to him was his quiet duplicate watching me in a

way that made me feel funny. It wasn't a bad feeling. Just different.

"She can handle it," a kid next to Rhodes spoke, his hair a vibrant red.

"I was searching for ears or a tail," I admitted. "You're a cat shifter right?"

The big kid started laughing as the small matching boys frowned at him. "Adyen stop it."

"It's a good question if you don't know shifters," the quiet twin stated. I flashed him a smile.

"What's your name?" I asked.

"Neo," he answered as his eyes went wide and super dark again.

"What about you?" I asked his twin.

"Athens."

"I like those names," I nodded approvingly and looked to the big guy.

"Adyen." He grinned. "Sorry for laughing, Princess."

"Queen," I demanded.

"Yeah, Adyen," The red head offered a cheeky smile. "Queen."

"Adyen, you can't be mean to me," I stated confidently. "I have to be nice to you and you have to be nice to me."

The big guy nodded as his ears turned pink. Someone came to stand next to me and I smiled up at the redhead.

"What's your name?"

He flashed a dazzling smile. "Taylor."

I nodded and then a thought occurred to me as I frowned.

"What's wrong?" Rhodes asked, his voice worried.

"I didn't even ask if you guys wanted to be my friends. I'm sorry." I spoke quietly, feeling stupid. No one really wanted to be my friend because I couldn't leave the castle. I didn't want my parents forcing friends on me.

"You didn't have to!" The boy with magic and dark eyes offered a smile. His twin nodded enthusiastically.

"He's right," Adyen stated softly. *"We want to be your friends."*

"Okay," I smiled and Taylor squeezed my hand.

"All right!" my mother said, laughed. *"Time to go eat, little one."*

I frowned but then looked at all the boys again. "Can we play after eating?"

My mom just offered me a smile and led me away from the boys. I wasn't positive what the True Heir Guard did but if I got to be friends with them, I'd be happy.

"Holy crap," I muttered as I looked up at Taylor's dark eyes. "How did I forget that?"

"Repression of memories," he sighed, "it was a traumatic night."

I nodded and placed my head on his chest as the nightmarish memories attempted to invade. I needed a distraction.

"I'm worried," I murmured. "I'm worried that I have no idea how to handle this coming battle."

"Well," he grunted. "The first part we should figure out is how long we have until it does."

I nodded and sighed. "What are the chances it won't be for another year?"

He chuckled, "I thought you wanted to fight Mario."

"I did," I paused. "As an individual. This is different, Taylor. I'm supposed to be protecting an entire kingdom."

His mouth tightened. "You've got this baby girl, we've got this. You know that no matter what happens you will always have us, right?" I nodded and snuggled closer to him as he kissed the top of my head. His long legs were spread out and I felt the entire beat pattern of his heart under my ear.

After a moment, a sound caused me to look up. Both of us

could hear someone walking and, before long, it turned into several people. I straightened as Taylor stood next to me, both of us wondering who the fuck was walking all the way out here. My magic purred happily as if she wasn't worried. Honestly, neither was I, but really. Who the fuck was in *my* training area? I'm Queen. I get to dictate a small clearing as mine, right?

"Oh, shit," a soldier laughed as he and three other men stumbled out from the forested area. They didn't seem drunk but they didn't seem all that bright.

"What are you doing out here?" Taylor's voice turned sharp and commanding. Was it wrong that I totally found that hot?

"Commander Taylor?" One of the men squeaked as all of them snapped to a weird military position. The corners of my mouth tweaked as I gathered up both our swords and wrapped an arm around Taylor. At first I cared about how my kingdom would take my relationship with my men. Now? I didn't really give a fuck. If they didn't like it, then I would hope they'd let me know.

"Your Majesty?" Another echoed as all eyes snapped to me. The men bowed. I smiled at that.

"Rise," I murmured and rested my head against Taylor's shoulder.

"What are you doing out here?" He demanded again.

"We came out here to train," one of them muttered.

"Not for SE guard," another admitted.

Taylor and I both shared a confused look.

"What for then?"

"We can't practice our magic in the normal guard area because Commander Travis stated that only natural born mages have that honor," the first admitted.

What? Excuse-a-freaking me?

"Who is this? This Commander Travis?" I demanded sharply as all the men paled.

"Travis," Taylor sighed, shaking his head. "I'm sorry you

gentlemen have been dealing with this. How long has this been going on?"

"It is really not a big deal," one of them stated. "In fact, you probably shouldn't mention it, if possible."

"How long?" I demanded.

"Since we joined."

Oh, no. That's some bullshit.

"Where is this Commander Travis?" I asked softly. Taylor's lips twitched as he seemed to come to a decision.

"Would you gentlemen come with us?" He asked, but it was totally a demand. I could hear how nervous the men were but they had no reason to be. The only one who was going to get hurt was Travis the asshole. I was practically skipping back to the kingdom.

This! This is the fun shit queens do.

I tried to not get ridiculously turned on walking into the SE training center but it didn't help that Neo stood with Athens on the sides where it seemed two men were sparring. Taylor was talking to the men probably trying to locate asshole McGee. I approached my two shirtless twins who currently looked like they belonged in GQ.

"Hey, baby." Athens winked and I blushed. I didn't care that the room was watching as he leaned down and gave me a chaste kiss. What I wanted to do? I wanted to go back to that fucking bathtub again. I shivered thinking about the slow deep pace so different from his playful personality. My eyes widened at the intensity of the expression on his face.

Note to self. Athens can be just as intense as Neo.

Speaking of Neo. I looked up since he was now behind me, his eyes glittering. "What are you doing?"

His lip twitched. "Me? Just looking over these two markings on your back. Now, I wonder, Gray. Why it is two instead of one. Has something changed?"

I narrowed my eyes at Athens. "You kissed and told!"

He let out a booming laugh as Neo nipped my ear. "Gray? He didn't have to tell me anything. I could hear your moans from the bed. Do you know how badly I wanted to join?"

"Why didn't you?" I spoke boldly as Athens let out a low sound and tugged my hair.

Neo tilted my jaw upward and pressed a hot kiss to my lips. "Next time, I won't hesitate."

"Baby girl!" Taylor called from across the room and gestured. He was so into drama it wasn't even funny. I turned my head in the direction he pointed. A feral grin flashed across my face as Travis sauntered into view.

"Fuck this guy." Athens muttered. "He's such an ass."

Travis, it sucks to be you, man.

"He's been in such a sour mood since our father fled," Neo rolled his eyes. "If the fucker wanted to be his son that bad I would have given it up."

My hand squeezed his because I knew how much he hated his father. Then I stepped forward and spoke. "Then you will love this."

"Your Majesty," the asshole stuttered as Taylor yanked him by his collar. I grinned. Travis paled.

"Commander Travis is it?" I asked as the whole training room went silent.

The man nodded and I sighed despondently. "I heard a rumor about you and I really hope, for your sake, it's not true, Travis."

"What was the rumor?" He asked quietly.

I stepped into his space and allowed my magic to wrap around his legs like vines before quickly bringing him to his knees. He grunted as Taylor snickered. I grasped the man's bearded chin and forced himself to look up at me. It really didn't matter how big or small you were when it came to magic.

"That you were not allowing human-made mages to practice

magic," I stated loud enough I could feel the tension in the air. It was my understanding that we didn't have a ton of non-natural born mages as it was but that did not excuse discrimination. There was nothing worse than choosing to not like someone because of a factor that they can't control.

For example, I have every reason in the world to hate elves. My adopted parents beat me. I was subjected to so many different forms of abuse that I had stopped counting. Now, only the scars showed the physical remnants of my pain. Their friends, co-workers, and families were all elves. All of them cruel. Yet, I don't hate elves. By all rights, I should, but instead I was filled with sadness towards those who had hurt me knowing it had nothing to do with what species they were and everything to do with what assholes they were. So. I really didn't see an excuse for discrimination, even in the face of a jaded past.

"I can explain," he started. I silenced him by putting a finger to his lips.

"Can I have all human-made mages step forward?" It was a command and they did. The training center was massive, nearly filled with over two hundred soldiers, and out of everyone it seemed to be a group of maybe thirty men.

We really needed to get some fucking women in the military.

It was truly upsetting, as a badass myself, to see the opportunity of a military career not given to women purely because of the way they were born. Every woman deserves a chance to be a badass whether they wanted to serve in the military or run their own business. Don't even get me started on how fucking amazing you have to be to run an entire household of insane children. I'm telling you, if a lot of men were as tough as the women in their lives we would be in a much different place within the universe' short history.

"Before I ask you a question, I want it to be stated very loud and clear that any attempted repercussion from their answers will be handled by me. Personally. I don't give a fuck what your bias is. What I *do* care about is having competent soldiers. Now, has Commander Travis ever told you that because you were non-natural born mages, you were not allowed to practice magic?"

It was quiet but then a man from earlier spoke up.

"It isn't just him. It's also Commanders Alexander, Wash, and Pickrett."

Fabulous.

I heard a curse as threatening magic soared through the air. I sighed. With a flick of my wrist, the magic user was coiled in tight cold ashy magic and let out a painful scream. Music to my ears.

"That was hot," Taylor admitted while kissing my head. I totally glowed under his approval.

"Now," I continued softly. "Raise your hand if you have ever faced discrimanation as a mage."

All of them. Good.

"Alright, so this is what is going to happen. Commanders Travis, Alexander, Wash, and Pickrett will all report to your section commander."

Yes, I knew that was Neo and Athens. I wanted Neo to handle them since his father was part of the problem. He deserved to decide their punishment.

The man looked practically gleeful. I should be worried about that, right? Oh well.

"I would like everyone that raised their hand to meet with the section as well. Athens will record the specific incidents."

Athens flashed a smile with a dirty wink and motioned for them to follow as Neo grabbed Travis by the arm and the other three trailed behind without protest.

"Now," I walked forward into the middle of the room. "Since it seems like there has been a bunch of bullshit going on, does anyone have anything else they'd like to report?"

Silence.

"If you would rather reach out to someone in private, please contact your section commander." Yes, it would be one of my five boys and you bet your ass I would hear about it. They could deal.

I turned towards Taylor and he offered me a sweet smile before leveling the group with a look. "Now that Athens and Neo are busy, I will be taking over training today. I don't care what you thought you were doing before but now you are doing combat training. No external weapons."

I didn't hear any complaints. I scowled thinking about how I had to use weapons but they didn't.

The door opened. Rhodes walked in followed by Adyen. The room shifted with tension.

Adyen chuckled. "Taylor, if they don't want to do that we can always run the border."

A general whisper and dissent sounded as the men began to spread out to do exactly as Taylor said. I couldn't look away from Adyen though and my dragon reached for me, his large arms enveloping me. His lips grazed my bite mark. I shivered as he unapologetically grew hard against me.

"Lil brawler, hearing you yell at all of them was hot as fuck," he graveled as he pulled my hips flat against his own. I gasped as he pulled on my lower hips.

So aggressive.

"Were you listening outside?" I murmured in a teasing voice.

"Absolutely." He dug his hand into my hair and nuzzled my neck again. He was so fucking big that he eclipsed me completely.

"You know with them so busy, we could slip away." I drew a hand up his chest.

"Kitten," Rhodes whispered in a riled, accented voice behind me. "You have an audience."

I leaned back into his chest, resting between the two of them. "Let them look."

Adyen rumbled appreciatively as Rhodes hid his chuckle in the crook of my neck. Taylor barked commands. I was comfortable between the boys. Cinnamon and ash mingled with Rhodes's expensive cologne sheltered me.

When the room's power shifted, my gaze shot to the side. Neo offered me an intense look filled with mirth while dragging someone towards me. The other three commanders stood looking terrified as my mage tossed this man on his knees in front of me.

"Tell her what you told me," he chuckled mirthlessly. It was a laugh that made me shiver.

"I didn't mean it," he hissed as his entire body trembled. "I just meant that things were fine before…"

"Me?" I grinned, finishing his sentence. I tilted my head staring directly at him. So much hate resided in those small beady eyes.

"We had everything figured out," he hissed realizing he was screwed anyway. "You don't even have military or combat experience. You are just a fucking bitch with a tight hole between her…"

Oh, you dumb shit.

I stopped my boys from beating him with a quick step forward and I grabbed the man's throat in a hard dangerous hold, his words choking off. I crouched down to look him right in the eye. My nails drew blood.

"You doubt my experience and ability?" I whispered softly. "Would you like a demonstration?"

He had fear in his eyes. He started shaking his head. I grinned and lifted him by the neck as he struggled. But my power was in charge and she didn't care what he wanted. I led him with all 5'2" of myself as the big asshole struggled to break free. The entire room cleared to the side as I released the man in a crumpled heap and stepped away.

"Stand the fuck up," Neo growled. Rhodes watched with a blank expression but I could see the anger in his eyes. Athens and Taylor talked quietly, amusement sparkling in their eyes. Adyen paced dangerously on the sidelines, his eyes nearly black.

"Your Majesty." Travis sounded like he was going to beg. I almost felt bad but then I remembered his crude comment regarding my body.

Fuck him.

"Stand up and prove to me that you are somehow better," I goaded. "Prove to me that, with all your experience, you are worthy to make the decisions I make."

The man looked green. He tried to move into position. I let him gather his substantial magic as his metal ability allowed him to attract several swords to him. Then he began to create a barrier of metal objects in defense. I felt a smile threaten my blank expression.

"Are you ready?" I asked with disinterest.

He didn't respond. I took that as a yes.

I sighed. "If the gentleman on the wall behind him could please move, it would be appreciated."

They scrammed as the man tensed.

Then without further prelude, I slowly let out my magic as I walked forward. I felt his fear grow. When I reached his metal border, my magic pushed the barrier pieces aside and melted into a path straight through any resistant elements. The man cursed and backed up as he stuck out a sword. I flicked my wrist and it fell to the floor. In a final defensive attempt, he started calling metal things to fly at me in the room, all of which were blocked by my magic with an almost boring ease. I backed him up against the wall and I held him with my power without breaking a sweat.

"Do you see what just happened?" I whispered softly. "That

was nothing to me. Nothing. Do not equate inexperience with lack of power. You could have been in this position for hundreds of years and you would never have the power I do. But none of that matters to me. Do you know why?"

He was shaking now.

"Because that doesn't make me better than you. Any of you." I spoke louder. "It doesn't give me the excuse or right to discriminate. So, why the fuck you think *you* have that right is beyond me. I don't care, though, I don't care about your bias because you are not going to be part of my military anymore. You are officially discharged, so take your asshole attitude and get the fuck out of here."

I released him and turned on my heel.

Rhodes offered me a look that made me hot all over, but I simply returned to their sides. Everyone watched as *Asshole Mc-I-think-I'm-Better-Than-You* trailed out of the training center.

"Back to work!" Taylor announced with a savage grin.

As the room exploded back into action I sighed and leaned my head on Rhodes's shoulder. He kissed my forehead. "You did good, kitten."

I offered him a smile feeling really good about today.

8

NEO

She had to know. *Right?*
She had to know I loved her.

I'd heard her say the words to Athens and I knew I wanted to say them to her. I was slightly concerned, though. I didn't want to push her. I didn't want her to feel pressured to say it back. I felt like those words weren't good enough for how I felt about her. I think I might have been slightly obsessed with our little queen.

My arms tightened around her as she yawned. We were taking an afternoon nap. Well, she was and I had told her I would as well just to ease her concern about being "lazy." We all had agreed she needed sleep, even if she wouldn't admit it. Honestly, if she hadn't demanded training with Taylor this morning no one would have woken her up. To be fair, she had no idea how early he had planned on waking her up. I had no idea how long it would be until Mario was at our door, so I figured she should get rest now rather than later when it might be too late.

The wind brushed into our room through the open windows as Rhodes shifted from where he sat on the couch, his legs crossed and eyes on a book. Adyen, Athens, and Taylor had stayed at training but I'd needed a break. I was still worked up over the fucking assholes my father had managed to surround himself with.

A meow sounded as Lunatic padded across the room with a flick of the tail. I had no idea how kittens were supposed to act but she seemed oddly aware for a cat. I needed to look into this more, I felt like I was missing something. Her gold eyes focused on me as she jumped on the bed and snuggled between Gray and me. Lord. I was actually enjoying this.

Then again, this was probably the most affection I'd experienced in my entire life.

I smiled because the stunning woman laying next to me had changed my life in so many ways. Her dark hair spread across her pillow. The silver crescent scar shimmered like diamonds on her skin. Those thick-lashed eyes fluttered as she murmured something. I didn't even try to stop myself from letting my eyes trail along her body covered in a comfortable overshirt. I muttered a curse because there was nothing more I would rather do than sink right into her tight warmth again. The woman was undeniably and unintentionally sexy.

"What are you thinking about?" A soft voice whispered as I looked down at Gray. Her deep red lips were soft and plump, making my cock harden.

I tipped her chin up. "I think you can guess."

"Paint me a visual, Neo. Maybe I can make it come true."

I groaned and her eyes flickered over to Rhodes. Not that I cared about him being there while intimate but maybe she did. The bastard looked over, a curious arch over his eyes. "Kitten, no one is stopping you from enjoying yourself."

Bastard.

My lips pulled into a grin as challenge entered Gray's eyes. "I don't want to disrupt your reading, Rhodes. I am being nice. I know you won't be able to resist yourself, even from all the way over there."

Gray.

I nearly chuckled because nothing drives Rhodes more insane than challenging his control.

His eyes solidified. "Don't you worry. I will be perfectly fine."

Gray bit her plump lip and I saw a dangerous glint enter her eye. I loved that she was becoming more confident in her sexuality. She lifted Lunatic from in between us and snuggled closer to me, her lips against my ear. The cat huffed and trotted through the closet towards our other rooms.

"What about you, Neo? Do you wanna play with me?"

Did I fucking ever.

Without any concern regarding Rhodes really, I pulled her on top of me with ease. I hadn't had a chance to enjoy her body fully since the last time had been in the haze of fury. Now, though? Well now the only thing blocking me was that damn oversized shirt.

"I'm always available to you," I whispered, wrapping her hair around my hand so she was forced to arch into me, her eyes dilating.

Yeah, sweetheart, I wasn't really planning on just playing.

"Oh?" Her voice was breathy and I drew her close, my mouth meeting hers. I nearly groaned at the taste of her lips against mine. The woman had the power to make my body harden painfully with just a soft kiss. She rolled her hips. I grunted against her lips as I felt her nipples harden against my bare chest. My other hand dropped from her hip to her silky smooth legs and dragged up.

"Nothing on underneath?" I purred gently as she let out a whimper at my tight hair hold, "That's dangerous, Gray."

"Why?" She whimpered as curiosity and need flashed in her eyes.

Was it wrong that I loved how innocent and yet fucking

seductive she was? It was an intoxicating mix. I began to kiss down her neck and nibbled on the skin there as I flipped her overshirt over her perfect ass, exposing her to the open air. Rhodes muttered a curse.

I nearly laughed at that but then I groaned as my hand skimmed her tight wetness. She trembled against me as I pet her gently knowing she was probably still sore from Athens. Then again, she was so fucking wet, I couldn't imagine it would hurt all that much.

"Neo," she moaned as I teased her entrance but didn't let my finger slip in yet.

I wanted to drag this out until she felt like she was going to cum from just a kiss. That was how worked up she got me. So it was fair. My finger trailed up her slit to where her clit lay. I gently teased it. She whimpered against my lips with urgent need. I loved watching her get all desperate like this. I knew I could fix it but it would feel even better if I drew it out.

"Come on sweetheart," I whispered, "you can handle a bit of teasing, can't you?"

She was very responsive so this was probably killing her. Yet, she nodded and I took her lips before slipping a finger inside of her tightness as a reward. Her moan made Rhodes curse. Somehow, that fueled me as well. It was fun punishing the man who thought he had control over everything and everyone in his life.

The truth? Gray was the only one in control and he knew it damn well.

I let out a groan as she began to rock back and forth against my cock as my finger fucked her slowly without relief. Her nails bit into my shoulders as she gasped and her body began to shake. I pulled my finger out and she cried out in frustration. With an easy movement, I pinned her underneath me and let my magic seep out. Now that we had more time, I wanted to truly play with her.

"Neo!" She gasped as my shadowy magic grasped her wrists and drew them above her. I smirked at her as I slowly kissed down her body, giving her a chance to pull back or say no. Instead, she arched her body towards me.

Good girl.

Her overshirt was easily removed with a slight tear down the center. Then her entire body was exposed to me. I could have gone to fucking heaven. She was so fucking beautiful. My teeth bit down on her flesh playfully as her noises made it all that much better. When I pulled her nipple into my mouth, I heard Rhodes stand up and I knew the fucker was probably removing himself to an even further place in the room.

Gray didn't even realize how much pain she was causing him.

"Please!" Her body wiggled as her legs fell apart and I let my tongue trail down her body until I was settled between her legs. My girl began to shift as if that would somehow make me start tasting her sooner than I planned. What she didn't realize was that I fucking loved every single moment of build up. I wasn't just into punishing others.

I met her heated, glassy eyes before I began devouring her with a lazy, yet deep pace. She cried out as I sucked her clit. I could feel her struggling to move her hands. I tightened the hold and lifted her closer to my face as my hands cupped her perfect fucking ass.

Her taste was the sweetest fucking shit I'd ever had. The slower I went, the wetter she got. I could have spent most of my life down there. Honestly, I'd be perfectly fucking content with my head buried between her legs forever.

"Damn it," Rhodes muttered as her eyes popped open. I looked up and knew he wasn't going to last much longer, his eyes completely focused on her bound arms and trembling, flushed body.

I wasn't even into controlling her but teasing was fun and I knew that position would drive Rhodes fucking crazy. Her little mewling noises had our controlled leader running a hand through his hair in a frustrated motion.

"Rhodes," she moaned. His control started to shatter.

I smiled as she arched up to meet his lips. After a brief kiss, I pulled her away with ease as Rhodes growled. My arm wrapped around her center as my magic tucked her arms behind her and between us. Rhodes's eyes flashed gold and I found myself wanting to break him.

Was that fucked up? Probably. Oh, well.

"Rhodes she needs you," I spoke quietly while nibbling her neck. "I'm not going to give it to her."

She let out a frustrated noise as I let a hand crawl between her legs and I gently strummed her clit. Then, I pulled away. She faced Rhodes on her knees, fully displayed, as I played with her in a slow torturous pattern. I knew he wanted her and I could see his animal taking over moment by moment.

"Please!" She gasped, while a shiver of need raced through her.

Rhodes let out a pained sound and my lips curled. I knew he was worried she wasn't ready to make that bond but let me assure you, she was ready. There was a sixth sense buried inside of me that was encouraging me to bring our group together.

"Fuck," he grunted and unbuttoned his shirt.

I let her loose just slightly as she yanked him forward. Their lips pressed together. Before I knew it, Rhodes had her turned so that her sweet body was facing me. I traced her lip with my thumb as Rhodes seemed to be trying to fight with control. So close.

"Neo," he snapped softly, "I'm not going to be able to do this without marking her."

Gray tossed her head back as I let my magic out to gently brush against her body. Specifically, her clit and nipples. I could see how close her body was to climaxing and I knew all it would take would be for me to slide right into her. Yet, somehow I found this far more satisfying. Pushing both of them. Punishing them. For what? I smirked. I didn't really have a good reason, did I? I didn't need a good fucking reason.

"Please, Rhodes," she whispered desperately.

His eyes met hers for just a moment before he let out a low growl and lost it. I'd never seen the man move so fast but, before I could blink, he was lined up with her entrance. It was fucking glorious watch them both break and her eyes met mine right as he slammed home.

Her climax was like the sweetest fucking music in the world.

Gray

"Oh, fuck," I whispered as Rhodes filled me completely and my entire body pulsated with pleasure. My eyes fluttered shut and my hand went behind his head to hold him to me. I could feel his lean body against mine as he tried to not move from where he was seated deeply inside of me.

"Kitten," his voice whispered. "I'm going to fuck you and then mark you. I hope your okay with that because I'm not positive I could fucking stop at this point."

I nodded because I wanted that. I knew our emotions were all messy but I had no doubt these men were important to me and this felt right. I cried out as he pulled out and then slammed back in. Another climax began to pulsate through me as a pair of lips pressed against mine. Neo.

"Oh, god," I whimpered as Rhodes began to fuck me in deep demanding strokes, my hands locked behind my back courtesey of his rough large hands. His head was tucked against my neck and he kept leaving small bite marks that sent fucking electric shocks to my clit.

"Do you like this, Gray?" Neo asked with a dark sexy glint to his eyes.

"Yes," I answered honestly. I was rewarded by his fingers moving deftly on my clit. Oh, my.

"Such a good girl," he commended while rubbing with the lightest pressure. "Letting him fuck you so deep like that."

Rhodes let out a deep rumbling sound of satisfaction as he began to pound into me so hard I had to place my head on Neo's chest, my cheek flush against his warm skin. He nibbled my ear as he quickened his pace on my clit and I found myself making noises that were so needy it was worrisome.

"Don't come yet, Kitten," Rhodes' dominant voice demanded. "Don't you dare come."

"Please," I whimpered as Neo kissed me, his tongue tracing my bottom lip after he nipped it.

"It will feel so good," Neo drawled. "Just hold it off sweetheart."

I couldn't. I began to tremble and Rhodes cursed as he began to guide my hips back and forth while my hands released and stretched out to touch Neo. The mage spoke in a rough voice. "Touch me, Gray."

Oh, but I did.

I couldn't accurately describe how it felt to be between the two of them. Rhodes filled me completely and pushed my body to where sweat dotted my skin while Neo teased me. It was fucking amazing. My hand wrapped around Neo's thick, familiar length and he let out a low, dangerous sound against my lips. I began to move my hand as Rhodes grew impossibly larger inside me.

"I can't wait," I whispered breathlessly. "I'm going to come!"

I felt everything inside of me shatter as my head fell back and Neo's release pulsed against my hand. His words came harsh and low as he growled out my name. I think I nearly blacked out when

Rhodes's teeth clamped down on the back of my neck and he exploded inside of me.

Everything in my body pulsed with power. As a whimper of relief broke through my throat as our bond snapped into place, the three of us became one. I felt my eyes flutter closed as I fell to the side but I never fell completely. Gentle arms cradled me.

The world was a comforting haze. A haze of mint and an expensive, exotic scent.

When warm water hit my body, I let out a pained groan at my sore skin but whomever was holding me never let go. Soft voices echoed around me. A soft, near purr under my head made me feel as though I was in a dream. I'd never felt this kind of contentment. I wondered if this was a mate thing.

"Oh, shit!" A familiar voice said, "What the hell did you guys do to her?"

Someone answered, but not the person holding me.

"He marked her." Adyen chuckled. "Good control, buddy. You waited all of one day."

The chest under me made a soft sound and I nuzzled against it.

"She probably needs food," Athens said lightly.

Taylor responded. "Already on its way up."

A soft meow encouraged me to open an eye. I snorted. It was very obvious that I was on Rhodes's golden chest. My gaze strayed to his scars as I gently reached for one of them. He let out a pained, yet loving sound as my eyes found...Lunatic?

"Let's leave the fam bam," Athens snorted and I felt the others leave.

"Now she thinks I'm her dad," Rhodes muttered and I chuckled.

Lunatic meowed openly while walking back and forth along the edge of the tub. I kissed Rhodes's chest and he hummed appreciatively.

"I am glad you marked me," I murmured.

He lifted my chin and his pale beautiful green eyes stared intently at me. "You're mine, kitten. I hope you like me - a lot."

I smiled and started to say something very different, but the door slammed open. Both of us snapped alert as Adyen began speaking. I couldn't understand a word but my peace had been officially shattered.

"Another attack?" I asked my reality popping back into full color.

Adyen's eyes darkened. "This time it was from within the kingdom."

"Where?" I whispered.

"The mage community." He spoke softly. "It was a non-natural born mage."

"The commander I kicked out?" I asked softly.

"No word yet," Taylor answered. "And sorry to ruin the honeymoon."

I turned and kissed Rhodes fully and deeply. He growled against my lips and pressed his forehead against my own. I was out of the tub and tugged a robe on, sprinting towards my closet. The other boys were getting ready and I tried to center myself but I felt incredibly off-kilter.

I tugged on a loose top with a corset and a pair of leather pants. My boots were laced up with the same leather as my quickly done braid. I froze in the mirror. My lips were red and swollen. My skin was flushed. My neck was covered in small love bites and two very large silver bites.

Because I needed more scars.

Fucking possessive claiming bites. I hated it. Yeah, that's such a lie. I loved it.

"Ready?" Rhodes asked from the door.

I blushed seeing him and instead of speaking, nuzzled his chest as he kissed the top of my head. Neo met my gaze with a cocky smirk. I narrowed my gaze and flicked his chest before kissing him gently. Sneaky teasing bastard.

"I can only guess what happened," Taylor sighed.

Athens flashed a grin as well. "I bet I can guess."

"Not the time," Adyen shook his head, exasperated, before lifting me with ease. I let him carry me through the dark halls of the castle because, frankly, I was still tired. My brain was still fuzzy and I was still cozy until I smelled the fire.

Instantly, my brain snapped awake and I jumped from his arms. It took us less than a minute to reach where the most recent explosion was being put out. Except it wasn't an explosion. It was a fire. I felt my eyes fill with tears as I watched a small mage family huddled together.

This made me furious.

"Get them a room in the castle," I demanded from any of them. "Did anyone…"

"No," Taylor answered in a hard voice.

"Was it him?" Thinking about how I had let that man out of my sight instead of keeping his biased ass on watch.

"Undetermined, but the shifters think they crossed back over the border," one of them responded as true pain lanced through me. I felt like this was my fault. Truly.

I knew it was him.

My eyes flickered with flames as I watched the house burn. I felt fury roll through me as I let my eyes wander toward the border and further, as if I could see Mario himself. The fucker needed to die. I turned back to my boys and spoke carefully.

"Up the amount of people on the border tonight," I grunted. "I don't trust Mario to not try and take advantage of this."

I walked away from the sight of the destruction before I had a chance to get any angrier.

When a pop sounded in the air, I was genuinely surprised to see Palo in front of me. Nevertheless, I kept walking and he continued to keep pace until I finally said something. He met my gaze when I asked him what he needed.

"A resource from within the Dark Fae realm has stated that Mario will attack within days, Your Majesty. I heard further news from the scouts farther north that they have begun traveling. It seems they are using portals to move closer to the border."

They were being predictable on purpose.

The hallway we were in was quiet, the only sound the crackle of the torches lining it. I nodded and met the gaze of a man of whom I still harbored an undetermined opinion. My words were out before I could stop them.

"What do you think I should do?" I asked quietly as if that would make the problem go away.

Palo's eyes widened slightly as he tilted his head. "You're asking *me* for strategic advice?"

"Sure." My eyes met his once more. "I don't know what the right move here is, Palo. Do I attack or wait to play defense? Do I put the city on lock-down and scare everyone or let them feel safe? Do I hunt down the fucker who just tried to kill a family? Or do I focus on training? I am truly at a loss here, Palo, I feel like there isn't a right answer."

The demon seemed to think for a moment before he spoke, choosing his words carefully. "I think I would focus on amassing a defensive structure. He would want to draw you out. I think you have a better chance if you take advantage of all the allies that are loyal to you."

He was right.

I nodded my head and deflated slightly. "Thank you. As for the info about Mario, please contact the required sources so the Red Masques are ready. I figure that Edwin and Byron aren't currently involved in day-to-day procedures."

Palo nodded and looked toward the other end of the hall. "Yes. They have been doing a lot of different things."

I chuckled and watched as my boys began walking down the hall. "Palo, you're treating Marabella right, I hope."

His eyes darkened and he spoke with sincerity. "I don't think she would allow for anything different, Your Majesty. On top of that, I know I made some poor choices but I do love her."

It was so honest and it made me smile.

"Good." I reached a hand out for Taylor. He offered me a tired smile and nodded to his brother. I finished my comment. "I'm rooting for you guys."

Adyen scooped me up and I tucked against him wide awake. I could feel that tonight was going to be a long night.

9
GRAY

"You need sleep." Adyen commented.

Sleep was for losers.

Also for actively functioning adults that were, as a result, able to focus on their shit.

So...totally not me!

I looked back down at the massive map I had of the three kingdoms. We were in my quarters, but I hadn't slept since the night before. Instead, my entire defensive plan was spread out in front of me as I played through scenarios of what they could do. I wasn't tired. In fact, I was so far from tired it was ridiculous. The espresso may have helped.

"*You* need to sleep," I chided and pulled my rubber band tighter as strands of hair fell out.

I could see him eyeing my ponytail but I had left one of my loose day scarves on the couch nearby to distract him. My lips pressed together once I realized it was gone. Such a little hoarder.

"Hey, big guy?" I asked, having noticed something.

"Yeah?" He wondered.

"What is this?" I pointed towards a small clearing of trees that were darker, and surrounded by a stream of water like an island.

"That," he tilted his head, "is the oasis for Pixies."

My nose scrunched. "Fucking Pixies?"

"They get a bad reputation," Adyen stated with humor, "honestly, they aren't even that terrible. Although they get a kick out of spreading rumors and causing mischief."

"Dude," Athens chuckled, looking sleepy and sexy with his eyes a bright metallic sheen. "They literally set fire to a passing carriage just for fun."

I snorted. "Any chance they would fight for us?"

Both men frowned and shrugged. "I mean, you could ask."

Athens nodded. "They may say yes. Who knows?"

I sighed and my lips twisted. Then without a second thought, I turned towards the bathroom to get ready for the day. My hair was darker and thicker than normal so I had to pull it back to make me feel more awake. I washed my pale features with soap and water and when the smell of coffee hit my nose, I finally perked up. I smiled as my handsome mage offered it to me with a cute smile. Athens. My handsome Athens.

"Baby, you look so cute." He teased.

I narrowed my eyes but suddenly Esme was laughing. I looked at my friend who had entered the room. She smiled broadly.

"What?" I frowned.

She shrugged. "Just nice to see you all cute and girly."

"Fuck you." I tossed up a tall finger.

"Are we doing that uniform thing you mentioned today?"

Oh!

"Yes," I smiled and looked to Adyen. "Can you contact Byron or Edwin? I want to see Vegas today if possible."

He kissed my shoulder as I shivered. Esme raised a singular brow and I bumped her hip as the two of us left the room. My boys followed behind but I could feel how sleepy they were. Me, though? I was suddenly good-to-fucking-go. I finished my coffee and began talking in a more upbeat tone.

"What if we changed the uniforms?" I looked at my friend. "Like, I love leather, right? I mean, who doesn't? But, still. I want, like, something more shiny."

"Yeah, and you could end up looking like a superhero," she chuckled.

"Oh." I frowned. "That would be weird."

"Marabella!" I greeted her, as my other friend entered the hall. She offered me a smile while ignoring the two men following her. Both of them talked quietly and narrowed their eyes at the guards on each side of the passage. My friend barely noticed as she stood next to me with an excited smile.

"Do you know how many different materials you ordered?" She asked with honest shock.

I cocked my head. "That was totally after a day of logicistical planning so I was feeling like I needed a change from all this fucking leather."

"What happened to Henry the VIII vibes?" Esme asked.

"I need it more chic though," I explained as we entered into a massive work room. My face split into a smile as I looked over all of the fabrics. Then I looked at my two friends. Both of them cringed realizing how long of a day it was going to be.

"Come on! That silk won't try on itself."

Athens

I could see the tension rolling off her from across the room. She was sprinting around enthusiastically, but I could see the stress. I worried about her getting too worked up. It didn't help that Vegas and Byron had just walked in along with two other women. My magic told me they were new mages and I could feel my mom's ink magic floating across their skin. I was happy to see the community was growing and not with assholes like our father.

"Baby," I drawled, "you're going to give yourself a heart attack with how excited you are."

Gray tossed me an eye roll as she continued to float around the room. Honestly, it was pretty cute and I found myself watching her intently. If I thought I loved Gray before there was no comparison now that the two of us had bonded. I could feel our magic intertwining with ease and I felt lucky that my brother and I would never have to be separated again.

"Any word on the border crossing yesterday?" Adyen asked as I shook my head.

"Nah," I sighed. "I have no idea how he did it. Except for crossing the wards at the border, his path was completely masked."

"He wasn't even that strong of a fucking mage," Adyen sighed.

Guilt surged through me because I knew the fucker had become radicalized and worked up due to my father. That family essentially almost died because of the asshole that created part of me. Sure, it probably wasn't super logical to feel that way, but I couldn't help it. The bastard was causing even more problems than we already had. Then Gray already had.

"What about this?" She opened up a long purple silk.

I shook my head. "Baby, you know that wouldn't work."

Her mouth pinched as she narrowed her eyes at me. "You don't know that."

"Yes, I do." I grinned as her eyes lit up.

"Oh?" She put her hand on a popped hip. "And please tell me, Athens, why this wouldn't work on the battlefield."

I stood up and walked towards her as those eyes flamed with fire. My hand shot out to grasp the fabric as I brought it in front of me. Then I ripped it with a quick movement.

"Shit," Vegas laughed.

Gray groaned, tossing her head back. "But you can do that with, like, anything. You are crazy strong."

I totally preened like a fucking peacock. My hands looped around her waist as I leaned down to her ear. "As much as I love the idea of ripping silk off you, I would probably suggest wearing something a bit more durable."

Her shiver enticed me to nibble her hair as her eyes flicked up at me. I wondered if we could sneak away without anyone noticing. Was that possible in a room that had only one door?

"You're distracting me." She tried to pull away but I didn't let her. Mostly because I was ridiculously hard. Instead, I turned her so she faced the room and sat down with her small frame planted in my lap.

"Have them try on stuff instead," I rationalized as all the women offered me grouchy looks.

"Oh, good point!" Gray exclaimed and began directing them.

I took the time to gently comb through her hair and braid it to expose her back and shoulders. My finger traced where my rune was. She wiggled as her magic caressed my fingers like a playful wind. My eyes traveled the expanse of her back and shoulders. I wanted to kiss each scar there but I wasn't positive she would let me. Instead, I placed a gentle kiss on her shoulder.

"Could you give me a massage?" She asked, rolling back her shoulders.

I was glad everyone was distracted because I turned her chin and raised a questioning brow. I would have to touch the area she was really sensitive about to do that. Her eyes warmed considerably.

"Please?" She asked, granting me permission.

My large hands practically enveloped her shoulders as their rough texture slid across her scars. Instead of tensing, she leaned back into me and I began to gently massage them but with enough force to cause her to break out in goosebumps. Her voice was light and happy, as if this wasn't a massive fucking deal. Adyen watched her carefully.

I think he wanted to make sure she ate because he kept pushing her tray closer and closer. It was going to end up on her fucking lap if he wasn't careful.

As the afternoon proceeded, I could see her growing more and more tired, something that seemed to be a general consensus. Vegas, the woman who oddly looked like our girl, had dark circles under her eyes, too. I felt like the poor girl was about to fall the fuck over. Byron had his eye on her and he continued to shift himself so that he was only inches away.

I think that Edwin and Byron's relationship with Vegas struck me as the most odd. You have to understand, because of Taylor and the mage community, I had known both of them essentially since childhood, Byron far more than Edwin. The blood mage had earned himself a rather sadistic reputation. While my brother and I had substantially more power, there was something to be said about the danger of fucking crazy people. The brothers qualified for that description completely. I hadn't confirmed it but I was fairly positive they killed for fun rather than necessity. So to see them treat someone with such affection and gentleness, was very odd.

"Athens?" Gray looked back and I offered her a soft smile. "Vegas is about to head out, but her sister and partner are going to get a tour from Esme and Marabella. Is it safe, you think, to leave the castle?"

Was it? Probably for most people except Gray.

I looked at Palo and he drew his eyes away from Marabella to meet my gaze. "Palo, can you go with them?"

Taylor stood as well. "I'll join. I need to talk to you about something, brother."

As everyone said their goodbyes, Rhodes shared a look with

Adyen. I frowned and Neo nodded towards Gray, her frame still as she looked out the window, indecision on her face. My gaze followed her own but I knew it was on the border. An intense and determined look came over her face that made me smile because I knew Gray would be just fine. She just needed to keep her spirits up and believe, without a doubt, that she would be able to defeat that bastard, Mario.

"Can we go see the Pixies?" She turned to look at the three of us.

"I should stay here," I sighed. I really didn't need to but I figured that both Adyen and Rhodes would appreciate some time alone with her. They were always so busy trying to keep things from imploding on us, they deserved a break. "Why don't you two go with her?"

Neo must have been thinking the same thing. "I wanted to check on a few things as it is."

Gray looked at both of us and nodded, seemingly having decided we were actually okay with it. She pressed a kiss to Neo as my brother's hand grasped her shirt just a bit tighter than normal. Talk about someone who needed more time with her. I knew damn well that he'd been the cause for Rhodes finally snapping. I also knew he would say it was about breaking or punishing them. I didn't buy it. I think Neo wanted our family to be happy and he knew she was the key to that.

The asshole was one of the best guys I knew and he didn't even allow himself to think that. I looked at my brother and came to the decision that it might do us some good to spend time together anyway.

"Will you be up when we get back?" Gray asked, wrapping her arms around my neck.

"Of course." I kissed her gently, "Now, go see those asshole Pixies."

I smirked as the three of them left. Neo walked over and he let out a tired sigh. I shot him a look and spoke quietly.

"I am worried about how biased the mage community has become." I muttered. "If people start to view this as a war between non-natural and natural born mages there will only be more internal fighting."

Neo sighed. "I know. We need to get an understanding of how they actually feel."

I froze and looked at him. "We should hold a large assembly about it."

My brother smiled. "That sounds like something mom would fucking love."

As we left the room my smile grew. He called her mom. I know he had before, but this time it was different. This time it seemed normal.

I wasn't lying when I said Gray was mending our family.

10

GRAY

"Rhodes," I groaned. "I know how to get off a horse." He let out a low grumble as Adyen chuckled. "Good luck there, lil brawler. He's just marked you as his mate. You could get a paper cut and he'd flip his shit."

I met Rhodes's pale green eyes and the bastard just shrugged as if to say 'sorry, not sorry.' I rolled my eyes as we began to trek towards the Pixie's oasis. The sky was turning deep twilight shades of purple and blue. The creatures of the night, from owls to crickets, had begun their song. My smile beamed as we came upon a curved stream and grouping of willow trees. All we had to do was cross over the creek.

"Nothing weird is going to happen, right?" I asked because you never really fucking knew when it came to Fae shit. Your perspective on what was "normal" started to alter drastically when trees started adjusting and shifting for your benefit.

Sorrrrry for being cautious!

"Weird?" Adyen chuckled while grasping my hand on his side. "We are about to go talk to Pixies about joining our war efforts against another Fae kingdom. Would you consider that weird?"

Point made.

I scoffed and jumped over the creek with an easy leap. Rhodes made a frustrated sound. I smiled. What? The man was even more of a control freak now that I was his mate. Of course I was going to fuck with him. Adyen, as if knowing his pain, simply offered him a shoulder squeeze and followed after.

Was it wrong that Adyen's humor about it made me want to complete mating with him also? You know, just so they can bond over what a pain in the ass I am.

Also… I really wanted to sleep with him. Bad.

The willow trees shifted out of the way like curtains. I stepped through from the small stones on the creek's shore to a stunning clearing. My mouth popped open in surprise as I took in the whole scene. Each willow tree contained these small glowing lights. The smaller shrubs and saplings contained these little wooden houses. I jumped slightly as a brilliant buzzing light shot past me. I began to realize that the small glowing lights in varying shades of pink, green, and blue were actually small, living creatures.

Holy shit, but the pixies were so small!

I had no idea how the hell they would help in the war effort since they were the size of my thumb nail, but I didn't want to miss an opportunity to meet them.

"How do we talk to them?" I asked Rhodes. His arms wrapped around my waist. Adyen seemed just as interested in the little creatures as me, his eyes shifting fluidly from gold to black. I think his dragon got frustrated sometimes, feeling as though he didn't get enough time to explore. It was a tad more difficult for Adyen to shift in comparison to Rhodes considering the massive difference in size.

At least the dragon had a sense of humor though. He was funny as fuck from what I'd gathered. Possessive, but funny.

"Our Queen," a tiny voice began as a small blue light began to grow larger in the center of the clearing, "does not need to ask. We are here to talk whenever she needs us."

My mouth popped open as a stunning, ethereal woman appeared in front of me. She was taller than me by far, nearly Rhodes's height, and dressed in a long silk dress that flowed around her. The most shocking factor, however, was her honest-to-god blue, shimmering skin that almost had a water-like texture to it. It shimmered like scales underneath the surface of the water and matched her deep, sapphire-colored hair. Honestly, I'd never seen anything like it. She offered me a small smile as if knowing what I was thinking about.

Her eyes traced where my crown sat and I was suddenly glad I wore it, feeling as though it somehow shielded me from this new experience. I mean, I'm sure I could kick their butts but I had absolutely no idea what type of power they had. There was just a general scent of magic that wrapped around the clearing with no singularity.

"Mina," Rhodes spoke formally. "It is good to see you."

"Child," she greeted and looked towards Adyen. "I hope both of your fathers are doing well."

Oh! So, she knew the council representatives? Also, how old was this woman if she considered Rhodes a child? I was totally going to bust his balls about that later.

"They are," Adyen answered. Rhodes nodded. I frowned slightly, reminding myself to ask Rhodes the state of his relationship with his father. He said those scars were from him but he didn't treat it like Neo had. My guess? The cigar burns had been some type of punishment. My other guess? That was the reason for Rhodes's need for control. It made me want to delve even deeper into my mate's soul. We had a lot to talk about still.

I figured this would be a good time to speak.

"I came here to see if you would aid us in the upcoming war with King Mario," I admitted bluntly.

What? It's not like I am known for my fucking finesse.

Mina's lip twitched as she walked forward before reaching out a hand. I gauged her posture and expression, not noting any aggression as my magic surrounded the two of us before I clasped her hand. Her eyebrows raised.

"You are far stronger than I expected little True Heir." She smiled happily. "Your parents would have been proud."

Oh, no. I did *not* have time to open up that package of emotions.

"Thank you," I responded honestly.

She continued, her eyes constantly on my expression . "As for King Mario, I am not certain you are aware but he was the conqueror who destroyed our realm and hoped to enslave us. Your mother found out about the migration of our kind into captivity. She negotiated for our freedom. I believe the trade was an expansion of the Dark Fae lands, resulting in a smaller kingdom for the Horde. The sacrifice that she made has never been forgotten by our people. So child, the answer is yes. Of course, we will help."

A small thankful smile tugged on my lips. I was just hoping they could all grow to be this large in size or else we'd have to be really creative with their place in this battle. Also, can we give it up to my mom? What a bad bitch.

"I do have one request," she stated.

I tilted my head and waited for her to continue. Mina spoke, "After Mario is… taken care of, I would like to open up the conversation of having a pixie representative on your council."

Well, that is actually really fucking reasonable considering what I assumed to be their large population. I nodded and came to a decision.

"I think that would be a good idea. Did you have a particular person in mind or would you want to serve in that capacity yourself?"

Mina let out a soft laugh. "Me? No. I am far too old and stuck in my ways. Instead, I would like to suggest my son."

Before she finished her sentence, another light of green glowing material grew to stretch out into the figure of a large man, nearly Adyen's height. My eyes widened because of several factors. The dude had green skin that was this odd metallic material that contrasted against the texture of his grass-like emerald hair. A pair of nearly silver eyes like his mother's met mine as he offered a smile.

"Marcellus," he offered and extended a hand.

I met it and he smiled pleasantly. Before I knew it, Rhodes had me back in his arms. Both Pixies smiled at his possessive behavior. All right. So, Pixies weren't bad, but they did seem a bit antagonistic.

"I would love to discuss adding a representative onto our council in order to be a voice for what you need. After everything settles down with the Dark Fae, please come to the castle and we will sort something out."

He nodded and I nearly laughed at my words. I was really fucking sure we would win, wasn't I? All right. In a weird way, that made me feel more confident than anything else recently. I mean, hell. If I wasn't sure of myself, how would anyone else be.

"We will ready ourselves and make our way to the SE guard for anything that happens from now on," Mina added.

"Thank you," I responded and after a head bow they were back to colorful zips of light. Marcellus, a green glow, brushed across my cheek as Rhodes let out a growl. I couldn't help but laugh.

The three of us began to walk our way back under the willows and across the creek as thunder cracked across the sky. Of course, it would fucking rain.

"Shit," Adyen cursed. "The twins are going to have their hands full if a storm is coming in."

"What?" I frowned.

He looked back up at the sky. "They are holding a mage town hall of sorts and I think they'd planned on holding it in the mage city center. It's going to become a cluster fuck."

"Go help," I spoke while also feeling pride at my two mages. I had a feeling I knew exactly what the town hall was about.

"Wait!" I grabbed his shoulder. "How did you know what they were planning to do?"

"Taylor saw them and let us know." He flashed a smile.

I gasped. "I want to be part of the secret conversations."

Rhodes chuckled. "Then we can't talk about you, kitten."

Adyen kissed me and took off by shifting, leaving me scowling at Rhodes who flashed me a smile. I grumbled as I swung up onto Midnight who was in a nuzzling fest with Rhodes's horse.

"Tell your horse to stop flirting with mine," I demanded.

"I think your horse is instigating this," Rhodes pointed out. It was true. Midnight was walking extra sassy and kept pushing her nose against his. Although, I still felt like his horse looked a bit too cocky, like he knew what he was doing.

Thunder and lightning exploded in the sky as we both shared a look. When we began to ride in earnest, I felt as though the castle was far further than I assumed. Christ. I was so about to get rained on. When the first spattering of rain hit me I urged Midnight to go faster but she wasn't feeling it and continued to go at a normal pace.

Come on, dude.

Ten minutes later, both of us were soaked. We had a bit of relief as we traveled along a thick, forested path until a massive boom of thunder shook the trees. Midnight took the fuck off.

Oh, okay. Now you want to go!

I leaned forward and hung on tightly, but I knew she was going too fast. She was spooked and as we took a turn I braced myself, my body sliding from her saddle. Fuck, this was going to hurt. I grunted as my body slammed right into a massive tree.

Stupid trees. Now you didn't want to move?

Rhodes's voice echoed around me but I couldn't open my eyes. I was at the base of a tree, groaning, blood dripping from my nose. Good. What I needed right now was a broken fucking nose. Honestly, fuck my life.

"Gray," a concerned voice echoed in my ears as Rhodes's scent surrounded me. I grasped onto him as I groaned in pain.

"Stupid fucking tree," I muttered as he let out a strangled laugh. His body was gone for just a moment before I felt fur brush up against me, causing me to look up. Fuck. Those teeth were massive yet I wasn't scared of his jaguar form. The fucker started to nuzzle me and lick my injury which would have been totally gross if it wasn't healing me at the same time.

Yeah, in case we all forgot… Rhodes has a healing lick.

Ha. I could go so many different directions with that.

"Thanks," I murmured as his soft fur body wrapped around me and his head lolled against my knee. He was fucking massive.

His golden eyes focused on my face. Despite how lethal he looked, the bastard was sort of snuggly. I used my nails to run through his fur and a low purr began to hum through his body. Honestly, I was feeling better now but very sleepy. The rain and thunderstorm didn't help because I felt like I was in bed listening to some meditative nature sounds. Rhodes didn't even attempt to get up so instead of worrying about everything that needed to be done, I closed my eyes.

Our problems would still be there in the morning.

Taylor

"Should we move them?" Athens asked, clearly amused. I think he and I were the only ones who found this even remotely funny.

Adyen and Neo had essentially had heart attacks when they'd seen Midnight return without Gray in tow. After the rather successful and eye-opening mage town hall, we had come across her horse and immediately began searching for Gray.

It had been fairly easy to find them.

There was a small forest pathway that they had clearly ridden through. I wasn't positive why they had stopped but the scene in front of me was something out of a fucking fairytale. Rhodes, the sneaky bastard, had shifted and wrapped himself around our Fae queen. Her dark hair was spread out around her sleeping form. The plants around them seemed to be bending and swaying to keep them comfortable. An owl had planted itself above them and in the late moonlight it was actually fucking beautiful. A small part of me warmed at their closeness. I think this god damn bond was making me a softie.

"Yes," Adyen sighed.

Before either of us could respond, a meow sounded and my eyes darted down to my chest as the other men froze. Our cute kitten escaped from my jacket and hopped onto the soft grass.

"You brought Lunatic?" Neo sputtered.

Athens started laughing and Adyen just fixed me with an incredulous look. How did I explain this?

"Alright so before the town hall, I went back to Gray's quarters for a moment and Lunatic was just staring at the door making me feel guilty. So, I brought her with me."

Athens started laughing hard enough to draw tears as the other two just stared at me. When the metal mage could finally talk he gasped. "Oh, Taylor, that is fucking great. I would have never expected you to be the pushover parent."

Fucking shit.

"I am not," I demanded his retraction of the obviously true statement. Lunatic let out a meow as if she agreed with the bastard.

Neo shook his head in disappointment as Adyen started chuckling. I followed his gaze and discovered Lunatic sitting in front of a sleeping Rhodes, her paw on his nose expectantly. One eye opened. A disgruntled huff came out of him as she jumped on his nose and crawled up his head towards Gray. This was some quality shit.

"Oh, hey, baby," Gray smiled as Lunatic began purring.

"Rhodes," Adyen spoke loudly, "you're getting sort of soft in your old age."

"Didn't even hear us approach," Neo noted.

Rhodes looked at us through narrowed eyes as Gray looked at all of us in surprise. "Oh, hello!"

"Baby girl," I grinned, "why are you guys out here?"

"I fell off Midnight and got injured so Rhodes healed me and we fell asleep," she rambled while standing up. Rhodes shifted and grasped Lunatic before she fell. Our leader groaned and stood up looking exhausted.

"I suppose I didn't realize how tired I was," Rhodes conceded.

Gray walked towards me and wrapped her arms around my waist before laying her head against my chest. I pulled her close and nuzzled my nose in her hair.

"Let's get back," Adyen suggested. The group of us began walking and the rain had pretty much let up. Although I could tell Gray was soaked to the bone from the storm.

"How was the town hall?" She asked as the twins offered surprised looks that she already knew.

"Adyen," I noted as she nodded.

Neo answered. "Originally, we had done it to gauge general attitudes towards non-natural born mages. What we found was even more interesting. It doesn't seem the mage community itself has a problem but, rather, the military. The most biased people we came across were either previous military or current military. I can only assume my father was to blame for that."

Athens continued, "Obviously, they have a right to their extremely stupid opinions, however we made it clear that if any comments or actions reflecting bias regarding non-natural born mage were reported, they would be dismissed."

I thought it was a fair solution.

Gray squeezed my hand. "How is it outside of the SE Guard? Have you talked to the Red Masques to gauge the problem?"

Both twins nodded and I spoke, "My cousins wouldn't allow that. However, it is possible it still exists. Why don't we take a visit to headquarters tomorrow morning? I heard Byron mention today that they would be training there. Vegas and her boys included."

"That's perfect!" Gray nodded. "Then we can see how they react to them because they are non-natural born."

Then a wicked smile lit her face.

"Maybe I can train with Vegas since none of you will go against me with just our natural magic," she drawled antagonistically.

All of us laughed, but no one denied it. She could think it was about whatever she wanted but, honestly, I'd seen her power in action and that shit was scary. I wasn't one to make a habit out of stupid decisions and challenging her magic would be stupid. Her magic was not the sweet cuddly version of Gray. It wasn't the feisty queen version either. It was just savage.

When we entered the castle and made our way up to her quarters, I could see the exhaustion in her face. Without even showering, she fell into bed and I watched as Rhodes crawled in next to her on one side with Athens and Neo on the other. Adyen stretched out at the end of the bed. I considered briefly sleeping on the couch. Then I said screw it and climbed into the middle of the bed, wrapping my arms around her center.

We really needed a bigger bed.

11
GRAY

"Vegas!"

I had a lot of fucking enthusiasm right now. For several reasons. One, I had drank four cups of coffee. Two, I loved shocking the ever living hell out of a special forces unit. All of them were offering me terrified and nervous looks, bowing down as if they were toy soldiers. Three, Vegas! As usual she didn't bow and I was glad of it. Despite our odd power dynamic, with being Queen and all, I considered her an equal, like my men.

I'd fucking die to see Rhodes bow. On second thought, that could end up being some sexy foreplay. As if knowing my thoughts, the jaguar rolled his eyes.

I practically tackled Vegas as her smile grew wider. It was clear when I'd walked in that she had been feeling awkward.

Never fear, friend! I am ten times more awkward so no one will even notice your awkwardness.

"Stand up!" I demanded of all the toy soldiers.

Vegas's eyes widened. "Are you training with us?"

I could feel my men gauging the responses of the mages in the room. Rhodes was speaking quietly to Edwin, most likely explaining our dilemma. Well, not a dilemma, per se. Just our need to make sure we didn't have bias assholes serving our realm. We really needed cohesiveness. I had a feeling that Mario was getting closer and from what Neo had heard from the scouts, his troops were making great time.

At least they were punctual.

The military on our end had been quietly getting ready and I could feel the energy in the Horde changing. Becoming darker and tenser.

"I figured it's better than training with a bunch of men that won't actually fight me."

Neo's power gripped the back of my long hair as he tugged antagonistically. I scowled at him. The man just offered me a dangerous smile. Scratch that. *He* might be willing. I feel like that could end in us naked, though, so maybe later.

He winked at me. Bastard knew me way too well.

"You may face the same problem here," Edwin admitted while holding onto Vegas rather possessively. I half understood that, though, because most of the men here were trying to get a look of her as it was. I don't think she noticed or cared. I don't know how she dealt with it. I would have been so fucking uncomfortable. Like how people stare at my scar but worse. I nearly shivered at the mere thought.

"No, I won't," I locked eyes with Vegas. "Because Vegas is going to fight me."

Her eyes brightened as she wiggled out from Edwin and nodded. "Let's do it."

My boys offered me concerned looks because of two reasons if I had to assume. One, they were probably concerned I would blow up the building and hurt everyone. Two, they didn't know what Vegas was. Neither did I but honestly, I was going on instinct here and instinct told me to trust her. She was possibly the only person I had ever trusted so automatically in my life.

It was some weird shit.

As Vegas and I spread out, I could feel Neo and Edwin wrapping us in a protective barrier. Not to protect us, of course but more to protect everyone else. Honestly, I had a moment of worry looking at Vegas but then my magic scoffed. I really had no idea if she could face me or not but my magic seemed confident, so I guess I was as well.

Then she lit up.

Her entire skin shimmered like dragon scales in a flash of red and orange before disappearing again. Her pale hair turned red with flashes of orange like a living flame. That was what she looked like...a bright flame. It was fascinating.

"Oh," I grinned. "I need to know how you do that. You are an enigma, my dear friend."

Really though. I wanted to be like the human torch. That shit was cool.

But then again I could turn people to ash and snap their necks with ease. I thought that was pretty badass. Plus, I had a crown.

Vegas spoke. "I've never sparred before."

I took a step towards her and offered my best advice. "It's instinctual, at least for me. You just have to react."

I hoped that was how her magic worked.

"React to what?" She was cut off as I sprinted forward and was happy to find I'd been right. Her body, in a smooth movement, gracefully landed at least ten feet away from me. My grin grew because I had a feeling this was going to be a fair fucking fight.

I'd always considered myself to be a blunt force fighter. I was quick and lethal. I would snap a neck before drawing out someone's death. I was like a wrecking ball. So, it was fascinating to go against someone who fought the opposite way. Her movements were almost languid and graceful as she avoided my movements and attempted to land a hit. My smoky power clashed with her flames as we collided again and again. It was beautiful.

"Never sparred, my ass." I jumped over her next attack and brought her to the ground. I grunted as she landed a hit and I totally pulled a bitch move by tugging her hair. She cursed and we started to get really fucking rough.

It was awesome. I had never felt more like a sister than in this moment. Siblings fought, right? I mean probably not with fire and ash... but it's gotta be similar.

She was mirroring me almost directly and it was fascinating to watch. I could see the pure excitement and elation on her face. I hadn't even meant to boost her confidence but I could see it happening. So of course, I tried harder to kick her butt.

I was such a good friend and teacher, pushing her boundaries and such.

I landed a hit to her stomach.

"Motherfucker," she hissed and knocked my legs out from under me with a whip of fire. I let out a low sound and grasped her arm, tugging her into me before tossing her away with an explosion of ash. She fell face first into the mat and let out a groan. My legs were tired and I groaned feeling as though I was finally getting a real workout in.

How long had we been sparring? This was so fucking insane. I loved it though. I could feel my body hurting and muscles tight. I was totally bleeding from my nose and my magic was cursing up a storm, throwing a middle finger at putting us in this state.

As a last moment the bitch pulled on my ankle as I stood over her. I actually fell on my ass and let out a chuckle. Well, then.

"Vegas," I groaned from where my back hit the ground after her last attack. "How the hell are you matching me?"

For real though, I needed to know if I was just getting weak or if she was just a badass.

"Gray," She turned over and fixed me with a look. God we

looked awful right now. "I can barely fucking move right now, but there is something you should know."

Obviously.

Unfortunately, I was left with a motherfucking cliffhanger because down came the protective shadowed walls. Instantly, I felt Rhodes's panic and my eyes shot up.

"Gray," He demanded my attention, "There has been another attack on the North border."

My heart squeezed as my magic coiled within me. I looked around and almost laughed at the horror-stricken expressions at our state. We must have looked bad. To be honest, Vegas looked like a cloud of ash had exploded on her. Her purple eyes moved around the room with a dark glint of amusement.

I totally loved her sense of humor.

I looked to Edwin and sighed. "Be ready tomorrow, I have a feeling this is one of his last small attacks."

I squeezed Vegas's shoulder and left with my men. The minute we were outside the castle, Neo began talking. "It was a different type of attack this time, if we can call it that. It also drew our scout's attention to them entering and exiting the portal as predicted. They don't seem to be in a rush, though, and didn't even bother hiding from our scouts. I would give it a day's time until they are here. Probably dawn in reality."

Fuck.

"What type of attack was it?"

"Dragons," Adyen grunted. "Not the shifter kind either."

So, that was how dragon shifters were made? Oh, god. Fae and dragons. Nope. I didn't need to know or imagine that.

Lies. I sort of wanted to know.

"They burnt all of the land right in front of our wards. The dragon's flames began burning and destroyed at least three miles within our border before SE was able to put it out," Rhodes stated.

"The ward plan is working though," Taylor mentioned. "They are going right there."

"So," I took a deep breath. "We have tonight to prepare."

"We are prepared, baby," Athens wrapped an arm around me.

I hoped he was right.

12

RHODES

My hands were strung together behind my head as I paced her private quarters. It was far past sunset and I couldn't help but worry that Gray had yet to fall asleep. Somehow, she was impossibly calm and I was freaking out. Not for the reason you'd assume which was that we were entering into a major war.

No.

I was losing my shit about Gray being in potential danger.

I know.

She was going to be fine. I knew she was. Rationally. My jaguar on the other hand? He really didn't care about being rational and was actually annoyed that I would even consider being okay with her fighting. I grunted as he let out an aggressive sound through my chest.

"Rhodes, honey," Gray looked up from the book she was reading with all the Zen in the world. I wasn't positive what happened between her panicked look after training to now, but something had snapped. She seemed perfectly at peace with tomorrow's events.

"You need to stop pacing," she commented, taking a sip from

her teacup that rested against her robe-covered legs. The woman looked like she was just enjoying a fucking Sunday morning tea. I truly didn't think I'd ever grasp the full extent of who Gray was as a person. She just changed so fucking often.

I loved it. It was chaotic and messy. The opposite of me and wildly attractive.

"I can't!" I snipped. "How are you not more concerned about this?"

She raised a brow at my tone and I grunted before sitting down. Lunatic pranced over to me and clawed my arm before curling up next to me. I was going to kill this cat, except she *had* grown on me. I still wasn't convinced she was a normal kitten. She seemed far too rational. Or, and this is a thought, I was losing my mind.

"No point in stressing," Gray shrugged as my eyes flickered to the mating bite I'd put on her. Male satisfaction pulsated through me as I smiled. At least there was that.

Gray was mine. My mate.

Taylor's snore had both of us looking over and then I was laughing. Taylor was in the center of the bed and both twins were on either side of him, squished together like a pile of pups. Gray smiled affectionately at the sight and looked toward Adyen, who sat near the open window. He looked equally as stressed as I was.

I had a million different questions I wanted to ask her. I wanted to know how she felt about tomorrow. About Mario. About our mating bond. Fucking everything. The woman drove me mad. At the same time, I didn't want to put her into a panic when she had so clearly found a point of peace.

"You're stressing her out."

I looked down at Lunatic, that was the clearest I'd ever heard her speak.

"You can't tell that," I responded with a frown.

Lunatic narrowed her gold eyes. *"Except she's my mom, so of course I can."*

"*You're a cat. You are smart enough, though to realize that she is not your actual mom."*

"No, shit," Lunatic growled through our connection. Although I had to admit, everyone did essentially treat her like a child. I mean heck, she even had her own little bed in the corner and everyone got super awkward if we were being affectionate and she trotted into the room.

She's a fucking cat. We shouldn't be worried about that. I think it was because I knew she could communicate like this.

"When did you start swearing?"

"I age more advanced than most and I've sworn most of my life."

"You are the size of a fucking orange. You haven't had much of a life before now."

"Just tell her that you aren't worried. Comfort her." She was fucking ignoring my statement.

"I'm not going to lie to her about my concerns."

Lunatic rolled her eyes, yes rolled, and stretched standing up. *"Fine I will."*

I would like to state for the record that I expected her to go and lay on Gray's lap. So, you have to imagine the pure unadulterated shock that went through me as Lunatic wiggled down onto the carpet and let out a meow.

Only to be encased in a soft white light that had all three of us watching in horror and fascination.

"What in the ever living fuck?" Gray muttered.

My mouth popped open because as the light faded away we were left looking at a girl about ten years old.

Oh. Shit.

Now I felt bad about swearing at her.

The little girl narrowed her vivid metallic golden eyes at me and pointed at Gray. "Tell her. Tell Mom you aren't worried about tomorrow. I shouldn't have to do your job for you."

"Lunatic?" Gray whispered, her eyes round with unfiltered shock. Adyen looked dazed and beyond confused. I was glad the others were sleeping.

"I would actually like to change that." The peppy little girl bounced and sat down on top of the coffee table between all of us. "I'm thinking Luna."

Silence.

"You're a cat shifter?" I asked quietly.

"No shit, Dad." She rolled her eyes.

Gray looked at her with raised brows and Luna caught her expression. "Oh, don't look at me like that. Dad has been the one cussing up a storm."

"Why didn't you change before now?" Gray whispered as Adyen started laughing.

Luna shrugged. "I hadn't had the energy because when you'd found me, I'd been on the street for weeks."

Oh, fuck.

"Stop swearing around her!" Adyen continued to laugh. "She even has a slight English accent. This is so freakin' funny." Yes, he did choose to not swear in that sentence. How nice of him. Fucking show off.

Luna narrowed her eyes at Adyen. "Last time I checked, you're equally responsible for the words I hear, Dad. All five of you swear. Actually, six. Mom you are terrible."

Gray legit blushed and leaned forward.

"So you are a cat shifter." She murmured, "How old are you? How did you get left outside? Are your parents alive?"

Luna sighed. "Yes and around ten years old although shifters age remarkably fast. Especially cats because we are better than everyone. As for my parents, they really don't matter because my Mom passed away forever ago and my Dad left me before heading to the Earth realm. So, here I am! You thought you only adopted a cat and you got a kid. Pretty neat, right?"

Oh.

"Well," Gray spoke and then her smile grew as Luna smiled back. "So, I'm like a parent and I didn't have to even get pregnant? That's some shit right there."

I see the swearing issue now.

"Yep!" Luna smiled. "On that note, I'd like siblings but not yet because now that I've had the chance to shift, I'd like to do some cool shit, post war of course. Oh, also I need a new bedroom because I have had to leave several times because of your gross adult stuff. I mean get a room or better yet, get me a room."

Now, I was blushing.

"Hey, Luna," Neo yawned as he walked over and messed up her hair.

What the actual hell?

"You knew?!" Gray exclaimed.

Neo tilted his head to the side. "I thought it was obvious. Granted, it took me a bit but once I considered it… it just made sense."

Athens was there then hugging Luna as she let out a small childish giggle. The girl was adorable. "Luna! You finally shifted."

"That's because Rhodes was acting like an ass," Taylor added.

Adyen tried to stop laughing. "How it is that everyone but Gray and the two shifters here didn't realize you were a shifter."

Luna shrugged. "Not sure. You guys are the adults."

"Wow," Gray whispered, amused. "This takes the cake by far in regards to the most surprising things in my life."

"Oh, talking about big life moments," Luna stood on the table top. A sense of overprotective paternal bullshit had me leaning forward to catch her just in case she fell.

"I want to fight tomorrow," she twirled on her foot. "I am super light on my feet and great with a thin sword."

"No!" Gray exclaimed with horror.

I saw her panic as the thin young girl crossed her arms and leveled her mom with a very familiar 'Gray' look. I couldn't help but smile because this was actually really cool. She looked nothing like any of us but that didn't matter, she was part of our family. Her white, like snow-white, hair was down to her waist and she was tanner than even myself. I honestly could not believe what I was looking at right now.

"Mom!" she frowned. "Aren't you the one always saying that women shouldn't be limited by age or their gender?"

Gray's mouth opened and closed as Athens chuckled.

"You are a kid," she explained, "I don't want you out there honey."

"I figured." She sighed flippantly. "That's okay. I have a better way to help. I was thinking since Aunt Marabella and Esme are probably not fighting, the three of us could bring all the children and anyone else who didn't plan to fight into the castle to keep them safe."

You know what, I was officially claiming this kid as mine. She was fucking smart.

"Thanks, Dad!" She stated with a genuine smile. Oh. I'd said that out loud.

I felt a smile curl on my lips.

Talk about a day! Shit, I was a dad.

Oh fuck. Now I really was worried about tomorrow. It wasn't just us adults anymore.

Gray

I couldn't sleep. I needed to be ready far before dawn and my mind was a million different places, not even including the panic of realizing I'm essentially Luna's adopted mom. The girl was fucking awesome though, so I didn't mind in the least. Her head was laid out on my lap as I gently petted her hair. She was a beautiful girl and I couldn't help but think about what would have happened if she had been left out on the streets any longer than she already had.

Her lashes were closed, like white, almost translucent feathers, and her thick, wavy, white hair was now all over the place. I swear her hair was heavier than she was. Her body was a bit too thin but I knew that would change after a time of living off the streets. After she'd fallen asleep, I'd had the boys do several things. One, explain to Esme and Marabella the plan regarding having those who weren't fighting stay in the castle. I felt awful because that hadn't even crossed my mind. Secondly, Luna needed her own room and space. The girl was smart and way older than her biological age. I figured that she would enjoy a space with a lot of different shelves and floors so I gave her the east tower. It would be like her own apartment and, if she shifted, she'd have the ability to climb wherever she wanted. The boys were arranging for some items as well as plans for the currently unused tower. I wanted it ready as soon as possible. And, yes, I totally arranged for some cat towers to be randomly stationed throughout our main living spaces and her apartment.

Wasn't this every cat mom's dream? I was a legit cat mom.

The boys were still passed out except for Adyen who was up as well. His eyes moved back and forth from the window to me occasionally. They strayed to Luna as a brow crease caused him to look very concerned. I had to assume he was feeling more pressure now that we had even more people to take care of. My eyes trailed the horizon and I realized I'd need to get ready soon. I looked back down at Luna and the soft breathing pattern that moved her.

If I didn't have a reason to kick ass before, I did now.

"Gray," Marabella spoke softly as she arrived about ten minutes later. Her dark eyes went wide as she saw Luna in person for the first time.

For the record, I'm really fucking glad that Lunatic could be shortened. That would have been so awkward. Am I right? Like, talk about shitty parent of the year award.

"She's stunning," Marabella offered. "I heard she's super funny, Athens was bragging up a storm about her."

Of course he was.

"I honestly had no idea," I murmured. "I mean it's amazing but I wish we'd sworn less. Also, acted a bit more like parents."

Marabella offered me a hug. "You guys have been great to her. Don't stress about it too much."

"You're right." I sighed and then grinned. "Let me just worry about this war instead."

"Wait!" Marabella grinned after a moment. "Does this mean she's officially the Horde's Princess?"

Oh man.

"Yeah," I grinned. "Make sure to freak her out by putting her in a bunch of dresses. Like big, I'm talking massive, cotton candy pink ones. But don't let her actually go out like that, not that she would. She strikes me more as a…"

"…jeans and t-shirt kind of kid," Luna mumbled before yawning. Truth. Currently, she was wearing a large hoodie and shorts from Marabella because she was the smallest out of all of us. When she'd shifted I had noticed the wear on her clothes.

"Damn," I muttered.

"Do I get a princess crown?" She asked looking at my pointy black one. "Because if I do, I want it to be gold and like a warrior head piece around my head instead of on top. Wait, I lied! Can I just have armor instead?"

Adyen grinned. "Gray, I blame you for this."

I smirked.

Guilty.

Luna sat up and walked towards the other couch before falling asleep curled up like a… cat. Christ. Marabella tugged my hand towards the bathroom as I looked at my exhausted and shaken expression.

Motherhood, man. Anyone else finding this ridiculously funny? I get to make those jokes now.

The serious part of me actually felt super strongly about the prospect of having someone in my care. I mean I'd had an awful childhood and it sounds like Luna had already been through a lot. I promised that I would try to make the rest of it amazing. I liked Luna as a cat, but as a child? My kid? I fucking loved her. Plus, now I had someone to back me up when the guys were being bossy. We could be a little badass mother and daughter team. I loved that.

Can we say matching outfits?

Marabella began to pull my hair up as I stared at myself in the mirror. I mean really stared at myself. From my pale skin to my darkening eyes, all of it was me. It was the same person that I'd seen the mirror for years. Well, I looked a bit more ethereal, but still Gray.

Except this Gray wasn't weak or beaten.

This Gray wasn't scared of a group of men revealing her identity.

This Gray wasn't scared of assuming her rightful place in the Horde.

This Gray was about to kill the one man who'd taken and changed everything in her life.

It was odd reaching the point that I had been reaching for and dreaming about for years. I know most little girls didn't daydream about murdering their parents' murderer. But. I wasn't most little girls and the bastard deserved it. Anyone who'd do that to a family deserved it.

While I'd always wondered if it was my place to decide and play God when it came to Mario, I'd realized the question no longer mattered. He needed to die and if I had that stain on my soul forever then I would gladly carry it.

My crown sat proudly on top of my head and I slipped into my custom made armor. Armor I had created quite a bit ago. I was still bitter that I didn't get to have silk on it.

Could I have a cape though? That would be cool.

The suit was silver and covered my body like a second skin, from the neck down to the laced-up solid boots. I nodded to myself in the mirror before walking back into the bedroom, the early dawn light was a pale grey spreading across my luxurious suite. I could hear my men outside but my eyes strayed to where Marabella sat tucking Luna into bed.

I really hoped that this wasn't the last time I'd see both of them.

I mean it wouldn't be, right?

I couldn't think like that.

"Luna," I whispered, sitting on the edge of the bed. A pair of bright golden eyes met mine and she offered me a hug. I tucked her head under my chin as my eyes met Marabella's tense gaze. After a shaky breath, I stood up and gave my friend one as well.

I left the room before I decided this was all too risky. That this could hurt my kingdom too much.

"Esme?" I asked as I stepped into the hallway. My friend looked at me with a small smile, her body wrapped in a robe as she talked quietly to Bobby. Palo spoke quietly to my boys, everyone seemed to have this quiet tension that was making me twitchy.

"Hey." Esme offered a smile.

"Take care of her," I spoke quietly and then looked to Bobby.

Hadn't it been two months ago that I'd been saying goodbye to them?

Bobby squeezed my shoulder and I breathed in as determination filled me. Without another thought, I turned and met Rhodes's gaze. Those eyes were a stunning gold and I knew he was close to shifting already. I nodded and, after a nod to Palo, we began to walk down the hall away from my little makeshift family. I couldn't help but look back to where Marabella stood in the doorway of the room where Luna slumbered. Palo and Bobby both were talking quietly to her as Esme offered me a worried look.

I hoped her worries were unfounded.

Our team was silent and my men were dressed in armor of their own as we silently moved through the halls of the castle. I could see families making their way through the gates and it seemed the migration had started late last night. I stopped one of the soldiers at the main gate.

"I want the city swept twice," I ordered sharply. "I don't care if they don't want inside the castle walls. You bring them anyway. I want this door and the outer gates shut. Do you understand?"

The commander nodded as Rhodes offered him a warning look. I trusted it would be taken care of. Midnight stood waiting for me with a silver saddle. My leg easily swung over as I mounted her and looked over the parade of military men making their way towards the clearing.

Without warning my men, I nudged Midnight and we began to move quickly through the hundreds of SE guards that were marching in perfect lines like toy soldiers. The commanders watched as the five of us galloped through their center lines and I noted there was a new commander that I hadn't seen before.

He wasn't SE and neither was his unit.

Marcellus.

The emerald colored Pixie offered me a head nod and I felt hope pulse through me. I knew Mario had more land but our army was more cohesive and larger in size. My people had something to fight for where Mario's men were simply oppressed.

I hoped to save some of their families.

I didn't want to have to rid the world of the Dark Fae or kill unnecessarily.

Honestly, the only person I wanted to kill was Mario.

The dawn was barely at its start and the air was misty, I moved faster than I probably needed to but there had been soldiers stationed over night at the clearing. I felt as though I should be there as well. If we were going to have a war then I was sure as hell going to be part of it.

The council representatives would be set up in a base camp further back and Laurena waved at me as I passed. The soldiers all stood and bowed their heads as we rode past. I wanted to tell them to stop but figured now wasn't the time to explain that modern politicians didn't require bowing so why should I? The clearing was massive and I stopped around fifty feet back from the wards as my eyes traced the forested landscape opposite me.

Nothing yet.

"The Red Masques are here." Taylor stated.

I looked over the massive army behind me as my gaze was drawn towards the east where a massive unit of men entered in a unified position, all completely in black. I felt a smile break across my face as I caught sight of Vegas in the center of it all looking wide-eyed but not scared. I felt bad because I'm positive this was overwhelming for her.

When she met my eyes, her determination shone through and I nodded her over. If she was the only one in this kingdom that could match me blow to blow than I wanted her right fucking next to me. I was surprised when her men didn't try to stop her. Maybe they had expected it?

As she approached I heard Edwin shout an order as the Red Masques covered the outside lines of my army. It was a very telling move and I realized just how dedicated this group was towards the Horde. They had no reason to be really, yet they were, and I would never forget that.

"Morning," Vegas offered me a small smile.

"I didn't sleep last night," I admitted quietly.

She agreed with a nod. "Neither did I. I can't believe I'm here."

"What do you mean?" I asked as she looked over the ward and forested area ahead.

"I mean, this past Halloween, I was just a college kid. Now, I'm here." She whispered and then shot me a smile. "It is pretty fucking cool."

"Vegas!" A voice shouted and I turned to see a group of eight making their way down the rows of soldiers. My trained professional men all paled and stepped out of the way. Then again, a lot seemed to fucking scare them.

"Tamara!" Vegas grinned. "Gray, this is Tamara."

Oh. This was the infamous Tamara and her men?

Then their power hit me and I whistled openly. Holy crap. Can we say demons?

"You must be Queen Gray," Tamara flashed a wicked grin. "I like you far better than Silas."

Silas. Fuck I hadn't said goodbye to him.

Not goodbye! Not a fucking goodbye. I would be back.

Still, I should have given him a hug or some shit.

"Nice to meet you," I smiled at the woman. Her bubblegum pink hair was in two pigtails on top of her head. The woman was wearing, and for the record this is not a joke, a cheerleading uniform. The skirt and top were black and in bold cursive letters was the word "Psycho."

The bitch had gotten that from Pinterest.

"These are my boys," she threw a thumb over her shoulder while chewing gum. I totally loved her. I mean she was wearing combat boots and had daggers strapped to her thighs. The bitch was cool.

Was that an upside down cross tattoo? All right. It was official. I loved her.

"Hi, Tamara's men," I nodded and all of them offered greetings but they were bickering about something internally. Their power not matching their bitching.

One of them spoke. "Tamara, you need to give me that list."

He was a smaller man with eerie dark eyes. Tamara produced the said list and offered it to him. He smirked and she rolled her eyes. They were sort of cute in a totally weird fucked up way.

"So the list…" I drew.

"He can't kill without it," she explained, "so I made a list."

"Of every single Dark Fae?" I tilted my head.

"Nah," She sighed, "I made it very specific. It was: 1) any Dark Fae that directly was threatening a member of the Horde 2) anyone that tried to hurt one of my friends 3) Mario. I know he is totally your kill, but I figured I'd throw it on there just in case the opportunity presents itself."

"Thanks," I nodded appreciatively.

"Is it weird I'm excited?" Vegas murmured.

I understood that though, I was fluctuating between hyped up and serious. It was an odd mix. When I went to respond, a pulse of power made me look back towards base camp. Vegas paled at something behind me. My eyes followed towards the forest border, the pulse of odd power forgotten, because he was here.

Fury sizzled in my veins as that motherfucker walked out from the trees on his white horse.

Mario.

13

GRAY

The bastard looked even worse than I remembered him. His body was massive and he sat on top of that white horse like a goddamn King. Piece of shit. My lips peeled back as his dark eyes met my own, that blonde hair faintly reminding me of silver. I hated this man so much. I wanted his body in ashes at my feet.

My skin heated up as the predator behind my eyes shifted.

Why was he smiling? The fucked up bastard took his time as his army marched behind him. His cocky smile had me feeling infuriated as Vegas stepped closer to me and spoke.

"This isn't right."

I knew she was right.

My eyes tracked over his posture and I breathed in the air around me. Something was hiding just outside of my reach. It didn't surprise me though, I knew he would play games. The man was too much of a son-of-a-bitch to do anything upfront and honest.

A coldness invaded my spirit as I narrowed my eyes at his gaze. He seemed confident but there was tension there. Tension I soaked in because I knew he was scared. His army was small.

This was a fucking suicide attempt. So, why did he seem so confident?

He stopped his lines right where the ward would have been if I hadn't weakened it. Perfect placement. So, what was wrong?

"I would agree with that." It was an honest response that lacked my true feelings.

"Gray," Rhodes's accented voice drew my attention. "There were troops attempting to come from the East border but we've intercepted them with the men already stationed there."

I turned to my jaguar shifter and his gold eyes met my own. I squeezed his shoulder but looked back at Mario. I was glad the East border hadn't worked out for them, but right now? That didn't matter as much, that just seemed like a well-placed distraction.

Our armies were fifty yards away from one another and I knew what was coming next.

Mario offered me a goading look and approached the downed ward as a sign of trust. I nudged Midnight forward as Adyen made a pained sound. There was a part of me that wanted to comfort him but the other, stronger part of me was possessed by my need for vengeance.

I wished that I could have saved everyone but the real target of this war, Mario, was using his army as a shield. He knew he would lose against me and the Dark Fae had no True Heir, so he had to be creative instead of facing me head on. If creativity meant sending your men on a suicide mission.

This *was* the man who encouraged suicide bombers though.

Behind me the power levels turned up and I felt it fuel me. The land around me came alive and Mario's eyes widened slightly at the disturbance. He could surrender. He should.

"This is a suicide mission," I spoke with a serious tone.

Mario's eyes flashed with a sickening light. "Good try, little girl. I'm not concerned about your band of misfits. Why don't you hand yourself over and spare yourself the embarrassment of defeat."

I snarled. "I am trying to save your people's lives. Don't make me do this Mario."

His lips pulled together. "I can't wait to see if you scream as pretty as your mother."

This motherfucker.

I couldn't wait to have his blood dripping from my hands.

"I am going to rip your heart from your chest." I let a dangerous purr into my voice as he seemed to get more excited.

It was dangerous to play war with a madman.

The screams and blood wouldn't be stains on his hands. They would be washable. Forgettable. Me, though? I would never fucking forget. I let myself absorb the significance of what I was about to do. I was going to kill. A lot.

Mario spoke softly. "Tell me, what do you think your little Horde misfits will look like in chains?"

The imagery he painted made my decision very clear. There were people counting on me and I planned on being what they needed. What was essential.

Before he could respond, a loud roar shook the land and my lips peeled back in a snarl. It took one moment of distraction. I had looked up towards the massive dragons ripping through the scene as they spewed black flames on my army.

Fuck.

Panic ripped through me but my eyes widened at the sight of Vegas's power lighting up. Her hands shot up and like once before at coronation, a black mirrored surface broke the damage. I knew any chance of peace was over at that point. Motherfucker tried to kill my people.

My eyes found Mario's as he slowly retreated and his army charged forward.

Motherfucker.

Instantly, men were on me. I soared off Midnight, gracefully landing as I nudged her and she sprinted back towards the base camp. A soldier collided with me and I laughed as he attempted to take me down. My hand twisted to grab his arm as I snapped it in half. His cries were the sweetest delight.

The savage in me was coming out.

Mario had men coming at me from all directions. I couldn't even take the time to go after him or check in on my boys. I was letting out my magic without a second thought. She twirled with delight as I let her ashy tentacles whip out and icy windows collapsed over the space I fought in. A large man came right at me with a sword and I snapped his neck, his body and sword falling into another man and killing him.

Dumbasses.

Someone grabbed the back of my neck and I grabbed the person's hair. My power pulsed through and ash surrounded me from whomever I'd just broken apart. Unfortunately, not all deaths were as neat and, before I knew it, I had to use raw force to kill these men.

My fist broke a chest cavity as someone attempted to slide a sword into my back. I twisted the man in front of me to take the brunt of the sword and was thanked by a massive explosion of blood. I could feel Rhodes's power as he let out a vicious roar that was echoed by Adyen in the skies. My confidence in the situation began to grow as I killed man after man. Body after body. I was covered in blood and ash as the cold, icy winds surrounded me in a dangerous hurricane.

Then, I felt it.

I grunted as my magic was pulled on, almost like a vacuum. I didn't need to fucking guess who was doing it but instead offered Mario a scathing look.

Asshole.

My power was still stronger than his bullshit though, and the only distraction from my mass slaughter was a massive dragon landing in front of Vegas. Who the fuck was that? I didn't have a chance to watch the individual confront her because someone tried to yank me onto the ground by my hair. That was some petty shit.

"Baby," Athens stood over me having sliced off the head of the hair puller. He offered me a hand and I grinned.

"Oh, watch out," I swore as he ducked and I blasted the man behind him with cold dark power. The man paled and then broke into smoky ashes.

Fucker tried to hurt one of my boys.

My eyes found Neo as he easily, and with a grin, slaughtered soldier after soldier. I could also see some mass commotion happening towards the back of the base camp. Now, why the fuck did I feel that was Tamara and her men?

A searing pain broke through me as a fucker stabbed me in the ribs. I growled and thunder cracked throughout the Horde. My power manifested from the land in the form of lightning. I couldn't help but smile as I killed the man who'd stabbed me and lightning began to strike down some of the assholes. Now, that was cool.

"Oh fuck," I was tossed off my ass and found myself falling face first into the rough, burnt ground. A heavy weight tried to press on my back. I used all my strength to throw them back as the heavy fucker cried out. My sword, rarely used, made an appearance while slicing through his neck. The splash of blood felt like cool water against my searing fury.

Vegas was there then, and her eyes were black as she shimmered with some odd fucking fire magic. I grunted as I snapped the necks of two more men before looking back at her. "Having fun?"

My ribs were radiating with pain but screw it. What was the point of war if you couldn't be light-hearted about it? Except

Vegas didn't find it funny and her eyes snapped to Mario, a nearly feral look crossing her face. Then my magic sparked in response to Vegas.

Vegas barreled towards Mario and the land responded to her, making me feel as though our connection was a live wire. Fury rolled across my skin from her and then the bitch lit up in purple flames. Legitimately.

"Holy fuck," Neo stated, fairly monotone actually, while killing five men at once.

That was hot.

I didn't have a chance to truly watch Vegas in action because I saw Rhodes jump onto a group of soldiers, maybe three, and bite down on their throats, ripping them out. Damn.

"She's fucking flying," Athens noted.

My eyes snapped up to find her, indeed flying above us with purple fucking flame wings. Oh no, Vegas. No secrets at all.

Cool, *friend*.

I was so holding a grudge for this.

"Gray," Taylor grasped my hand and turned me so that I narrowly avoided someone. His red smoky power surrounded us and instantly, a group of ten in front of us, were all dead by a dagger lodged in their throats. I had no idea where this many weapons came from.

"You know," I drawled while kicking someone so hard in the chest they flew twenty feet back. "I am getting real fucking tired of not killing the person I actually want to kill."

Almost as if my prayers were answered, Mario's body fell five feet from mine as Vegas soared above. I wish I could have spent more time on the fact she had fucking wings.

"Mario," I sang as he tried to stand up but my speed was too quick and I stepped down into his chest. Something cracked as he cried out.

All around us the screams of war echoed and I couldn't tell

whose blood it was that stained my land. All I did know? I was at my wits' end with this asshole.

"You finally did it," he grinned with bloody teeth. "You have me in your grasp. But tell me Gray…"

Pain lanced through me as my connection with Vegas rocked with horror. My eyes shot up as I realized she was on a fucking dragon. What the hell?

"He took her," Mario chuckled while wincing in pain. "Your friend is gone, Gray. So will your entire family be. You think we didn't prepare for this? Do you think Colliard didn't think this through? You kill me and your entire castle goes 'boom.'"

No.

I kneeled down and my hands tightened around his throat. I could see the blunt truth in his eyes. Was he being truthful? No. I didn't believe that. I couldn't believe that.

Whether it was true or not. It was enough. Enough to distract me for one fateful moment.

A blow hit my head so hard that my cry echoed throughout the space. I fell limply to the side. Mario's eyes filled my vision as he began to squeeze ever so tighter and tighter.

"Now, say bye-bye to all your friends, Gray." He whispered.

No.

My eyes fluttered shut as he began crushing my windpipe. I tried to fight. Tried to struggle. But nothing came except blackness. Spots clouded my vision and roars echoed around me. The entire earth shifted with power as I felt the scene burst.

Explode.

I couldn't tell you if it was with power or physically.

Everyone in my castle would be in danger and no one knew.

I wish someone knew.

My consciousness faded and I was left with one thought.

I never told all my men I loved them.

14

NEO

"Neo," Athens spoke.

I didn't respond, though. I had nothing to say that would be helpful or positive. In fact, I was far more likely to lose my shit. This was my father's fault. This was Mario's fault. This was even my fault. Gray was gone.

They had fucking took her.

The slaughter of the Dark Fae didn't matter and burning their bodies wasn't nearly as fun without Gray. I know. I know. Dark and all, but it was true. My eyes trailed over our camp as the first night set in. Who the hell knew how long it would take to get there, or how long she would be in his deranged little castle. It wasn't only her, though. It was also Vegas, Gray's friend.

She was gone and it didn't make it easy when the commanders of the SE guard and the Red Masques lead team were essentially checked out. This was why we had solid section commanders, so that I could sit here and zone the fuck out.

"This is important." his voice was sharp. "Come in the tent now."

My lips pursed together as I grunted and followed him in. Instantly, my eyes went wide.

"Luna?" I hissed.

Athens grunted and walked towards our... daughter? Yeah, that was weird.

Her eyes were livid and she looked a bit like Gray in that moment. How had she even gotten out of the castle or to our travel camp? I'd seen her what, twelve hours ago and she'd promised to stay home.

"You guys are losing your shit." She muttered. "So, I decided I'd have to come with."

"You are ten," Athens scolded. "A war camp is no place for you."

She narrowed her eyes but ignored him. "Now, we need to keep it together. I know you are stressed but this is *Mom* we are talking about. She's going to be fine. She's a tough cookie."

How was this little girl so relaxed?

Her eyes trailed over the two of us and our lack of response. Without another word she stalked from the tent and we both followed.

Yeah, we wouldn't be getting dad of the year award.

"Luna?" Adyen snarled. She huffed and entered their tent as Rhodes, looking sick and pale, met her gaze with wide eyes.

"I get you both are going through mate withdrawal," she chided, "but like I just told the twins, you need to pep up. There are people counting on you."

"What are you doing here?" Rhodes demanded.

She rolled her eyes skyward and muttered something. "Can you listen to what I'm saying?"

"Is grounding her a thing?" Adyen asked authentically.

Luna huffed and turned around to walk out. Now all four of us followed after her and I was really starting to see why dads found sons easier to handle than daughters. This girl was easily walking all over us and the worst part? We were letting her!

Then again, she was also right about what she was saying, so it was hard to argue.

"Luna?" Taylor grunted from the fireplace as she put her hands on her hips.

"Don't ask me why I'm here," she huffed, "you five need to go have your little meeting or whatever in order to pep up. We have three or so weeks ahead of us if my calculations were right. Then again, Mom's maps are so old, but still you guys need to get it together."

One of Vegas's men chuckled and I shot him a look, silencing him.

"Come on!" Luna exclaimed and Taylor stood up.

I think all of us were resigned at this point.

"All right, gentlemen." Rhodes sighed. "Let's at least go talk. Luna, I want you to go to bed. You can sleep in one of our tents and we will crash on the floor or something."

She waved us off and sat down at the fire.

Then like the saps we were, we went to have the talk our daughter suggested.

I really needed to read a book on this parenting shit. I think we were doing it wrong.

Luna

"Stubborn bastards," I muttered.

My head shook, annoyed. Don't get me wrong I loved my dads, but they were stubborn and grouchy. I had easily snuck in with their bags in my shifted form and they'd been so distracted they didn't notice. Clearly, Mom and I needed to teach them how to be stealthy.

I smiled thinking about my mom.

It probably sounded silly because I'd really only known her for about two weeks, but I really felt that way. She'd saved me. I was starving and almost died. I had actually gotten distracted by her because I recognized her as our new Queen, then that damn wagon almost hit me.

She had cared and loved for me since then even without knowing I was a shifter. My mage dads had figured it out easily and so had Taylor. Rhodes and Athens somehow hadn't noticed. I really had no idea how Rhodes missed it since I was freakin' talking to him!

It was pretty funny that I got to blame them for my swearing. Unfortunately, I had been swearing and exposed to a bunch of stupid adult shit for the past two years. That's what a crappy orphanage and being homeless gets you. Luckily, a lot of people will take a kitten in for the night.

"You swear a lot," a voice noted.

My eyes snapped up as the man across the fire offered me a look. His hair was about as bright red as the fire, sort of like Dad T's.

"You're one of Vegas's husbands right?" I perked up because I was actually really bored. I wouldn't tell them that but war was sort of boring when the actual fighting part was missing.

The man chuckled. "Not yet, but soon."

I nodded and looked around the camp noting everyone's down energy. A massive wolf, larger than myself, walked past me towards the man. I tilted my head and the movement caused the wolf to look back at me. I wanted to hiss at him even though I'm sure he was a perfectly fine man. But he was a wolf! Cats were much better. I hopped up and walked back through some of the other tents.

The wind was cool and I looked down at the super cool outfit Marabella had dressed me in. Yes, before you ask Esme and Marabella had supported this idea and packed clothes for me into Rhodes stuff. Once again, no idea how he didn't notice.

My little leather outfit consisted of hunting pants and a velvet jacket with laced up boots. I looked just like my mom. I loved that. Esme had even given me a smaller light weight sword that Dad T had apparently requested for me before they went to fight the other morning.

I was sort of disappointed he hadn't noticed it on my hip.

It was pretty fabulous.

When I bumped into a form a bit taller than my own, I grunted and scowled. My eyes followed up and up until I was looking at a boy maybe just a bit older than myself.

"Watch where you are going," I demanded.

The boy scoffed as he stepped back, his scent smelling oddly like a shifter. He was dressed in a military uniform but carrying several shields. Was he a helper of some kind? That was sort of cool actually.

"Who are you to tell me that?" He frowned. His eyes were what Mom would call a vibrant blue and his hair was dark and messy. It was actually really pretty, but most boys didn't want to hear that.

"Luna," I stated easily, walking into the light of the camp more. I could not believe my mom had named me Lunatic.

Bitch move, bro.

God she'd feel so bad though if I ever said that.

My original name had been… Gertrude. I know. Ah! It was terrible. I liked Luna much better besides I'd never gotten used to the other because my real father had just called me "girl."

I noticed the boy was offering me an odd look as his cheeks darkened slightly. I frowned. "What?"

He opened his mouth and closed it immediately. "Nothing, I was just surprised to see a girl here."

Typical.

I smiled. "Well, here I am. What's your name?"

He hesitated but then spoke. "Jude."

I liked that name.

"Well," I swayed on my tip toes. "Do you want help with those, Jude?"

He tilted his head and it reminded me of a wolf. I didn't mind it much on him, though. It made me feel safe. I put my arms out and he laid the smallest shield in my arms. I nearly scoffed.

"You smell good," he stated awkwardly, as if upset.

"Huh?" My forehead wrinkled.

He flushed and started walking away. I followed because I had to know what he meant. Didn't curiosity kill the cat? Ha! I am so funny.

"I just meant you smell nice. Like a rose or something stupid like that." He muttered.

"Thank you, Jude." I said sweetly. "So, what are you doing helping out with all this?"

"My older brother is one of the commanders for the Red Masques. His boss's wife was one of the women captured."

Oh!

"Apparently they aren't married yet," I stated, remembering enough to know that Edwin was in charge and in love with Vegas. That was what my mom said.

"Huh," he muttered as he shook his head. "Adults are weird."

"Right?" I chuckled as we stored the shields.

A loud laugh made both of us pause as a few soldiers swayed towards their tent. When they caught sight of us I felt my metaphorical fur bristle.

"Ah!" One of them pointed at us, "Look at these two, aren't they just cute?"

"Come here, boy!" One of them demanded. "We need more ale."

"I don't have ale." Jude sighed.

"Go get some!"

"Stop yelling." I growled and stepped in front of him. "Go get your own damn ale."

Silence.

"What the hell did you just say, little bitch?" One man growled, stepping forward. I refused to move. Mom wouldn't have.

A low rumble behind me made me feel better as Jude wrapped an arm tightly around my shoulder. "Back off, James, my brother is going to be pissed."

"Your brother is-"

"I am what, James?" A deeper voice asked as a man in his mid-twenties stepped forward.

"Commander Cannon," The drunks cringed.

"Both of you to Commander Valerio's tent, *now*."

I sighed and leaned back into my friend's side happily. I looked up at Jude to find him already staring at me. For whatever reason, I felt shy and that was messed up. Women like mom and me didn't do shy. It was what she always said.

"Jude?" His brother frowned.

"Cannon!" Jude burst into speech. "She was just helping me and then they started with us, she tried to defend me so I couldn't let him hurt her."

Cannon's lip twitched as he looked away for a moment before speaking. "Girl, what tent are you staying in?"

"With my dads," I offered a smile.

"And where is that?"

I shrugged. "Wherever Neo, Athens, Rhodes, Taylor, and Adyen are."

Both boys froze as Jude turned me with wide eyes. "The SE guard heads are your fathers?"

I shrugged and popped my "p" in a hearty "Yep!"

"Maker!" Cannon grunted, "Let's go you two."

Jude seemed to make a decision because he clutched my hand and walked ahead of his brother. I smiled at him and the two of us raced ahead of one another but still kept in contact.

"How old are you?" I asked.

"Twelve." He grinned as if proud. "You?"

"Ten," I huffed, "but my birthday is in January, so I'm almost eleven."

When we reached the tent with all the familiar scents of home, Jude ignored his brother's words of pause and brought me in. Instantly, all five of my dads looked up as Cannon entered behind us.

"Hey, guys." I chirped and swung Jude's hand. Cannon began recapping and I noticed Jude didn't seem afraid in front of my dads. I liked that. He was brave like me.

"Are you done?" I asked Cannon politely.

Athens chuckled as Cannon grunted.

"This is my new friend, Jude," I squeezed his hand. All my dads looked at him.

He offered a bright smile that I thought was really nice. "It's good to meet all of you. I'm Cannon's little brother."

Silence.

Adyen muttered a curse then and narrowed his eyes at Athens. "I'm blaming you for this."

"Me?" Athens scoffed. "Neo is much more the type to do something like that."

Something like what?

"I *so* don't want to deal with this yet." Taylor groaned. "Don't we get like forty years first?"

Rhodes just tilted his head and spoke directly to Jude. "Why do you want to be friends with Luna?"

"Rude," I growled as he chuckled.

"Not as a bad thing little one." He smirked. "Just want to make sure he knows that you are a Princess. Like, a legitimate one."

Oh.

"I promise to keep her safe," Jude spoke clearly as Neo's grin grew. He didn't smile much so it was nice.

"Oh, hell." Taylor muttered.

"Fine," Rhodes stated softly. "For tonight though, you need some sleep, Luna."

I nodded and turned back towards Jude. I pulled him into a big hug and the giant picked me up and squeezed me. It was a great hug.

"Tomorrow?" I smiled.

He nodded and looked at my dads. "Thank you."

Huh? Before I could ask, both boys were gone. I turned back to my dads.

"You know he's a wolf shifter right?" Adyen hedged.

"Very cool." I nodded but moved on. "How are we doing with the 'pep' train?"

Athens chuckled and looked down. "Well, if we weren't unified before we are now."

"That's good, right?" I yawned.

"Why don't you shift and get some sleep," Rhodes suggested.

I shifted in a flash, a warm glow surrounding me before I was tiny again. I meowed and jumped up on Taylor's lap as he grumbled and placed me on his shoulder. I sighed and after Neo pet my head gently, I fell into a deep sleep.

I wasn't positive why they were unified now, but I was glad.

Plus, now I had a brand new friend.

15
GRAY

"Vegas," I groaned and she turned her head to the side offering me a pained look. The two of us had been in this god damn cell for at least a week now. Our eyes adjusted to the dark room and cold winds that howled through the small window across from us. It also kept spewing rain water all over us which was some bullshit.

"I know." She grunted as her eyes strayed to the man she'd just killed.

Mario, and his son, Victor, had fucked up. Victor, who was apparently Vegas's deranged stalker, had suggested putting us inside holding cells with cuffs that cut off our power. Which it did. Well, it cut off mine, I should say. Vegas's seemed just fine and continued to react defensively to any guards trying to hurt us.

I was thankful for her because it was stopping both of us from torture if I had to correctly interpret the malice on their faces. I felt fucking useless.

For once in my life my confidence waned.

I felt as though I'd let everyone down and risked everything for nothing.

Mario wasn't dead. The castle could be decimated by now. I

couldn't even start to think about my friends, my Luna... my people. They could all be dead. My men could be dead or injured. I was in prison without powers and Vegas was trapped alongside me. Honestly, it didn't help that they weren't feeding us anymore.

I mean, shit.

You burn a few guards to death and the punishment is no food? That seems harsh.

Mario didn't come down often and I think he was livid with Victor. Victor who swayed from sadistic asshole to total bitch every other day, much to Vegas's annoyance. She kept trying to convince him to let her out but Mario always seems to step in at the wrong fucking time.

At least Mario couldn't get to either of us right now and my powers had nothing to do with that.

That? That was all Vegas.

"This fucking sucks," I commented softly.

Vegas chuckled and rolled her head to the side. My face was twisted up with frustration and pain. Pain because I was still injured from battle and my power wasn't letting me heal. I was really fucking hoping that didn't mean I was mortal. I mean how did that shit even work?

Vegas grew serious and spoke quietly. "Gray, I have something to tell you. Something that I know Mario will bring up whether I want him to or not."

Honestly, I'd completely forgotten about the secret of her power because I'd been so thankful it was working. Never in my life had I been comfortable being reliant on someone and it was humbling. Where Vegas struggled with feeling confident in her strength, I struggled with others being strong for me. Talk about an ironic fucking turn of events.

"I know," I spoke gently because I didn't want to rush her.

"I grew up in the Horde."

Excuse me?! Huh?

Then the craziest and most honest words came from her mouth. Truth and clarity rang in her tone and I was compelled to listen despite the unbelievable nature of it.

"I was created by Nicholas, an alchemy mage, a sorceress upon creation around twenty-one years ago. One of the only ones currently alive. I was unaware of this of course, until the night or your coronation, but I'll get to that. You see, my initial hesitancy came from the fact that the person who ordered my creation was...your mother."

Pain lanced through me at the thought of my mother. I felt a wisp of power across my cheek as if she was here brushing my hair back. Yeah. Maybe I'd lost too much blood.

I focused on her so that she would continue.

"She wanted to create something or someone that would be able to be a weapon for you. Someone so powerful that they could match you. But not just that. When your mother created me I became attached to her so that even in her death she was able to contact me, informing me that I have a larger purpose within the Fae lands."

There was so much to fucking unpack there but the most major was that she had fucking talked to my mom! Like, holy shit.

"You talked to her?" I demanded.

Vegas looked pained. "Yeah, I should have explained that better. When we were taken into the dreamscape by Victor, your mother saved Booker and me from some creepy white scaly creatures. She appeared. Your mother said that I had a larger purpose. And that message you got from Palo? The advice? It was from her. She seemed to be right. This was much larger than I could have ever expected."

I believed her. I believed she was a sorceress. I believed that she'd talked to my mom. I just believed in her. I smiled because something truly special occurred to me and it fit like a puzzle piece.

"Our mother," I whispered.

Vegas looked at me wide-eyed. "What?"

I smiled in disbelief. "Our mother, she created me and created you. We are sisters, right? It's why we have such a strong connection."

Her eyes lit up with hope like mine before she deflated a bit. "I was built to be a weapon."

"No," I stated truthfully. "It sounds like you are much more than that. Go on, though."

Also, cool, Mom. No pressure but "Vegas you will change all of the fae realms."

Vegas smiled softly. "I was sent away from the Horde when you disappeared. I grew up with both Byron and Edwin, living at their residence with Nicholas. He sent us to the Earth Realm for our safety. I was placed in a foster care safe house with a human who understood the delicate situation. The Ivanov brothers began to gather my circle of ten and I ended up growing up with them."

Well, that made *way* more sense. Her boys weren't just crazy, they were also bound to her through magic.

"Circle of ten?" I asked.

"They keep me grounded and protected."

I tilted my head because I could tell there was more to be said. "Why are you telling me this? Besides Mario?"

"You mentioned that you felt bad about bringing me into this," she frowned, "and I need you to understand that this would have happened whether or not you and I met."

"What?"

Honestly, I was now confused.

"Mario had sent Victor over to find me, knowing that I was a sorceress. Unfortunately, the bastard got all creepy and before I knew it, Edwin had announced we had magic and shit."

I whistled in surprise. So Victor wasn't *just* a creepy stalker. It also explained things even more.

"Well, shit. That explains why you are so strong."

"I'm sorry I didn't tell you sooner, I just needed to work through it. I needed to understand it." Her words were filled with guilt.

"Hey!" I demanded her attention. "Don't worry about it. It's not like I have told you everything about my life."

As in most of my horrific childhood.

"But this could have affected your decisions," she closed her eyes with a sigh.

"Vegas." I spoke again as she looked at me. "Knowing this only makes me happier I've met you. We are in this together and if anyone can get out of here, it will be us."

Vegas's eyes grew big and filled with emotion. I reached through our cells as if we could hold hands. I smiled and felt my amusement spark at a thought.

"We are totally a badass sister version of Bonnie and Clyde," I muttered.

"I love that!" She let out a solid laugh.

I laughed, too, because shit! I had a sister. That was fucking awesome.

Adyen

We were so close yet my body and chest hurt. I could feel the mate withdrawal cracking through my system. Rhodes was far worse but we were trying to keep a brave face for our men and Luna. I wish we had been able to simply portal to their castle but then their wards would have given them warning to our arrival.

I didn't want them to panic and do something irreversible to Gray or her friend Vegas.

It was becoming obvious that both girls were located in the

cells downstairs and only yesterday one of Vegas's men had been able to see that through his dreams. Apparently, his ink ability had been manifesting differently than normal. The main aspect? Gray and Vegas were alive in the cells under the castle and apparently there were others as well.

My eyes followed the late sunset as I rubbed my chest. Not being around my lil brawler hurt. A fuck ton. She was everything to me. How had I not told her how much I loved her yet? When I found her little ass, I planned on saying those words as soon as I could.

"You're freaking me out over there." Luna stated, narrowing her eyes from across the fire.

I almost barked out a laugh because the girl was honestly growing on me. Mostly because of how bold and refreshing she was.

Just like her mom. I missed Gray.

"How so?"

"You look all emotional," she cringed. A laugh in the distance made her snap her head to the side. I nearly rolled my eyes as Jude offered her a stupid grin.

Kid was going to kill me.

Don't get me wrong, I liked Cannon despite not knowing him well, and Jude seemed okay. I knew their friendship was innocent and probably completely healthy...but, they were still young, so of course it was simply lighthearted right now. What happened when they got older, though? I mean I didn't plan on letting our kids date until they were like fifty so this was going to be an issue.

It wasn't even a maybe issue either. The wolf shifter literally looked at her with enough adoration to make most mate couples look bad. It was authentic and refreshing, though. It was how love should be without people acting like idiots about it.

"Stay close," I noted as Jude offered me a serious nod and took her hand.

At least he was polite.

"How's Rhodes?" I asked quietly as Taylor took a seat next to me.

His eyes stayed focused on the two kids as he spoke. "He's sleeping right now but I can tell it is draining him. They should have been together for far longer before being apart for more than a week, even."

I grunted. I knew that well.

My mouth opened to say something when a familiar thread of magic invaded our space. Taylor and I both looked up to face Edwin. His jaw was tense but he spoke quickly.

"We need to leave tonight." He stated. "We will leave camp set up here with a small unit, but if we leave now, our arrival will be early tomorrow evening."

"You want to leave our camp a day's worth away?" Taylor demanded softly.

"Safe enough distance away so that it isn't destroyed but close enough that we won't worry about some of our less-seasoned soldiers," he sighed.

The kids.

Of course.

I nodded. "All right. Let's do it."

"Really?" Taylor raised his brows. "We are leaving to go get her? Like tonight?"

I smiled. Yeah, we fucking were.

Then I was going to claim her little ass as my mate because I was done waiting.

16
GRAY

"**G**ood morning!"

I let out a curse as Vegas met my gaze with a frustrated look. That was the voice of pure irritation and neither of us were in the mood to deal with it. Victor's footsteps were loud on the stairs. Even after four weeks of coming down here, he had yet to figure out the third step from the bottom was wobbly.

Dumb shit.

I circled my ankle but the cuff around it held tight. I was soaked head to toe in cold water and my hair was matted. I had yet to sleep or eat in forever and my wounds still throbbed in pain. I think my body had no idea what to do with itself. Honestly, I was impressed that they had been able to create a cuff to hold me and then annoyed because why couldn't they just have used iron?

The minute I got home I was taking a long ass bath.

If I got home. If there was anything left of my home. Fuck. This sucked.

"Little flame," Victor sang in his gross whiny voice, "won't you come out and play with me?"

The man had a split personality and we'd seen two elements of it. One was sadistic and rude on some days and one overly sweet and pathetic. It looked like option number two was our lucky draw! I watched as Vegas narrowed her eyes at him but I could tell it was hard for her to look at him. She said he looked just like one of her boys. Bandit? I think. He was the scary one.

I honestly couldn't focus enough to see the similarities. I was hungry.

Hungry Gray was not a good version of me.

"Victor, honey, if you get these chains off me we can have all the fun you want."

I laughed at her tone as I shifted in the pooled rainwater. My breathing felt rough and I wondered if the sword that stabbed my ribs had gone too deep and punctured something. Honestly, I felt more awful than I'd ever felt in my life. That was saying something. Part of it was because I wasn't healing and instead just sitting in pain and hunger.

I could not overemphasize the hunger part.

"Really?" He asked her with big eyes.

"Absolutely," Vegas snarled.

"Victor!" Mario snapped. "Back away."

My lips peeled back at the bastard's voice and I attempted to summon my magic. It failed, as usual. It was worth the effort at least. "Fuck off."

"Don't be so distraught," Mario sang amused.

"Hard to be in a good mood right now, asshole," I growled as my magic sizzled under my skin. It was so fucking frustrating to have magic and be unable to use it.

"Well," he stopped and met my gaze, "we have good news then. Both of you will be attending a wedding tonight."

No. Absolutely fucking not.

"Whose wedding?" I barely managed.

"Little Gray." Mario chided. "Do you remember when you

watched me murder your bastard of a father and rape your mother?"

Bastard. Who the fuck says that shit? My chest tightened and pulse pounded.

"Of course you do!" he chuckled. "Anyway, you see, that day I was attempting to arrange for your marriage to Victor. I found that you were betrothed to the Light Fae prince. Of course, I was furious, so I killed them. Now, frankly, you are far too strong to keep around so once I have taken the Horde, I plan on killing you. So, my son will be marrying your little sorceress and hope that is enough of a help to control your band of misfits."

"Why?"

Her question was a solid one.

"When she dies, the power from her will either fill you or her death will drain both of you. Either way, it seems like a good compromise because either way you are in our control. My control." I really didn't think that was how that worked, but far be it from me to correct King Mario.

"Father," Victor whispered.

"Shut up!" He roared as his son flinched. "I am giving you what you fucking want."

"Well, if you're asking for my opinion, I'm not really a marriage type of girl," Vegas goaded quietly.

Victor's eyes widened. "I'll be a good husband."

"How about you and I talk about this alone." She flashed a smile.

"Not now," Mario growled before fixing us both with a look, "I will send someone down to aid you in getting ready. After all, I'm sure your wedding day is important."

Well, shit.

"This is our moment to escape," I murmured.

Vegas nodded. "I know. Do you think we can do this?"

"I think that if anyone can do this, it's us." I smiled at that concept.

When the door opened the asshole guards brought forward two women, one with a smooth dark complexion and one with pale light hair like Vegas. Both were crying.

"Let's go, ladies." The guards shoved them into each cage with a bundle of whatever they had with them.

"My Queen." The woman in front of me whispered, causing me to still. I allowed her to help me undress from most of my clothes as I tried to recognize this woman. I didn't know her though.

"You have to trust me," the woman whispered so quietly it was nearly inaudible, "this won't actually work."

What wouldn't work? The woman held a bottle of dark liquid and I heard Vegas's helper explain. "You have to take it. You will be drugged out for about six hours and your magic won't work."

I felt Vegas's panic and knew she may freak out. It wasn't time yet. The woman in front of me kept an honest and truthful gaze on me. I made a warning sound at Vegas and she met my gaze. The look we shared had her calming down and really looking at the woman in front of her.

My nose scrunched up as I swallowed down the grape-flavored bullshit.

"Chambers. Now!" The guards hissed as we were led out.

My magic felt good now that they had taken the cuffs off of us, assuming the potion had stopped our magic. I had to hold back from using it as one of the guards grabbed Vegas's arm. I prayed she wouldn't go nuclear because there were far too many people at stake for us to make a singular escape.

We had all heard the cries of prisoners down here.

"So much friendlier now." He grunted. "You didn't think we wouldn't want to play with you, did you?"

Pig.

I hissed as he knocked her knees and a strangled sound came from her throat. He only grinned and brought a knife up to where he held her hair in a tight twist.

Oh, hell no.

"We wouldn't want this getting in the way, now would we?" he chuckled.

The door flew open but it was too late. The knife sliced her silver hair as it cascaded in a waterfall around her to the floor. Oh, shit.

"Vegas?" I whispered. "Are you okay?"

"Feel lighter already." She murmured with a fury in her eyes I'd never seen before. Honestly, it was pretty fucking cool.

We were ushered upstairs and I didn't have to hear the warning from my woman to know we couldn't run yet. "Don't run yet. We have people stationed everywhere but we want to affect the most damage so we have to do it at the ceremony. That is if we want to be free of these bastards."

As we entered into a suite, Vegas was rushed to the bathroom and my woman turned towards me. She spoke softly. "My name is Brenda, Your Majesty."

I smiled softly at her. "Thank you, Brenda. For all of this."

"I need one favor," she begged, "when we are successful, we need you to free everyone in these dungeons. All real criminals are executed or in power. These are women who refused to do what they were 'expected to.'"

Now, that made me furious.

"Of course," I nodded. She offered me a damp rag and small water bowl. I was a hot fucking mess. There was no way around it. Apparently, since I wasn't the bride, I didn't get a full bath. Brenda helped wash off most of my wounds and since I was just in a lace slip undergarment, she gave me a change of clothes as well as a god awful brown dress.

Horrid.

"I'm not going to try to brush through this." She admitted, looking at my hair.

I barked out a laugh and we tied it on top of my head in a knot. My cheeks were gaunt and I still had streaks of dirt on me, as well as ash. Small blessing, though? I was able to use the real toilet and then also brush my teeth.

Vegas, dressed in a white gown, with her choppy hair offered me a look that was filled with dark humor and something far more insidious. Oh, why did I not see this wedding going well? My magic whispered against my skin with a coy grin as if thrilled she would be destructive with us.

A knock on the door had all of us jumping.

I hated being jumpy.

"Little flame?" Victor, personality number two, demanded. "Come out."

Vegas's eyes went wide as tears pricked with emotions far too complicated for my state of exhaustion. He tried to comfort her but she pulled away.

Only a moment later, we headed down to the first wedding I'd ever been to.

I grabbed Vegas's hand for comfort as we entered the massive overcrowded hall. My vision blurred as Mario began speaking. The minute his voice crossed my ears I felt myself grow furious and sharper, like the real predator had come out to play.

"So glad that you could join us!" Mario leered. "Everyone please welcome Queen Gray of the Horde and Vegas the Sorceress."

"My son," Mario motioned to where Vegas went to stand with him up front. I hissed as Mario grasped me. I was tempted to just kill his ass right here and now. Honestly, though, I knew my magic was limited from pure exhaustion right now so I couldn't mess up the timing.

The creepy music selection made me groan. Mario gripped me

tighter as he started to buzz with excitement. I watched Vegas's eyes grow wide as if something was wrong.

Shit.

I knew what this felt like. Come on! Focus, Gray!

Oh, no.

"Mario!" I growled, "You cannot bond them!"

Mario laughed and grasped my shoulders, shaking me, before letting my body fall as I collapsed into a pile. I chuckled a soft pained laugh. Oh I was going to kill this fucker. I snarled and stood up approaching Mario in his distracted state. I moved fast.

My hand was a millimeter from his neck before he turned, grasping my neck in a tight grip while hitting me in the ribs. I cried out and I could no longer hold back.

The magic, restrained inside of me for four weeks, exploded. A massive explosion of dark smoke and ash collided with brilliant fire from Vegas, glass shattering. A volcano-like energy swirled and attacked the Dark Fae that wished us harm.

Victor's screams matched others and I needed to hear this one.

"You motherfucker." I finally lost it and punched Mario right in the chest, his chest cracked as he lost all momentum of power. His head snapped back as he fell to the floor crying out.

Always punch first, am I right?

I grasped his throat and bore down on him as those dark eyes flashed with fear. I squeezed before I changed my mind.

"You are too weak, little girl!" He let out a wild strangled laugh.

I'd show him weak.

Fuck you, Mario.

"You deserve this," I snarled and snapped his neck with ease. My hand buried down into his chest as my nails pried out his heart. I had promised I would.

I hadn't even realized I was crying until I was slamming the organ into the marble steps and staring down at his very dead body. The blood just poured around me and relief filled me. I had killed him.

Visions of my mom's suffering and my father's death flashed before my eyes. He'd killed them.

He had killed them and I had sought vengeance.

There may be people who think I should have let him live and to that I say "Fuck you."

No. He was an evil motherfucker.

The doors opened, and as my back began to burn *I knew,* my men were here.

17

GRAY

The room burned around us and I simply looked at Vegas, drawing closer. "You know, I didn't imagine your wedding this way."

She chuckled and helped me up. Vegas let me lean on her and I cringed as the gash on my side began to bleed openly again. I knew my body was trying to heal but I was asking a lot of it. We must have looked like a sight. Covered in blood and ashes with fire burning around us in our wedding dress and bridesmaid dress.

Vegas snorted. "You imagined my wedding?"

"Of course, once we became friends I started wondering just how one would pull off an eleven-person wedding. I have some great color ideas if you were wondering. None of them include the fucking bridesmaid dress I have on right now."

I'd already decided my dress would be emerald green. I know. Call me picky, but I was Queen and I deserved it. Hm. Maybe I just needed my own wedding.

Oh god. I flushed thinking of the boys.

"If it wasn't for being Queen, you could probably be in the fashion industry." Vegas admitted.

Aw.

"You think so?" I hummed "You know we could start our own fashion industry here, but it may be important to bring cars over first."

Someone coughed and we both looked at the scene in front of us. Dead Dark Fae. The women who had helped us were smiling, along with other women dressed in black. The SE Guard and the Red Masques staring wide-eyed. Then my men and hers. Well. This was a lot to deal with.

"What happened?" Rhodes's voice was rough as tears threatened. He looked awful. I felt bad thinking that but it isn't like I looked any better.

I hugged Vegas before she limped over toward her men. "I'll go explain, go see your men before they rip you away from me and I have to kill them."

Not that I had the energy to.

I spoke roughly. "I need guards to help the women here to release the prisoners downstairs. Additionally, if we could clear the bodies that would be nice."

Other commanders barked out orders as I faced my five men with a tired sleepy smile.

"Baby?" Athens's eyes turned massive and filled with pain.

"Hey." I offered a hand and he gently pulled me close as tears started to track down my skin.

The handsome amazing man began to whisper his love to me as he held me for a minute too long because Rhodes tugged me from him. I faced him as those eyes turned into a pale green. His thumb stroked my mating bond and I offered him a stupid sweet smile.

"I missed you," I whispered roughly.

"Kitten," he mumbled and wrapped his arms around my shoulders and head so that we were buried against one antoher in a perfect silence.

"Baby girl, if I don't get a kiss I'm going to lose it," Taylor groaned as Rhodes let out a relieved chuckle. I turned and my demon grasped me gently and pressed his head to mine.

"Why hadn't you healed?" He asked roughly.

"I was locked up with a cuff that restricted my powers."

I heard several rough growls and dark sounds from the other men.

Taylor's lips pressed to my forehead as he spoke sweet words. "I can't live without you, Gray, please don't leave again. I know it wasn't your fault but I can't lose you."

I kissed him to stop him rambling and offered him a sleep smile. I groaned as a rib popped back into place and Adyen hissed, turning me. His eyes looked over me as he frowned. My mouth opened to tell him I was fine but instead he kissed me.

I sighed into it and then he spoke against my lips.

"I love you, Gray."

A glorious fucking smile broke over my lips.

"I love you, too. I love you, Adyen."

His dragon let out a soft rumble and I offered him a goofy half-lidded smile as I tugged the silk tie from my hair as the matted locks fell. I tucked it into his hands and his eyes grew glossy.

Finally, I turned to Neo.

Neo watched me with an intensity that had my heart throbbing a million miles an hour. The other men began talking to soldiers asking questions as Neo brought me into his embrace. I tucked my head against his chest and he just studied my face for a moment.

"Maker." He mumbled. "Gray, I am in love with you. So painfully in love with you."

Oh.

I blushed and let a small shy smile come onto my lips. "Yeah?"

His eyes sparked. "Yeah."

"I love you, Neo. I love you so fucking much."

Then the bastard kissed me.

A question occurred to me and I pulled back. "Neo, the castle, the kingdom, is everyone…"

"All alive and all safe," he whispered softly.

Oh, thank fuck.

"Wait until Luna…"

"Mom!" A voice cheered and I felt my eyes widen.

"What the hell?" I muttered as a head of snow white hair bounced around her and those gold eyes met mine.

"Good to see you too." she grinned. "See? I told them you would kick butt."

Once I started laughing, I couldn't stop. I pulled her into a hug and pressed a kiss to her forehead. A singular moment passed and everything fell into place.

Mario was dead and my family was together.

Everything was perfect.

Now, why did it feel like I was forgetting something?

EPILOGUE
GRAY

It was the day before Christmas as I busied myself in my brand new office that overlooked the massive yard where SE trained. I could see my men out there even as the soft snow began to fall. Everywhere within the Horde, lights lit up the streets in honor of the winter season. It was beautiful.

In the past few days, after portaling back home thanks to my brother, we'd been relaxing and trying to reconnect. My injuries had healed and after a very long bath I was feeling far more myself. Adyen was upset about my weight but he had me eating enough I was sure I'd put it back on. Until then? I was wearing a few pairs of smaller leggings and oversized sweaters.

I was over leather for a bit.

When the men had told me of their success with the rest of the battle, I'd been proud. I had also been happy to report that the all-female assassin group in the Dark Fae had recovered all the Dark Fae women that had been put in prison. They were an anti-government group originally and named themselves the Obsidian Butterflies. We had yet to talk about how their kingdom would go forward but I don't think anyone was rushing anything but sleep and food right now.

I loved sleep.

Despite feeling better there really felt as though I was forgetting something. After Christmas, I had plans to start forwarding the Horde in technology and making sure all communities were represented. I had a lot to do and some of those things were my men.

Not like that... pervert.

Yeah. Okay. It was totally like that.

So, why did I feel so forgetful?

"Mom!" Luna sang.

I smiled because the boys had told me all about Luna and her boldness. I was thrilled she stood up for what she wanted but I had a feeling we were going to have to keep an eye on her.

"In here, honey." I responded as Neo and Athens, as if knowing I was creeping on them, looked up at me.

Rhodes and Adyen were running drills while Taylor finished a weapons tutorial on something they'd found in the Dark Fae lands. Everyone looked happy.

"You have a letter," she entered the room all cheerful smiles and wide eyes. Why did she look so happy? Ah, never mind.

Jude followed in after her and offered me a polite smile. Mark my words these two would be trouble. As in, my daughter would make him a trouble maker.

"Hello, Your Majesty," He bowed and Luna rolled her eyes.

I took the letter and Luna spoke. "We are going to go sledding. Do you need me to stay until you read it?"

I opened it and shook my head as the two of them bolted out. My brow furrowed as the sigil cracked open and the parchment unfolded gracefully.

My mouth popped open as pure shock filtered through me.

"Baby girl?" Taylor frowned as he walked in all dusted with snow and cute.

I swallowed and put the letter down.

"What is wrong?" He demanded.

"The Light Fae will be here in four days for my wedding to their True Heir."

"Fuck."

Well said, Taylor. Well said.

18

BONUS SCENES

MARABELLA & PALO

Marabella - 2 years prior

For the third time this week I made my way through the library. I tried to tell myself that this was the shortcut to my chambers but it actually added ten minutes to my nightly journey. I also could have flown there. Yet, here I was at 9 p.m., walking through the library as my soft day slippers pressed into the old wood and the smell of parchment filled my nose. It was peaceful.

It wasn't that I wasn't allowed to be in here. I was. Except, normally the "help" avoided it because of *him*. Who is 'him' you ask. Well, he's the dragon. That's not true. He's a demon, but everyone avoids him because the library is his space and apparently he is mean. Really mean. I had never met him so my curious eighteen-year-old mind didn't care about his reputation. I had to see for myself.

I wanted to see him. I was trembling with nerves as I traveled through the massive three-story tall rows of shelves. While my primary mission was to see him, I was getting distracted. I couldn't help it. I had grown up in a massive family and despite being loved, I learned to be quiet. Quiet and curious. Always flying around to do something on my own.

Except it was lonely and working in the palace wasn't as glamorous as I imagined. I hadn't needed this job. My family came from wealth and status. They were known for being scholars and intellectuals. I wanted something different for myself, or at least to be somewhere different.

I wanted to actually help problems not just write about them!

My thoughts had strayed so I was truly shocked when I slammed right into a very hard wall. I cursed in my native tongue and rubbed my head looking at the base of the wall. Except it wasn't a wall. It was a pair of large leather shoes that set my heart pattering.

The scent of vanilla tickled my nose along with a smoky afterthought. My eyes ran up his body starting from legs encased in dress pants that followed up to a full suit. I figured I should really absorb all of this if I was going to die.

Man, what a sight before I died though!

The man was much larger than myself. His shoulders were nearly twice the size of mine. I let my eyes finally stray to his face and I gulped at the intensity I saw there. Except, I couldn't be scared. The man was beautiful. His jawline was clear cut. His skin a stark shade that highlighted his crimson hair. I trembled slightly, my body curling in just a bit, as I fought the urge to fall into his arms. Which was messed up, of course, because I didn't know him. A pair of black eyes, fathomless in nature, met mine and my owl perked up and looked at him with interest.

That was bad.

"Sorry," I squeaked.

Yep. Look at me being brave.

His head tilted like the predator he was. "What are you doing here?"

Oh, his voice was beautiful. It reminded me of a soft, dark song filled with smooth tones and depth. It electrified my skin.

"I wanted to see if you were as scary as everyone said," I blurted out before turning pink. Did I mention I couldn't lie? My body trembled slightly under his power which was like red smoke that thickened around us. Except, instead of hurting me it seemed to surround me protectively.

His reaction was not what I expected. The demon's lip twitched in a millimeter smile as he stepped closer, wrapping a finger around my hair.

Oh shit, I was going to pass out.

"What's your conclusion?" He whispered, his voice tickling against my skin. I could feel myself falling into him and my heart began fluttering as my hands fell from where I held them against my chest to lay on his. Was I pushing him away or just the opposite?

Was he scary?

I considered his question.

"I think you're intimidating," I answered honestly, "but not scary."

His eyes sparkled. "What's your name, little lamb?"

"Marabella," I whispered breathlessly.

He tested my name on his tongue. "So, Marabella, what is the difference between the two of those?"

My toes curled in my slippers as I once again replied. "I don't think you would hurt me."

Instead of laughing at me, a softness invaded his eyes and he rubbed a thumb along my jawline thoughtfully. I shook. He spoke quietly as if worried he was scaring me.

"You're right," he said softly, almost under his breath, "I wouldn't hurt you."

My shaking stopped and I found myself loving his gentle

hold. I swallowed and tried to be more bold. "What's your name?"

"Palo."

I liked that.

"Well, Palo," I grinned softly. "It is wonderful to meet you."

His eyes studied me for a minute before he seemed to remember something, stepping back but keeping his hands on my arms. I waited to see what he would say.

"Do you have any interest in the Earth Realm?"

I tilted my head. What an odd question.

"Well," I frowned slightly and looked at him. "I'm not sure. I don't know much about it."

"Tomorrow," he stated slowly as his lips pressed into a barely-there smile, "you should come back tomorrow, little lamb, and I can show you some things I've been working on."

"I'd love that," I smiled softly.

"Then tomorrow," he said as his lips touched my forehead and the demon disappeared, leaving me feeling like I'd run a marathon. I couldn't help but smile as I left the library.

Mission accomplished.

See? I was brave.

Palo - The next day

What was I doing?

I shook my head as I watched the library through my open office door. She probably wouldn't even show up. Why did I even *want* her to show up?

She is only the most beautiful woman I've ever met in all the realms I've traveled.

It really isn't a big deal. No harm, no foul. Except it *was* and I couldn't get over how right she felt pressed against me. I fiddled with my pen and felt everything still as a figure appeared in the door.

"Hey, you." She offered me the sweetest smile as if I wasn't an asshole.

"Marabella," I spoke her name as her cheeks turned pink. With all the comfortability in the world she came and sat right across from me, her hair like golden wheat falling out of her ponytail. There was a candle lit on my desk and her features looked fucking gorgeous in the shadowy light.

"Palo?" she asked softly.

I snapped my eyes back from her glowing complexion to her dark eyes. I sighed, "Sorry, lamb. It's been a long day."

Her mouth parted as she frowned. "What happened?"

I considered not saying anything because frankly no one had ever asked. I had documents I could show her and a million other things that would fuel that curiosity in her eyes. Instead I answered and for the first time, I forgot about the work I needed to do.

"See my brother…"

Marabella - 6 months later

"Palo!" I sang out as I walked into the library. It had been only six months since I'd met my demon and I'd never been happier. At home, with all those kids, I'd always been forgotten. Not with Palo though. The man listened to every word I said. As usual, I walked through the library and went right to his office. Without knocking I opened the door and paused.

Oh.

Palo looked up from where he sat in his office chair, which wasn't unusual, and my eyes met hers. *She* wasn't usual. Who the heck was this lady? She was sitting on his desk and when the door opened she sneered at me.

"Palo, honey, who is this?" She asked her voice rough. She was beautiful though. They looked right together. They made sense.

I met Palo's gaze and those eyes filled with something I didn't understand as he swallowed with difficulty looking at a file that this woman held. I think I knew what he was going to do before he did. It didn't make it hurt less and his reasoning didn't make me feel better. I loved how much he cared about knowledge, really, but he chose it over everything. It didn't surprise me when he chose it over me as well. She clearly had something he wanted.

"She's nothing," he stated, his voice gruff.

My heart stopped and I felt like I was going to pass out.

Nothing.

I'm nothing.

Our friendship? Nothing. Staying up late together every night? Nothing. What about when he carried me to my chambers because I fell asleep? Or when we both fell asleep looking over a set of documents and I woke up with his arms around me? Or when, during the holidays, he bought me this stunning, yet delicate necklace?

Nothing.

Was this one-sided then?

Clearly.

"What is her problem?" The woman scowled because I'd clearly stayed for too long. I met her gray gaze without looking at Palo.

"So sorry to interrupt," I offered her just in case she was someone important. "He had a message from King Silas and I was sent to inform him that it would be in his chambers."

"Oh," the woman nodded. "You work here, then?"

And he's essentially royalty. Yeah. Sometimes I wish I didn't work here because then my family's status might be enough for him. Not that he'd ever admit to that but this woman was pointing out the clear issue.

I licked my lips and offered her a forced smile. "Exactly. Just a worker. Sorry to interrupt."

The woman nodded and I turned.

"Wait." His voice gave me pause but I knew it would be bad. "Please close the door behind you."

Fuck.

I shut it gently and tears welled in my eyes. My body shifted without permission and I let my wings expand out, taking me to the ceiling of the library. I rested my own form in a small corner and tried to sleep. My clothes slipped from my beak as I used them as a makeshift nest. My chambers weren't safe anymore, not after I found one of the guards over my bed. So I had been sleeping here.

Palo had made me feel safe.

But now I was nothing to him.

Palo - Minutes later

I listened to Trinity's voice and compared it to Marabella's soft cadence. When I heard wings flapping through the library, pain lanced through me.

What the fuck was wrong with me?

"Hey, listen." She smiled and handed me the file. "I would love to finish this over a drink. Do you have time tonight?"

"No," I responded immediately, making her jump. I slipped the file away and Trinity stood up with a scowl.

"You just needed the info, didn't you?" She snarled.

"Yes." I sighed. "You knew that."

With that, the second woman tonight slammed my office door on their way out. Well, Marabella hadn't. My little lamb had gently closed it before disappearing into the night. My head pounded at the thought of what an asshole I was. Who the fuck does what I just did? What the fuck have I done?

"She's nothing."

She's fucking *everything* and that's the problem.

Clearly I suffered from self-destructive tendencies.

I was obsessed with Marabella and there was no way she would want to deal with that. Maybe it was better that she hated me. I closed my eyes thinking about how perfect her body felt pressed against me. How those massive dark eyes and wheat-colored hair filled my constant dreams. Fuck. I couldn't stop thinking about her.

Obsessed. I was fucking obssessed.

This was a mess.

I'd just hurt my little lamb. That was so fucking wrong. I was the one who stopped her from getting hurt. I was supposed to keep my little lamb safe because she was mine. Demons were known for being possessive but I'd never felt it until she came into life. Immediately, I had started calling her mine. Mine to protect. Mine to care for. Mine to love. Ever since that first day I'd been the big bad wolf keeping my little lamb safe.

Not anymore.

I stood up and locked up my office. I'd deal with all of these documents tomorrow. I practically jogged towards her chambers hoping that she was still up. When I got to her small door in the workers quarters I felt a snarl pull at my lips.

What the fuck?

A guard, low ranking, was opening her door. I stepped closer and watched as the man looked around and swore. Shaking his head he turned around and I closed the door, locking both of us in.

"What the fuck? Oh shit!" The asshole paled.

A very dark feeling filled my chest. I had no idea where Marabella was but I had a feeling that she hadn't been sleeping here for a bit. My power leaked out and wrapped around the guard as he started blabbering.

"I was just checking, man, I was worried. A sweet thing like Marabella..."

His words cut off as I snapped his neck.

It did nothing to cure my bloodlust. I had bigger issues though. Where was she?

My eyes closed and I did something I promised I never would do. I tracked her. My demon growled low in my throat as I let my instinct take over as I neared the library. I walked in and before I knew it I was climbing the massive ladder that led to the storage room.

I felt everything go still inside of me at what I saw.

She looked like fucking Thumbelina. Her soft hair was spread out everywhere and she was wrapped up in her clothes on a pile of soft fabric that sheltered her like a flower. Had she been living up here? Fuck. How had I not caught onto that?

Without thinking, I easily lifted her and jumped down with ease, landing without a sound. Her breathing was even but a small frown marred her brow. When we entered my chambers, I laid her on the bed and moved towards the chair near the fireplace.

Fuck.

How long had she lived there? How long had that bastard been scaring her? Hurting her?

I must have made a noise because a pair of large dark eyes blinked open at me. Silence permeated the area and when she spoke her voice was empty.

"What am I doing here, Palo?" She whispered.

"I moved you here." I stated as pain flashed in her eyes. "How long have you been sleeping up there?"

"Past few ni… you know what? I have nothing to say to you." She stated and stood her body in only a sheer slip. I could have fucking died and gone to heaven with that vision in my head.

"Sit down," I commanded softly.

I had to admit, I was a bit of a control freak and super demanding. Marabella, for whatever reason, Maker bless her, put up with me and just offered an eye roll when I did something crazy. Usually.

"No!" She growled and I felt myself still. She had never been this upset. I'd fucked up. I didn't even know how to fix this. I hadn't ever had a formal relationship beyond a one night stand.

"I'm nothing," she stated with tears in her eyes, "remember? Well, workers that are nothing don't sleep in aristocrats' chambers."

I tightened my hands on the chair because I was a second away from snapping.

"It wasn't like that," I whispered, feeling a sensation of pain pulse through me that I'd never experienced before. This wasn't our dynamic. She was all soft and sweet while I was a cold and demanding bastard, except to her. Usually.

"Yeah?" She laughed with no humor.. "Whatever you say. I get it. Knowledge is more important than anything else."

Her body was by the door and I nearly strapped her to the bed to keep her here.

"I.."

"Next time you're in the library, Palo?" Her tears spilt over her cheeks as she spoke. "You should read a fucking book about how to be a good friend."

The door slammed shut and I felt my heart break.

What the fuck was happening to me? She was right. I was a terrible friend.

Marabella - 1.5 years later

I hated that I had to walk through here today. After a year and a half, I still hated this place. Every time I saw Palo it hurt, but today it was my actual job to inform him of something. Since that night, he'd tried to talk to me several times. It was stupid. Everytime I ignored him and it didn't help that he was making my life lonely. He literally warned everyone off me, mostly men, so I was just fucking alone. All the time. What an ass.

I knocked on the door and as it opened I nearly laughed. How fucking ironic.

Trinity.

She looked down at me and I maintained her eye contact instead of thinking about Palo being a few feet away. I swallowed and spoke.

"Sorry to interrupt, ma'am," I offered a smile. "I have a message for Palo, but I can…"

"Get out."

Oh, good. What a fucking asshole.

"Trinity, get out." Palo stated softly as my eyes shot to the ground to hide my surprise.

"What?" she hissed. "Why?"

"Because I fucking said so," he ordered sharply, "I need to talk to Marabella, so leave."

Now I was positive there was something wrong with me because that commanding tone was a total turn on. I totally felt my heart flutter so I also got angry. I was furious with him.

"No. Really. Don't," I muttered but Trinity slammed the door and I was stuck.

His office looked different. There was no order to it and everything seemed messy. His hair was longer and he looked… sad? I felt my heart squeeze.

"The message is from your brother…"

"I don't give a fuck about the message, lamb," I stilled as he caged me against the wall in a move faster than a blink. My heart fluttered and his dark eyes tracked my pulse for a moment. I forgot what it was like having him this close. What it was like breathing in his scent.

"You should. It is about…"

Then his lips were against mine and I gasped into his mouth. Pure pleasure exploded through me and his vanilla smoky scent wrapped around me in greeting. I shivered as I curled into him and his body dominated me with ease. As if it was meant to. As if I was meant to. It was so easy to let him take control. My first kiss was now his.

I know. I was such a freakin' loser. Who was twenty and just having their first kiss? Someone sheltered most of her life.

"No." I pulled back as tears filled my eyes. "You do not get to take my first kiss. Not now."

His expression was heartbreaking as he placed his forehead against my own, his arms shaking with tension. It was so easy to ignore his constant attempts at communication when he wasn't right here smelling like vanilla. They *had* been constant, for the record. Week after week.

"Marabella," he spoke in a rough voice. "Please."

"Please what?" I tried to ignore how my lips tingled.

"Forgive me," he whispered softly. "I need you back in my life."

"No. You don't get that back. You hurt me, Palo. You hurt me really fucking bad. You treated me like I was nothing," I whispered in a hushed tone.

He groaned as if in pain, rubbing his nose against my hair. "You are everything, not nothing. That's the fucking problem." Then his temper spiked. "I'm not sorry about that kiss, I'm glad it's your first one, lamb. It's mine and you're mine."

Tears spilled over as I shook my head. "Stop."

"Please?" His voice took a begging tone as he grasped my shoulders.

"I don't trust you to choose me over work," I spoke softly.

His eyes darkened and he buried his nose against my neck, "I promise I will do whatever…"

"Friends."

"What?" he asked softly.

"I said 'friends.' You can be my friend."

Mostly because if he didn't stop talking, I was going to give in.

A small smile broke onto his lips. "Thank you."

Without another word I turned and left. I'd never given him the message but it hadn't been that important anyway.

Palo - Queen Gray's coronation

I was close to killing every single guard here. I watched as Marabella gracefully walked down the hall in front of me in that damn dress that Gray gave her. Every head that turned toward her made me growl like the possessive bastard I was.

She was *mine*.

We might still be just friends but she had started wearing the necklace I gave her nearly two years ago, so she's mine. That's final. I really was grasping at straws when it came to her. I needed something from her. I felt like a fucking dog begging for a bone.

"Lamb," I caught her shoulders gently as she looked up at me expectantly.

"Yes?" She arched a graceful eyebrow. How did this woman get sexier every day? I wanted to taste those lips again. My gaze drew down to them and I nearly groaned.

"We need to talk," I demanded.

Her lips pulled into a smile. "We are."

I pulled her into a tiny corridor and pressed her against the stone wall, eclipsing her smaller frame. Her breathing quickened as she watched me with a clear challenge. The woman was making me mad.

"Marabella," I said softly. "I can't keep doing this."

Her eyes warmed and she looked over my expression. "Alright."

"Alright?" I frowned.

"Yes," she said softly. "If you can't do this anymore, I understand."

I growled. "You know I don't mean it like that, woman. I want you Marabella. I want you more than any fucking piece of knowledge or social connection. The kingdom could go to hell-"

She touched my lips and I didn't hesitate. Her sweet mouth was inexperienced and I found I loved that. I grasped her neck and she let her head fall back as I devoured her lips. God, I loved her. I was going to lock this woman up. She was mine. *Mine.*

The word was like a chant in my head.

This is what happens when your demon loses control.

Marabella - Nearly a week later

Tears welled up in my eyes as I walked home. The rain was soaking me and the Horde had a nasty winter chill that had crawled up out of nowhere. Gray had given me the night off so Palo had planned a date for the two of us. The bad part?

He didn't fucking show.

No word. Nothing.

I wrapped my jacket further around me as if it would keep my heart and stomach from hitting bottom. When I walked into the castle, I sighed and moved towards my quarters feeling not only rejected but exhausted. I didn't want to play this game with him anymore.

I wanted someone who looked at me like Gray's men looked at her.

Or how Vegas's group obsessed about her.

I just wanted someone.

My room was larger now with a fireplace and massive private bathroom. I changed out of the wet clothes and locked my door, crawling into bed as I watched the flames crackle.

No word. Nothing.

Nothing.

Nothing

The word still taunted me.

When I eventually fell asleep I felt as though my heart was breaking all over again. I hated how much power he had over me.

Palo - A few hours later

I stood in front of her door and put my head back to rest on the opposing wall.

Maker. I just couldn't get this right.

I knew, even if I explained that I'd had to talk to Edwin and Byron, she would still doubt my commitment to this. I couldn't blame her.

Did I even bother to knock?

When I raised my hand, the door opened and there stood my sleepy little owl. Her eyes were dark and lips pressed together. She didn't say a word.

"I'm not going to make excuses," I stated softly. "It was an emergency regarding Edwin and his team."

"I believe you," she stated softly.

But?

"I believe you, but that doesn't change anything for me. I can't be with someone who doesn't view me as a priority."

"Lamb," I whispered.

She shook her head. "No. Thanksgiving is tomorrow, Palo. I don't want to get into this. You and I are over."

A low growl came from my chest and before I knew it, I had

her frame pressed against the opposing wall with her scent wrapping around me. I pulled back a tiny amount.

"We are never done or over," I demanded, "I fucking love you. I can't let you go."

Her eyes filled. "You love me?"

Had I never said it? Oh fuck.

"Yes," I stated softly.

She shook her head. "This is too much. I need time."

"But.."

"Time," she whispered and I let her go.

"You don't get to ignore me," I whispered. "I will do anything for us to move past this, but you can't ignore me. Or I'll end up doing something crazy like tying you to the bed."

Her lips tilted but she spoke softer words. "Like I said, time."

Without her permission, I kissed her lips and pulled back. She turned pink and before she could slam the door in my face, I walked away.

I clearly needed to move some things around. I had a bigger priority than work now.

Marabella.

My little lamb.

PSYCHOS

BLURB

I had thought the hard part was over.

Mario was dead and my vengeance was achieved. However, the past was still causing problems, namely in the form of the Light Fae. Yeah... them. Remember how I am supposed to be getting married to their True Heir? That wasn't going to happen. I needed to find a solution and fast before my men lost it. That isn't even including all my responsibilities as Queen of a post-war Horde kingdom! How am I supposed to reform such an archaic system?

It seems the new year is going to be a busy one. At least, I have my sexy guard and adopted daughter by my side! There will be a wedding this year but it wasn't going to be with the Light Fae heir…

Fantasy RH Our bad*ss heroine and guardians swear a lot. As well, please be advised that the book contains darker themes including assault, PTSD, and violence. Additionally, sexual themes are suitable for mature audiences +18.

PROLOGUE
COLLIARD

I clenched my fists, trying to restrain the anger pulsating through me. My own sons! My own fucking sons betrayed me and chose to follow their Queen. A Queen that didn't deserve to be on the throne in my mind. Her prior absence from the kingdom was not something that needed correcting. Even worse, she kept a familiar relationship with human made mages. The swine of the mage community that should be violently sought out and eliminated. We needed to keep our blood lines pure and she was going to ruin that.

It was why I had supported King Mario.

Now the bastard was dead and I'd barely escaped into the Light Fae lands, my seething anger pushing me forward towards the only possible solution I could see towards getting my sons back and my community back under control. No one would support her as Queen if she began another war with the Light Fae for breaking her marriage contract. Something I knew them to be very set on. They deserved to know what a lying whore their son's future wife was.

Although, that seemed to be a common trend throughout most women didn't it? I refused to see the Horde fall into such a quicksand trap of allowing human made mages and women to have equal voices within my community. If the shifters wished to have female representatives then they could, but not in my house. Not in my goddamn community.

The moment I got my hands on Neo and Athens, I would beat them until they were within an inch of their life. I didn't care how powerful they assumed they were. I was still their father and I wouldn't let their betrayal go unpunished. I snarled nearing the large castle of the Light Fae, the heat of the bright sun beating down on me. I was exhausted and my pride was rightfully injured, having no choice but to run from the disgusting spectacle at Mario's castle.

He had let Gray beat him. He had lost his own son and had died at the hands of the false Queen. Even her sister, the abomination of magic and sorceress, had managed to come out mostly unscathed. I should have known backing him was a risky chance though. The man had been draining magic from his entire kingdom… that type of effort could only result in instability.

"State your business," A Light Fae guard demanded his eyes narrowed.

The entire kingdom was far too lush and dramatic for my taste, the buildings made of marble and an ocean of water surrounding the white castle. Their gates were open to all, allowing me to cross over the water by a long bridge to where I stood now, in front of this guard.

"I am here to see His Majesty," I explained quietly. "I have news that is pertinent to them regarding a contract with the Horde."

His eyes widened a bit as he held up a finger and moved towards another guard, their voices quiet. I didn't want to use my magic but if I had to it would turn into a rather bloody affair pretty quickly. My shoulders relaxed as guards walked down the castle pathway and the first one spoke.

"We will escort you in."

"Thank you." I kept my chin held high despite probably looking worse for wear.

The closer we got the larger my smile became. This was the first step to taking back my power and getting that whore off the throne.

1
GRAY

The parchment crinkled under my fingers, the seal of the Light Fae kingdom a pale yellow and broken in half. I inhaled looking over the contents of the letter as shock filtered through me. How had I forgotten? How the hell had this slipped my fucking mind?

Here I had been minding my own business, enjoying that Mario was very dead and that Christmas was tomorrow… only to have this land in my lap. *This* being the letter that reminded me of the teeny tiny little problem that all of us seemed to have overlooked. *Gods! Couldn't we catch a break?*

I mean truly in the past few months, I had assumed my rightful place on the Horde's throne and fought an entire war that left me in captivity for a month. I really felt as though I deserved some time off… but hey, that's just my opinion. It seemed like the fates had a different plan for us and I was mad at myself for forgetting about the current dilemma.

"Baby girl?" Taylor frowned as he walked in, his crimson hair dusted with snow and his eyes vivid green against his pale skin. I took a moment to appreciate how sexy he looked before putting the letter down and shaking my head. I needed a distraction, and in walked the perfect one. Except, Taylor wasn't going to let go of this. He would want to know what was going on.

"What's wrong?" He demanded stepping forward and touching my shoulders in a small soothing motion. *See what I mean?* After being locked away in that fucking dungeon, I craved their touch. All five of them. I leaned into him and absorbed the physical comfort.

"The Light Fae will be here in four days for my wedding to their True Heir," I mumbled quietly.

"Fuck."

Well said.

"I can't believe I forgot about this," I looked up at him and saw a dark possessive light filter through his eyes before he tugged me against him. I inhaled his familiar scent before wrapping my arms around him, both of us thinking it over. Then he broke away and went towards the door as I shook my head following after.

"Taylor," I warned as we walked down the hall away from my office. The entire grandiose hall was decked in festive decor, from the top of the arched ceiling to the deep red runner we walked on. I had never been one for holidays, keeping it simple with Esme and Bobby usually, but after Thanksgiving and everything with Mario I craved the festivity and closeness it would bring out, we all needed it.

Each large stone edged window we passed showcased the light snow that was falling over my kingdom. I could see the SE guard training occurring in the courtyard within the castle walls and knew that Taylor had just come from there, his lean tattooed warrior body unfortunately covered in a long sleeve shirt and dark pants.

Wasn't it my right, as a Queen, to request that he walks around shirtless always? I scowled at the thought of other women and men seeing him without a shirt. Never fucking mind.

"We have to tell them," He stated his jaw clenched and his body tight from the tension radiating through him. His demon flashed behind his eyes and I had to be careful not to poke or prod it out. I tried to walk ahead of him but he kept pace with me and wouldn't let me get far ahead.

"After the holidays." I stated, trying to keep the stress from my voice. "You know how bad it is going to get if they have four days to think about this. Let's just enjoy the ball tonight and Christmas morning. Please, Taylor?" See! I was even saying fucking 'please'!

He chuckled softly, with a sexy edge, and offered me a look. "Sorry baby girl, but I love my body and Adyen will snap me in half if he finds out I hid this from them."

"Bastard," I muttered as he intertwined our fingers and led me towards the outside pavilion. I scowled at the holiday decor we passed because somehow my holiday season had turned stressful. That shouldn't be a thing, holidays should be a time for family, friends, and celebration. I had thought that with Mario dead I would be left feeling relieved… and I did. Except now real life was slapping me in the face. I had to now focus on not only being a good Queen to the Horde but somehow bringing the archaic kingdom into the new modern world. That wasn't even including the fact that we had members from the Dark Fae trying to rebuild their kingdom, something that I was in part responsible for since I had killed their King. I didn't want to reabsorb their kingdom though, I had enough things to worry about. This was all without considering the very real commitments that existed… like this damn marriage contract. Now, they plan to show up here in four days for a wedding that will not be happening. *At least to me.*

Although, I wouldn't be opposed to marriage, just not to the True Heir…

Plus, I had plenty of men in my life and if my instincts were correct, the Light Fae Heir, didn't want to marry me or any other woman. I was determined to figure out a peaceful solution to this but I was concerned that my broody and possessive mates may make that difficult.

Before Luna and her friend Jude had dropped off the letter, I truly assumed I would be having a relaxing afternoon. Oh yeah! That's right, Luna. I'm a mom! That's right folks. Luna? Yeah she wasn't a kitten. Nope she's a nearly eleven year old child that believes I am her mother. A role I actually oddly enjoy. I'd never considered myself maternal, but lately I have been feeling very comfortable with the idea of settling down.

Parenting wasn't easy though and I truly had no idea what to enforce and how to treat my adopted daughter because she was so confident and self-sufficient. Already she had Jude, the younger brother to Cannon, a Red Masques commander, that followed her around with devoted attention. Did I put a stop to that? Why the fuck would I if she liked spending time with him? I couldn't claim she was too young to be friends with boys, because… well that was stupid and the girl had survived on the streets alone for some time now.

I frowned at that thought. *My poor Luna.*

My final problem? The Dark Fae weren't the only lingering result from our war. We have one missing person. Neo and Athens's father seemed to have disappeared. That worried me on several ends because not only was the man a biased asshole who hated everyone but natural born mages, but he was a traitor. One that had allowed Mario to attack my coronation ball. I felt very protective over our delicate peace and I refused to let him disrupt that. My hope had been that he had died during the chaos of war but the more likely case was that he was hiding somewhere. My hope was that it's somewhere in a dark cave with bats, *no... bears*, bears would be better.

"Kitten?" Rhodes rose a brow as we stepped down the stairs into the fresh cold snowy air. Taylor helped me slip into a long emerald green jacket while untucking my dark silky hair. My clothes, an oversized sweater and leggings, were still a bit loose but I had been steadily gaining weight back since captivity. My magic was constantly healing me and even my hair, which had been turning matte and dirty, was now shiny and far past my waist. It was like Mario had never occured. I had given up on ponytails officially as well because *someone* kept stealing my hair ties. God damn dragon bastard.

"Hey," I smiled up at my jaguar mate. His pale green eyes, streaked with gold, flickered down to my neck and the half hidden mating mark he left on my skin. My body involuntarily responded to his heated gaze, my core heating up as Taylor muttered a curse, burying his nose in my hair. My other hand reached up to string through his hair as I went to explain to Rhodes, in a peaceful relaxed way, what was going on.

"What's wrong?" He asked as Taylor looked up at him and they did that weird mental connection thing. *If only I could be included in these little silent talks.* Taylor's lip quirked at my mental prompt but the bastard kept it to himself even though he had the ability to pass thoughts between the group of us. Asshole.

Instead of letting me explain, my demon simply stated, "Gray got a letter."

Rhodes's blonde brows dropped as he wrapped an arm around me and brought me against him so I was pinned between the two of them. I was momentarily distracted because frankly the man was sinful. He was lean muscle with shoulders nearly twice my size and he walked with a predatory grace that was sexy in its own right. His golden hair was tied back and those short golden hairs on his face shaped a neat beard. The man was stunning, especially today, with the snow drifting and leaving diamond like flecks in his beard and hair. He looked as magical as he was.

"Regarding?" His english accent tickled across my ears as I nuzzled into his chest slightly, Taylor's front against my back. I tried really hard to not rub against his hardening cock but the man was sex on a stick. His hands gripped me tighter, closing in the space between us, as he muttered something before answering.

Don't do it.

He did it.

"The Light Fae will be here in four days for a wedding. True Heir promised to True Heir."

Rhodes stilled and I let out a total squeak as his arm tightened and a low predatorial sound came from his throat. *Yeah.* Shifters were a bit unpredictable. It didn't help that I'd been ripped away from the man right after mating. Except for this afternoon, he hadn't left my side in the past week and the hard control freak had been softening into a more loving and affectionate man. Mind you that was just around me and the man had gotten more, if not equally, as possessive as Adyen, so it wasn't all flowers and hearts.

Then again, Adyen and I hadn't officially mated so who the hell knows what he would end up like!

"I'm sorry?" Rhodes demanded clarification. I pulled back or tried to but he growled and plastered me to his chest. Fuck.

"You better tell them to head the fuck back home," Adyen's snarl echoed through the space as he walked towards us. Taylor chuckled softly against my neck. Fucker.

"*I* didn't tell them to come here!" My demon goaded. "No one told them the contract was off."

I thought Adyen was going to lose it. "Gray," Adyen's voice was deep and near pleading, his dragon right under the surface. *My poor dragon.*

"Adyen," I remind him gently, "I was in prison for nearly a month. I had completely forgotten about this ridiculous marriage thing." *As if I'd actually want to marry the guy.*

The large man offered me a near pout which was fucking hilarious considering the man was nearly 6'5 and looked like a bronzed god. His short dark hair was covered in snow and those honey eyes were filled with frustration and heat. I wanted to pull him down and kiss those perfectly sculpted lips that continued to stay in that adorable pout.

Outside on the training pavilion probably wasn't a great time for a foursome, right? Yet that didn't stop my blood from heating and my center tightening at the imagery flashing through my mind.

Taylor barked out a laugh at that as I scowled and elbowed him. Adyen stepped closer and grunted, "I know."

After a moment, "Why now?" Taylor's voice was far more serious than previously.

Fantastic fucking question.

"Colliard," Neo sighed approaching us, his eyes intense on me, "if I know my father, he went to the Light Fae for protection and ratted on your 'extra marital affairs.'"

I snorted at his indifferent bored tone. His dark onyx eyes, heated like melted metals, glinted as he showered my body with a look filled with desire and lust. His dark skin and sharp fade looked stark against the white snowy field. I let my eyes wander down his tight workout clothes and found my pulse quickening. When I looked back up at Neo's gaze it was filled with satisfaction and a small pleased smile decorated his lips.

"You think so?" Athens groaned walking up, no one clueing into the eyefucking Neo and I had been partaking in. Except for him, of course and I could see the glint of retribution in his eyes. The man was going to get me alone at some point today, mark my words. *Can't fucking wait.*

"Yes," Neo determined.

"We should send scouts out to send them home before they arrive," Rhodes muttered with a slight growl.

Just then, Luna's laugh echoed throughout the court yard and all of us suckers immediately searched the grounds to find her.

Overbearing much? A head of snow white hair, pulled up in wavy tendrils and decorated in snow, danced in the wind as she easily walked towards us, her gold eyes lit up with amusement. She was dressed in all leather with a velvet riding jacket… followed by three boys? Was it just me or was her following growing? *I'm too young to get grey hair.*

"I do not look forward to the day when she gets old enough that I have to start threatening our own guard," Taylor shook his head.

"Luna," Adyen stated, his voice deep and rolling, "aren't you supposed to be helping Esme?" *And not with three boys.* That was what he really meant.

Her nose twitched as snow landed on it and she shook her head. "Can't Dad, I have new friends to show around."

Rhodes straightened as all of us looked at the boys behind her. Jude was familiar and had a hand on the small of her back, his eyes filled with amusement compared to the other boys. I'd give the wolf shifter this, he was a confident kid. His dark hair was in direct contrast to my daughter's and he stood slightly behind her like a protective shadow. I nearly shook my head, this couldn't be going anywhere good in the future.

"Who are you?" Taylor demanded of the others, I nearly snickered at his upset tone.

One of them stayed silent as the other stepped forward with a hand. "Jackson, Commander Taylor, my brother is in the Red Masques."

Oh. This was just getting more and more fun.

Jackson looked slightly older than Jude, maybe two years, putting him around fourteen. His hair was a white blonde and his eyes, that kept darting to Luna, were a clear almost icy blue. I frowned trying to determine the faint smell of copper tinging the air.

Oh gods. He was a blood mage. I could see the tattoo peeking out from his long sleeves. That was all I needed around Luna! I mentally chided myself for being biased because not all blood mages were psychos. Just Vegas's men.

"And you?" Athens prompted as Neo tilted his head, studying the two other boys.

"Stop embarrassing me," Luna growled as Adyen chuckled.

"Marcus," The quieter boy said, stepping forward slightly. The kid was dangerous looking, his eyes dark with learned caution, but, hey, I wasn't one to judge. Still… No kid that age should look that haunted or dangerous. Hadn't that been me though? Hadn't I killed my adopted parents right around a similar age?

The kid was taller and far bigger than the others, despite being around the same age. He had a scar that traveled from his eyebrow down to his jaw line and was only interrupted by his nearly black eyes against his olive skin tone. A dark wavy mess of hair surrounded him like a dark hood. His skin was already littered with tattoos and there was a wild air to his energy.

I looked at Luna, her lips twitching as she batted her long lashes at me innocently.

Right. *I've got your number kid.*

"Where are you from?" Taylor asked quietly.

"Where am I from or what am I?" Marcus asked his hands tucked into his pockets as he spoke. *Damn, this kid has balls talking to him like that.*

"The quicker we do this the faster we can eat." Luna bounced on her toes while offering her reminder.

Marcus smiled slightly before answering. "I was born in the Demonic realm but I don't know what I am exactly, besides part mage. I had been imprisoned in the Dark Fae realm until recently."

Oh.

A pregnant pause caused all of us adults to feel like shit

because it was clear this kid had been through some shit. Luna grabbed his arm and shook it, "Food, Marcus. Food is very, very important to me."

He let out a bark of laughter and shook his head. "Alright Princess, lead the way."

Jude grumbled about something as Jackson followed after like an excited puppy. The four of them went off to wherever they were going... what the heck had that been? "I think we may need to move up that 'worrying' timeline."

"She's only ten, she shouldn't even be talking to boys until she's like 50. And *Princess?* Did you hear that? Where does that kid get off calling her that? I already don't like him." Rhodes muttered as I grinned.

"So the Light Fae?" Adyen resumed the conversation after moving his narrowed eyes from their retreating figures.

"I will tell them the contract is off but let's at least try to figure out a solution beforehand. I would rather not tell them to fuck off and lose an ally if there is another option. As we know, the True Heir doesn't want to marry me. In fact, I would guess that he'd be far more interested in my brother."

"Really?" Rhodes asked.

I nodded and then we snapped our heads to the side hearing a fight break out. One of the recruits called to Adyen, but I was already there watching as the literal brawl took place. A few people stepped away from me not realizing I had appeared nearly out of thin air. Well, in their perspective at least.

When we had liberated the Dark Fae kingdom, we had allowed anyone who wished to seek refuge here. The Obsidian Butterflies, the anti-government group that helped overthrow Mario, were now aiding in reconstructing the kingdom as a whole. Their prized member had been locked up in the dungeons for years on end and once released, had refused to stay in those lands. I couldn't blame her, so we had offered her a place with the

SE. I would have told her to fucking relax instead of fighting but she refused to do so.

Maize was a bit strong headed.

"If you *ever* call me that again I will snap your neck." Her voice was dangerous from where she straddled the bleeding man underneath her. His breathing was rough and face purple from her grip on his neck. I could feel the pure fae energy rolling off her and her wings expanded out in a black and diamond white butterfly pattern, causing everyone to step back.

You see. The issue with Maize was that she was poisonous. If she wasn't completely in control of her magic, she could kill someone with barely a whisper of a touch. I wondered what had made her lose her cool this much, I thought about interfering but I'm sure the man probably deserved it. As I said, she was known for being calm and collected.

"Okay," The man gasped as she released his neck and he started coughing. She stood and retracted her wings, watching him with contempt as he scuttled off. When she turned towards me I could see the tips of her ears pinken slightly.

Maize was very much what you would expect a pure fae to look like. She was nearly 5'8 with long, lean, sinewy muscles that were almost ballet like in nature. Her dark hair was at her shoulders, recently chopped off post imprisonment, and her features were perfect in a stone like way. Her lips were a deep red and eyes a reflective cat like silver. There was a haunted darkness to her entire aura, and here I thought I had taken the cake for that.

Her clothes were new, black leather pants and boots, with a half top of leather that Esme no doubt ordered for her. My daughter, Athens and Neo's mother Laurena, and my best friend had all gotten quite close with the haunted woman living in our castle. I had kept my distance in respect for her time to heal but she really seemed like someone I would get along with. I briefly categorized that she had a fresh tattoo coiling up her waist that no doubt came from Laurena. If I wasn't mistaken, which was possible since I didn't want to stare, I was nearly positive it was a scorpion wrapped around her. Something about that struck a chord with me, because if I had to imagine her as a type of creature, scorpion or possibly a poisonous spider would make the most sense.

"Your Majesty," She stated in greeting, her head dipping.

"Walk with me," I commanded quietly, wanting to get her out of the circle of men surrounding her. I know, *way to be over protective over everyone Gray.* The two of us walked out of the group of soldiers and despite our silence it wasn't uncomfortable. We were at the archery grounds before either of us spoke.

"I'm sorry about that…" She stated.

"He was probably an asshole," I stated quietly.

Her lip twitched as she nodded. "The lot of them have decided they don't like me very much I'm afraid."

"What did he call you?" I asked curiously as her jaw clicked.

"He accused me of being an enemy of the state essentially," She shook her head. "I let my temper get the better of me. I had no allegiance to the Dark Fae when I lived there as a free individual and my hatred only grew every year locked up, so to infer *that…* it just made me upset."

Her words were honest and I could see the truth radiating from her. Maize struck me as someone who didn't play games. Someone that laid everything out in perfect clarity so as not to have confusion. I liked that about her. In my book that made her trustworthy.

"The SE can be idiots," I stated quietly, "but you are going to face that in most military branches here. Resentment for the Dark Fae runs pretty deep. If it gets too bad, there are other options."

She gripped the railing we leaned against looking over the snowy forest ahead of us. "I want to give it a chance…"

"Just let me know if you ever want to move to the Red Masques," I offered with a small pat to her hand. Her eyes met mine and she nodded. I knew that the woman had a good sense of humor because Luna had told me about it. But today? Today she seemed lost in a different universe.

"Gray?" Marabella's voice sounded as I turned to find my lady in waiting and good friend. I could see distantly that Bobby, my familiar, and Palo, Taylor's brother, stood waiting with her from a distance away.

"What's going on?" I asked her noticing her eyes were dark but amused.

"The dress tailor is here for the ball tomorrow, for final fittings." She grinned.

My lips twitched as I looked up at Maize, "Oh good! You don't have a dress for tomorrow, do you? We need to get you one, come on. You are perfect for dressing up, you're like a model." I loved clothes and I could tell Maize was a bit overwhelmed by my outburst, but to her credit she followed after me.

Maybe she would find out shopping could be her therapy as well?

2

RHODES

I wasn't positive how we were supposed to celebrate Christmas Eve but this seemed like a damn good start. Silas, who had officially been deemed the Horde's event planner, had once again gone all out and was rewarded by Gray's enthusiastic hug. Which had my jaguar growling in my ear, which was fucking ridiculous since it was her brother… but he didn't care. At all.

Gray had complained that I was being a bit overbearing and I was thankful that was all she'd fucking noticed. I'd been going crazy since we mated and then she was fucking taken from me. I felt like killing any man that looked at her and half the time was tempted to lock her up in her bedroom. It was bad. Really fucking bad. So being described as 'a bit overbearing' was perfectly fine with me.

The entire room, a large fireplace lit den, was decorated with garlands and ornaments. Silas had charmed the entire ceiling so that glass ornaments rotated in a slow starry sky of red, gold, and green. The massive, very real, tree took center stage with leather couches, tables of food and wine, as well as family and friends were spread around us. It was a smaller group than the ball tomorrow night and personally, I preferred this. I wanted to be as close to Gray as possible, which isn't as easy to do in a larger crowd.

Gray was talking to Marabella and Esme, her normally serious and intense expression relaxed and happy. I loved seeing her like this, it made me feel like I was doing something right. Her dark hair was getting longer and longer, and tonight her fair skin was head to toe in a deep crimson color. Despite having lost weight, which scared the shit out of me considering how small she was, I couldn't deny how fucking sexy she was. Her pert curvy ass was like a magnet for me, always pulling me in and I desperately wanted to carry her out of this room. I thought I would have been able to maintain a level of control in my emotions once mated. How stupid that had been.

I needed to tell her how much I loved her.

I wasn't fantastic with being romantic. I knew I wanted Gray though and I knew I loved her. I also knew I wanted to marry her, something that had hit me right in the fucking gut when I had heard about the Light Fae coming to the Horde. If Gray was getting fucking married it was to us.

"Dad?" Luna asked as my eyes snapped down to her. I nearly rolled my eyes at her three disciples following her around but tried to play nice. See? I could be pleasant.

"Yes?" I asked as Gray looked over at us. The woman's hearing was far better than any shifter I knew.

"We are going to go outside, will you tell Mom?" She chirped, trying to slip past me. I grabbed her little shoulders and set her back in front of me. I narrowed my eyes at the three boys behind her who looked suspiciously expressionless.

"Why?" I asked as she sighed with a muttered curse. I would have told her not to swear, but I was very much not the person to give that lesson.

"We just want to play in the snow," She offered an innocent grin.

"Actually," Marcus drawled, "my brother is outside, and I need to see him tonight. I told her she didn't need to come with me." I had to admit my first thought was that I appreciated his honesty.

I narrowed my eyes at my kid as she narrowed her gaze at Marcus's honesty. He kept his gaze on me and I begrudgingly had to confess I sort of liked the kid. Sort of. "Why don't you bring him up here instead?" *Did I really just suggest that?*

I guess. I had. You know, it was probably a smart idea because telling Luna no with some things was like telling Gray no. You could repeat yourself till you were blue in the face and it wouldn't matter a damn bit. I examined my daughter's hard set jaw and frustrated expression before looking back at Marcus.

I could tell Marcus came from nothing. The other two both were part of the system, mainly from The Red Masques, but Marcus came from nothing, a lot like Luna so I didn't have to wonder why they got along so well. His eyes widened at my words and after looking down at Luna, he nodded and slipped past me. She tried to follow and I stopped her.

"He'll come back, come on Luna." Jude offered her a small smile.

"He wouldn't want to miss out on the food anyway." Jackson joked as she sighed and followed after them to wait for their friend.

"That was nice of you." Gray's voice was soft against my ears as I looked down at where the woman had appeared in front of me, my arm wrapping around her waist easily. I could see her pulse, relaxed and slow, right near my mating mark. The scar made me irrationally happy because it signified that she was mine. My mate.

"What are you looking at?" She teased, her arms wrapping

around my neck as I looked back up into her tri-colored eyes that were thickly lashed.

"You." I murmured, leaning closer and pressing a soft but intense kiss to her lips. A shiver worked through her and I nearly groaned at how good she smelled. I wanted to eat this woman up. Instead of backing away like she sometimes does in public, she deepened the kiss and I tightened my grip on her causing a whimper to come out of her lips.

"Rhodes," She spoke against my lips and I knew exactly what she needed. I pulled back just enough to see Adyen offer me a nod in reference to keeping an eye on everything. I had no idea how he was dealing with having the mating bond on her without wanting to fuck her senseless. I pulled her hand gently as we moved down a nearby hall that spanned and turned around many dark corners.

"Where the hell are…" She didn't have a chance to ask because I pushed her up against the stone wall around the corner and gripped her waist.

"I need you." I growled against her lips as her breathing grew fast and she pulled back to lift a hand behind her neck. I was confused for a moment before her dark red dress fell to the floor and I let out a pained sound.

Gray had nothing on but a pair of black lace panties and her heels. I let my eyes crawl over her perfect skin and tightening nipples. I was calm and measured, before I wasn't and I was attacking her and pressing her into the wall. My hands gripped her thighs and I picked her up to wedge her against the wall. My lips attacked her neck as she moaned at the feeling of my hard cock pressing against her wet covered center through my pants.

"Rhodes please," She cried out as my lips crawled down her skin and I pulled a nipple into my mouth as her hands tightened in my hair, the diamond peak cool in my warm mouth.

Normally I would have taken time to tease her more, instead I used a hand to undo my dress pants and pulled out my painfully hard cock. I ran the tip against her wet center, snapping her panties with ease as her head fell back. I didn't waste time and impaled her against my cock, her cry loud and echoing against the stone. I didn't even bother trying to stop it. I groaned at how fucking good she felt wrapped around me. She was trying to suck the fucking cum out of me as I bounced her on my cock, my growl against her neck nearly feral as I bit down.

"Fuck." She gasped. "You're so fucking big."

"Are you trying to make me come?" I growled, increasing my speed to the point that I could feel the sweat breaking out against her skin as I screwed her into the wall. I pinned her with my hips as I drew her arms above her head and plastered my lips against hers. She gasped against my mouth and the noises she was making were turning me into a mad man.

"God damn it, Gray," I snarled, "those noises are going to kill me."

"As long as you keep fucking me." She gasped out as I barked out a pained laugh slamming into her, deep and at a slow pace, causing her body to tremble as her pretty eyes started to roll back.

"Rhodes," She whined, "please go faster."

I slowed down and smiled against her neck, glad to have control back. She growled, her nails biting into my shoulder. I slammed into her as she cried out my name but I refused to speed up. Her hand gripped my jaw and she demanded my attention. "Please."

After two more hard thrusts I gave in because I could practically feel myself ready to explode inside of her. I started to pound more rapidly and she came on me at least twice before I bit down on her neck and exploded inside of her, my jaguar producing a low predatorial sound from my chest, half purr, half growl.

For just a moment the two of us were suspended. I could feel her shaking slightly and I turned my head from where I was against her breast, her eyes focused on me and her entire face flushed with color.

"Fuck," I groaned. "you're so beautiful, kitten."

"Rhodes," She whispered, causing me to straighten slightly.

"Yeah, kitten?" I murmured.

"I love you."

My smile grew as I hardened fully inside of her again and dipped my lips down to hers. "I love you so fucking much, Gray. I'm sorry I didn't say it sooner. But I do. I've probably been in love with you since you tried to choke me out in that classroom nearly four months ago."

Gray barked out a laugh, her eyes sparkling as she clung to me tighter. She wiggled against me and I buried myself deeper inside of her, still hard as she whimpered. I was tempted to keep her trapped like this. Impaled by my dick and stuck against the wall. After a few slow thrusts, I pulled out as she scowled at the loss of contact. I helped her step gently back onto the floor, those damn stilettos probably left bruises against my ass, much like the ones my fingers probably left in her thighs. I slid the dress up her silky skin and clasped it at the top, leaving her looking still put together.

Her long dark nails wrapped around my still hard member and I let my head fall back, as she sucked on my neck before squeezing me and backing away. I narrowed my eyes at her, wondering how long I had to go back into the party for before I could kidnap her again. Once dressed, I drew her into a deep kiss before tucking her under my arm to go back into the party. I loved that she smelled like me now. Let all the unwanted fuckers know exactly who she belonged to.

Adyen was waiting for us by the hallway leading directly into the room and his eyes darkened on her, as his dragon let out a low sound. I grinned because it was only a matter of time before his dragon demanded he claimed her. After a hand squeeze she detached from me, sauntering past Adyen with a wink as I stepped up next to my second in command adjusting my cufflinks.

"Sorry mate," I drawled, not sorry at all.

Adyen chuckled and shook his head. "No, Rhodes, it's fine, because I'm about to ruin your fucking night, *mate.*"

We both walked out into the room and instantly my eyes were on the center of the room where Luna and Gray were. Except Luna wasn't paying attention to her, she was paying attention to the tallest boy in front of her.

"Is that…" I asked quietly.

"Kai?" Adyen chuckled. "Yes. It is. Apparently, that's Marcus's brother, they were separated until recently." *Ah, fuck.*

Now, I wasn't one to judge. But this kid was a piece of shit. He was not only a known thief but he was a fighter in one of the local rings. None of that would have really mattered to me if he wasn't holding my daughter's hand. What the fuck was going on around here?

"Why?" I snarled to Adyen as he shook his head drawing a hand down it.

"Apparently," He shook his head, "they have known one another for quite some time."

Jude was scowling next to them and Gray was offering Luna an odd look. Then the five of them were leaving the room, Gray looking confused and meeting my gaze. I was there in a second cupping her cheek.

"What the fuck was that?" I asked quietly.

Gray frowned and I followed her gaze where the five of them were talking in the hall, Luna's eyes tearing up as she hugged Kai tightly. What the fuck was going on? Gray spoke, "Um… apparently they know each other. I guess they'd been separated, and she didn't realize he was alive after this fire at a shelter they both had stayed at…"

"You know he's trouble, right?" I spoke quietly.

Gray sighed. "I can't judge any kid who is just trying to survive."

I wish I were that good of a person, I kissed the top of her head and tilted her chin up. I realized Adyen was talking to the twins and Taylor, so I took a moment to broach a topic.

"Gray," I spoke quietly. "After the Light Fae…"

Her eyes sparkled up at me as if my next words were very important. I exhaled because I wanted to partially demand that she marry us but I would never demand anything from her. I needed her to want to marry us and I almost wished she'd bring it up. I needed to say something though, *but then* Esme was calling her over.

"Later?" She asked quietly.

"Later." I confirmed while walking towards the others.

"Why do you look so serious?" Athens asked, offering me an amused look.

"How the hell are we going to bring up marriage to Gray?" I muttered, feeling a bit confused. This wasn't a normal situation at all.

All four of them froze.

"Well shit."

Well stated, Taylor.

Gray

Christmas Eve had been, by far, one of the most enjoyable holiday experiences I'd had to date. Although, now that I had my family I hoped that would change. I hoped we could make every year this special. I inhaled thinking over Rhodes's question after he was interrupted before finishing.

I knew what they wanted to talk about.

My hands gripped the window ledge of my bathroom tightly before sliding down to wedge myself comfortably in the open air.

I could see the entire Horde from here. I could see all four sectored communities that surrounded the castle and further out. I could see the forest where the Pixies lived and the massive gothic estate that Vegas and her men resided in. My lips pressed up thinking about how their Red Masques party was no doubt still in full swing. I wasn't positive if it was just that I felt older or what, but I could not party how the group of them did.

Right now, my crown was off though and my skin was only clothed in a small blue silk robe. I felt free and more relaxed. Don't get me wrong, I loved being Queen but it wasn't easy by any stretch of the imagination. My fingers rolled over my shoulders as I memorized the scars there, the ones that would litter my body for the rest of my life.

A small smile tilted my lips as I thought about how far I'd come in a matter of months. I'd gone from a woman hiding from her past and unable to be touched without some level of discomfort to *this*. To have taken my rightful place as heir to the Horde and being in a healthy relationship with people that I trusted. It was a fucking insane twist that I would have never expected.

I knew the extent of my PTSD was still there. Still buried and would probably surge to the surface under different circumstances, but I felt better equipped to handle it now. Plus, I wasn't the only one who had their demons and if Rhodes could live a healthy life after the trauma his father induced by burning cigars into his shoulders, I felt like I could as well.

A shadow crossed behind me as a smooth deep voice spoke against my ears, arms wrapping around me. "Kitten, come to bed."

I looked up at Rhodes and his stunning mint colored eyes as I nodded, moving back through the window. He picked me up, wrapping his arms around me as I looked over at my bed seeing both the twins in there. I slipped into the sheets as Athens offered me a sleepy smile, his arms wrapping around me tightly before burying his head against my stomach. Rhodes moved behind me and my eyes fell to Neo where he was propped up on his elbow watching me. I reached out a hand to rub it over his jaw line and he leaned into it, seeming to take comfort from my touch alone.

"I love you." I whispered as a smile broke onto his face and he surged forward kissing me and causing my head to spin before pulling back.

It was pretty fucking easy to fall asleep after that, my thoughts drifting into less real concepts and a more dream like state. I could only hope that tomorrow would go as seamlessly as Christmas Eve had.

3
GRAY

"Matching dresses?" Esme stated, looking amused as I stood getting ready in the mirror. My dark hair was pulled back in an intricate braided top, exposing the diamond like crystals that lined my hairline. Was it just me or were my ears a bit pointier than before?

"Yes!" I grinned, "Well, not exactly, but the point is that we are all wearing metallics. Come on, Esme, you know you were going to wear gold anyway."

My friend narrowed her eyes, tapping her cigarette on the window ledge, that was blowing cool refreshing air into my suite. Luna was already dressed in a silver gown like myself and Marabella was even playing along wearing a rose gold dress that fell off the shoulders. I watched as my friend muttered a curse and walked into the bathroom to change. *That's what I thought.*

She could bitch and moan all she wanted but the woman had planned to wear gold anyway, she just didn't like being told what to do. It was why we were friends.

"Mom?" Luna asked as Marabella and I both looked at her, those blonde brows pinched on her tan face. I knew Marabella came from a large family but she'd confessed not feeling very important, ever, feeling somewhat lost among all of the other siblings she had. Despite that, I could tell she had missed having siblings so once she'd relaxed a bit, she had instantly clicked with Esme and especially, Luna, who she treated a lot like a little sister.

"What's up?" I asked sitting next to her knowing something was off and had been since yesterday. Despite her age, Luna seemed far older to me than ten. She had the maturity of someone who had been on their own for quite some time, with the lighthearted nature of her youth.

She sighed and looked up at me. "I don't know what to do."

My brows raised as Marabella handed me two diamond earrings to slip in, my other piercings along my ears already placed. Luna looked thoughtful for a moment and then I smiled as she began. "Okay, so let's say… I had a friend."

"You do have those." I pointed out, amused.

She rolled her eyes, "Funny, Mom. The point is, this friend was gone for a bit and I thought they were gone forever so I made new friends… some of those new friends don't like that he's back. I don't know what to do because I am torn between telling them to deal with it and understanding why they are frustrated… and I just don't know."

I squeezed her shoulder and spoke, "I am going to take a guess that Jude and maybe Jackson aren't happy that Marcus's brother made an appearance?"

Her ears tinted and she sighed. "Or something like that. More Jude than anyone."

I nodded and took the glass of champagne that Marabella offered me as she pulled up a stool to sit and relax. I was really glad she was becoming more comfortable around me because I wasn't joking when I said that the woman was one of my closest friends. I would tell her that she didn't have to work for me but I think she enjoyed organizing everything… She was a bit crazy about organization.

"I think," I took a sip, "that if Jude is your real friend that he should understand that you have enough room in your life for him and Kai. Maybe he needs to hear it from you though?"

She blinked at me in thought and smiled, pulling me into a hug and sprinting towards the door. I watched in confusion as she slipped out and both Marabella and I shook our head. Now, some people may have tried to tame her because royalty didn't usually run through the halls… but I wasn't that Queen. Or mother. I ripped the heart out of my enemy, who was I to talk about social niceties? If someone had a problem with it then I was right here, waiting for them to fucking say something to me about it.

"Okay!" Esme stated dramatically walking out in a stunning gown, "This is perfect, Marabella, how have you not gone into fashion yet? You have such a good eye for this."

My owl shifter friend shrugged but smiled at her work. Esme really did look stunning, her dark curls and eyes, highlighted by the gold flecks spread through her hair against her dark skin. The dress cinched at the waist in a corset like bodice and flowed out in a skirt but still maintained tight sleeves.

Before anyone could say anything, the door echoed with a knock and Marabella shook her head muttering under her breath. I moved my hand in a swish motion as it opened to reveal Palo. I swear the man stalked her. To be fair she didn't seem to mind but he really was very overbearing. His model angular face was highlighted by the black suit he wore and crimson red hair, his dark eyes roamed over her before he groaned and breathed in for patience. Marabella offered me an amused smile right as Bobby walked in. Robert, as Marabella preferred to call him, was not only my familiar but one of my closest friends, his blonde hair and brown eyes were warm against his green suit tonight and without pretense he picked Marabella up and spun her.

"Let's go, I wanna get her a shawl or something," Palo scowled. I nodded to Marabella as they left and Esme took her seat. I was glad the group of them seemed to have worked out their differences but she and I needed to have a longer discussion about that at some point. I wasn't positive I was ready to forgive Palo for making her so upset and screwing with her originally.

"I really need to find someone."

I raised my eyebrows at her, "Didn't you say you were going to be eternally single?" As a lion shifter Esme was fairly dominant as a person, so human women hadn't really cut it for her. Now that she was in the Horde though, maybe she would have better luck?

"Yes, yes," she waved her hand dismissively, "but everyone else is happy and in love, I should probably give it a shot, see if it is all that it's cracked up to be."

I snorted and then the doors opened to reveal my dragon. I smiled up at him as his eyes trailed a heated molten path across my skin and I shivered, my toes curling in my stilettos. Esme groaned, "See! I'm out man, I have to go find someone. Pronto." She was gone then and Adyen walked over, kneeling down in front of me, caging me against the velvet couch I sat on.

"You are so beautiful." He growled, his lips pressing against my jaw and then tracing my scar, making me tremble. "How did I get so lucky?"

Now I must be getting fucking soft because instead of saying the very apt sarcastic response of *'I don't know, how did you?'* I went with a soft kiss on the lips and responded with, "You're lucky? I've got five amazing men that I love, who somehow love me back."

"It's easy to love you, Gray." He spoke his voice deep and caressing.

A bit of insecurity, buried deep, had my lip dipping slightly. It was stupid but hearing that made me feel a bit emotional. I had never been easy to love. I had been hated by my adopted parents and even at the academy I'd been difficult. So hearing that Adyen found me easy to love had my eyes prickling slightly. His brows shot up as he tilted his head, grasping my jaw gently.

"Sorry," I sniffed, running my hand over the back of his neck. "I have no idea why I am being so emotional, I'm blaming the holidays."

He chuckled and pressed his forehead against mine, running a thumb against my cheek as a tear fell. I moved closer to him, bathing in his warmth and security. After a comfortable loving moment, a clearing of the throat had both of us looking up to where Silas stood. My brother offered me an awkward smile and I stood, walking over to my vanity where I lifted my dark crown on top of my head and confirmed that I didn't have makeup streaked all over my face.

"Silas." I spoke in greeting, as my brother offered me a small smile, I put my hand on his shoulder. I had been livid at Silas when he had first shown up and while I still found him annoying, because let's face it... he's my brother. Brothers are annoying. I had also gained an appreciation for him. He wasn't nearly as frustrating or lazy when he was doing something he loved like event planning.

"I want to thank you for putting this all together," I smiled authentically, "you're very good at it."

He smiled and ran a hand through his hair as Adyen walked next to me, his hand on my back. Silas spoke, "I didn't realize I would enjoy it so much... but I didn't have much time to explore what I did like before you took over. You are far better at this than me."

I didn't disagree *but* that reminded me of something. "Hey, Silas?"

"Yeah?"

"What do you know about the Light Fae's True Heir?" I inquired.

His ears turned pink as he shrugged. "Why? Not much. I

mean we've talked a lot but... I don't know." *Talk about a rambling sentence!*

"I don't want to marry him." I explained easily, his eyes widened. "It is going to break the contract and I need to find a solution. Do you have anything that you think would work? Anyone you know he would want to marry from the Horde?"

His eyes darkened as he sighed. "I would assume he wants to marry you."

I shook my head. "No he doesn't."

"Did he say that?" Silas looked at me expectantly.

"Didn't have to," I chimed. "I don't think he is into me or any other woman."

Now, I knew damn well the Horde was archaic and probably had sexist and homophobic citizens in spades. However! I was neither of those things so I had no issue speaking freely about it.

Silas coughed, clearing his throat. "How do you know that?"

I examined his tense jaw, yet hopeful expression and spoke freely. "The same way that I know you are into him."

"I'm not," Silas shook his head, his eyes shooting to Adyen as my dragon sighed rubbing a hand on my back.

"Alright..." I sighed. "Well, then help me find some male that you think he would be interested..."

"No!" Silas barked out.

I grinned. "You need to make up your mind."

My brother cursed but didn't have a chance to respond as the doors to the ballroom opened and I walked out into the massive festivities taking place. Ah! He had done it again. Do you ever see those Pinterest photos of the elaborate ballrooms where everything seemed to be sparkling with light? That was how grandiose the celebration was. Silver and green covered every surface and massive, nearly twenty foot trees stood in the corner of the room so that it was the first thing you saw when you walked in. It seemed that nearly everyone had arrived.

"Baby!" Athens grinned as the man picked me up and spun me, my laughter authentic as I pressed a kiss to his full lips.

"You look stunning." Neo spoke from behind me sending a shiver up my spine, making me dig my nails into Athens's chest.

"You're just trying to butter me up." I leaned back tilting my head up at the massive man. He let out a deep rumble and kissed me gently, causing me to shiver as Athens's hands tightened around my waist.

"I'll do something to you alright." He growled against my ear.

I shivered wondering just how long was socially acceptable to stay at my own celebration. *I've been here long enough, right?*

Luna

Mom was right. I just needed to tell Jude that this wasn't a 'one or the other' situation.

At almost eleven, I'd been through a lot. A lot of things that I preferred not to think about. I had been kicked as a kitten when I tried to hide under the bushes in front of someone's house, all I had tried to do was find a home. I'd been starved and had to hunt bugs. I had been alone. Well, never completely alone because there was always one boy who was always there.

I had told Kai to leave me alone, but he never listened to me.

Most nights, I had found myself at the shelter nearby in the shifter district of Horde. That was where I met Kai and when he had decided, at only three years older than me, he would try to provide for me. Something I did not need, although I have to admit, I never rejected it when he brought back stolen food for both of us to eat in a dirty corner of the shelter.

I sat with my dirty knees pulled up to my chest, my pants way looser than they had been a bit ago. My head was pounding and the few bugs that I had managed to eat this afternoon weren't doing anything to keep the human side of me sated. I didn't want to stay a kitten though, because kittens got hurt. Often and a lot. I had a bruise on my rib from when some asshole kids had thrown rocks at me. My eyes hurt, tearing up, at the pain in my stomach and how mean people can be. I guess it was better than the other looks I would get from some of the boys at the shelter. That was why I was hiding up here, in the attic where no one else went. I pulled a blanket, from one of the boxes left up here, and curled in on myself.

It couldn't have been much longer before the creaking of a door opening, had my eyes flashing open. A boy, who looked older than me, seemed to search the room before his shoulders relaxed. I watched in envy as he carried a small sack of what smelled like food towards the wall across from me. Maybe I could change into a kitten, maybe he would share some with me. I swallowed and kept my head down refusing to ask for help.

"Do you want some?" His voice was soft and had me jumping, so much so that I hit my head into the stone wall behind me. I groaned as I put a hand over my head and didn't bother answering him because of course I wanted fucking food.

I heard him stand up and my body tensed shrinking into the wall. I growled meeting his gaze. "Don't come near me."

His dark eyes froze on me, searching my face, and some expression I didn't understand crossed it. He sat down a few feet away and opened up his bag, holding up a wrapped piece of bread making my eyes tear up. Alright, I usually was way tougher than this but I hadn't eaten in two weeks. Not anything real. Water, a little, but not food.

"Come on," He urged. "please?"

I sat up slightly and leaned forward, my hand curling around the bread before I pulled it back. I waited for him to follow it with something, for him to tell me that I owed him. But he just started to eat from a bag of what smelled like peanuts. I tucked my legs underneath me and began to slowly eat the bread, trying to not hurt my stomach in the process.

"What's your name?" He asked me quietly.

"I don't have a name." I muttered, not wanting to tell him my real one.

"I'm Kai." He offered softly his dark hair looking nearly as dirty and messy as my own. "I'm going to call you... peanut."

A laugh escaped me before I could scowl. "I hate that."

"Alright, Peanut, sure you do." He flashed me a smile and I felt the tension release from my shoulders. I shouldn't have trusted him as much as I did already.

After that first day, Kai had always been by my side. He had always been there when I needed him and I had always been there for him. Even when he acted like an idiot.

"You can't keep doing this!" I pointed out, sitting on the cleared off bed we had set up in the attic. Kai was scary enough that he was able to keep most people out of our space. Although, a lot of the little ones, who were 5 or 6, would come up here and I never minded that.

"I will until we have a better option." He mumbled his head against my leg from where he was slumped on the floor. My fingers soothed through his hair as I cleaned the awful gash he had on the side of his face. I swallowed feeling everything inside of me rebel at the idea of him getting hurt like this.

"I need to find a job." I mumbled.

"You're ten," He offered softly. "no one is going to hire us, seriously. You're tiny, Peanut."

I growled under my breath. His lips pressed to my hand as he closed his eyes. "Besides, I've got you. I'll always take care of you, you know that."

A small smile lifted on my lips because I did know that. I knew Kai would always take care of me no matter what. I just wanted to be able to take care of him too. He was the only person I had in this sad little world.

That was why a small part of my heart broke when I thought he had died. Alright, the part wasn't very small at all. I'd been distressed enough that I'd stayed in kitten form until Mom needed me. Healing physically and emotionally from everything I'd been through.

Nearly two, almost three months ago, before mom had found me, a fire had burnt down the shelter. Mages had been yelling things about the place sheltering half breeds and a bunch of other cruel words. I had escaped, but Kai had gotten lost in the chaos, pushing me towards the door while helping some of the little ones down the stairs. No one had been able to find him in the ruins of the building or any personal items we'd had, I had to swallow the truth that he was most likely dead. I had never felt pain like that.

Except he wasn't. He wasn't dead. When he walked into the room with Marcus last night, I had nearly stumbled and fell to the floor. If it hadn't been for Jude I would have probably done so because it was like seeing a ghost. I was so relieved, which of course freaked me out.

I could understand why Jude was upset, but he didn't understand, just because Kai was important to me, didn't mean that he wasn't. I had never expected to have so many friends so fast, when I'd been on the streets by myself and in the shelter, the only person that had ever talked to me was Kai. It was hard being prey. Because that was what a kitten was, no one wanted to be around you because you were essentially useless. That was why the part mage and part we-have-no-idea boy had confused me.

Where Jude was someone I could always rely on to have fun with and to be on my side, I could count on Kai to always be there. Even when I told him to leave me alone. That was why I couldn't understand where he had gone. Why did he leave me? I tried to not let those thoughts plague me too often because if I let them grow I became more and more upset. Then there was Jackson. Jackson was funny. He made me laugh a lot and I liked his smile. Even Marcus was becoming a close friend. He had felt familiar to me and now I understood why, having been so close to his brother. The two of them were very different though, where Kai was sharp and very smart. Marcus was quieter than him and more dangerous. I liked Marcus a lot, he seemed like a good friend to have.

Looking around the ball, I didn't see any of my friends and the people I did see my age tended to offer me not so nice looks. There was a group of girls that were the daughters of the SE Guards and they put their noses up at me as I nearly snarled at them. I'm sorry but who was wearing a crown? Not them. I was thrilled when Mom suggested we match.

Finally, I found Jude being yelled at by Cannon. Alright, *yelled* was a bit dramatic but my friend, dressed in a dark blue suit, stood across from his brother that had this stern look on his face. Immediately I was making my way across the room because while I knew Cannon meant well, that was my friend and I wasn't okay with him being spoken to like that.

"Jude," Cannon's voice was sharp and demanding, "you have to stop this."

"I'm not going to stop hanging out with her," My friend growled, my kitten side perking up at the sound of his wolf's growl, "She's my friend. So she's mine. Being a Princess doesn't change that."

"Edwin," Cannon paused looking over at a figure that had joined them, I couldn't focus on that and I'd nearly reached them. "You can't go hanging around with a Princess."

I stepped right up next to my friend and growled, "Stop telling him that, he's my friend." I leaned against Jude as he wrapped an arm around me protectively. "He's my friend. I'm a Princess, as you keep emphasizing, and if I want him, then he's mine."

Cannon's eyes widened as he muttered a curse. The man next to us spoke, "Sorry to interrupt…"

"Commander Edwin," Cannon started looking surprised, "you know my brother, Jude, and this is Luna, Princess of the Horde."

I snapped my head up towards the orange eyed man with shadows around him and realized I knew him fairly well actually. "You're one of Vegas's husbands right? Mom loves Vegas. I need to go say hi to her now that I'm not a kitten." I thought I heard one of the men say something about Vegas not being married, but I wasn't very focused on that. Husbands? Boyfriends? What's the difference if you love someone? Labels don't matter if both people are committed to one another. I had heard Mom say that to someone recently, but I couldn't remember who.

"She's a cat shifter, they adopted her not knowing that was the case." Cannon explained and I scowled at the knowledge he was imparting. My life, stay out of it, dude. *As if they would have turned me away if they knew, not hardly.*

"So," I looked up at my friend. "Are you ready? I found the perfect place to throw them from."

Jude frowned for a moment and then grinned realizing I was trying to get him out of this damned conversation. Mind you probably not the best excuse since it sounded like we were doing something bad, but oh well. Cannon stepped forward out of the corner of my eye and Jude snapped his head in his direction, letting out a growl. It stopped Cannon cold in his tracks as he offered a slight hand raise in an attempt to look peaceful. I grinned and pulled his hand as we left the adults to the adult stuff.

"Thank you for that." Jude stated quietly.

I nodded and pulled him towards a table, my dads frowning at me as I tossed them a smile and moved on. We sat down and I tried to speak but Jude spoke first.

"Sorry, Luna," He mumbled. "I didn't mean to get mad yesterday."

"Jude," I spoke softly. "Just because I'm friends with Kai doesn't mean I'm not friends with you also. You're just different friends."

Jude offered me a confused expression, "But what if he doesn't want me to be friends with you? You would have to pick then."

I shook my head and squeezed his hand. "I promise you we will always be friends. I refuse to choose between you."

"None of that!" Dad T chimed, walking past us and tapping our hands. We both pulled away and I have no idea why but Jude's face turned bright pink.

"Where are the others?" I asked Jude.

He looked around, "Should be here soon, Marcus was trying to convince Kai to come by, he seemed nervous about it."

I nodded, "He doesn't like the SE guard much, he's a pretty well known thief around the Horde… but it was just food, plus he gave it to me most of the time."

"He did?" Jude frowned. He didn't like talking about my life before this. I couldn't completely blame him, thinking about him in trouble, or *any* of my new friends, left me with a weird feeling in my chest, it was very uncomfortable.

Before I could answer him, I heard my mom calling me over. I stood up and placed a hand on his. "Come find me when you find the others?" He nodded and squeezed my hand, as I turned to walk across the room a bit to where my mom and Vegas stood. Oh! Good! I could finally say hi to her and not as a kitten.

"Vegas!" I chirped as a pair of bright purple eyes turned on me and widened. It was clear my mom had explained the situation but she probably had been having a hard time believing it until now. Post battle, no one but her men had been allowed close to her. I looked over her dark red and black dress and realized that she and my mother really did look alike, not in their hair or eyes but they were almost the exact same height and their faces were very similar. If Vegas had kids would they be considered my cousins? That is sort of neat. I was growing a larger family every moment of the day.

"You're Lunatic?" Vegas tilted her head, "The cat? The one that was like the size of my fuckin… sorry, *freakin'* hand? That's insane. I mean, seeing you and thinking about… I just can't."

I grinned, "Luna, you can call me Luna. But yes! I am very much the same cat."

"I just don't understand how…" She muttered.

My mom fixed her with an amused look. "That is what gets you? After all of this? Her being a cat shifter is what blows your mind?"

Before any of us could say anything, the doors opened and in walked my mom's friend Tamara and her men. She was dressed in this bright green spring dress and I had to admit, I was sort of wishing I had worn something a bit brighter now. Maize wore silver like mom and I, her eyes on our group as she approached. I loved Maize. She was a bit different but I admired how strong she was. Despite warning me several times, I had practically begged her to tell me about how she had survived in Mario's dungeons. I could see the woman was in pain and despite worrying about telling me about the experience, it seemed to make her relax a bit. I liked that I could help people like that. I found myself smiling, feeling really lucky to have so many strong badass women around me.

The Christmas ball seemed to fly by after that and I really enjoyed it. Mostly because I was able to spend time with my family and friends. It was odd that such a little thing meant so much to me but I'd been alone for so long. The only downer? Kai never showed up. I mean, I wasn't exactly surprised because Kai being at one of these events was nearly as odd as Marcus at one of these events. Although the latter had shown up.

When the party started to get later *and* louder, my parents sent me to bed as my other friends went home. I walked back to the East Tower feeling a bit down. It didn't help that I knew the Light Fae would be here tomorrow and the peace my family was feeling would be severed. I really hoped mom had a plan for that because I had overheard my dads talking and I knew they wanted to be the ones to marry Mom. I'd never been to a wedding before so I had to admit, I was a bit excited.

After changing and letting my hair down, I sat on my balcony curled up under a blanket watching the snow drift off the roof above me. The East Tower was a massive structure in which I had a space that started one story up from the gardens but spanned up four stories, so the main room had a beautiful spiral staircase and a large lounge area with a constantly burning fireplace. My bedroom was all the way up on the fourth floor and if I was feeling too lazy to walk up the stairs, I fell asleep on my chair near the fireplace. Sometimes though, I would shift into my kitten form and jump from ledge to ledge, just for the fun of it. It was a perfect space and one I absolutely never expected to have. Closing my eyes, I let the winter weather brush over my skin, inhaling the freshly fallen scent of snow and pine. A small sound had me smiling.

It goes without saying that I knew Kai pretty well so when I saw a shadow making its way across the snow-covered lawn before scaling the wall, I knew it was him. I wondered how he knew where my room was but I had a feeling that was his brother's doing. Marcus paid attention to details like that. I think he had an entire map of the castle in the forefront of his mind. He easily looped himself up from the garden and landed on the railing, a one story feat that had me feeling a bit impressed. His eyebrows shot up to find me waiting. It had just been a feeling but it was exactly what I would have expected from my friend.

"Peanut," Kai landed softly on his feet and paused before

walking over to me, crouching down so that we were eye level. I watched him quietly, not fully knowing what to say.

"I go by Luna now." I explained softly my cheeks blushing at his closeness. I should have gotten used to it by now but that was before I realized how much I cared about him.

He flashed a smile knowing how much I hated my original name. "You're still peanut to me." I hoped I was taller than him one day, just to prove I wasn't small like a peanut.

I spoke quietly after a moment, examining his familiar face. "I'd thought you died, Kai." I was honestly surprised by the amount of emotion in my voice and a bit embarrassed. Trying to push the sadness away, I wrapped my arms closer around me.

Kai examined my expression before coming to sit next to me, pulling me against him and forcing me to release my hold on myself. His voice was soft and familiar. "I'm so sorry, Luna."

"What happened?" I asked softly, my cheeks blushing further despite not knowing why. He shook his head as pain flashed across his face. I nodded, knowing he would probably tell me eventually, before closing my eyes, leaning against him. We'd fallen asleep like this countless times before.

"Are you going to disappear again?" I asked quietly.

Kai was silent for a few moments before he shook his head. "No, I'm going to stay."

I closed my eyes and the sleepiness from the busy holiday hit me hard. I wondered if he would be here in the morning. I wondered if he would actually stay.

Marabella

"I need to check on her before I go to sleep." I told Palo and Robert. Well, the latter was already sleeping and his handsome tanned face looked so relaxed. I smoothed a hand over his golden hair and looked back up at Palo.

His eyes were dark and I blushed finding him a bit intimidating still after all this time. Since the night of our cancelled date, Palo had seemed to become more and more intent on proving how serious he was about this. I mean he was nearly attached to me at the hip. I blushed further thinking about Robert, Palo and I in bed together. Nothing had really happened… well, I mean things had *totally* happened, but I still hadn't slept with either of them. It wasn't that I didn't trust Robert, I just didn't know him well. Plus, I still had trust issues with Palo. I felt like they were fairly well deserved considering ditching me on a date and the other bullshit he'd put me through.

My body disagreed though, for the record, as well as my owl. Both didn't understand my hesitancy and were practically begging me to move things along.

"I'll come with you." He spoke softly as he grabbed my hand gently. I followed after my demon and realized that I hadn't seen him in his office for some time. In fact, ever since the war with Mario had ended and we'd saved Gray, things had been relatively calm for all of us. With the arrival of the Light Fae though? That worried me. A lot.

"You don't think the Light Fae are going to be an issue, do you?" I asked softly.

Palo examined my face and offered a small smirk. "Are you asking if my brother and his team mates are going to let Gray marry someone else?"

"I mean, if she thinks it is the right choice…"

"Won't matter to them." He stated as we approached the East Tower. "They will follow Gray till the ends of the realm, but give her up? No. I don't imagine they would be comfortable with that."

I pressed a kiss to his cheek as I slipped into Luna's private chambers, a chill rolling over my skin at the feel of the balcony doors being left open. Wrapping a shawl, from one of the hanging hooks nearby, around my shoulders I approached the doors. My eyes widened at what I'd found.

A young boy, I believe his name was Kai, was sitting with a sleeping Luna, his eyes snapping to mine in realization. His voice was worried as he spoke. "Please don't tell the guards, she knows I am here. We were just talking before she fell asleep, I didn't want to wake her up."

If it had been anyone else I would have called the guards regardless but after hearing Luna earlier? I believed his story. I opened up the balcony door wider and his eyebrows shot up, as he adjusted Luna and lifted her toward the couch. He laid her down and placed a blanket around her before sitting in a chair next to it so he could continue brushing her hair. I locked the balcony doors and offered him a warning look, but he just nodded earnestly. I had to admit this was pretty flippin' cute. After a look back at his closing eyes, I made a note to leave extra blankets in here because I had a feeling the boy would be back. I frowned also thinking about where he would have been sleeping if not with her. Where did Marcus or he stay? I would need to bring that up to Gray, I knew she would understand my concerns.

I had heard the rumors about Kai, but I also knew that survival instincts were strong. You did what you had to do and I didn't blame him for stealing.

"You look thoughtful." Palo remarked.

I nodded and looked up at him. "How does someone join SE guard training?"

He smirked. "Are you interested, lamb?"

"I'm serious," I nudged him gently.

"You apply," He added softly.

"I want to put in applications for Marcus and Kai, if Gray approves it," I whispered. "I think it would do them well."

"Did Luna bring it up to you?" He asked, confused.

"Something like that." I mumbled.

After searching my face, he nodded and tugged me down a different hallway, "Let's stop by my office and I can draft up two applications."

Perfect.

Now, let's just hope Gray agreed.

4
GRAY

I woke up with a long delicious stretch only to find myself caged between two very impressive bodies. I squinted open my eyes and realized that I had landed myself a Rhodes and Adyen sandwich. Talk about luck, am I right? I smiled against Rhodes's golden, muscular, chest as I arched my back and pressed my ass against Adyen's hardening cock, his chest rumbling even in his sleep. It was past Christmas but couldn't I still get a present? Namely one that included riding Adyen's dick? I was Queen after all.

"Gray," Adyen growled against my neck, "you better stop it."

"Or else…" I drawled as Rhodes let out a dark chuckle, his large hand smoothing over my breast and creating a shiver to break out over my skin. A small moan escaped from my lips as Adyen nipped the skin of my shoulder right on the mating bite mark he'd placed before the war. I tilted my head so that it was completely exposed to him and he sucked the skin, making me cry out a little as I felt my center explode in heat, his hard erection pressed firmly against my ass.

My hand wrapped around Rhodes's hard cock as he hissed and pressed a searing kiss against my lips. I rubbed myself against

Adyen looking for any sense of relief. His hands slid around my hips as he yanked up the loose shirt I wore, my bare ass exposed as the cool air hit my wet center causing me to squirm. I let out a small whimper as Adyen's fingers pulled apart my legs so that he could run them through my slit, the feel of them rough and hot against me. I whined in need against Rhodes's lips, that were demanding a lot from me, and I wrapped my hand tightly around his now bare, impossibly hard, cock.

"Please," I begged Adyen looking back at him as Rhodes moved down my body and began to nip and kiss the skin down my chest until his teeth were tugging on my nipple, his hand replacing Adyen's on my clit.

Adyen's voice was rough and dark against my neck. "Please what, Gray?" *Bastard knew exactly what I wanted.*

"Please fuck me." I met his gaze and he snarled, biting down on my shoulder as if the action somehow curbed his growing frustration. Honestly, it just turned me on more. I jumped as his hot, long erection pressed right against my ass, released from the boxers he had slept in.

"Fuck, kitten," Rhodes looked up at me from where he was toying with my abused nipple with his tongue. "you are soaking my fingers."

Adyen's chuckle was soft and dangerous against my ear as he pressed my back forward and angled the tip of his cock right at my entrance. I hissed as he pressed in slightly causing my entire body to tense in anticipation. *Oh holy shit, he was big.*

"Adyen…" I totally went to warn him that he may not fit.

The bastard slid right in balls deep as I cried out his name and Rhodes quickened his fingers work on my clit making me tighten around him. Fuck he was massive. My dragon grabbed my hair in a tight hold and pulled back, exposing my neck and fucking me from behind as Rhodes teased the front of me. I was cuming in seconds as I moaned out my release, feeling my core explode in molten heat as my magic wrapped around both of them. My back burned and I could feel the fourth tattoo of Adyen's rune being filled in. A sense of satisfaction filled me because of the claiming process and my magic offered me a salacious wink.

Suddenly, I was flipped over so that I was on top of Adyen, my legs sliding to either side of him. His large rough hands pushed my hips down, filling me to the brim, as I tried to adjust to how large he was, including my hips trying to accomodate for his large muscular body I was now riding. Once he started pounding me though? Any thought but pleasure went away, my eyes fluttering closed in relief as I came around him, his thrusts becoming faster and far more wild.

Rhodes's lean muscular body pressed up behind me and his familiar hard length pressed between my ass. A very sauve squeak, I'm positive, came from my mouth as he wrapped my hair in his hand and Adyen paused his movements. I was left feeling like we'd gone from 60 to 0, leaving me trembling with adrenaline and feeling needy and wanting.

"Kitten," Rhodes demanded his words crawling across my skin, "tell me I can fuck your ass." His blunt words had me practically gushing as I slid further down Adyen, his responding growl and tightening of his hands, making me know he felt it.

"Yes." I whimpered trying to move my hips as Adyen stopped me. Rhodes's fingers swept across my pussy where I was practically split in fucking half by Adyen, as he brought the lubricant to my back entrance, circling it lightly. My body tightened in anticipation as goosebumps broke across my skin and my nipples tightened.

"Say it," Adyen demanded, his cock somehow grew even larger inside of me.

I looked up into a pair of golden eyes and arched my back so that his cock was nudging my entrance, "I want you to fuck my ass, Rhodes."

A dark smile took over his face and I screamed out a 'fuck' as he slammed home, my head snapping back as I let out a moan of pure pleasure. I felt so fucking full and being caged between their two hard bodies was equisite. It felt so fucking right. Adyen's lips covered my nipple as the two of them began to fuck me deep and hard, not waiting for me to adjust.

Honestly, I had no idea what language I began crying out in as my moans grew louder, but as they quickened their pace my body went limp with pleasure, losing track of the pulses of pleasure working their way through me. This had to be some crazy fucking shifter stamina because I had no idea how they were keeping this up without having cum yet.

"Fuck," Adyen groaned. "I'm going to cum way too fast, with her tightening and squeezing me in a fucking vice grip like that..." *Too fast? Ha!*

Rhodes let out a pained chuckle from over my shoulder. "You should feel her ass, mate."

Now why the fuck was it so hot that they were talking about me like that? It gave me a burst of fucking energy and I began to bounce as white hot pleasure seared through me. I could feel the two of them were only separated by a thin membrane with how tightly they were squeezed inside of me. Both of their hands were gripping and touching some part of me, their mouths licking or biting my skin and I swear to you, this was their attempt to fuse us into one being.

Rhodes let out a deep growl, losing any control he had, as he began to pound into me from behind, Adyen's grip tightening on me. I exploded from the sensation of my clit rubbing against his toned body as Adyen bit down right on his previous mating mark, exploding inside of me roaring out my name.

Rhodes followed, his slap across my ass loud and sharp, as he finally buried himself deep inside of me before cuming. My body was limp with pleasure as a haziness filled my vision, my magic shimmering around us, happy to have officially claimed another of our mates. My body was still recovering from having Rhodes in my ass so I could barely contain how it wrapped itself around their magic in a soft embrace. Not that I would want to.

Rhodes was holding himself up above me, but his cheek pressed against my back. Both were still hard and buried inside of me, our breathing rough and our bodies, well mine at least, fucking exahusted. It was a good exhaustion though. I felt sated and happy.

"I don't even know what to do after starting my day like that," I murmured with a soft laugh. "I love you both so, so much." Holy shit. I blinked and tried to exhale and inhale like normal, overwhelmed by what I felt for them.

Adyen let out a soft hum. "I love you too, lil brawler."

"I love you, kitten." Rhodes nipped my skin and after another relaxed moment, they pulled out and Adyen lifted my body up. My eyes closed and the next thing I knew I was in a bath of warm steamy water pressed against Adyen's chest and my legs captured on Rhodes's lap.

Now this? This was how you started your fucking day.

Adyen

Gray was tucked between the twins now, who had shown up only minutes ago, wanting to sleep in late today. Well, those were Athens's words, I think Neo was just trying to get as close as possible to Gray. I understood the feeling fully. Taylor was sitting on the couch, drinking coffee and flipping through a massive book. My guess was that he was attempting to distract himself from this bullshit. All of us were attempting to avoid the impending situation. I looked at my mate, her long lashes wet from the bath and skin flushed. I swallowed down the possessiveness coursing through me… or tried to. It was far worse now that

I had buried myself deep inside of her, my cum painting the inside of her fucking womb. I understood how archaic that shit was but ask me if I care.

I didn't.

Rhodes buttoned up his shirt and once we were dressed we headed towards the hall. Not before I pressed a kiss to her forehead though. My dragon offered me a low snarl at leaving her side but in order to keep her ours, I had something I wanted to fucking handle. Gray had been through being a goddamn prisoner of war, having a conversation with Silas was the least I could do for not only saving our kingdom by taking her rightful place but for making my life one hundred percent better than I could have ever expected it to be.

So yes, it was time to have a conversation with Silas.

Gray would marry the fucking Light Fae heir over my dead, god damned, body. Don't get me wrong, it wasn't personal against him, but if he tried to marry her I would snap his neck no questions asked.

I smiled thinking about the first day I'd met her, sitting in that rose garden with a pouty scowl on her face after punching Bobby. I had not expected her. I hadn't known what to expect but a woman who breathed pulsating energy and smelled delicious enough to devour, wasn't it at all. I could have imagined a thousand different ways how this could have ended up and I had to admit, I was beyond thankful that this had been the result.

I had learned a lot about Gray in the past few months, but there were two things that stood out to me as of this morning. Two elements of the complicated entanglement that was Gray. *One.* She had a very strong sense of loyalty. The woman would die for the people she loved. *Two.* She didn't like to break promises. This was a fucking promise she would need to break, though. If she didn't want to do it, I would force the situation somehow. I would not be able to handle seeing my mate in the arms of someone else, even if it was just for show. It was different with my brothers because… well, I had been with them my entire life. There was trust and respect there.

Especially with Rhodes.

If I had to call someone my best friend, outside of Gray, it would be Rhodes. While our backgrounds hadn't been nearly as severe as the twins, it hadn't been particularly happy either. Both of us had grown up with the pressure and prestige that came with being True Heir guards and having fathers as representatives to our entire community. I was thankful because my father hadn't handled things like Rhodes's had, his scars being very literal. In a way I was glad that Gray and him shared that though, because being abused in any form wasn't something that went away. It seemed like the two of them healed each other. It was slow moving but I could see the change there.

My family hadn't been terrible, they'd just been indifferent. My father served the crown and used his children when he found it necessary. Both him and my mother would then forget about me until the next time they needed something. It was something that I had always been envious about when it came to Rhodes and the twins. It was fucked but even though their parents were mean to them… I'd been jealous about the fact that they got *any* attention, even negative, from them because mine acted like I didn't exist unless they needed something.

At the time, I hadn't let it bother me much, once we were paired as a team and in training, none of us looked back. We became a family. In retrospect though? Well, it made me realize that I never wanted to subject our children to that. I wanted our kids to always feel loved, no matter what the outside world was like. I suppose that was one of the many reasons why the Luna situation was so fascinating yet welcomed at the same time. Unintentionally, Luna had forced all of our hands into moving 'us' along. She had brought us together as a family by calling us

'Mom' and 'Dad' when we were distracted by Mario. Now, that the war was over it was easy to see just how perfect we fit together as a unit.

I couldn't help but let my mind wander to Gray being pregnant. My dragon offered me a somewhat eager look at the prospect and I nearly rolled my eyes. I smirked though because I knew Gray's pregnancy would be a bit crazy. She was no doubt going to be an amazing mother, but she would be crazy overprotective, and that's coming from me. Then again, when I took the time to consider bringing a little life into this world… yeah, maybe I would be the crazy protective one, or hell, all of us would no doubt. I honestly, couldn't believe these thoughts were crossing my mind because before Gray they had been essentially nonexistent.

"He's going to be defensive." Rhodes ran a frustrated hand through his wet hair.

"Don't give a fuck." I shrugged indifferently. I didn't. He could be defensive, angry, throw a fucking fit and it wouldn't matter. This conversation was happening. We continued down the halls and turned the corner, nearly running over Marabella.

She let out a squeak and backed up, paper in her hands crinkling. Her eyes were wide and she looked excited about something, we both stopped.

"I am so glad I ran into you two!" She chirped and thrust papers into our hands.

I frowned, realizing it was an SE Application… for Kai. I flicked my eyes over to Marcus's application in Rhodes's hand. What the fuck was this?

"They want to apply?" Rhodes clarified looking a bit surprised. Marcus didn't surprise me but Kai sure as fuck did.

"They don't know," Marabella explained. "Palo and I were thinking, since both boys are living in an orphanage, and well let's face it, one of them is known for trouble and the other looks it, we were thinking structure would help. Especially after everything Marcus has been through."

I sighed looking at Rhodes. I knew that it was selfish but having two boys around our daughter that she was clearly fond of annoyed me. Yet, I didn't disagree. As an adult I knew the structure would be good to get them off the streets. As a soldier, I knew those boys were practically made for fighting. I had an idea of what they were a mix of exactly, but until we had them in training it would be nearly impossible to determine.

"What made you think of this?" I asked, narrowing my eyes realizing we were in the East Tower, the wing's door to Luna's suite only a hall away. She spoke softly while looking towards Luna's door.

"They were so peaceful." She murmured. Both of us were striding towards the door, and slipped in. I nearly groaned at the sight in front of me. I knew this kid was going to be a fucking problem. Rhodes went to say something but I shook my head, examining the scene in front of me.

On the large velvet coach in the bottom floor of her room, Kai was stretched out sleeping with Luna curled up in a white fuzzy ball on his chest. His hand was protectively wrapped around her. What the fuck was he protecting her from? If anything she needed protection from him! I looked to where Marcus was stretched out on the floor, both of the boys looking exhausted. I felt a small tug of pain at that because no kid deserves to live in survival mode.

See? I'm not a complete asshole. I turned as the three of us walked out.

"I'm not sure when Marcus arrived." She explained quietly. "But the two of them have been like that all night."

"Why didn't you wake them up?" Rhodes demanded.

She seemed to stand straighter to defend her position. "Because I think it's harmless, at least at their age. I'm not cruel enough to put them back out on the street either. Listen, I know the reputation Kai has but I've also heard how both he and Marcus talk to her. I'm telling you there is nothing to worry about. With that said, I think that this is a great solution. They can continue their friendship while having a place to sleep, eat, and something to fill their time with."

I muttered and shook my head in disbelief at what I was going to say. "I think I have to agree with you."

"Adyen?" Rhodes rose a brow in shock and I grunted. "Think about how we felt about Gray when we first met her, even when we were younger on her birthday. I think Marabella is right, I think that it is better to have a solution than freak out and make Luna feel like she has to walk on eggshells around us."

"I don't want him in that room though, either of them." Rhodes muttered before folding the papers and tucking them away. "Fine, I approve the fucking application and tell them both."

Marabella nodded and walked back towards the door without another word. I shook my head but I didn't disagree. I partly wondered what we would have been like if the six of us had never been separated. We would have still ended up here but it would be different no doubt.

"Let's go talk to Silas." I muttered feeling exhausted.

"We have to stop that." Rhodes motioned towards the room.

"Let's see what Gray thinks, remember Luna isn't exactly a normal kid. If she feels safe with them it's probably for a good reason." I grunted.

"How are you saying this?" He demanded. "You of all people!"

I sighed, fixing him with a look. "You know what happens when we try to tell Gray to not do something?"

"She does it anyway." He growled.

I am sorry but I was finding this fucking funny. The man was losing his cool as the days went on, I found myself smiling. "Exactly, so what do you think Luna would do?"

He sighed at that. "Fucking ridiculous." I nodded towards the other wing, where we would find Silas. He followed after me muttering in annoyance. I tried to refocus on the task at hand.

Silas. I grunted. Silas had been a terrible king. Like I mean absolutely fucking awful. He was far better serving in the capacity he did now. I knocked on his door as we approached the massive intricate wooden piece. As Silas opened it, his eyes widened in surprise at the sight of us this early in the morning.

"Good morning." He frowned.

"We need to talk." Rhodes demanded quietly as he searched our faces before sighing in realization. He stepped back and let us in, leading us towards the seating space of his suite. I sat on the same couch as Rhodes facing Silas.

"So," He asked innocently, "what do we need to talk about?"

"You know as well as I do, that you and the Light Fae's true heir have been having an affair for over two years now. The SE intercepted *several* of your letters, before you deny it. So why are you giving Gray a difficult time about this marriage?"

Silas's expression turned into near heartbreak as he ran a hand through his long hair. "Because, even if the Horde somehow transformed into being more progressive, the Light Fae? They are not and they would never consider the alliance since we can't produce heirs."

"That's bullshit, he's immortal and you are as well, you don't need heirs." Rhodes stated quietly.

Silas leaned back and opened up his palms in a pleading gesture. "I don't know what you want me to say? I would absolutely love if I got a fucking happily ever after. But that's not going to happen. He's already stopped returning my letters, you can't really call it an affair when it's been mostly over letters…" He turned an obvious shade of red. "*Mostly.*"

"What if we could get you two alone to talk it out?" Rhodes asked quietly.

"Doesn't solve the problem gentlemen, no one is going to approve the marriage. Hell, you're one to talk, do you think the people are going to be okay with the Queen's guards marrying her?"

I couldn't fucking deny that fact. It drove me crazy that we were in some odd fucking limbo. Rhodes growled as I stood up, both stepping towards the door. *I was very much done with this conversation.* I spoke, looking him straight in the eye. "I'm getting you two in the same room together, we have to work something out because they are not getting married. As for people not liking our situation… there's a large difference between you and us."

Silas chuckled darkly. "What's that?"

"I don't give a fuck if they don't like it."

5
GRAY

Right now, I was sort of wishing for a snow storm. Maybe just a baby one? The Light Fae army had been spotted crossing the border which meant they were, at most, forty minutes from the castle. It infuriated me. *This entire notion infuriated me.* I was standing in my office looking over the contract in question as I listened to the sounds of the castle being switched from Christmas decor to elegant themes of navy blue and silver, with elements of pale yellow for our visiting guests.

I really hoped to put off official talks until tomorrow, a large feast was planned for tonight to celebrate their arrival and in their celebratory state I hoped we could arrange for Silas and the True Heir to meet. I wasn't positive about what had changed but Adyen stated that Silas was very eager to agree to the plan, making me feel very positive about today actually.

Apparently I'd missed a lot, because Luna had run into my room stating that she was furious at Rhodes and Adyen. When I asked why she turned a bright red and stated that they were trying to 'take away her friends.' Marabella had offered me a look and explained calmly that she thought it was a good idea to make sure the boys had somewhere to sleep. Luna had quieted at that note and stalked back out.

Marabella had proceeded to explain how she'd found Kai and her, and then the addition of Marcus this morning. Frankly, it didn't bother me that much but I agreed with the move to make sure that the two of them were a bit more busy than they were currently. I would never admit to any of them, but I thought it was all very cute.

I rubbed my eyes, for once wishing I wasn't in elegant silver heels that lace around my ankles. I was wearing a dark blue gown that was tight around my chest with long sleeves and a full bottom. It was very conservative and not something I'd normally wear *but* it was very Queen-like.

"Baby?" Athens strode in and I looked up, unable to not smile at him.

"They're almost here? Or have you come to tell me that they have turned back?" I asked with a hopeful note. Maybe, they weren't coming?

Athens offered me one of his cheeky smiles and curled his large hand around my neck, tilting my head back to lay a kiss on my lips. His familiar scent relaxed me and those massive muscles felt wonderful under my fingers. This man was a personal dosage of Xanax.

"Tell me this is going to work out, Gray." He mumbled, and I could hear the insecurity in his voice. My metal mage still had some serious abandonment issues he was working out but I would never leave him so he didn't need to worry about that. Then again he may be a bit doubtful of that considering I'd left for nearly three weeks when we'd first met.

I would never do that again. My brow dipped as a memory crashed over me.

I entered my East Coast estate, settled as a massive stone structure against the cliffs of the Atlantic. The entire place was perfectly maintained but it was cold and unfamiliar. Pain severed my chest as I thought about how comfortable my room had felt this morning, waking up surrounded by them. Then my magic had pushed me to run. Not only from them but from my familiar and Esme. Hadn't Bobby said only the other day that he was going to lose me soon? Apparently, it was far sooner than expected.

"Miss?" A soft voice asked as I looked towards a woman who didn't look surprised by my presence. I placed my bag down and offered her a small smile.

"Hey." I whispered. "Do you mind taking this to my room? I am going to curl up on the couch for a bit."

"Should I make you dinner?"

Thinking about food nearly made me sick, I shook my head and kicked off my shoes. My personal exile was already feeling like a massive mistake. I tucked myself into the side of the luxury couch and sighed. This was for the best. This was for the best. I kept that on repeat in my mind.

Maybe I would convince myself.

It hadn't been for the best. In fact, when I'd come back and Rhodes had stormed over to me across the academy's yard, I had been thrilled. My little heart had started beating a million miles an hour and I'd been tempted to throw myself into his arms and sob. Instead, I had attempted to be strong. Attempted to maintain some distance… until he showed me his scars. That had done me in and I felt the wall between us breaking as I left him into my world, unable to rationalize parting from them again. That was when I realized how screwed I was when it came to these guys.

"Gray?" Athens's voice pulled me from the memory. "Where did you go?"

"We are going to figure this out." I promised seriously as he searched my face. I continued, "I will not be marrying him. I can promise you that."

His smile grew as he nodded, seeming appeased momentarily.

Athens let out a small hum, looking over my face before a possessive light filtered into his onyx silver speckled gaze. I met his lips eagerly as he dipped down and began to devour my lips in a slow almost intoxicating pace that was so different from the normal playful tone that he maintained.

A familiar voice, coming from the door, sounded and interrupted us. "You're right, you won't have to marry him if we can play this right."

Palo offered us a frustrated look as if our kissing had somehow disrupted his schedule. I was very glad the man had dropped his attempt at being charming like he had originally done when I first met him, it was very much not his thing. Athens chuckled against my temple as Neo followed into the room. My alchemy mage wrapped an arm around me, tugging me from his brother with a grin as I melted against him. The man nibbled my neck as I attempted to focus but Athens had this mischievous look in his eyes I didn't completely trust.

"What do you mean?" I asked Palo wondering if he had thought of something that we had not.

All three of us watched as Palo's hands shifted through the copy of the massive document before finding a page he had clearly studied often in his own office. I watched as he took the quill that was poised next to my favorite picture of Adyen, Rhodes, Luna and I curled up in bed together. I really needed more photos of us. That was my New Year's resolution! I would take more pictures, I was sure the boys would love that. I smirked imagining how annoyed they would be.

Esme had taken a ton of photos during Christmas and she was trying to find a way to develop them now. The Horde was very difficult to live in sometimes, considering the mix and match of technology.

"I mean," he pointed to the phrase that was so tiny I had to squint, "there is an actual clause in here that says, the marriage contract is valid *'unless agreed null and void by both heirs.'*" My smile grew as I tried to not jump across the desk and hug the man.

This meant that all we had to do was arrange for Silas and Rainer, the True Heir, to meet for sure.

"How hard is it going to be to actually get them into the same room? I know that would be ideal but there are a million different reasons this could fail." I asked curiously.

Neo spoke with a soft chuckle, "I think you may find that they very much *will* most likely want to meet. They've been talking for some time now."

Well at least that is confirmed.

I nodded. "Perfect. Let's make that happen post-feast tonight, until then I need you two to remind the others to play nice. I am not going to marry the man but I need to act like it until then."

"No!" Taylor growled from the doorway causing me to jump just a little bit. When the fuck had he showed up? His lip twitched and let me know he had heard that thought. He stepped into the room and walked over to me, tipping my chin back.

"I can't handle you being within touching distance of him." Taylor stated bluntly. I tried to not smile because *when had he gotten so possessive?* We all remember when Taylor and I first met, right? It wasn't exactly best friends at first sight. I couldn't help but love how protective and possessive he'd become over me. Don't get me wrong, the bastard was still crazy and did insane shit, but he also was pretty damn cute.

I sighed and looked at both twins, they didn't seem to disagree in the least. I looked at Palo and he put his hands up, excusing himself from being the voice of reason. Instead he left the office muttering under his breath. Probably about Marabella, he was also a bit obsessive where she was involved.

I leaned against the desk, breaking away from them and sitting my butt on the edge of it. "I'm not sure what you guys want me to do, *really.* I am not about to treat Rainer like shit just because I don't want to marry him. He's not into me, so all of you need to chill out so this works, and please, for the love of the gods, keep Adyen and Rhodes from freaking out."

"Why would I freak out?" Rhodes asked as he entered, his eyes a pale green that crawled over my body. All of them were dressed in official armor and I had to admit, being around them was absolutely intoxicating. Who knew I would be so turned on by armor and intense warrior men.

Said no woman ever.

"Gray thinks it would be a good idea if she keeps up appearances by acting as if she is going to marry the Light Heir tonight," Neo murmured, pulling me into his chest so that I couldn't maintain a distance from them. His lips pressed to my forehead as Taylor narrowed his eyes at my injured lip where I had bitten it by accident. He stepped into my space and grasped my jaw gently looking frustrated.

Rhodes spoke, "No. I can't handle that, Gray. I understand if you have to be polite but I can't see you touching him, all civilized behavior will be out the door."

"Why would she be touching him?" Adyen snarled from where he appeared in the door. That was about when I gave up. I sighed crossing my arms as Adyen started to go off on a tangent that was only made worse by Taylor amping him up. I think I stood there for about five minutes trying to think about something that would distract them from this wedding.

Oh!

"Hey guys," I chimed as if they weren't talking about killing Rainer, "so after all this nonsense with the Light Fae, what are we doing about our wedding?"

Bingo.

All five of them stilled and snapped their gazes towards me as if I had spoken a foreign language. For the record, I hadn't. I swallowed down any insecurities, reminding myself how they felt, as I crossed my arms waiting for their response.

"Wedding?" Athens asked, his eyes wide and darkened with heat. Huh. Who knew that weddings could turn people on? I hadn't.

I looked over them and their shocked faces, "Well, yeah, I figured we were going to get married… I mean we don't have to…"

No one offered me an answer, their mouths open, so I straightened myself, "Well, once you snap out of this, let me know our plans." I was out of the room then, sliding past Adyen, his dragon releasing a low rumble. The massive steps leading from my office were large and stone, twisting and turning until they reached the throne room. I didn't hear anything behind me which made me smile, knowing I had shocked them into silence. It was sort of awesome.

I wish I could tell you that I was looking forward to this feast, like the other two, but what I really craved? A good glass of wine and some de-stressing.

For the record, I wasn't very worried about their reaction or lack there of vocally regarding the wedding. For several reasons I suppose. One of them, despite not saying it to Taylor, I knew that these men loved me. I smiled softly, I loved them probably more than they would realize *but* I did know how devoted and loving they were. *They were my favorite psychos.* I had also heard them talking about asking me to marry them when they thought I was distracted.

I loved Vegas but I wasn't one to wait around waiting for someone to purpose to me. I wasn't a very patient person to begin with. Although to be fair there were a lot more of them to consider. In the end, I hadn't even asked them to marry me. I had just assumed because it was a safer route. Right? Alright now I was a bit nervous. Hopefully, saying it out loud would distract them in a positive way so that we could get through tonight. When I reached the doors leading to the throne room, I found Luna and Esme waiting, talking quietly. The latter helped me into my silver cloak and adjusted my crown, my brother showing up seconds later.

"You look nice!" I noted to my brother, his dark almost purple hair pulled back in a long braid and his entire black outfit spotless with dark purple accents.

He grunted offering a frustrated look that made me smile. I looked around and saw my boys making their way down the stairs while maintaining a quiet conversation, that made me laugh. All of them snapped their heads up as I stared at them with open amusement, which had half of them scowling. Instead of commenting on it I straightened and as they announced the Light Fae into the hall, Rhodes and Adyen stepped up next to me.

"We're talking about this later, kitten." Rhodes growled as Adyen hummed in agreement, coming out far more like rolling thunder in his chest.

"Maybe," I whispered as we walked through the arch, "maybe I am offended by your lack of an answer."

I wasn't.

I searched the hall, noting how beautiful it was, the elegant navy and silver complimented by the pale yellow. The marble white flooring and walls drew attention to my massive dark throne that highlighted the centre stage. Everyone's eyes snapped from the Light Fae royalty to us and luckily, I was able to monitor my reaction. *Holy shit, they'd brought everyone.*

The entire hall was split half between dark blue and silver, the other a pale gold and white. I kept my face neutral as I stood in front of the throne that was placed up higher than the table set aside for all of us to eat at front and center of the hall.

I was really thankful for Silas right now.

My brother began to talk, his voice professional and loud, as he greeted the Light Fae and made a lengthy metaphor about unity and the symbolic nature of alliances, without once mentioning either of our names. That was a skill. My eyes drifted towards my betrothed and I offered him a small smile, his eyes relaxing a bit at something he saw in my expression. As a True Heir the man was very powerful and I could feel it drifting off him, similar to the King and Queen, his parents.

There was tension in his form and the moment he looked away from me his eyes were back on my brother. I swallowed down a bit of emotion because it was very clear that their communication had far surpassed the level of 'friendship' a bit ago. Despite my annoyance with my brother, I wanted the two of them to have their happily ever after. Not just because it served my purpose either. Honestly, their connection just pushed me further to make this work.

Rainer looked nearly as though he was heart-broken, his expression filled with sadness and his hazel eyes nearly black. He was a beautiful man, his skin a deep burgundy with thick dark braids that were adorned with gold accents, and if this was a different situation, in a different life, I would be happy about marrying someone like him. I mean, I'm still against arranged marriages, I'm just saying that this could have been far worse. He was a good man and it helped that he was handsome.

After a bit my feet began to hurt, so I shifted uncomfortably as I tried to maintain a pleasant expression. My brother, right on time, announced that Rainer could step forward and I moved a step down to meet him, his bow low as he grabbed my hand. Our magic meeting and offering each other pleasantries.

"Queen Gray," He stated, his voice soft and pleasant.

"Rainer," I smiled, "good to see you again." He went to pull away but I clasped my other hand over his and leaned closer.

"Be in the East Wing at midnight tonight, there are things we need to discuss," I spoke quietly. "Trust me." His nod was immediate and he pulled away, his eyes flashing to Silas. 'We' would consist of my brother and him. I trusted Silas to be able to express the plan and idea moving forward. The only possible issue? I suppose if Rainer didn't want to marry him but if I was going to take a guess, I would say that wouldn't be an issue.

Immediately after our greeting, music started up and he led me towards the table where I sat next to Rainer, with Silas on his side and Rhodes on mine. The rest of my men were lined up behind me and I relaxed the moment that Rhodes's hand touched my leg, his eyes understanding but a bit vulnerable.

I needed this to be over. I hated any of my men not knowing where we stood, it made me extremely uncomfortable.

The food was fantastic, although unfortunately my appetite was lacking because of all the wedding talk that the Light Fae King, Axion, and Queen, Elena, were determined to entertain us with. As the moments went by and the two of us, meaning Rainer and I, had drunk more wine, I felt Rhodes get more frustrated with their talk. Hell, I could practically hear Adyen's possessive rumbling behind me.

"Oh!" Elena smiled, "and we can't forget, once you two settle down, we can find a place maybe on the Elven lands? For a vacation spot for our family, hopefully you two will start giving both our kingdoms little heirs…"

I was about to lose it but then Taylor was there, his hands on my shoulder as he spoke against my ear, "Gray, you have to make them stop, please, baby girl? I can't handle it. Adyen is about to fucking lose it and I don't trust Rhodes either. You have to change the conversation or step away."

Offering a nod I stood as if he had just said something very important to me, "If you don't mind, I'll be right back. Please excuse me."

I turned and walked past the twins, both of them looking tense and uncomfortable as I heard Silas take over the conversation.

Taylor placed a hand on my lower back and the moment we were through closed doors I was pressed against the hard stone wall, my demon bearing down on me.

I was not complaining.

Taylor's scent wrapped around me and my fingers curled into his crimson hair as he pressed his forehead to my own. "I can't handle that, baby girl." He growled pressing his lips to mine. "I can't handle them talking about a fucking wedding and especially you having his fucking kids. I want to hurt the fucker and he hasn't even said anything."

"Taylor." I pressed my lips to his lightly as I grasped his face to look into his eyes. "After this dinner is over, it will be like it never happened. You know I'm yours. If I am marrying anyone it's the five of you, no one else. I promise."

His bright green eyes flitted between each of mine before he spoke quietly. "I love you Gray. I need you, baby girl. Tell me you're mine. I can't go through this entire fucking dinner without knowing you're mine."

"Of course I'm yours." I purred running my hand down his leather armor until I reached the ties of his leather pants and his hardening cock. "I don't want you to worry about that, Taylor."

"Tell me," He whispered, pressing his lips against mine, nipping it sharply.

"Tell you what?" I can't help the small smile on my lips.

"What I want to hear." He growled as I unlaced the leather ties and loosened them enough to have access to him. All of him.

"What is it that you want me to say?" In a swift movement I turned him, his back against the wall, as I sunk to my knees and looked up at him. Instead of an answer he let out a dangerous sound and I pushed his leather pants down low enough that his massive cock bounced out and I immediately gripped it in my hand, offering him a small smirk at his growl.

"Gray," He rumbled as I licked the rim of his cock, the precum a salty explosive taste.

"I love you," I whispered, he groaned and then hit the stone wall behind him with his fist as I took him completely into my mouth and down my throat. I began to slide his length in and out of me as my tongue wrapped on the underneath of his cock, his hands finally gripping my hair tight enough that tears stung my eyes. My movements were slow, and every time he tried to take control, I stopped dead. Eventually after my teasing he hit his breaking point, I was deep throating him when he pulled me off him and took me to the ground.

Mind you, we were *right* outside the banquet hall.

"Better stay quiet, baby girl," he growled, flipping my dress up and snapping my lace boyshorts, tossing them to the side, "wouldn't want your *fiancé* hearing." The word fiancé sounded like a curse in his mouth and I would be lying if I said it didn't turn me the fuck on.

I let out a hiss as Taylor wasted zero time burying himself deep inside of me, his hands pressing on my thighs to open me up to him. My back arched as I pulled him down to me, needing his lips on mine so I didn't scream. I knew we were making a bit of noise but I couldn't help it. The way he was taking me on the floor like he couldn't wait to be inside of me had me soaking wet and the harder and longer he fucked me, the louder I got. Not even his hand on my mouth was able to stop my moans, luckily I could also tell the music had gotten louder post dinner so maybe they wouldn't hear.

I didn't really fucking care.

"Gray," He groaned, pumping into me and filling me completely, making me clench around him, "I love you so much, baby girl."

"I love you more." I gasped as he sucked on my neck, no doubt leaving a massive hickey. Possessive bastard. Any sarcastic retort was gone though as he began to fuck me senseless, my body shaking as a hand wrapped around my throat. I let out a cry as he pulled my bottom lip between his teeth and bit down, the taste of my blood between us. I exploded around him and after another few hard thrusts, Taylor growled and buried himself deep inside of me, climaxing with a possessive snarl.

Well then.

"Think they heard us?" I grinned as my demon pulled back his eyes sparkling with a sated yet simmering heat. There was amusement there and a smug glint. Bastard.

"I fucking hope they did!" He growled nipping my injured lip before helping me up and adjusting my dress. My crown was tilted, my dress wrinkled, and my lip bleeding. I felt fucking amazing though. I wrapped my arms around him and Taylor nuzzled my neck, whispering softly in the Horde language, a bunch of sweet shit I would usually punch him for.

"Alright, baby girl," he whispered, as his hands were crawling along the final tattoo on my back that had now been filled in, "you ready for the next few hours?"

I pulled back, catching my reflection in the mirror, and using a simple glamour to make myself look put together and back to normal, despite his scowl. "Are you ready?" I asked back, more concerned about his reaction.

My demon shrugged, opening the door. "Guess we will see. Heads up, if someone dies it's because I wasn't ready." I couldn't help but laugh at that. I fucking loved Taylor.

6
NEO

One thing left to do.

The night was nearly over and this was an essential aspect of making sure all of this bullshit ended. I couldn't handle the concept of Gray being someone else's on a good day and today was not a good fucking day. I didn't want to leave her in the hall but my mission was simple: walk with Silas to meet up with Rainer to make sure things went smoothly. It was maybe five minutes until midnight and the two of us walked in silence, Silas vibrating with tension.

You know, in retrospect, I was probably not the right person to go with him.

I mean I wasn't exactly known for my emotional range. Trying to figure out what to say was a bit of a dilemma to me but I tried to imagine what I would do if my brother was dealing with something similar. I almost smirked at that, I couldn't wait till I told Athens that I was pretending I was talking to him. He would, one hundred percent, be offended that I thought he needed to be talked through shit.

"You know," I started, "you don't have to do this. Gray believes that you want Rainer, if you don't, walk away from this.

No one will blame you. After all, we aren't trying to create another unwanted marriage."

Silas snapped his head toward me, "It's not that. I do want this. Very much so."

"So why do you seem upset?" I asked curiously.

"Because, there is a chance he may not want me." Silas whispered looking beyond frustrated. Ah fuck. See? This was not my ball park.

"Want my opinion?" I asked curiously.

"Yes," he whispered as we reached the foyer of the East Wing.

"From what I've seen," I spoke honestly, "that isn't going to be an issue."

"Silas?" A voice echoed softly before he could respond. I stepped back slightly as Rainer appeared in the room, both of them looking at one another with wide eyed concern and honestly sort of heart-breaking expressions.

"I am going to leave you two to talk." I noted turning on my heel but neither of them were listening to me as Rainer crossed the room and pulled Silas against him. My lips pressed up into an actual smile as I turned and walked away.

That went far easier than I expected.

The halls were quiet until I came to the cross section, where I could see the East Wing. I saw someone walking along the shadows and I shook my head, slowing my walk that way. What I came upon made my chest hurt just a bit, because Luna was hugging Kai, his mouth dipping into a sad grimace. The two of them looked fucking miserable. We hadn't heard back about his decision from Marabella, only Marcus, so I had an idea of what this was about.

"Luna?" I asked as she jumped and Kai offered me a tired and sad look. I wasn't positive if any of the others had a clue on what Kai was but his magic was very strong. The type that would do well in the SE guard if developed. My guess? He was some type of hybrid because he wasn't anything I'd come across before and that goes for his brother as well.

"Dad," She sniffed as I realized she was crying.

"What's going on?" I asked Kai.

He spoke honestly, "I am leaving town, probably going to the Light Fae lands. I can't stay here."

Luna gripped his shoulders, "Just join the SE, you would have somewhere to live and be with your brother."

"If I may," I asked, curious about the situation. "why haven't you accepted the offer?"

He winced and ran a hand through his hair. "I have stolen from nearly everyone in the Horde, or close to it. The SE Guard knows me and I imagine that their reaction will be worse than yours. I would rather live alone and on the road than be harassed everyday."

He was right, they would. I respected the establishment I was part of but there was, no doubt, really shitty people. I examined Luna's heartbroken face and I realized that I was about to make four people in total very happy today, this shit was exhausting. My own mother would roll her eyes at that thought for sure.

"Kai, come Monday, I want you to report to training. Your brother and yourself will be given a place in the castle, seperate from the SE guard dorms. You both can apprentice separately under my brother and I. I have a feeling as it is, that your magic is going to require special attention anyway."

Luna's face broke into a smile so I continued before she could explode into confetti. "I will make sure that no level of harassment occurs as long as you agree to two promises."

Kai nodded slowly looking nervous. "Which are?"

"I don't want any more of *this*," I started looking at the two of them, "especially at night. I'm not saying you can't be friends, before you object, Luna. When they aren't training you can hang out all day, but let me make myself clear, I do *not* want *anyone* in your room at night. You're both too old for that not to mean something more, understand?"

Luna nodded looking confused because I doubt she understood what I was saying, the message was more for Kai who offered a sharp nod. It wasn't that I thought the kid had nefarious intentions, really. His feelings seemed pure enough towards her, *but* I remember what I was like around his age and it only got worse as I got older. Far better to stop it now.

"Secondly, no more stealing." I stated simply.

"I stole mostly to survive." He explained quietly.

"I'm guilty too then." Luna chirped. "He gave most of the food to me."

Kai turned bright red and I was very much secured in my choice. "Well, there are worse reasons to steal. Off to bed now, Luna. Go on."

She hugged Kai quickly and turned into the room, leaving me with the kid. I nodded toward the stairs and he followed, both of us pausing as Jude appeared at the top of the staircase turning bright pink. *Christ.* I shook my head and pointed towards the ballroom.

"I was just concerned." Jude growled out, looking at Kai.

"I would never hurt her!" Kai spat out at Jude. I felt myself nearly roll my eyes as I put a large hand on the back of their heads, pushing them along.

"Both of you are going to make sure you never hurt her, or else," I noted stopping myself from a full threat. They were just kids. Just kids. I kept reminding myself so I didn't threaten them as I would an adult.

"Yes, Sir." Jude muttered and Kai nodded. Both of them walked ahead and started arguing more as I shook my head. Passing one of my head guards I fixed him with a look.

"Do me a favor and post two guards outside of Princess Luna's room." I explained.

"For how long?" He asked curiously.

"Till she's sixty-something!" I shook my head as he chuckled but began giving orders. *Who knew someone could be so damn persistent at twelve and fourteen? It was fucking ridiculous.*

As I came back into the ballroom I offered Rhodes a nod, and I saw relief fill him. I stopped by my mother's table and she offered me a smile, kissing my cheek. I was thrilled to have her back in my life but I was still getting used to it.

"Everything okay?" She asked softly.

I sighed, "It's been a night for sure."

She squeezed my shoulder reassuringly. "I have no doubt you six will figure it out."

With that I walked towards Gray, her eyes filled with lightness. I offered Taylor the conversation regarding Luna through my memories and I saw as he offered it into everyone else's minds. Even Gray raised her eyebrows in surprise. Before I had a chance to comment on it, an odd feeling ran up my spine and I looked around the room.

A low rumble broke from my chest as a bad feeling settled in my chest. Fuck. I hated not understanding these odd random premonitions I had. It had been fairly recent development that left me frustrated more often than not. I wasn't positive if it was because of my connection to Gray, or just a later development of my powers.

"Everything okay?" Gray asked quietly as I examined her face. She didn't need any more stress.

"Absolutely." I said with a small smile, moving to stand next to her. I was really hoping it was nothing.

7
TAYLOR

The evening was nearly over and I was feeling far better, partly because I could smell myself on her skin. I wanted her to let down that damn glamour so I could see the marks I'd left on her skin. Instead we continued to act professional and I could feel the tension relax from my body when the Light Fae hierarchy went to their quarters for the night. Gray had Neo go with Silas, just to make sure the two of them met up. It was clear that the trip had been successful and I couldn't describe the relief I felt at that. I could see the weight being lifted from her as well and it was clear to me, as well as everyone else, that Gray also hoped that it would work out in order to secure her brother's happiness. Despite not admitting it, I knew she loved her brother. He might annoy the fuck out of her but Gray never let go of those that she cared about.

Much like the rest of our family it seemed. I had no idea how Luna had developed that trait. I was a bit shocked to watch the memory play across Neo's mind and to be honest, I didn't disagree with his choice but it did surprise me. He was usually rather violent, but instead he'd taken a peaceful compromise.

"Remind me to never set up an arranged marriage for our children." Gray spoke from where she was sitting on her throne with us around her, our eyes on the massive ballroom floor. "Also remind me, keep Luna busy."

"She wants to join the SE Academy." I noted softly.

Gray's eyes lit up, "I am very torn about that. Part of me loves that idea and the other part of me worries, about… well, anything relating to her." I nodded in agreement.

Those boys had better watch themselves. I remember exactly what I was fucking thinking about at thirteen and Luna doesn't need to be around that. *She's not even eleven yet for fuck sake.*

"That reminds me, kitten. While we're talking about our future kids." Rhodes circled around so that he was standing in front of her. "What was it you were saying about marriage earlier?"

Gray blinked her massive dark eyes innocently, "Marriage? I said kids, who said anything about marriage?"

"You would have kids with us but not talk about marriage?" I winked in a teasing tone.

Her smile at that was amused but ultimately sly. "Are you admitting that you want to have kids with me?"

"I would love to put a baby in you." I let out a low rumble as her eyes darkened with heat. Really though. My demon fucking loved the idea of knocking her up. It was totally unhealthy.

"Please try to focus?" Rhodes reminded us as we both sighed and looked up at our control freak.

"What about marriage, sweetheart?" Gray goaded going back to his question.

"Baby," Athens complained. "we just want you to repeat what you said earlier."

Neo shook his head while he ran a hand along the back of her head, massaging it slightly so that she became more relaxed. Adyen looked grumpy as fuck and I could tell he was trying to ignore the conversation and failing. Gray stretched her arms up, her breasts pressing against her dress and making me want to rip it down the middle. I nearly growled thinking about how tight and wet she had been only hours ago. Couldn't I just have her climb on top of me so she can ride me right in the middle of the throne room? Was that too much to ask?

"Oh yes!" She chimed, looking playful. "I asked what we were doing about our wedding."

"You want to marry us?" Adyen asked immediately as she arched a brow.

"Well…" Right as I was about to hear the fucking answer I wanted, the room shook and an explosive sound echoed through the halls blasting open the doors. Immediately, I was up and had Gray wrapped in my arms as we watched the smoke clear.

No one. There was absolutely no one there. No army, no group of guards waiting. *What the fuck?!*

SE Guards started to scramble and search the space as Adyen began shouting orders. Without asking her, I led Gray from the room and towards her private quarters. Oddly enough she didn't argue and instead there was a tension running through her, as if she knew something I didn't. As we walked quickly up the staircase, I found myself very happy that Neo had stationed guards outside of Luna's room. I had no idea what the fuck was going on but this shit needed to end. We deserved some goddamn peace and quiet. When we reached the fourth flight, her hand hit my chest and she backed me up against the wall despite the silent hallway. We were right outside her suite yet she kept us from making that final turn. When I went to ask, she placed a hand over my mouth. I tried to extend my senses but then several things happened at once.

First, Gray's magic shot out to shield us and trap me from movement. Secondly, the hallway suddenly rocked with another explosion that without a doubt came from her room. I snarled as a figure darted out from the smoke and attempted to run past us. Gray's arm snapped out to grab them by the arm, snapping it and slamming them against the floor, causing the figure to cry out. His magic faltered as hers moved from me to wrap fully around his, vibrating with furious anger.

"You are such a fucking bastard!" She growled and my demon snarled at her endangerment. The smoke cleared to reveal *fucking Colliard!*

Oh, you have got to be fucking kidding me.

"*Your Majesty.*" He sneered as he darkened into a shade of purple from lack of oxygen. I couldn't believe I had looked up to this man as a child. For someone who used to be held in such high regard, the man looked like total shit. He had not only lost weight but his face was covered in sweat and dust. He looked fucking awful.

"Colliard." Her voice was a soft hiss. "This was by far the stupidest fucking mistake you've made in your entire life. By far more even than being a traitor to my kingdom. Why? Why the fuck did you come back?"

He snarled and tried to move but my boot came down right on his pelvis. I had no doubt Gray had it but hey, just in fucking case right? Colliard cried out and I smirked as Adyen rounded up the stairs, his eyes landed right on him and I saw fury pass over his face. Without asking for confirmation, the man grabbed Colliard, his dragon no doubt in charge, before slamming him up on the wall. I didn't wince when I heard his head hit against the stone but I didn't imagine that it felt very good.

"You dumb motherfucker!" He growled. "Neo, go make sure we have a cell open until we know what we want to do with him." Neo's eyes filled with malice from where he had arrived on the staircase.

Adyen continued, "Are there anymore god damn bombs? Better yet, were you working with anyone else?"

Colliard's eyes were filled with fear as he spoke softly. "No one else, just me." He said it as if it was a bitter thing. As though he was surprised he didn't have followers. "It was just the two."

"Gray?" Adyen looked at her as I realized I was locking Gray into place protectively, her eyes on my face as she cautiously watched the two of us, probably worried that we would end up going all caveman. I was pretty close to it.

"Lock him up until we talk, make sure to search the entire castle anyway." She commanded and her body vibrated with tension. Adyen didn't waste time, grabbing him and walking down the steps, away from our view. The silence felt tense and I kissed her neck as she let out a long exhale, relaxing back into me. Rhodes appeared as I heard Athens decide to follow Adyen downstairs, his voice low and dark at his father's obvious arrival.

"Are you okay, kitten?" Rhodes asked softly, grabbing her jaw.

"Yes," she whispered and shook her head, "fucking bastard, I should have known." Her eyes suddenly widened with horror. "Luna? Is she okay?"

"She is completely fine, do you want me to bring her here or have her stay in the East Tower."

"East Tower." She spoke and he left us, her head falling forward as she shook it. I lifted her easily and she didn't even protest, making me know she was exhausted.

"Are you okay? Really, baby girl?" I whispered softly feeling very concerned about her.

"No." She whispered, looking pale. "What if we'd been asleep? Or Marabella had been in there? Or Luna had been in there, still in kitten form?!" I could see panic overriding her and I knew Gray had a hard time not being able to protect everyone at all times. It was why she probably kept people away for so long, because when Gray loved, she loved with everything she had.

"Everyone is okay." I whispered and began walking her down the stairs, knowing that she did not need to see the explosive mess that was her suite. "Plus, now we can build a room that fits all of us."

Gray offered me a small smile and clung onto me just a bit tighter than normal. It filled me with warmth and made me feel like we had finally found that balance. Although I was positive that I was willing to do anything and everything for her, was that balanced or obsessive? Maybe a bit of both. It seemed to run in the family.

As we entered the massive hall, I noticed that some had sustained wounds from shattered glass and broken up pieces of marble. One of those overseeing it was Palo. I didn't see Marabella or Bobby, but I made my way over there. Gray stopped and talked to people as she passed trying to ensure that everyone was indeed alright. I approached my brother.

"You're hurt." I noted quietly as Palo fixed me with a look. While good at hiding it I could smell his blood and wound on his shoulder from shattered glass. I also knew he was a stubborn bastard and wouldn't ask for help. Hell, most likely he wouldn't even pull it out until he was alone.

"I'm fine." He stated softly.

"Come on." I nodded towards the corner of the room and the tables there. "Let me help you."

My brother and I had always been sort of close, but we were so different and there was a natural distance that came along with that. I'd been jealous I hadn't had his brains, because it meant that I'd been chosen for the SE position, something I hadn't wanted at the time. He'd been bitter about always being alone, which was something he clearly grew up to enjoy. He was still my brother though, despite being a moody unstable asshole.

"Is everyone else alright?" I asked regarding our family, as Palo nodded and followed me, mind you looking very disgruntled, towards the table. He sat with his back facing the room as he took off his jacket wincing. I studied the embedded glass and sighed.

"This is going to hurt like a bitch." I stated bluntly and braced his shoulder pulling it out swiftly, without breaking it which caused him to let out a low growl. The glass fell to the floor and I took a dining napkin and dipped it in some water, wiping blood away from the wound.

"Thanks." He muttered as I watched the wound begin to heal.

I offered him a grin and clasped his other shoulder. "That's what I'm here for, brother."

Palo looked surprised by my statement but just nodded as we both stood. Gray walked over and met both our gazes before noting his shoulder.

"Everything okay?" She asked quietly.

"I'm fine." He nodded and then walked toward Marabella and Bobby.

"Is he?" Gray asked, looking concerned.

I cupped her jaw, "As fine as Palo can be." My cheeky smile had her rolling her eyes.

"What now?" She asked curiously looking around.

"Now? We figure out where everyone who is without a room is going to sleep." I kissed her temple, and then added, "And we figure out what to do with that bastard downstairs."

A snarl broke through her lips as she nodded. "I think I have the perfect punishment for him."

I bet she did.

8
GRAY

Exhausted was an understatement. Honestly, right now I was close to telling the Light Fae to go stick it where the sun doesn't shine because I had bigger fish to fry. The suite we were staying in tonight was smaller, but I found I didn't care as I soaked in the bathtub, my eyes closing as I nearly fell asleep. I had so many issues to resolve in the morning. Colliard. This marriage contract. Just a lot to deal with and right now I was sort of hoping that I could sleep for twelve hours. We could have the meeting tomorrow evening instead, right?

Probably not.

Dipping my head under the water, I rinsed out the lavender conditioner and opened my eyes. I wasn't very surprised to find Neo there, his gaze watchful and filled with pain. Reaching for him, his hand intertwined with mine easily.

"Gray," He whispered, looking furious. "I am so sorry that he has ever been part of this equation."

"Hey," I gripped his jaw, stepping out of the tub and wrapping a towel around myself, "none of that is or was your fault, Neo. He's a bastard and you are far better than him, you have been from the start."

He swallowed offering a small nod before lifting me from the steamy bathroom, and he carried me towards the large bed. Athens laid there his eyes dark and watchful as Neo let my towel drop, leaving me very naked and between the two of them.

The serious tone of the room had any teasing comments that had existed on my tongue disappearing. Instead, my mouth was busy being devoured as Athens pressed a searing kiss to my lips. His fingers gently rolling over my clit and my soaking pussy. I shivered as I felt Neo's magic crawl over my skin and press my legs open, his hot breath against my center.

"You are so beautiful," Athens murmured, kissing my jawline and along my silver scar. I let out a breathy moan as Neo ran his tongue against my slit, causing me to arch against his brother, who was now kissing and nipping along my neck. Their mouths were teasing on my body as I gripped the sheets trying to create some sort of friction but Neo just chuckled softly, stilling my body with his grip and keeping it under his control.

"Please," I whispered as Athens tongue swirled around my nipple, refusing to actually touch it and making me want to cry out in frustration. His large hands gently gathered my wrists and pulled them up as metal cuffs formed from the bed frame, keeping me completely exposed and at their will.

"Let me know if you want them off," He murmured but I cried out Neo's name as he sucked on my clit, making my legs shake and a climax build. It was right fucking there. Then the bastard pulled away his eyes sparkling with dark intent.

Neo spoke softly with a smug grin, "Were you about to cum, Gray?"

"Yes!" I nearly scowled as Athens tugged off his shirt and then his pants, making my eyes dart down to his massive cock, pressing against his boxers.

Neo nipped my hip causing me to look back down as he offered me a cheeky smile. "You didn't ask to cum though."

"I have to ask now?" I narrowed my eyes but my body disagreed because I could literally feel myself growing wetter as his fingers worked their way in and out of me, his tone turning me on. Slowly but building in sensation, making my body turn pink and my nipples harden into painfully tight buds.

"Although it may be difficult with something in her mouth," Athens pointed out with a chuckle as I felt his cock nudged against my lips and I couldn't help but let my tongue dart out. He groaned as I opened my mouth and Neo chuckled at my whimper as he pulled away. I would have looked up but Athens had control of my head and before I knew it, a soft silky material was covering my eyes as Neo nipped my ear and disappeared again.

Without being able to see my senses exploded and I could only imagine Neo watching me writhing with need while I sucked off his brother. Athens let out a low growl as I took him completely into my throat, my eyes tearing a bit at the sensation.

I moaned around it as he held himself deep in my throat, his grip tight as Neo's impossibly hard cock pressed right against my folds, sliding back and forth in my wet heat. He groaned, "Fuck you are so wet, Gray. I could cum from just thinking about how fucking tight you are."

Athens pulled back as I gasped for air, my lips popping open only to welcome him back in. Neo pressed in slowly, his pace almost gentle despite how much he was pushing my body to accomodate for him. I let out a cry around Athens as Neo pushed in fully, his thrusts deep and hard as Athens began to match it, both of them using me completely to satisfy themselves. My body was shaking with the need for release and this time when I hit the peak, Neo pushed me past it by biting down on my nipple. Heat exploded in my center and the wait had me nearly seeing stars in relief. Fuck. They could use me every single day if that was how it was going to feel. I was shaking in relief.

"Bad Gray," he snarled, "you were supposed to ask."

"Hard to with Athens in my throat," I mumbled as Athens chuckled surging forward again.

"True." Neo conceded, "Brother, maybe she needs you elsewhere."

Oh shit. I hadn't thought this through clearly.

My handcuffs disappeared but Neo grasped my wrists as he righted me so that I was now straddling him, his cock so deep inside of me I was convinced he was touching my womb. I was panting with need and they seemed to be purposefully torturing me as Athens appeared behind me, his hand wrapping around my throat.

"Do you want this, Gray?" He snarled. "Do you want both of us filling you completely?"

"Yes!" I whispered eagerly. My cry of Athens's name was authentic as he pressed against my ass and slid in, my body tensing at how large the two of them were. I could feel tears soaking my face as pleasure exploded in my center, making me feel nearly euphoric.

Then they started fucking me. Whatever pace they'd been going before had been with great restraint. My voice nearly went hoarse as they started pounding into me, their fucking twin sandwich making my covered eyes roll back as their grips tightened into brusing holds. I was barely holding myself up as Neo grasped my jaw and spoke.

"Open up," He whispered and I did, another cock pressing right against my lips. *When the fuck had he gotten here?* Taylor's magic wrapped around me as he slid into my throat and pulled at my hair going to the opposite of their pace, making me feel like I was being tugged in a million different directions. There was no controlling it. I gave into it and the climax that blasted through me, making me nearly pass out.

"Fuck!" Taylor snarled in a dangerous tone, moving faster. "It is so fucking hot watching you deep throat me, baby girl."

I heard Athens roar out my name and tighten his grip on my throat as he exploded inside of my ass and Neo followed quickly after, his grip bruising and demanding. I cried out around Taylor as he slammed in deep, filling me completely. I swallowed instinctually as Taylor spilled into my throat and I could feel any energy I had left seeping from my body. I was ready to collapse.

Neo disappeared from under me as a pair of warm hands positioned me over their cock. My voice was a whisper as Rhodes kissed my lips, not giving a fuck about Taylor having been there. "I can't."

I really thought I was about to pass out.

"Sure you can, kitten." Rhodes purred as my entire body heated again. My magic was in heaven. As he slid inside of me and began to bounce me up and down his cock, my body reacted and tightened, causing me to let my head fall back in pleasure. *Fuck. This felt amazing.* Adyen's mouth was there then, against my neck and he pressed behind me, his cock feeling very daunting as he lined up with my ass. As he eased inside of me, I began to roll my hips and I actually was thankful because the two of them kept a slow yet impossibly deep pace.

It was intoxicating and I lost track of time, also pretty damn sure I would never see again, the dark silk felt very familiar and it was soaked with tears of pleasure. I gasped out my release as my nails broke Rhodes's skin, I could feel the other hands on my body as they touched every single sensitive part of me. My magic was alive and dangerous, the tattoos on my back searing as electrical shocks went through my body like pulses. I cried out something unintelligible as both of them finished, their teeth finding their mating marks and filling me with more cum, probably enough at this point that it was going to just spill the fuck out of me.

My body was like jello as I slid onto my side and I didn't

bother opening my eyes when the blindfold came off. Unconsciousness consumed me and I fell into it easily.

Athens

She was so fucking beautiful, it was actually painful to look at her. Which I could. Literally all night. Her flushed and passed out form pressed between Adyen and Taylor as I walked out from taking a shower, ready to figure out what the fuck to do about this entire mess. Neo was showered as well and Rhodes was in there, set on coming with us.

We really hadn't planned on any of what had just happened but the minute we started fucking her, I felt like I couldn't stop. I had honestly never lasted that long in my life, I was impressed by myself, and I had been practically choked by her tight ass. I could see my bruised finger prints on her and that made me irrationally possessive.

When the others had walked in, that shit had just happened and considering how sated she looked, it seemed to have been the right move. Gods. Couldn't I just get back in fucking bed with her?

"Are you ready to get this shit done with?" Neo asked softly.

"Yeah," I nodded. "Rhodes, you good?"

The man dried off his hair and slipped on his shirt, about as casual as we could get in just athletic wear. That was fine, I didn't need to look nice for what I was about to do. The three of us walked out of the room and down a few sets of stairs. I was just going for closure. I kept saying that yet the closer I got, the more furious I became.

When we finally reached the dungeons, the guards stationed there offered us salutes and let us pass through. Rhodes stayed outside the main door. "Just call if you need anything."

The two of us entered into the hall where our father was being held, alone and in the dark except for the pale light shining from the small window in the door. Neo growled quietly as our father came to stand at the bars so we could see his eyes.

"Boys," He offered a hopeful look. "have you come to bail me out?"

Was he fucking joking?

"Why the fuck would we bail you out?" Neo tilted his head. "You betrayed the Horde and nearly fucking killed my future wife tonight. If anything, I should kill you right now."

Our father had a terrible temper and I could see him turning red in the face. "You've always been a horrible son, I should have left you with your fucking mother."

"But you didn't," I spoke softly. "you left me instead. Then you beat the son you *were* lucky enough to have."

My father snarled. "You have no idea what your fucking talking about, I didn't touch him."

"Liar!" Neo whispered his voice menacing. "You are such a piece of shit. I have no idea how I looked up to you. I can't wait until you hear your verdict tomorrow."

We had an idea of what Gray was thinking but it wasn't for certain yet. Neo was gone then, probably unable to stay in the room without killing him. I watched my father as he turned his attention to me.

"Athens," My father begged, "I understand that I made a mistake choosing him. I should have never done that. What can I do to make it up to you? Can we start over?"

I walked closer and spoke softly, "No. There is nothing to start over. You never chose me and you never will because you only choose yourself. I don't need you."

As I was turning to walk away he snarled, "This is why no one fucking chooses you!"

I chuckled, "No, that is where you are wrong. I have someone that chose me."

Leaving him in that dark, and probably filthy, cell felt liberating and Rhodes offered both of us nods as we walked back up towards the West Wing. In the mess of the incident, we had been able to track down everyone, including Luna. She'd been so fast asleep she had barely heard the incident which I was thankful for. What had happened tonight, should have never occurred.

When we reached the room, we found Gray awake which was odd but she was freshly showered and sitting on the window ledge. Both of the other guys were still sleeping, her eyes met ours as she offered a small smile.

"I didn't think you would be awake." I commented softly, as she stood up and wrapped her arms around my neck.

"We need to decide where to send him." She whispered.

Neo grunted, "I don't give a fuck, you can kill him if you want to."

She squeezed his hand and I settled her on my lap as the four of us sat around the fireplace. The woman's body recouped so fast, and I could practically feel her buzzing with lively energy. I loved it.

"I want to send him to the Elven realm." She stated softly.

Rhodes chuckled, "He may flourish there."

She hummed. "No, I don't think so."

The Elven realm was in a word, excessive. There were no rules in the Kingdom of Day so it was filled with horrible acts. Everything from stealing to public sex were celebrated, and crimes, even murder, were considered daily occurences. It was the place where most of the other realm's citizens went to lose themselves. Being a prisoner there would be horrifying.

"Why not the Kingdom of Night?" Neo asked quietly.

The Kingdom of Night was a smaller rouge branch that had broken off. It was extremely successful and wealthy, but very exclusive about who it invited in. I said, "King Adriel would no doubt be thrilled to get a hold of him."

"I know," Gray sighed. "but he doesn't deserve such a normal treatment."

Her eyes then looked over both of our faces. "If you're okay with that?"

"As I said before," Neo stated, "fuck him. Do what you want."

"I'm okay with it." I agreed softly.

Gray nodded and then offered a small smile. "Alright now we can go back to bed."

"Which reminds me, we need a bigger one." Rhodes noted.

Gray hummed in agreeance as I carried her over to the bed, her small cuddly form curling around a pillow. Those thickly lashed eyes closed and I found myself looking out the same window she had. Contentment washed over me.

I hadn't been lying, I had found someone who would chose me, every single fucking time.

My eyes traced over Gray and an idea popped into my head as I met Rhodes's gaze. I nodded towards the door and he followed, hopefully after tomorrow she would never again question how much we chose her too.

9
GRAY

My body was deliciously sore as the dawn light began to filter through the windows. I could feel the soft pillows under my head and I stretched out realizing I was very much alone. Rubbing my eyes, I sat up and blinked taking stock of my body. Despite being tired, I felt oddly good and I had to wonder if that had anything to do with my men. Crazier things had happened and our bond always gave me a bit of a high. Looking around, I instantly broke into a soft smile. In the early pale blue light of the morning, my entire bed was covered in dark blue flower petals that led off my bed and towards a door leading to a smaller part of the temporary suite. I slipped off the bed, wrapping a robe around my oversized shirt and sock covered feet.

Despite knowing how stressful today was, there was an underlying current of excitement. This was it. This was when we stopped having to overthink everything, stopped having to plan for issues. This would be my closure and fresh start. I pushed open the door and found myself in a warm room that had a crackling fireplace and rose petals everywhere. Walking to the center of the room, I knelt down to pick up a small blue box.

Instantly my eyes started watering as I opened it to reveal a stunning emerald cut diamond ring. *Holy crap. It was freakin' massive!* I was shaking as I stood and turned to find all five of them kneeling with smaller boxes in tow.

Maybe this was a dream? This had to be a dream. My throat felt thick and my eyes were warm as hot tears trailed down my face. When had I become such a crier?

"Guys..." I whispered but Rhodes only stood, beckoning me forward, and I walked into his space as he pressed a gentle kiss to my lips. I was totally crying but I would never admit that to anyone, even under the threat of death.

"I love you so much, kitten. I want to spend the rest of my life loving you, and hopefully you want to do the same thing," Rhodes whispered as he kept my gaze, slipping the large engagement ring onto my finger and then opening the other box. I couldn't help the smile that broke through at the smaller diamond band that had a sapphire stone center. He slipped it right onto my finger as a wedding band.

It was beautiful, but what meant even more to me were his words. I went up onto my toes and grazed his lips gently. "I love you, Rhodes." I did. I loved him so much it hurt. I loved how serious and controlled he was around others and how he seemed more free and wild around me. I loved his smile and his terrible swearing habit that we shared. Shit. I just loved him.

Taylor, the impatient bastard wrapped his arms around my waist and dipped me into a kiss, my skin breaking out into shivers as he stole me from Rhodes. His emerald eyes were bright and dangerous as he nuzzled his nose against my throat. I could see the emotion running over him and he was oddly quiet and serious as he slipped a small band on my finger.

"Ours," He whispered, kissing my finger and I mouthed *'I love you.'* I thought I caught his eyes tearing up a bit as I looked down at the thin diamond band with a center ruby. His kiss was soft and languid, distracting me before Athens chuckled and pulled me towards him. What? I could totally spend all day kissing the man. He was sexy as all hell, but more than that, Taylor challenged me. He pushed me and made me better. Hell, I must love him if I keep letting him pick me up and carry me places.

"I love you, baby." Athens whispered with a playful smile. "Will you marry us?"

"Oh, now you ask?" I grinned as he nipped my lip and slid his ring, of all pure diamonds, onto my finger. All of them were stacking perfectly in line with the emerald cut engagement ring. I hadn't realized how symbolic the ring would feel to me but as each band was added, my heart filled and I found myself nearly shaking with energy and joy.

"Say yes!" He demanded with a smile, running a hand along my waist.

"Yes." I whispered as Neo stood his eyes serious and filled with so much depth and heat that I found myself shivering under his appraisal. He took my hand and placed me in front of him, his massive body shadowing mine as he wrapped his arm around me.

"You are my entire world." Neo spoke, his voice rough as his ring, with a center onyx stone, slid onto my slightly shaking hand.

"I love you." I cupped his jaw and he pressed his forehead to mine making me feel almost light headed. I couldn't imagine a world anymore where I hadn't met the twins, where the two of them didn't fill my day like the sun and moon.

I couldn't control the happy tears as Adyen pulled me into his arms, his dragon rumbling through his chest. "Don't cry, lil' brawler." He mumbled.

"Happy tears! I promise." I fanned my eyes as he examined my face and broke out into a small smile.

"Be ours forever?" He whispered, slipping a diamond band with an emerald center stone onto my fingers.

"Absolutely." I whispered as he picked me up and landed a

big kiss to my lips making me moan into it. Adyen. I had totally wanted to punch him when I first met him, but now? Now I wanted him forever. For keeps. He was so fundamental to my life. I was thrilled to have someone like him, despite being overprotective. Which even though I never admitted to, I sort of loved.

"Oops!" Marabella's voice rang out and I grinned whilst I peeked over Adyen's shoulder as Esme bumped right into her, both looking very shocked in the early morning. You know I probably should have considered they would be here early to get ready.

"Oh my god!" Esme smiled, after a silent moment between the eight of us. "Is this what I think it is?"

"Christ..." Rhodes chuckled as I nodded. Her squeal had me laughing as Adyen put me down and she tugged me into a hug. I found myself smiling like an idiot. I honestly couldn't tell you how much time passed between talking to them and taking a moment alone with each of my boys. I couldn't get over how beautiful the gesture had been and I had to wonder how long they'd been planning it.

"I would have never expected this!" I admitted to Rhodes as he cupped my jaw and looked over to where Athens was laughing at something Esme was saying. Marabella had ordered breakfast and coffee so we were all celebrating. I smirked thinking about how it was essentially an engagement brunch and I was totally still in my PJs.

"It was Athens's idea." He stated softly. "We were going to wait to give you the rings until after today, but I brought them with me last night, you know, just in case… considering the explosion I'm thankful I had. After talking to his father, something must have inspired him because he convinced me that we should do it before not after. I had no real argument because frankly I've wanted this ring on your finger for a long time."

I nuzzled against his chest with a smile and looked at the ring. "It's beautiful."

Rhodes's lips on my head had me relaxing into him as everything turned into a peaceful ocean inside of me. No more tension or stress. There was a finality to my thoughts and it was good because today was not the type of day for indecision.

It wasn't until sunrise fully hit that I had to get ready, kissing all of them enthusiastically as they went to go prepare the room. It was a blur as Marabella fixed my hair and Esme helped me get dressed, my focus on the concepts of wedding and marrying them.

Holy shit. I was fucking engaged.

"Marabella," I whispered as she smiled at me in the mirror. "I'm fucking engaged."

"I would say you're married by the looks of that ring!" She teased. She was right, they should have just done the full thing and placed a wedding band on my finger as well. Although I feared I was running out of space on my hand.

My hair was braided back as she placed the crown on my head. Esme helped me slip into a pale blue dress that fell off my shoulders and was loose around my body, adding a bit of softness to my overall look. I didn't take off the ring because frankly, there was no going back from what happened this morning. My men had been confident enough that this would work out, so much so that they put a goddamn ring on it. I wasn't about to take them off. They felt like a shield in the upcoming battle I was sure to face. One that I was going to win come hell or high water.

I left the room, and found Rhodes waiting for me. His official armor and dark silver and navy cloak made him look especially handsome this morning. Or, and this was a very possible outlook, I was just crazy about the man.

"You okay?" He whispered as he smiled at the ring still on my finger.

"More than ready to get this over with." I spoke softly inhaling. "I am going to force this day to be a good one even if it takes all my effort."

"I have no doubt, kitten." He smoothed a hand over my back causing my toes to curl.

As we approached the throne room, I didn't wait to be introduced because besides the guard it was just the Light Fae, council representatives, and my brother. I sat down, at the edge of the throne's seat feeling anxious to get this over with. Rhodes announced they could rise and then called for the SE to bring in Colliard. My eyes flickered over to the twins and I could feel the anger and betrayal through our bond towards their father. Not an ounce of regret though.

The previous council representative knelt and I had a total mental Queen of Hearts moment. Very *off with their head!* I wasn't that cruel though. I spoke loud enough that it was commanding but not so much that I felt as though I was purposefully making a show of this. I just wanted him gone and so did the rest of my kingdom no doubt.

"Former Council Representative Colliard," I announced, leaning back slightly, "you have been accused and found guilty of treason against your country, adding in opposing war effort as a spy, and two accounts of terrorist attacks. How do you plead?"

The man's eyes rose as he winced at my gaze and then looked to his sons, his eyes darkening, as something that looked a lot like regret filtered over his expression. "Guilty." He spoke, stunning me a little.

Well, that made it easier.

"For punishment of your crimes, you are exiled from the Horde and will be placed in captivity within the Kingdom of Day as a prisoner. Your sentence is ten decades. *If* you've survived past that, you are welcome to attempt to leave. Although, you will not *ever* return here." I announced as fear entered his eyes.

I watched as my twins looked down not wanting to pay attention to his pleas as the guards pulled him up and took him to be portalled the fuck out of my kingdom. I inhaled and shook my head. Rhodes called next for Palo with the contract, who was acting as an intermediary between the two parties. After all, one of the main issues with this as it stood, was that this was a transaction.

The Light Fae King spoke, "Before we begin, I want to apologize to Your Majesty, we had no idea that we had taken the information of a traitor. We assumed that he was a messenger because he had shown himself as one. We were only attempting to answer your 'call' and maintain the status of the contract, not to rush you."

I inhaled feeling the truth radiating off them. "I am happy to hear that, unfortunately I fear that you may have made the trip in vain."

The Queen frowned in confusion. "What do you mean?"

I went to speak but Silas stepped forward slightly as Rainer watched him. Rainer then nodded and also stood. I tilted my head, watching curiously as both men came to stand facing the two parties.

"We have something we need to talk to all of you about." Rainer stated boldly.

"Well…" The King motioned with his hand and I heard Athens try to hide his chuckle.

Silas intertwined his hand with Rainer and both of them looked at one another before addressing everyone's stilled and surprised reaction. Fascinating. It was like I wasn't even part of what they were talking about. It was brilliant.

"We got married last night." Silas stated, and my mouth popped open.

Holy shit!

"You what?!" The King thundered as the Queen squeezed his shoulder.

Rainer spoke, "I have been trying to tell you for years that this arranged marriage wasn't going to work out."

"You said you were in love with someone from the Horde!" His mother exclaimed looking at me as if I was somehow going to be furious about this. I kept my face blank so I didn't start dancing around.

"I am." Rainer kissed the top of Silas's hand. "Which is why I married him last night."

The King looked at me. "Your Majesty, we had no idea, I am sorry…"

I raised my hand and offered a soft smile. "I think that this should be a lesson, no? That arranged marriages are a bit outdated. The contract is void in my mind but not our alliance. In fact, I think this may actually better our alliance."

"How?" The King looked shocked.

I smiled at Silas. "Look how happy the two of them are, my brother being happy? That makes me far happier with this alliance. Forced marriages are almost never successful as it is."

The Light Fae seemed shocked and I walked down to the King and Queen placing a hand on their shoulders. "Do not worry about our alliance, I make you a promise that as long as you treat us with the same kindness and fairness as we treat you, we won't have any issues."

"So no wedding?" The Queen stated looking a bit shocked.

My lips quirked up. "Well no one said that did they?"

EPILOGUE I
GRAY - FEBRUARY (2 MONTHS LATER)

I hadn't been lying to them. We had held a massive ceremony for the Light Fae heir, Rainer, and Silas, both of them saying official vows in front of the entire Horde. Their wedding was blessed by, you guessed it - me! I wouldn't admit it but I totally cried and Silas in his true fashion had somehow transformed the entire hall overnight into their decided wedding colors of pale yellow and silver. It had turned out beautifully and now the two of them were very happy on a honeymoon in the Earth realm. I couldn't remember the name of the tropical island but Vegas had recognized it.

Vegas who was currently standing behind me adjusting my hair as Marabella continued to steam my dress. I closed my eyes thinking about the other wedding that had occured in the past two months, not that there had only been two, I mean it must be 'getting married' season because I had been to at least six or seven it felt like. See? Having friends was rough, man. So many fun things to do and so little time.

Marabella hummed, her hair was pulled back and a soft satin dress in navy draped over her frame. Unsurprisingly, the moment the stress of the contract ended, Palo and Bobby had proposed to her. The same night Silas and Rainer were actually married. The three of them had been married the following week and surprise surprise, she had found out she was pregnant already. Now, it may be because of her small frame but I swear to god the woman looked four months pregnant. It suited her well though, a constant smile on her face.

I had been a bit sad to lose her as a constant force by my side, but I had understood when Palo and Bobby decided to purchase a larger estate further from the city. The amount of happiness I felt for them was uncomparable to be honest. It made everything inside of me inflate with happiness and that so wasn't my style. Although, it was becoming more difficult to maintain my badass attitude as time went on. There was too much love and happiness inside of me.

"Mom?" Luna called sweeping into the room.

Like Marabella and Vegas, I'd had her wear navy, but hers was tulle and honestly made her look a bit like a cupcake. It was fucking adorable. Something she would no doubt be furious about… but come on. She's also been training with the SE academy despite not actually attending it. I'm sorry but I didn't want my now eleven year old daughter in an academy of all boys. No doubt she could hold her own, but why not have the best of both worlds? Train like the little badass she was but still come and sleep in the castle safe and sound every night.

If you were wondering, her shadows were very much still present. In fact, the only reason they weren't behind her right now was because the room was guarded in preparation for today. I looked over my face and couldn't help but smile at how I looked. I had kept my makeup light and neutral with white tones that matched the snow that was still very much present outside.

"You look beautiful!" Vegas beamed as I squeezed her hand.

"I have the bubbly!" Esme announced walking in, her dress a sparkling pink champagne. After all, as the maid of honor she had to stand out.

That's right, today *I* was getting fucking married!

She popped the bottle and poured a glass for me and herself, even offering a mini cup to Luna. I grinned as she made a sour face at the taste of it.

"Let's get you in the dress!" Marabella grinned pulling down the sparkly, sexy dress that I had decided to wear. I know. I probably should have worn something more Queen-like but frankly, I was only getting married once in my entire life. I was going to wear my dream wedding dress.

I slipped off my robe and Marabella helped me step into the crystal bodice and skirt. It looked like one of those Victoria's Secret corsets with the ribbing and the jewels. The neck dipped low but attached over my shoulders in a romantic swoop. The initial skirt was short but then over it was a massive, slightly see through, tulle skirt that made it look more ethereal than fully sexy. Honestly, I had never felt better in a dress than I did in this one. Vegas helped me tie up the diamond stilettos I slipped on, and I did a little bit of a twirl as everyone around me babbled slightly with enthusiasm. Luna's hand closed around mine as I smiled down at her, happy to have found the little nugget. I couldn't imagine life without her.

"Wait! Last piece," Marabella noted and placed a personally designed crystal crown that wrapped around my forehead and adorned my dark hair with diamonds. After leaving me, she had gone into the fashion and jewelry industry with Esme. Despite the slow moving progress to enhance the Horde's technological progress, they were doing very well.

"How are we doing here?" Bobby's voice sounded as Marabella wrapped her arms around him.

"Ready to get married." I offered a smile as my familiar came up to me and pulled me into a hug. I couldn't help but be thankful that I wore waterproof mascara as my eyes teared up a bit. Damn these emotions.

As we made our way down a private corridor, my nerves hit me as I found myself getting almost hyper with excitement. It wasn't like I hadn't been with these men for what felt like forever already, but still it was nerve wracking. More so than normal when I had a ton of eyes on me.

"Silas?" I asked as we made it downstairs and he flashed a smile, looking far tanner than before.

"Gray!" He pulled me into a hug. "You look stunning."

"I thought you weren't going to be here?" I couldn't help but smile.

"You think I would have missed your wedding day? How would I have made sure everything went as planned?" He winked as I raised my brows and we began to line up, the hall silencing with the start of the music.

Luna hugged me before stepping forward with Jude by her side, the two of them made their way down the massively long hallway, meeting the door before Palo and Marabella followed. My lips pressed up into another smile as I sighed, finally feeling like everything was fitting perfectly into place. Vegas walked down the aisle with Edwin and I could hear them both talking in low amused tones. I loved the two of them together despite never having thought that would work out, considering how stubborn both of them could be. It probably helped that there were so many of them. Esme and Bobby followed as Silas offered me an elbow, the realization of what for quickly dawned on me.

"You're going to walk me down the aisle?" I whispered.

"I know you don't need me to and that no one is 'giving you away', but I would love it, if you would let me?" He spoke softly looking a bit insecure.

"I would love that." I admitted, very seriously.

The music changed signaling our entrance, and the crowd all looked towards us as a bright blush filled my face. Gods dammit. I never blushed. I couldn't help it though and I was partly distracted by the gorgeous decorations. Everything was white, crystals and diamonds. The runner was a dark blue silk and up front I could see the wedding party to either side of the five men waiting to marry me.

Shit. I was so lucky.

All five of them were wearing navy blue tuxedos with champagne pink bow ties. The colors really came together and as we made our way into the throne room, I realized that there were accents of blue and pink everywhere between the white. I swallowed as Rhodes offered me a smile. My eyes teared up a bit. See? I was becoming such a little bitch.

From the moment that I reached the top of the steps, and the five of them circled around me in a semicircle, time seemed to slip away. Laurena, who had been thrilled to do the ceremony, read the vows and I turned so that I could repeat each of them as my men each slipped their individual rings back onto my finger. *Esme had been right, they were wedding bands!* I even was able to get out part of the ceremony in the Horde's language and a small vibration of magic filled me as my tattoos sparked with energy, the room's candles growing brighter upon my words.

I think everyone broke out into laughter when I essentially threw myself at Rhodes and he kissed the shit out of me. I should have felt awkward about kissing each one of them so intensely with an audience, but I couldn't lie, I didn't give a flying fuck.

Trying to express the distinct satisfaction that filled me was almost impossible. My little family of six, seven including Luna, was feeling far more complete as each day progressed. This ceremony though? This sealed it. I let tears of happiness break away down my face as the hall exploded into a chorus of cheers and the pure joy surrounding us was tangible. I now felt like *I* was the one that was about to explode into confetti.

It was hard to remember why I had ever wanted to punch these men, they were so perfect.

EPILOGUE II

GRAY

The windows of our bedroom were open wide, allowing a fall breeze to break through the massive suite that we had designed specifically for ourselves. After Colliard had destroyed the first, we used it as an excuse to create something absolutely spectacular.

The dome shaped room was pale silver and navy, with a massive bed made for six plus any little ones that decided to join us. I shook my head as I slowly rocked the little peanut of joy in my arms, kissing the top of his dark auburn hair. *Reaghan.*

Had I only had him two months ago? How in the heck was he getting so big already? His dark eyes blinked up at me and I nuzzled my nose against his. I slipped on my slippers and padded over to the couch, relaxing into the velvet material, the afternoon sun playing against the carpet.

"Kitten?" Rhodes called, his voice exhausted. A smirk grew on my face. Sucker.

"Yes?" I offered a smug grin as my shifter walked in, blonde hair a mess, and paint all over his face. Over his shoulder was our five year old daughter Willow. Now, that girl knows how to freakin' sleep. Where Reaghan reminded me of a mix between

Adyen and Taylor, Willow was all the twins and Rhodes. Don't ask me how that happened, I'm blaming magic. All I can say is that the little nugget had stunning dark hair, rich olive skin, and bright mint green eyes. She was also already showing the characteristics of being a mage. I think Rhodes was hoping for a naturalistic one so that she was a shifter like Luna.

"How does she move that fast?" He asked astounded, placing her passed out form on our bed before saunterring over to me.

I grinned knowingly. "She's five, honey. You took her to paint, with *other* children. What did you think would happen?"

He grunted and crouched down, his eyes lighting up as Reaghan grasped his massive finger with his own little hand. "How's our little guy doing?"

"Sleeps way better than she did." I pointed out.

It was true, after our wedding we'd gotten pregnant that following spring. It wasn't by accident if you were wondering, in fact, it had been a really devoted effort. It had all started because the following Christmas, Rhodes had all but almost beat up one of his own guards. To be fair the man had been drunk and had been making comments about me that weren't… polite? That seemed like a good word. He was an asshole. He was being a fuck dick and Rhodes had to put him into his place. But it was like the straw that broke the camel's back because the very next day they'd started talking about starting a family and shit just escalated.

Taylor had been right on board, thrilled at the concept which probably surprised me the most, but he was always a bit of a wild card. Rhodes had brought up the idea so our control freak was on a goddamn mission to get me knocked up, nearly as bad as the twins. Both of them made, and continue to make, constant efforts to spend all day inside of me despite my responsibilities. I literally missed several important meetings because they'd kept me in bed. The most extreme? Adyen. I had no idea what had gotten into the crazy bastard because all of the sudden it was essentially the 'fill Gray up with as much cum as possible' mission. Yeah, I probably didn't encourage it by going off my birth control almost right away and telling them that. What? I had been eager to start a family and we'd been settled for a bit, it just made sense.

None of us had really been surprised when we found out we were pregnant a few months later.

Now, nearly six years later and our little family is growing. I didn't admit it because Adyen always got particularly worked up about it... well, all of them did, but I was hoping to have quite a few kids. I never thought mothering would be for me, but creating such a positive experience felt almost healing for my shitty childhood.

"Baby girl?" Taylor called out as Athens chuckled, both of them walking in and pausing, their eyes on Willow. Knowing how energetic she could be they didn't want to risk waking her up, so they walked over silently and kissed my forehead and greeted our little one.

"What happened to you, bud?" Athens flashed a cheeky grin as Rhodes scowled.

"I like your makeup..." Taylor tried to keep a straight face at the bright pink paint on his lips. I couldn't help but let out a laugh. What? Seeing Rhodes all worked up was fucking hilarious! *Sorry...*

"Mom?" Luna whispered, popping in with Neo and Adyen following her. It was clear the three of them had been training because my daughters hair was muddy and all over the place, her hand taped up, probably from rubbing it raw on that sword she used daily. The girl had become absolutely lethal while somehow maintaining everything that made Luna... well, Luna. At just a bit over seventeen, she towered over me at 5'7" but still looked very small and as elegant as a cat, using her balance and reflexes as an advantage in fighting. Neo admitted, despite not wanting to tell *her*, that she was probably the best fighter they had. Neo also knew that if he said that to Luna it would be all over the kingdom after she gave her friends shit about it.

I think the girl was more popular than me. Scratch that, I absolutely know she was more popular than me. As the six of them talked, I watched as Willow blinked open her massive eyes meeting my gaze with a bright mint leaves version of hers. In a flash of a movement, she was jumping on Neo's back and he caught her mid air, making sure she didn't hurt herself.

"Daddy!" She hugged him and Rhodes scoffed because Willow totally had a bit of a favorite. She loved Neo. She loved all of them, but she had grown super attached to Neo. Luna offered Rhodes an understanding pat on the shoulder as I grinned. Luna then left, calling that she would be back later. I had no idea what she was up to half the time.

"What's on the schedule for tonight?" I asked curiously.

Neo spoke with a smile as Willow tried to climb over his shoulders like a monkey. She was a freakin' wild child, I swear. "Tonight is the anniversary of our meeting, Esme is picking the kids up."

I smirked and looked at all of them, Athens offering me a wink.

"How do you know it won't end like how you first met me?" I raised my brows.

"Yeah, Gray?" Adyen smiled, "You think that is going to work out for you?"

"Maybe?" I mumbled kissing Reaghan's forehead.

"Don't worry, baby girl." Taylor teased. "We just want to show you exactly what we wanted to do the first day we met you."

A shiver rolled down my spine as I looked up at him with a smirk.

I was not about to say no to that.

ENDING NOTE TO READERS

Finishing Gray's story was a bit emotional for me because despite being a shorter series, it was one of my favorites. Queen Gray, our badass MFC, was my very first character in my first novel *Savages*. I am thrilled to be able to release it right after my author-versary and I can not wait to hear what all of you thought about the conclusion to Gray's story of vengeance, adventure, and love.

To those who are looking forward to Luna's story? I have a surprise for you! While the title is not set in stone, I have attached a preview to the start of her future series. *Enjoy!* Follow my facebook group, Sinclair's Ravens, for more updates and cover releases.

SNEAK PEEK

A PIXIE'S ECLIPSE IN BOOK 1 OF THE DAUGHTER OF ARTEMIS

Luna

"Jude!" I demanded from my precarious position on one of the many small ledges in the East Tower. "You leave my room, right flippin' now! You are not welcome here." My voice was sharp and I kept my chin high, demanding that the wolf shifter listen to me.

Jude let out a low frustrated growl as Jackson chuckled flipping through one of the massive books I kept on my coffee table. I briefly examined Jackson's dimpled smile and tried to avert my eyes. Dangerous sexy blood mage. He fixed me with a sexy look as if knowing my thoughts. "What about me, Luna? Can I hang out here?"

I narrowed my eyes at the icy blue eyed mage, his white hair slicked back, to expose a stunning perfect face. It was unfair. "You are just as bad, Jackson." His large arms, lean but chiseled, were decorated in dark mage runes. He was wearing his Red Masques uniform but his coat was undone and he looked, as usual, perfectly content in his own skin.

"I don't understand why you are so upset." Jude growled. He had been doing that a lot recently. The taller and bigger he got, the more massive his shadow over me grew. Protective, overbearing, insane and very handsome. I used to think Jude was level headed then right around the time I turned sixteen, he got way more protective over me. Now, he growled a lot and had issues understanding why I got upset about certain things.

Well, I wouldn't let him wait in suspense, I was more than fucking willing to explain what was upsetting me. I jumped off the balcony, landing as both boys made worried noises, the pads of my feet making no noise as I straightened myself to my lean height of 5'7". I searched Jude's deep blue eyes and his dark messy onyx hair. The man was devastatingly gorgeous.

I noticed his eyes ran over my usual outfit for work of leather thigh-high boots over leather pants, with a velvet jacket that was unbuttoned to show off a snow white shirt that matched my hair. Honestly, his staring made me feel a bit better. However, the real problem was that at eighteen Jude was way too attractive, and twenty suited Jackson far too well.

"You know I hate her." I waved my hand dismissively and walked over to the large open balcony window. I could easily see the SE Guards training down below with two of my dads and I offered a small wave to a few of the guards that looked up. Honestly, I loved the SE Guard. I knew that they were a bit rough around the edges but honestly, they were pretty cool.

"I don't enjoy talking to her." Jude explained softly from behind me. I held my breath, afraid of my reaction because *holy hell!* I was getting more and more attracted to him everyday. Both of them. These overly muscular men shouldn't be around me. Maybe, I should have never become their friend.

"Well," I turned and looked at him, "clearly you do because you either wanted to go out with her or you were too nice to say no. Either way, you are dating the enemy and we can no longer be friends." Also, I was a bit terrified I would scratch her fucking eyes out. Michelle was doing this on purpose. I knew she was.

"That's rough!" A deep rolling voice stated. I snapped my eyes to the door as I smiled, Jude letting out his usual annoyed sound. Marcus looked amused, those dark eyes glinted, and his full lips pressed together trying to hide his smile. At twenty something, he was massive and his dark cut off shirt showed off his massive arms that were covered in tattoos. His dark, rich, wavy hair hung to his jawline and my eyes found his dark black gaze set in his olive skin tone. There was a white scar that traveled from his eyebrow down his jaw line, matching his wild energy.

If Jude was traditionally handsome and Jackson was stunning, Marcus was lethally beautiful. I loved his roughness. I often wondered if his rough looks would translate in bed. I mean… I could only imagine what being under him would feel like. No literally, I could *only* imagine it. I'd been so friend zoned it was pathetic.

But Gods, could I look and appreciate him because the man just did it for me.

"Shut it!" Jude snarled.

The three men were best friends, but Jude often wanted to fucking kill Marcus. Not nearly as much as Kai mind you but they really pushed his buttons. I walked around Jude as he tried to reach me, my movements too fast as I shook my head. No. I didn't want his hugs. Marcus lifted me easily and I tucked my head against his neck, unable to stop myself from nuzzling it slightly, his chest letting out a low rumble.

"Put her down," Jude demanded. "Luna, we need to talk about this."

Jackson chuckled. "Mate, just tell Michelle that you won't go out with her."

I smiled against Marcus's neck as his rough hand ran up and down my spine, his lips pressed to my forehead. I was extremely comfortable around these men and I hoped, dreamed maybe, that once I had turned eighteen things would change. They hadn't so far, for the record.

"I can't." Jude grunted, and jealousy boiled under my skin as I shook myself. I stiffened and pulled back as Marcus tried to plaster me further against him. I wiggled down and turned to face Jude, no longer feeling like teasing him.

"If you really like her, then go out with her." I said softly my gold eyes probably darkening with frustration and sadness. "I don't like her but I get it if you do."

Something clicked as he sighed. "Luna it isn't like…"

A flash of gold had me sprinting towards the window. I heard Marcus shout something but I leaped through the air, my feet pushing off the window's ledge as my dad's shifted dragon form flew past. I landed right on his back with perfect agility. I gripped his scales as he let out an amused huff and soared over the training center before landing, steam rolling off both of us. I slid down and shouted my thanks as I strode confidently towards two of my other dads, Athens and Neo, both watching me with amusement. Well, Athens was smiling. Neo offered this small lip twitch that was essentially laughing for him.

"Good Afternoon, my wonderful devoted guards!" I offered a princess wave to the men I passed as they chuckled. I grinned, pulling out my sword and turning to meet Taylor's sparing hit. He grinned and I shook my head at his surprise attack.

"You're getting old, Dad." I warned as I ducked away as he attempted to ruffle my hair. I am positive it was a mess as normal.

"What are we doing today?" I asked the four of them as Adyen joined us. He barked out a command as the guards snapped their heads away from me. I didn't blame them. I was a bit unusual to look at. White hair. Gold eyes. It was a bit intense.

"You're supposed to be with your mom and Willow!" Rhodes walked over with an amused smile.

"Shh!" I hissed. "That's nearly as bad as asking me to babysit Reaghan. I love the kid but I've got shit to do, come on!" Willow was my nearly eight year old sister and my baby brother Reaghan was a little nugget at almost two. Still we didn't exactly have much in common at this age. I know it's surprising, right?

Athens chuckled. "Are Esme and Gray with the personal shopper?"

A horrified shiver worked through me as I nodded. "They tried to put me in heels!" I growled. "Can you imagine what they have planned for my birthday ball? Which I don't understand since my birthday has already passed… but I am far more useful here! *Fighting*! Have me do something helpful at least? I can kick most of their asses… scratch that Kai and Marcus aren't here, all of them. I can kick *all* of their asses!"

My face heated a bit thinking of Kai and I wondered where he was today. After he left my room this morning, he hadn't mentioned where he would be going. And no, it isn't like that. I wish… But ever since Kai had come back into my life, despite countless times being told not to, he slept in my room. After a while, even my Dads gave up. It wasn't like that between us and we had grown up falling asleep together on the streets so it just felt natural. I loved waking up in his arms.

Neo grinned. "Actually, Luna, that is a wonderful fucking idea."

"No." Adyen warned.

"He needs a lesson in humility!" Neo led me past all the guards as I bounced with a bit of energy. As I had gotten older, the boys I had trained with had become men and all of them had started looking at me differently. Honestly, I didn't mind. You know who did mind? Jude. Jackson. Marcus. Kai. They all minded a fuck ton.

"Eldon!" Neo snapped as the Pixie commander's son turned to face us. His cocky smile slipped away and I couldn't help but smile. I liked the man despite his massive ego. Everyone else in my life seemed to have a distinct distaste for him.

He was older than me by nearly six years and you could tell he thought himself better than nearly everyone in his field. His eyes were a stunning aquamarine and his skin was nearly iridescent with styled blue hair. The man was a piece of fucking artwork. Like one of the classics.

"Yes?" He asked, looking cautious.

"You are running training loops with Luna." Neo grinned as the man became infuriated.

"I asked for harder…"

"Now," Rhodes urged.

I stepped up as the clearing opened up and I pulled my sword out easily, facing him and raising a brow. Eldon looked over me with a frown. "You sure that you want to do this, Princess?"

I winked in return. "Never wanted to do something more in my life."

Ten minutes later, the Pixie was on the ground with my boot at his throat and my sword over his head. I grinned as his eyes darkened, seemingly shocked at what had just happened. "You're actually very good Eldon, I enjoyed that greatly."

I offered a hand and he took it, his look of anger turning into something else as he stepped up closer to me. He looked down at me and I nearly shivered at the predatory flair there. *What?* Scary was hot.

"Luna." Kai's voice was sharp as his warm hard chest appeared behind me. Eldon met his gaze and looked back down at me, shaking his head.

"Good spar." I noted, stepping back as Kai's fingers tightened around my waist. He was always like this. Very possessive over me. Jude and Jackson's magic seeped into the area along with Marcus as I sighed.

Then Eldon did something unexpected, he pulled my wrist

forward, enough that Kai grunted and lost hold on me. "Get a drink with me tonight, Princess?"

I swallowed and pulled back looking over his face, no cocky smile in place. "Time?"

"Six? Outside the castle gates?" He asked softly.

"Deal." I turned as I realized that training rounds had broken out around us. I didn't believe my fathers were oblivious for a moment despite pretending to be. They let me fight my own battles and I appreciated that.

"What was that?" Kai demanded as we walked away, his eyes dark and his hair far longer on the top than the sides. Once we got closer to the castle, I couldn't stop him from lifting me up as I growled. The other boys were following after in heated talks.

"What was what?" I arched a brow.

Kai's grip tightened on me as his eyes flashed down to my lips. "What were you talking about?"

I sighed and fixed him with a look. "I'm getting a drink with him tonight."

His dark eyes widened as possessiveness overtook his face as he let out a low dangerous sound. "Absolutely not."

"Why?" I asked, feeling annoyed.

Then he did something completely unexpected. Kai dipped his head and sealed his lips to mine.

Oh shit!

EXCLUSIVE BONUS SCENE
EARTH REALM - GRAY

"This is your fault, kitten. I told you this was a terrible idea." Rhodes muttered, looking all worked up and handsome, his golden hair falling in his face which was very unlike my serious in control husband. It sort of made me want to tease him even more. I rolled my eyes as Adyen let out a small growl at Rhodes's blame game. Really, dude? You would have thought after all these years the man would have calmed the heck down -- but no. That would have been far too much for me to ask for.

To be fair, I had caused this situation but I didn't regret it.

You see, currently, we were in a small suburb of Denver in our massive estate that I'd purchased simply for the use of this year. I know, you're probably wondering, what the hell I am doing in the Earth realm. It was pretty simple actually.

We had needed a break from the Horde.

Being a Queen was hard work… I mean really hard work. I knew the kingdom would be fine without us for a year and we still were planning to go back for Thanksgiving, Christmas, and the like. I really didn't have hopes for my husband's well-being if he was like this and it was only October. I had thought our trip had been going fairly well plus it was giving the kids some perspective.

I didn't want to call them spoiled... but they were. Well, except Luna but she was all grown up doing her own thing. She had promised to come out here though so I was excited about that.

But yes, my children were adorable, perfect, and spoiled. They were sweet as can be and funny as all hell but because of their fathers, they had never even questioned whether something would be available to them or not. I didn't help either. Honestly, I wouldn't have wanted it any other way. I loved making sure they were happy and always loved.

I thought that experiencing a different perspective and place in the world would be helpful and healthy for them -- I'd even chosen a half supernatural and half-human school district for them to attend. This brought us to our current issue and why two of my husbands and I were standing on the front porch watching the scene unfold in front of us with very different emotions.

Willow would be turning eighteen soon and I think that reality was hitting everyone very differently. Me? I thought she had turned into a brilliant and stunning young woman. No really, I wasn't just saying that as her mom. While she had the upbeat personality of Athens, her *slight* control issues due to Rhodes and Neo had made her the top of, well, everything in the Horde. Here seemed to be no different and if the number of people here for the Homecoming pre-picture party told me anything, she was very popular. I didn't think her father was a fan at all. To be fair neither was her little brother Reaghan.

It may have also had to do with her dress... it was honestly beautiful. Our daughter had gotten my height coming in around only 5'2 and her hair was a dark wave that fell all the way down to her waist. She had chosen the literal dress I would have picked for her and I was thrilled to see that she seemed so confident in it. It was pale jade green with a tight sweetheart neckline and a tulle skirt that showed off her long legs with sparkly gold shoes. She looked like an adorable cupcake but somehow her father's found it entirely inappropriate... I could only imagine how prom season was going to treat them.

I smirked as Willow offered me a frustrated look from across the yard before going back to smiling at her date. Her date, Texas, was staring at her with near adoration and completely ignoring the glare that Taylor was offering him. I didn't think many people noticed because they were milling about taking pictures, eating and drinking before the limo came to take the group of twelve to the dance, but I totally saw it. Reaghan, who was soon to be in high school, stood next to him with a scowl that almost matched perfectly. I couldn't help but offer my two-redheads a smile because it was pretty cute. Taylor narrowed his eyes at me and I wondered if I'd be punished for that.

I hoped so...

"I'm going to save her," I announced and walked off the porch ignoring sounds of protest, my eyes searching for Athens who I found playing with triplets. No. I didn't want to talk about it and neither did my vagina. Shit was painful but I survived and now Saint, Adeline, and Emmy were here and ready to cause trouble which was why Neo was helping Athens scoop them up whenever they left the large playset we had to the side of the house. *I had been done having kids.* No really. I wasn't like some other women, cough cough Vegas and Marabella, who loved being pregnant. It was fun but I couldn't kill shit when I was. Something that was all my mates and not me in the least. I would still kill shit but they got weird about it. Luckily I was immortal so while I totally wanted to have more kids, I was a fan of taking a tiny... A few year break. I mean, we literally had forever and I wasn't about to have ten flippin' kids in like ten years. You know?

The triplets had been a surprise and now in second grade, they were... energetic to say the least. At least it was fairly easy to tell them apart considering one had blonde hair, and the other two brown and red respectively. They were adorable, despite our son Saint hating that word. He was adorable though and he looked literally just like the image of Rhodes where our daughters tended to look far more of a mix of my husbands like the other children.

"Honey," I smiled at Willow, her death glare making me smile. *We all know where she got that look from.*

"Do you want a picture with Texas?" I asked, waving my phone.

"Yes please," She smiled looking excited at the perspective. Willow had discovered Instagram and the amount of pictures I had taken of her was extensive but oddly fun to do.

As they backed up my son frowned, "Mom, now they are standing too close together."

"Dude!" Willow scowled. Her date chuckled, making her blush, and he, thankfully for his safety, kept a polite hand on her upper back as Taylor relaxed slightly. Good move kid. I took a few photos of them and when the limo pulled up, I told her I would send them her way and gave her a hug.

"Behave," I warned as she rolled her eyes but nodded. *So much sassiness.*

Taylor narrowed his eyes at the kid but shook his hand probably wanting to say something but not risking it. Last time one of us had done that, Willow had gotten… angry. It had proved her temper was by far the same as Taylor's which was amusing as hell.

Reaghan sighed, "He's going to be trouble, I can just tell."

I laughed and messed up his hair. *This kid.*

I wandered towards the twins as they both looked up, seemingly thrilled to see me. Freakin' weirdos, I literally hadn't gone more than twenty feet from them… alright, it was a bit cute.

"Mommy!" Emmy offered me what I called the *world's most perfect smile* as she jumped on me. I pulled her closer and kissed her temple loving that she smelled like sunshine, her dark hair messy waves.

"Mommy, Daddy won't let me go on top of the playset," Saint snarled, narrowing his eyes at an unmoved Neo. It was good that I had Neo around because he seemed to be the only non-pushover. Well... most of the time, except with Willow but I think it was because they bonded over gardening.

Yes. I know, it was adorable. Willow had started gardening at a very young age and ever since then he had offered to help her with the heavy lifting. It had turned into a massive bonding thing and I'd taken a million photos of how cute they were. Willow had ended up being an elemental mage, her magic very much focused on earth and water. It was pretty damn cool actually.

Reaghan on the other hand was a shifter. There was no waiting to wonder since the kid had literally shifted into a dragon around five when he sneezed too hard. Adyen had been literally thrilled and now they would take practice flights whenever Luna and Rhodes went to go train near the Pixie forest. Yes, the two nut jobs still trained constantly.

"That's because it's dangerous," Adeline said, her white-blonde hair perfectly still with a bow in it. Adeline was adorable and would no doubt probably bring the Horde to its knees with that look she always gave. It was like the little girl was secretly forty and had absolutely no issue telling you what you were doing wrong. She also was a huge cuddler and loved reading at night. I blamed Athens since he would read practically a million books to her and never said no.

The three of them were little demons and it was clear as day to Taylor. I didn't really know what to look for but he assured me it would be more noticeable as they got older. I didn't really care what they were as long as they were happy and healthy but it was cool to have such a diverse family.

The car pulled up the driveway as Marabella parked her...

massive minivan. They had decided to come with us and I had no idea how the woman looked like she slept so well because she had, and no this is not a joke, twelve children. My eyes widened as six of her little ones jumped out running towards my triplets and I stepped back not even wanting to get in the middle of that insanity.

Marabella, wearing a peasant top and jeans, hugged me, "Everyone ready to go?"

Bobby, Palo, and her were going to a movie together -- yes, that was as funny as it sounded. I was thrilled though because I totally needed a bit of a breather and some alone time with my men. I loved my kids but they made it hard as hell to have sex whenever we wanted. Bobby was laughing at something Adyen said and Palo was talking to his brother. I was glad that Taylor and his brother had gotten so close, it made our family impossibly larger. No really, we tried taking a family vacation once with Vegas's clan, yes I am calling it a clan, and ours along with Marabella and Palo. It had taken a massive commercial size jet to get us all to Bali together. Totally worth it though.

"We should have more kids," Athens stated quietly as they drove away, after twenty minutes of getting all ten in the car. I turned my head towards him as he chuckled at my no doubt horror-struck expression.

"Oh no," I wiggled my finger, "You don't have to push them out. You have no idea how much that shit hurts. Next time make smaller babies and I'll consider it, Reaghan was almost ten pounds!"

"I could see a few more, especially so they are all young together," Rhodes agreed.

"Come on, li'l brawler," Adyen teased, biting my ear as I shivered.

"Plus what if they are mages," Neo even added.

I dipped underneath Adyen's arms, "Nope!"

"I am hearing 'yes, I want to have sex all night and see what happens'," Taylor grinned tossing me over his shoulder as I let out a laugh. His hand came down on my ass as I squeaked and he walked through the front door.

I smiled at my boys and their commentary as he carried me towards our bedroom. More kids or not, my life was absolutely perfect and I knew it was because of my sexy mates. My sexy mates who were amazing husbands and fathers…

Alright, fuck it, why not one or two more!

M. SINCLAIR
INTERNATIONAL & US BEST SELLER

M. Sinclair is a Chicago native, parent to 3 cats, and can be found writing almost every moment of the day. Despite being new to publishing, M. Sinclair has been writing for nearly 10 years now. Currently, in love with the Reverse Harem genre, she plans to publish an array of works that are considered romance, suspense, and horror within the year. M. Sinclair lives by the notion that there is enough room for all types of heroines in this world and being saved is as important as saving others. If you love fantasy romance, obsessive possessive alpha males, and tough FMCs, then M. Sinclair is for you!

Just remember to love cats... that's not negotiable.

ALSO BY M. SINCLAIR

Vengeance Series

#graysguards

Book 1 - Savages

Book 2 - Lunatics

Book 3 - Monsters

Book 4 - Psychos

Complete Series

The Red Masques Series

#vegasandherboys

Book 1 - Raven Blood

Book 2 - Ashes & Bones

Book 3 - Shadow Glass

Book 4 - Fire & Smoke

Book 5 - Dark King

Complete Series

Tears of the Siren Series

#lorcanslovers

Book 1 - Horror of Your Heart

Book 2 - Broken House

Book 3 - *Announced soon!*

The Dead and Not So Dead Trilogy

#narcshotties

Book 1 - Queen of the Dead
Book 2 - Tea Time with the Dead
Book 3 - *Announced soon!*

Descendant Series

#novasmages

Book 1 - Descendant of Chaos
Book 2 - Descendant of Blood
Book 3 - Descendant of Sin (*coming soon!*)

Reborn Series

#mayasmages

Book 1 - Reborn In Flames
Book 2 - Soaring in Flames

The Wronged Trilogy

#valentinasvigilanties

Book 1 - Wicked Blaze Correctional

Standalones

Peridot (Jewels Cafe Series)

Collaborations

Rebel Hearts Heists Duet *(M. Sinclair & Melissa Adams)*

Book 1 - Steal Me

Forbidden Fairytales *(The Grim Sisters - M. Sinclair & CY Jones)*

Book 1 - Stolen Hood
Book 2 - Knights of Sin
Book 3 - Deadly Games

Join our Group on Facebook The Grim Sisters Reading Group.

STALK ME... REALLY, I'M INTO IT

Instagram: msinclairwrites
Facebook: Sinclair's Ravens (New content announced!)
Twitter: @writes_sinclair
Newsletter: Link
Amazon: M. Sinclair
Goodreads: M. Sinclair
Bookbub: M. Sinclair
Website: Official M. Sinclair Website

Printed in Great Britain
by Amazon